SCORCHED EARTH

DANIELLE L. JENSEN

TOR PUBLISHING GROUP

NEW YORK

SCORCHED EARTH

Maps by Jennifer Hanover

A Tor Teen Book
Published by Tom Doherty Associates / Tor Publishing Group
120 Broadway
New York, NY 10271

www.torpublishinggroup.com

EU Representative: Macmillan Publishers Ireland Ltd, 1st Floor, The Liffey Trust Centre, 117–126 Sheriff Street Upper, Dublin 1, D01 YC43

The Library of Congress has cataloged the hardcover edition as follows:

Names: Jensen, Danielle L. author
Title: Scorched earth / Danielle L. Jensen.
Description: First edition. | New York : Tor Teen, Tor Publishing Group, 2025. | Series: Dark shores ; 4
Identifiers: LCCN 2025016255 (print) | ISBN 9781250290823 (hardcover) | ISBN 9781250290830 (ebook)
Subjects: CYAC: Fantasy. | War—Fiction. | Diseases—Fiction. | Good and evil—Fiction. | Romance stories. | LCGFT: Fantasy fiction. | Romance fiction.
Classification: LCC PZ7.1.J4558 Sc 2025 | DDC [Fic]—dc23/eng/20250529
LC record available at https://lccn.loc.gov/2025016255

ISBN 978-1-250-29084-7 (trade paperback)

First Tor Teen Trade Paperback Edition: 2026

Printed in the United States of America

10 9 8 7 6 5 4 3 2 1

PRAISE FOR *SCORCHED EARTH*

"Jensen tosses readers right back into the action. . . . A big, bold send-off for beloved characters." —*Kirkus Reviews*

PRAISE FOR *DARK SHORES*

"Richly woven, evocative, and absolutely impossible to put down—I was hooked from the first lines! *Dark Shores* has everything I look for in a fantasy novel: fresh, unique settings; a cast of complex and diverse characters; and an unflinching boldness with the nuanced world-building. I loved every word."

—Sarah J. Maas, #1 *New York Times* bestselling author

"The book grabs readers from the beginning with its stellar world-building and multidimensional characters. . . . A gripping introduction to a new series." —*Kirkus Reviews* (starred review)

"This epic first installment in a new series from Jensen features stunning world-building, a vivid cast of secondary characters, and a steamy slow-burn romance between two exceedingly competent and compelling heroes. *Dark Shores* is not one to miss."

—*Booklist*

"This is a lush, imaginative world, and as the focus shifts between Teriana and Marcus, it becomes clear that the readers are only getting a glimpse of its complicated history and mythology. . . . Their secrets don't, of course, stop Teriana and Marcus from embarking on a steamy romance, and fans of Rutkoski's sigh-worthy *The Winner's Kiss* and the high-stakes sea adventure of Levenseller's *Daughter of the Pirate King* will want to know where Marcus and Teriana journey to next." —*The Bulletin of the Center for Children's Books*

"The plot's twists and turns and fantastical elements add to the allure of this thrilling story. Exhilarating fantasy-adventure romance for fans of Tricia Levenseller's *Daughter of the Pirate King*, Alexandra Christo's *To Kill a Kingdom*, or Natalie C. Parker's *Seafire*. Readers will eagerly await the next book in the series."

—*School Library Journal*

ALSO BY DANIELLE L. JENSEN

THE DARK SHORES SERIES

Tarnished Empire (prequel)

Dark Shores

Dark Skies

Gilded Serpent

THE MALEDICTION SERIES

Stolen Songbird

Hidden Huntress

Warrior Witch

The Broken Ones (prequel)

THE BRIDGE KINGDOM SERIES

The Bridge Kingdom

The Traitor Queen

The Inadequate Heir

The Endless War

The Twisted Throne

SAGA OF THE UNFATED

A Fate Inked in Blood

A Curse Carved in Bone

For Melissa Frain:
I wouldn't have made it to the finish line without you!

NORTHERN CONTINENT
GENDORN
DERIN
Deadground
Helatha
Alder's Ford
Liratora Mountains
Wall
Mudaire
Abenharrow
TWISTED SEAS
MUDAMORA
Obarri
Rotahn
ANUKASTRE
THE DOLDRUM
TALTUGA
THE ENDLESS SEAS
EOTEN ISLE
Serlania
Revat
GAMDESH
Emrant
Rita
Uncharted Lands
ARINOQUIA
Aracam
Galinha
SOUTHERN CONTINENT
KATAMARCA
THE BARRENS

SIBERN
The Teeth
FAUL
DENASTRES
THE EMPIRE
THE ENDLESS SEAS
CELENDOR
Celendrial
Padria
ATLIA
SEA
F THE
DEAD
PHERA
TIMIA
Hydrilla
BARDEEN
SIBAL
CHERSOME
THE BARRENS

SCORCHED EARTH

1

KILLIAN

Night was coming, and with it, the monsters.

Killian's shoulders burned, every muscle of his body shuddering from exhaustion. His clothes were drenched with sweat from rowing all through the day on a lake that seemed as vast as an ocean, albeit as smooth as glass.

He needed to find cover.

With darkness, and no fog to conceal the tiny boat, it was only a matter of time until the deimos found them and all the wrath of Rufina's army descended. A fate Killian was desperate to avoid, but one the corrupted in the boat with him reached toward.

Lydia was barely recognizable. Each passing hour since they'd escaped, the rage and hunger in her eyes had grown. Black windows to the underworld that he couldn't bear to look into, because this was not Lydia.

This was not the girl he was in love with.

Except that it is, a voice whispered from the depths of his soul. *That she contained that part of herself doesn't make it any less her.*

Gods, but he hated that dark truth. Needed to silence it, except to do so meant silencing himself.

If she contained it once, she can contain it again. She's strong.

A sentiment he prayed was true despite much proof to the contrary. Three times she'd broken free of her bonds. His clothes were a shredded mess from all the strips he'd torn off to secure her incredible strength and to gag her to keep her from crying out for Rufina's aid. In the space of hours, she'd gone from desperate to kill to the queen of Derin to seeing Rufina as her savior.

All because of the hunger that consumed every part of her.

He wanted to blindfold her. Wanted to hide from that malevolent gaze that set off every instinct in his soul, demanding that he fight. Demanding that he kill.

"I'm heading to shore." He eyed the shadowed coast. "We need to find some form of cover for the night." Against his will, Killian's gaze flicked to Lydia's face.

She was watching him, tangled dark hair clinging to her face.

Gone was the maddened, frenzied creature, and he almost wished for it to return, because now the dark pits staring at him were full of calculation. Cunning. She was waiting for a moment of weakness, waiting for an opportune time to strike, which removing her from the boat would surely give her.

"I'm not giving up on you," he said. "You can fight back against the Corrupter. I'm going to help you."

Killian waited for some sign that the goodness in her was still there. A gleam of hope that he could cling to. Instead, a feral smile curved up around her gag, Lydia's teeth gleaming red from where fabric cut into her mouth.

Kill her.

Killian jerked his gaze back to the dark coast, sucking in a mouthful of air. *Just row*, he told himself. *Your focus needs to be on evading the deimos.*

The sun burned lower and lower behind him, illuminating what he first thought was a mangrove swamp but then realized was a dead forest. Trees of every sort jutted out of the murky water, their branches skeletal and barren of life but for the putrid fungus growing on their rotting bark. Finding a gap wide enough for the boat, Killian rowed beneath the dead canopy just as the sun's glow faded below the horizon.

He paused in his rowing to catch his breath as the boat drifted deeper.

The moment night fell, the fungus on the trees came alive, glowing a deep green that provided just enough light to see by. The density of the tree trunks forced him to draw in one of the oars and use the other as a paddle, slowly weaving deeper into the dead forest and, he hoped, closer to land. The smell grew sulfurous and strange, and in the shadows of the trees, small shadows crawled, though they froze the moment his eyes fell upon them.

Then the water stirred.

Killian stopped paddling as a large form swam toward them, then under. It struck the hull of the boat, rocking it violently, and he held his breath, waiting for it to attack.

But the creature only moved on, reptilian tail drifting side to side as it continued down the path from which they had come. Lydia shifted her weight, and Killian tensed, but she made no move to test her bonds.

Not yet, at any rate.

He didn't know if pressing onward was the right thing to do, for everything about this forest was *wrong.* Everything felt touched by the Corrupter. He was certain that daylight would reveal the same black veins as stretched across Mudamora. Veins that stole the life of everything they touched. The product of tenders—those chosen by Yara to have power over the earth—whose marks had been tainted by the underworld.

The thought brought Malahi to mind. She was perhaps the last uncorrupted tender on the continent, which meant the last person capable of reversing the tide.

If she still lived, that was.

He'd found unexpected allies in Agrippa, the defected general of Rufina's armies, and Baird, a giant marked by Gespurn, but while they might have succeeded in their mad scheme to get the Queen of Mudamora out of Helatha, the half of Rufina's army not pursuing Killian would be on their heels. Agrippa was resourceful, but there was only so much one man could do against all the tools Rufina had at her disposal.

It is what it is, he told himself. *There is nothing you can do to help them right now. Focus on staying alive.*

Yet he felt paralyzed with indecision, the weight of Lydia's gaze making him want to scream. Making him want to lash out, because where were the Six? Why had they abandoned their marked so easily? Not just the marked, but the whole of Mudamora.

A shriek sounded overhead, and Lydia stiffened. Killian threw himself on top of her, pressing his gloved hand against her mouth to silence the scream that would summon the deimos patrolling the skies.

Because in denying Lydia the chance to steal life to ease the hunger burning inside of her, Killian had become her enemy. And the enemy of her enemy was her friend.

Her body jerked back and forth beneath him, and Killian prayed the cloth he'd wrapped around her hands stayed in place.

She'd gotten her hands on him once. Had stolen life from him in the few seconds before he wrenched away, and the memory of the sensation made his skin crawl.

"Shhh," he whispered even as he felt her face press against him, trying to bite him around the gag. "They'll move on soon enough."

She only struggled harder. Made desperate mewling sounds.

"Stop." He pressed his face into her matted hair. "I need you to fight this. Need you to come back to me."

As the thud of the deimos's wings faded, he let go of her. Lydia's voice was garbled but clear enough for him to understand as she said, "I hate you."

It wasn't the first time she'd said it, but each time was a twist of the knife embedded in his gut. It was the hunger that drove the words, not her heart, but if she didn't master the darkness in her, how long would it be until the hunger consumed her entirely? Killian didn't acknowledge the vitriol, only retrieved the floating paddle and carried on deeper into the forest.

The trees grew denser, although equally dead and rotten, forcing him to backtrack and find different routes inland. Making him question whether there was a route to solid ground or whether he'd be forced to head back to the lake with the dawn. Or worse, get stuck and be forced to wade through the fouled water containing who knew what sort of creatures.

Though none more dangerous than the one he'd have to carry in his arms.

"Shit," he growled. "Shit, shit!"

Lydia only chuckled around her gag, the sound making his stomach turn. Killian opened his mouth to tell her to be quiet when a light ahead caught his eye.

Not the eerie green glow of more fungus, but the yellow flicker of lamplight.

How had Rufina's men found them? How had they moved so quickly?

Then a voice reached his ears.

Not the sharp bark of hunting soldiers, but the soft, wordless song of a woman.

Killian hesitated a heartbeat, then paddled closer, a large hillock appearing through the trees. There was a small cabin atop it, the glowing windows flung open so that the occupant's song could spill forth.

Lydia tensed, seeming to dislike the voice. Yet there was something about it that drew Killian nearer. Jumping out, he hauled the small vessel out of the water and then hesitated. He didn't want to face the unknown with her trussed over his shoulder, but neither did he trust that she wouldn't find some way to escape in his absence.

Cursing under his breath, Killian checked that the fabric he'd wrapped around her hands was secure. Then he lifted Lydia into his arms, gritting his teeth as she thrashed. "Be still."

He ignored her scowl as he carried her up the spongy slope to the cabin. The smell of woodsmoke overpowered the sulfur of the dead forest, and the grass beneath his feet was lush and alive. An island of life in a swamp of death. Killian fought the urge to walk faster.

The cabin was small and made of roughly hewn logs, but lace-trimmed pink curtains hung in the window, and the voice . . . Something about it soothed his battered soul. Flipping Lydia over his shoulder, Killian reached out to knock on the door, only for it to open, revealing an old woman with a long grey braid over one shoulder. The weight of her presence was something he'd only felt once before in his life, when he'd received his mark as a child.

Killian fought the urge to fall to his knees.

The stooped old woman smiled at him. "Come inside, dear ones. I've been waiting for you."

2

TERIANA

"Where is Marcus?"

All three men stared at her. Well, two men plus a boy, because for all Austornic was legatus of the Fifty-First legion, he was thirteen years old. That he was skinny as a rake and his forehead only came up to Teriana's chin didn't help his cause when it came to treating him seriously.

Commandant Wex cleared his throat. "Gone."

Teriana drew in a steadying breath that did next to nothing to calm her nerves. She'd slept not a wink since Marcus had shattered her heart and abandoned her in Senator Valerius's villa last night, all her hours dedicated to piecing together exactly what had happened from the bits of information she'd gleaned from Austornic's men, who were just as keen to gossip as the Thirty-Seventh.

Central to what she'd learned was that Legatus Hostus of the Twenty-Ninth had been tasked with hunting Marcus down.

Marcus had told her dark things about Hostus. Austornic's men had told her worse. The legatus of the Twenty-Ninth was not only a sadist, but apparently also a *cannibal*, and more than a few of his men had adopted his proclivities. Each time she blinked, Teriana saw Hostus's green eyes. Felt his hands on her as he'd restrained her, his breath hot. The line his knife had scored down her neck was still sore. *There will be a reckoning for this.*

"Be more specific," she said between her teeth.

Neither answered. Which was so gods-damned typical. There were dozens of players in this political mess of power games, all with agendas she couldn't begin to keep straight, but despite the fact that Teriana was at the heart of it all, everyone wanted to keep her in the dark. For her own gods-damned good.

To keep her *safe.*

The only thing they had told her was that blame for everything fell at the feet of Lucius Cassius. The proconsul of Celendor aimed to rule all of Reath and did not care whether he had to blackmail, murder, or subjugate everyone he crossed paths with to do it. Cassius had tried to have Marcus and his family murdered, but Marcus had killed the assassins. One, apparently, by caving in his skull with a marble statue—the description of which Teriana could have done without. All of which had been quietly cleaned up by his mother and sister while his father argued Marcus's case in the Senate, because apparently Cassius was trying to claim Marcus's unsanctioned departure was treason and deserving of execution.

And it was not yet midmorning.

Teriana's scowl grew, but beneath her anger, panic loomed. "At least tell me if he's safe."

"Domitius convinced the Senate that while Marcus's choice to depart against orders was impulsive and deserving of reprimand, that it is not treason," Valerius finally said. "A stern letter will be drafted. The precise language is currently under debate."

A stern letter.

Teriana tucked a loose lock of hair back into the wrappings holding it off her face, already sick of the bureaucracy. Knowing that was all she'd get from Valerius, she shifted her glare to Wex. Marcus's mentor was unreadable, but she suspected the man who ran the legion school of Lescendor had a soldier's opinion of politicians. What's more, she *knew* he had a soft spot for his library mouse. "Does that mean Hostus will stand down?"

Wex exhaled slowly, then said, "No. With Hostus's men dead by Marcus's own hand, the Twenty-Ninth will be on the hunt with vengeance in their hearts. There was bad blood between them before and this will only have made things worse."

"But as long as Marcus makes it to the stem here"—Teriana held up her roughly sketched map showing the xenthier stem that led from Celendor to Bardeen—"before Hostus's men, then there is no catching him. They won't pursue him through the Bardeen stem to Arinoquia. Correct?"

Wex's eyes flicked to Austornic, who shifted uncomfortably because the location of the stems was supposed to be a secret.

"Marcus showed me a master document with all the mapped and unmapped stems across the East. Your men only confirmed what I already knew." Not entirely true, because while Marcus *had* shown her the map, it had only been for a moment. But the pretense had been enough to loosen the lips of Austornic's primus on the matter.

"Teriana," Austornic said gently, "sharing that particular map is considered—"

She gave him a flat stare, and he broke off.

Wex circled the library, occasionally taking sips from the glass of cucumber water in his hand. "This is a good lesson for you, Austornic. You're used to functioning within the confines of Lescendor, where everyone plays by the rules. Not so in the real world, where the rules are broken for any number of reasons. Where the players on the board are not pieces of marble but human beings with their own goals, ambitions, and"—he glanced at Teriana—"lusts motivating their moves."

She scratched her chin with her middle finger, but rather than taking insult, Wex gave her a sad smile. "Hostus might well hold the distinction of being the cruelest legatus in active service. That said, he's no fool. He was trained to have contingencies in play, which means that he'd be prepared for Marcus to escape. Prepared for him to head to Bardeen. Which is why Marcus"—he tapped her map—"didn't take this route."

The palms of her hands turned cold. "But it's the fastest route to Bardeen."

"No," Austornic said. "It's just the most direct."

"Madness." Valerius shook his head even as Austornic walked to the map of the Empire framed on the library wall, running a hand over his shorn dark hair as he considered it.

"Why madness?" Their reaction made her stomach roil with tension. "You think he'll make a mistake? That Hostus will catch him?"

Visions of Marcus being dragged before the Twenty-Ninth's legatus filled her mind's eye, and it was all Teriana could do to keep from vomiting as her imagination supplied all the awful things Hostus would do to him.

"There are options." Austornic's eyes moved over the unlabeled map as though it bore every xenthier stem that the Empire had ever found, which, in his mind's eye, it obviously did. "But I can't find a path with less than eight jumps."

"Impossible." Valerius ran a hand through his thinning blond hair. "The strain is too great for anyone to bear. He'll die if he tries."

Die?

"It's been done," Wex replied. "It's not impossible, else I wouldn't have allowed it."

What had been done?

"The rule of three." Austornic's voice rose above the other two. "Never more than three jumps in a row."

"What are you talking about!" Her words came out in a shout.

All three exchanged looks, but it was Austornic who answered. "Traveling through xenthier takes a physical toll. I'm sure you are familiar with the sensation of dizziness and disorientation, yes?" When she nodded, he continued, "There is endless speculation in the collegium as to the mechanics of xenthier, theories about the impact on the body from extreme acceleration and deceleration that I won't bore you with, because you only care about the consequences."

"Thank you for sparing me."

"Each time you travel is like taking a minor knock on the head. Something easily recovered from. But if one travels through paths in quick succession, each knock on the head compounds on the next. Like being hit over and over, with obvious results. The rule is no more than three jumps in the space of a week to avoid lasting harm. What Marcus is doing is akin to a battering ram to the skull."

"Does he know that?" She pressed her fingers to her own skull, feeling phantom pain within it. "Never mind. Of course he knows."

"It's possible he came up with a path with fewer jumps that allowed him to reach Hydrilla before the Twenty-Ninth," Wex said. "There are hundreds and hundreds of paths across the Empire, and puzzles always were his strength. It's equally possible that he determined it couldn't be done and has gone to ground somewhere in the Empire."

Except Marcus didn't believe in the word *couldn't* when it pertained to him, which meant he'd have done it, risks and all. "But you said others survived many consecutive jumps?"

But before any of them could answer, a servant appeared at the door with a tray bearing a folded note. Valerius crossed the room, snatching up the scrap of paper, his already grim expression darkening further as he lifted his eyes to meet Teriana's. "Cassius has agreed to meet with you."

3

MARCUS

"What's wrong with him? Why is he getting worse?"

Titus's voice cut through the haze, but Marcus kept his eyes squeezed shut. The fog thickening his thoughts refused to clear, made worse by a throbbing ache in his skull that made Marcus want to curl in on himself. Made him want to hide from light and sound, because they made the pain so much worse.

He had only vague memories of what had occurred since he'd woken in Titus's camp without his armor, the letter Wex had given him, or any of the other proof that he'd been in Celendrial. He'd faded in and out of consciousness, but the same dream repeated, of Titus leaning over him and whispering, *I might not be able to stop the Thirty-Seventh from having their revenge on you. They're angry, Marcus. And they're not the same legion as when you left.* Every time he regained consciousness, his first thought was, *What has happened to them?*

He hadn't been moved from the floor of Titus's tent, and he vaguely heard the sounds of legionnaires breaking camp, the air smelling of wet ash as they doused cook fires. Marcus's name was mentioned often, but not half as often as another word.

Deserter.

"It has to be a head injury, sir. From when he was beaten."

"You said his skull wasn't cracked!"

"It's not, but he's got a black eye, so we know he was hit. Head injuries can be unpredictable like that."

"No," Marcus tried to say, but it only came out as unintelligible noise.

"Fix him!" Titus snarled. "You're a fucking surgeon—do something!"

"There's nothing to be done, Titus! Not even Racker could fix what's wrong with him. He's a dead man, sure and true."

A dead man.

The weight of that pierced through the haze, the burden of failure making Marcus want to scream.

"Shit!" Titus raged. "Shit shit shit! If he dies, the Thirty-Seventh will blame us!"

"Why? They'd have killed him anyway."

"Because it's different!" Titus's voice was like knives in Marcus's brain. "They need to be the ones to kill him. It has to be them. Don't you see?"

Merciful silence.

"How you choose to manage the complexities of this situation is up to you," the surgeon eventually replied. "But he's not going to survive the journey to Aracam. By your leave, I've other patients to see to who I can actually treat."

"Go!"

The surgeon saluted and departed.

"There's irony to this, you know," Titus said.

Marcus first thought the comment was directed at him, but then it struck him that the language Titus spoke wasn't Cel but Arinoquian. "All the times I've tried to kill him and now I need him alive, so he'll die to spite me. Felix won't believe that I just happened upon him. He'll think I've had him locked up somewhere all this time, and instead of cheering me for delivering their piece-of-shit deserter, they'll come for my blood."

"Better to dispose of him then?" asked a vaguely familiar voice. "Burn the body?"

"Too many of my men know he's here. I'll never keep it a secret." Titus's footfalls were like thunder as he stomped around Marcus. "Why does everything go wrong?"

Marcus forced himself to crack open one eye. An old man with the mahogany skin of a Gamdeshian stood with Titus. The same one who'd been present when Marcus had first woken in Titus's tent. But the pain forced him to close his eyelid again to hold back the stabbing light.

"He may yet live." The Gamdeshian's voice was soothing. "Do not give up on all you have gained, young master. You are the commander of a great army, and soon you will be the one to lead the Empire to victory over these lands."

"You're only interested in the reward you'll get for aiding me," Titus replied sourly. "But know this: if I go down, so do you. Get some water in him and keep him alive." Commands given, Titus spun on his heel and marched away.

Hands grasped Marcus's body, rolling him, and then fingers peeled back his eyelids. Light and pain stabbed them, everything a blur.

When his eyes focused, it was to find the Gamdeshian kneeling before him. He was old, skin heavy with wrinkles and brown hair heavily laced with white. His left ear sagged beneath the weight of the silver rings piercing it, and his dark brown eyes gleamed with intelligence.

"I am Zaide," the Gamdeshian said, pressing his hand to his chest. "Advisor to the legatus."

Why does Titus have a Gamdeshian as an advisor? Where is Ereni? "How did I get here?" Marcus's words were slurred.

Zaide's head tilted, eyes scrutinizing Marcus's face. "You've no memory?"

His vision split into two. Then three, and Marcus shook his head to focus it, only for knives of pain to stab him in the skull. "No."

"You were found a few miles from here," Zaide said. "In civilian clothing."

That . . . that wasn't right. Wasn't possible. "You're lying. You stole my armor. My possessions."

"Why would I do such a thing?" Zaide's frown was confused but his eyes gleamed far too bright. "I didn't even know who you were until the legatus's men recognized you. The Cel all look the same to me."

"Liar." Marcus tried to make his voice clear, but it was so slurred he could barely understand himself. "Who are you?"

"It is you who are the liar," Zaide replied. "All the legatus's men agree on it. Liar. Traitor. Deserter. They've been saying it since you disappeared." He cupped a hand behind the silver rings of his ear. "Listen."

Deserter.

Deserter.

Deserter.

His head felt on the verge of exploding, each thud of his heart like thunder, the pain so bad that tears ran down Marcus's cheeks. Yet even through the fog, it was clear to him that he was being framed. That when he'd stumbled out of the xenthier and fallen unconscious, it had been the Forty-First who'd found him. And when no one had come through the xenthier to provide Marcus a witness to his story, Titus had decided to take advantage. This man Zaide was nothing but a creature Titus had paid to give credence to the story when it was presented to the Thirty-Seventh. When it was presented to Felix, who had every reason to believe that Marcus had deserted to be with Teriana.

The risk to Titus was next to nothing, because when the truth came out that Marcus hadn't deserted, it wouldn't be Titus's hands that were bloody from Marcus's execution.

It would be the Thirty-Seventh's.

"They say the girl you abandoned them for was a beauty beyond measure." Zaide patted Marcus on the cheek, each impact a hammer against his skull. "It is known that love turns even the cleverest of men into fools. Perhaps the Thirty-Seventh will take pity upon you for your weakness. Perhaps its legatus will forgive you for your mistakes. Perhaps in the time it will take us to reach Aracam, you'll find a way to talk yourself back into power. But then again, perhaps not."

"It won't matter if I'm dead." The words came out as incomprehensible noise.

Zaide gave him a pitying look that didn't reach his dark eyes. "Death will come for you, legatus, but there is enough life left in you to survive a while yet. You've fought death too long and hard to surrender to it easily, and I think suffering is an old bedfellow."

Marcus tried to answer, but his mouth couldn't seem to form words.

Shouts of alarm abruptly filled the air of the camp, and then horns bellowed.

Attack. The camp was coming under attack.

Zaide leapt to his feet, a growl of anger that made Marcus's skin crawl pouring from his lips. His eyes snapped to Marcus, and it was like staring into the darkest depths of night.

"Keep breathing, legatus," he commanded. "He has purpose for you yet."

Then without another word, Zaide raced out of the tent, leaving Marcus to sink down into darkness, his last thoughts for Teriana.

I'm sorry.

4

KILLIAN

The weight of being in the presence of one of the Seven rendered Killian speechless, but he carried Lydia into the cottage, Hegeria shutting the door firmly behind him.

"You can put her there." She gestured to a small bed made up neatly with a patchwork quilt. "Tea?"

"Do you have anything stronger?" he croaked, carefully setting

Lydia on the bed. Her eyes were still black pits, and she watched the goddess intently. He'd hoped she'd grasp at the chance that Hegeria could free her from the hunger, but those eyes suggested Lydia saw the goddess as a threat rather than salvation.

Hegeria sniffed in disgust, then shoved her long white braid over her shoulder. "Falling into the bottle during moments of adversity is a slippery slope, Killian. Especially when you need your wits about you."

Feeling profoundly chastised, he said, "Tea would be lovely."

"Help yourself to a biscuit." She gestured to the plate sitting on the small table, then put the kettle on the stove. "You'll feel better with something in your stomach." When he hesitated, she added, "I made them myself while I waited for you."

The last thing Killian wanted to do was be rude to a goddess, so he sat on one of the small chairs and took a biscuit, and swiftly discovered that Hegeria had the same feelings about sugar as she did about strong drink. Forcing himself to chew and swallow, he watched as she circled the table to kneel next to the bed. "Careful," he warned, rising to his feet, but Hegeria waved him away.

Ignoring Lydia's glare, the goddess curved a hand around her cheek, the gesture as tender as a grandmother's touch. "Oh, dear one, he has his claws in deep." She sighed. "I warned you this would be a hard road, but even I didn't foresee this moment."

Ice pooled in Killian's stomach at her dismay. "Can you help her? Can you break the Corrupter's hold on her?"

"Yes." Hegeria dropped her hand from Lydia's cheek. "And no."

It felt suddenly very hard to breathe.

"I cannot take away her mark. But what she chooses to do with the powers she has is her choice." Turning her head, she met his gaze. "As it is *your* choice, for do not believe for a heartbeat that my dark brother does not reach out his grasping hands to take *all* of our chosen."

Killian had felt that touch. Felt the compulsion. "She's beyond choices. I don't think she can see her way clear of him. I don't think she even cares to try. The . . . the *hunger* for what she takes is too overwhelming. It's only getting worse."

Lydia was watching them. Listening. Killian's instincts flared a heartbeat before Lydia lunged at Hegeria, snapped bindings falling away from her reaching hands.

Hegeria had Lydia by the throat, though he hadn't seen the goddess move. Not squeezing but holding her in place with the terrifying strength of a god.

Lydia clawed at her arms and tore the fabric of Hegeria's dress, but the goddess's face was impassive. "She is not yours," she said, and it echoed through the cottage like thunder. "Release your hold and crawl back amongst the villains where you belong!"

There was nothing human in Lydia's scream as she ripped away her gag. The sound was both fury and agony, and though it might be the death of him, Killian tried to go to her.

Only to find himself fixed in place, unable to move. Unable to do anything but watch in horror as the love of his life writhed in the grip of a god.

Hegeria's eyes pooled into inhuman voids, all colors and none. "Release your hold!"

"She is mine!" a voice that sounded like breaking glass said from Lydia's lips. "You have lost her to me, sister!"

"Not yet," Hegeria said between her teeth. "Not ever!"

Lydia opened her mouth, and inky black smoke poured from her lips. The mass of smoke swirled around the room with a shriek of rage, then it exploded outwards.

The power holding Killian released him, and he fell to his knees as tiny pieces of the cottage rained down, slivers of wood slicing his exposed skin. Ignoring the pain, he scrambled upright. Lydia was limp in Hegeria's arms, both of them panting in exhaustion. But the sight of her green eyes filled him with relief, even as his instincts screamed that it wasn't over.

"He's not going to let me go," Lydia sobbed. "He'll never let me go."

Hegeria ignored Lydia, her focus beyond the ruin of her cottage. Killian looked upward, and his heart broke into a gallop. The sky was full of oily black smoke, circling in an ominous and vast cyclone above their heads.

"Take her." Hegeria pushed Lydia into his arms.

She was boneless and limp, chest rising and falling in rapid pants as though she'd been running. Killian lowered her to the ground. "He's coming," she whispered. "Killian, the Corrupter is coming. You need to go. You need to run!"

"I'm with you to the end." He pulled her close and pressed his lips to her forehead. "No matter what the end."

The cyclone descended, and with it came the awful howling. Like a thousand, like *ten* thousand, tortured voices all shrieking their agony.

"Steady now, Lord Calorian!" Hegeria's skirt brushed his elbow. "If it is a fight he wants, a fight he shall have!"

A stream of black mist broke away from the cyclone, flying toward them with a piercing wail. Hegeria lifted her hand, and the mist exploded with a concussive blast that made his ears ring.

But the Corrupter was not so easily defeated.

Stream after stream lanced toward them. Hegeria met each one with her own power, the noise deafening and the ground shaking. The attacks only increased in frequency, the air a blur of blackness, the goddess's jaw tight with strain.

She was losing.

Losing to the Corrupter, and Killian's mind recoiled from the reason. From the truth that the Corrupter's influence had undermined the faith people had in Hegeria. In all of the Six. With his own eyes, Killian was witnessing the consequences.

Hegeria staggered and fell to one knee. She struggled upright, blocking a dozen attacks in a matter of seconds.

But one got past her flanks.

Killian watched with helpless horror as the oily stream of blackness struck Hegeria in the side. A cry tore from her lips as she fell, the earth shuddering as though it were a tower that had fallen, not an old woman.

Pushing herself upright, Hegeria blocked another attack. But as though bolstered by having landed a blow, the cyclone birthed a dozen streams of blackness, all racing together.

Killian held Lydia tighter and closed his eyes. *Please,* he silently begged the higher power he served. The god who'd given him his mark. *Please, Tremon, do not leave her to fight alone.*

When he opened his eyes, it was to discover not salvation but the streams of the Corrupter's power drawing closer, the air so cold his breath misted around him. All the light in the world seemed to disappear in shadow, and then—

Five columns of white light burst through the darkness, the ground shaking as five figures landed on the ground. Killian blinked away tears from the sudden brightness, and his breath caught as his eyes latched on a familiar armored form. "Tremon?"

The god who'd marked him gave him a wink, then reached down a hand to pull Hegeria to her feet. "Sister."

"You took bloody long enough," she muttered. "As is your habit."

Tremon laughed, then turned to face the attack, the rest of the Six forming a perimeter around Killian and Lydia. They were human in size but had the presence of giants, beautiful and yet terrifying to behold. The pressure formed by their presence made it almost impossible to breathe, Killian's heart stuttering in his chest as his eyes skipped from Tremon to Madoria to Gespurn to Lern to Yara and back to Hegeria.

The Six had not abandoned the world.

Far from it.

Seething with rage, the cyclone descended in a screaming wrath of darkness but was met by a brilliant glow of light as the Six lifted their hands. Killian threw himself over Lydia, closing his eyes and covering his ears as the might of the gods collided. The ground shuddered, as though Reath herself cringed away from the violence of the moment.

Then all fell still.

For a long moment, Killian didn't move. *Couldn't* move, if he was being honest with himself. Then he managed to push up on one elbow. Lydia stared with wide eyes, the half-moon tattoo stark against her blanched skin. "Is . . . is he defeated?"

"It is a battle won in a war without end," Tremon answered. "For a time, our brother will need to rely on his chosen to do his fell deeds, as it should be. The toll of battles between the divine is too great for it to be otherwise."

"Reath weeps." Yara pressed a palm to the ground, even as Madoria closed her eyes and said, "The sea is in turmoil."

Gespurn, who looked for all the world like Agrippa's friend Baird, snorted in disgust. "We should not be here." Then he disappeared in a swirl of white mist. Lern and Yara simply vanished, yet as Madoria began to dissipate, Lydia reached forward to catch hold of the goddess's dress of seaweed. "Teriana. Is she all right?"

Madoria smiled, teeth white against her midnight skin. As she leaned down to cup Lydia's cheek, her multitude of braids clicked as seashells and bits of coral knocked together. "Her road is as difficult as your own, child, but Teriana is exactly where she needs to be."

Then she dissolved into a froth of water that swirled away on the breeze, leaving them with Tremon and Hegeria.

Killian dragged himself to his feet, helping Lydia upright. Only to stagger as Tremon pounded him on the back. "You've done good work, boy. Far cry from the smart-ass little brat who fell off his pony." As Killian met the god's fathomless eyes, Tremon grinned and drew his finger through the air, parting it like shears through fabric to create a slash of brilliant white. Tremon reached into it and extracted a familiar sword, handing it to him. "Your father is proud of you, Killian."

Then he disappeared.

Killian stared at his father's sword, which he'd left with his lieutenant, Sonia, for safekeeping before he'd left for Derin. He was so overwhelmed he couldn't speak. His father's last words to him had been that he was a disappointment, and the weight of that had sat on his conscience ever since. To know that his father was watching, that he was proud, meant more than Killian could ever begin to explain.

"It is far from over," Hegeria said. "Enemies approach from all sides, for even in the lands where we have been forgotten, there are many who reach into the darkness. And my brother always reaches back." Gripping Lydia's shoulders, the goddess gave her a tight smile. "You will never lose the temptation, dear one. All we've done is given you the freedom to fight it."

A battle won. But not the war.

Hegeria rounded on Killian. "You cannot fight the enemy alone. Your companions flee south toward Anukastre. Find them."

Then she was gone.

5

TERIANA

"This is utter madness, Teriana." Valerius tossed Cassius's note onto the table. "Might as well walk into a dragon's den and bare your throat. Your mother would gut me like a fish if she knew I'd allowed it."

"I don't need your permission or your protection," Teriana snapped, but in truth her bravado was false. Every part of her wanted to fall to her knees and scream at what she'd been told. *You can't help him,* logic tried to whisper. *Focus on those you can save.*

Lydia's father pulled a white cloth from the folds of his toga and wiped away the sweat that had formed on his brow. He'd lost the awful jaundice that had plagued him before she'd taken the legions west, but he still did not look healthy. "Perhaps you might share what you aim to achieve by meeting with Cassius. Because if it's to gain the freedom of your people, you are wasting your breath. Cassius wants them as leverage, not only against you but against Marcus. For, rest assured, Cassius will assume he's alive until he has concrete proof otherwise."

Her eyes welled with tears, but Teriana swallowed her grief. "Leverage only works if you have the ability to employ it. With the paths we found deemed nonviable by the Senate, Cassius has no way to control what Marcus does or doesn't do in the West. Nothing's changed."

A lie, because nothing was the same and might never be again.

Valerius gave a grim shake of his head. "Cassius leaned on semantics to get out of being held to the agreement with you. The fact of the matter is that while the terminus in Sibern is most certainly nonviable midwinter due to the extreme cold, the genesis stem in Bardeen *could* be made safe. It's just a matter of quashing the latest rebel leader and her forces and bringing Bardeen back to heel. That could be accomplished by spring, at which time the Sibern terminus can be accessed. And Cassius will, once again, be able to use his leverage."

Gods but Teriana hated that she was a weapon to be used against Marcus by their enemies.

"You speak of quelling Bardeen as though it were a simple thing," Wex said. "Once the rebels learn where the stem at Hydrilla goes and who is on the end of it, they will make our lives very difficult indeed."

"It was the Thirty-Seventh that broke the back of the last Bardenese rebellion," Austornic murmured to Teriana. "It's said that the Bardenese still curse Marcus's name, for it was he who captured Hydrilla."

Judging from his dark hair and the light brown hue of his skin, Austornic was Bardenese by heritage, but she heard nothing of the nation in his accent. If she closed her eyes, the boy would have sounded as patrician as Valerius himself. Yet she couldn't help but wonder if he felt anything for the nation that gave him his blood.

"Marcus's list of enemies is long and dangerous." Valerius took a long drink of water.

Teriana's pulse quickened even as her throat tightened. *We are enemies, Teriana*, Marcus's voice whispered in her head. *And while you might think you love me today, one day soon you are going to come to hate me.*

Teriana didn't *think* she loved him. She knew she did. But she was also furious at him for leaving her behind. Yet the anger was not enough to drown her fear of the future Marcus foresaw, in which he believed her love would turn to hate.

Realizing the trio was watching her, she said, "I know Cassius isn't just going to hand over my people. Which is why I'm going to negotiate with him."

When they all frowned as though she'd spoken gibberish, Teriana added, "I have leverage of my own."

"This is too dangerous by far." Valerius again wiped away the sweat, reminding Teriana that his health was not good. "I've already lost Lydia. I won't lose you to Cassius as well."

"Be wary of making accusations, my old friend," Wex said. "While we all know that Cassius is the culprit in your daughter's disappearance, there is no proof. No witnesses. No . . ."

He trailed off, but they all knew the word the commandant had avoided. *Body.*

Grief swelled in Teriana's stomach. "I spoke to Marcus before the assassins attacked. I asked him if he knew anything about what had happened to Lydia. If Cassius had harmed her. He said that all he knew was that Cassius had been using Lydia to win the elections. That Cassius didn't trust him with details, so . . ." She tried and failed to remember Marcus's exact words. "If something happened to her, he didn't know anything about it."

"Of no great surprise," Valerius said. "Using legion resources for a personal assassination is not the sort of risk Cassius would take." For all his voice was steady, Teriana felt the weight of his disappointment. During the endless months that she'd believed Lydia had betrayed her, Valerius had been burdened with growing certainty that Lydia hadn't run away, but rather had been murdered. Worse still, he'd been powerless to do anything to strike back at the man who'd killed her.

But Teriana was not powerless. Whether he wanted to admit it or not, Cassius needed her. If he wanted to keep her, he was going to have to pay for it.

6

LYDIA

A cold wind blew over Lydia. She shivered, taking in the shattered remains of the cottage spread across the empty hillock, the only evidence of the battle between the Six and their dark brother.

That, and the absence of the wild hunger that had consumed her heart.

Except in its place, a riot of emotion was threatening to drown her as she struggled to come to terms with what she'd said. What she'd done. What she had *become.*

Drawing in a ragged breath, Lydia twisted on her knees to look up at Killian. His dark hair clung to the side of his face, olive skin smeared with dirt. "I am so sorry," she croaked. "Killian, I am so sorry. I'm so sorry. So—"

He pulled her against him, silencing her rush of words. "Do not apologize." His breath was warm against her ear. "It's not your fault. Everything you did was because the Corrupter had his claws dug into you, so the blame is his."

Lydia desperately wanted to believe him. But that would require lying to herself.

She'd made the choice to open the door to the Seventh god for the sake of the strength that it would give her, which meant she was responsible. She was to blame. Every time Lydia blinked, she saw the carnage that had been left in her wake when she had gone down into the dungeons in Helatha. With every breath she took, she remembered the flow of life that had flooded into her as she'd drained men and women to dust. With every heartbeat, she remembered trying over and over to do the same to Killian. The words that flowed from her tongue had been evil and spiteful but still very much her own, because a large part of her wanted to keep the power that came from the dark side of her mark. In the moment, she'd resented Killian and Hegeria for forcing her to give it up.

The Corrupter's claws had been pulled free of her, but the door back to him was still there. Still tempting Lydia with all that lay beyond, her fingers reaching for the handle as her eyes focused on the rich glow of life surrounding Killian, the press of his skin against hers making her ache with the need to *take.*

With a start, Lydia wrenched out of his grip, then pressed her fingers into the mud. "I . . . I can't," she whispered, knowing that it was no explanation. "Please don't touch me."

"Lydia?"

Sensing him reaching for her, Lydia cringed away. "I'll hurt you."

"Not anymore, you won't," Killian replied. "Hegeria broke his hold on you."

Her eyes stung with shame and grief, no part of her wanting to confess the truth, but neither was she willing to risk him by lying. "She broke his hold, but they couldn't take away the part of me that opened the door to him in the first place."

Killian didn't answer, and though cowardice pleaded she look anywhere but at him, Lydia forced herself to lift her head. He was sitting in the dirt next to her, elbows resting on his knees, brown eyes on the sword Tremon had given him. His father's sword. A line of blood ran down his stubbled cheek from where he'd been cut during the explosion, and his hands were marked with scrapes and bruises from escaping Rufina. No doubt he had worse beneath his clothes.

Yet rather than feeling compelled to take off his shirt and heal him, all Lydia saw was the rich glow of life made sweeter by his mark. All she felt was the desire to take it, to feel the flood of ecstasy as his life bolstered hers, making her strong. Her heartbeat accelerated, her breath turning to rapid little pants, and it took far too long for her to notice that he was watching her, dark eyes grim.

"I heard what Hegeria said." His voice matched his eyes. "There is darkness in everyone. But if it were impossible to control, the Seventh wouldn't be warring against us. He'd have already won."

"It's more difficult for me," Lydia snapped, irrationally angry that he thought it was so easy. That he thought she was like him, never straying from the right path.

"The Six stepped onto the mortal plane to give you back your freedom to choose what to do with your power, Lydia." Killian climbed to his feet. "Don't squander it."

There was little she could say in response. Lydia stood, straightening her clothes and looking anywhere but at him.

"There is little chance that Rufina's scouts aren't aware we're here, and I suspect they will arrive soon enough. We need to go." He started down the hillock to where the boat was pulled up on the ground. "Hegeria said that our companions are on the run south, which must mean that Agrippa and Baird successfully got away with Malahi. We need to find them and get out of Derin."

"How are we going to do that?" she asked. "It will be like finding a needle in a haystack, never mind that Rufina is hunting for the same needle. Aren't we better off making our own way?"

"We came here to rescue Malahi because we need a tender to drive back the blight. All of this, all that we have endured, has been to achieve that goal." When she was silent, he added, "Are you really willing to leave her with Agrippa? For all he seems to have turned on Rufina, I haven't forgotten that he once led her armies. Nor that he was once part of the Cel army that holds Teriana prisoner while they conquer Arinoquia. The only thing I trust about that man is that he'll look out for himself first. We need to get Malahi away from him before he sells her to the highest bidder."

Shame filled Lydia, for though he was right that Malahi had always been the priority, she'd not spared one thought for the fate of Mudamora's queen since learning that Agrippa and Baird had spirited her out of Helatha. Her every thought had been for rescuing Killian from Rufina's dungeons, and since then, her every thought had been for herself. "South, then?"

"Into Anukastre. That has to be Agrippa's plan."

"But isn't Anukastre a death trap?" She climbed into the boat. "Why would he go there?"

From what she knew, the nation that shared a border with both Derin and Mudamora was a desert that almost never saw rain. But worse still were the Anuk themselves—nomads who were uniquely capable of surviving in the wasteland's extreme conditions and who were notoriously willing to slaughter anyone who crossed into their lands. They raided Mudamora almost constantly, their favored target the Rowenes gold mines along the border. Gold mines that Killian had spent months defending in violent conflict, which had earned him a name among the Anuk, most especially with Xadrian, the Crown Prince of Anukastre.

Unbidden, the memory of being trapped with Killian on a boulder in the middle of a flash flood of debris filled her mind's eye. Of standing between the Anuk's deadly storm of arrows and Killian, Xadrian screaming at his men not to shoot, lest Killian pull Lydia down with him. The Anuk wouldn't hurt her because she was marked by Hegeria, but they'd be more than delighted to take revenge against Killian.

"Agrippa will go into the desert because there's no other choice," Killian said, interrupting her thoughts. "There are only so many ways in and out of Derin and they will all be watched. My guess is that Agrippa is banking on Rufina's belief that the border with the sand kingdom guards itself."

Lydia nodded, mostly because she didn't believe Hegeria would lead them astray. "That doesn't explain how *we* are going to find them. The border is large, and once they reach the desert itself . . ."

"First we get out of this swamp and find horses and supplies," Killian answered. "Then we worry about finding them."

There was a clipped tone to his voice that suggested he wished the conversation to be over, and Lydia's tongue fell silent even as her imagination went wild as to what was going on in Killian's mind.

Gods . . . what he must think of her.

Bad enough that she'd lost control in such a horrific way, but knowing that she still could barely control the dark half of her gift? Lydia bit the insides of her cheeks, trying to curb the burning sting of tears in her eyes.

She had not thought this was how it would go. She'd been so certain that she would be able to embrace the Corrupter's power while she needed it to free Killian from Rufina, and then would be able to shove it away. Bury it beneath a mountain of will and never unleash it again.

Whether she'd underestimated the Corrupter's control or overestimated her own strength, Lydia could not have said. Only that the desire to reach out and *take* clouded her every thought, Killian's proximity much like having a glass of water set in front of an individual who has just stumbled out of the desert. The desire to take hold of it was—

Her breath caught, because her hand was stretched out toward him. She shoved it into her pocket.

Killian had noticed, though he said nothing.

"You should tie me up," she whispered. "So that I don't hurt you."

"No." The word exited his lips like a cracking whip. "Unless you want to spend the rest of your life trussed up, you'll learn to control it. Or live with the consequences."

Then he put his back into the oars and rowed them through the night.

7

TERIANA

The sun was high in the sky and scorching hot when Teriana and Valerius set out to meet Cassius. The narrow paths were shaded by ancient trees growing to either side, the air thick with the scent of stone pine and cypress, yet within minutes, Lydia's father was breathing hard, sweat dripping down his golden skin. "Are you well?" she asked. "Should I send a servant for water?"

"Well as I ever will be." He wiped sweat from his brow.

It had been his fear of his own mortality that had driven Appius Valerius to betroth Lydia to Cassius. Fear that his nephew and heir, Vibius, would mistreat her. The thought drove Teriana to ask, "Where is Vibius?"

Valerius was silent for a long moment, then he shrugged. "He's been confined to an institution, I'm afraid. He requires daily care and it is not expected that he'll recover."

Teriana blinked.

"After I discovered he was conspiring with Cassius, I exiled him from my home. Lo and behold, no sooner was he absent from my life did my health improve."

"He was poisoning you?"

Valerius nodded. "So it would seem. I disinherited him after I found out, and all that I have will go to a distant cousin when death finally claims me. But as I continued to search for Lydia and became more convinced that she'd met a dark end, I had one of the retired legionnaires in my service track him down and put him to question. During the removal of his testicles, Vibius confessed that he'd been dosing my wine."

Teriana felt the blood drain from her face, because this was not the confession she'd anticipated.

"He unfortunately fouled himself during the conversation with my guard," Valerius continued. "That's not the sort of filth you want in an open wound, and he succumbed to infection that went untreated for a shocking length of time before he was brought to the physicians collegium for treatment. They did what they could, however the infection seemed to have gotten into his head and eaten away at his mind, so now all he does is jabber and drool. My sister, of course, was devastated, so I spared no expense for his ongoing care. Tragic, of course."

"My sympathies." What else could she say? Though Appius Valerius was educated, cultured, and considered one of the more altruistic senators on the hill, the Cel were the cruelest people on all of Reath. Some of them just hid it better than others.

They carried on past ancient walls covered with ivy and eventually approached Cassius's estate. Legionnaires stood at the gate, but at their approach, a lean servant with a pinched mouth met them. "Greetings, Senator. With regret, you must be searched before I may allow you to enter. I'm afraid that there are many who conspire against our gracious consul, and caution must overrule manners."

Teriana said nothing as one of the legionnaires stepped toward her. His armor was stamped with a 29 and she clenched her teeth in preparation for the worst, but he only performed the task with dead-eyed efficiency before nodding at the servant. Another legionnaire did the same to Valerius, scowling as he extracted three separate knives from the folds of the senator's clothes.

"One can never be too careful," Lydia's father said with a bland smile. "There are many unsavory individuals in Celendrial's streets these days, I'm afraid."

"The Twenty-Ninth is making short work of those who step out of line," replied the legionnaire searching Valerius.

"Yes, well, sometimes the cure is worse than the disease." Valerius motioned at Teriana. "Come along, dear. We do not wish to keep the consul waiting."

They moved onto the property, Teriana taking it in lest she need to make a quick escape. Where all the other patrician villas were full of old-growth trees and lush gardens that had been tended for generations, Cassius's grounds were barren of life. It was all stone pathways, marble statuary, and elaborate fountains. Cold and devoid of history. A fitting location for the villa that had been erected at the center, which looked more like a political building dedicated to the administration of taxes than a home.

Valerius's lip curled as though he smelled something foul, and he muttered, "Garish eyesore," along with a few other choice insults toward Cassius's taste, though he fell silent as they reached the entrance.

The door was plated with gold, the metal gleaming in the sunlight, but under the hand of the servant leading them, it swung open on silent hinges. A rush of icy cold surged out, dragging gooseflesh to Teriana's skin as she'd not felt since her trek across Sibern. She gritted her teeth and stepped into the dimly lit building. Valerius moved to follow, but the servant blocked his path. "The consul has requested that you remain outside while he meets with Teriana, Senator. Refreshments will be brought to you."

"The audacity—"

Teriana lifted a calming hand. "It will be fine. I'll be fine."

Valerius grimaced but only clasped his arms behind his back as the door swung shut behind her, the dull thud echoing through the cavernous space.

Much like the exterior grounds, Cassius's home was barren of life and color, though there was no doubt that he'd spent a small fortune on the construction. Carved busts graced every alcove, the sconces held oil lamps made of the highest quality glass, and the tiles underfoot were an elaborate mosaic of greys depicting the Cel dragon. Her footfalls echoed no matter how softly she trod, and Teriana found herself rubbing her arms against the growing chill. "Did he build his house out of solid ice?" she muttered. "It's bloody freezing in here."

The servant glanced at her as though she were mad, then said, "Quality construction keeps out the heat. The consul employs only the finest."

In truth, the temperature seemed not to touch the man, nary a goose bump on his bare arms while Teriana was shocked that she couldn't see her breath.

They pressed deeper into the villa, each step causing dread to pool deeper in her stomach. *You can do this,* Teriana reminded herself. *You know what he wants. Know how he thinks. And you have a plan.*

None of which prevented her heart from stuttering as the thin servant stopped before a heavy door. He knocked once, and at a muffled acknowledgment from within, swung it open.

Teriana took a deep breath and stepped inside. Her fear rose to a dizzying frenzy, but she drew in a deep breath and focused on the man before her.

Cassius lounged on a divan before a table of lacquer and gold, a delicate glass of wine held in one hand. The consul of Celendor was of perhaps fifty years of age, his short brown hair combed forward, and his blue eyes small and closely set. He wore the clothes of his office, a tunic and toga, with leather sandals strapped to feet that were strangely smooth. As though some poor servant had spent hours scrubbing and polishing his soles until they were as devoid of calluses as a newborn babe's. Teriana found herself staring at them, not realizing that Cassius had risen until his feet started moving.

"Teriana, you are a vision." He circled the furniture, and she held her breath as he gripped her shoulders with overly warm hands, then kissed both her cheeks. His lips were moist, and she fought the urge to scrub her sleeve over her face as he pulled back, eyes raking over her. "It is easy to see why Marcus has thrown caution to the wind. You are a rare beauty indeed, although not to my particular taste."

"Too young?" She lifted one eyebrow even as every instinct told her to *run*.

"Too defiant." He chucked her gently under the chin, leaving a smear of what she fervently hoped was masseur's oil. "But in an ally, I admire your sort of spirit."

"Oh, we're allies now, are we?"

"That's why you're here, isn't it?"

Teriana rubbed her hands up and down her arms, knowing she was out of her league. Knowing that he was probably ten steps ahead of her. But that didn't mean she couldn't get what she wanted from him. "I'm here to make a deal with you."

"We already have a deal."

"I have a deal with Marcus and with the Senate." She lifted her chin and met his eyes. "I want to make a deal with *you*."

"I'm intrigued." Circling back around to his divan, Cassius perched on the edge. He picked up a bottle of wine and filled two glasses. "Sit. Drink."

Teriana sat on the chair on the opposite side of the table but didn't pick up the glass.

Cassius chuckled. "Don't worry, my dear. I learned many years ago not to, pardon my crassness, shit where I eat." Picking up her glass, he took a sip and then smiled. "See? Perfectly safe."

The last thing she wanted to do was drink anything he served, but Teriana also understood this game. She had watched her mother negotiate difficult deals all her life, and one always needed to be gracious right up to the point one was not. Picking up the glass, she took a sip from the side that didn't have his mouth print, then set it back down. "You have good taste in wine."

Cassius drank from his own cup, then pressed a finger to the side of his nose. "Would you like to know a secret?" Without waiting for her to answer, he said, "I have no palate for wine. Whether the bottle is swill or the costliest vintage, it makes little difference to my tongue. One of my failings, I'm afraid."

Picking up the glass again, Teriana swirled a mouthful across her tongue. "The Lastura vineyards in Atlia. You could feed ten families for a year on the cost of one bottle that you don't appreciate."

Cassius smiled. "Shameful, isn't it?"

The expensive wine turned sour on Teriana's tongue, but she refused to be baited. She was here for a reason, so it was time she got to the point. "We both hold the power to give one another what we each most want. I propose a trade."

"I'm listening."

"I want my people freed. You want secure routes to and from the West so that you can send more legions in pursuit of conquest. Routes better than Bardeen and Sibern."

Cassius sprawled back on his divan, letting out a sigh. "It's not much of an offer, I'm afraid. Another path from Arinoquia to Atlia has been found."

Her heart lurched, and it was with a shaking hand that she picked up a report that he gestured to. Her eyes skimmed over the words, which detailed finding the bodies of dead men floating in the middle of a lake by fisherman. They'd borne the fresh tattoos of path-hunters and each had a sealed letter from Titus. Teriana's hand stopped shaking. "What good is a path that leads to the bottom of a lake? That's even *less* viable than a path to the middle of Sibern."

"Lakes can be drained."

"Not before the next election." She set down the paper. "Care to reconsider my offer?"

Cassius sighed. "You've already made this deal, Teriana. If you knew the location of viable xenthier paths, you'd have already given them to Marcus. For as much as he's thrown caution to the wind for you, I suspect you've done much the same for him."

Her throat tightened, but Teriana made herself say, "There are many things I haven't told him."

"Really?" Cassius rolled onto an elbow, his eyes glimmering with delight. "So much dishonesty between you two lovebirds. So many secrets. Though I suppose that's what one gets when one sleeps with the enemy."

Teriana bit down on her desire to demand Cassius reveal what he knew about Marcus's secrets. "Not in Arinoquia, but in other nations, there are xenthier stems that have been bricked up for generations because they posed a threat. I can name at least three where it is rumored that screams emanate from behind those brick walls at the same time each year. It's said that they are screams from the underworld, for no one knows the language, but I reckon that it's Cel pathhunters who have found themselves entombed."

She paused to allow the shock to sink in.

Yet it was not horror that filled Cassius's gaze. It was *desire.*

Sitting upright, he dug into a stack of paper on the table and pulled out a map, which Teriana recognized from their first meeting. The meeting where her nails had been ripped off her fingers to get her to talk. The map still had streaks of her blood on it. "Where? Show me."

Picking up her glass of wine, Teriana took a mouthful, then leaned back in her chair. "Quid pro quo."

He made a noise of disgust. "I'll not release my prisoners based on rumors, girl."

"Obviously." A bead of sweat trickled down her back as she stared at those bloodstains, remembering how easily she'd been broken. Knowing that there was little to stop Cassius from putting her to the question again to get the information out of her, and this time Marcus wasn't here to intervene. "I want you to call off the hunt for Marcus. Call off your assassins."

Cassius threw back his head and laughed. "That's how you'll spend your capital, Teriana? On a Cel legatus's life?"

"Yes." She watched him with flat eyes, content for him to believe that the request was motivated by sentiment and not strategy. Content to allow herself to believe the same even as her heart wept, because the greatest danger to Marcus right now was himself.

"Why?" Cassius refilled their glasses. "Marcus is a bad man, Teriana." Spreading the rest of the pages on the table out before her, he shook his head. "So much harm. So much death. All enacted under his orders, and all detailed here in his own hand in reports he sent back to the Senate during prior campaigns. Look!"

Teriana glanced at the pages, recognizing Marcus's handwriting, then looked away. "I know what he's done. There's not a soul in the Empire who doesn't know, and the West is swiftly learning his reputation."

"You don't know the half of it." He eyed her for a long moment. "I think if you knew what a nasty creature he truly is, you'd beg me to put him down. Marcus is a villain of the first order, Teriana. Wherever he goes, he leaves death in his wake."

A band of tension closed around Teriana's chest. Cassius was most certainly manipulating her, but part of her couldn't help but wonder if she didn't know the full extent of what Marcus had done in his life. "If he's such a villain, then why do you want him dead?"

"Why do you believe I want him dead?"

She huffed out a breath. "I don't know, maybe because you sent assassins to the Domitius villa to kill him?"

"Hostus's doing, I'm afraid. He and Marcus have bad blood from their time together in Bardeen. Conflict between commanders is quite common, unfortunately. Like roosters in a ring, they try to peck each other's eyes out."

Teriana bit the insides of her cheeks, despising the amusement in Cassius's piggish gaze. "Cut the crap, Cassius. We both know that Hostus doesn't take a shit without your permission, which means you gave him that order. Most likely because you want Marcus out of the way to allow Titus to take control of the mission."

"Titus is inexperienced. Why would I want him in command?"

"Because he's your son."

Cassius smiled. "You need to learn to play at life like you do at cards, Teriana. Information, and secrets, most especially, are valuable commodities that one should hold back until they can be most effectively played, not thrown down on the table in wild abandon to elicit a reaction. Or lack thereof."

His voice was serious, but Teriana could feel his mirth. The sudden urge to scream, to cry, to rage threatened to overwhelm her because Cassius was so damn good at making her feel powerless. "Enough. Deal or no deal."

Silence stretched, the room growing colder by the second.

"It's not a deal I can make," Cassius finally replied. "Hostus's men are in pursuit, and there is no way to reach them in time to tell them to stand down. Marcus will either beat them to Bardeen or he'll die on their blades. It's possible he's already dead. Either way, I'll not negotiate with collateral I don't have. Name another price."

She'd known he wouldn't commit to it. Couldn't commit to it, and his refusal to do so gave Teriana some confidence in her belief that he'd be honest in answering the question she really wanted answered.

"What happened to Lydia? I know she didn't run away. I want the truth."

The room was so cold now that Teriana was shaking, her skin a mass of gooseflesh. Cassius swirled the wine in his glass, eyes distant, considering. "You want to know Lydia's fate," he murmured. "She means enough to you that you'd give me this information?"

"Yes," Teriana replied. "I think you had her killed once she'd served her purpose. Tell me how and where she met her end so that she can be put to rest in peace."

"Yet what you offer will bring the exact opposite of peace." He set his glass down on the table. "Are you sure this is a bargain you wish to make? Because you will not like what I'm about to tell you."

"Yes." She clenched her hands at her side, dread making her gusts twist. "Spit it out."

Cassius shrugged. "As you like. I was not present, but her murderer informed me that she was drowned in the baths and put down the drain into the underground river. I'm afraid her body is quite unrecoverable. Of course, if you try to use this information against me, I'll deny it. There is no proof of my involvement."

I hate you I hate you I hate you. Tears flowed down Teriana's cheeks, but she forced herself to deliver on her half of the bargain. "All three entombed xenthier stems are in Gamdesh."

Cassius's eyes flickered shut, his tongue passing over his lips as though savoring the moment. "Interesting how all three are in the biggest military power of the West."

Steady, she told herself. *You won't get what you want if you mess this up.* "I'm sure there are others, but Gamdesh is the center of trade. It's where the *Quincense* did most of its business, so I know it best." Her lip quivered. "Next deal. In exchange for you releasing my people, I'll travel through the Bardeen stem back to Arinoquia and share the precise locations with Marcus."

Cassius shook his head. "No deal. Firstly, he might already be dead. Secondly, there is nothing to stop you from running the moment you're through that stem."

"The Thirty-Seventh holds my ship and crew prisoner."

"So you say."

Teriana allowed consternation to rise to her face. "Fine. I'll give the information to whoever is currently in command, Marcus or otherwise. Also, I'll travel with the legion you send to reinforce them, so I won't be able to run."

He eyed her, his suspicion palpable. "A legion is a costly asset. Sending one now is an unnecessary risk given that a handful of men are enough to secure *you*."

It was her turn to shrug. "Your choice, Cassius. The deal is my people's freedom in exchange for me giving the exact locations of the stems. But for free, I'll throw in a warning. Two legions won't be enough to take any of the locations, especially not under Titus's command. As you say, Gamdesh is a force to be reckoned with, and the longer you take, the more time they have to prepare. Because I assure you, by now they know all about the Empire."

Wheels turned in the depths of his cunning eyes. But there was power in using the truth in one's schemes, and it was no lie that it would take more than two legions to prevail against the might of Gamdesh. No lie that the jewel of the West knew about the Cel threat and was preparing for the incursion. And Cassius knew it.

"As delightful as this little negotiation has been," he finally said, "I don't feel compelled to make any concessions. You are already bound by your agreement with the Senate to provide this information, and that same agreement states that viable paths to and from the West need to be secured before your people will be released. You have no ground to stand upon."

Teriana rose. "Let me know if you change your mind. I'll be staying with Senator Valerius."

She turned to leave just as the door opened and Cassius's servant appeared. The sour-faced man walked past her to his master's arm and whispered something in his ear. She caught "Timia by way of Alsium . . . Hostus is determining potential . . . can't be done in less than ten."

Teriana reached the door.

"Wait."

She smiled, then schooled her face to blandness as she slowly turned. "Let me guess. The men Hostus had waiting on the road didn't catch Marcus. Because he didn't go that direction."

Cassius spread his hands wide. "Apparently not."

"I've heard that there are hundreds of xenthier paths crisscrossing the Empire. So many different ways to get anywhere he wants to go."

"It's not that simple. Multiple jumps—"

"Are like being cracked over the head, I know."

"Ten—"

"Was the number *Hostus* came up with." The corner of her mouth curled up in a smirk. "But remember who you are hunting. Hostus isn't going to catch him. You know it. And I know it."

"Dominus," the servant whispered, "we can consult the commandant for potential—"

"I don't think you're going to find Wex to be particularly helpful," Teriana interrupted. "Also you may want to discipline Hostus for his failure. Thanks to his botched assassination, you have a wild-card legatus who knows you tried to kill him about to rejoin his *very* loyal legion."

Silence.

"What do you think Marcus is going to do?" She stared him down. "What will be his first action when he's back with the Thirty-Seventh?"

"For your sake, and that of your people, you should hope he does as he's told."

Her teeth were chattering, but Teriana managed to say, "Alliances are formed when mutually desired goals need to be achieved, but also when shared obstacles need to be overcome. You know I have influence over Marcus. I know that the Senate dances to your drum. Give me what I want, and I'll return the favor in kind."

Cassius's face revealed little, but his choice of silence rather than an immediate repartee told her that he, at least, believed Marcus was a threat. A threat that she had the power to mitigate.

"I'm not giving up my leverage over you," he finally said. "I'll free fifty of your people, plus you'll travel through the Bardeen stem with the Fifty-First legion. They are convenient and the least valuable by virtue of their age."

"One hundred of my people, which must include all the children, loaded onto a Maarin ship before I leave. I want to watch them sail away."

"One hundred, including all the children, on one of your ships before you depart." Cassius downed the rest of his expensive wine. "But only if you agree to a timeline. I want viable paths capable of transporting legions with acceptable levels of risk within six months."

Her heart skipped, then sped. "And if I don't meet your deadline?"

"Then I execute ten of your people for each month of delay."

Six months.

Teriana's eyes moved to the map, latching on to the port city of Emrant along the border of Arinoquia and Gamdesh. It wasn't so very far from the legion camp in Aracam, but would fifteen thousand legionnaires, a third of which were only *thirteen years old*, be enough? "He'll need a fourth legion."

Cassius shrugged, and it was not lost on her that there was no other ruler in the world who could shrug about five thousand trained soldiers. "Easily done . . . for a cost. Let's see . . . fifty executions for every month of delay?"

They were bartering with lives, but what else could she do? Teriana stared at the map, calculating what she knew about Gamdesh's Imperial Army. The legions had ships. Chests of gold. Alliances with the Arinoquians, and likely one forthcoming with Katamarca. They had Marcus, who everyone said was the greatest military strategist alive. "A year. And I choose my hundred. *And* I want them to set sail today."

"I'm happy to allow you to choose. All six hundred, including the children, are in Celendrial's prison; their ships are in the harbor. But I cannot concede on the timeframe. Elections, and all that."

"You are keeping the children in prison?" Bile burned her throat, but Cassius only shrugged again and said, "I suggested Lescendor for the young ones, but you weren't amenable. Disappointing given that we prefer to see our ranks representing every province under Celendor's control."

"The Maarin people aren't one of your *provinces*."

He refilled his glass and took a long mouthful. "Soon enough."

Six months wasn't enough time, not with the stakes so high. Yet to refuse would mean her people languishing in Celendrial's prison for who knew how long. The adults could endure, but the children . . . "I need to see my people. Then I'll decide."

Cassius smiled. "I thought you might say that."

8

TERIANA

Teriana waited until they were back in Valerius's villa, in the library filled with books and scrolls that would be the envy of any collector in the world. In the library that had been Lydia's domain, where she was ever to be found hunched over an obscure passage with ink staining her fingers. But never again. "She's dead. I'm so sorry."

Senator Valerius sat down heavily on a chair, elbows resting on his knees, eyes blindly staring. "I knew. In my heart, I knew, but . . ." A sob tore from his throat, and Lydia's father buried his face in his hands.

Teriana's face remained dry, as though all the tears she had in this life had been used up, leaving dry wells in her eyes even as her heart fractured with grief.

"How?"

"Drowned," she said softly. "Apparently the baths have an outtake tunnel that leads underground."

"Oh, my sweet girl." The words sounded ripped from his throat, like the truth had shattered him entirely, and Teriana knelt next to Lydia's father to take one of his hands.

"We'll have vengeance," she whispered. "Maybe not today or tomorrow, but the day will come when there will be a reckoning."

"It will not bring my girl back."

It wouldn't. Not doing her level best to strangle Cassius had been one of the harder things she'd ever had to do, but there was no room for impulsiveness. Only cold strategy. It made her understand why Marcus was the way he was.

Valerius squeezed her hand, then, to her shock, slid off the chair to sit on the floor next to her. She'd known him all her life, for he and her mother had been friends, of a sort. But Appius Valerius was a Cel Senator. As rich and powerful as any king or queen. More so, in a way, given Celendor's might. It had meant that no matter how close she'd been with Lydia, the respect her father had commanded had demanded a certain distance. Certainly not sitting on the floor of a library hand in hand.

"There is something I need to tell you, Teriana," he said. "Pieces of information that both your mother and I chose to keep from you, and from Lydia, that you should know. Secrets that . . . no longer need to be kept."

Her heart skipped, then sped, not only because of the gravity of his tone but because her *mother* was involved.

"The story you've been told was that Lydia's mother was a stranger to me. A nameless pregnant woman who died in the gutter, whose child I took pity upon. But that is not the truth. I knew her—knew her well—although it had been long years since we'd last spoken. Her name was Camilla."

That . . . was no great revelation, but Teriana remained quiet, sensing the story was far from over.

"We met by chance in our youth. I was quite entranced by her, if truth be told, but she saw me only as a friend. A friend whom she eventually trusted enough to confess she was not from the East, but had rather come here by accident, or impulse, I suspect, via a xenthier stem originating on the far side of the Endless Seas. From a kingdom known as Mudamora."

All the blood drained from Teriana's face, only to be replaced with a swift flood of elation. "I knew it!" she cried. "I knew that was where Lydia was from. It was written all over her face. But . . . who is Lydia's blood father? If Camilla was here . . ."

"She went back." His smile was sad. "She'd searched for years for a route back to the West, as did I using my significant resources, but there were only whispers. Rumors. Nothing I deemed safe enough for her to risk, so I took it upon myself to befriend a Maarin captain. Your mother."

He gave a soft laugh. "Tesya was like you when she was younger. Willing to break every rule, so it was easy enough to convince her to take Camilla back to the West. They remained friends, and Tesya would bring me letters from Camilla when she could."

The shock of what he was telling her rendered Teriana mute, because no one, *no one,* had held to the mandate that East must not meet West more than her mother.

"It is the crime of youth to think that the old never have secrets, the crime of the old to think that the youth will never discover them," he said. "At any rate, through our correspondence, I learned that Camilla had wed. To a king, no less. I yet held a torch for her, so I took the news rather poorly and ceased correspondence. A petty choice that I came to regret."

Camilla. A king. "Oh gods," Teriana whispered. "Oh gods, Queen Camilla Falorn?"

"Yes." He sighed. "I ignored her letters for years, but it was still me she came to when she was mortally wounded and needed aid. 'Care for her, Appius,' she said. 'Keep her safe.'" He rested his head in his hands. "I failed her."

Teriana's throat felt thick, the story too much to take in, but the part that stuck was . . . "Lydia is Kitaryia Falorn."

"Yes." He lifted his head. "Your mother came to Celendrial to tell me that Camilla was missing and presumed dead, only to discover that I already knew. She said that dark forces desired Kitaryia dead, and together we decided it best that I raise her in Celendor where such forces have little power. Here she'd be safe. Which she was, until my fear for her future put her in the hands of a monster as bad as any that hunted her in Mudamora."

In her own fears for Lydia's future, Teriana had tried to pull her in a direction equally dangerous. "That's why Mum wouldn't let me help her. Why she was trying to keep us separated."

"Yes." He stared, unseeing. "You both thought we weren't paying attention, but we were. Knew that it was only a matter of time until you told her the truth, and her questions would demand answers we weren't willing to give." He shook his head. "Maybe that would have been better. For her to go back to where she belonged. Maybe she'd still live."

For so long, Teriana had believed that she had been the one to instigate everything that had happened. That she'd been the one to open the door between East and West. Now she realized how short-sighted that had been, the tangled web of connections across the seas far greater than she could have imagined.

A knock sounded at the door.

Valerius climbed to his feet, fixing his clothing before he said, "Yes?"

Austornic opened the door, and though his face bore no emotion, the young legatus radiated excitement. "The Senate supports Cassius's proposal to send reinforcements to join the Thirty-Seventh and Forty-First. The Fifty-First will travel to Bardeen tomorrow, then make the crossing to Arinoquia." His brown eyes met Teriana's. "All that's left to decide is whether you'll be joining us."

* * *

Given Celendrial's size, its prison was rather small.

Not because the city lacked criminals, but because in Celendor, the vast majority of offenses were punishable with death. It was something of a sport to them, and hangings were viewed as a suitable family outing, though the peak form of entertainment was held in the stadium, where hundreds of prisoners would be put onto the field with wild animals of every sort. Teriana had heard that if you survived the animals, you would earn your freedom.

She'd also heard that no one ever survived.

Cassius had sent instructions to meet him at the prison, where he'd make arrangements for her to speak to her people. From her vantage point next to Austornic, the familiar blue sails of a Maarin ship were visible in the harbor. It made her think of the *Quincense*, the ship that had been her home all her life, which she hadn't seen in far too long. Except this vessel had Cel sailors moving about the deck making it ready, the sight making her uneasy because it meant Cassius was certain of what her decision would be.

"How long will it take to reach Arinoquia?" she asked.

"We'll leave at dawn," Austornic, or Nic, as he'd told her to call him, said. "I've already sent messages ahead, and what we need will be gathered and ready for us in Hydrilla. That's the fortress city near to the xenthier stem."

"I know where it is."

"Unfortunately, it's very time-consuming taking a full legion through a path, as we can only go one at a time. But four days, give or take."

"You'll want to banish vagueness from your vocabulary," she said mechanically. "Marcus likes accurate answers."

Nic didn't answer, and Teriana knew what he was thinking. That there was every chance Marcus was dead, which would mean it was Titus whom he'd be serving beneath.

"Does it make you nervous?" she asked. "The uncertainty of what you'll be walking into?"

"Yes." Nic met her gaze, brown eyes serious below his helmet. "But less nervous than the very certain fate we'd be facing if we were stuck with Hostus."

"Sir," Pullo said, the primus and his men guarding their legatus much the same way Gibzen always did with Marcus. "The consul approaches."

Sweat pooled beneath Teriana's breasts as she caught sight of an approaching litter, eight men straining to carry the red and gold monstrosity. Men of the Twenty-Ninth walked in escort around it, and her stomach tightened as she recognized the familiar cloak and helmet of a legatus. Hostus was with him.

"Don't let him provoke you," Nic murmured, and his men all gave tight nods, though Teriana was fairly confident the advice was for her.

The litter stopped before her. Cassius's skinny servant climbed out and then helped his master exit.

"Good, good, you're here." Cassius straightened his garments before striding toward her. "All is in order for you to meet with your people and make a decision about our agreement. Hostus, would you serve as my representative inside? I'm afraid I have no tolerance for the smell in these places. It clings."

"Of course, Consul." Hostus gave Teriana a smile that was all teeth as Cassius climbed back inside the litter. The Twenty-Ninth's legatus was well into his twenties, white-blond hair cut short, his emerald eyes vibrant against his golden Cel skin. A face to inspire sculptors, she had no doubt, but from the moment she'd met him, Teriana had sensed the monster lurking within.

Hostus clapped Nic on the shoulder so hard that the boy staggered. "Wait out here, puppy."

"No." Nic's voice was cold, but though he showed no visible signs of nerves, Teriana could sense his apprehension. She suspected Hostus could as well. "The Commandant's orders are that I am to remain with Teriana at all times, under full guard."

"Don't you trust me to take care of her?" Hostus's gaze was feral, his smile still showing far too many of his white teeth. "I'm starting to feel a little hurt, puppy. First you abandon my care to tie yourself to the Thirty-Seventh's apron strings, and now you throw doubt upon my ability to manage a prisoner."

"Feelings are irrelevant," Nic answered. "I'm following orders."

"He's coming with me," Teriana snapped. "If for no other reason than to keep me from cutting your throat." She patted the hilt of the knife at her waist. "I've still got the blade I took from you."

Hostus met her stare. "Let's see how well that little thing serves you in the dark, girl." He gestured to the building. "Shall we?"

The prison was cool, and as Teriana's eyes adjusted to the dimmer light, she frowned in confusion. Rather than rows and rows of cells, as she'd anticipated, the prison appeared exactly like one of the state buildings. All columns and high ceilings, the tiled floor sparkling clean, and the domes painted with scenes of marching legions. Banners of red and gold hung from the walls, and it was incredibly quiet.

"It's underground," Nic said softly. "The upper level belongs to the administrators and the warden, and this is their entrance. There is another one for the prisoners."

Underground.

Teriana swallowed her nausea as Hostus strolled past, leading them down the main corridor before stopping in front of a heavy door flanked by six legionnaires with the number 29 stamped on their breastplates. He muttered something to them, and one extracted a thick key and unlocked the door. Hearing the clack of legion-issue sandals behind her, Teriana glanced over her shoulder to see more of the Twenty-Ninth following them in, weapons in hand.

"My people aren't to be harmed." Panic rose in her chest because she realized she hadn't been specific that the hundred be *alive* when they set sail. It was just like Cassius to look for such a loophole.

"As long as they are peaceable, they won't be," Hostus replied. "I'm merely being cautious."

There was zero chance she'd trust Hostus at his word, but Nic gave a small nod of affirmation that partially eased the tension in her chest.

Then the door swung open.

A wave of *stink* washed over her, and Teriana recoiled, gagging. It smelled worse than a legion camp latrine, for it was tinged with vomit and . . . *rot*. As though not everyone in the prison below was alive.

"Gods." She pressed her sleeve to her mouth and ignored the dark glares the legionnaires gave her, because her people were trapped in that horror. She tried to shove past Hostus, to sprint down into this underworld to find them. To help them. But Hostus's hand latched on her wrist.

"There are protocols," he murmured, the bones of her wrist grinding beneath his grip. "*Walk*."

Then he pulled her through the entrance. The staircase was wide and made from square-cut stone blocks, sconces filled with burning oil both illuminating the space and filling it with a haze of smoke that mixed with the miasma of human waste as they descended, passing yet more legionnaires as they circled into the bowels of the structure. Behind them, the door slammed shut.

Teriana's heart throbbed with the same speed it had when she and Marcus had been chased by wolves across Sibern, her ears now filled with cries and moans of pain and despair, the stink so terrible her eyes burned.

"You get used to it," Hostus said with a chuckle, maintaining his grip on her arm. Nic and Pullo followed behind them as they reached the bottom of the stairs.

A corridor lined with steel bars stretched out before her. She peered into the darkness, dread filling her at the sight of dozens and dozens of holes in the ground. Perhaps four feet in diameter, they looked like wells with bars overtop, except they didn't contain water. Weeping emanated from the space, and she clenched her teeth against the sourness rising in her throat at the thought of being kept in the tight, dark space for days. Months. Gods, it was possible some of the prisoners might have been in there for *years*. "If my people are—"

"They're not," Hostus interrupted. "Those are for individuals who have done truly despicable things, not sad little sailors who put their faith in the wrong girl."

Her chin trembled. "Seems a fitting place for you."

Hostus's laugh echoed through the prison. "None of those holes are deep enough to contain me." Pulling his gladius loose, he ran the blade along the metal bars with resounding clangs, shouting, "It's bath time, you filthy ingrates!"

There were dozens of the Twenty-Ninth on duty around those holes, and all of them moved on cue. Teriana blinked back tears, refusing to watch what they were doing but unable to drown out the splashing and cries of distress from the prisoners. Nor the acrid smell.

"This is not acceptable, Hostus," Nic said between gritted teeth. "I will raise this with the Senate before I depart."

Hostus broke off his laughter. Dropping Teriana's wrist, he whirled, catching the boy by the throat and slamming the young primus against the bars. Pullo moved to interfere, but more of the Twenty-Ninth were on them in a heartbeat, knocking him back. Two of them stepped close to Teriana, eyes cold as snakes as they backed her away.

"You aren't going to say a thing, puppy," Hostus whispered. "For if you do, you won't wake up tomorrow in your camp, but rather in the bottom of one of these holes. Be assured, I *will* choose a prisoner who will be delighted for your company."

Knowing that any intervention on her part would only make things worse for Nic, Teriana twisted on her heels and broke into a run. Her boots smacked the stone floor with heavy thuds, Hostus's curses chasing Teriana down the corridor. The cells full of holes fell away, replaced with large rooms filled with men and women chained to the wall, but none of them were her people.

What if this had been a trick?

What if they weren't down here, and this was merely a perverse way to lock her up in prison?

What if . . .

Her thoughts trailed away, not because of the scowling men who'd stepped from their posts to intercept her, but because beyond them, in a large cell, were familiar faces.

"Let her pass," Hostus ordered, though she barely heard him as she walked up to the bars, gripping them tightly as she stared inside.

Dark-skinned faces stared back at her, Maarin eyes all swirling grey seas of misery, though some lightened to a faded blue as she was recognized. "It's Teriana," many of them whispered. "Teriana of the *Quincense*. The Triumvir's daughter."

Most of the men were shackled by the ankles, but though the women and children were unbound, they had no more freedom of space with the number of them stuffed into the chamber. They were filthy, clothes ragged and stained, and faces gaunt with hunger. Many looked ill, others bearing injuries that oozed with infection, and in the corners, some forms were still.

This is your fault, her conscience whispered. *This would never have happened, if not for you.*

Abruptly she felt the brush of warmth against her cheek.

Hostus was watching her.

His lips were slightly parted, his breathing rapid—relishing her misery in a way that caused her to recoil.

"This is almost as good as cutting you open," he whispered. "Shame Marcus isn't here to enjoy his part of this horror show."

Don't let him provoke you. Nic's warning filled her head, and Teriana swallowed down the mouthful of saliva she'd been about to spit into his face. "I want to speak to them."

Disappointment that she hadn't reacted filled his eyes and he blew out an irritated breath. "On your bellies," he ordered. "By orders of the Consul and Senate, one hundred of you are to be granted liberty. That is, if Teriana agrees to the price."

Murmurs filled the air, her people all obediently falling to their bellies as one of the guards unlocked the bars. Teriana pushed past him, filth squishing beneath her feet as she moved into the cell. Though her people remained prone, heads turned to regard her, waiting.

She didn't know what to say.

Did not know what words could possibly make this situation better, given she stood polished, clean, and well-fed while they suffered. Nothing she'd endured compared to this, and she wanted to scream in rage at Madoria for choosing her as her champion against the Cel, for she'd failed so miserably.

Yet seeing her people like this also brought clarity as to her purpose, and Teriana turned to Hostus. "Tell Cassius we have an accord. Six months."

Hostus smiled, the answer seeming to please him. "Then you may choose your hundred."

"I've negotiated for the freedom of one hundred souls." Her voice was hoarse. "The rest to be freed when I fulfill my obligations to the Senate. I negotiated for all the children, but I think the rest should not be my decision."

"But that was the deal," Hostus crooned. "It *must* be your decision, Teriana. You must personally choose each one. And I'll personally cut the throat of anyone who opens their mouth to assist you."

Her hands balled into fists, nails cutting into her palms, every part of her wanting to lash out in violence.

Except that would be giving him exactly what he wanted.

"Fine." Her mouth tasted of copper, the insides of her cheeks bleeding where she'd bit them. "If I touch your head, please go to the door. The legatus's men will escort you above, where you will be brought to the ship waiting for you in the harbor. They have committed to your safety as long as you do not invite violence. Please don't give them an excuse."

Hostus chuckled. "Or do."

Fresh blood filled her mouth as she bit down on her cheeks again, but Teriana forced herself to proceed, touching the heads of two young girls, as well as that of their mother, whose arms held them to the ground. As the woman slowly rose, Teriana finally saw past the grime. It was her cousin, Elyanna. Her own gods-damned flesh and blood was imprisoned in this place and she hadn't even known it.

"Get moving!" Hostus barked, and Elyanna jerked, eyes midnight storms of fear as she clutched her daughters against her and edged out of the cell, casting a terrified glance back at her husband. Though she hated to do it, Teriana moved past him to touch the head of a woman, who held a baby, then an elderly man, as well as the boy Nic's age who clung to him tightly. Tears trickling down her face, she moved through the prone forms of her people, touching the hair of those younger than her, as well as one of their parents or grandparents.

"That's forty-five," Hostus said when she was through, his voice bored. "Pick up the pace, Teriana. I haven't got all day."

She stood frozen in place, eyes skipping from person to person, realizing that she was not only choosing who would live, she was also choosing who would die if she didn't make her deadline. How could she pick one over the other? Did she choose the elderly, for they were least likely to survive, or did she choose the young, for they had their whole lives ahead of them? Panic made the world spin, and she started to reach for the second mate of one of the ships, only for the man to turn his head away from her.

She froze, realizing a second later that he was making the choice for her: *not him*.

All around her, the strong, both men and women, were turning their faces away from her, guiding her hand without whispering a word. She heard Hostus's hiss of irritation that they were stealing the pleasure he took from watching her suffer. Teriana ignored him, instead walking among her people, taking their guidance. The elderly. The ill. The injured.

The god marked, of which there were three.

"You're at ninety-six," Nic said from where he stood next to a glowering Hostus. "The others have already begun to make their way to the harbor."

Scanning the remaining men and women, she stepped toward a massive man with biceps as thick as her thigh. He recoiled, giving a slight shake of his head, but she said, "You will protect them." In quick succession, she chose three more known to be fine fighters, giving them the same instructions.

"Finally," Hostus muttered. "That was tedious. Get out of there, Teriana, I'm late for my midday meal."

She didn't want to leave.

Didn't want to abandon her people in this miserable prison under the guard of Hostus's men. Wanted instead to exchange herself for one of them, because if anyone deserved to be here, it was her.

But she doubted Cassius would let her off so easily.

"Stay strong," she said. "I will free every last one of you, I swear it."

"Don't make promises you can't keep," Hostus drawled. "Not even Marcus can do what you committed to do within six months, which means at least some of these *brave* and *self-sacrificing* sailors are destined for the gallows. Or the stadium."

Her stomach filled with unease as every eye in the prison shot to her. Six months felt like an eternity to keep them imprisoned, but if Hostus said otherwise, then . . .

"It can be done," she swore to her people as one of Hostus's men caught her by the shoulders. "I can do it. It's possible. I'll get you out."

Her words echoed hollowly down the hallways as the legionnaires dragged her away, but it was the ones inside her head that were the loudest.

What have I done?

9

TERIANA

Austornic hadn't waited for dawn, instead ordering the Fifty-First to break camp immediately after the Maarin ship full of her people had disappeared on the horizon. Whether it had been in anticipation of the mission or the desire to be away from Hostus, Teriana couldn't have said, but she breathed more easily once they were gone from Celendrial. Easier still when they reached the first xenthier path from Celendor to Bardeen. The feeling of disorientation as she stepped out amongst the towering redwoods of the southern nation weighed more heavily upon her now that she knew what it meant.

"I know you're supposed to forget everything about who you were before you went to Celendor, or at least never bring it up," she said to Nic as they waited for the legion to pass through. "But—" She broke off, because Pullo and the rest of Nic's bodyguard were all waving their hands at her to be silent. "Never mind."

"I was a product of the legion's early campaigns on the coast of Bardeen," he responded, tone flat. "Whoever my mother was, she gave me over to be a ward of the state and I was raised in an orphanage. I've no notion of the identity of my father. When I turned seven, I went to Celendor with all the other male wards my age. The only Bardenese thing about me is the way I look, and the Fifty-First is the only family I've ever had. My loyalty is to them."

His life had been one of hardship, and yet Nic had remained kind. It made her think there was more to his blood than just his looks, but she said nothing more.

A matter of hours brought them to Hydrilla. Teriana shivered, the chill air of Bardeen harsh in comparison to Celendrial, then glanced at the fortress atop the hill. The walls were decorated with crimson and gold banners, and patrolled by countless legionnaires, but some sixth sense confirmed what she'd been told about this place. It was not safe. Not secure. Not entirely under the control of the Empire, despite the Thirty-Seventh and the Twenty-Ninth having won a great victory here over four years ago.

"It's a very famous siege," Austornic told her as they passed in the fortress's shadow, the long line of the marching Fifty-First stretched out behind them. "Won as much by guile as force, in that only a few men, led by the Thirty-Seventh's then primus, Agrippa, turned the tide. He's the Thirty-Seventh's only deserter, did you know that?" When she didn't answer, he continued. "Hostus was supposed to be in command of the siege, but in the final hours, he was replaced by Marcus. It's considered Marcus's first major victory, though it's well-known at Lescendor that Hostus had been taking credit for his strategies long before that."

He carried on with his explanation of events, but the world fell away as Teriana imagined what it had been like for the Bardenese to look down upon the camp of ten thousand men set on their destruction. What it had been like to starve with no way to escape. But it also gave her hope that her own strategies would not end in total calamity. For while the Bardenese had been conquered four years ago, every day since, their resistance had grown.

"The rebels are now led by a *girl*," Nic grumbled, his opinion of that very fitting for a thirteen-year-old boy. "The spies haven't been able to learn much about her, although it's rumored that she fights with a gladius marked with the 37. Probably stolen from a casualty when they were here. At any rate, they raid and attack supply lines and merchants, necessitating everything and everyone to be under heavy guard at all times. It's entirely disrupted trade and cost those in power a great deal of money, which has the entire Hill in a frenzy. Many calls to send in a few legions to purge the country, because the only thing they value in Bardeen is the lumber."

"What is a bit of genocide in comparison to being deprived of redwood furniture?" She looked up at the towering sequoias that were sacred to the Bardenese.

"Patricians don't take well to being deprived of *anything* they want," he answered. "But there isn't a legatus alive who doesn't dig in his heels over being sent here." He scanned the branches above, shaking his head. "I think there are places in the world that refuse to be cowed."

Teriana prayed the West was one of them.

"Will we go straight through without delay?" she asked.

"Unless there is a compelling reason not to."

Working her jaw from side to side, Teriana said, "There is something you need to know." She'd been holding off on revealing this particular concern but could delay no longer.

Nic gave a world-weary sigh. "Oh?"

"The Thirty-Seventh obviously knows we went missing but they don't know why," she said. "Marcus had some concern that they'd think—"

"He deserted?" Nic gave a sharp shake of his head, cursing under his breath with words a boy his age had no business knowing. "If they believe that, then he might already be dead. You should prepare yourself for that."

"How do I prepare for that, precisely?" Just the thought of it made her sick.

Nic was quiet for a moment, then he said, "His death wouldn't change any of your goals, only how you'd go about achieving them. Consider how you wish to secure your people's freedom if you lose the leverage you have with him. Set aside emotion and think about it logically."

Seeming to reconsider his words, Nic added, "Fortunately, Marcus is aware of the complication, so he'll plan accordingly."

"How is that possible? There is no chance that the terminus stem isn't under guard."

"With luck, it will be the Forty-First. They'll be less emotional and hear him out."

That won't be luck, she thought, but kept it to herself and adjusted the pack she carried. Valerius had ensured she had everything that she might need, including having the woman who'd served as Lydia's maid rebraid Teriana's hair. The woman wasn't half as deft as Teriana's aunt Yedda, but she still felt more herself with the multitude of braids hanging down her back, her collection of hair beads all carefully woven into them. She had fresh clothes, trousers of buttersoft leather, a blouse of fine blue silk, and a snug leather bodice that kept her breasts in place. Her boots were also new, which was why she was currently nursing a blister on her right heel, but they matched the belt to which she had the knife she'd stolen from Hostus fastened. The pack held spare clothes and various other sundries that she might need that the boys of the Fifty-First most definitely did not.

They walked over a bridge, and Teriana noted that downstream the water had been diverted away from a large excavation of earth and stone. In the mud surrounding it stood a group of older legionnaires and a centurion, who saluted as Nic approached. Not for the first time, she was struck by how strange it was to see a grown man deferring to a child, but rank was rank, and Nic was a legatus, even if the top of his head only reached the other man's shoulder.

"We received word that the Thirty-Seventh's legatus traveled through this stem recently," Nic said. "Can you confirm?"

"He did, sir. The legatus showed no hesitation despite our intelligence indicating the terminus was unknown," the centurion said. "He told me that the path was mapped and that he wished to inspect the genesis. I thought it strange that he was alone, but I wasn't about to tell a legatus what he could or could not do. Then the Twenty-Ninth showed up, shouting at us to stop him. They put on pursuit into the tunnel, and it came to blows before they came back up and said he'd gone through the stem. They were angry, but gave no explanation, only departed."

Nic's face was bland as he lifted one shoulder. "There was some miscommunication within the Twenty-Ninth. You were right not to impede the legatus, for his orders are of the highest priority."

"Figured as much, so the engineers accelerated the excavation. It's mud up to the knees, but you won't be crawling down a tunnel."

"For which you have my gratitude," Nic replied. "It will be seeing a great deal of future traffic."

"Was he well?" Teriana interrupted. "The Thirty-Seventh's legatus? Did he seem all right?"

The centurion's eyes narrowed but Nic said, "Well?"

"No," the centurion said. "He looked like right shit, if you pardon my saying so, sir. Half of what he said was slurred like he was drunk, but he didn't have the stink of booze on him. Something wrong with him?"

Breathe breathe breathe.

"He's fine," Nic replied. "Merely some concern he's brought a flux with him, so we'll stock our medics accordingly."

"They made it, then?" the centurion asked. "The Thirty-Seventh is on the other side of Reath?"

Nic didn't answer, only gave the man a look that said that such information was above his rank, and the centurion flushed. "Sorry, sir. All is in order, whenever the Fifty-First is ready to proceed."

"Good." Nodding at the centurion, Nic moved past him down the excavated slope to where the glittering black spike of xenthier protruded from the ground, his bodyguards—every one of them shorter than Teriana—following at his heels.

"So this will take us to the far side of the world," Nic said softly.

Teriana didn't answer, knowing that he was speaking to himself. She'd told him, his officers, and his engineers everything she knew about the location of the terminus, including the scaffolding that had been set up when she'd last been there. "If that's been removed, it's a big drop," she'd told them. "Survivable if you land well and roll, deadly if you don't."

"Protocol would have demanded they ensure the safety of all who might travel through," an engineer had grumbled, to which Teriana had laughed. "We won't be in the Empire anymore, my friend, so be wary of leaning on protocol. We're just as likely to find a bed of spikes as scaffolding."

The boys had all shifted uneasily, then turned to the discussion of mitigation. She'd suggested they shove a wagon-load of pillows through the stem to cushion the potential hard landing, and while they'd dismissed her suggestion as lunacy, she had heard some muttering about her idea after her back was turned.

Now the moment to take the step through was upon them.

"This is not how it's done," Pullo groused. "Paid path-hunters are supposed to go back and forth several times to ensure the terminus is safe and secure before legion transport."

"You know as well as I do that such a thing is not yet possible," Nic said. "Until the lake in Atlia is drained, the only mapped path back suitable for human travel has a terminus in Sibern, and it's the dead of winter."

For all the path from Arinoquia to Atlia was stymied by a large body of water, Teriana's skin still crawled with the certainty that it was not a matter of if but when that the Empire would *make* it viable. Even if such a thing were not possible, it was still a route of communication. For the Empire, information was power.

Nic continued, "You think the Senate is going to allow us to sit on our laurels while we wait for certainty that this path is safe? No. We'll be back under Hostus's command, and I, for one, would rather dive headfirst into the unknown than salute that prick."

Teriana could hardly blame him, for the memory of her last conversation with Hostus made her shiver. "This isn't over, little girl," he'd said to her before she'd left to go with the Fifty-First. "There is no place in the world that I can't find you—remind your lover of that when you see him, if he's still alive. I have a new dining set that I had made specifically for serving him up rare."

She'd been so bloody terrified that she'd nearly thrown up on his feet, but had managed, "I'll pass on the message," before scuttling into Nic's care, his face as green around the gills over Hostus's words as her own.

But now Hostus was a distant fear, whereas the very real threat of an uncertain xenthier loomed right in front of her. There was no turning back, though. She'd made a deal with the enemy, and if she backed out of it, there were still five hundred of her people locked in his prison to pay the price.

"So what's the plan?" she asked Nic, just to say something, because Teriana *knew* the plan. Had watched how they'd methodically gone through the first path on their journey. Knew that Pullo, as primus, would go through first with a dozen of his men, secure the ground; then the rest of the legion would slowly filter through, along with their supplies. All very regulated and orderly and so very, *very* Cel.

"I could be leading them to their deaths." Nic pulled off his helmet to wipe sweat from his brow. "We've no certainty of what is on the other side. None."

"Marcus is there, now," she reminded him. "If nothing else, it will have motivated them to ensure the terminus is fit to receive travelers."

"Right." Nic strode forward and closed his hand over the xenthier, winking out of sight.

"Shit!" Teriana shouted, the sentiment echoed by his bodyguard. Not thinking, she raced after him, grasping hold of the cold crystal.

Everything turned white, her mind feeling as though it disconnected from her body, and then she was gasping in a mouthful of warm, humid air. She stumbled, her feet thudding against stone, and then a hand closed on her arm to steady her.

Nic.

They stood together on a stone platform, but Teriana took nothing in because she was too busy screeching, "That was not the—"

Her words cut off with a muffled *ooof* as someone slammed into her back, knocking her forward. Then another and another, Nic's bodyguard coming through the xenthier to land in a tangled dogpile on top of the platform. Which wasn't very Cel-like at all.

"Stand down!" Nic barked as she disentangled herself from the boys, grumbling that a better order would have been to stand up. But then she heard the distinct sound of a gladius being drawn, then another and another.

Nic had his weapon in hand, as did Pullo and the others, their bodies tight with tension.

And that was when the smell hit her.

Rot.

Shaking her head to clear the lingering dizziness, Teriana tried to climb to her feet but Pullo's hand forced her down with surprising strength. "Stay low," he hissed. "The terminus isn't secure."

Fear thrummed through her veins as Teriana peered through their legs, her breath catching as her eyes fixed on the body of a legionnaire sprawled across the ground, flies buzzing above his still form. "No."

A scream tore from her lips, and Teriana shoved between the boys, stumbling down the ramp to the ground and falling to her knees next to the body. It was bloated and grey, the stink beyond words, and with shaking hands, Teriana rolled him over.

The legionnaire's face was ruined beyond recognition, but the 41 embossed on his breastplate was clear as day.

It wasn't Marcus.

But there were other bodies. A dozen corpses sprawled within eyesight. Once the Fifty-First saw them, their remaining innocence would be destroyed. "Stop!"

The boys all froze, and Teriana scrambled between them and the corpses. "Stay back! Don't look!"

Pullo frowned at her, then muttered something to his men, who pressed onward, ignoring the bodies in favor of establishing a perimeter. They were nervous, a hint of fear on their faces, but none of them hesitated.

Nic caught hold of her arm. "We've another twenty minutes before the rest of the legion will begin coming through," he murmured. "Twenty minutes on our own."

What if she'd brought them into a death trap?

Teriana's hands turned to ice as she surveyed the jungle around them, which was too quiet, like the animals and insects were all holding their breath. "What do we do?"

Bending down, Nic picked up one of the fallen Forty-First's shields, handing it to her. "We hold our position until we are reinforced. Pullo knows his business, so we keep our mouths shut."

The grip was covered in dried blood, but Teriana closed her hand around it and held up the shield to cover her torso as Nic tugged her back toward the xenthier's scaffolding.

"I'm sorry," she whispered. "I brought you here."

"By virtue of being born second, this was always in our cards." His brown eyes skipped over the fallen men. "You have nothing to be sorry for."

"You're just children." Children who had now seen the reality of the future they faced in mangled corpses being consumed by rot and flies. "This is no place for children."

"Tell that to the Senate next time you meet with them," he answered. "But for now, keep quiet."

Teriana obeyed, staying crouched behind the shield, the only sound the drone of flies and the thunder of her heart. Her eyes jumped from corpse to corpse, part of her still terrified that Marcus was among them, but it was impossible to tell. It seemed like an eternity before Pullo backed toward them, face blanched but hands steady as he crouched next to his legatus. "The attack didn't come from the xenthier," he said. "Looks like their camp was hit first. The guards are all dead at their posts and there are signs of where they tried to form up before being overrun. Eighteen dead, all Forty-First, and if they took down any of the enemy, the bodies were removed. No signs of life, ours or otherwise. Should I scout farther afield?"

"No," Nic responded. "Hold."

Pullo lifted his hand and made a series of gestures that Teriana knew were orders, then he said, "No arrows, all blade work and fists, looks like. But some of the bodies . . . They're wearing Forty-First gear but they're old men. You know anything about the Forty-First recruiting, Teriana?"

All the blood drained from her face, terror rising in her heart as she realized what had happened here. "It was one of the corrupted who did this, Nic."

She'd told the boy about the corrupted during their journey from Celendor to Bardeen, and though he'd heard her out, Teriana had known he hadn't believed her. If his beliefs had changed upon seeing this carnage, the young legatus didn't show it. "Hold positions. All that matters is keeping this ground secure for reinforcements."

Every second felt like a lifetime as they waited, Teriana's skin crawling whenever a fly landed upon her, because she knew what the wretched things had been feasting upon. Then footsteps thudded on the scaffolding, and Pullo was on the move. Running up the ramp, he barked orders at the arrivals, and though their hearts must have filled with fear, the Fifty-First obeyed with no hesitation.

Hundreds, then thousands of legionnaires exited the path, the area around the terminus swiftly deemed secure enough that she and Nic were able to move about. Teriana forced herself to look at each of the bodies to make sure they weren't Marcus as Pullo led her and Nic to the Forty-First's camp, which was torn apart and splashed with blood and gore.

For all the Fifty-First had been trained for this, more than a few of the boys vomited at the sight, the stink and horror and adrenaline more than they could bear.

"Here's one." Pullo pulled the cloak covering the face of the corpse down to reveal a wrinkled face splattered with blood, the eyebrows above his unseeing eyes as white as snow.

Even so, Teriana recognized him because of the tattoo of a bird on one of his biceps. "His name is Florius. Absolute shit at cards. He's . . . eighteen."

"Eighty seems more accurate." Pullo covered the corpse again. "Are you suggesting one man did this, Teriana? Took down *eighteen* trained legionnaires without injury?"

"Injury means little to the corrupted. They just steal life," she said. "They use it to heal themselves."

"Fuck me," the young primus muttered, and she had to curb the urge to tell him to watch his language.

"They've been dead for some time, judging from the decay." Nic surveyed their surroundings. "Any sign of Marcus?"

"No, sir. But the timing of this couldn't be coincidence."

"Logbook?"

"Still looking, sir."

Numb, Teriana moved about the camp, seeing that they'd been in the midst of cooking dinner when they'd been attacked, the pot of food overturned and rotting into the mud. *Where are you?* she silently asked. *Are you safe?*

A foolish question, because how could he be?

"Sir! We found it!" One of the boys ran up, handing Nic a leather-bound book smeared with blood. As he opened it, a letter fell free to land on the ground. Bending to pick it up, Teriana read the contents. "It's signed by the Commandant," she whispered. "Marcus was here."

Nic was reading the last record, his expression grim. "Marcus arrived but was unconscious. The centurion sent a messenger to Aracam requesting medical aid from the Thirty-Seventh, as well as reinforcements. He noted his intent to transport Marcus to Aracam on the heels of the messenger. That's the last record."

Tears burned in her eyes. "Where is he? Did the corrupted take him?"

Had the corrupted been Ashok?

The Thirty-Seventh had hunted the corrupted who'd kidnapped her but never found a trace of him. Except not for a heartbeat did she think he'd abandoned Arinoquia, and there was no doubt in her mind that if Ashok had been given the opportunity to take revenge against Marcus, he'd do so.

"The attack may have come after Marcus left with the escort charged with transporting him," Pullo said. "It's rained since, so any tracks on the trail leading east were washed away."

"What do we do?" It was a struggle to breathe, because this was all so much worse than Teriana could have predicted. Marcus not just sick, but potentially in the hands of one of the corrupted.

"We know the Thirty-Seventh is in Aracam." Nic snapped the ledger shut. "We bury the dead, then we march to meet them."

10

LYDIA

As dawn lightened the sky in the east, Lydia rolled onto her side in her bedroll, the thick carpet of moss soft beneath her. Frogs croaked in the nearby stream and the air was thick with moisture, though it was not half as oppressive as the swamps surrounding the lake. Everything here was alive, birds chirping in the trees and a woodpecker creating a racket as it attacked a tree. It might have been peaceful, but Lydia sensed Killian's eyes upon her from where he was preparing breakfast, so tension sang through her. He didn't speak, and neither did she.

But the tension said everything.

It had grown every day since they'd left the ruined cottage in the swamp, making their way south during the day and seeking the deepest cover during the night. She was afraid to sleep, terrified that if she let down her guard the urge to *take take take* would overwhelm her. It was the cruelest fear, because she loved Killian. Desperately wanted to go back to that moment before they'd entered Helatha and he'd kissed her. Memory filled her mind with Killian's voice. *From the moment you walked into my life, my heart, my soul, belonged to you, even if my sword did not. And I'd say that I felt torn in two because of it, but that would be a lie, because every moment I've spent with you has felt right.*

If she had her way, every moment forward would be spent in his arms, but instead she was considering asking him to tie her to a tree at night so that she could get some rest.

Unless you want to spend the rest of your life trussed up, you'll learn to control it. Or live with the consequences. His chastisement filled her head, his tone shifting from grief to frustration to condemnation with each passing day. Though she knew it was her subconscious and not Killian saying the words, Lydia still felt as though she were failing him.

Part of her wished that it *was* him repeating the words. That condemnation would turn to hatred and that he'd put his sword through her heart, ending her misery.

For misery, this truly was.

Though the air was temperate, she was plagued with nausea and sweating, barely able to eat, lethargy taking turns with hyperawareness. All her energy went toward both keeping up with Killian and keeping herself from killing him. Keeping herself from killing the horse she now rode. Keeping herself from killing every living soul they came across.

Which was mercifully few.

A terrifying mercy, for the absence of civilians had them both unnerved. They passed endless towns and villages devoid of human life, meals abandoned half eaten, laundry half hung on the lines. As though everyone who'd lived in them had dropped what they were doing at the exact same moment, with no evidence as to where they'd gone. Few animals remained, and Killian always took the time to set free those trapped in barns and stables so they could make their own way.

In one of the abandoned homes, Lydia had found a pair of spectacles that modestly improved her vision, as well as new clothes. Dark wool trousers and a white blouse, the only thing she retained of her stolen garments the leather corselette and her boots. Being mostly free of the trappings of one of the corrupted had made her feel more like herself until she'd found Killian examining a water glass with black sediment on the bottom. He straightened as she came in. "Look at this."

Every part of Lydia wanted to believe it was only grit from well water, but as she examined the glass, there was no denying that the black wasn't particles of dirt, but something that shifted and moved. Sentient and terrifying.

Blight.

"Rufina's killing all her people, isn't she?" Lydia whispered softly. "Building another army?"

"We've seen no evidence of blight in the land here." Killian bent closer to examine the swirling blackness. "Which means it's been transported from Deadground. Put in well water purposefully." He shook his head. "Explains why the animals won't drink from the troughs. They can smell it."

"Where are the blighters?" she asked. "How is it that we've seen not a one?"

Killian didn't answer, only went outside and walked to the edge of the town, pointing to the faint tracks. "They're heading south."

Neither of them spoke, but sickness of understanding filled Lydia's chest. An army, yes. But an army built for a specific purpose.

Catching Malahi. And catching *her.*

That had been more than a day ago, and they'd still seen no sight of blighters or their companions.

Coming around the fire, Killian set a bowl of porridge on the ground near her rather than handing it to her directly. "Eat quickly. I'll get the horses ready."

Lydia stared at the bowl, knowing that his behavior was a reaction to her own. Every time he came too close, she recoiled, and she could only imagine how that felt. Especially after what he'd said to her after Hegeria's battle with the Corrupter. *I'm with you to the end. No matter what the end.*

Killian disappeared between their horses, and Lydia squeezed her eyes shut to control the swell of tears. There had *always* been tension between them, from almost the moment they'd met, but it was twisted now. Corrupted, Lydia supposed was the right word, for how else did one describe a situation where you both loved a person and wanted to kill them? A relationship in which all you wanted in the world was to fling yourself into the person's arms but knew you couldn't because instead of kissing them, you'd steal years of their life from them?

"I hate this," she whispered in Cel because she needed to say it, needed to unleash her frustration lest it overwhelm her self-control. "It's not fair."

"Did you say something?"

"I said I'll be right back." Lydia walked into the trees and descended into a ditch to relieve herself, only to draw up short at the sight that greeted her. Taking a few steps farther, she paused and said, "Killian, you need to see this."

He approached, although she didn't fail to notice the healthy distance he kept between them. He blew out a breath of air between his teeth at the sight. "It seems Hegeria put us on the right track."

At the bottom of the hill were five bodies wearing Derin army uniforms, as well as one in the black leathers of a corrupted—less its head. Bushes with lush white flowers had grown in a thicket, partially obscuring them from sight. At least from any who might fly overhead. The bushes were nothing special, except for the fact they were the only plants in sight that were in bloom. The work of a tender, sure and true.

Killian hurried down the slope, Lydia following with more reluctance, for flies buzzed around the pools of congealed blood. "Look." He pointed to a body where the head was entirely caved in. "No human has the strength to do this in one blow. There's no doubt that a giant made this kill. And here." He extricated the corrupted from the bushes. "You can see how the opponent went for the spine to immobilize her, then reversed to take off the head before she had time to heal the injury. That takes skill, which suggests Agrippa. Given it's winter and these bushes are the only things in bloom, I'd say they still have Malahi with them."

Killian's excitement faded as swiftly as it manifested, and he abruptly kicked at a rock. "We spent the night with these corpses right next to us when we could have been in pursuit. We should have caught them by now."

"At least we know we're on the right track."

"Every moment we spend searching for Malahi is a moment we could be spending getting back to Mudamora, Lydia. You can bet the blight is spreading, never mind the army Rufina is obviously creating for another invasion. We have no time."

As if she didn't know that. "Can you track them?"

"Maybe. Get the horses."

Lydia clambered back up the slope, shoving the rest of the gear they'd accumulated into the saddlebags. Both horses pinned their ears at her approach. Lydia could hardly blame them, but her anxiety rose as Killian called for her to hurry up. "Easy, easy," she mumbled to the animals as she put on their saddles and bridles, both showing the whites of their eyes as they tried to pull away. "I'm not going to hurt you."

"Lydia! Let's go!"

Her skin flushed with frustration, and with a jerk, she hauled both animals in the direction Killian had gone.

"They only have one horse," he muttered, eyes on the tracks. "We should be able to outpace them. Just hope that they won't put up a fight over giving Malahi back."

It was not lost on Lydia that Killian felt responsible for everything that had happened to Mudamora's queen. He felt responsible, or at least complicit, and not at all pleased to have left her salvation in the hands of a Cel legionnaire who had recently been commander of Rufina's armies.

Taking his horse's reins, Killian swung into the saddle and heeled the animal down the path. Leaving Lydia to climb awkwardly into the saddle of her mount as it tried to sidle away from her. "Stop it," she snapped at the animal, her spectacles sliding down her nose. "Stand still!"

It only snorted and tried to back away, sensing her rising anger and lessening control.

With a snarl, she flung herself into the saddle, and the horse broke into a gallop as though it could outrun the monster on its back.

Within moments, she caught up to Killian and his horse, and her focus became all for staying in the saddle as they wove through the dense forest, following the trail left by their companions. Even without skill at tracking, Lydia noticed when the singular set of hoof tracks turned to two. Then three.

Then four.

And then it became impossible to tell how many horses were in pursuit.

Fear rose in Lydia's chest. It drove back the incessant hunger, as well as the nausea that came with denying it, because Malahi was the reason they'd come to Mudamora. They needed a tender to cure the blight consuming Mudamora. If Rufina captured or killed her, everything they'd done, everything they'd endured, would be for nothing. The Corrupter would have won.

Lydia urged her horse for more speed.

Wind whipped her hair, and the gaps in the trees revealed dark clouds swirling in the distance. Not the same swirling blackness of the Corrupter descending, but unnatural, nonetheless. Lightning burst downward in precise bolts, and she shouted, "That has to be Baird! He must be using his mark to manipulate the weather."

Killian cast a glance over his shoulder, giving her a tight nod before laying his reins against his exhausted mount's shoulder.

Faster.

Lydia bent over the neck of her horse, then touched the hilt of her sword with one hand. How much good she'd be able to do with it, she didn't know, but if Baird was resorting to manipulating the weather, it meant the situation was dire.

Above, the clouds swirled and surged, but between rolls of thunder, Lydia heard a familiar sound that chilled her to the core.

Deimos.

Whether it was because of the darkness provided by the storm or that their riders had given them no choice, the creatures were braving the sunlight. Worse still, there were at least two of them.

Ahead, the trees ended at the crest of a slope. Killian drew up his horse, Lydia's mount sliding to a stop next to it. Down the steep hill was a meadow that was alight with flame, and smoke billowed on the violent wind of the storm. A tiny, hooded figure clutching the reins of a rearing horse stood on the road, a man and a giant flanking her. A dead deimos lay smoking in the charred grass, a victim of the lightning. But encircling the trio were a dozen soldiers led by a woman clad in black leathers, long dark hair spilling down her back.

Lydia's heart lurched. *Rufina.*

The thunder from the storm had hidden the noise of their approach, so neither group had noticed them yet. But as the lightning had ceased, the wind carried Rufina's voice to Lydia's ears.

"I'm not pleased with you, Agrippa," the Queen of Derin said. "You stole my favorite toy."

"But I left you with two better ones." Agrippa smirked, the wind whipping his brown hair this way and that. "Or did you lose them, too?"

"Kitaryia can run back to the far side of the world, and it won't matter." Rufina lifted one shoulder in a graceful shrug. "She has welcomed my master into her heart and serves him now. If she's not already been the death of Killian, it's only a matter of time."

"I always did think they were destined for a tragic end," Agrippa replied. "But they're not my problem."

Rufina took a step closer, only for lightning to lance down from the sky, exploding the dirt before her. She froze.

"No closer, Your Grace," Agrippa said. "Or you'll find yourself in the same position as your mount." He jerked his chin toward the smoking deimos corpse.

"What do we do?" Lydia whispered, only to discover Killian lifting the bow he'd found at one of the abandoned towns, nocking an arrow and taking aim at Rufina.

"We end this," he whispered, then let the arrow loose.

It flew through the air, aim sure and true, but just before it struck, Rufina spun and snatched it from the air. Brush crackled behind Lydia, and she turned to find two women in homespun dresses standing behind them. Their skirts were covered in vomit, their feet bare and stained, and they were very, *very* dead.

"Blighters!" she gasped, only for the women to drop to the ground. Both had arrows embedded in their eyes.

Killian lowered his bow, but quick as he'd been, the damage was done.

"Why won't you just die, Lord Calorian," the Queen of Derin called up the slope. She watched them with midnight eyes rimmed with flame, her skin pale against the black leather clothing she wore. To Lydia's eyes, she glowed preternaturally bright, but even without her gift, the youth of Rufina's face betrayed that she was drunk on stolen life. "I grow weary of our encounters."

"Then let's make this our last." Killian dug in his heels, shooting his remaining arrows at Rufina's soldiers as he galloped down the slope. Dropping the bow, he pulled his sword.

Instead of raising her own weapon to fight, Rufina turned on her heels and ran.

A deimos swooped from the sky, and she leapt onto its back, taking to the air. As she did, Lydia heard it.

In the back of her mind, she'd thought it noise from the storm.

But it wasn't thunder. It was marching feet.

Hundreds, no, thousands, of men and women ran in lockstep through the trees, their faces blank.

As dead as the two women on the road behind her. And infinitely more in number than they could fight.

Her horse reared and Lydia dug in her heels. "Run!" She galloped down the hill. "Blighters!"

"Get on the horse!" Agrippa roared at Malahi. Instead of listening to him, Malahi dropped to the ground and pressed her hands to dirt.

The ground shook, and Lydia's mount nearly lost its footing. Nothing before her explained the tremor, so she risked a backward glance.

The trees were moving.

It was unlike anything she'd ever seen. Anything she'd known possible. The trees grew and wove together, branches twisting around each other and creating a wall running as far as she could see in either direction.

Yet it came at a cost, for Malahi slumped into Agrippa's arms.

Pulling her horse to a stop next to Killian's, Lydia stared at the wall. It shuddered as the blighters slammed into it, and she held her breath, half expecting for men and women to tear their way through it.

But it held.

Killian rounded on the remaining Derin soldiers. "I suggest you run."

The men appeared ready to take that advice when deimos screamed overhead, three descending, including the one that bore Rufina.

"Baird!" Agrippa shouted. "Kill them!"

"I've told you, little man," the giant shouted back, shaved head gleaming with sweat, "my aim isn't that accurate!"

The deimos landed with heavy thuds. One screamed, wings stretching out wide, and Lydia's terrified mount reared. She toppled backward and landed in the dirt.

"An interesting display." Rufina drew her sword, which she used to gesture at Malahi, who had roused. "This is why you're so precious to me, Your Grace. Not all of the marked are equal, and with your power, the blight will stretch across even the Endless Seas."

"I'll die first," Malahi hissed as Agrippa helped her upright.

Rufina laughed. "Brave words from the girl who hid from me beneath her bed. I remember how you screamed when I dragged you out by your ankles, Malahi. I remember how you wept when I cut open your face, and every time after when we'd look at your ruined beauty in the mirror."

"Do you remember the moment I gave in?" Malahi lifted her chin. "I will never bend to your master. Never."

A wave of shame washed over Lydia, but she shoved it away, because Rufina was only buying time. Malahi's wall was impressive, but it was only a matter of the blighters circling around the edges. The dead could run forever and not falter.

They needed to escape, and quickly.

Killian must have come to the same conclusion, because without warning, he galloped straight at Rufina.

What happened next, Lydia couldn't have said, for the other deimos and its corrupted rider flew directly at her.

She flung herself out of the way. Scrambling for her fallen sword, she caught a glimpse of Agrippa and Baird exchanging blows with the soldiers while Rufina's mount prowled up behind Killian from the rear.

"Look out!" she screamed, but the moment of distraction cost her as the corrupted who'd attacked her struck again.

The impact of the woman hitting her was akin to being struck by a battering ram, driving the wind from her lungs and sending Lydia's sword flying from her grip.

They rolled across the ground, the corrupted ending up on top of her, and Lydia had no chance to react before the woman's hands were on her throat. Choking.

Taking.

Lydia's scream cut off as the corrupted squeezed her throat. She couldn't see Killian beyond the deimos and didn't know if he was alive.

You're weak, the voice that plagued her whispered. *You love him, but you're too weak to fight for him.*

Lydia clawed at the woman's hands, but the corrupted only laughed, breath hot as she leaned down, her eyes infernos. An inhuman voice poured from her lips: "You're mine, Kitaryia."

Lydia's blood turned to ice. She knew the Corrupter's voice all too well because it was the voice that spoke every fear in her heart.

I'm not, she tried to scream, but no sound came from her lips.

The corrupted smiled, revealing stained teeth. "I will make you strong. I won't leave you to stand alone as Hegeria did. I will make you the queen you were destined to be."

No no no!

The pain in her throat was excruciating, life pouring from her into the other woman. In the distance, Killian roared her name.

"He stands alone," the disembodied voice said through the corrupted woman's lips. "The Six have left him to die. Look."

Killian fought both Rufina and her deimos, each taking turns attacking.

"You could kill them both, if you wanted," the voice crooned, breath hot against her ear. "Or you can allow them to kill him. Choose."

Lydia chose.

Her hand latched like a vise onto the woman's wrist, and with all the desperation burning in her soul, Lydia *yanked.* The woman's eyes widened in shock. Her lips parted just as Lydia drained the last of her life, and her body exploded into dust.

Lydia saw only red.

Felt only *need.*

With speed not meant for this world, she flung herself at her fallen sword, swinging it at the forelegs of the deimos between her and Killian. It shrieked as its limbs severed, falling, blood spraying, but Lydia already raced toward the other deimos.

It tried to take flight, but Lydia was faster.

Flinging herself onto the creature's back, she wrapped her arms around its neck as it rose in the air, teeth snapping at her leg.

Lydia only dug her fingers into its leathery skin and *took*.

The desperate creature flew higher, trying to shake her free, the battle a blur of shapes as bolts of lightning danced through the sky.

Then the ground was rushing up to meet her.

The dead deimos exploded into pieces of brittle bone and dust as it struck, the impact snapping Lydia's arms. She barely felt the pain, the excess of life the sweetest pleasure as it mended her body, making her whole.

And so very powerful.

In her periphery, Rufina bolted, a blur of black racing from the fight. Lydia considered pursuit, but then her eyes fixed on the gleaming beacon of life that stood before her. How had she not noticed before how bright the queen of Mudamora shone?

"Lydia!" Malahi gasped, taking a step back. "Don't. Please don't."

Lydia took a step after her, then another, closing the distance.

"Please."

In the back of her mind, Lydia heard her conscience *screaming* that Mudamora needed Malahi. That this young woman was their salvation. But louder was the hunger, and it whispered, *All Malahi has ever caused you is grief.*

"Lydia . . ." Malahi lifted the knife in her hand even as Lydia's muscles bunched, readying to attack.

She'll hesitate, the voice instructed. *Take her life now.*

Lydia took a step—

Only for something to strike her in the back with violent force. The ground rose up to meet her, and for a heartbeat, everything went dark.

11

KILLIAN

The speed at which Lydia moved told Killian everything he needed to know as she attacked the deimos, but there was nothing he could do with Rufina pressing him hard.

Their swords clashed in a symphony of steel, it feeling to Killian as though they picked up from where they'd left off the last time they'd fought. A battle that never ended, because they were too evenly matched.

Then the queen of Derin skittered backward and said, "Malahi will never break, which means she is no good to me." Her laugh was cruel. "So I'll let Kitaryia do my dirty work."

She turned on her heel and *ran*.

Logic demanded Killian pursue. Rufina was the heart of all the horror consuming Mudamora, and killing her would end it.

But his instincts demanded he turn around.

Lydia stalked toward Malahi, who took one step back. Then another step.

"Lydia, no!" He broke into a run, but Agrippa was closer. Was faster.

Horror stole the breath from Killian's chest as the other man swung his blade, the steel slicing through Lydia's spine. "No!"

She fell, and Killian howled, wordlessly skidding to his knees before her. He'd lost her. He'd lost her.

"Get back!" Hands caught hold of his shoulders and tried to pull him backward. Killian lashed out at Agrippa, clipping the other man's jaw.

"She's not gods-damned dead, you fool! Get out of reach!"

Killian's hackles rose, and he slowly turned his head. Lydia was reaching for him. Reaching, and dragging herself toward him as her severed spine slowly knit together.

"Kill her!" Agrippa shouted. "You don't have much longer until she heals!"

He couldn't.

He wouldn't.

"Fight it," he pleaded. "Please, Lydia. You know you can fight this."

"She can't." Agrippa froze as Killian pointed his sword tip in the legionnaire's direction. "I've seen them like this. They can't control themselves. She's lost!"

"She's not!"

"If you let her recover, she's going to kill you! And then I'm going to gods-damned kill her!"

Killian ignored Agrippa, locking eyes with Lydia. "You can control this. You've done it before." *With the help of all the Six.* "You can do it again."

She went still.

"You have beat back a *god*," he whispered. "Who else in the world can claim such a thing? The answer is no one because no one else is *you*." Killian swallowed hard. "So many people love and depend on you. Teriana. Finn. Sonia." Were the flames around her irises fading or was it just his wishful thinking? "Me, most of all."

Her leg twitched. Behind him, Agrippa said, "Malahi, get on the horse. Baird, take her and run. I'll deal with this."

"Go with them, Agrippa!" Killian snarled over Malahi's protest that she wouldn't leave.

"No. I'm not leaving one of the corrupted to hunt at my heels. Some things are too dangerous to be left alive."

Killian opened his mouth to tell the other man that if he tried to harm Lydia, he'd find himself run through with Killian's sword, but then Lydia spoke. "By that logic, he should put *you* down, legionnaire. Soldier of the Empire. Soldier of the Corrupter. How much death have you left in *your* wake?"

"Numbers beyond count," Agrippa answered. "But I'm not about to fall on my own blade over it and leave Malahi, who alone in this company has killed *no one*, to be murdered because her sworn bodyguard is too damn lovesick to do his job!"

Killian clenched his teeth, the barb stabbing through panic and fear, and he fought the urge to look over his shoulder at the queen in question.

"Better she be protected by someone like you, Agrippa?" Lydia crooned. "The man who has always chosen to be the villain?"

Agrippa tensed, and Lydia smiled. "Who was she? Who was the Bardenese girl? How much worth were your promises to protect *her* when the Thirty-Seventh laid siege to Hydrilla? Or does her corpse rot beneath Bardenese redwoods?"

Names and nations that meant nothing to Killian, but he could feel the anger seething from Agrippa as he snapped, "Silvara? I hate to disappoint, but hers was the last face I saw before I was whisked to this side of the world, and she was *very much* alive. Knowing her as I once did, she's likely grown up to be a thorn in the Empire's ass and in little need of anyone's protection, least of all mine."

"Whereas helpless little Malahi makes you feel relevant?"

Agrippa's scowl darkened.

"I wouldn't count on him too much, Your Majesty," Lydia said with a soft laugh. "Once he learns the Thirty-Seventh is on the Southern Continent, I suspect he'll go scampering back to them." She pressed fingers to her smirk. "And now he knows."

Agrippa was silent. Killian risked a backward glance over his shoulder to find all the color drained from the other man's face, his blade tip lowering. "The Thirty-Seventh is in the West?"

Killian's instincts flared, warning him, but not fast enough. Lydia regained her feet in a flash, lunging at Agrippa, but as she did, roots exploded from the ground beneath her, wrapping around her body in a thick net and pinning her to the ground. Killian staggered, struggling to keep his own footing on the shaking ground, the horses shrieking in panic.

Agrippa grinned. "Malahi's not helpless. Far from it."

Rising from where her hands had been pressed against the charred earth, Malahi drew back her hood and approached. Not Lydia, but Killian.

Though he'd seen her briefly in Helatha, Killian had not at the time fully appreciated the horror that had been enacted upon Mudamora's queen. Her skin was sallow, the shadows beneath her eyes so dark it made them appear sunken. Her once lustrous blond hair had been roughly cut, though patches of it were gone entirely, her scalp scabbed where the hair had been ripped out. All her fingernails were missing, and her hands were covered with livid scratches. But worst of all was the livid wound stretching from her hairline to her chin that had been badly stitched together.

Malahi had been tortured, and for all Killian wouldn't change his choice to go after Lydia at Alder's Ford, there was no denying that *none* of this would have happened to Malahi if he'd done his duty and remained at her side.

There were no words that could undo the harm done to her, but still his lips parted. "Malahi, I—"

She held up her hand. "Don't. I have no interest in hearing it. What is done is done, and I desire to focus on the future, not on the past, because it will be in the future where we win or lose this war against evil. I refuse to go toward that battle with someone I can't trust to put me first at my back. Therefore, Killian Calorian, you are released from your obligations and oaths to me. In truth, you were never free to give them, for you were sworn to Princess Kitaryia Falorn—Lydia—long before you and I ever met. I am grateful for all that you have done to liberate me from Ru—" Her voice caught, and she swallowed hard. "From Rufina. But your path is no longer at my side; it's at Lydia's."

Shock radiated through Killian, but Malahi allowed him no response as she turned to kneel before Lydia.

"Malahi . . ." Agrippa reached for the queen with the obvious intent to pull her back, but he stilled as she cast a slight smile over her shoulder.

"What happened to me not being helpless?"

"Doesn't mean you don't make bad choices on occasion." He

grimaced. "I said I would have your back as long as you needed, so at your back is where you will find me until you tell me to piss off."

Malahi's smile grew, then fell away as her focus returned to Lydia, who had stopped struggling against the implacable vines. "You were right."

Lydia said nothing, only watched the queen.

"In those brief moments we spoke in Helatha, I claimed a higher road in my refusal to betray Yara's gift to the Corrupter's influence and you said that doing nothing was also a betrayal. I hated you for saying that. Hated you for so many reasons, if I am being honest. But in the days since, I have come to see that you were right. We have both acted in ways that have given our enemy power, you in a desperate attempt to be strong, and me in conceding defeat. We have both erred."

Killian said nothing, didn't so much as move, for Lydia was listening.

"I didn't want to fight," Malahi said softly. "I wanted to hide. To crawl back under the bed in my prison and slowly fade, because I felt as though everything about me that had value had been destroyed. I was weak. Broken. *Ugly.*"

Agrippa made a noise of protest, but Malahi held up a hand to silence any interruption.

"All those things are true," she continued, "and yet Rufina has pursued me at all costs to try to get me back. Why would she do so if I held no value? If I could not make a difference to Mudamora? Perhaps it is strange, but seeing proof of how much Rufina values me allowed me to value myself. I am weak, broken, and ugly, but I am not yet defeated."

To Killian's horror, Malahi reached out and clasped Lydia's hand. He lunged to pull her away, but Agrippa blocked his path. "If she wants help, she'll ask."

Lydia's eyes fixed on the hand holding hers, but Malahi's battered fingers showed no sign that Lydia was draining any of her life.

"I think you keep allowing the dark part of you to take control because you believe you are weak. Because you know you aren't a warrior. Because you think it's the only way to protect those you care about," the queen said. "Yet ask yourself this, Lydia: Why would the Corrupter give his enemy a tool that made them stronger?"

Silence hung in the air, the tension as thick as the smoke from the fires that still burned around them. Then Malahi's hand began to heal, the scratches disappearing and the torn nail beds becoming whole.

Lydia let go of Malahi, her chest rising and falling with rapid breaths, and her eyes . . .

Were once again green.

Relief flooded Killian's veins even as Agrippa muttered, "Fuck me, she did it." Which *she* he meant, Killian didn't know, and didn't really care, because Lydia was herself again.

"I'm sorry," Lydia said hoarsely. "I . . ."

"Don't waste breath on apologies." Malahi pressed her healed hand to the earth and the roots unraveled from around Lydia's body, disappearing beneath the ground. "The enemy sees you as a threat, and it can't just be because of your name. We need to discover what it is they think you can do."

"She can heal people infected with blight." Killian blurted out the truth. "Lena was infected, and Lydia saved her."

Malahi's eyes widened. "How?"

"It's only possible in the short time between infection and death, and it nearly killed me." Lydia climbed unsteadily to her feet. "But it's why I think a tender might be able to do the same thing for the land, we need only figure out how."

It bothered Killian how easily she dismissed her own value, refusing to recognize that she'd accomplished something no one else had even tried. Why didn't she see that as the strength it was?

"This is all wonderful news," Agrippa interrupted, catching Malahi's wrist and tugging her away from Lydia. "But there are several thousand corpses hunting for a way around that wall, and once they find it, they'll be in pursuit. Perhaps we might save conversation for later, when we have put them off our trail."

"I'll catch the horses," Baird muttered. "Foolish animals can't have gotten far."

Malahi swayed with exhaustion, and Agrippa immediately caught her elbow and steadied her, the pair speaking quietly as he led her away.

Killian watched them for a long moment, then said to Lydia, "I knew you were struggling, but not once in the past days have you said that you didn't have it under control. Why didn't you tell me?"

"Because I was ashamed." She looked anywhere but at him. "The Six themselves pulled out the Corrupter's claws, but a big part of me wants to fall back into his control. I know what Malahi said is right, that allowing my mark to be corrupted makes me weaker, not stronger, but it doesn't feel that way in the moment. It makes me feel invincible."

"Agrippa proved otherwise." His tone was flat, and Killian winced, knowing that he wasn't helping. Hegeria had said that this would be a lifelong battle for Lydia, but a big part of him had been certain that the worst was over. Had been convinced that the memories of what she'd done, what it had been like to be under the Corrupter's influence, would be enough motivation to keep her from slipping up again. But he'd been wrong. "How can I help?"

He took a step toward her, but Lydia took a quick step back.

"I need space," she whispered. "I . . . I can't be tempted. Not yet."

Unbidden, Killian's eyes moved to their companions. Agrippa lifted Malahi into the saddle of the horse Baird had caught before swinging up behind her. Malahi leaned back against him, and a flood of envy ran through Killian. Not for their closeness, but for how easy things seemed between them. Something as simple as touch, which they took for granted and yet was forbidden to him and Lydia, the stakes her sanity and his life.

Killian's hands balled into fists, the urge to curse and shout and slam his fists into *something* nearly overtaking him. All he wanted to do was help her, yet the best thing he could do for Lydia was to stay away. "I understand."

"It's not fair."

There was bitterness in Lydia's voice, and he noted her hands were as tightly fisted as his own.

"The only reason we haven't been together is because of the obligation you felt to Malahi. The guilt you felt over her being imprisoned. But not only did she free you, she seems to have forgiven you," she said. "Yet the gulf between us feels bigger than it was before. It's my fault, and I—"

"It's not your fault." He reached for her, then caught himself and shoved his blood-smeared hands into his pockets where they could do no damage. "You'll learn to control it. It will get better." *Please let it get better.* "I will be at your back, come what may."

Lydia wiped at her eyes, then gave a tight nod.

I love you, he wanted to say. *I will always love you.*

But sensing that the admission would only make both of them feel worse, he said, "We should ride. Night is coming, and we need to have good cover before more deimos take over the skies."

12

MARCUS

"He's dying, sir."

"Keep him alive! We're almost to Aracam!"

"He's had six seizures in as many hours. He might still be breathing, but he's never going to wake up, sir. His brain is pulp."

"Fuck! Go, then! And consider yourself demoted, you incompetent sack of shit!"

Marcus could hear them, but he could not move. Could not open his eyes. Could not speak.

There was nothing but sound and pain.

"Shit!"

"Might I make a suggestion, young master?"

"Unless it's a way to keep him alive to deliver to Felix, I don't want to hear it, Zaide."

"It is, young master. We have medicines. Your healer . . . *surgeon*, yes? He would not take my advice, but desperate times call for desperate measures, would you not say?"

"Do it. I don't care what it is—do it. If it works, I'll have that useless shit flogged for not listening before."

Through the pain, Marcus felt hands grasping him. Someone forced his mouth open and pouring something down his throat, the noise of Titus cursing like knives in his skull, but then even pain slipped away as his mind fell away into nothingness.

It was akin to the feel of a xenthier path, except instead of brilliant white, all was black. An endless, ceaseless void and Marcus silently screamed, because to remain like this would be the greatest torment ever devised. An endless nightmare from which there would be no escape, and he screamed and screamed and—

Opened his eyes.

"See, young master," the old Gamdeshian crooned even as the excruciating pain in Marcus's skull began to ease, his vision clearing to reveal the ancient man leaning over him, hands cupping Marcus's cheeks. "Your Eastern healers know nothing."

"Watch your tongue, Zaide, for such slander against the Empire will see it cut out." Titus shouldered Zaide out of the way and leaned over Marcus to look him in the eye. "Though for these results, I will forgive it."

"You are benevolent, young master."

Titus ignored the old man, catching his balance against the side of the rocking wagon as it bounced over a rut. "Welcome back to the land of the living, Marcus. Just in time to return you to your men."

Marcus coughed, his mouth tasting foul and every part of him aching, but he could move and see and—"This isn't going to work, Titus."

The younger legatus roughly patted Marcus's cheek. "You dug this hole yourself, *sir*. But truly, I do wish you the best. Zaide, get him up and put a hood on him. I want Felix to have the grand reveal."

Climbing to his feet, Titus jumped out of the wagon. "Get this thing moving faster," he said. "He's awake but I don't know for how long."

Marcus couldn't help but wonder the same thing. For while the pain was diminished, his head still throbbed, and nausea still pooled in his stomach. Realizing the Gamdeshian had a firm grip on his wrist, he jerked free of the man.

Zaide only grinned at him, white teeth gleaming. "You will live long enough to die, legatus."

Before Marcus could answer, the Gamdeshian pulled a hood over his head.

Think.

He had no idea what the man had given him to bring him back to consciousness, likely some stimulant he'd pay for later, but this might be the only moment he had with a relatively clear head to come up with a way through this. A way to explain to Felix and the Thirty-Seventh what had happened before they beat him to a pulp for desertion.

While there had most certainly been witnesses to his arrival through the xenthier, Titus clearly had them under strict orders to keep their mouths shut. His armor was gone. As were his weapons, gold, and the letter Wex had written him with proof he'd been in Celendrial. Eventually, path-hunters would come, but by then, it would be far, *far* too late.

Think.

But he could not focus as he heard familiar shouts of codes and orders, the wagon slowing its pace. Though the sack obscured his vision, Marcus didn't need his eyes to know they'd entered a legion camp. Not with the familiar smell of smoke and sweat and shit. The bark of centurions giving orders. The laughter of men around fires.

The ever-present tension of an army ready to fight at a moment's notice. And a certain quality to the whole mix of it all that told him this was the Thirty-Seventh's camp.

The wagon stopped moving, and rough hands pulled him out. Marcus landed in a heap on the ground, then was dragged to his feet, his knees struggling to support him. The same hands shoved him into a walk, and his head swam with dizziness.

How long did he have until Zaide's medicines wore off? How long until the endless darkness returned?

"Find Felix," Titus called from behind him, and hands pulled Marcus to a halt. "The Forty-First has a gift for the Thirty-Seventh, and I think it best that he be the one to unwrap it."

Sickness twisted Marcus's gut, because his history with Felix was more likely to be his damnation than his salvation. Echoes of their last conversation filled his head, drowning out the curious murmurs of the legionnaires watching on.

Since we've been children, I've protected you, Marcus. Lied and deceived and murdered to keep you alive and to achieve your ends. And for what? What do you give me in return?

Apparently not the one thing that you want.

Hateful words cast when he'd believed that it was Felix who'd betrayed him, Felix who'd given over Teriana to Ashok, Felix who'd put the Thirty-Seventh at risk by conspiring with the enemy.

But it hadn't been Felix, it had been Cassius's piece-of shit-son, Titus, and anger chased away Marcus's fear. Every part of him wanted to hurl accusations at Titus, but that was coin one could only spend once, and Marcus had played the game too long to waste it now.

Footsteps approached, the distinct purposeful rhythm a punch to the stomach because he'd know Felix's stride anywhere.

"Why are you here, sir?" Felix asked. Marcus clenched his teeth, the sound of his friend's voice after all this time threatening to shatter his composure. "I was under the impression you were focused on dealing with the inlanders. My last report is that they attacked your camp."

"It was nothing more than rattling of spears and banging of drums," Titus replied. "Given the importance of the prisoner, I thought it a better use of my time to deliver him to the Thirty-Seventh myself."

Silence stretched, and Marcus felt Felix's eyes on him, heard the slight intake of breath as his friend realized his identity.

Marcus clenched his teeth, waiting for the distinct snick of steel as a gladius was drawn, but instead, Felix said, "You have our gratitude, sir. As this is Thirty-Seventh business, we will take him from here." A hesitation, then, "Bring him to command."

Relief flooded Marcus's veins. Felix was going to give him a chance to speak, to explain himself, to—

"I'd suggest that the prison is a more appropriate destination," Titus said. Catching hold of the hood concealing Marcus's face, Titus wrenched it away, then kicked Marcus in the spine.

He sprawled at Felix's feet, tasting mud and worse. Yet it was tempting to remain in that position, for the alternative was to look up and face the consequences of all that he had said. All that he had done. While he was no deserter, neither was Marcus innocent, and even if he made it through this alive, there would be a reckoning.

Get up, he ordered himself, ignoring the pain and nausea and fear that demanded otherwise. *Face this on your feet.*

It was awkward with his arms bound, but Marcus got his knees beneath him. Then his feet. Mud dripped down his face as he straightened, the rising tide of angry voices making his pulse roar as his men recognized him. Legionnaires he'd led most of his life bent to pick up rocks, their faces flushed with fury, and he couldn't blame them. It had been he who'd brought them to this place, whom they'd followed without question, and they all believed he'd abandoned them for a girl.

It was the worst form of betrayal, and the only thing standing between him and being beaten to death by his own men was the friend he'd all but stabbed in the heart.

He met Felix's gaze, then immediately wished he hadn't, for his friend's blue eyes blazed with an awful mix of fury, shock, and grief that was barely kept in check. Men pressed closer all around them, the air tasting like violence, and Marcus knew that Felix wanted to unleash them. Wanted to pick up a rock and strike the first blow. The final blow. Anything to find respite from the hurt Marcus had caused him.

"He was found in civilian clothes near our camp." Titus's voice was measured, but his glee shone as bright as his polished armor. Titus would relish watching the Thirty-Seventh slaughter him, because it would clear a path to uncontested power. "He was injured when we found him. Black eye, bruised ribs. It seems Teriana grew tired of him and gave him a beating. He denies desertion and has wild claims about his whereabouts, but we have been unable to confirm his words. I suggest you give him the benefit of explaining himself before you take action."

The clever bastard was doing his level best to ensure he couldn't be blamed for any of what came next.

The din of shouts calling for his death grew. "Fucking traitor!" someone screamed, and Marcus flinched as a rock glanced off his arm. Then another hit his shoulder, sending a spike of pain lancing down his fingertips.

But he kept his eyes fixed on Felix's. "I didn't desert," he said. "You can hear me out or kill me and hear the same story from the path-hunters who will soon arrive. Your choice."

"No one knows better than me how easily you lie, Marcus." The muscles in Felix's jaw stood out in stark relief. "That the same story comes from someone else does not make it the truth. It only means you've manipulated them into believing it so."

Another rock struck. Then another, and the chance for Felix to stop the violence was nearly past. His ears were full of the promise of death, his nose with sour sweat and his own coppery blood, but Marcus didn't blink as he said, "Your choice, Felix."

The world seemed to stand still, balanced on the edge of a knife blade, and Marcus braced himself for the pain.

Felix lifted one hand. "Hold."

Only a lifetime of training made the men obey, and even so, Marcus felt their anger pushing against the order like a storm against a seawall. Felix sensed it too, and he glared at the surrounding men.

"Back. The. Fuck. Up!" he roared. "We have fallen far in this place, but not so far that we have forgotten the rule of law. He will be heard, and if his words fail to convince me, we will have his blood! Now get back to your duties before I have the lot of you flogged!"

The men reluctantly retreated a few paces, but Marcus's heart didn't slow its rapid *thump, thump.* Not with the whole camp seething with the barely checked violence of men who'd been raised as killers. Men who believed vengeance against him was their right.

Servius appeared, his large friend refusing to look at him as Felix said, "Lock him up. Keep him alive until I'm ready to hear him out." Then he gestured at Titus and said, "If you would, sir," before turning on his heel and striding toward the newly built stone structure at the center of the camp.

"Don't speak," Servius said, grabbing hold of Marcus and shoving him forward. "Don't say a bloody word, or on my life, I'll gag you with an ass wipe. I don't want to hear your excuses. Don't want to hear your reasons. And I sure as shit don't want to hear your lies—you can save those for Felix, though I think you'll find him less tolerant of them than he once was."

Marcus said not a word as Servius forced him through the rows of white tents, the scowls of the Thirty-Seventh coming from all sides.

Only for Gibzen to step into their path.

"You should never have come back," the primus hissed, drawing his gladius. "Not after what you did. Not after you chose that Maarin whore over your own brothers!"

"Unless you want your ass whipped raw, you'll put that away," Servius barked. "Legatus's orders."

"But he—"

"I know what he did, Gibzen." Servius jerked on Marcus's arms with enough force that his feet lifted off the ground. "Go find yourself a rock and wait for Felix to give the order."

The primus slammed his gladius back in its sheath, then spit in Marcus's face as he passed. "Traitor!"

Marcus said nothing, spittle dripping down his cheek as Servius dragged him toward a thick stone structure.

The legions had been busy in his absence, the prison built in the Cel style they'd been trained to use, every block perfectly cut and fitted together, the floor set into a mosaic of smaller stones. Gleaming steel formed the fronts of each of the cells, and as Marcus stumbled down the center hallway, a familiar face appeared from behind the bars.

"Marcus?" Quintus pounded a bruised fist against one of the bars. "I knew it! Knew that unless you were dead, you'd be back. Knew you hadn't deserted, but those shitstains wouldn't listen!"

"He didn't come back," Servius snapped. "Titus's men caught him."

Quintus went still. "Teriana?"

Her name was a knife to the gut, tearing down the walls Marcus had built up around the emotions he felt for her. And the lies he'd told to her.

"Wasn't with him," Servius snapped.

"Is she alive?"

"She's in Celendrial," Marcus answered, because he could see that Quintus cared, and rewarding that was worth Servius slamming him sideways against the bars like Marcus was no more than a ragdoll.

"I said, be silent!"

Stars filled Marcus's vision, everything spinning, but he heard Quintus say, "Celendrial? Shit. How?" before he was hauled out of earshot.

Servius unlocked the cell at the far end, then threw Marcus inside. He stumbled over his own feet and fell to his knees, nearly colliding with the shit bucket before he caught his balance. The bars slammed shut behind him, and Servius crossed his arms as he moved to stand in front of the cell opposite.

From down the hallway, Quintus shouted, "I told you that she wouldn't abandon her ship! I told you that something happened to them!"

"Quintus, shut up or I will cut out your tongue and shove it down your throat!" Servius roared, his voice reverberating through the stone structure.

Marcus winced at the noise. His head throbbed, exhaustion weighing him down, for adrenaline was not enough to overcome the hunger and deprivation Titus had inflicted upon him. Still, he risked asking, "What has Quintus done to deserve being locked up?"

"What hasn't he done would be a shorter list." Servius gave a sharp shake of his head, then leveled a finger at Marcus. "I told you to be quiet."

Easing to his feet, Marcus sat on the cot and watched his friend stew, knowing that Servius hated the silence and would feel compelled to break it. The muscles beneath Servius's brown skin flexed, his jaw working back and forth, brow creased with a scowl. Sure enough, only a few moments passed before his friend crossed the corridor and gripped the bars. "Do you have any idea of what your desertion did to the Thirty-Seventh? Do you have any idea what a mess things have been since you went running off into the sunset with Teriana?"

"I didn't—"

"Be quiet!" Servius rattled the bars, face darkening with anger. "I'm doing the talking!"

Silence stretched, then Servius spun away, turning in a circle before gripping the bars again. "We've lost one hundred twenty-four of the Thirty-Seventh since you've been gone."

Marcus's skin turned to ice, his stomach hollowing. "How?" he asked, though what he really wanted to know was *who*. Whose names were now struck from the ranks of the Thirty-Seventh with the word *deceased* written next to them.

"Titus ordered us to press into the interior. There are things in there. Creatures and . . . and we don't know what. We find men slaughtered if we find them at all." Servius let out a ragged breath, shaking his head. "It hasn't gone well under Titus's command, but without the Senate's approval, Felix is only acting legatus. What could we do?"

Rise up.

The thought screamed its way into his head, instantly to be dismissed, for following the chain of command was so instinctive to his men that they did it as naturally as breathing. Marcus's hands fisted because without his protection, everything he'd feared would happen to his legion had come to pass. "Why the interior? It was never the target."

Servius spread his arms wide. "What else? Xenthier. We all knew you dragged your heels in the search for reasons of your own, but Titus raced after every rumor like a rat terrier. He wants the glory of conquest, and that's not happening with only two legions. Not against a target like Gamdesh. We needed a route back to secure more resources."

"There is a genesis in the abandoned city," Marcus replied. "But the terminus is in the middle of Sibern. Don't send anyone."

"You don't give orders. Not anymore."

Servius's voice was frosty, but Marcus didn't miss the way his friend's jaw had tightened. They'd found the stem in the collapsed temple.

"Whomever you sent is likely in the belly of Sibernese wolves. Or frozen, given that it's the depths of winter."

Curiosity flickered in Servius's brown eyes, but all he said was, "Good thing Titus doesn't trust us, then. Sent two of his own." Servius seemed to be gathering his thoughts, trying to determine truth from fallacy. "You . . . you're saying you have been in the East?"

Marcus didn't answer.

With a few pieces of information, the seed was now sown, curiosity a far more powerful creature than the full story itself. He could see the questions forming in Servius's eyes, each of them undermining the truth that the Thirty-Seventh had come to believe about his desertion.

Except, in the end, it didn't matter what Servius thought. The decision of whether Marcus lived or died was in Felix's hands. "How has Felix held up?"

The question had slipped out, and while Marcus was tempted to blame exhaustion and his rattled brain for the error, the truth was that he was desperate to know Felix's state of mind.

Servius was quiet, and that alone made Marcus's stomach plummet. Yet it fell lower still as his friend said softly, "He had half the legion hunting for you. Refused to believe that you'd desert, especially with

Quintus ranting that Teriana would never abandon her people. He was convinced you were in the temple when the floor collapsed and went through the xenthier involuntarily. Was all any of us could do to keep him from ordering an entire century of men after you. But then—"

Servius broke off as the sharp clack of legion-issue sandals against stone filled the building, his gaze going up the hallway.

"I'll speak to the prisoner now." Felix stepped in front of Marcus's cell. "Alone. Take Quintus with you—I've no interest in his incessant need to involve himself."

Servius wavered, appearing ready to argue, but then he slammed a hand against his chest. "Yes, sir." With no further comments, he disappeared from view.

A lock clicked and hinges creaked, then Quintus was shouting, "She wouldn't have done it! Wouldn't have left them! Don't believe the lies, Felix! No matter what you think of him, Teriana wouldn't have—"

There was the sound of a fist thudding against flesh, then Servius's muttered, "Shut your bloody gob, Quintus," and the thump of the door shutting.

Leaving Marcus and Felix alone, the only sound the rising storm of Thirty-Seventh voices outside the prison calling for his blood.

13

MARCUS

Neither of them spoke, the silence stretching, and for Marcus's part, it was because he didn't know what to say.

Felix took hold of the bars and leaned his weight against the cell. He wore his old armor, the breastplate scratched and dented in a few places, including across the embossed 37. Given his friend's commitment to maintaining legion standards, that meant he'd seen recent combat. His fair hair was freshly shorn, but his golden skin was shadowed with exhaustion.

Felix looked him up and down, then slowly exhaled. "Doesn't look good for you. They're calling for your blood."

"That's not their call," Marcus answered. "It's *yours*."

Felix's eyes locked on his, then, in a flurry of motion, he let go of the bars and slammed his palms against them with a loud bang. Leveling a finger, he said, "Fuck you, Marcus. Don't you dare dump this on my feet as though I created this mess. You did this. *You.*"

His tongue was frozen in his mouth, his brain nothing but noise. Though Marcus knew he should say whatever it took to buy himself time for path-hunters to arrive and prove where he'd been, all that came out was, "I'm sorry."

Felix huffed, then looked away. "Yeah, I bet you are. There's something about having to beg for your life that makes every man sorry for the choices that got him there."

"No," Marcus said. "I'm sorry for what I said to you before I left to go inland. You didn't deserve any of that from me."

The silence stretched, the tension between them thickening enough that Marcus struggled to breathe. Then Felix said, "What difference do you think that makes? Do you think any of them care that you said shit to me and now you're sorry? They're not angry that you're an asshole, they're angry that you deserted. I'd say apologize for that, except we both know that you'd be spitting into the wind."

Marcus bit the insides of his cheeks, not bothering with denials. "Ashok, the man who was working with Urcon, told Teriana that it was one of my men who'd betrayed her location. Whoever it was wanted to be rid of her, wanted things to go back to the way they were before she joined our camp, and he paid Ashok in gold to do the job. I'd been trying to figure out who the traitor was. Teriana suspected Titus, but I—"

"Thought it was me." All the color had drained from Felix's face. "You thought that I'd set up the men guarding her to die, just to get rid of Teriana? Thought that I put the Thirty-Seventh at risk, just to have her killed? Thought that I betrayed my best friend and commander, just because my *fucking feelings* were hurt?"

All the reasons, all the justifications, that had once made perfect sense now felt like lunacy. "Yes."

Felix leaned against the bars, his eyes on the floor, and Marcus's chest tightened as his best friend's jaw trembled.

"It was bad enough when I thought you were angry that I was against you and Teriana. Bad enough when I thought you'd chosen her over me." Felix lifted his face. His eyes were red, gleaming with unshed tears. "Now I wish I could go back to thinking that, because the truth is so much worse."

"I'm sorry."

"Stop." Felix scrubbed his hands over his shorn scalp. "I . . ."

As Marcus watched, his friend turned his back to the cell, then slid down the bars to sit on the floor, face pressed to his knees. "I hate you for this. I hate you so much."

Not as much as Marcus hated himself.

His mouth was dry, but he said, "Teriana was gambling with the men while we were in the interior, and one of them had a newly minted gold dragon with Cassius's likeness on it. It triggered her memory of the coins paid to Ashok by the traitor, which were the same mint."

Felix went still. "Those weren't in circulation when we left Celendrial."

"No, they weren't," Marcus replied. "But of a surety, Cassius had access to them."

"Titus."

"So it would seem." Marcus moved so that he was sitting with his back to Felix, as he had times beyond counting, though he knew it was not just steel bars that rested between them. Every inhale brought the familiar scent of leather and soap, of sweat and steel. "But I don't have any proof. I . . . I don't trust myself to see clearly anymore. Not about this."

Outside the prison, the Thirty-Seventh screamed their rage. Their hurt. Marcus closed his eyes and listened, grief and guilt filling him. They'd suffered in his absence. Suffered because of the mistakes he'd made, and there was no way to undo that. No way to bring back the dead.

"Tell me what happened."

Marcus drew in a ragged breath, composure wavering because even though Felix didn't have to, even though he surely didn't want to, his best friend was going to hear him out. "We left camp so that Teriana could tell me her theory about the coins," he said. "But we were set upon from above by a tiger. We ran and it pursued, chasing us into one of the temples. The floor collapsed, revealing the xenthier beneath. It was dragging the rubble into it, but we couldn't climb out because there were inlanders in company with the tiger. People capable of changing into beast form, though I didn't know it until later. They were going to kill us, so we took the only chance at life and went through the stem. To Sibern."

With the rage of the Thirty-Seventh a rising tide in the background, the story poured from Marcus's lips. The trek across Sibern. The passage down to Celendrial. His encounter with Hostus, conversation with Wex at Lescendor, and fateful meeting with Cassius and the Senate. The attempt to assassinate him at his family's home and then his flight through the xenthier stems to beat his pursuers to Bardeen. Very little did he leave out, only things that he'd die before revealing, and if Felix questioned any of the gaps, he did not say so.

His friend was quiet for a long time after Marcus had finished, then he said, "You could've disappeared. Could've left this life behind. Why didn't you?"

Teriana's voice filled his head. *I love you and I want to be with you, but the only way that's possible is if you leave this life behind. Will you do it? For me?*

"She wanted you to, didn't she?" Felix asked, seeming to see inside Marcus's thoughts. "But you said no? You said you needed to come back?"

He could hear the hope in Felix's voice. The need to have some of the hurt undone with the knowledge that when it had come down to it, Marcus had chosen the Thirty-Seventh over Teriana and freedom.

Lie, logic screamed at him. *Tell him what he wants to hear.*

Except Marcus was tired of deception. Tired of juggling a life so interwoven with lies that to pull one out would see the whole mess come falling down around him. "I didn't get the chance to answer her, because that was when Carmo caught us, rendering the question moot."

Silence.

"If he hadn't come just then, what would you have said?"

Marcus closed his eyes. "I would have said yes."

A loud bang made Marcus jump. Then another and another, the legion throwing rocks against the building as they screamed for justice. Whatever control Servius had outside was hanging on by a thread. A thread that was going to snap, whether Felix wanted it to or not.

"I should despise you for that," Felix said quietly. "Yet finally seeing proof that you're capable of caring, even if the care was not placed where I might have liked, makes it impossible to hate you for that choice."

Another loud bang, then the heavy clack of sandals on stone, and Servius appeared. "It's chaos, sir," he said. "Gibzen's lost his head and is riling them up. They'll not accept anything other than blood, and they won't wait for your judgment to take it."

Marcus hadn't been raised to believe in fate, for the Cel thought such things pagan nonsense. Yet with all he had seen, he had to wonder if there was something to the idea. Had to wonder whether he'd dodged death too many times, and some higher power had decided this would be the moment. And that he'd pay for all he'd done tenfold.

Felix cursed, then pressed his fingers to his temples. "He's telling the truth, Servius."

How had he ever believed that Felix would betray him?

Felix was loyal. Not because Marcus deserved it, but because that was the sort of man his friend was.

"Felix . . ." Servius gave a slow shake of his head. "You know how he—"

"Lies? Manipulates?" Felix climbed to his feet. "I know better than anyone, which means that I know he'd never make up such a wild story with endless places to get caught out. He and Teriana escaped an attack by fleeing through xenthier that took them to Sibern."

Servius sucked in a breath, then let it out slowly. "All right. But where is the proof?"

"I had new armor," Marcus answered. "A letter from Wex. But I passed out after coming through the stem in Bardeen, and when I woke up in Titus's camp in Galinha, it was gone. I can only assume he got rid of it."

"So no proof."

There was uncertainty in Servius's gaze, but also worry that Felix's conviction was misguided. Worry that Marcus had manipulated old sentiment to achieve his ends. He didn't blame Servius for thinking that. "No proof until the Senate sends path-hunters. Perhaps not even then, for Cassius will no doubt instruct them to go straight to Titus."

Servius crossed his arms. "Then the writing is on the wall, Marcus. Felix believing you isn't going to save you from the Thirty-Seventh. They believe you deserted and that all they have suffered since is your doing."

It *was* his doing, even if he hadn't intended it.

"I'm not allowing them to kill him for a crime he didn't commit." Felix took the keys from Servius and unlocked the cell. When Servius made a noise of protest, he said, "Think, Servius. Titus tried to drown him during the crossing in an attempt to secure command. It was apparently Titus who gave away Teriana's location to Ashok, his goal to undermine Marcus's authority. Now he's destroyed all proof Marcus isn't a deserter so that the Thirty-Seventh will murder him, ensuring his authority remains uncontested. We can't let him get away with it."

"I don't see how we are going to stop him."

Servius had to shout the last because the noise outside was deafening.

Thousands of legionnaires chanted Marcus's name, but where once it had been to honor victory, now it was to demand his death.

Marcus remained sitting on the floor of the cell, listening to Felix and Servius argue about what to do, knowing how this would go. Knowing that even if he had proof, it wouldn't be enough to save him, because there was no hate more intense than one birthed from love. If his friends tried to stop what was to come, they'd be painted by the same brush as he was and killed for their troubles.

Leaving the Thirty-Seventh entirely at Titus's mercy.

Rising to his feet, Marcus swayed as dizziness hit him. He rested a hand against the wall of his cell until his vision cleared. Then he said, "Let's get this over with."

Felix broke off in his argument. "Pardon?"

"You think they won't realize you tricked them?" Marcus asked. "You think they won't kill you for it?"

His friends were silent, then Felix said, "In all the years I've known you, I've never once seen you give up." His voice shook with anger. "If this is all it takes to get you to lie down and die, I fail to see why you bothered coming back at all."

"To play my last card." Shoving aside his exhaustion, Marcus squared his shoulders, knowing that he needed to make a choice. Knowing that he couldn't save everyone. "Above all things, a good legatus protects the lives of his men, and that's what I'm doing now. You are going to take me out there and give me to the Thirty-Seventh. Then, with them at your back, you are going to take power from Titus and find those gods-damned xenthier stems so the Maarin can be freed."

Felix went pale. "But—"

"As a last favor to me: please free the *Quincense*," he said. "Tell them Teriana is with Senator Valerius in Celendrial. Also . . . tell Yedda to tell her that I'm sorry."

For all that he'd done. And all that he would be leaving undone, for he knew they would cause her grief in equal measure.

"I'm not letting them kill you for a crime you didn't commit!" Felix shouted. "I'll tell them you're innocent. That proof is coming!"

A loud *bang* echoed from the front of the building, and Servius grimaced. "They're pulling out the door."

Marcus's heart hammered, sweat dripping down his back, and he gripped Felix's shoulders. "They are past reasoning with, and you know it. If you stand with me, they'll kill you."

"So be it. I'm not condemning you."

"Pull!" Gibzen's voice filtered through the door. "Heave, you lazy sons of bitches!"

They had seconds before the decision was made for them.

Drawing in a ragged breath, Marcus pressed his forehead to Felix's. "I know I never said it. I know I never showed it. But I've always cared, and I'm sorry that you've spent all these years believing otherwise." Squeezing his eyes shut, he gripped his best friend hard. "I won't order you to do this, but for the sake of all that we have been through together, please promise to see this through."

A tremor ran through Felix, and Marcus heard him swallow hard before he said, "Yes, sir."

"Thank you."

The door on the building exploded outwards, light pouring in right as Felix twisted Marcus around, gripping his wrists. "Let's do this, then."

Gibzen rushed in, a dozen men on his heels, all with rocks in their hands. They slowed at the sight of them.

"Not only will you be fixing that door, you'll be digging shit holes for the next year for this behavior," Felix barked. "Outside. Now!"

Clearly having anticipated a different reaction, Gibzen blinked. "What are . . . Are you condemning him?"

"Obviously." Felix's voice dripped with irritation, and he shoved Marcus down the hall. "But this is legion justice, not satisfaction for your personal grudges. Now outside, or you'll be digging those holes *after* I have you whipped for insubordination."

Gibzen's eyes narrowed, a low growl exiting his lips, but he slowly backed up out of the building. Whether it was vestiges of discipline or the promise of blood to come, Marcus didn't know, only that the primus's eyes were feral with rage.

And . . . *grief*?

Marcus met Gibzen's gaze for only a heartbeat before Felix dragged him past the other man, but the intensity in his expression was unnerving. Marcus had known they'd be angry, but this . . . this was infinitely worse than he'd imagined.

Forcing his eyes to the muddy ground, Marcus said under his breath, "Never tell them the truth. They can never know." It was bad enough for them to believe he'd betrayed them. Worse still for them to discover he was innocent after the rocks and fists had flown.

Felix didn't answer, only pushed him through the ranks of shouting legionnaires. Men he'd known since they were children at Lescendor. His brothers. The Thirty-Seventh was his family, but he hardly recognized them as they screamed *deserter* in his face, their hands already clutching rocks they intended to use to shatter his body.

His fear rose, for Marcus had seen deserters executed before. When the Thirty-Seventh were done, he'd be nothing more than bloody pulp mixing with the mud. *You will do this,* he ordered himself. *You will show no weakness.*

Because if he did, Felix might crack. If his friend broke, the rocks would turn on him as well.

Breathe. Just breathe.

They had reached an open space the legion used for training. Felix's hands were like ice against his skin, his arms trembling, but he forced Marcus to his knees.

Stepping in front of Marcus, Felix held up his hand, and a lifetime of training caused the men to fall silent. "Legionnaire One Five One Nine, you have been found guilty of desertion. Do you have any final words?"

He met Felix's gaze. "We do not fall back."

The mass of men surrounding them snarled and seethed, their faces barely human. Their desire for blood barely checked.

Marcus allowed them to fade to a blur, keeping his eyes focused on Felix's face. Seeing the tears pooling in his blue eyes, though his voice was steady as he said, "Then you are sentenced to death at the hands of those you betrayed."

Bending down, Felix prised a fist-sized rock out of the mud, and relief tempered Marcus's growing terror. Felix would make it quick, so that all else that was done to him would cause no pain.

The Thirty-Seventh was a mass of barely checked violence waiting for the command. Waiting for the order to enact the justice they believed they were owed. Marcus prayed to this world's gods that they'd never learn otherwise.

I'm sorry, Felix mouthed to him, tears running down his cheeks. Marcus gave a tight nod, then closed his eyes.

And a familiar horn blew.

14

LYDIA

They rode hard until the sun was low in the west, stopping only from time to time so that Malahi could use her mark to erase their trail, which explained in part how the three had evaded capture for so long. When they'd put acceptable distance between themselves and the horde, they finally stopped for rest.

"The deimos will be out in force soon enough, so no light, no fire." Agrippa loosened his horse's girth but kept the saddle in place. In case they needed to make a quick departure, was Lydia's guess, so she did the same with her mount, the animal eyeing her warily.

"They may be already," Killian muttered. "Given they were in the air midday, there must be a way to make them fly, even when the light hurts their eyes."

"That *way* is called asking them, though they are notoriously mulish," Agrippa replied. "Their humanity isn't overly intact, but they understand orders just fine."

"Pardon?" Lydia demanded, even as Killian said, "Humanity?"

"They don't know." Malahi was perched on a rock and cloaked by shadows. "Of which you are well aware, so don't pretend otherwise."

"You do enjoy ruining my fun, Majesty." Agrippa removed his saddlebags, carrying them into their camp. "The deimos are corrupted shifters. Men and women with Lern's mark who spent so much time in animal form that they lost themselves to it. Doesn't matter what animal they favored, this is what they become, and from what I know, they can never change back." His gaze flicked to Lydia. "Though I suppose it's possible. I'm just an Empire soldier, so what do I know about gods and such."

Lydia bit the insides of her cheeks, hearing the double layer of slight against her. For all she'd reined in the impulse to give in to her darker half, Agrippa quite clearly didn't trust her and kept himself between her and Malahi at all times. But rather than resenting him for it, Lydia found herself appreciating his caution. Agrippa, at the very least, would do what was required to keep her from harming anyone.

Unlike Killian.

Unrolling her bedroll, Lydia cast a glance at Killian where he was feeding the horses, grief threatening to drown her. They were finally free to pursue the love between them, but there wasn't a chance she'd risk touching him. Even with her focus at its sharpest, she'd be tempted. Not just by her mark but by him, because gods help her, he was the most beautiful man she'd ever seen. With lust burning through her veins, there was no chance she'd be able to maintain any level of control.

Killian believed she would master her darker impulses.

But what if she didn't?

What if their fate was to spend their lives together but out of reach? Unified in purpose and soul but unable to show it? How long until their love turned to bitterness and bitterness into hate?

Her eyes burned, and turning to Agrippa, she asked, "Will you bind my wrists and tie me to a tree?"

"No," Killian snapped. "We are done trussing you up like a prisoner."

It was tempting to remind him that he'd done just that when she'd been deep beneath the Corrupter's hold, but instead Lydia said, "I need to sleep. I can't sleep if I'm afraid of losing control of myself and killing my friends."

"If it makes you feel better," Agrippa said, "we aren't friends."

"Agrippa." Malahi's voice was cool. "Do not be an ass to her."

"Can't help it." He grinned. "It's part of my charm."

"It's not."

"And yet . . ." He gave Malahi a wink, and though it was too dark to see clearly, Lydia sensed Mudamora's queen was blushing.

Jealousy roared into her, anger rising that they'd flirt and make light of her circumstances right in front of her. Lydia's lips parted to inform Malahi that Agrippa's flirtation meant nothing at all because he was a womanizer and whoremonger who would cast her aside as soon another pretty face came along. He was probably only flirting with her because she was Queen of Mudamora *and* the High Lady of House Rowenes, which made her the wealthiest woman on the continent.

Instead, she said, "Did you love this Silvara?"

Agrippa's smirk fell away, his hazel eyes darkening, and in Cel, he said, "You're not improving my opinion of you."

"I'm not trying to," she answered, using Cel as well. "But I know you, and I don't care to see you take advantage of her."

"Given not hours ago you were ready to steal every drop of Malahi's life, I think your motivations here are much less selfless." Agrippa held out a hand to Baird. "I need your belt."

"Use your own." Baird's accent was terrible, but it appeared Agrippa had taught him some of the Cel language. "Her wrists are skinny, so it should suffice."

"Apparently I need my belt around my waist to keep my trousers in place."

Smoothing out his blankets, Baird said, "A chain and padlock couldn't accomplish that."

"Enough." Malahi climbed to her feet. "You will speak in a language that everyone present understands, or you will not speak at all. In fact, unless you two have kind words for each other, you will keep them to yourselves. We have enough adversity in our lives without arguing over petty issues."

"How do you know my issues are petty?" Agrippa reached out lightning quick as Baird flopped down on his bedroll, yanking the giant's belt free.

"Body language is universal."

Agrippa huffed out an annoyed breath, then approached Lydia. She held out her wrists, and he stared at her bare hands for a minute before tugging gloves from his belt and tossing them to her.

"Thanks," she muttered, pulling them on. Killian went back to caring for the horses, his jaw tight with displeasure.

"If it comes to it," she said softly, "kill me. Please."

Agrippa expertly bound her wrists before her with Baird's belt. "He'll stop me. He'll die before allowing anything to happen to you." He looped the length around her back and through her own belt, limiting her range of motion. "You're overestimating me if you think I can stop him."

"You stopped me."

"You can't fight worth shit, and corrupted, in general, tend to leave their backs exposed." His mouth twisted. "Sorry. I know you're trying. But I've spent years around those with corrupted marks and only the old ones have any control. In my experience, control only makes them more dangerous."

Moving to retrieve a length of rope from a saddle, he fastened it around the tree with several highly complex-looking knots, then came back to her. "To answer your question, I was sixteen when I met Silvara. As you surmised, it was during the siege where we, along with the Twenty-Ninth, captured the rebel-held fortress of Hydrilla in Bardeen province. She was in the camp of followers who served the needs of the legion. A laundress, but unbeknownst to me, also a rebel. As to whether I loved her . . ." He trailed off as he fastened the other end of the rope to her belt. "I hated her for a long time after we parted ways. Now I understand why she did what she did, and also why I deserved it."

"Sorry," she mumbled. "I shouldn't have brought it up."

"It's in the past." He checked the knots again. "That should slow you down a bit if your dreams get the better of you."

"Thank you." She awkwardly lowered herself to her blanket, sensing Killian's scrutiny although he said nothing.

Agrippa walked over to Malahi and sat next to her. Though he was slightly shorter than Lydia, Agrippa was broad of shoulder and heavily muscled, and Malahi seemed tiny next to him. Agrippa rooted around in his saddlebags and extracted a packet of jerky. He gave Malahi a large piece, then said, "Was what you said about the Thirty-Seventh true or was it just a ruse to disarm me?"

This was dangerous ground. Telling Agrippa that the Thirty-Seventh was in the West *had* been effective in disarming him, but it had also potentially been a mistake on her part. If he chose to return to the legions, he'd bring with him an incredible wealth of knowledge that would aid the Empire in its conquest, and Agrippa had proven that he was willing to switch sides. But . . . she also remembered what he'd said about desertion. The legion might just kill him without taking time to discover his value, and Agrippa had to know that. She warred with what to answer, but then Killian came up to the group with his own bedroll and said, "It's true."

Silence stretched, broken only when Baird said, "Well, shit."

"This was the army you told me about?" Malahi asked. "The one you'd been with since you were a boy? That you were separated from when you fell through a xenthier? The one whose mark you have on your chest?"

Lydia couldn't help but wonder what else the pair had discussed during their flight across Derin, for it seemed Agrippa had held little back.

"Yeah." Agrippa sighed, then added, "The Thirty-Seventh Legion of the Celendor Empire."

"This was where you fled to, Lydia?" Malahi asked. "Or, I suppose more accurately, where Queen Camilla fled to with you as a baby?"

Malahi was filling the silence to give Agrippa a moment, Lydia could tell that much. "Yes. She was injured by Rufina during her escape through a xenthier stem, and she died on the streets of Celendrial. I was taken in by a senator, which is like a very powerful lord, and he raised me as his own daughter."

"I assume the Thirty-Seventh came through the Bardeen path?" Agrippa's voice remained toneless. "Path-hunters mapped it?"

"I was gone before they departed," Lydia answered. "But I've a friend in a Maarin crew who told me that the Maarin were blackmailed into taking the Thirty-Seventh and Forty-First legions into the doldrums where the greater ocean paths are hidden." It was her turn to swallow hard. "If they've since learned about the path you took, I could not say."

Silence.

"How did *you* come to return to Mudamora, Lydia?" Malahi asked. "Was it accidental or purposeful?"

"I suppose that's a matter of perspective." It felt strange to discuss her history in such a forthright manner, as it had always felt like something that needed to be secret. Which perhaps was true, but . . . "I was not considered marriageable to anyone of good breeding given that I was not Cel by blood, so when a senator named Lucius Cassius offered to wed me, my father accepted, despite my protests. Cassius used my father's influence to win the consulship. That's . . . I suppose it's the same power as a king, though it's elected by citizens and is limited to two terms in office . . ." She trailed off, suspecting that no one was tremendously interested in the political structure of Celendor. "After he'd won, I no longer held value to him, so he arranged for the Thirty-Seventh's legatus—commander, that is—to murder me."

"Marcus is dead?" The first hint of emotion since this conversation had begun filled Agrippa's voice. Shock and . . . *grief*?

"No. He's alive." A sneaking suspicion that what she was about to say next would be a blow caused Lydia to hesitate before she said, "He tried to kill me, and no doubt thinks I'm dead since—"

"Bull fucking shit!" Agrippa shouted, on his feet in a flash, not even seeming to hear Baird's cautioning words that shouting was not advisable. "Marcus wouldn't do that. You're lying."

Killian was on his feet as well, and Lydia noted his shadowed arm had his sword half drawn.

"I wish I were," she responded. "I was put down the drain in Cassius's new baths, which led to an underground river that dead-ended in a xenthier stem. My choices were to risk an unknown path or die down there."

"Marcus would not drown some girl because the consul didn't feel like marrying her," Agrippa snapped. "You're mistaken."

"I'm not. I was introduced to him personally at the elections. My height, golden brown hair, blue-grey eyes, scar across his cheek."

At the last, Agrippa stiffened.

"If it helps, he took no joy in it," she said. "I believe Cassius was blackmailing him in some way, although in truth, since the conquest of Chersome, the Thirty-Seventh's reputation has been . . . dark. The Senate holds several Maarin ships and their crew as prisoners, and the Thirty-Seventh have my best friend in their *care*, forcing her to aid them."

"Triumvir Tesya's daughter," Killian said.

"Teriana?" Malahi gasped. "Oh, gods. This . . ." Her voice hardened. "All this has been going on, and you both *knew* and said nothing? Why has Celendor crossed the Endless Seas? What is their goal?"

"Conquest," Agrippa answered. "Chersome was the last nation in the East not under the Senate's thumb, and with it defeated, they have set their eyes across the seas. The Empire is as bad as the blight for turning things into its own."

"Arinoquia, perhaps, but they can't think to stand against Gamdesh," Malahi said. "The Sultan has a standing army of twenty thousand soldiers, led by Princess Kaira herself. They'll crush them."

Agrippa began to laugh, quietly at first and then louder until Baird cursed and punched him in the side to shut him up.

"What precisely is it that you find so humorous about this?" Malahi demanded.

"My numbers are old, but you probably have fresh information, Lydia. One hundred forty thousand in active service?"

"One hundred fifty thousand." She drew her legs up, resting her chin on her knees. "And Cassius was of a mind to expand the ranks training in Lescendor."

"Right." Agrippa exhaled a shaky breath. "One hundred fifty thousand trained soldiers. For clarity, I don't mean the pathetic excuses for soldiers that fill the ranks of most *standing* armies, but men who have been living and breathing the art of war. All under command of one of the most gifted commanders to ever live. If Marcus was the legatus I once knew, there might be hope, but if what Lydia says is true and he's lost himself, then may the gods have mercy on every soul on the Southern Continent."

No one spoke. No one even seemed to breathe, the only sound the whistle of wind through the trees and a deimos screaming its frustration in the distant skies.

"I'll ask since we're all wondering," Killian eventually said. "What is your intent, Agrippa? Are you planning to return to your brothers in arms?"

"Well, it would be pretty stupid for me to admit so if I were," Agrippa replied. "Because I can only assume you'd stab me with that half-drawn sword rather than allow that to happen."

It was Malahi's turn to stiffen, and Lydia heard the queen's intake of breath to speak but Agrippa beat her to it. "No, it's not my plan. For starters, they think I deserted, which means if I walk into camp, they'll beat me into a pulp with rocks and fists, and never stop to wonder if perhaps there's more to the story. Two . . . I've been on the wrong side for too long. Fought for the wrong reasons, to achieve the wrong things. Even though it's starting to look like doing so will mean almost certain death, I'm of a mind to die fighting for something right."

"Same," Baird said. "For what it's worth."

Agrippa gave his friend a nod.

"Does that mean you're our resource?" Killian pressed. "If it comes to it, and the Empire pursues conquest in earnest, will you advise us on how to defeat them knowing that your advice will mean the deaths of those you once called friends?"

"My advice would be that you can't defeat them so we should all get very drunk and do debauched things until the bitter end." Agrippa sighed. "But in lieu of that, yes. I'll tell you what I know. Though I did as much for those in Arinoquia while they nursed me back to health and it doesn't seem to have done them much good."

In the darkness, Lydia watched Malahi's shadow reach out and rest her hand on his arm. How Lydia wished she could take such easy comfort from touch, for the conversation had turned an already grim situation so much grimmer. "It's not a coincidence, is it? That Rufina's armies marched at the same time the Senate set its sights on the West?" She hesitated, then added, "Rufina said that you'd told her about Celendor."

Agrippa huffed out a breath. "I told her any number of things so that she'd continue to think I was too valuable to kill, but as far as I know, she wasn't conspiring with the Cel Senate. She merely liked the way they did things."

"She said that you opened her master's eyes to a world of opportunity, for her master looks back at those who gaze into the darkness, whether they know his name or not." Then, lest it seem as though she were casting blame, she added, "Hegeria seemed well aware of the Celendor Empire, so I cannot think the Corrupter was unaware of its nature, but it does suggest to me that perhaps—"

"The Corrupter has influence in the Empire?" Agrippa snorted.

"Seems a stretch given that paganism is a crime in Celendor. We erase it everywhere we go, so you can best bet they are pulling down god towers and silencing any reference to the Six in Arinoquia."

We. Lydia tensed at the proof Agrippa had not entirely disassociated himself from the Empire.

"Urcon, the ruler of Arinoquia, sold all the Arinoquian healers to my father," Malahi abruptly said. "Quindor told me it was so, and if he bought healers, it's possible he bought other marked. Which means . . ."

"Most of them are dead." Lydia thought of the tenders in Deadground, who might as well have been.

"I think it no coincidence that Arinoquia was stripped of its marked just before the Cel legions arrived," Killian muttered. "Still care to claim the Corrupter isn't influencing actions in Celendor, Agrippa? Because it seems to me that your old legion is just another one of the Corrupter's weapons."

"They're not—" Agrippa sucked in an audible breath, then was silent for a moment. "Don't get it in your head that they're some sort of monsters set on chaos and destruction. They're just men who have been given no other path in life but war. They won't have chosen this because they don't get choices. Even Marcus is beholden to the whim of the Senate."

"Much like the majority of Rufina's army had no choice but to fight," Baird said, expression cloaked in darkness. "Doesn't mean they won't work to achieve dark ends, if only to protect their own necks."

"Shit." Agrippa jumped to his feet, kicking rocks so that they went sailing into trees. "*Shit shit shit*!"

"As alarming as this development is," Malahi said over the sound of his cursing, "the threat of this invading Empire is not our most pressing concern, for they are not the threat closest to hand. We need to put our minds to escaping Derin and making it back to Mudamora, where we can rally our forces. We should give all due warning to Gamdesh, but I can't help but think that the Maarin will have already done so. For all we know, the collective armies of the Southern Continent may have already driven the Empire's legions back across the seas."

"You only think that because you don't know them," Agrippa growled. "You only think that because you don't know *him*. The only way the Thirty-Seventh won't win any fight they choose to pick is if Marcus is *dead*."

15

MARCUS

The horns sounded again.

"Those are legion horns!" Felix shouted. "Scout reports! I want an explanation for why there is another legion on our doorstep, and no one fucking noticed!"

Someone shoved through the masses of the Thirty-Seventh, bellowing, "Empire banners and marks of the Fifty-First."

Austornic's legion.

Marcus released a ragged breath, but didn't move a muscle, for not one of the men had dropped the rocks they held in their hands.

"Fall to command," Felix roared. "He's not going anywhere, but your chance for vengeance will be lost if this is an enemy trick. To arms!"

Training took over, and the Thirty-Seventh was once again the well-oiled machine Marcus had created, moving without hesitation to defenses even as more scouts brought reports confirming that the army on approach was, indeed, Cel in origin. Was, indeed, the Fifty-First.

"Stay down," Felix said under his breath. "I don't want anyone to get any ideas if they see you on your feet."

Marcus's knees ached from kneeling in the mud, but he did not so much as twitch as the gates to the camp were opened wide and a group of young legionnaires with a 51 stamped on their breastplates marched inside, the crimson and gold banners they carried flapping on the wind. They came to a halt, fists slammed against chests, and then they parted to reveal Austornic.

He wasn't alone.

All the world fell away as Marcus took in Teriana, her black braids swaying as she moved, her eyes turbid seas of distress. His chest filled with every emotion, the swirling storm inside him making him want to be sick.

No.

She can't be here.

She can't. Be. Here.

"Fifty-First Legion of the Celendorian Empire reporting to duty, sir." Austornic gave Marcus a smart salute with no regard to the fact that Marcus was in civilian clothes and on his knees in the mud.

"We bring new orders from Consul Lucius Cassius and the Senate, as well as an update on information that has changed since you met with them last week in Celendrial."

The entire camp went still, the only sound the faint whisper of Austornic's words being repeated through the Thirty-Seventh.

Marcus barely noticed, his eyes all for Teriana and the same questions repeating in his head. *How is she here? Why is she here?* Her lips parted as though to answer his unvoiced questions, then she shook her head and remained fixed at Austornic's elbow.

Felix's hand closed on his wrist. A knife sliced through the ropes binding him. His knees screamed as he eased to his feet, muddy water dripping from the clothes he wore. Marcus ignored the discomfort and cleared his throat before shouting, "Show the Fifty-First an appropriate welcome!"

Silence.

Then Felix slammed his fist to his chest and bellowed, "Hail the Fifty-First!"

The Thirty-Seventh seemed to take a collective breath, then unleashed a deafening roar of, "Hail the Fifty-First!"

Austornic inclined his head. "Hail Thirty-Seventh. It is our privilege to join you on this historic mission."

From behind him, more than five thousand young voices screamed, "Hail Thirty-Seventh! Hail Forty-First!"

His legs were shaking beneath him, but Marcus looked to Servius. "See to it that the Fifty-First are well accommodated. It is the Senate's wish that we complete their training, and they are to be treated with respect." Motioning to Austornic, he added, "I'll take your report in the privacy of command."

Marcus turned toward the fortress at the center of the camp and started walking.

No one acknowledged that he'd been a hairsbreadth from being stoned to death by his own legion. No one said so much as a word. As his eyes fixed on Titus, who stood encircled by his men, Zaide at his side, Marcus didn't hesitate. "Coming, Titus?"

"Yes, sir." Though Titus's voice was emotionless, he radiated frustration and trepidation.

"Let me kill him." Felix spoke so softly that only Marcus heard, and it was a struggle not to say yes. A struggle not to take the knife belted at Felix's waist and embed it in Titus's face over and over until he was unrecognizable.

But that would be a mistake.

The Forty-First was loyal to their commander. If he killed Titus out of turn, they would retaliate, and he'd have a fight on his hands. Though he knew that Titus was guilty, Marcus had no concrete proof. To take down Cassius's son, he needed his accusations to be ironclad. Yet Marcus couldn't help but murmur, "Soon enough."

Felix led Marcus inside the stone fortress. As they passed the guards on duty, all Thirty-Seventh, he said, "Officers only. No exceptions. No interruptions."

"Yes, sir." They both saluted sharply, though their faces were pale beneath their helmets. Rattled. With his legs barely holding him up, Marcus knew how they felt.

Just as he knew the only person that his men would actually prevent from entering was Teriana. His heart gave a few unsteady beats as they blocked her path, Austornic ordering his men to keep guard over her, but Marcus didn't look back. Couldn't look back.

"Welcome home," Felix said, the doors embossed with the Cel dragon swinging open in front of them.

Created using Cel-style construction, the interior was blissfully cool and dry, the architecture the familiar blend of beauty and function. "Rastag did good work," he said, recognizing the hand of the Thirty-Seventh's engineer.

Felix grunted an affirmative. "We were able to use the same quarry that was used for Aracam. Good stone, he says. The camp's drainage system is also well underway."

"That should please Racker. The damp breeds disease."

"Nothing pleases Racker."

"Truer words never spoken."

It was such a bland conversation given what had just happened, and though it was his tongue that was doing the speaking and his ears the listening, it felt as though he were watching from a distance. A sense of surreality struck him because he was alive, he was in the Thirty-Seventh's camp, he was back in command of a mission to conquer the western half of the world.

And Teriana was here.

Why? he screamed in the depths of his mind. *Why did you follow me?*

They reached a pair of doors manned by two guards. Both men saluted, then opened the doors to reveal the center of the legions' command.

Marcus stopped in his tracks, his lip curling in disgust at what he saw.

Rather than the austere and functional setup he'd left behind, the command room was lavishly decorated with thick carpets, heavy wooden furniture, and an excessive amount of red velvet and gold thread. Blowing out a slow breath from between his teeth, he said, "Amarin—"

"It will be put in order for you, sir," his servant's familiar voice said, and Marcus turned to find the older man standing behind the group of legionnaires, a uniform folded in his arms. Amarin's bronze skin seemed to have gained wrinkles, his hair more silver than brown. "It is good to see you back with the Thirty-Seventh again, sir. You'll have everything put right in no time."

The surreality abruptly vanished and Marcus felt his mind dragged back into the moment, the insulation of distance vanishing even as the weight of all that *had* happened and all that *would* happen pressed down and down. Moving into the room, he sat heavily on one of the chairs, Felix, Austornic, and Titus taking seats.

"I unfortunately bring bad news," Austornic said. "When we arrived from Bardeen, we discovered everyone stationed at the terminus camp was dead."

"What?" Titus was back on his feet in a flash. "Those are my men!"

"Attacked *when*?" Marcus asked, unease building in his chest. For while he wouldn't put it past Titus to order his men to lie, the Titus he knew wouldn't stoop to killing his own men just to keep a secret. But much had changed in the time he'd been gone, so who was to say what lengths Titus would go to secure his power.

"After you arrived." Austornic extracted Wex's missing letter, setting it on the table, along with one of the leather-bound logbooks the centurions used. Its cover was stained with blood. "Evidence that the Forty-First witnessed you coming through the stem, sir. Unconscious and deemed xenthier-sick by the centurion in command."

Evidence that Titus had lied about where Marcus had been apprehended. Austornic hadn't said it, but he didn't have to. Everyone in the room heard the accusation.

Marcus didn't move to read the logs, instead watching as Titus snatched up the book, flipping to the last entries, all the color draining from his face as he read, because it was concrete proof of his deception.

Marcus held his breath, waiting for the other legatus to begin casting blame. To backtrack his way out of the hole he'd dug. Instead, Titus said, "Felix, did one of my men bring word that Marcus had arrived from Bardeen?"

Felix picked up the book and read the logs. "No. We've had no word from the terminus camp in some time."

Silence.

Marcus said nothing, watching Titus's nostrils flare, the pulse at his neck rapid, then he stormed out the door.

"I think we have grounds to arrest him," Felix said. "This is damning proof that even the Forty-First can't contest."

This was exactly the proof Marcus needed to bring down Titus, but through his exhaustion and aching skull, his instincts were screaming a warning. "Not yet."

16

TERIANA

"Officers only." The legionnaires on guard crossed a pair of spears in front of her as Marcus, Felix, and Nic pressed into the building without a backward glance, Titus following.

Breathe, Teriana told herself. *In and out. Nice and slow.*

The admonition only seemed to make the overwhelming anxiety she'd felt since coming through the xenthier a thousand times worse. The adrenaline that had kept her going through the rapid march was fading and taking her strength with it. With a thump, she sat down in the middle of the steps.

"You look like you need a drink," a familiar voice said, and she looked up to find Quintus approaching. Her friend wore his usual tunic and sandals, his blond hair long enough that he risked discipline, but it was his grey eyes that caught her attention, for they lacked their usual spark.

"Who let you out?" one of the guards demanded.

"I let myself out," Quintus answered. "Seemed a bit unnecessary for me to remain locked up given that it's been proven I was right all along."

Quintus flopped down on the stones next to her, then handed over a bottle of what smelled like rum. Teriana gulped down several mouthfuls, and whether it was the rush of alcohol or Quintus's presence, she didn't know, but emotion rushed over her like a burst dam.

Snatching up a small rock, she hurled it at one of the legionnaires on guard behind her, his eyes widening as it bounced off his breastplate. "I hope you feel awful!" she shrieked at him and his equally surprised fellow. "I hope you feel like assholes!"

Spinning on her heels, she balled her hands into fists as she faced down those of the Thirty-Seventh watching on. "You're all *fucking morons!*" she screamed at the top of her lungs. "Did you honestly believe he'd leave you? That he'd desert his family? Do you have any idea what he went through to get back to you?"

No one answered, their eyes on the mud.

"I hope you feel sick!" Picking up a handful of muddy pebbles, she hurled them at the onlookers. "I hope you can't sleep tonight or the next night or the next, because you're drowning in guilt over what you almost did!"

"Easy, Teriana." Quintus wrapped an arm around her shoulder. "They know they were wrong, but the worst didn't happen. He's fine."

"No, he's not." She rubbed her temples. "Quintus, he went through eight xenthier paths in a row."

"That's not possible. He'd be dead."

"But that's what he did." In a voice too low for anyone but her friend to hear, she explained what had happened in Celendor.

"Shit." Quintus rested his elbows on his knees. "I have no idea how he's standing, much less talking. The collegium have done studies, paid desperate men and women to do exactly what you're describing, and after five jumps, most of them were so addled in the head they couldn't form a sentence. A handful survived but most were dead within the week."

Marcus looked deeply unwell, but there was no denying that he was both standing and coherent.

"He has to have figured out another route," Quintus said. "He's bloody good at puzzles, so it makes sense. There is no other way he could be alive, Teriana."

Just then, Titus exploded out the fortress doors. Ignoring both of them, he leapt down the steps, face murderous as he headed into camp.

"Looks like someone got news he didn't like," Quintus murmured. "I'll bet—"

He cut off as Felix appeared, expression grim.

"Follow him," he said to Quintus.

Her friend cleared his throat. "I'm not leaving Teriana unguarded, sir."

"She's with me." Felix motioned for Teriana to follow him back inside. He was silent as he led her through the fortress into a room with a narrow cot and shut the doors behind them. "Sit." He gestured to the small table with two stools next to it.

They took seats on opposite sides, Felix resting his elbows on the maps strewn across the table's surface, eyes fixed on the places they detailed. Dark shadows marked the golden skin beneath his blue eyes, his jaw muscles tight with tension, cheeks uncharacteristically marked with stubble.

"In case you need to hear it from me, Marcus didn't desert," she said quietly.

"I know he didn't. He told me everything that happened, including that it was Titus who conspired to have you kidnapped. Titus's days are numbered, although I don't think he quite realizes it yet."

A mix of bewilderment and anger filled her chest. "If you knew, then why were you about to execute him, Felix? If you knew he was innocent, why were you going to allow the Thirty-Seventh to kill him?"

"Because he told me to." Felix lifted his face. "We looked, Teriana. Hunted and searched, but . . . with the way Marcus had been acting and with his relationship with you something known by the entire legion, everything pointed to desertion." His throat moved as he swallowed. "Even I came to believe it because there was no proof otherwise. The anger we all felt . . ." He trailed off, shaking his head. "When Titus got his hands on him, he knew that the Thirty-Seventh would not see straight when Marcus was dragged into camp. Knew that we'd lift up stones and fists, and if the truth later came out, he'd be able to hold up his hands in innocence, for we'd be the guilty ones. It nearly went exactly as he planned, because the Thirty-Seventh went mad when Marcus was brought into camp. There was no reasoning with them, and instead of allowing me to secret him out of the camp, he ordered me to allow him to take the fall. To not interfere, because he wanted me to take control away from Titus, which wouldn't be possible if I was complicit in his escape. I—"

His voice cracked, and without thinking, Teriana reached out and took hold of one of his hands. From the first moment they'd met, she and Felix had been at odds because of Marcus, yet they were also united by the burden that came with loving him. She knew better than anyone the toll these past hours, these past *months*, must have taken on him. "Cassius's control of the Empire is absolute, Felix. He's well on his way to creating a dictatorship hidden behind a puppet senate, and Titus is his most powerful tool in the West. You need to secure leadership of these three legions, because once more paths are secured, Cassius will unite forces with Titus and will wield as much power as he does across the Endless Seas. The only way to temper him is to remove Titus from control and limit Cassius's influence."

Felix's eyes narrowed, and he pulled his hand out of her grip. "Is that your play, Teriana? To use us against the Empire?"

"That's a bigger ambition than what I can lay claim to," she answered. "My goal is to free my people from Cassius's prisons. To free my ship and crew from *you*. There's only one way to achieve that goal, and that is to give Cassius what he wants: safe routes to and from the Empire that will allow him to exercise control. Bardeen is in the middle of an uprising, and the middle of Sibern is obviously no better. Cassius used the risks of both locations to deny my people liberty. I need to find paths so secure that even he can't dispute that I've fulfilled my deal."

"You *do* understand that with secure paths he can send another ten legions? Fifty thousand trained men, all supplied by the breadbaskets of the East."

"I know."

"You'll sacrifice the autonomy of the West for the sake of six hundred Maarin?"

"Five hundred," she corrected. "Cassius released one hundred of them onto a ship as a token of goodwill. But to answer your question: Yes. The remaining five hundred are in Celendrial's prison under Hostus's *care*. So I'll do what I have to."

Felix's jaw tightened at the mention of Hostus, but his voice was cool as he asked, "Goodwill for *what*? What did you give him?"

"I have a good idea where to find terminuses for paths coming from the Empire," she said. "I promised Cassius to give the information to whoever was in command, Marcus or otherwise." Drawing a map in front of her, Teriana stabbed a finger down on a dot along the coast of Gamdesh. "There's a tomb of sorts in the middle of Emrant, entirely walled in with no entrance. Has been there since recorded memory. But rumor has it that annually, voices speaking a gibberish language can be heard shrieking from inside. The Gamdeshians believe they are voices coming from the underworld. My guess is that if you crack open the stone walls containing it, you're going to find the bodies of a lot of Empire path-hunters."

Felix's golden skin blanched ever so slightly as he imagined the horror of that sort of death, then he said, "Why didn't you bring this up before?"

Because I was unwilling to betray Gamdesh. "Because you were never going to be able to move against Gamdesh with only two legions."

"And your solution was to bring us the greenest legion in the Empire's arsenal? The Fifty-First are *children*. They need two years more training before they see real combat."

She shrugged. "If you're trying to make a power play, you don't bring in people who outrank you. Plus, if I didn't bring them, Cassius was going to give them to Hostus to finish their training, which means they are *grateful* to be here, and that is to your advantage."

Felix was quiet, then he said, "All well and good, Teriana. But answer me this: why did Marcus leave you in Celendrial?"

A question she'd asked herself a thousand times over. "What reason did he give you?"

He regarded her in silence, refusing to bite, so it was her who caved first.

"He said it was because he loved me." The words sounded as though they were dragged over sandpaper as they exited her lips. "But that it needed to be over between us. That it had been a mistake. That we were enemies, and that one day I would come to remember that, and I'd hate him. That he didn't want to see it happen."

"He's undoubtedly right. Yet here you are."

"Here I am," she agreed, feeling impossibly hollow and alone.

"Why? Why didn't you remain in Celendrial with Valerius? You could have provided the information to the Fifty-First and accomplished the same result. Is it because you won't accept that it's over between you? Did you chase him across the world to try to get him back?"

Her face burned hot with humiliation. "No! I . . . It's . . ." Teriana bit down on her stammering because the truth was so very complicated. "In exchange for the freedom of one hundred of my people, I had to commit to a deadline for finding the paths. Six months for success, or Cassius will start executing the rest. This is my responsibility to see through. That's why I'm here."

When she'd said those words in the heat of the moment the night Marcus had fled Celendrial, they'd felt just and powerful. Yet saying them now, Teriana felt childish. Foolish. Because what exactly would she contribute other than information she could have written in a letter?

But rather than mocking her, Felix only scrubbed his hands over his head. "Six months?"

She nodded, his reaction confirming Hostus's opinion on the aggressive deadline. That it might well be impossible to make.

Panic rushed into her like a rising tide, and Teriana drew in a steadying breath, only to nearly jump out of her skin as a fist pounded on the door.

"What?" Felix demanded, and a heartbeat later, it flung open to reveal Quintus's panicked face.

"We have a problem."

17

MARCUS

Marcus fixed his eyes on Austornic. The boy was yet another issue needing to be addressed, but he didn't have the energy for it when all he wanted to do was collapse on a bedroll and sleep for a week. "We'll talk," he said. "But I have to get this camp in order first. Have your men stay out of the way of trouble or they'll have cause to regret it."

You sound like Hostus, his conscience whispered, and Marcus pressed fingers to his throbbing temples.

"Yes, sir. But—"

"It can wait."

Rising to his feet, Marcus pulled off the filthy civilian clothes he still wore, but as he reached for the red tunic that Amarin had brought, Austornic said, "It can't wait. There's more information about the attack on the terminus camp that you need to know. I didn't want to say anything about it with the others present, because Teriana indicated that aspects of what she told me were . . . confidential."

Marcus went still, hand resting on the clean garment. "What information?"

"About the nature of the attack." Austornic quickly described the scene as the Fifty-First had found it. "Teriana believes the attack was perpetrated by one of the individuals known as *the corrupted.* I . . . Well, obviously it goes against all of my training and beliefs to accept the existence of gods, much less individuals who are granted special powers by them, but I can provide no other explanation for why we discovered men who appeared well into their eighties bearing the mark of the Forty-First tattooed on their chests. She also mentioned the name Ashok."

Anger filled Marcus's chest like cold fire.

Was Titus's desire for power great enough that he'd make another deal with Ashok that included killing his own men to silence them? "She was certain?"

"Yes, though you can ask her yourself if you doubt me."

Marcus wasn't ready to talk to Teriana. Wasn't ready to be in the same room with her. That was why he'd left her in Celendrial, and with every breath he took, Marcus was aware she was now in this very camp. "I don't doubt you."

"Did you see who took you from the terminus camp?"

"I remember coming through the stem. The next thing I knew, I was in Titus's tent barely able to think from xenthier sickness."

"How many jumps?"

"Six." He shook his head. "No, seven."

Austornic was staring at him, a peculiar expression on his face. Like he wasn't entirely certain Marcus was quite real. "You should be dead."

He should. Had been fairly certain that he'd been about to breathe his last. And yet . . . "Maybe it's coming."

Everything that had happened in those first days had been a blur, except for Zaide. The old man's face was burned on his memory, his mind picking away at it, unable to let it go. Zaide, the Gamdeshian. Just as Ashok was Gamdeshian.

Not caring that he wore only undergarments, Marcus bolted across the room.

"Sir?"

Ignoring Austornic, he shoved open the doors. Zaide's ancient face dominated his mind's eye, the old man's dark eyes too clever by far. Marcus had long suspected that Urcon, the tyrant who'd terrorized Arinoquia, had been nothing more than Ashok's puppet. But no one had seen someone of the corrupted's description in Urcon's company, which meant he'd used agents.

"Sir?" Austornic was calling after him, the guards who'd been outside the door following him, but Marcus paid them no mind. The stone was cold beneath his bare feet as he stumbled down the hallway, his head throbbing. Pushing open the fortress doors, he nearly fell down the steps as the bright sunlight stabbed into his eyes.

"Sir?" Hands caught his elbows, steadying him, but Marcus brushed them aside. "Where did Titus go?"

"Toward the mess tent, sir."

Marcus broke into a run.

If Zaide was Ashok's agent, it meant he was a witness to all of Titus's dealings with the corrupted. A witness that Titus had a vested interest in silencing.

A commotion was coming from the mess tent, hundreds of men standing outside, the delineation between the two legions clearly visible.

As were the weapons in their hands.

It would seem that news of Titus's apparent duplicity had spread.

Shoving into the tent full of shouting men, Marcus elbowed his way through the ranks to the front where food was served, mutters of his name rising on a swell. When he finally broke into the open space, he found Titus with his naked blade pressed to Zaide's throat.

"Stand down." Marcus injected force into his tone despite feeling ready to pass out. But he couldn't allow Titus to kill this man.

This witness.

Titus ignored him. "Who are you working for?" he growled at the old man. "Who killed my men?"

"I work for you!" Zaide pleaded, the silver rings decorating his ears glittering in the light as he shook his head. "It was your own men who found him passed out in the brush, master. You know this, for it was they who carried him into Galinha."

"Liar!"

Seeing Titus's intent, Marcus lunged, catching hold of his arm and hauling him back before he could kill the one man who could bear witness to his crimes. The one man whose testimony would allow Marcus to put Titus on the gallows.

"This is not how we're doing this, Titus," he snapped. "Stand down, or I'll have you restrained. Either way, I'm not allowing you to use him as your scapegoat."

"Scapegoat?"

"You knew I came from Bardeen."

"No, I did not." Sweat was running down Titus's forehead, his usually unflappable composure fracturing around the edges. "Obviously I regret not taking you at your word, Marcus, but everyone thought you'd run off with Teriana. *Everyone.* Every man here knows you're a good liar, every man here knows that you can put on a show, and I thought that's all it was. That things had gone sour with Teriana, and you were doing whatever it took to get your old life back." His jaw worked back and forth, and he added, "I've worked hard to make progress on our mission, and I didn't want all of it to go to waste. Didn't want to go back to setting up house in Arinoquia with no mind to achieving the goals set to us, which I knew would be what you'd do. So if the Thirty-Seventh chose not to believe your bullshit and put an end to you, well . . . I wasn't going to shed any tears." He squared his shoulders. "But I didn't lie. And I sure as shit didn't kill my own men to cover that lie. My only fault is trusting this vermin."

Wrenching out of Marcus's grip, Titus leveled his gladius at Zaide. "I will have the truth from you."

"I am but an old man," the Gamdeshian pleaded, then reached out to catch hold of Marcus's wrist as though he'd protect him. "I helped you, master. Nursed you back to health."

Marcus tried to pull his arm free, but the man was shockingly strong; the bones of his wrist ground beneath the old Gamdeshian's grip. "Get your hands off me."

"Marcus."

Teriana's voice caught his attention and Marcus turned to find her standing next to Felix, eyes black-tossed seas of terror, her whole body shaking.

The tendons in his wrist screamed beneath Zaide's grip, but Marcus couldn't pull his eyes from Teriana's terrified face, her chin quivering as she said in Bardenese, "Corrupted."

18

TERIANA

An icy shiver coursed through Teriana as though the breath of the Corrupter himself had brushed the back of her neck. Her pulse fluttered like a caged bird in her throat, fear freezing her tongue in place.

The man who'd kidnapped her and held her prisoner all those long months ago had been young, his hair inky black and skin smooth, but the moment Teriana heard the old Gamdeshian speak, there'd been no doubt in her soul who he was.

Ashok.

And he held Marcus's bare arm in his grasp.

"Get your hands off me!" Marcus snarled at the corrupted, trying to shake him loose, but Teriana saw what he did not. Ashok's eyes pooling black, a ring of flame beginning to glow around them.

Already stealing Marcus's life.

"Marcus!" Her mind raced for a way to warn him that wouldn't alert Ashok that he'd been discovered. Latching onto a language there was no chance Ashok spoke, she said, "Corrupted!"

Marcus's eyes widened, but Felix reacted faster.

In a blur of motion, his gladius was in his hand and swiping through the air. It bit into Ashok's forearm, severing it in a spray of blood that struck Titus in the face, blinding him. Marcus fell back. His head cracked against Felix's breastplate, and the whole tent turned to chaos.

Ashok shrieked in agony and fury, moving with incredible speed as Felix closed in for the kill. The corrupted snatched hold of Titus by the throat, using him as a shield to block Felix and the other encroaching legionnaires. Titus struggled, but with each second that passed, the corrupted grew younger.

And Titus older.

"He's killing him!" she cried. "He's draining Titus's life!"

Titus fought to get free, but Ashok wrapped his wounded arm around the legatus's waist, binding his weapon to his side. Teriana screamed as she watched the corrupted's forearm healing, growing, reforming first wrist then hand even as Titus's face morphed into a near replica of his father's.

But Ashok didn't stop there.

As he backed against the tent wall, Titus's face wrinkled and sagged, his muscular body deteriorating under his armor until what slumped in Ashok's arms was a wizened old man, the corrupted young and whole again.

It had happened in seconds.

Ashok plucked the gladius from Titus's grip and sent the legatus toppling to the ground, now possessed of speed and strength that only a warrior marked by Tremon himself could face. He grinned, eyes fixing on Marcus, and Teriana screamed a warning.

Only for Ashok's eyes to bulge in shock, the tip of a gladius protruding from his forehead.

Howling, the corrupted pulled himself free of the blade. Blood poured down his face as he whirled to face the long slice that appeared in the canvas.

Quintus stepped through.

He was already swinging as Ashok reached for him, and her friend chopped the creature's head clean from its shoulders.

Ashok's body fell to the ground with a thud. Blood flooded from his severed neck with *one, two, three* great gouts before his heart went still.

For long seconds, no one moved, and then Felix was shouting orders. Marcus pulled away from the protective circle that had surrounded him to fall to his knees next to Titus, rolling the now ancient man onto his back. "Get Racker!" he shouted.

Oh gods.

Titus was still alive.

Teriana rushed toward him, trying and failing to ignore the decapitated head on the ground. Which was impossible given the corrupted's lifeless face was *aging*.

Titus wheezed, "What did he do to me?"

"You know damn well what he did," Teriana snapped. "You knew he was Ashok, which meant you knew exactly what he could do. You just didn't think your own dog would bite you."

"Ashok?" He stared at her, rheumy eyes filled with such confusion that Teriana wondered if the corrupted had also stolen his wits.

"Yes, Ashok," she said. "Unless you've forgotten the man you conspired with to have me kidnapped. The man who threatened to send me back in pieces if Marcus didn't retreat from Aracam. The plot that nearly saw the legions trapped between two armies. Remember that?"

Next to her, Marcus let out a slow breath, but she didn't care if he was annoyed with her outburst. What she cared about was that even on his deathbed, Titus was still gods-damned *lying* like he could somehow get out of this alive.

"You think I—" Titus broke off in a wheezing cough that shook his fragile body. "No," he finally gasped out. "Wasn't. Me."

"I know it was you, Titus," Marcus said. "Ashok was paid with Cel dragons, which I forbade being brought across the seas. Dragons that were stamped with Cassius's visage, which were not in circulation when we left. To whom else would Cassius give them but his own son? You put your own legion at risk in your quest for power."

Titus studied him for a long moment, then he asked, "You truly believe I'd do something that *stupid*? You really think I'd risk my men just to make you look bad?"

Unease prickled across Teriana's skin, because if not Titus, then who?

Racker chose that moment to arrive, the surgeon uttering several colorful curses at the sight of Titus. Kneeling next to the legatus, he pressed fingers to his throat, then gave Marcus a shake of his head. "He's dying."

If the revelation terrified Titus, he didn't show it. "From the moment we met, you thought the worst of me, Marcus," he whispered.

"Was it because *he's* my father? If you want the truth, I hate him. He murdered my mother."

Teriana tensed, it suddenly dawning on her how little she truly knew about Titus. That he was Cassius's son was no secret to anyone, yet not one of them had ever asked for his opinion of his father.

"No. It's because you're manipulative, backstabbing, and power-hungry," Marcus retorted.

"And you're not?" Titus let out a wheezing laugh that turned into gasps for air. "Every legatus fits that description, even the puppy they've sent you to train. It's how we get to the top."

"But you made it personal," Marcus said in a low voice. "I know the gold came from you, Titus. I know if I have your tent searched that I'll find the rest of it. Do you really want your last words to be lies?"

"You'll find more gold in my tent." Titus's skin was blanched pale. "I won't deny that. But I'm no traitor to pay the enemy to do my dirty work. I paid one of *your* men to spy on Teriana for me." Titus sucked in a rattling breath. "He *hates* your girl, Marcus. *Hates* you breaking the rules. Can't say I'm shocked he risked his own brothers, but it wouldn't have been to ruin you. It would have been to give you a chance at redemption."

"Who?" Marcus demanded. "Give me his name, Titus, or I swear that I'll have you buried in the latrines."

Titus grinned, his gaunt face twisting in a way that made Teriana cringe. "Kiss. My. Ass."

It was as though the defiance stole the last vestiges of his energy, for the second the words passed his lips, Titus's eyes rolled back in his head and his body began to shudder. "Tell my father . . . tell him. Tell him that—"

What final words Titus wished passed on to Cassius died with him, for only a rattling breath exited his lips.

Then he was still.

Racker reached forward and drew Titus's eyelids down, but no one spoke. Teriana looked around, finding the tent had been cleared of nearly all the men. Lev, who was Titus's second—now the acting legatus—was the only member of the Forty-First remaining. He stared at the corpse of his commander, then cleared his throat. "What are your orders, sir?"

Silence stretched, the tension in the tent so thick it was hard to breathe.

"Arrange for him to be buried with full honors," Marcus eventually answered. "Mark him in your books as a casualty of war, dead at our enemy's hands."

"Yes, sir." Lev stooped, picking up Titus's fragile body, but then he paused. Looking down at Marcus, he said, "I . . . I don't want to be in command. I don't have the stomach for it."

Marcus's face was emotionless as he regarded Titus's second, then he said, "Felix will lead the Forty-First until such time as the Senate can address the chain of command. You will serve as his second."

Relief flooded the young man's eyes. "Thank you, sir."

At Marcus's nod, Lev departed, Racker following with mutters about examining the body.

"This isn't how it's done," Felix said quietly. "The Forty-First needs to be under the command of one of their own."

"He'll rally." Marcus rubbed at the back of his skull, wincing. "Until then, they need a steady hand, and I need certainty that they'll do as they're told."

No one spoke, and Teriana took a moment to note who remained in the tent. Marcus and Felix. Servius and Quintus and Nic. Ashok's headless corpse.

Marcus swayed as he rose to his feet, and Teriana reached to steady him, but he jerked away, refusing to look at her.

Hurt stabbed her heart, although this was exactly what she'd anticipated from him. Marcus had drawn a line in the sand, and he would not take her leaping across it with grace. But neither would she take his behavior lying down. "I need to speak to you."

"Later," he muttered. "Servius and Austornic, I want everyone busy with something. Drills. Patrols. Cleaning gear. Running laps. I don't care what, just not sitting around. The last thing we need is three legions with too much time to gossip." The pair saluted and left, and Marcus turned to Felix. "What are the chances the real traitor still has some of that gold?"

Felix tipped his head side to side. "It's possible. But just as likely that it's made its way into circulation. I can have the centurions run searches. Give them a list of contraband, including coinage, which might give us a few leads."

"Do it now," Marcus ordered. "Word will spread soon enough, and if he's smart, he'll get rid of any dragons he has left. We need to catch him before that happens."

Felix shifted, eyes flicking to Teriana and then back to Marcus. "Yes, sir. I'll have your guard wait outside the tent for when you're finished up here." Then he spun on his heel and strode out.

Teriana's heart was racing, her pulse loud in her ears. Countless times during her journey back to Arinoquia, she'd practiced the speech she'd give when this moment came, but all those words seemed to have abandoned her. Still, she couldn't lose this chance. "Quintus, do you mind giving us a moment alone."

"I'll—"

"Quintus will remain." Marcus's eyes were fixed on the ground between them.

She blinked. "This isn't the sort of conversation that needs an audience. I want to talk to you alone."

"No."

"Why?"

"Because I don't want to be alone with you!" He finally looked at her. His blue-grey eyes were swollen and bloodshot, one still bruised from his fight with Carmo in Celendrial, but it was the edge of panic in his voice that made her chest clench. "It's not appropriate," he added, as though that made things any better.

"So, I'm to be your . . . *escort*?" Quintus rocked on his heels. Though he'd been the one to kill Ashok, he was almost devoid of blood splatter, whereas Marcus was covered in it. "Here to keep you two star-crossed lovebirds from falling into bed together again?"

"I said that you would remain, not that you would speak." Marcus crossed his arms over his bare chest, scowling. "Stand there and be quiet."

Quintus rolled his eyes, and as though to be contrary, sat on one of the benches with his bloody gladius rested across his knees.

Teriana felt abruptly unsteady, legs weak beneath her. "I want you to explain yourself."

Marcus stared at her, then said, "You want *me* to explain *myself*? Perhaps we might start with an explanation of why you and the Fifty-First are in Arinoquia."

"Because I met with Cassius and that was part of the deal. Which you might consider thanking me for because if we hadn't arrived when we did, there wouldn't be enough left of you to fill a jar!"

Silence stretched.

"You met with Cassius? What . . . what did he say?"

"A lot of things," she snapped. "But so did I."

Marcus's jaw worked back and forth, but it was not words of gratitude that emerged. Not that she'd expected them.

"You entirely ignored my instructions for you to remain with

Valerius in Celendrial and then brought a child legion to Arinoquia with you."

"You're not my commander." Her temper shoved aside her nerves. "You have no right to tell me what to do. You have no authority over me."

"You're right, I'm not your commander," he spat. "I'm your captor. And you're my prisoner. Which means I have total authority over you."

"Don't you dare." She closed the distance between them. "Don't you dare reduce what's between us to *that.* Not after what we've been through together. You don't get to tell me that you love me and then run away with no greater explanation than your belief that I'll *someday hate you.* It's not good enough."

"To protect you, that's why!" he shouted. "I had Hostus's men on my heels, knew I was going to risk turning my brain to jelly with the number of stems I had to go through. Never mind riding without an escort through rebel territory in Bardeen, plus traveling through a dubiously mapped xenthier stem into yet *more* enemy territory. You were safer in Celendrial. Safer with Valerius. Most certainly safer with an entire ocean between the two of us."

All of that was probably true, but it was the last part . . . She rose onto her toes so that they were eye to eye. "So after endless months of keeping me as close as possible for my safety, it's suddenly better for us to have an ocean between us? Why?"

"You know damn well why."

"No, I don't." Her eyes prickled. "Explain it to me. And don't give me the shitty reason that we are enemies when you know that from day one we've been allies against the common threat that is Cassius. Something happened in Celendrial that changed everything for you, so tell me what it is. The Seventh take my soul, but maybe whatever it is will change everything for me."

Marcus blanched, then looked away. The muscles in his jaw flexed as though he were warring with his thoughts, then he said, "I spoke to my sister. She was disgusted with my choice to take up with you. Called it immoral. She was right. I'm a grown man, the commander of legions, and you're a seventeen-year-old girl who is also my prisoner."

A tear slipped down her cheek because it was all starting to make sense. She knew his sister had influence over him. That he cared what Cordelia thought about him. "Eighteen."

His eyes shot to hers. "Pardon?"

"I turned eighteen while we were in Sibern," she murmured. "I didn't think about it because we were running from wolves."

Marcus's brow furrowed. "I . . . I didn't know that."

Quintus snorted in disgust. "You don't even know your own girl's birthday?"

Rounding on Quintus, Marcus leveled a finger at him. "I changed my mind. Wait outside."

"All right." Quintus got to his feet. "But if I hear any funny business, I'm coming back in."

When they were alone, Marcus reached for her, then seemed to realize what he was doing and took a quick step back. "I'm sorry. I know I hurt you, but it's for the best. This will get violent and ugly, and if you remain with us, people will blame you. Whereas if you stayed away, you'd just be another of the Empire's—"

"Victims?" she supplied, then wiped tears from her face.

Marcus only exhaled, seeming to dislike the word as much as she did.

"Teriana, this is my life. My hands . . ." He trailed off, staring down at his crimson-stained palms. "The blood on them is beyond what you can ever comprehend. I'm already hated. Already reviled by nations of people. Already the villain. I could have mapped enough stems to see your people freed and been the one everyone blamed when the Empire poured across the seas, but now you've gotten yourself tangled up in it again. And for what? What do you bring to this campaign that is worth the destruction of your reputation?"

"I know where the stems are." She stared at the 37 inked in black on his muscled chest. "Or at least, I have some strong guesses. Now that you have more men, you can secure them." She swallowed hard. "My promise to deliver that information to you secured the freedom of one hundred of my imprisoned people, including all the children. Cassius allowed them to take one of our ships and set sail. I did that, not you."

Silence.

Marcus cleared his throat. "What was the catch?"

"A deadline." Teriana swallowed the lump in her throat. "We have six months to find viable stems, after which time, Cassius will hang one hundred of my people for each month that passes."

Marcus went very still, and his reaction made Teriana feel like an idiot. Like she'd made the biggest of mistakes. But her people's children were free. That was worth it, wasn't it?

"Six months?"

"Yes."

Marcus scrubbed a hand over his hair, heedless of the blood. "Where are these stems?"

"The nearest is in Emrant." She knew Marcus had memorized the maps of the Southern Continent. Yet still she said, "On the coast near the border between Gamdesh and Arinoquia."

"I know where it is." Stepping backward, he sat down heavily on a bench, resting his elbows on his blood-smeared knees. "It's a major port city. The Gamdeshians won't give it up without a fight."

Her hands turned clammy. "We can negotiate. They might give us access to it rather than go to war. You have fifteen thousand legionnaires—that's a lot of men."

"A third of whom are children I'm expected to finish training, not fodder for Gamdeshian catapults. As to the Gamdeshians giving it up without a fight, that's madness, Teriana. If it's a good path, I'll be able to use it as a supply line straight back to the Empire. Food. Weapons. Gold. Legions. Every resource I could possibly want, and the only way to cut the line would be at the genesis. I've heard a fair bit about Princess Kaira of Gamdesh. Once she learns I'm after that stem, she'll march her armies in defense of that city. To take it within six months means it will be a bloodbath, and we won't even know if it's worth it until it's over."

It had to be worth it. It had to be.

"You said *stems*. Plural. Where are the others?"

Her tongue felt dry and thick as she told him the locations, his slow exhale telling her what she already knew. That they were even *more* difficult targets. The compulsion to apologize nearly overwhelmed her. Instead, she said, "They were keeping my people in Celendrial's prison. Children, *babies,* locked in cages, all under guard by the Twenty-Ninth. Agreeing to the deadline was the only way to get the hundred most vulnerable free."

Silence.

Slowly, Marcus lifted his head. "You made the only choice you could. Cassius holds all the cards." He rose to his feet, moving to stand before her. "I'll get it done. But I need you to promise you'll stay out of it. And away from me."

A knife to the gut would have hurt less.

"If you wish, you may join the *Quincense* for the duration of the campaign. If you prefer to remain in this camp, you can share a tent with Quintus, as he seems content to resume his duties as your bodyguard. I will not involve you, and you will refrain from attempting to involve yourself in any capacity."

Her lips parted, but echoes of her conversation with Felix filled her head. *Did you chase him across the world to try to get him back?* "If this was your intention," she said, hating the way her voice shook, "then why did you bother telling me that you loved me? Because if it was a lie intended to soften the blow, it did the exact opposite."

Outside the tent, the noise of thousands of men undertaking busywork filled the air, but Teriana barely heard them, her focus on the sound of his breathing. On the rapid rise and fall of his chest. On the sharp intake of breath he took as he started to speak and then bit down on the words. Though it was only seconds, it felt like a lifetime had passed before he said, "It wasn't a lie."

He took a half step toward her, and for a heartbeat, it was as though they no longer stood in the mess tent but were back on the riverboat in Celendrial, when they belonged to no one but each other.

"Why give me everything and then take it away in the next breath?" She brushed away the tear that rolled down her cheek. "It would have been better if you'd said you were over me. Bored of me. Hated me. Wanted someone else. Anything but what you chose to say."

Marcus's brow furrowed, but then he shook his head, expression hardening.

Already he was walling himself back up, emotion vanishing from his face, from his eyes, until all that remained was the prodigal legatus.

"Because to be loved by someone like me isn't a gift, Teriana, it's a curse."

She flinched, looking away even as she fought the urge to scream that Cordelia Domitius was responsible for this. Her cruel words were making him talk and act like this. The list of people Teriana hated was short, but Cordelia had earned a place right next to gods-damned Lucius Cassius.

"Will you be joining your crew or remaining in camp?"

"Remaining," she answered between her teeth, her fingernails cutting into her palms as she warred between anger and grief. And because she had no intention of giving him the last word in this, Teriana added, "I'll tell Quintus to find us a tent," then walked out.

19

MARCUS

Breathe. Just breathe.

Marcus could feel one of his attacks looming, rising on a tidal wave of panic, exhaustion, and illness, and he sat down on a bench, sucking in mouthfuls of air.

Why hasn't Cassius told Teriana the truth about Lydia? That had been Marcus's first thought the moment she'd revealed meeting with the bastard, quickly followed by horror that she'd walked alone into the dragon's den. Except further consideration made the consul's strategy clear to him. Cassius had sunk his teeth in for the kill, but much like the bite of the dragon that adorned every banner across the Empire, it would not bring a quick death. It would be a slow and excruciating one. What Marcus had done to Lydia was leverage, and Cassius intended to use it to make Marcus dance to his tune.

His breathing was taking on a wheezing tone, and Marcus squeezed his eyes shut. *Not now. Please.* Because part of him knew that if his illness came for him today, he didn't have it in him to fight it.

"Sir?"

Marcus twitched, his eyes snapping open to focus on Gibzen. The Thirty-Seventh's primus had entered the tent, the uncertainty on his face unfamiliar in its rarity, for Gibzen was confident even when he was wrong. "Yes?"

The other man approached, then to Marcus's horror, dropped to his knees before him. "I want to say that I'm sorry, sir."

He stared at the top of Gibzen's head, black hair shorn nearly down to the scalp. "For what?"

Breathe.

"I . . . I *spat* in your face. And the rocks . . ." Gibzen lifted his head, and Marcus could tell that he clearly weighed the former a far greater injury than the latter. "I'll take whatever punishment you care to give me for what I did. I was wrong to doubt you."

Marcus did not want to deal with this now. Could not deal with this now. "It's fine. Get up. Thirty-Seventh don't grovel."

Gibzen scrambled to his feet, hands behind his back at attention. "Yes, sir. Sorry, sir."

"At ease." Marcus tried to mask the wheeze in his voice. "Was there anything else you needed?"

"Teriana stormed out snarling at Quintus about how they needed to find a tent," Gibzen said. "That right, or do you want me to see about getting her a room in the fortress?"

"No, that's right."

"Fair enough. Racker said he wants Ash—Uh, the . . . what's the word? Corrupted?" Gibzen's gaze was on Ashok's corpse. "The body. You know how Racker likes to play around with corpses."

Pot, kettle, Marcus thought, well knowing the primus had his own proclivities when it came to the dead, but he kept his mouth shut. Being forced to think about practicalities was calming his mind, which was the first step in maintaining his ability to breathe. "That's fine. Have a few men bring it over."

"Will do. We should also get you cleaned up, sir. Looking like your usual self will help morale by showing the men everything is as it should be."

Nothing was as it should be.

"Titus had Rastag put a proper Cel bath into his fortress, and since he ain't going to have need of it, being dead and all, might as well get use from you."

"Your sentiment for the fallen is as inspiring as always," Marcus muttered, but he didn't argue as Gibzen hauled him to his feet, steadying him when the world spun.

"Walk on your own," Gibzen said. "Doesn't look good if I'm helping you."

Marcus forced his shoulders to square, then started toward the exit. Outside, the camp was a flurry of centurions screaming orders in their typical overaggressive way. All three legions were an organized scramble of men falling to command, though everyone stopped what they were doing to salute as he trudged past. Gibzen's men formed up around him, eyes watchful. It struck Marcus that none of the men under Gibzen's command were the same as when his previous primus, Agrippa, had held the role, and he frowned, disliking that for reasons he couldn't quite articulate.

Climbing the steps to the fortress nearly sapped what remained of his energy, but he managed to make it down the corridor, Gibzen moving ahead to open a door. Marcus stepped inside, where he paused.

It was indeed a proper Cel bath, a basin large enough to fit ten men at the center, simple fountains recirculating water from each of the four corners. The tile was set in a mosaic of reds and golds, columns held up a ceiling painted in a simple fresco, and light poured in from a glass skylight high above.

He hated it.

"Looks like it belongs in some senator's villa. All we're missing is some good Cel girls."

"Have someone find me Amarin," Marcus said. "I need . . ." He trailed off because the list of things he needed was too long for his sluggish mind to begin to wrap around. The back of his skull ached from cracking against Felix's breastplate when Ashok had attacked, the injury compounding all his other problems.

He only half heard Gibzen give the orders as he peeled off blood-splattered undergarments, tossing them aside and walking into the pool. It was blissfully cool, the filtered water clouding to a rusty hue as it rinsed away blood and sweat and filth. He sank beneath the surface, but in the silence, Teriana's voice filled his head. *Why give me everything and then take it away in the next breath?*

It was because it had been the only truth he could give her in the endless sea of lies.

His lungs burned, demanding air, and Marcus surfaced to find Amarin having appeared. His servant was in the middle of a tug of war with Gibzen over a tray, the latter winning by virtue of youth and size. Gibzen circled the pool with the tray. It contained a pitcher of water, food, soap, and a razor.

"Racker indicated that you need bed rest," Amarin said, glaring fiercely at Gibzen. "That if you don't get it, you're liable to die."

"I'll get him to bed after he's cleaned up," Gibzen muttered. "Don't treat him like some sort of invalid."

"You're accountable for at least some of his injuries," Amarin snapped. "Though I see you've come groveling back, you nasty creature."

Gibzen turned dark eyes on Amarin, and Marcus held up a hand. "Enough. What was done cannot be undone, and I've no interest in casting blame. I'll sleep when I'm fed and washed, and when I wake, I hope it is to find everything back in order, most particularly in command."

The standoff continued a few heartbeats, then Amarin gave a curt nod and left the room.

Gibzen opened his mouth, but Marcus shook his head. "I don't want to hear it."

The primus shrugged and took up a post near the door, hand resting on the hilt of his gladius. "So . . . it took you to Sibern?"

Marcus gave a short nod, then began to mechanically shovel food into his mouth to avoid conversation, washing it down with mouthful after mouthful of water. His stomach roiled under the unfamiliar onslaught, but he ignored the pain.

"See any of those wolves the Sibernese boys are always yapping about?"

"Yes. They hunted us between shelters."

"They as big as they say?"

A flicker of memory filled his mind's eye: glittering eyes, hot breath, and white fangs. "Yes."

Gibzen whistled. "Kill any?"

"One."

"How did you kill it?"

The tone of Gibzen's voice raised the hackles on the back of Marcus's neck, and he turned his head to regard the man. Gibzen's dusky skin had a sheen of sweat on it and his lips were slightly parted with anticipation, the grip on his weapon so tight his knuckles were white. "Does it matter?"

Gibzen shrugged and looked away, hearing the real question in Marcus's words, which was *Do we have a problem?* "Nope."

The legions were full of men like Gibzen. Men who enjoyed killing the way other men enjoyed sex, strong drink, or narcotics. Men who thrived on the violence of conflict and war as it served their lusts well. It made Gibzen good at his job, but Marcus had personally set rules of conduct for him. Rules, he was beginning to suspect, that had perhaps not been adhered to in his absence. "I want everything back in order, Gibzen. I want everything to be exactly as I like it to be."

"We'll ensure it, sir."

Marcus relaxed slightly. Abandoning the rest of the food in favor of soap, he set to work ridding himself of blood and filth, the only sound the tinkle of water coming from the fountains.

Except his mind more than filled the silence.

The overwhelming chaos of problems fought for supremacy in his skull, ricocheting from the casualties his legions had taken to Teriana's presence. From Titus's revelation that the traitor was still at large to his guilt over Lydia's death. From the lies he'd told Teriana to the absolute certainty in his heart that he loved her above all else.

Around and around. The only thing it kept recoiling from was the deadline he now faced. *Six months,* Teriana's voice echoed in his skull, only to be drowned out by Lydia screaming for her life.

Focus! he snarled at himself. *Make a plan!*

His mind only raced in circles. Faster and faster, and logically he knew that the only thing that would help him see straight was sleep, but the thought of sleeping with all these problems in the air was unpalatable. "I wish Agrippa were here."

The statement came from nowhere, yet even as the words slipped from his lips, Marcus knew it was a truth that had always been, even if he'd kept it buried.

"Why?" Gibzen's tone was clipped. "He deserted us for a Bardenese chit. I hope he's rotting in a shallow grave somewhere."

Because he's the only one who could lead as well as me. Marcus kept the thought to himself, though it expanded and grew, rising on the tide of his turmoil. If Agrippa were still the Thirty-Seventh's primus, Marcus could have passed out and slept for a week, certain in the knowledge that Agrippa would run the legion just as well as him.

Possibly better.

"Don't you find it strange," he said to fill the silence, "that we never heard another word about him? He was never intended for a quiet life, would have risen to the top of any situation he found himself in, but not a whisper."

"Because he's probably dead." Gibzen's tone was frigid. "That girl likely got sick of his yapping and cut his throat. What difference does it make, anyway? You're better off without him. He was always arguing with you. Never falling to command."

"When he argued, he was usually right," Marcus muttered, picking up the razor. "He always got the job done."

Gibzen snorted. "Agrippa always did his level best to make you look bad because he never got over that you came out on top, and he didn't. I hope that prick's dead and I hope he died hard."

As Gibzen spoke, the coldness in his voice turned to venom. The two had never gotten along, but Marcus hadn't realized Gibzen held a grudge that seemed to go beyond the animosity earned by Agrippa's desertion. Which possibly explained why not a single legionnaire who had served in Agrippa's hundred remained under Gibzen's command, all of them either dead or under the leadership of other centurions. As he soaped his face, Marcus briefly considered pressing the primus, but what was the point of digging into the past with so many other problems facing him in the present?

Not the least of which was the traitor in their midst. Gibzen had ever been loyal, in his fashion, and his hatred for those who were not had been well proven. Plus who better to track the culprit down than his own personal bloodhound?

Lifting the razor to his cheek, Marcus debated how to approach this as he scraped the blade over his skin.

Only to hiss as his unsteady hands betrayed him.

"Let me help you with that, sir." Gibzen circled the pool to kneel behind Marcus. "Can't have you walking around looking like you shaved drunk."

"It's fine. I'll—"

Gibzen pulled the blade from his grip. "Agrippa wasn't loyal. Nothing matters more than loyalty."

Marcus didn't answer, his attention all for the blade Gibzen was expertly scraping along his skin. Swallowing carefully, he finally said, "I've reason to believe that someone in the Thirty-Seventh betrayed the location of your men when they were escorting Teriana back from Galinha."

Gibzen's hand paused. "Why do you think that?"

"Because Ashok told Teriana as much. He had Cel dragons newly minted with Cassius's face that the traitor had given him as compensation."

"*Traitor.*" There was anger in Gibzen's voice.

"Yes. Never mind that the idiot got your men killed, his actions caused a change in strategy that nearly resulted in the Thirty-Seventh being caught between two armies. I thought it was Titus, but before he died, he denied it. Said he'd brought the gold but the only thing he'd used it for was paying one of my men to spy. He wasn't a traitor."

Gibzen scraped the blade up the side of Marcus's throat. "You sure Titus wasn't lying?"

Marcus closed his eyes, remembering the look in Titus's dying eyes. "Yes. He was guilty of many things, but not this."

"Did Ashok give Teriana a description of the individual?"

"No." Marcus held his breath as the blade passed over his jugular. "Only that whoever it was held a grudge against my relationship with her and desired things to go back to normal. Ashok thought we all looked the same."

Gibzen huffed out a breath. "So it could be anyone? You have no idea who the man might be?"

"Unfortunately not." Out of the corner of his eye, Marcus watched as Gibzen wiped clean the razor, then set it on the tray. "But I want you to find him for me. I can't have a traitor in my legion."

"Want me to kill him?"

Marcus shook his head. Climbing out of the bath, he wrapped a length of toweling around his waist. "No. I want him brought to me because this is personal."

"Yeah."

Hand resting on the hilt of his gladius, Gibzen walked to the door and opened it, nodding at the men standing guard outside before taking the lead down the hallway. Marcus followed, legs feeling like lead, every inch of him aching, and he watched with dull eyes as Gibzen checked his room.

"Head hurt?" Gibzen asked.

"Everything hurts."

A flash of emotion played through the primus's eyes, and he dug into his belt pouch, then held out a vial.

Marcus took it. Recognizing the etchings, he said, "You shouldn't have this."

Gibzen shrugged. "Racker's cheap with it, especially with my men. I only give it to them when they're really hurting."

A flicker of irritation passed through Marcus that the surgeon would deny men in need out of personal spite between him and Gibzen. "I'll talk to him about that."

"Nah. You take it, then we'll all be on the right side of the rules."

Staring at the vial, Marcus slowly nodded.

"Get some sleep, sir," Gibzen said, opening the door to where the rest of his men stood. "We'll watch your back."

The others murmured their agreement, and Marcus nodded at them, wishing they all stood outside his familiar tent and not a room in a fortress that felt far too much like Celendor for him ever to be comfortable.

As he set the vial down on the table, his eyes skipped over a rack holding his old armor, which Amarin must have squirreled away, though the weapons with it were all new. Turning down the lamp on the table, he crawled onto the cot and shoved the pillow onto the floor. Faint light from the fires and torches in the camp filtered in through the window above, which was little more than an arrow slit—Rastag was too engrained in warfare to have been swayed by the need for beauty.

Go to sleep, he told himself, squeezing his eyes shut. *You need to rest. You need to be able to think clearly.*

Except in the silence, the problems reared even as his skull ached.

One hundred and twenty-four of the Thirty-Seventh are dead.

I paid one of your men to spy on Teriana for me.

Why did you bother telling me that you loved me?

Six months.

It was the last problem that took over, finally shoving aside all else with its terrifying magnitude. Six months to find paths, and his only good lead was a terminus in Gamdesh. Six months to capture a major port city from the most powerful nation in the West.

Six months.

If he failed, one hundred of Teriana's people would head to the gallows for each month that passed.

You'll figure it out, he told himself. *This is what you do. This is what you are best at. This is who you are.*

Just get some sleep!

His panic refused to listen, refused to grant him respite, and with an exhale of frustration, Marcus sat up and set his feet on the floor.

You don't need it.

Yet the vial was suddenly in his hand, though he didn't remember crossing the room. The glass was etched with a familiar symbol, the liquid within holding the power to drive away both pain and consciousness with a few drops.

Marcus warred with himself, but it was a short battle. With shaking hands, he opened it and measured three drops onto his tongue, then tucked the bottle where it wouldn't be immediately found, between the mattress and the cot.

The light above blurred, his vision splitting into two, then three. He lay back down and pulled the blanket over his legs as blackness poured into the room, filling his eyes, and dragging him down, down, down until the world fell away.

20

TERIANA

"I don't know what you see in him." Quintus held open the flap to a tent so Teriana could duck inside. "Other than looks, I suppose. He's got no sense of humor, he's an asshole, he has the emotional range of a bowl of overcooked porridge, and he didn't even bother to ask when your birthday was. That he's in the running for the prettiest man in the legions really does not make up for all that."

"I don't want to talk about it." In truth, Teriana had no idea when Marcus's birthday was, either. She stared at the interior of the tent, which contained nothing but a single bedroll atop a wooden platform to keep the occupant out of the mud. Though it appeared Quintus had tracked in plenty, tidiness not one of his competencies.

"Because you know I'm right." His eyes narrowed. "Please don't tell me it's because he's that good in bed? Is that it? I mean, you never really know someone until—"

"Quintus." She rounded on him to tell him to drop it, only to suck in a deep breath when she found her friend staring at the smears of blood on his shaking hands, his golden skin blanched. "Are you all right?"

"Fine."

He was most definitely *not* fine, and a wave of guilt flooded Teriana as she realized the extent of her self-involvement. Catching hold of his hands, she pulled him down onto the bedroll, then grabbed a waterskin and rag. She scrubbed away Ashok's blood, Quintus's hands shaking beneath her grip. "He's dead," she said quietly. "You killed that monster, and he can do no more harm."

"What more harm could he do? He already destroyed my life."

Quintus hid his grief over his separation from Miki so well that there were times that she forgot how much he was hurting. How hopeless he felt at ever being reunited with the one he loved, for every odd was against it.

"Your life isn't destroyed." She put more water on the rag, then set to work cleaning the dried mist of crimson on his right arm. "The end is in sight, and just because Marcus is being an ass to me does not mean he's forgotten the deal he made with you." Her throat tightened, and she swallowed. "Six months and this will be over. You'll get Miki, join up with me and the *Quincense*, then we'll all drink rum on a white sand beach."

How long until all those beaches are stained red in the war you started? her conscience whispered. *How long until there is nowhere left on Reath that knows peace?*

"I've dreamed about killing Ashok every moment since he threw Miki against that tree." Quintus studied his hands. "I've imagined a thousand ways of killing him. Imagined using all the training the Empire forced upon me to make him suffer. Imagined how I would feel watching the light go out of his eyes, and how it would change everything. Now he's dead, and it has changed nothing."

Her hands stilled, her tongue frozen, because what could she say? What comfort was there to give when vengeance was hollow?

"I think it's because while Ashok might have been the one to hurt Miki, he wasn't the true villain," Quintus said softly. "It was one of ours who betrayed us. One of ours who considered getting rid of you worth the lives of his brothers."

Teriana went still, every instinct in her body screaming *danger*, something she'd never felt around Quintus before despite knowing he was a killer. And that he was very good at it.

"You knew it was someone in the legions who betrayed our location, didn't you?"

"Yes," she whispered. "Ashok told me while I was prisoner that it was one of Marcus's men who gave him our location. The traitor paid him in Cel gold to get rid of me, going on about how I'd been nothing but trouble. That Marcus was making a fool of himself chasing after me. How everything would go back to normal once I was dead. Ashok didn't identify who it was. Said you all look alike, but that the individual idolized Marcus." Seeing his lips part to speak, she added, "Obviously it sounded like Felix, and that's who Marcus was convinced it was, which is why he was such a prick to him. Except I thought it was Titus *pretending* to be Felix and that he was trying to discredit Marcus using me." She blurted out the rest of the explanation. "But you heard Titus while he was dying. He said the gold had gone to one of the Thirty-Seventh to spy on me."

"Yeah," Quintus said, voice cold. "I heard. Fascinating as it all is, that's not the explanation I'm looking for. I want you to explain why you kept this from me. And it better not be that Marcus told you to keep your mouth shut, because we both know you don't take orders from him."

Teriana ran her tongue over her lips, heart pounding. "Because you'd have killed Felix. Or Titus. Maybe both."

Quintus's blue eyes were frosty as a Sibernese morning. "No, I would not have, because I know neither of them is stupid enough to have done something like this. Both Felix and Titus are top military strategists, and whoever betrayed us clearly didn't think about the fallout of his actions. Which Marcus, of all people, should have considered, but when it comes to this, I don't think he can see the forest through the trees."

Said that way, it made perfect sense. Made Teriana feel like an idiot for leaping to conclusions, even if Marcus had been leaping right beside her. Drawing in a slow breath to calm her heart, she said, "I'm sorry I kept it from you. I should've told you, but I was so focused on how it impacted Marcus and me that I never considered how it impacted you."

He stared at her for a long moment, then sighed. "Yeah, all right." Reaching for his bag, he dug around and extracted a bottle, taking a long mouthful before passing it to her. "Here."

The rum burned down her throat, and Teriana closed her eyes, the tension fading from her shoulders.

"I listened to your conversation," Quintus said.

It was a struggle not to wince, but her friend continued, "Don't worry, your secrets are safe with me. But . . . six months to take a critical trading port city from the mightiest nation of the West is quite the commitment."

"Every time someone says that it feels like less time."

"Because it is." Quintus grinned. "Each passing second is one. Second. Less. Time."

"You're obnoxious." Moving so she was sitting next to him, Teriana leaned against her friend's solid shoulder.

"I can't believe you brought us babies as reinforcements."

Teriana scoffed, then took a mouthful of rum. "Just because they aren't bitter old drunks haunted by dreams of campaigns past doesn't make them *babies*."

"Well that's just mean." Quintus kicked a piece of his armor that was discarded on the ground next to his pallet. "They will have to fight, though. You understand that? You understand that in coming here, many of them will die before they shave for the first time? They'd have been kept out of the thick of it if they'd stayed back East."

"They were going to be given to Hostus to complete their training. Having had the pleasure of meeting him, I think the battlefield is preferable."

"Shit." Quintus winced. "Fair enough."

"It's not even possible, is it?" she finally asked. "That's why Cassius agreed to it. Because he knew that six months would come and go, and that he'd have license to murder my people until they were all dead."

Quintus was quiet for a long moment, the bottle moving back and forth between his hand and hers as he thought. "I don't know Cassius, so I can't speak to his rationale. What I do know is that if there is anyone who can do it, it's Marcus. This is what he *does*, Teriana. He's a solver." Quintus turned his head to look at her. "But don't for a heartbeat think that means you'll like the solution he comes up with."

21

MARCUS

A hand roughly shook his shoulder, and Marcus cracked one eye, finding Racker's face mere inches from his. "You're an idiot." The surgeon's dark brown eyes gleamed with anger "You deserve to be dead."

"Noted," Marcus rasped, his mouth dry as sand.

Shoving himself up on one elbow, he blinked to clear his vision, annoyed to discover that Racker, Felix, Amarin, and Servius had all entered his room without him waking. "What time is it?"

"Noon."

Cursing, Marcus tried to stand, but Racker shoved him back down on the cot, surprisingly strong given he was skinny as a rail. "Sit. I've heard all about your *genius* choices, and according to every study done by the collegium, you should be a mindless body on the floor. That you're alive is one of the greatest strokes of luck I've ever seen. That you are coherent is a bloody miracle that I can't begin to explain."

Marcus didn't disagree, but the last thing he wanted was anyone to question his capacity to lead. "It was much worse previously, but I'm fine now."

"Headache? Dizziness?"

"No," Marcus lied, because the room around him was swimming. "I'm fine."

Racker held up one of his specially designed lamps with mirrors that shone light through a narrow hole, the beam stabbing Marcus in the left eye and making him wince. Racker scowled. "You're normally a better liar, sir."

"Careful, Racker. I'm in no mood."

"When have I ever given a shit about your mood?" Racker handed his lamp to Amarin. "You're not fine. At best, you are looking at weeks of recovery. At worst, you may never recover, and the headaches, dizziness, and sensitivity to light will forever plague you. If I thought you'd listen, I'd tell you to spend the next week in here, in the dark. Except you never listen."

"Then don't waste your breath." Marcus pushed him out of his way and rose. "I've work to do."

"You also have well-trained minions and a legion sick with guilt that is desperate to please," Racker snapped, using his superior height to loom. "Let them do what they do so that when you're actually needed, you can do what you do."

Except with only six months to achieve the impossible, that time was now. "I'm fine. Felix, report. Amarin, something to eat. Servius, I know you have more important things to do, so do them."

Racker leveled a finger at him. "You're not immortal. If you don't show some level of care, you'll be no good to anyone. You should be dead. That you are not must be by the grace of the powers of this land, so I would not tempt their ire with stupidity." Then he strode from the room.

Unbidden, a blurred memory of Zaide . . . no, *Ashok* filled Marcus's mind, his hair snow white and face ancient as he said, *You'll live.* Had the corrupted done something to bring Marcus back from the brink of death? According to Teriana, each god granted a specific power, and individuals could only be marked by one god. Hegeria's gift was healing. The Corrupter's was death.

You could ask her.

He shoved away his mind's suggestion. Shoved away all thoughts of Teriana because he needed to focus.

Except his heart cared nothing for focus, plaguing his vision with images of Teriana's face as he'd pushed her away, her eyes dark storms of hurt at his words.

"He's right that we have everything sorted," Servius said. "I don't think anyone will question if you choose not to attend the funeral."

"I'll attend," Marcus muttered. "Give me an hour."

Felix waited until their friend had left, shutting the door behind him before he said, "Nic says that just before he left, he learned that one of the stems Titus sent hunters through terminates in Atlia, albeit at the bottom of a lake. Not viable for travel until the engineers can drain it, which is a good year's worth of work, but we can send messages through it in the meantime. I'd suggest that we inform the Senate you are back in command and request additional reinforcements by way of the Bardeen stem. If we're going to do this, then we need to do it right."

Marcus took a mouthful of water, disliking not being the best informed. "Let me think on it."

Felix shifted his weight from heel to toe and back again, his unease obvious. "It's good to have you back in command, Marcus. I know you like the politics, but for me, it's the purest form of misery. That said, Racker's right. Better you rest now so that you can do the heavy lifting when you're needed."

There was no one he trusted more than Felix, yet the lie still slipped from his lips. "I'm fine." Partially to keep his friend from pressing and partially because he was desperate for answers, he asked, "Did the centurions' search turn up any evidence as to whom Titus was paying to spy on me?"

"Not enough to make accusations," Felix answered. "I spent last night going through reports on the contraband they found on their men. More than a few had Cel coinage on them, but it was mostly silver and copper. A handful had dragons, but none with Cassius's face on the back. And before you ask, I personally inspected all the officers, and the results were the same." He cleared his throat. "Titus had a small chest of gold in his tent, which I confiscated without argument from the Forty-First. They . . . are taking my interim leadership better than I'd anticipated."

"I suspected they might. So whoever was on the take either spent the coins or had the wherewithal to hide them outside of camp." Not entirely surprising. "I've set Gibzen the task of hunting down information. He always seems to know everyone's dirt."

Felix tensed. "You're willing to trust him? In case you've forgotten, he was leading the charge to beat you to a pulp for desertion. I was anticipating that you'd request a demotion for his behavior. A demotion, for the record, that I'd support."

Felix had never supported Gibzen's promotion to primus in the first place, so this was no revelation. "That's one of the reasons I trust him for this. He volunteered for punishment, but instead, I gave him an opportunity to make it up to me. You know how his brain works—doesn't like owing anything to anyone. He'll feel compelled to deliver. Doesn't hurt that it was his men who were killed and injured as a result of the traitor's actions."

"Agrippa's men."

Marcus blinked, then looked to Felix askance. "Pardon?"

"The men Gibzen had watching over Teriana the day she was kidnapped were the last of the men in Gibzen's century who were chosen by Agrippa," Felix said. "Probably because they were the only ones you could reasonably trust around her. Now his hundred men are fully of his selection. The nastiest dogs in the Thirty-Seventh, and every one of them was behind Gibzen with stones in their hands, eager to cave in your skull. That's your bodyguard."

That fact should have alarmed Marcus, but it didn't. Instead, the idea that his back was guarded by men who cared so much about loyalty to the Thirty-Seventh that they'd been willing to kill anyone who betrayed it made Marcus feel not only safer but validated in his choice to put Gibzen on the hunt. "Have they been out of line?"

"No."

"Have they been doing their duties?"

Felix sighed. "Yes."

"Then we have our answer," Marcus said. "I'm not punishing them. They didn't do anything wrong."

"Marcus—"

He cast a sideways look at his friend, cutting him off. "I know what Gibzen is, Felix. He might be a mad dog, but he's *my* mad dog and has been since we were in Lescendor. He knows better than to bite the hand that feeds him." Then, because he didn't want to be at odds with Felix, he added, "If he steps out of line, we'll revisit this conversation. But not today."

"Fine."

Amarin chose that moment to return, sparing Marcus any further arguments as he set to eating food he had no appetite for while listening to Felix's update on less confidential matters, which was a mixture of good and decidedly bad. Titus had carried on the negotiations Marcus had started with Katamarca, securing an alliance with the nation's queen. Except he'd also gotten greedy and broken Marcus's carefully forged alliance with Ereni. The Arinoquian imperatrix was now allied with the inlanders she'd once fought against. The combined force was what had cost so many legion lives when Titus had pressed inland. There was more information, endless information, and his head began to pound as he mentally compiled a list of things that would require his attention.

But first Titus needed to be put to rest.

"I want *everyone* not on duty assembled for the funeral." Marcus took his weapons belt from Amarin and buckled it on himself, using the opportunity to secret the vial of narcotics into his belt pouch so Amarin wouldn't find it. "Titus will be treated with every respect. He was an ass and none of us liked him, but he was no traitor."

"Understood." Felix stepped outside, his mutters of *mandatory* and *will have their asses whipped* filtering through the doors as he gave the orders. When he returned, he asked, "What are your plans for Teriana?"

Her face flashed into his mind, passionate and beautiful, making his heart feel like a weight in his chest.

"I gave her the choice of remaining in the camp as our guest or sailing to the island where her crew is staying to be with them. She chose to stay."

"In a tent with Quintus?"

"That was the agreement." Taking his helmet from Amarin, Marcus pushed it down on his head, the smell of steel filling his nose as he motioned for his servant to depart. When he was alone again with Felix, he added, "Along with her commitment not to attempt to interject herself into our strategy. And to stay away from me."

"That's going to be difficult given that she's one of our best resources."

"Not anymore." Marcus gripped Felix's shoulders, the room spinning around him. "It's over between Teriana and me. I should never have allowed it to happen in the first place."

"Why?"

The question wasn't what Marcus had anticipated, and his words stumbled over each other as he said, "For obvious reasons."

Because I killed her best friend and I hate myself for it.

Felix was silent for a long moment, then he said, "If it was over, you wouldn't have given her the choice about staying or leaving. She'd be on a ship taking her both out of sight and out of mind. Instead, you gave her the choice because you knew which one she'd make. Knew that she'd choose to stay. Because it's not over."

Was that true?

His fingers tightened on Felix's armor. "I need it to be over."

"Then send her away."

Horns blared outside, urging the men into their ranks, and Marcus dropped his hands from his friend's armor. "We should go."

For a moment, Felix looked like he was going to say more, then he lifted one shoulder. "Let's take Titus for his last march."

* * *

Legion legati who were killed during service were usually brought back to Celendor to be interred in the monument near Lescendor. That was not possible in this instance, so the decision had been made by the Forty-First to cremate him. All three legions had arrayed in neat ranks on the large open space beyond the ridge overlooking Aracam where the Thirty-Seventh had battled and won against Urcon's mercenaries. The Forty-First's officers carried the litter bearing the body to the pyre of fuel-soaked wood, Marcus, Felix, Austornic, and their various officers walking behind it.

Marcus had given a speech, listing Titus's deeds and accomplishments, not insulting the Forty-First with false sentiments when all present knew the truth. Yet as the pyre was lit and Marcus watched the black column of smoke reach up to the sky, he considered what would be said when he finally fell. To have his existence summed by an account of his career. The nations and armies who'd fallen before him, the peoples who'd been forced into indenture, the children he'd left in his wake to grow up as orphans.

A legacy of death.

After an appropriate amount of time, he nodded to Felix, who gave the quiet orders for the men to return to duties and for certain officers to carry on with them into Aracam.

Marcus strode toward the city, Austornic at his right and Felix at his left, the others close enough for conversation. Though much of his focus was consumed by walking in a straight line, his balance still off kilter, his eyes drifted over the city they'd captured what seemed a lifetime ago. The skyline now only held a singular black tower, which he'd been told couldn't be damaged by any tool in their arsenal. None of the towers should have been damaged, but he suspected that Titus had been intent on doing all the things that Marcus had not so as to prove himself superior. Or, perhaps, to prove himself to his father.

Whom he hated.

It weighed upon Marcus more than he'd expected that Titus had been, at least emotionally, at odds with Cassius. Mostly because he hadn't known. It struck him that Titus had been right that Marcus had immediately cast him in the role of adversary for no reason more than that he'd been Cassius's son. That he'd never bothered to truly get to know the younger legatus, and had certainly not mentored him, as he should have. He'd forced Titus into the role of enemy from the moment they'd met, so was it any wonder that the younger man had made moves against him? Was it any different than how Marcus had behaved when he'd been under Hostus's control all those long years ago?

How much differently would things have gone if he'd given Titus a chance? If he'd taught him as he had been supposed to? If he'd led the Forty-First with the same care and consideration he did the Thirty-Seventh?

They reached the gates to Aracam, passing into streets full to the brim with people going about their business.

"You were right about trade opening up after Urcon's death," Felix said. "Aracam has grown into quite a hub, though we've had more problems since parting ways with Ereni. She and Titus did not see eye to eye."

"Problems?"

"Violence." Felix took off his helmet to wipe sweat from his brow before replacing it. "Every morning our boys find bodies in alleys, and we've had to double patrols to deal with the fights that seem to break out over nothing."

"That's to be expected given the influx of individuals from different nations." Marcus examined the bustling shops lining the streets, the patrons not just Arinoquian, but every nationality, half the languages spoken unfamiliar to his ears.

"Agreed, but it's not fights between strangers," Felix said. "It's friends turning on friends. Wives murdering husbands only to be murdered by lovers. The whole damn city just seethes with . . . anger isn't the right word. I don't know . . . animosity, I suppose."

"It might behoove us to mend fences with Ereni, then." As he spoke, the black tower twisted, then leaned, the eyes carved into it glowing. And they were watching him.

Marcus blinked, and the tower was back in place, solid and inanimate. He shook his head to clear it, then added, "Do we know where Ereni is?"

"More or less. But she's sent the heads of our last two messengers back to us, less their bodies."

The tower leaned again, seeming to reach down to him, and Marcus staggered sideways, colliding with Austornic and nearly knocking the boy over.

Felix caught his arm. "You all right?"

"The tower—" He broke off, seeing the black tower was as it always was. Unease spooled in his stomach, because headaches were one thing. Seeing things was quite another. Austornic was staring at him with suspicious eyes, so he swiftly said, "Why didn't Rastag pull down the Seventh tower?"

"Oh, he tried." Felix shook his head. "Used up half our stores of black powder trying to blow the base, ropes to pull it over, and even dug into its foundation. The damn thing seems to grow out of the ground itself and is made of stronger stuff than even xenthier. Same in Galinha. I'll show you."

The marks of the Thirty-Seventh's engineer's attempts were made visible as they entered the wide swath of space that had once been encircled by the towers. Cobbles had been torn up around the black tower, the excavation extensive. Walking to the edge of the pit, Marcus stared down. The strange black stone did indeed run deep and seemed entirely unmarred by the explosives. Stronger stuff than xenthier, indeed, for the crystal paths *could* be destroyed with black power, the right timing, and a healthy dose of nerve. "Leave it," he said. "It's not worth our time or resources."

His eyes landed on Gibzen, who had climbed down onto the scaffolding and had a hand pressed against the black stone. "Gibzen!" When the primus didn't respond, he repeated, "Gibzen!"

The other man started, then looked up at him. "Yes, sir?"

"Get out of there!"

Marcus turned back to his officers, but the motion threw his balance off. His shoulder slammed against Felix's with a clank of metal, and several of the men frowned. Not giving them time to comment, he said, "I will not waste breath on preamble, especially given that most of you are fully updated."

They all nodded.

"We have learned about potential routes terminating in Gamdesh, the closest of which is in Emrant." They all knew the maps as well as he did, so there were nods all around. "Except the Gamdeshians aren't going to allow us control of a port city without a fight."

"We can't take them on with three legions," Lev, Titus's second, said. "At least, not without an unpalatable number of casualties. Especially not if we wish to maintain control over Arinoquia."

"Agreed. However, we have the capacity to request reinforcements through the stem that terminates in the Atlian lake." Marcus made a note to ask Rastag if he was familiar with the lake and could give his own estimates on how long it would take to drain. "We will also request reinforcement. As to whether the Consul will choose to send another legion, only time will tell. Until then, we will pursue other tactics. The Maarin have ensured the Sultan of Gamdesh is aware of the Empire's . . . *reputation.* If we leverage what they've been told of our military capacity, they may be willing to consider diplomacy, especially given the alliance that Titus cemented with Katamarca. Allowing us access to the paths for the purposes of trade would prevent it from coming to all-out war. The Gamdeshians don't know the stems in Bardeen and Sibern are inadequate. For all they know, we have the whole of the Empire's military force at our beck and call."

"Except if they call our bluff," Austornic argued, "we'll have told them our exact goal and target. They'll begin the process of reinforcing the city, and we'll have lost the advantage of a surprise attack."

"Diplomacy first." It was a struggle to suppress his annoyance that the boy was pointing out the obvious flaw in the plan. Especially given that Marcus couldn't reveal his actual intentions.

Austornic crossed his arms. "I think it's a mistake."

Giving the boy a warning look, Marcus said, "I need translators literate in Gamdeshian and Katamarcan for correspondence."

Austornic's lips parted. "Teriana—"

"No. She is not to be involved, is that understood?"

"Is that wise?" Servius asked. "Not only is she fluent *and* literate in all these languages, but she also personally knows these rulers. Obviously there are some . . . ah . . . complications, but from what I've heard from the Fifty-First, her interests are aligned with ours. Seems prudent to use her as a resource."

"No," Marcus repeated. "That is an order. She is not to be involved, and if I discover that *anyone* has violated that order, I'll have the skin lashed off the perpetrator's back."

Servius whistled through his teeth. "Fine, fine. I'll see who has mastered the language, but if your missive to the Sultan is full of spelling errors, that's—"

"Servius . . ."

His big friend fell silent but scuffed his sandal across the paving stones to show his displeasure.

"You've a lot of work to do," Marcus told him. "The Senate didn't send the Fifty-First here to watch the Thirty-Seventh sit around campfires drinking and gambling. Put them to work. And Felix, arrange a meeting with Atrio. Dismissed."

His officers started to depart the square, including Austornic, but Marcus leveled a finger at the boy. "You'll stay."

"Yes, sir." The young legatus crossed his arms behind his back, face expressionless as he stared at Marcus's breastplate.

Once the other officers were out of earshot, Marcus said, "I'd like to discuss your choice to question my strategy in front of the others." Out of the corner of his eye, the black tower leaned again, but he forced himself not to react. "I would have done the same thing when I was your age. Though I am now starting to understand what a pain in the ass I was to every legatus I served beneath."

Austornic's cheeks colored but he said nothing.

"So full of clever ideas and an ego that demanded they be deployed, never mind that those in command might have alternative plans in play. Never mind that I might not have all the information. Never mind that every legion is a different beast that can only be predicted by those who know it well." It felt hard to stand steady, the square swimming out of focus, and Marcus broke off to take a drink of water from the skin at his belt.

It didn't help, but Austornic was watching him with narrowed eyes, so Marcus continued. "It was no wonder that I was the way I was, given that I was told ad nauseam just how clever everyone thought me to be. Trotted before the Senate at age twelve to listen to the most powerful men in the Empire exclaim how I was the most brilliant mind to ever graduate. A strategic genius destined for greatness. The prodigy of Lescendor." Marcus remembered how he'd once loved that title and now hated it. "My arrogance when I went into the field was a thing to behold, but I quickly learned that plans that were perfect on paper rarely worked out that way in practice. I learned that by getting men injured. Captured. Killed. Because I was a *child* and having every campaign in the Empire's history memorized did not make up for *experience*."

Austornic's jaw tightened, the boy chafing at being reduced to his age. Marcus remembered what it had been like when Cassius had done the same to him before the Senate. Yet he also was aware that part of the reason Cassius kept getting the better of him was that the Consul had been playing the game for longer.

"I want you to think," he continued, seeing Gibzen again approaching the black tower. Climbing onto the scaffolding and down into the pit. "I want you to come up with ideas and strategies. But you will bring them *to me*. I'm not Hostus to take credit for your work, because I don't need to step on your back to make a name for myself. You can question me when it is appropriate. You can disagree with me as long as you agree to obey. But if I catch you meddling behind my back, putting the lives of my men at risk, I will lock down your legion until such time as I can send you back to Celendor. Do you understand?"

"Yes, sir. Understood, sir."

"Good."

"By your leave, sir, I'd see to ensuring my men are in order to begin their duties."

Marcus nodded, watching the boy salute and then depart, full well knowing that Austornic's desire to prove himself smarter than Marcus would only have grown on the heels of the speech.

Going to the edge of the pit, he scowled at Gibzen. "What are you doing? I told you to get out!"

"I've never felt anything like it," his primus mumbled. "It's like glass. You should touch it."

Marcus didn't want to touch it. Didn't want to risk climbing onto the precarious scaffolding when he could barely walk in a straight line, but all of Gibzen's men were watching. If he showed even a hint of weakness, they'd smell it.

Taking a deep breath, he climbed down onto the scaffolding, immediately feeling a temperature change from the raw earth at his back. He eased across it to Gibzen's side and reached out a palm to touch the tower.

Only to jerk back with a curse. The black rock was as cold as ice. Pressing his palm against the stone again, Marcus drew in a breath. The noise and stink of Aracam fell away and his blurred vision came into focus. The pain in his skull retreated, and for the first time since he'd fled through the xenthier stems, he felt himself again.

Almost himself.

Withdrawing his hand, Marcus stepped back and the pain resumed.

"Beautiful, isn't it," Gibzen murmured, but that that wasn't the word that came to Marcus's mind as he looked up at the black length of shiny stone.

"Tell Rastag to let it be," he said. "It's not worth our resources. Now get out of this hole, primus."

Gibzen obeyed, falling in next to Marcus as they walked through the city, saying nothing every time Marcus bumped into him.

To break the silence, Marcus asked, "Have you made any progress finding our traitor?"

Gibzen gave a sour grunt. "More challenging than anticipated. Seems as though Titus used his father's gold to pay for a few things, including company. Talk is that several of our boys won the coin off the house in one of Aracam's better brothels but had the wherewithal to have it melted down. Our cause ain't aided by the fact the Fifty-First is being paid with new mint and they're giddily spending their wages. Losing, more accurately, because the pups are bad at cards and can't hold their drink."

Marcus exhaled a long breath, adding the Fifty-First's conduct to his list of troubles. As if he didn't have bigger concerns than his men impressing all their bad habits on the boys. "Find another angle, then. Reasonably, it's someone who works guard duty on the command tent, which means he's probably one of yours."

"I've lost more than a few in recent months." Gibzen's feet splashed in a puddle as they walked. "Might be whoever you're looking for is already dead."

Titus's voice filled his head. *He hates your girl, Marcus. Hates you breaking the rules. Can't say I'm shocked he risked his own brothers, but it wouldn't have been to ruin you. It would have been to give you a chance at redemption.* Not how one would speak about a dead spy. "I don't think we're going to be that lucky. Look to those who have voiced anger about Teriana."

Gibzen barked out a laugh. "I hate to be the bearer of bad news, sir, but that's about everyone. Got any other ideas?"

A wave of frustration rolled through Marcus, not because of the jab at Teriana, but because if this had been Agrippa, he would have figured out a solution himself rather than asking Marcus to do his job for him. "I gave you a problem, Gibzen. Solve it."

They had nearly reached the gate when Quintus approached.

"A word, sir."

Unease filled him. "Where is—"

"Sleeping."

"What do you want?"

Quintus stepped closer. "She's sick with worry about her people being stuck in a prison run by Hostus."

A vise of guilt tightened around his chest, but Marcus didn't answer.

Quintus glowered at him. "I don't disagree with your choice to keep your distance, but unless you've got a heart made from the same black rock as that tower, you might consider easing her fears about your intentions. Because if she doesn't know your plans, she'll make plans of her own."

Irrational anger replaced his guilt, but Marcus bit down on it. "I don't involve civilians."

Quintus's eyes darkened, a reminder that he was the deadliest assassin Marcus had in his service, but all he said was, "Teriana's not a civilian. She's your girl, even if you refuse to admit it."

Then he twisted on his heels and strode away.

"Quintus needs some discipline," Marcus vaguely heard Gibzen say, but that was the furthest thing from his mind.

It seemed a lifetime ago that he and Teriana had held each other in the darkness of his tent and whispered words of building trust. How it would be the foundation of everything between them, sturdy and unshakeable. They'd built a palace upon that foundation, little knowing that it was not trust they'd built upon but lies, everything beautiful and pure set to crumble the moment the truth was revealed. A desperate part of him wanted to preserve that palace, to protect it at all costs, yet he was afraid of what it would do to her if it crashed down upon her head.

Better to push her away so that she wouldn't be crushed.

She's your girl.

Teriana would never be his. Could never be his, and yet some greedy part of his heart refused to give her up even if keeping her close was hurting both of them.

Then, out of the corner of his eye, the glint of gold caught his attention. The shop was a goldsmith's; a hulking man with a cudgel stood guard out front. Ignoring him, Marcus stepped up to the window, looking through the glass to a display of fine jewelry. Aracam was an absolutely ridiculous location for such a shop, for few Arinoquians had risen high enough from the ashes of Urcon's oppression to afford such goods, so it was no surprise the shop was empty. For that reason, Marcus would also bet all the gold in his camp that the man had been placed here by Queen Erdene to show off the skills of her nation's craftsmen in the belief there'd be interest in Celendor. The Katamarcan ruler was playing the game.

His eye caught on a pair of gold earrings shaped like tiny ships, the embellishments jewels and enamel.

Reaching for the handle of the shop, Marcus said, "Wait here."

Gibzen threw up his hands, but gave the order to those forming their bodyguard, the noise of their protests muffled as the door slammed shut behind him. A tiny man with black hair leapt up at the sight of Marcus, the stool he'd been sitting on falling over. "My lord legatus," he blurted out in heavily accented Mudamorian. "It is an honor to have you in my shop."

"I'm not a lord, only a soldier," Marcus answered him. "Legatus is fine. Did you craft all of these?" He gestured to the displays.

"Yes, my legatus." The craftsman's eyes skipped from Marcus to the window, where Gibzen no doubt stared through the glass.

"Do you take commissions?"

"From you? Of course, my legatus! It would be an honor!"

Resting his elbows on the counter, Marcus drew a piece of paper and charcoal stick in front of him, his brow furrowing as he sketched, drawing up details from his memory, adding touches from the set of pastels sitting on the table. He swiftly finished his sketch by indicating the scale of the project and how it would be worn.

"You have skill," the man said, bobbing a bow at Marcus as he took the paper and examined the sketch. "Few can claim such a talent for creation."

"It's wasted on me, I'm afraid." Marcus knew his real talent was destruction. "Can you make this in gold?"

"It would be an honor to demonstrate to you the talent of Katamarca's artisans." The man bowed deeply. "When do you wish it completed by?"

"I trust you'll find the balance between quality and speed." Reaching into his belt pouch, Marcus extracted ten Cel dragons and placed the heavy gold coins on the table one after the other. "Is this sufficient?"

The man's eyes bulged, then he shook his head. "I cannot accept payment, my legatus. It would be my honor to gift this to you."

"I pay my debts, as does the Empire," Marcus said, watching the man stare at the coins, then slowly lift his head, the message received. "Have it delivered to my camp when it's completed."

Inclining his head, he turned on his heel and exited the shop.

"What did you buy?" Gibzen demanded furiously.

Marcus paused in putting his helmet back on, slowly lowering it as he fixed Gibzen with a stare. "Pardon?"

The primus's cheeks colored, and he looked away. "We just got you back and already you're taking risks you shouldn't."

Marcus moved so that they were nose to nose. "I need a bodyguard, Gibzen. Not a nursemaid."

The primus's eyes shifted sideways. "Yes, sir. Sorry, sir."

"Back to camp."

22

KILLIAN

Killian watched Agrippa tie Lydia to a thick pine tree.

"You're not doing her any favors," he muttered. "She can't spend every night for the rest of her life tied up, and once we reach Anukastre, you'll be out of trees."

"You're quite right, Lord Calorian," Agrippa snapped. "I'm *not* doing Lydia a favor. I'm doing *myself* a favor so that I can get some gods-damned sleep without fear of having the life drained out of me while I dream. As far as the tree situation goes, I'll truss her up like a pig for a solstice feast once we're in the desert if that's what is required."

Lydia nodded as though this made perfect sense, and Killian had to curb the urge to scream in frustration that this was her solution. And frustration with himself for not being able to offer anything better.

"It allows me to sleep," she said. "The last thing I need is to become so exhausted that I can't control myself."

"Which is fantastic, because it means I won't have to bear the lifelong guilt of having killed you. Baird, shift over, would you." The giant moved from where he'd been sitting next to Malahi, and Agrippa took up the position.

"Don't pretend you'd shed any tears over my death." Lydia accepted the jerky Baird pulled from his pack to toss to her.

"I would," Agrippa retorted around a mouthful of food. "Also I'm an ugly crier, so let's avoid it."

"Did I actually hear you admit you aren't good at something, little man?" Baird said. "I think that's a first."

"It's a short list but crying is first on it. I get all pathetic and red in the face, so I avoid it at all costs. And don't call me that. I'm not short, you are all just abnormally tall. Except for you, Majesty."

He smiled at Malahi, who rolled her eyes and said, "I knew there was a reason you rescued me, and there it is."

They all laughed, Lydia included, and Killian hated it. Hated that they were joking about murdering Lydia, which he knew Agrippa would do without hesitation or the slightest bit of remorse. Hated that Lydia seemed to almost welcome that inevitability, because it felt to Killian as though she had taken the first step toward giving up. He didn't know how to protect her from that.

You've already failed her. Just like you failed Malahi. Just like you failed Mudamora.

Killian shoved away the thought, focusing on brushing mud from the horses' legs, but it was insidious, seeming to infect every part of him.

"What's eating you up?"

Killian twitched, not having heard Baird approach. The giant was shockingly silent when he wanted to be. "I don't find Lydia's death something to laugh about."

"I reckon you don't." Baird patted the horse's neck. "Though if it helps, none of them do, either. Agrippa doesn't want to hurt the lass, Killian, but he's also committed to Malahi's safety, and Lydia's a threat to that. The ropes . . . it's the only solution he has to offer, and that he's joking about it only means he hates it."

It was hard to argue with that, but Killian was too pissed off to let it go, so he said, "What happened between them before we met up? Why is Agrippa so set on watching Malahi's back?"

"What happened between them is their business, but as to Agrippa's motivation . . ." Baird trailed off, eyes on the midnight sky as he thought. "We were there when Rufina brought Malahi into Deadground. We had to watch as Rufina tortured Malahi to try to get her to grow the blight, but Malahi refused. Agrippa . . . To say that he admired her understates his feelings because it goes beyond that. Malahi did what he couldn't when she stood against Rufina. He hated every moment of leading that bitch's army, hated what he was doing, but he saw no other way through. Malahi revealed a different path, and given the chance to follow her light out of the darkness, he took it. Which you should be glad for, because it has allowed you the opportunity to focus on Lydia."

"I am." Even if his focus had amounted to nothing. "He's better at it, anyway."

Baird gave a soft laugh that reminded Killian of his father, then the giant said, "Well, for one, he was trained to do it. He served as a bodyguard to your new nemesis in the south before they parted ways. Two, he's well suited to it—likes to do it—whereas you prefer to lead soldiers into battle. Agrippa wants Malahi to be his only focus."

"I want Lydia to be my only focus, but instead of keeping her safe, I've done nothing while she's been trussed up like an animal."

Baird's thick hand moved to rest on Killian's shoulder. "Have you stopped to consider that this might be less about you and more about the girl in question?" When Killian didn't answer, the giant said, "Malahi isn't a fighter, but more than that, she doesn't want to be. She's not got a violent bone in her body, but there are a good many people who wish violence upon her. She needs someone to be her shadow, who will do what she can't—what she won't—and Agrippa is capable of filling that role in every possible way. Except you know as well as I do that Lydia doesn't want to be protected—she wants to be able to protect herself. What she needs is an ally who will stand back-to-back with her in every fight. Even the ones she has with herself."

Everything the giant said made sense, though Killian felt no more like an ally than he had a protector. "Gods, you remind me of Bercola," he muttered. "All my wisdom coming from giants."

"Bercola?"

"The giantess who served as my bodyguard when I was a child, and then stood as my friend after that." Until she'd sided with Malahi and nearly killed Lydia. "I miss her."

The air filled with a heavy silence.

"She wouldn't happen to be near sixty years of age? A warrior of the highest caliber and as beautiful as a sunrise after the darkest night?"

Killian blinked, envisioning Bercola with her shaved head, colorless eyes, and frame like a tree trunk. "Yes," he hazarded. "That description fits."

"I don't suppose we'll be seeing her when we return to Mudamora?"

"It's probable she's with my family," Killian answered. "Why?"

"Because she's my wife." Baird gave a morose sigh. "You go get some rest, Killian. I'll take first watch tonight."

Wife? Killian gave his head a little shake as he walked back to where the others were setting out their bedrolls, barely more than shadows. He picked up his own bedroll, about to lay it out when he hesitated, his eyes on the slender shadow that was Lydia. She lay with her back to the others, wrists bound to the tree, and though she wasn't moving, he knew she wasn't asleep.

What she needs is an ally who will stand back-to-back with her in every fight.

Picking up his blanket, Killian walked over and put it down behind her. Lydia turned her head. "What are you doing? You need to be out of reach."

"If you move or tense, I'll feel it." He flopped down next to her so that their backs were pressed together. "I'll be able to warn the others."

"But you're in easy reach."

He was abundantly aware of that given the heat of her body against his, the tight curve of her backside pressed against the small of his back. "I'm also in possession of a god mark that will allow me to react quickly if something goes wrong." He was quiet for a moment, then added, "I know you don't trust yourself right now, Lydia, but I hope you still trust me."

Her whole body was rigid with tension, the silence so heavy he felt reluctant to breathe. Then Lydia whispered, "With my life," and relaxed against him.

The words made Killian's chest swell, but there was no escaping the dread lurking in the back of his mind that the worst was yet to come.

23

TERIANA

Sitting in Quintus's tent, Teriana squinted in the faint light, trying and failing to write a letter to her aunt Yedda.

There were a million things she needed to tell her, not the least of which was that she was alive, because she had no idea if her crew had been informed that she was missing, and no one in either legion seemed inclined to tell her.

None of them seemed inclined to talk to her at all.

It seemed an eternity since she'd last seen her ship. Her crew. Her family. Closing her eyes, she imagined the vessel running on the wind, blue sails taut, spray filling the air. At sea was where she was meant to be, but the vision felt faded. As though the time she'd spent apart from all that she held dear had lessened their hold on her mind and heart, which made the guilt she felt all the worse.

Drumming her fingers against her thigh, Teriana stared at the blank page, then started detailing the facts of what had happened, leaving out anything that was best communicated in person.

Or not at all.

Teriana didn't know whether her crew had heard the rumors about her and Marcus, but if they had, she could only imagine what they would think. Part of her wanted to scream that it was only because they didn't understand, that they didn't know him, that the situation was complicated. Yet despite all of that, most of her people would see her falling in love with a Cel legatus as a betrayal. Maybe they'd turn their backs on her, as her mother had.

Maybe she deserved it.

I've secured freedom for a portion of those captive in Celendrial, but many remain imprisoned. They will be released when xenthier stems are found that are to the Senate's satisfaction. Mum is still safe in Senator Valerius's care, and he assures me that she is well.

She mused over whether to tell her aunt that she'd been given the opportunity to rejoin her crew but decided against it.

I wish it were possible for me to see you, but I hope that we'll be reunited, permanently, sooner rather than later.

Her eyes flicked up to where Quintus was reading a book, a bottle of rum sitting next to him.

If you are able, please find an injured legionnaire named Miki. He was hurt keeping me safe, and I owe him my life. Please let him know that I'm sharing a tent with Quintus, who is doing well but misses him terribly.

Teriana

Folding it up, she shoved it into her pocket to give to Servius for delivery later.

The camp, which had been empty while the legions trained on the plains outside, was now filled with voices and chatter. Though she'd heard Servius had assigned the Fifty-First labor-intensive duties, they still seemed flush with energy, groups of them racing through camp with a ball, playing some form of game.

"Did you used to play games like them?" she asked Quintus. "The Thirty-Seventh, I mean."

Setting down the battered volume, he glanced out the open flaps of the tent. "Yeah, at first. Not after Hostus took command. Under his leadership, the Twenty-Ninth made us do everything while they drank, gambled, and whored, so there wasn't much time left for fun. And *fun* was always on their terms. Here." He handed her the bottle of rum.

She took a mouthful, watching as the boys, dressed only in mud-splattered undergarments, ran and laughed, the older legionnaires watching with amusement and occasionally kicking the ball back when it went out of play.

Then a ball soared directly at her.

Reflex made her jerk sideways so that the ball flew into the tent rather than hit her in the face. After the ball followed a sprawl of boys, the lot of them landing on top of the ball in front of Quintus. Her friend did not look amused. "You little shits."

"Hello, Teriana," Nic said from the bottom of the pile. Crawling out from under his men, he handed off the ball to the other boys, who closed the tent as they departed, leaving their mud-smeared legatus alone with her and Quintus.

"What's this about?" She exchanged a confused glance with Quintus.

"After Titus's funeral we had a brief meeting with Marcus in Aracam where he gave all the officers orders not to speak to you about his plans." Nic sat cross-legged. "Said anyone who did would have the skin whipped off his back."

Marcus giving such an order shouldn't have hurt, but it did. Because apparently he needed her so far removed from his life that he refused to tolerate anyone he knew having anything to do with her.

"Marcus doesn't make idle threats," Quintus warned. "You get caught, you'll not be able to sit a horse for a month, *sir*."

Nic shrugged. "I won't get caught."

"Just so you know," Quintus said, "Servius has eyes on the back of his head for misconduct."

"They're more interested in the Forty-First. We're just children." The irritation in Nic's voice was palpable despite that being an unarguable fact.

"What did you want to say to me that's worth the risk of pissing off your boss?" Teriana asked.

"Marcus plans to try to use diplomacy to try to get the Gamdeshians to give him control of Emrant peaceably. He thinks that they know enough about the threat the Empire poses to concede the city rather than risk all-out war."

Teriana blinked. "There is no chance they'll agree to that. None. It would be lunacy to give Emrant up without a fight, and Kaira, in particular, doesn't give up *anything* without a fight."

"So you think the strategy is weak?"

"I—" She glanced to Quintus, who shook his head. "I struggle to imagine Kaira agreeing to it. And the Sultan doesn't counter her military advice."

"We'd be revealing our target if we pursue diplomacy. How do you think Kaira will react?"

Teriana bit the insides of her cheeks. "I suppose logically it would allow her time to bring in reinforcements to defend the city."

"Which would make our fight all the more challenging? Higher casualties?"

"I . . . I suppose, yes." She was no military strategist, but that seemed logical. "Except Marcus knows all this. It was the first thing he said when I told him the stem was in Emrant. It has to factor into his plan somehow."

"When I questioned him, he told me 'diplomacy first,'" Nic said flatly. "There's chatter around the camp that going through so many xenthier stems damaged his thinking. That he's not coming up with a better strategy because he can't. Or worse, that he's lost his nerve."

"Careful now, puppy," Quintus warned. "Those are fighting words, and you and yours can't back them up."

"I'm not looking for a fight," Nic retorted. "But I'm not putting my men at risk for the sake of blindly following a commander who has lost his edge and will give up his greatest advantage in the hopes that posturing will spare him a fight. A commander who refuses to use his best resource"—he pointed at Teriana—"because he was foolish enough to break the rules and get involved with her. Tell me I'm wrong, and I'll piss off. Except I don't think I'm wrong. Not when he can't even walk in a straight line, he's so addled."

The world was spinning, and Teriana realized she'd been holding her breath. Sucking in a mouthful of air, she willed her heart to calm and said, "I don't think Marcus has lost his nerve."

"Well, there's always the chance he doesn't care about not meeting Cassius's deadline."

She didn't believe that. Refused to.

"Unlike Marcus, I was in Celendrial's prison with you," Nic said. "I saw what you saw, and your people are still there, still being pissed on, starved, and beaten by Hostus's twisted legion. Are you sure you're willing to risk them being stuck there until they are executed because you put blind faith in the ex-lover who might not be capable of strategizing further than a path to the latrines?"

Quintus drew back his arm, obviously intending to punch Nic in the face. She caught hold of her friend's wrist. "Don't."

"You aren't serious," Quintus snapped. "Marcus is an asshole, you'll get no arguments from me on that, but he's proven himself more times than I can count. The Thirty-Seventh would follow him into fire if he said it was the right path, because he's never wrong!"

"I'm not denying that he earned his reputation," Nic shot back. "Except he shouldn't even be breathing after that stunt. He looks awful. He would have fallen twice today if Felix hadn't caught him."

"He's exhausted." Quintus wrenched his arm out of Teriana's grip, looking ready to fling himself at the boy. "Give him a bloody minute to recover. Also, keep in mind that he might not be telling you his actual plan. Have a little trust in your commander, *sir*."

Gods, she was so dizzy. Why couldn't she remember to breathe?

"I want to trust that Marcus has a better plan than this," Nic said. "I want to believe that I can trust him with the lives of my men. But I can't do that if he keeps me in the dark."

"It's his prerogative to keep you in the dark." Quintus narrowed his eyes. "It doesn't matter if you like it. There's nothing you can do about it."

"I can send my own messages to the Senate," Nic retorted. "Explain the situation and request reinforcements that include someone who can take over command. Or—" He scrambled away from Quintus's reaching hand, her friend looking ready to throttle him. "Or Teriana can get the information out of him. If she can talk to him and get the truth, if she feels he's on the right course, I'll trust her."

"He won't talk to me, Nic." Teriana's eyes stung, and she blinked rapidly, unwilling to cry in front of this child. "He's made that clear. I don't think you should undermine him by going behind his back, but I also don't think you should rely on me to get the information you need."

Silence stretched, then Nic said, "Cassius told me that you were the key to controlling him, and I hated that. Hated that the legatus who had been held up before us as the ideal could be controlled by *lust*."

"You might understand that better when your balls drop, puppy," Quintus muttered.

"But at least then your involvement made sense," Nic continued, ignoring Quintus. "You had a purpose. Whereas now, I don't understand why you came at all other than to sit in Quintus's tent, drinking, gambling, and crying into your pillow while the rest of us work to save your people."

Her cheeks burned hot. "Get out. Get out, or I'm going to let Quintus drown you in the latrines."

"Fine." Nic tossed a letter on her lap. "This was attached to a crate in our supplies. We have it set aside where the other legions won't find it. If you want it, ask Pullo and it's yours." Then he pulled a gold coin out of his belt pouch and tossed it on top of the letter. "Or you can buy yourself another bottle of rum."

He gave a sharp whistle, and a heartbeat later, the mass of Fifty-First tumbled past the entrance of Quintus's tent, shouting and laughing. Nic flung himself into the midst of the muddy boys, stole the ball from one, and raced off with it.

Taking a deep breath, Teriana opened the letter.

Teriana,

I've included this gift in the hopes it aids you in achieving our mutually desired ends.

Lucius Cassius

"What does it say?" Quintus asked.

Teriana crumbled it angrily in her fist. "Nothing I'm interested in. Cassius's *gifts* always come with strings attached."

"Austornic is an obnoxious little shit!" Quintus snarled, then he locked eyes with her. "Don't even think about it, Teriana. You promised not to get involved, and allowing a child with grand ambitions for his military future to convince you to break that promise would be a mistake."

"Except I am involved!" Growling in a mix of frustration and misery, Teriana pressed her fingers to her temples. "Nic wasn't wrong about my people, and what does it say about me if I sit in your tent playing cards and drinking rum, trusting that others will save them?"

"Sometimes doing nothing is better than doing the wrong thing." Quintus frowned and grabbed her arms, giving her a gentle shake. "Breathe, Teriana."

She gasped in a breath. "It feels like I've forgotten how. Who forgets how to breathe? What's wrong with me?"

"Nothing's wrong with you." Her friend pulled her against him, and Teriana inhaled the scent of the cheap soap the legionnaires used, the familiarity relaxing the tension that had every muscle in her body twisted into ropes. "If you weren't losing your head, I'd question whether you had a heart, given the position you're in. But you're only going to make things worse for yourself if you get in the middle of it."

Quintus was right. She knew he was right. Yet a seed of fear that hadn't existed before had been planted in her heart. "What if Nic's right? What if . . . what if Marcus isn't okay?"

Quintus was silent, and the seed of fear began to take root. She'd seen Marcus rubbing at his head, the obvious pain he was suffering, the slight stagger to his walk. What if he'd pushed too far? What if he wouldn't get better?

"Give him a few days to recover," Quintus finally answered. "Don't jump to conclusions."

Yet Nic's words sank into her soul, making her feel sick with her near uselessness in a situation where she was supposed to have been one of the most powerful players of all. "Do you think Nic's right?"

Quintus crossed his arms and scowled. "No. I think Austornic had grand ambitions for what his role would be and is acting out because Marcus stomped on his dreams."

"But what if he is unwell?" she asked, her voice barely audible. "What if that's part of the reason he won't speak to me? Because he knows I'll see right through to the state he's in."

"Marcus broke things off while you were still in Celendrial, Teriana. So whatever his reasons are, they predate his jaunt through all those xenthier paths." Reaching over, Quintus took her hand. "This is just a baby legatus trying to flex his muscles and gain control he hasn't earned. Marcus was *just like this* at that age, although I'm only now appreciating how obnoxious it was for our minders. Do you want me to tell Felix that Nic is meddling?"

"No," she said. "I don't want him punished."

"We might be doing him a favor in the long run," Quintus said. "If he reaches a little too far in his ambitions, it could cause us all a fair bit of pain."

She stared down at Cassius's crumpled note. "Not yet."

"More rum?" he offered, holding out the bottle.

Teriana shook her head. "I need to visit the latrines, and then I'm going to sleep."

He winced. "You sure you don't want to use the trench this time? Your shed is looking awfully foul."

"Better filth than hanging my ass out in the open for everyone to see."

"I can chase them all off, but it's your call." Belting on his weapon, Quintus led her out of the tent, the light rain turning heavier as they wove toward the rear of the camp. Darkness had fallen, the Fifty-First seeming to have finally settled their antics, and the only sound was the faint boom of thunder and chatter around campfires.

The stink of the latrines greeted her long before her eyes picked out the trench in the darkness. Ignoring the handful of men standing before it doing their business, she stalked toward the small shed that had once been allocated for her personal use.

"I'll wait here," Quintus said. "If you start to succumb to the stink, shout and I'll rescue you."

"Thanks." She unhooked the lantern hanging outside the shed, then pulled open the door, bracing herself for the filth.

Instead, she was greeted by a naked woman perched on the disgusting bench.

"Hello, Teriana," Astara said softly in Gamdeshian, pushing long dark hair back over her shoulder. "We thought that you were dead."

"I'm surprised *you're* not dead, lurking in this mess." Teriana wrinkled her nose at the disaster the legionnaires had made of her outhouse during her absence, though her comment was mostly to cover her shock. Though this wasn't the first time the shifter had approached her, Teriana had not realized Astara was still watching the camp. "Why are men so revolting?"

"Shut the door."

Teriana pulled it shut behind her, flipping the latch before turning to face the shifter. The prior time they'd met, Teriana had not had a lamp, so this was the first time she'd seen the other woman clearly. In her early twenties, Astara was pretty, with large brown eyes framed with lush lashes, soft brown skin, and a figure that would make anyone look twice. Skulking about was hardly necessary, because Teriana had no doubt the legionnaires would have happily allowed her into camp. "How much do you know about where I've been?"

"I've heard the chatter," Astara answered. "They know I see well, but they don't seem aware that my hearing is also excellent. Especially in the dark."

An unexpected sense of resentment made Teriana clench her teeth, for it was yet another piece of information she'd have to choose whether to keep secret or not. The endless dilemma of being on both sides of a conflict, and she hated it. Hated the way it ate at her soul and kept her perpetually on edge. "Then I won't waste my breath. Why are you here?"

"To find out the Cel commander's intentions."

"We aren't precisely on speaking terms right now, so you would be better off eavesdropping on his men."

"Ah, yes. Lover's quarrel." Astara's tone was full of condemnation that made Teriana want to shove the woman down the hole in the bench into the shit below.

"Whose side are you on, Teriana? Because, I confess, it's difficult to tell. First you beg help of Gamdesh in defeating this incursion, but then you fall into bed with the Cel commander, disappear with him for many long weeks, only to return with yet another legion. Albeit a legion of children." Her pretty face twisted with disgust.

Teriana felt her temper snap. "You want to know whose side I'm on, Astara? *Neither.* I'm stuck in the gods-damned middle is what I am. Five hundred of my people are locked in a prison under the control of the cruelest man I've ever encountered, and if the Empire doesn't get what it wants within six months, they will start executing them. I'm my people's only hope, so it's *their* side that I'm on."

"Given that necessitates aiding your blackmailer, it amounts to you being on his side." There was no sympathy in the woman's voice. "What are five hundred lives compared to the millions in Gamdesh?"

Teriana squeezed her eyes shut, seeing the faces of her people shackled in the prison, Hostus's laugh filling her ears. "They are *everything* to me. Gamdesh has Kaira, and you, and an enormous army with a fleet to rival any in the world. All my people have is *me*."

"No good ruler puts the few over the many."

"I never said I'm a good ruler," Teriana retorted. "But I do try to be a good person, and my peoples' deaths are certain if I don't act. Whereas what fate might befall Gamdesh is unknown. I won't condemn my people for an unknown, and if you have a problem with that, you can kiss my ass."

Astara tensed, and Teriana cursed herself for locking the door latch, because the shifter was nothing if not dangerous. Then a thought occurred to her. "Why are you so certain that Gamdesh is where the Empire's eyes will turn? Katamarca is a far easier mark."

The woman didn't answer, and Teriana didn't know whether to laugh or cry at this silent confirmation of her theory about the terminuses in Gamdesh. "You hold the key to my people's salvation, don't you," she said softly. "You hold it in your hands, the ability to save those innocent lives, yet you will do nothing."

"Sometimes sacrifices need to be made."

Teriana's body quivered. It felt like she stood on a great precipice, warring between the decision to jump or to keep clinging to the edge. Except Teriana always jumped. "I think it is Gamdesh that needs to make a choice. These legions are the weapon I'll wield to save my people, and if you stand between me and Maarin liberty, the blow will fall harder than you can imagine. Now if you don't mind, I really need to pee."

Yanking down her trousers, Teriana relieved her aching bladder, then pulled her clothing back into place. Ignoring the stunned shifter, she flipped the latch on the door and exited the outhouse into the darkness of night.

24

LYDIA

Pressed against Killian's back with Agrippa's gloves on her hands and his knotwork binding her tight, Lydia fell into the first deep sleep she'd had in longer than she cared to remember.

Yet it was unfortunately short-lived.

It was still darkest night when Agrippa shook Killian's shoulder, waking her as he did. "The blighters are about a half hour back from us," he said under his breath. "They're moving south. Doesn't look like they're actively hunting, but if one sees us, they all see us."

"Shit." Killian sat upright. "I'd hoped we'd put more distance between us and them."

"They don't sleep. Don't eat." As Agrippa spoke, he started untying Lydia's bindings. "They don't feel any pain as their bodies break down from the abuse of endlessly running, and if they fall, they'll crawl. We can't outpace them."

"So what do we do?" Lydia asked.

"I think we need to get behind their lines," Agrippa answered, though his eyes were on Killian. "Thoughts?"

"Are there enough gaps between groups of them for us to get through?" Killian asked, and when Agrippa shook his head, he asked, "Do they look up?"

"No, they aren't concerned about the deimos."

"Would trees work?"

"Yeah. We'll have to abandon the horses, though."

"What are you talking about?" Lydia whispered as Agrippa unfastened the rest of her bindings.

"We'll hide in the trees while they pass," Killian said.

"I'll wake the others." Agrippa hesitated, then said, "Malahi doesn't do well with being woken up unexpectedly. Rufina used to set upon her whenever she slept, so she associates waking with violence. I'll try to keep her from screaming, but be ready to ride and ride hard if she does."

Heart hammering, Lydia gathered up her bedroll, though her eyes followed Agrippa as he approached Malahi and Baird. The Queen was buried in blankets, her back pressed against Baird's, but one of Agrippa's knives was gripped in her right hand.

Agrippa glanced skyward, then murmured, "Malahi."

She lurched upward with a gasp, slashing out blindly with the weapon, her lips parting. Agrippa only ducked under the blade, his hand pressing to her mouth to silence the rising scream. He pulled Malahi against him, restraining her easily, and Lydia heard him whisper, "Easy, Your Grace. It's just me. You're safe. You're safe."

They were the exact opposite of safe, but to Lydia's surprise, Malahi stopped fighting. As Agrippa dropped his hand from her mouth, she whispered, "I'm sorry."

"You've got nothing to be sorry for." His arm curved protectively around her back. "Always better to wake up fighting than not wake up at all." He was quiet for a heartbeat, and then he said, "I'm sorry I left without telling you."

Lydia twitched as Killian touched her arm. "Get everything packed. I'm going to set the horses loose so that they run ahead of us and hopefully throw off the trail."

She swiftly gathered their things, heart in her throat because every time she blinked, visions of the blighter horde filled her mind's eye. To willfully allow themselves to be surrounded by so many seemed like madness, but so did riding day and night without rest to stay ahead of them.

Baird was heaving himself up a thick tree while Agrippa lifted Malahi to grab the branches of another. Under Malahi's touch, the branch moved, pulling her higher, and Agrippa scrambled up after her with ease.

Killian lifted the saddles up for Agrippa to wedge out of sight, then he strode to where Lydia waited. "Do you need a boost?"

Given she'd never climbed a tree in her life, she nodded, and he lifted her so that she could reach a thick branch. She slung a leg over it, then reached down a gloved hand to him.

Killian jumped, hand locking on hers. Though Lydia was nowhere near as strong as when she gave in to the Corrupter, Hegeria's mark was no small thing, and grinding her teeth, Lydia bore his weight until he caught hold of the branch with his free hand.

Together, they climbed higher and deeper into the tree, and then fell still.

Not a moment too soon.

In the distance, the noise of hundreds of footfalls grew louder and louder, brush crunching beneath feet as the dead civilians of Derin marched across the countryside. Lydia allowed her mark to take hold, but while her companions glowed with life, the blighters were midnight shadows of *nothing* as they moved closer, then beneath the branches of the trees.

The smell of old blood, urine, and vomit drifted up from the horde, the stink almost making her gag as she silently counted them, losing track after a thousand. Lydia's body ached from keeping entirely still. She was afraid that even the tiniest movement, tiniest sound, would attract their attention, but they only pressed onward. The front-runners seemed whole and strong, but those that followed tripped and stumbled. As they drew closer, Lydia saw many had visibly broken bones, falling when their legs gave out only to crawl forward on hands and knees.

Despite seeing with her own eyes that they were dead, nothing more than corpse puppets commanded by the Corrupter, the scene still made Lydia's throat burn with bile. She could only imagine how her companions, who could not see that the blighters were dead, felt to witness the horror.

Minutes passed. Then hours.

Yet it felt like eternity as they waited for the last crawling members of the horde to pass them by, dawn illuminating the blighters as they slowly moved into the distance. Only then did Killian climb down, checking their surroundings before softly calling out. "I think we're in the clear."

Lydia clambered down, relieved to finally move her stiff muscles.

"That bitch killed them all." Agrippa stared at the trail of footprints the blighters had left. "Killed her own people to create another army for no other purpose than to hunt us down."

A snuffling filled Lydia's ears, and she saw that Baird was weeping. "Three years I spent in Derin, and I can attest these people didn't deserve this." He wiped at his face. "Most were born to these lands and were doing naught but trying to survive beneath Rufina's tyranny, and the tyranny of every demon who came before her."

Agrippa didn't answer, only stared into the distance, his fists clenched. Lydia could feel the anger seething from him. The guilt. For the first time, she felt certainty in her heart that he was truly on their side, if for no other reason than that they fought against Rufina. She met Killian's eyes, and he gave a nod of confirmation before saying, "Does this change the plan?"

"There's a reason why Derin is as isolated as it is," Agrippa replied. "Twisted seas and a coast made of swamp to the west. Liratoras to the east. Icefields to the north. Desert to the south. At least with Anukastre, there's safety on the other side, which you can't say for the rest. Plus the deimos can't tolerate the heat, and Rufina herself won't risk following on foot, which makes the sand dunes mighty appealing."

"Except she knows that's where we're going," Killian said. "All those blighters aren't just going to disappear. We're going to have to get past them at some point."

"The Eyrie, most likely," Baird muttered. "With any luck, they'll all just walk over the edge."

"Edge?" Lydia asked.

Baird and Agrippa exchanged long looks, and the latter said, "We still set on south?"

Killian's eyes went distant, then he nodded.

"Right." Agrippa rocked on his heels. "Well then, as we walk, allow me to tell you about the edge of the world."

25

MARCUS

Marcus rubbed at his temple, his head throbbing, but he ignored it in favor of drawing a piece of paper in front of him. Tapping a pencil against his chin, he wrote: *To Her Royal Highness, Princess Kaira.*

He stared at the line for a moment, the words splitting into two, then three, then scratched it out and wrote: *General Kaira.*

Writing in Cel, he detailed the Empire's belief that a terminus stem was located in Emrant and the Senate's desire for it to be opened to traffic for trade, which would be mutually profitable for both nations. He finished with a few sentences explaining the Senate's hope to achieve a peaceful and lasting alliance with Gamdesh.

Lies.

A sudden chill passed over him, and Marcus shivered, reaching for his cloak right as a knock sounded at the door. "Come in."

Atrio stepped inside. Dressed in standard legion kit, the good-looking young man appeared much like any other man in the Thirty-Seventh but for the fact that his dark brown hair was longer than regulation. Yet beneath the armor was a more significant difference in that he bore no legion tattoos on his brown skin. Chosen for this duty before graduation, he'd not been marked with a legion number as the rest of them had been, and he'd also had the tiny identification number that had been placed upon him when he arrived at Lescendor removed. Atrio was a chameleon who learned languages at shocking speed, his ability to mimic accents and mannerisms almost unnatural. He'd also been deployed in civilian garb to Gamdesh within days of their arrival in the West, where he'd remained until recently, making him one of Marcus's most valuable resources.

"Sir." Atrio saluted and removed his helmet.

"How do you fancy returning to Gamdesh?"

Atrio shrugged. "I got a girl in a port town just north of Emrant. She thinks I work on merchant ships that trade down the east coast of the continent. It's just a matter of me sailing into her harbor with a gift or two from my travels."

What made the spy good at his job was his ability to create relationships, but Marcus had never envied him his many false lives. Though if Atrio worried about the broken hearts he left in his wake, he never showed it.

"What's her name?"

"Astara, sir. She lives in the garrison in a fortress known as Imresh north of Emrant. I was working to find my way inside before I was recalled by Titus, but the Gamdeshians have Imresh locked up tighter than the virtue of a Senator's daughter. It's where Kaira is stationed, and I'd hoped to get eyes and ears on her."

Marcus frowned. "Don't get too close to Kaira. Her instincts are . . . *acute*."

"That's well known, sir. And to be frank, no concerns there. Kaira's one for the ladies, and besides, Astara might tolerate my absences, but she doesn't tolerate me looking sideways at other girls. Given she can turn into a giant hawk, I do my best to remain on her good side."

Marcus blinked. "Pardon?"

"Sorry, sir. I'm used to you knowing more than I know myself. Everyone is, which is likely why no one has mentioned her."

Marcus's teeth clenched, because he was also used to being the best informed. "Perhaps you'll do me the service of rectifying my ignorance."

"Of course, sir. There are people in the West with special powers gifted them by the gods, and—"

"I'm aware of the god marks."

"Right." Atrio rocked on his heels. "At any rate, Astara is marked by the god Lern, so she can turn into an animal. A hawk, specifically. She works for Kaira as a spy."

A shifter spy.

Atrio patted the helmet under his arm. "Astara is why I keep this on. She spies on our camp regularly, and her eyesight is keen. She comes and goes, but I heard her wings overhead earlier."

There was so much information Marcus didn't know, days and days of reports to read, but he didn't have time.

"Do you know how quickly she can make the journey between Aracam and Kaira's fortress?"

"She's fast," Atrio answered. "Anything that can be seen, you best be sure Kaira knows about, and then some. Felix keeps men on the walls whose sole duty is to try to shoot her down, but Astara knows their range."

"She a talker?"

Atrio blew out a breath of frustration. "No, unfortunately. I had a room in the village outside of the fortress and she always came to me. Everything I know about Astara's duties I discovered through looser lips, and that isn't much. Though she's often in Emrant, Kaira returns every night to Imresh. Must be worried about assassination attempts, because the garrison in that fortress has twice the number of men they need."

"If there is opportunity to learn more, do so. But I've a bigger priority for you." Marcus swiftly explained about the walled-in terminus in Emrant. "I want certainty that it's good before we take steps to secure it."

"How do you want me to do that?" Atrio asked. "If it's walled in, as you say, then my guess is the city guard will have something to say about me taking out a piece of said wall to determine whether it's a tomb for ill-fated path-hunters."

"I want you to listen."

Atrio's eyes widened. "Listen for . . . for screams? With respect, sir, that's grim given it's unlikely we could rescue them in time."

"Not screams." Marcus explained his plan, the corner of Atrio's mouth turning up in a half smile.

"Clever."

"It's only clever if it works, you know that."

"Yes, sir."

Marcus shoved his draft letter in front of the spy. "Can you translate this?"

The spy read the letter, then swiftly scribbled a translation on another scrap of paper. "You know the Gamdeshians won't agree to this after what Titus did to the god towers in Aracam and Galinha, right?"

"That's my problem, not yours."

Atrio shoved his helmet down on his head, then saluted. "I'll get underway quick like, but it might be a day before I sail out of Aracam. There are spies from every nation in the West in the city now, and this will all be for naught if I'm discovered."

"Be safe." Marcus watched the spy depart before taking both letters and holding them to the lamp flame, knowing that Atrio would reveal at least some of what he'd written over drinks around the fire tonight. He tossed them in the bowl on the table, watching the paper burn before drawing another page in front of him.

Writing swiftly in Gamdeshian, he explained Teriana's situation, the threat to the imprisoned Maarin, and the requirements for setting them free. *The Senate requires pathways that are safe and secure for trade, but with your cooperation, we can fabricate a pretense that I hold the stems under legion control. Once the Maarin are freed, I will withdraw from Gamdesh's territories. It is no permanent solution, for the Senate will soon discover my duplicity and remove me from command, but it will buy you time while also saving the lives of your Maarin allies. Lest there be any confusion, if you refuse to work with me now to save the lives of Teriana's people, you will war with me later.*

He signed the page and sealed it with wax stamped with Celendor's dragon, the creature staring up at him with mocking eyes.

The Senate would hang him for this, of that there was no question. But Teriana would be free. Her people would be free. And if all worked as he intended, it would aid those allied with his sister and her husband who were trying to wrest power from Cassius, because the voting citizens would not support a consul behind such a costly failed campaign.

Marcus stared at the wall, allowing himself a moment to imagine Felix receiving a message from a newly elected consul ordering the legions to withdraw to Celendor once summer arrived in Sibern. Not quite the dream he'd hoped for but better than the alternative.

Yet he still needed to plan for the alternative, because it was not lost on him that everything hinged on Kaira agreeing to his scheme. Her willingness to set aside the not-undeserved prejudices against his character that the Maarin would have revealed to her. Her willingness to risk Gamdesh for the sake of five hundred souls. It was a roll of the dice that he desperately hoped would work, but he'd not gotten this far in life by not planning for failure.

And planning for that failure necessitated communication with the Empire.

It had to be done. Not only because he needed Wex for his contingency plans to work, but because if he didn't send communication soon, Cassius would only send someone capable of forcing the issue through the Bardeen stem. The Empire had its claws dug into the Southern Continent, and pretending otherwise would do no one any favors. Picking up his pen and dipping it into the ink, Marcus drew a fresh piece of paper in front of him and began to write an update. He then moved on to a directive of specific instructions for Wex to undertake in relation to the potential stems in Gamdesh, the Commandant the only one he trusted to correctly execute the work.

When he'd finished, Marcus retrieved wax wrapping, which he used to carefully protect the letter from the water it would be immersed in, along with a water-tight box painted brilliant red that would bring the missive to the surface of the lake. Strategies taught to all legions, for termini were often located beneath water. Then he sat staring into space, his head throbbing, each pulse saying *six months.*

"It's time enough," he muttered. "Kaira's reputation is good. She'll agree to this for the sake of the Maarin, if nothing else."

The "nothing else" being the thing he did far better than diplomacy.

Picking up the letter to Kaira, he considered how best to deliver it to her knowing that it would surely be read by any messenger.

She spies on our camp regularly, and her eyesight is keen.

The room swam as Marcus stood, forcing him to grip the table until he could see straight.

You just need sleep.

Marcus packaged the letter with wax wrapping then tucked it into his belt pouch before picking up the box containing the message to Wex. Leaving the command room, he handed the box to one of the guards. "This needs to be delivered through the stem mapped to Atlia. Extra security to ensure no interference."

"Yes, sir."

Continuing on through the fortress with Gibzen and the rest of his guard at his heel, Marcus left the building, ignoring the vertigo that joined his headache as he descended the steps. The camp was quiet, only a few men sitting around fires, the Fifty-First all abed as per the curfew imposed upon the younger legion if they weren't on duty. Striding through the camp, he ascended the wall that encircled it, the guards on duty saluting at the sight of him.

Approaching the centurion, he said, "I understand that we are under watch by a rather large bird. How often does she circle overhead?"

The man scowled. "Astara, you mean? She's here tonight." He gestured to his shoulder, which had residue of what Marcus strongly suspected was hawk shit on his armor.

"Perfect." Marcus took the loaded crossbow that the centurion had resting against his shoulder. "I need to borrow this."

"She keeps well out of range, if you're of a mind to shoot her."

"I intend to use her as my messenger." Rain fell from the cloudy skies, moon and stars obscured. Cognizant that hawks were daytime hunters and that her vision in the dark was likely little better than his own, he cleared his throat and then shouted in Gamdeshian, "Astara, are you with us tonight? I've a message for your general!"

A shrill shriek filled the air, the volume speaking to the size of the bird above, which was likely more than capable of killing an armored man. Ignoring the faint thrill of fear that thrummed through his veins, Marcus extracted the letter and fastened it securely to the crossbow bolt. He could feel the curious eyes of all the men on duty, along with those in the camp who were awake to hear him shouting at the sky.

"She might not catch it just to piss you off, sir," the centurion said. "That's her personality."

Marcus shrugged. "Then I'll send it by ship, and she can explain to Kaira why it took ten times as long to reach them. Her choice."

Wings flapped high above, and holding the crossbow so that it was pointed at the sky with a trajectory that wouldn't see it coming down on their heads if Astara proved difficult, Marcus released the bolt. Then held his breath, sucking in air only when his ears caught the crackle of claws catching wax wrapping, the hawk shrieking to indicate success. Only, rather than heading north, she continued to circle above.

Watching.

"I want a report on all her habits," Marcus murmured. "Daily logs of sightings by every centurion. I want to know how fast that woman can fly."

"I'll spread the word, sir."

A sudden wave of exhaustion rolled over him, along with the need to close his eyes and escape from everything for a few hours.

"I'm done here," he said to Gibzen, blindly following the primus as he led Marcus down from the wall and through the camp. He barely saw the men saluting him as he passed, his attention so fractured that he nearly walked into Gibzen's back when the other man abruptly stopped.

"Move!" the primus snarled, and Marcus stepped sideways to find that Gibzen was facing off with Quintus and Teriana.

Quintus gave a smile that was all teeth. "Say pretty please."

Gibzen lifted a fist, and Marcus caught his arm even as Teriana hauled Quintus to the side.

Their eyes locked, and the sudden compulsion to fall to his knees before her and beg forgiveness swept over him. To say whatever he needed to say to have her back.

You're being watched. And you don't deserve forgiveness.

He tore his eyes from hers and trudged down the boardwalks that kept the camp out of the mud until he reached the fortress, where he headed straight to his room. Dismissing Amarin, he left his armor and clothing in a pile on the floor, and then crawled onto his cot.

It was better this way.

Sleep, he screamed at himself. *Just sleep.*

Yet he couldn't silence his mind, couldn't stop the throbbing ache in his skull, and the desperation to escape it made his heart hammer and breath race until he could take it no more. Scrambling to his feet, he fell to his knees next to his pile of clothes, digging into his belt pouch until his fingers found glass.

One drop.

Two.

But when he tried to shake out a third, nothing came.

It doesn't matter, he told himself. *You don't need it.*

The pain in his skull receded but his mind remained restless, circling through every nightmare he faced until dawn lit the sky, and the first order he gave was to Gibzen.

"I need more."

26

TERIANA

Teriana had slept poorly, but as dawn rose, she had a plan. Astara and Kaira might not be willing to help her, but she had other allies. Holding the gold coin that Nic had given her above Quintus's barely awake face, she said, "Let's go into Aracam and spend this."

His eyes focused on the gold. "It's awfully early. But I suppose we don't have anything better to do."

He took her to one of the finer establishments in Aracam, which of course meant that it was full to the brim with off-duty legionnaires—in this case, Forty-First. "You sure this is wise?" she asked, surveying the tables full of men drinking and playing cards, barmaids and prostitutes moving among them.

"Better them than the Thirty-Seventh," he said. "They're still quite testy about you being the cause of Marcus's disappearance, and they've taken to heart his decision to give you the cold shoulder. The

Forty-First is mostly interested in lying low. Also, they are worse gamblers, which means we might come out ahead."

Sighing, Teriana went to the bar and waited for the owner to notice her. The building was made of stone, as were all the structures in Aracam, the roof low enough that anyone much taller than her had to stoop. The walls were stained with soot from the poorly vented hearth in the corner, and Teriana didn't fail to notice the pale rectangles on the wall that had obviously, until recently, born hangings. Likely depictions of the Six, removed at Titus's behest. The owner finally took notice of her and approached.

The woman was tall, her silver hair shaved at the sides and back, the rest gathered in a long tail. "Two things," she said in Arinoquian, placing the gold dragon on the bar. "The first is that drinks are on me until this is spent. The second is that I want to get a message to Ereni."

Quintus made an aggrieved sound but otherwise held his tongue.

"The alliance is broken. Their commander"—the bar owner jerked her chin at the off-duty Forty-First—"broke it. The Cel showed their true colors. They don't want alliances and trading partners; they want to possess everything on Reath."

"I'm not asking to speak to her on behalf of the Cel," Teriana said. "I want to speak to her on behalf of the Maarin."

The woman shrugged. "I'll let it be known, but Ereni answers to no one." Then she lifted her voice and spoke in broken Cel, "Teriana of the Maarin is buying you all the drinks tonight."

Heads turned in their direction, the legionnaires lifting their glasses and cheering her name.

Quintus led her to a table, the men making room for them, and she fell into the old rhythm of life with the legions. Laughing and drinking and gambling, but it felt as though she were outside of herself watching a performance, her mind all for other things. Even so, Teriana could see the changes in the Forty-First. They had an edge they hadn't before, more scars and eyes that had seen too much and would see plenty more. She could tell that Titus's death weighed upon them, and though she wanted to ask how they felt about Felix taking on the role of legatus, which was not how things were done, she kept her mouth shut.

Though it was only late morning, they grew rowdier with every passing hour, the doors flung open to allow in a breeze lest the smell of men grow overwhelming. She and Quintus both won more than they lost, amassing coin but keeping favor by buying food because their companions were testier than she remembered about losing, aggressive and accusatory, though the tension didn't seem specific to her and Quintus.

They were in the middle of a game when Quintus abruptly rose. "I need to piss." He leveled a finger at her. "You don't leave this room."

She nodded, but once he was out the front door, she folded. "I'm getting another drink."

Moving to the bar, Teriana leaned her elbows on the polished wood, glad for the shadows of the corner in which she stood.

Then a familiar voice said, "You're back."

Ereni rested her own elbows on the bar next to her, silvered blond hair falling around her stooped shoulders.

"Bold," Teriana murmured. "They all know your face."

"They know the warrior's face. The imperatrix's face." Ereni lifted a walking stick. "Not the old woman's face. And old women aren't threats."

"That's not been my experience." Teriana took a sip from her drink. "I'm sorry for what has happened. It's not what I intended."

"Isn't it, though?" When Teriana didn't answer, Ereni added, "You brought them to these shores, girl. Have aided them at every turn in their conquest, and now you weep when you see what your actions have wrought? You let the beast out of its cage with delusions that you could keep it on a leash, and now that those delusions are shattered, you say 'this was not what I intended'?"

"Don't forget that you agreed to the alliance with them," Teriana answered softly. "Were happy to allow them free rein if they deposed Urcon. So are your tears worth any more than mine, Ereni?"

"A mistake I will never forgive myself for. Life was hard beneath Urcon. It's worse now. So many succumbing to injury and illness bred by the Empire, more still to hunger, for there are no healers left, no tenders. Faith in the Six diminishes, and with its loss, the gods give no marks. Titus's men pulled down the god towers in Aracam and Galinha, destroyed the shrines in every village where they found one, and threatened to cut out the tongues of anyone who invokes the gods." Her mouth twisted. "But the Seventh's tower remains, lording over our skies. I think that tells you all you need to know and more about who these men serve."

"They serve no gods, Ereni, you know that." Teriana couldn't keep the frustration from her voice. "That's why they tore them down in the first place. They'd have taken the Seventh's towers down as well if they could figure out how. Only they're too strong."

"And why is that?" Ereni plucked Teriana's glass from her hand

and drained the contents. "The gods' strength comes from the faith of the people, Teriana. You know this. The Seventh's strength comes from those who look into darkness to achieve their ends. These boys may not see themselves as serving a god, but they serve evil and that feeds the Corrupter. Look around. Can't you feel it?"

Teriana's skin crawled as she looked around the bar, the Forty-First not seeming happy with their hours of leisure but sullen and angry. In the corner, two men began shoving each other, only the bellowed threat of a centurion keeping it from coming to blows. She'd thought the tension the result of Titus's death.

Except what if she was wrong?

"I'm running out of options, Ereni." She swiftly explained her people's worsened situation. "Gamdesh has no interest in helping me, and I think you have no interest in helping me, either. Which means, in order to save them, all I have left are these legions."

"I will not help you if it means aiding the Empire's conquest," Ereni said. "The inlanders, who *we* once conquered, have set aside old animosities because they know much of Celendor from one who walked the paths before. They say that the Empire must be repelled at all costs or it will destroy all that we hold dear, and there is no denying the recent proof of that claim." She was quiet, then added, "I think Marcus understands that the alliance between us and his legions is burned to ashes, and that is why he's not bothered to make overtures."

That, or he hadn't thought of it. Teriana wasn't sure which was worst.

"I wish I had an answer for you," Ereni continued. "I wish I saw a way to free your people that was worth the cost. But I do not. It may be time for you to concede that you have lost that battle and look toward winning the war for all the other Maarin who live free in the West. For in continuing to give aid to the Empire, you put their lives in jeopardy."

"You want me to just let my imprisoned people die? Let them hang, despite being wholly innocent?" The faces she'd left behind in the prison marched across her mind's eye, and Teriana's chest tightened so painfully that she couldn't breathe. "You want me to abandon them?"

"Sometimes the hardest choice is the right choice." Ereni squeezed her arm. "I grieve for you, Teriana. Truly. But you cannot win this."

Hefting her walking stick, Ereni stooped across the bar toward the exit, none of the legionnaires paying her any mind. Not even Quintus, who passed her on his way in.

"I want to go to the beach," Teriana said to him. "I need to be in the sea."

He shrugged. "All right. All the gold is spent, anyway."

They wove through Aracam and then down a well-traveled path to the beach. Teriana pulled off her boots and stepped into the warm white sand.

"You doing all right?" Quintus asked, scanning the sky. "You got awfully quiet."

"Fine." A lie, but she didn't want to tell him about her conversation with Ereni. "You heard anything about Miki lately?"

"No." He kicked the sand with his toes. "I was going to try to bribe one of the sailors that makes runs to the island to deliver a letter, but I can't afford the going rates. It's gold or nothing, apparently."

She rounded on him. "Why didn't you tell me? You could have used that gold dragon Nic gave us. Instead, you let me spend it entertaining the Forty-First."

Her friend shrugged, eyes again on the sky, not even the obvious heartache that was plaguing him distracting him from his duties. "Was yours. It's fine. I'll win some more at cards. It's my own fault for spending it all. Bad legion habit to spend it as soon as you get it, because you can't spend it when you're dead."

That made a painful amount of sense.

Taking a handful of her braids, she picked out one and began to unravel it, extracting a bead made of solid gold set with a small emerald. One she'd bought for herself years ago that held no sentimental value. "Here."

Quintus glanced at the proffered bead, then shook his head. "I'll figure it out."

"He's my friend, too," she said. "It would make me feel better to do a bit of good for once. Take it."

"You're a dirty negotiator." He plucked the bead out of her hand and then carefully tucked it away. "I'll pay you back."

"Pay me back by one day escaping with Miki to live the life you always wanted."

He rolled his eyes. "Fine. Go have your bath. Keep something on in case the Fifty-First get curious."

Discarding most of her clothes, Teriana waded out into the gentle surf, then plunged beneath. The water was clear and warm, and it occurred to her that she didn't remember the last time she'd swum in the sea. It made her feel strong and whole, washing away her concerns even as it removed the filth of camp life.

Yet when she emerged, reality slapped her in the face as she heard Quintus snarl, "Back up!"

Wiping water from her eyes, Teriana saw him on the beach with his gladius leveled at a hooded figure, but as she watched, the woman lowered the hood, revealing dark skin and a familiar face. One of the hundred she'd freed from Celendrial's prison.

"Shit!" Teriana swam swiftly to shore. "Quintus, it's fine! I know her! She's my cousin!"

He didn't lower his weapon, and as she stumbled up the wet sand, he said, "Keep your distance until I check her for weapons."

Elyanna scowled as he checked her over, Quintus removing several sharp knives before he gave Teriana a reluctant nod.

"Gods, it's good to see you safe." Teriana closed the distance between them, noting that the other woman's eyes were storm-tossed seas of grey, her cheeks hollowed from months of captivity. "Your daughters? Are they well?"

"In Taltuga by now," Elyanna answered. "We sailed immediately to the greater ocean path because no one trusted that the Cel navy wouldn't pursue us, but once in the West, I came here to find you."

Teriana's shoulders slumped with relief. "Part of me had feared that seeing you sail away was too good to be true."

The other woman made a noncommittal noise, eyes looking Teriana up and down. "They said you were a legion prisoner. You don't look like a prisoner."

It struck Teriana then how she must look. Well-fed and healthy, floating on her back in a turquoise sea, only a single bodyguard, who clearly cared only for her welfare. Whereas Elyanna had endured endless months of imprisonment with her young daughters, suffering misery that Teriana couldn't begin to imagine. "Not all shackles are made of steel. They know I'm not going to run."

Her cousin was silent for a long moment, then she said, "Does the legionnaire understand our language?"

"Yes, but I trust Quintus. He won't betray my confidence."

Rather than easing Elyanna's concerns, Teriana's words only seemed to make them worse, the stormy water of her gaze now almost black with fear.

"What's happened?"

Silence.

Quintus sighed, then took a few steps back. "Make it quick so you're not seen."

"Everyone knows the deal you made with the Cel," Elyanna said. "The freedom of our people in exchange for paths suitable for legion transport. They all believe you struck a bad bargain. That the cost is too great."

Teriana's hands turned cold despite the heat of the sun. "Do you?"

Twin tears trickled down Elyanna's cheeks, and she shook her head. "No. My husband's in that prison. My crew." A soft sob tore from her lips. "The rest of our people already see them as casualties of war. Except they aren't even dead!"

Reaching out, Teriana took her cousin's hand and drew her down to the warm sand.

"No one is willing to take any risks to save them," Teriana said. "Not the Gamdeshians. Not the Arinoquians. And now you tell me that our own people won't even help?" She clenched her teeth. "I feel . . . I feel like I'm the only one who is fighting for them. The only one who doesn't believe any loss acceptable."

Elyanna's grip tightened. "You're not. There are other Maarin who believe we need to do what we can to save them, but we are the minority."

Silence stretched between them, the only sound the soft roar of the sea.

"Every waking minute, I dig through my mind for a solution that doesn't necessitate giving Cassius what he wants, at least for the interim," Teriana confessed. "I hunt for a way to save Maarin lives that doesn't cost threefold in Gamdeshian deaths. Only I can't see a way through."

"What will you do?"

"I don't know."

"If you—" Elyanna sucked in a deep breath, then blurted out, "If you pleaded with the legatus not to go after the stems, told him that you were willing to accept the losses, would he do what you asked?"

In truth, the thought had never occurred to Teriana, because not once had she been willing to let her people die without a fight. But Teriana forced herself to consider the question and eventually gave a small nod. "Yes. Marcus would free my ship and let me go my own way." Facing the other woman, she said, "Except that's no victory for us. The doors are open, whether we like it or not, and getting Marcus executed for the sake of a few months of peace changes nothing. Cassius will only send more legions and a nastier legatus to pick up the reins, and the invasion will continue. Sacrificing our people accomplishes nothing. The battle will have to be fought, one way or another. There is no running from it."

"But can we win it?"

"I don't know." Hearing Quintus's soft whistle of warning, Teriana pulled Elyanna to her feet. "What I do know is that we can't hide from it. You should go."

Her cousin nodded, pulling up her hood and retrieving her weapons from Quintus. "I don't know if the path you're on is the right one, Teriana, or if you will damn us all. But it was you who won my children freedom from that nightmare, so I will give you fair warning. You've been named a traitor. They say you are on the side of the enemy because of sentiment between you and the Thirty-Seventh's legatus, and that you act in his best interests. Watch your back, cousin."

Without another word, Elyanna hurried down the beach and out of sight.

"You all right?" Quintus asked in a low voice.

"No." Never had she felt more alone in her life. Chest aching, she pulled on her clothes. Paper crunched in her pocket and Teriana withdrew it, smoothing out the wrinkles. Taking in Cassius's familiar cursive.

Teriana,

I've included this gift in the hopes it aids you in achieving our mutually desired ends.

Lucius Cassius

Nothing that Cassius offered up freely would be a good thing. Except when you were drowning, you could not be particular about whose hand drew you out of the water.

Biting at her bottom lip, Teriana said, "Let's go unwrap Cassius's gift."

27

LYDIA

"Well shit," Agrippa muttered. "This is going to be a problem."

An understatement if Lydia had ever heard one, because as far as her eye could see in either direction stood a wall of blighters five deep.

"This escarpment isn't on any map I've ever seen." Killian looked east and then west before shaking his head, and as Agrippa opened his mouth, he added, "I know, Agrippa. Map or not, it is clearly here, just as you said. It just never ceases to amaze me how little we know about what resides within Derin's borders."

"Well, you can color the Eyrie on your maps when you get home," Agrippa quipped. "Runs near the full length of the border between Derin and Anukastre."

Impressive in and of itself, but the scarp itself had to be at least five hundred feet high, and beyond, the great dunes of Anukastre stretched below them like a golden sea.

"There are a handful of these outposts." Agrippa gestured to the fortification in the distance. "There's a pulley system that lifts a platform up and down the scarp. From experience, I can tell you that down isn't that much easier than up. It's not well made, but there is little need to go out into the desert, so no one has ever bothered with improvements. We considered it as an alternate launching point for the invasion of Mudamora, but then we mapped the stem to Deadground. Given that the Anuk's prince, Xadrian, was making short work of every scout I sent into the desert, we went with the path of least resistance."

"Is it possible to climb down it?" Killian asked.

Agrippa hesitated, glancing between Lydia and Malahi. "It's a tough climb, especially without rope. Five hundred feet, give or take. You're probably the only one who could do it, though Lydia we could just toss off the side, and she could heal whatever damage would be inflicted by the fall."

She rolled her eyes at him, and despite the gravity of the situation, Agrippa laughed before tugging Killian forward so that they could continue to discuss the obstacle before them, Baird following after them.

Lydia took the opportunity to stare back the way they'd come. The terrain had shifted as they'd traveled south, growing more arid. It was hot during the day but chill at night, and water had grown scarce. The ground here was dry and rocky, the only foliage spindly pines and dry brush. The ground crunched beneath her feet as she shifted, and the raven that had been cawing loudly above them fell silent.

"How are you coping?" Malahi asked. "I've been wanting to ask but I didn't want to press."

Lydia examined her hands, which were still concealed by the gloves Agrippa had given her. She almost never took them off. "It's tempting to say better," she replied. "Except I've not really been put to the test. All we've been doing is following the blighters."

"Well," Malahi murmured. "That's not *entirely* true."

Lydia's cheeks warmed. "Agrippa ties me up every night."

"And Killian sleeps right next to you." The corner of Malahi's mouth turned up. "I have eyes, you know. Once we're through this, I can keep Baird and Agrippa occupied if you care for some time alone."

After everything, it should have felt awkward talking to the other woman about this, but it didn't. So Lydia admitted, "I'm afraid if I lower my guard, that I might hurt him." She bit the insides of her cheeks. "What if I accidentally take years of his life from him, Malahi? I can't put them back in. It's like . . . slowly murdering him."

"He'd stop you." Malahi's eyes drifted to where the men still argued. "Killian loves you, Lydia, but he doesn't have a death wish. And he's more than capable of taking care of himself."

Malahi's words did nothing to alleviate Lydia's concern, so she changed the subject. "Perhaps I should be creating some alone time for *you*."

The Queen's cheeks turned bright pink. "Agrippa's only being kind to me because of what I went through. I think he feels guilty because he served Rufina for so long, and this is his way of making up for it."

"Is that what you think?" Lydia smirked.

Amber eyes shot to hers. "I know you think the worst of him, Lydia, but Agrippa's never once done anything inappropriate." Nudging a rock with her shoe, Malahi added, "He makes me feel safe. Maybe that won't last forever, but while it does, I'll take it."

Baird crawled back over to them. "I'm in disgrace for leaving you alone," he said to Malahi, forcing his bulk between the two of them as he added, "They're too busy rejecting each other's ideas to come up with a plan."

Lydia frowned, watching Agrippa building something with sticks and grass only for Killian to shake his head and knock it over with a swipe of his hand. "Baird," she asked, "have you seen this pulley system?"

"A few times." The giant wiped sweat from his brow. "Agrippa always made me do the pulling. He's a bit lazy when he can get away with it."

"What does it look like?"

"It's a big bucket." Baird frowned. "Hangs from an oak frame with rope as thick as my arm to pull it up and down. It can only fit three men on account of the weight."

"The ropes might snap?"

Baird shook his head. "Only one man can work the pulley system, and any more than three people and it's too heavy. Agrippa had a good number of criticisms about the design, but I wasn't particularly interested."

"There are five of us," Malahi said.

"Neither you nor I are very heavy," Lydia replied.

"But Baird weighs enough for three."

"And is as strong as four."

"Fair point."

The giant coughed. "I think the issue is not how much I weigh but rather how we get past the blighters defending it. All it takes is one of them seeing us and then the whole mass of them will come running."

"So the most critical thing is them not seeing us." Lydia tapped a finger on a tree root, her eyes locked with Malahi. "Is it possible?"

The Queen of Mudamora's eyes were distant as she held her hand to the root, but then she nodded. "Yes."

Agrippa and Killian chose that moment to return. "It's not possible," Killian said. Agrippa nodded in agreement, then added, "We need to backtrack. Steal some rope. A lot of rope."

"Lydia and I have decided on a plan," Malahi interrupted, and at Lydia's nod, she added, "This is how it's going to go."

28

LYDIA

The good plan no longer seemed so good as Lydia stared into the small tunnel that Malahi had carved underground using the roots of trees. It was dark and narrow, and at the end of it was a fatal drop.

"I hate everything about this," Agrippa said. "It's a terrible plan."

"I'll go first," Killian said, probably to be contrary, and without waiting for an answer, climbed into the narrow tunnel.

Lydia waited until his feet disappeared, then crawled after him.

It was tight and dark, the earth slightly damp and the roots rough beneath her hands as she gripped them to drag herself along. Malahi had carved the space with a mind for Baird's bulk, but she could only imagine how arduous it would be for the giant to get through.

As she progressed, the light from behind faded until Lydia could see nothing, and she allowed her gift to take over her sight, the brilliant glow of Killian's life appearing before her.

With fear flowing heavy in her veins, she almost instantaneously felt the urge to *take.* To crawl up behind him and find some bare stretch of skin to press her fingers against so that sweet life would flow into her veins, making her strong. Making her a force to be reckoned with.

No! she silently snarled, withdrawing from her power so that all she could see was blackness. *I won't.*

But it was so hard to resist. Like trying not to breathe, and Lydia forced herself to focus on the feel of the ground beneath her. The sound of Agrippa behind her, the ex-legionnaire bitterly complaining about his dislike for tunnels because *nothing good came from them*. Malahi would be next, then Baird.

"Are we close?" she asked, needing to break her own silence.

"No," Killian answered. "But I can see the light of the opening. Keep going."

Bits of dirt rained down on her hair, and Lydia cringed, praying to Yara that the tunnel would hold. That they wouldn't all meet their end buried alive in a grave of their own making. Praying that this would work because crawling backward would be next to impossible.

Then she found she could make out the soles of Killian's boots, a faint glow visible around his outline.

"Be quiet," he said under his breath. "We don't want them to hear us."

The only sound was the moan of the wind, the thousands of blighters utterly silent.

Killian rolled onto his back. In one smooth motion, he pulled himself out the opening and then disappeared from sight.

Panic ripped through her veins, and Lydia scrambled forward. She poked her head out of the opening, a wave of vertigo washing over her as she looked down.

And *down*.

Five hundred feet seemed more like a thousand, the rocks at the base terrifyingly far away.

"Stay there," Killian whispered, and she looked to her left to find him clinging to the rock face. With practiced ease, he worked his way up to where a large wooden structure dangled just below the edge. Her heart surged into her throat as he leapt from his perch on the cliff to grab the edge of the bucket, hanging for a moment before he quietly crawled inside. Then it slowly began to move.

Each creak and groan of the pulley made her cringe, but the focus of the blighters was on the plateau, not the scarp face below. Lower and lower, the bucket descended, Killian stopping it when it was level with the opening.

But most definitely not within reach.

"You're going to have to climb out," he instructed, securing the ropes so that his hands were free. "Then climb closer so that I can reach you."

Oh gods.

"Right." She eased outwards, every bit of her consumed by terror. She didn't know how to climb, didn't know where to put her hands or feet. Everything she touched seemed insecure and liable to collapse beneath her weight, but Lydia managed to edge out so that she was clinging to the rock face.

"Just work your way to the right," Killian said. "Then you'll need to twist around and jump. I'll catch you."

Simple instructions.

Seemingly impossible feat.

Lydia swallowed hard, sweat running down her back as she cautiously moved to the right. Testing each handhold. Each toehold. Wondering if her mark would allow her to survive such a long fall.

A glance downward told her that was unlikely.

A hot wind buffeted her clothing, the grit it carried sticking against her skin, and Lydia looked over her shoulder. In the distance, a dark wall filled the horizon.

Sandstorm.

"Keep going," Killian whispered. "You're almost there."

To her left, Lydia heard Agrippa reach the end of the tunnel, his soft curses telling her exactly what he thought about the situation. She ignored him and edged farther right.

"There," Killian instructed. "Get a good hold with your toes and left hand, then twist and jump toward me."

This was madness. Absolute gods-damned madness.

"You can do it. I'll catch you."

And she trusted him.

Sucking in a deep breath, Lydia let go with her right hand. Twisted. Then jumped.

For a heartbeat, she was weightless, then Killian's arms were around her, hauling her into the bucket. Adrenaline coursed through her veins, the lack of outlet making her shake as she watched Agrippa ferry their supplies from the opening and toss them to Killian, showing no concern for the fall below him. At least, not until it was Malahi's turn.

There was no mistaking the tension in the ex-legionnaire's jaw as Mudamora's queen carefully climbed out. Malahi cleverly extended the roots to provide her with handholds as she followed Agrippa's whispered instructions. He kept close to her side as she moved to where the bucket dangled.

"Killian will catch you," Lydia heard him whisper. "Just jump toward him as hard as you can. It's not that far."

"But it's awfully far to the ground," Malahi hissed. "This is insanity."

"Was *your* plan, lovely. I'm just following your orders."

Malahi muttered an incredibly colorful curse that drew a grin to Agrippa's face, then she twisted and leapt.

It was almost worse watching the other woman jump, and Lydia clenched her teeth, gripping the sides of the bucket. Yet Killian caught her easily, setting her next to Lydia. The tight quarters forced them together, and Lydia tensed at the feel of Malahi's life in such close proximity. Malahi didn't seem to notice, her face pale as she watched Agrippa leap with ease into the bucket, brushing aside Killian's offer of assistance and bodily forcing himself between her and Malahi. "You have control, Lydia?" he asked her. "Or do you need me to tie you up?"

"I'm okay."

He nodded, but she didn't fail to notice how his hand remained on his weapon as they watched Baird drag himself out of the opening. The passage through the tunnel had taken its toll on the giant, the fabric of his shirt stained with blood where his shoulders had been scraped, his face slick with sweat. Yet once he was out, he climbed as easily as Killian or Agrippa, twisted, and—

The rock supporting one of his feet snapped away right as he jumped.

Agrippa and Killian lunged, grabbing the giant's wrists.

"Oh, gods!" Malahi gasped as the bucket swung violently away from the cliff, rotating, then slamming with a loud *crack* against the rock.

Lydia's eyes snapped upward, every part of her praying the blighters hadn't heard. Except then as one, hundreds of them stepped to the edge and looked down.

Time seemed to stand still.

Then the blighters started to jump.

Not knowing what else to do, Lydia unhooked the rope from where it was twisted around a metal bar to hold it in place.

The bucket dropped.

Malahi's shrill scream filled Lydia's ears as the bucket plunged, blighters falling all around them, hands grasping.

"Grab the rope!" Agrippa shouted, and Baird flung himself at the blur of rope that would be their only salvation. The giant howled in agony, blood and flesh spraying as the rope burned away his palms.

Help him!

Without thinking, Lydia lunged, clamping her hands on the backs of his forearms, shoving life into him. Watching her own skin age as she healed his flesh only for it to be frayed away time and again.

Yet Baird didn't let go.

The bucket's plunge slowed, allowing Killian and Agrippa to grab hold of the rope. Eventually, it came to a stop, the bucket swaying back and forth.

"Are you all right?" she asked Baird. "Your hands?"

He gave a tight nod, and she pulled away, feeling a swell of need to take back what she'd just given.

"You two are never allowed to come up with plans together," Agrippa hissed, his breathing rapid. "Never."

"We need to get down." Killian alone seemed unrattled by their near death, his eyes fixed upward. "More of them are getting ready to jump."

No sooner did he say the words did deimos shrieks cut the air. Leather wings appeared overhead, black-clad corrupted riding on their backs.

"I'll get us down," Baird muttered. "You keep them off us."

The bucket resumed its descent, Baird's jaw clenched as he eased the group toward the ground, which was still two hundred feet away. The wind had increased in violence, the bucket now swinging side to side, and Malahi said, "Not to add to our problem, but is that a sandstorm?"

The storm to the south had intensified, now a wall of sand rising higher than the escarpment itself.

"Baird, can you do something about that?" Agrippa demanded, nocking an arrow in his bow.

"I need my hands," the giant answered between his teeth. "Need to be able to concentrate."

"It will blow the deimos off of us!" Killian shouted over the rising wind. "Give us a chance to escape into the dunes!"

"We aren't equipped to survive a storm like this!" Agrippa loosed the arrow, and the deimos that had been diving toward them twisted away. "The sand will strip flesh from bone if we don't find cover!"

Yet even if they made it to the bottom, there was no cover to be had. Only rocks and sand and dry brush. They didn't even have a tent, having been forced to abandon most of their equipment when they left the horses.

The bucket slammed against the rock face, sending it spinning, and a deimos tucked its wings into a dive.

Agrippa tried to shoot it, but his arrow went wide even as the rider climbed on top the saddle, eyes like voids ringed with flame.

"She's going to jump," Agrippa warned, and then the corrupted was leaping toward them. She caught hold of the rope above, then dropped, hands reaching.

Only for Killian's blade to slice one of the woman's hands from her wrists.

"Get down!" Agrippa flung himself on top of Malahi, Killian's blade whistling over his head as he battled the corrupted, blood spraying from her severed wrist.

Lydia dropped, trying to give him space, but it was a tangle of legs and limbs, Baird desperately trying to lower them while Killian fought to keep the woman's other deadly hand away from them.

Agrippa pulled a knife and stabbed the woman in the kidney, but she only shrieked and yanked it free, using it to slash at Killian.

He blocked the blow, then dropped his sword, the bucket swaying wildly as he grabbed hold of the woman and tossed her over the edge.

The corrupted's scream was lost to the howl of the wind, but Lydia didn't have time to look to see if she'd survived, because another corrupted leapt into the bucket.

Killian punched the man in the face, but rather than trying to fight him, the corrupted turned and plunged his knife into Baird's back.

The giant screamed, barely keeping his grip on the rope. Killian stabbed the corrupted repeatedly, and then Agrippa caught hold of the man's legs and heaved him over the edge.

"Lydia, help Baird!" Malahi cried. "He needs you!"

It was all too easy to rise, pushing past Agrippa to place her hands on Baird's arm. Except rather than life flowing from her to him, Lydia wanted to take everything that he had left. To consume the life of one of the god-marked and erase the weakness within herself.

"She's going to turn!" Agrippa shouted, but then Killian was in her face. "You can do it. You can save us all."

A deimos slammed against the bucket, its teeth snapping, forcing Killian to turn to fight.

Baird was shaking, his eyes fixed on hers, and the fear in them made Lydia sick. The wind was full of grit, stinging her eyes and making her skin burn, a mere suggestion of the violence that would soon descend upon them.

Except that wouldn't matter if they splattered against the ground.

You can do this.

Reaching for the hilt of the knife, she yanked it out and then flooded the giant with all the life she had to give. The bucket spun round and round, Agrippa and Killian banging into her as they fought back deimos and corrupted. Lydia's heart fluttered in her chest.

She couldn't breathe. Couldn't see. Could only feel herself falling . . . falling, then nothing at all.

29

KILLIAN

"Lydia!"

He screamed her name as she collapsed at their feet, her hair white and skin weathered as a woman thrice her age.

"She's breathing," Malahi said, even as Agrippa shouted, "Stay away from her! If she rouses, she'll be desperate!"

The last of the deimos slammed into the bucket, teeth reaching for Baird. Killian stabbed it in the eye, sending it spinning out of sight into the carnage below.

"We're almost down!" Baird roared.

And then the storm struck.

The pain was incredible, as though Killian's skin was being scoured from his face and eyes scratched from his skull.

He couldn't breathe.

"Get down!" Agrippa bellowed in his ear between coughs. "Cover your face! I'll help Baird!"

Killian dropped, fumbling for Lydia's still form. She was faintly coughing, so he tore off a strip of his shirt and wrapped it around her face before doing the same for himself. It was still like breathing dust, but the burn of sand striking him was diminished. Catching hold of Malahi, he shouted, "Is your face covered?"

"Yes!"

The howl of wind intensified, drowning out all sound, but he could feel the others shaking as they coughed violently.

He had no idea how much farther down they had to descend. Nor any idea of what they'd do when they reached the bottom.

The bucket twisted violently in the wind. Killian clenched his teeth, praying to the Six that the rope would hold.

Then Lydia stirred.

His mark had been quiet but now screamed *danger.*

He didn't know how to help her.

Protect the others. That's what she'd want.

Hauling Lydia against his chest, Killian held her tightly against him, her arms pinned by his. "We're almost down!" he shouted. "I'll get you more space soon!"

He could sense her inner battle. Weakened as she was, if she decided to fight him, he'd be hard-pressed to contain her without help.

But he didn't want to ask for it. Agrippa would protect Malahi at all costs, and trapped in a confined space as they were, the other man might choose to cut his losses.

"We're almost there!" He wasn't sure if that was truth or lie. "Hang on!"

Lydia strained against him, and Killian's arms shuddered to keep hers in place. *Please,* he prayed to the Six. *Help her.*

Except he knew they wouldn't. It had been one thing to throw off the Seventh's active hold, but this was a war Lydia was fighting against herself.

The bucket jolted to a stop, the impact of it striking the rocky ground jarring his spine. Trusting that Agrippa would take care of the others, Killian spilled them both over the edge of the bucket. His back struck something squishy and wet, but then they were rolling down an incline.

Lydia pressed her advantage.

Wrenching her arms upward, she broke his hold, rolling away from him. And he couldn't gods-damned see. Couldn't hear any sounds she might make over the roar of the storm.

But she can see you.

Climbing to his feet, Killian ignored the coughs wracking his body and gave in to the sense gifted to him by Tremon.

What if she goes after the others?

She won't. It's you she wants.

How he knew, Killian couldn't have said, only that he was turning, his arms rising to take the impact as Lydia slammed into him.

They grappled, rolling across sand and rock, slamming against the corpses of blighters and corrupted alike.

Her hand latched around his throat, but she was still wearing gloves. He heard her scream of frustration above the wind. Killian ignored it and caught her wrist, rolling her facedown and then pinning her arms to her sides.

Every breath was a struggle, sand worming its way under his clothes, scratching and burning. If he died, there'd be nothing to stop her from turning on the others.

Think think think.

What had he seen when he'd looked down? A stone platform. Endless sand and rock and . . . a small stone structure next to the platform.

Now all he had to do was find it.

Keeping his arms around Lydia, his hand locked on his own wrist, Killian heaved to his feet, hunting for his bearings.

The wind was rebounding off the escarpment, billowing in all directions like a cyclone. Cautiously, he moved backward, praying he'd hit the cliff wall rather than wander into open desert.

His foot caught on a corpse, nearly causing him to fall, but Killian pressed onward. His lungs ached from coughing, his arms shaking from restraining the thrashing Lydia. If he hadn't already been weeping tears from the sand, he'd have wept for joy as his back slammed against rock.

Allowing his mental map to guide him, he eased down the rock face until he guessed himself behind the platform, then he started forward until he reached the smooth stone.

Going by feel, he worked his way to the left side of the platform, then forward until he collided with a structure. As they edged around it, he found the opening, relief filling his chest as his boots found steps leading down.

He started the descent, praying that nothing worse than sand and dust would greet them at the bottom. His boots met a flat surface, and with the wind no longer blasting him in the face, he used the back of Lydia's head to pull down the strip of fabric covering his eyes.

And was greeted with blackness.

With his arms preoccupied with Lydia's squirming, there wasn't anything he could do about the light, but he'd endured worse than sitting in the dark for a few hours.

With Lydia in his arms, Killian explored the space and swiftly determined that it was nothing more than a small chamber that had been carved out of the bedrock, either for the storage of goods or as a shelter against storms. Leaning against a wall, he slid down so that he was seated, Lydia on his lap.

He squeezed his eyes shut, coughing up sand and grit while she thrashed, drumming her heels against his shins.

"Don't," he growled back at her. "I'm not going to let you go, Lydia."

She didn't answer, only smoldered with rage and frustration.

Killian felt himself sinking into despair, but Baird's words filled his thoughts, and instead he said, "Do you remember when we were sneaking into the sewers to help Finn take care of the orphans? How many children do you suppose you healed? Had to have been at least a hundred."

"For all the good it did." Lydia's voice was low, once again carrying the cruel edge that it'd had when they were in the rowboat on the lake. "Emmy's dead. She was poisoned by blight and spent her days telling everyone how *you* failed to protect her."

"Wasn't her doing the talking, though, was it?" He shifted, his ass already going numb against the rock. "Was the Seventh."

"Doesn't mean it was a lie."

A shot of guilt fired through him, but Killian forced it away. "What is your goal in saying these things? Is it that you think I'll get angry enough to make a mistake so that you have the opportunity to kill me? Or are you trying to provoke me into killing you myself?"

"Have you ever considered that I might just be saying what I really think?" she snapped. "Because I assure you, Killian, that the things I say are a small fraction of those that pass through my mind."

He *had*, in fact, considered that. "There is a difference between a thought crossing your mind and it being what you truly believe."

"Whatever makes you feel better."

Part of him wished Agrippa were here, if only for the fact that the other man would relish the verbal sparring, whereas it made Killian miserable. "I know that I've not been what you needed," he finally said. "In truth, I've been so consumed with my own anger that it's been hard to see anything else."

"Are you angry because I'm not being a sweet girl that you can imagine marrying?" Her tone was saccharine and mocking. "No one wants a murderous monster to mother their children." She hesitated, then said, "Though perhaps your concerns are *baser* than that."

He ground his teeth but refused to rise to the bait. "Anger at myself, is the answer. My purpose is to protect you, but I've done a terrible job of it."

"Perhaps I should enlist Agrippa," she said. "Seems to come naturally to him. Either that or he's not willing to allow his golden goose to come to harm."

Against his will, Killian's jealousy flared. "Malahi suffered because of my commitment to you."

"Malahi did her level best to get me killed, and I've not forgotten that. Though to her credit, she was probably smart to try to put me down."

"Stop."

"*No.*"

She strained against him, and he tightened his grip, then used his teeth to pull down the fabric covering her face. "My point for bringing up the tunnels is that I remember how you recovered your strength from the life that was all around us. From those in the shelters."

"The only thing living near me is *you.*"

"Not true. Our companions are nearby."

"Perhaps they're dead."

Agrippa was too clever to be killed by a storm. "Even if that's the case, it only means that there are nine more corpses above us, many of which were marked. All that life spilled out into the world, and I know that you can take it into yourself. You don't need to kill me to recover your strength."

"Quite right," she breathed. "I don't."

His instincts roared a second before she broke free of his grip. Killian flung himself sideways, but she was on him in a flash, gloved hands pinning his wrists to the rock, her knees to either side of him.

"Do it, then," he said. "If this is what you want, then take it."

He could feel her breath against his throat, smell the scent of her hair as it fell against his face. Knew that there was no escaping her grip unless he killed her, which he refused to do.

Yet Lydia hesitated.

It was the voice that whispered in his dreams that said, "I'm tired of wanting what I can't have. Tired of giving my heart nothing so that it is consumed with want for everything."

"What have I ever refused to give you?" he asked, not knowing exactly what it was he was offering, only that he'd give up his soul for the sake of her, so what was his life?

But as she lowered her face, Lydia didn't take anything, only brushed her lips against his. "This."

She hadn't pushed back the darkness, he knew that. Knew that the woman kissing him stood on the edge of a blade, but maybe that was all right. Maybe that was who she was, and to be with her, he needed to accept that every kiss was a risk. Every touch was a gamble. Maybe there was no better woman for him.

"Yours," he murmured. "Until my last breath."

Lydia's lips found his again. Not a brush but a kiss so fierce it hurt. Her tongue was in his mouth, the taste of her making him want more even as his heart throbbed with fear that his last breath was coming.

Except she wasn't taking.

Her gloved fingers flexed around his wrists, grip strong enough to bruise, but her lips kissed lines of fire down his jaw, then his throat, his pulse no longer roaring with fear but with want.

Gods help him, but he needed this. Needed her. Because what they'd had so far wasn't enough. Not for Lydia and not for him, and Killian would risk everything to have it.

She let go of his wrists, and he rolled her over, ripping off his coat, shirt, and gloves, casting them into the darkness. He kissed her, then bit her bottom lip, the moan that pulled from her mouth unleashing something primal in him.

He jerked open the buckles on the leather corselette she wore. Lydia lifted her shoulders to allow him to pull off the garment, and though he could see nothing in the blackness, his memory delivered him what his eyes could not. Pale skin and long lines, pert breasts that peaked in the chill of the air.

"Touch me," she breathed. "I need to feel you."

Because her gloves were still on.

He debated removing them, then abandoned the thought as her leather-clad fingers trailed down his arms, his chest, his back, every part of him wanting to strip her naked and take her in a way he'd thought of more times than he'd ever admit.

"I love you." He traced a finger down her sternum, over her flat stomach to the belt of her leather trousers. As he unfastened it, he lowered his lips to her breast, hearing the intake of her breath as he kissed the tip of it. "And you are mine. Every part of you, light and dark."

"Just as you are mine," she breathed, whimpering as he kissed her stomach, his body aching to take her. To claim her. To lose himself in her.

Lydia's gloved hands tangled in his hair, her long legs wrapping around his waist and pulling him against her, drawing a sound that was half growl, half plea from him as she ground against him. "Are you sure?" he asked. "Are you sure this is what you want?"

"Yes." The word came out in a gasp. "I want this. I need . . . I need . . ."

She trailed off, and it didn't matter, because he knew. Felt the same blinding compulsion to cross a threshold they'd stood on the wrong side of for too long. All they'd had was words, but words had no place in this moment of ragged breaths and touch, in these heartbeats consumed by sound and sensation that he prayed would last forever.

Then the scrape of a boot caught Killian's attention. He twisted toward the stairs to see a figure holding a blade outlined by muted sunlight.

"Well, this is a pleasant turn of events," Agrippa said. "I was quite confident that I was going to find you drained into a husk of a man, but here you are, expending the adrenaline of a near-death experience in a much more productive fashion. Well done."

"I am going to kill you!" Killian snarled, pulling Lydia against him so his body concealed hers from their laughing companion.

"Well, you might have to fight for that privilege," Agrippa answered. "Because the storm is near spent and judging from the activity atop the escarpment, it won't be long until we have thousands of walking dead back on our trail. Now shall we?"

30

MARCUS

In the days that had passed since he'd dispatched the letter with Astara, it was all Marcus could do not to stare at the sky every time he stepped outside, eyes hunting for the shape of the giant hawk returning with a reply.

Kaira will agree. She won't abandon the Maarin.

A thought that repeated through his head day and night even as he prepared for the alternative.

"Letter via the Bardeen stem, sir." Gibzen set a carefully packaged formal missive on the table. "You need anything?"

Marcus picked up the sealed tube, opening it to find a message written in Wex's familiar hand. A list of genesis codes, dates, and times. Atrio should almost be in Emrant, which meant the timing would work out perfectly.

At the bottom of the list, Wex wrote,

This is an expensive and risky experiment, and one strictly forbidden by the Senate after the debacle with the Nineteenth. It will be coming out of your budget, Legatus, not mine, and if it goes badly, you will be the one to take the fall. I look forward to hearing the results.

Wex.

Marcus smiled, then tucked the letter into his belt pouch for safe keeping. The Nineteenth Legion had accidentally set off explosives at a minor transport genesis in northern Celendor two years prior, the fatal and costly consequences buried in paperwork and propaganda, but Wex wasn't one to allow one idiot's mistakes to ruin a good strategy for all. Being of the same mindset, Marcus typically would use colored smoke for this task, but given the stems in question were entombed, it had to be noise. Something loud enough to be heard through rock but not so violent as to cause alarm, so he'd settled on firecrackers. Specific patterns to be repeated throughout specific dates, and Marcus had no doubt that Wex had needed to buy up the supply of every fireworks maker in Celendrial for the task. Atrio would hear the pattern, note the date, and the results would tell Marcus exactly the genesis stem that led to Emrant.

In theory, at any rate.

The experiment wouldn't be needed if Kaira cooperated, because once she cracked open the tomb, all the dead path-hunters she'd find inside would have information about where they'd come from. But if she didn't . . .

She will. She won't abandon Teriana's people.

But if she didn't, all the work that Titus had put into securing an alliance with Katamarca would prove its worth. All that remained once he had his target confirmed was a formal request for more reinforcements, which in truth, he suspected were already mustering at Hydrilla.

A formal request I'll never make, because Kaira will see the merit of this plan.

Marcus stared at the map before him, head still aching mercilessly, every part of him looking forward to the midnight hour when he could silence the pain and his parade of anxieties for a few hours.

It was then that he noticed how cold it was in the room, his skin prickling. As he looked up, it was to find Gibzen still standing next to the table, watching him.

There was a strangeness to the other man's gaze, and Marcus asked, "Have you discovered anything more?"

Gibzen handed him a page. "Men who were on guard duty in the time leading up to when Teriana was kidnapped. I put a mark next to the ones who don't like her."

The list was so messy it bordered on illegible, half the names misspelled, and nearly all with a mark next to them. "Why is your name on this list?"

With a mark next to it, no less.

"To be thorough, sir. It's not personal, but I don't like her much. She tried to bribe me once to keep something from you, and that never sat right."

"What did she want kept from me?"

"Her wanting to talk to Miki and Quintus alone, sir. I though it risky, given that Quintus wasn't in the finest mood. Turned out to be nothing, but rubbed me wrong."

Nothing, indeed, and Marcus scanned the list again, but no one leapt out at him as having acted strangely. Which made it yet another dead end. "Keep digging."

"Yes, sir." Gibzen departed, and Marcus swore the cold left with him, the air returning to the usually muggy heat of Arinoquia.

Only for Austornic to appear.

The boy came around the table, then handed Marcus a crumpled letter with a familiar wax seal. "Fell from the sky."

Marcus's heart broke into a gallop, his pulse a dull roar in his ears as he examined the seal.

She'll agree.

She has to agree.

She won't abandon Teriana's people.

Cracking the wax, he fought to keep his fingers from shaking as he slowly opened the letter.

You, and the Empire, can kiss my ass.
Kaira

Marcus stared at the writing, reading it over and over, searching for a message within the message that contained a different answer than this.

But there was nothing.

His head throbbed so painfully he could barely think, and Marcus dropped the page to press fingers to his temples, the room suddenly too bright.

Vaguely, he saw Austornic pick it up, though he didn't read Gamdeshian.

"I take it diplomacy has failed," the boy said. "Now we have to go to war against an enemy who knows our precise target and intentions. So what is our new plan?"

"I don't know," Marcus muttered, even though he very much *did* know.

Once Atrio confirmed the stem in Emrant, Marcus would take it by force. Hundreds, if not thousands, would die, with more succumbing in the trail of starvation and disease that war left in its wake. He would win, because he always did, but the cost . . .

Marcus rested his head in his hands.

"We need a plan." Austornic slammed the page down on the table. "We've spent time and resources we didn't have on this."

Anger rose in his chest that this *child* dared to criticize him. A boy whose knowledge of war was limited to books and practice blades and drills. "Do you think I'm not aware?"

"Then why did you bother? Because don't tell me that you truly believed the Gamdeshians would agree to this."

"Maybe"—Marcus slammed his palms against the table—"because instead of sending me a legion of men, Cassius sent me *you*. I need men who can fight; instead I have children that I need to feed and clothe and mind like a gods-damned nursemaid. Go find a ball to occupy you and your playmates, boy, and leave the matters of war to those old enough to understand the consequences."

Silence hung heavy in the room.

"I'm not sure a day went by at Lescendor that I didn't hear your name." Nic's voice was cold. "The prodigy held up as the golden standard that every one of us was desperate to achieve. Everyone idolized you. Everyone wanted to *be* you. I came here believing I'd be following a commander who held to the highest standards of conduct only to discover you are no better than Hostus and the rest, holding everyone to the rules except yourself. So drunk on your own power that you think you can do whatever you want and damn the consequences to everyone else."

"And?" Marcus's voice dripped venom, and he hated himself for it. Hated how the idealistic boy he'd once been had turned into the villain he now was.

"And you're a fucking disappointment," Nic answered. In a swirl of crimson cloak, he departed the room, the doors shutting with a loud thud.

Shoving aside his chair, Marcus went to the sideboard and extracted a bottle of wine, tearing the wax seal from the top and downing several gulps. His eyes fell on the circle of wax affixed to the side, which bore the symbol of a galloping horse. Vintage from House Calorian in Mudamora. Killian Calorian's family estates, but though he was curious about the man, Marcus could not waste time thinking about commanders on other continents. He returned to his chair, drinking from the bottle as he stared at Kaira's letter.

He did not want this war.

Did not want to slaughter his way northward.

It's who you are, a voice whispered up from his thoughts, and a sudden waft of cold flowed over him. *It's what you do.*

A knock sounded at the door. "Yes."

One of his men entered carrying a tiny box. "A delivery from a Katamarcan goldsmith in Aracam."

He set it on the table, eyes flicking to the wine bottle, then he departed.

Marcus studied the box for a long moment, then took a mouthful of wine. And another. The horse on the bottle appeared to move, mane and tail rippling in the wind, head tossing.

Like it was taunting him.

With a sudden fit of rage, Marcus hurled the bottle against the wall.

31

TERIANA

Teriana collected the crate from Pullo after she'd met Elyanna on the beach, but the sight of the contents had only filled her with red-hot fury, and she'd shoved it into the corner of Quintus's tent.

"We can sell this stuff," he'd suggested, rooting through it. "It's worth a fortune."

"That would only invite questions as to why I have it," she'd retorted, knowing in her heart that the real reason was because with every passing day that the legions did nothing but train while Marcus avoided her at every turn, that she might grow desperate enough to use it.

"Has he said anything more?" she'd asked Nic when she'd managed to get him alone near the latrines.

"No." The glare on the boy's face had been something to behold. "All he gives the men is busy work. All he gives the officers is admonitions of patience. If he has other schemes, I don't know of them."

It was desperation that had driven her to write a message to Killian explaining the situation, begging for whatever aid he might be able to give her. It had cost her a golden hair bead to get it past Servius to a merchant ship heading north, and in truth, with the mutters of dire circumstances in Mudamora, even her old friend likely wouldn't be able to help her imprisoned people.

And every day that passed was one day closer to Cassius's deadline. One day closer to a hundred of her people being executed because she'd failed in her promise to them.

* * *

She had only one avenue left.

One.

Which was why she was staring at the crate in the corner when Quintus pulled aside the tent flap and crawled inside.

"Two updates. First is that a letter from the Empire came by way of the Bardeen stem. Second is that the giant hawk just dropped a sealed letter in the middle of camp," Quintus said. "Nic's bringing it to Marcus, so we may have answers soon enough."

Teriana didn't allow herself to pray for deliverance at Kaira's hands, because there was no chance that the princess would concede so much.

Kaira would not help her.

Ereni would not help her.

Her own people would not help her.

Which meant the only allies she had left were the army surrounding her and the man who commanded it.

Stepping out of the tent, Teriana watched the fortress. She didn't have to wait long. Nic shoved open the flap of her tent, skinny form quivering with anger. "The Gamdeshians declined to concede the city to us," he said as he reached her. "I can't begin to imagine what madness drove Marcus to even try, but he can no longer hide behind that travesty of a plan."

"Did he say anything about next steps?"

"He said he doesn't know what he's going to do." Nic's hands were fisted, every part of him seething frustration. "Then he told me to go find a ball and some playmates. I fucking hate him. Everything they ever said about him is a lie."

"I'll do it." The words jerked out of Teriana's mouth, surprising her as much as they surprised Nic, whose mouth dropped open.

He quickly recovered. "I can get you past the guards at the entrance, but you'll be on your own after that."

"I'll be ready."

* * *

"Gibzen is off duty." Quintus ducked back into the tent. "Just saw him heading into Aracam with a few of his men. Which isn't to say those standing guard now are going to let you by, but the chances are better." He looked her up and down. "On second thought, the odds might be fairly good. You clean up nicely, my friend."

"This isn't going to work."

"If it doesn't work, then we'll know for certain that Marcus's brain has gone to mush."

Before she could lose what limited confidence she had, Teriana ducked out of the tent and started toward the fortress. The silk of her skirts tangled around her legs, and her feet ached in the high heels on the delicate shoes, but she strode past gaping men as though this were how she dressed all the time.

Nic fell in alongside of her. "I cannot believe that I've spent half my life learning military strategy and *this*"—he gave her a look—"is my first move."

"I don't like it any more than you do."

"Hopefully it works." He frowned. "It wouldn't work on me."

Teriana was too nervous to be insulted. Her hands curled into fists, nails digging into her palms, because this felt *wrong.* Marcus trusted her, and she was exploiting that. Yet she also knew that she'd stepped into the arena with the most powerful individuals alive, and the stakes were high. She couldn't afford to hang her hat on morals when everyone else in the game seemed devoid of them.

Teriana swallowed hard as she drew closer to the doors, the guards to either side straightening. But Nic's presence at her side seemed to quell any questions they had, and they swung open the double doors, allowing them to enter.

Once inside, Nic said, "Good luck," then turned left down a side corridor, leaving her alone.

Teriana didn't answer, only focused on keeping the narrow heels beneath her feet steady on the tile as she walked down the hallway, the *click, click* deafening. Ahead, the doors to the command room were shut, two of the Thirty-Seventh out front. Their eyebrows rose at the sight of her, and one said, "What's with the dress?"

"Apparently the Senate included gifts for me in the Fifty-First's supplies. Unless you think this outfit was meant for you?"

Both guards laughed, shaking their heads.

"Is he in there?"

"Yes," one answered, "but . . ." He exchanged a weighted look with the other guard, who shrugged.

"Did he give orders not to be disturbed?"

"No, but . . ."

"Then let me through." Pushing between them, Teriana shoved at the door. It swung open more easily than she'd anticipated, and she lunged to catch the edge to keep it from slamming into the wall, nearly falling as her heel bent sideways.

Flustered, she carefully closed the door, and then took a deep breath and turned around.

Marcus sat at the far end of the table, head resting in his hands, a bottle sitting next to him. "What do you want?" His voice was low and rough.

Teriana's pulse roared, sweat dampening her palms. "Do you want me to leave?"

He jerked upright, eyes widening at the sight of her. "Teriana. I . . . Apologies, I thought you were—"

"I pushed past the guards at the door, so don't take my presence out on them."

He didn't answer, only watched as she walked down the length of the table toward him. His eyes were red-rimmed, the grey-blue hazed with far, *far* too much wine, but there was no denying the *want* in them. The heat in his gaze sent a thrill dancing over her skin and made her realize that part of her feared that Marcus no longer wanted her. Feared that he'd committed to the end of their relationship so thoroughly that he'd erased all sentiment for her from his soul.

"The Senate sent me gifts." She lifted the wrist that bore a heavy gold bracelet. "A touch impractical."

His head tilted, eyes roving over her with a strange mixture of longing and loathing. "Clothing is a method of assimilating the conquered," he said softly. "Are you conquered, Teriana?"

"No." She pulled off the bracelet and dropped it on the table. "I'm not."

"Then why are you wearing it?"

"To be polite to Nic, as he delivered it."

Marcus's eyes narrowed, the wheels of his mind turning, albeit slower than usual. Or so she hoped.

"What did he want in exchange?"

Apparently not *that* much slower. Teriana's confidence wavered, because as she'd anticipated, wine and lust were not enough to turn Marcus into a fool. He knew her well enough to see through any lies she might spin, no matter how well crafted. Which meant she was better off deploying the truth. "He's worried that, in trying to escape Hostus, he's dragged the Fifty-First into something worse. Since you won't tell him otherwise, he asked me to discover your intentions."

"Why would you agree to be used in such a fashion?"

"Because I'm also interested in your intentions."

She'd reached the end of the table, the silk of her skirts brushing the legs of the heavy chair he sat upon. Marcus was no longer watching her, his attention instead fixed on a box on the table before him, but she didn't miss the way his fingers flexed on the arms of the chair.

"You could have asked." He coughed to clear his throat. "No need to dress up like a senator's mistress."

Anger rose in her chest. "Really, Marcus? Because you made it quite clear that I was not to come near you and was to stay out of your plans. You were a right prick about it, if we are being honest."

"By all means," he muttered, words slightly slurred. "Let's be honest. That is bound to go well."

She huffed out a breath at his sarcasm. "At least have the decency to look at me while I'm speaking to you."

Marcus didn't move. Didn't so much as twitch.

Teriana's anger burned hot. Gods-damn him for acting like this—like a petulant toddler. She kicked violently at the back leg of his chair. The chair twisted even as she lost her balance on the stupid heels, only Marcus catching hold of her hips keeping her from breaking her ankle, though she still yelped as pain lanced up her leg.

"Are you hurt?"

His hands were icy through the thin silk of her dress, but it was his eyes, which were squeezed shut, that held her attention. The desperateness in his expression melted Teriana's anger into grief, and her voice caught as she asked, "Why won't you look at me?"

He didn't answer, only jerked his hands away from her hips to grasp the arms of the chair again.

"If you ever cared anything for me, then you'll prove it and look me in the eye." Her whole body shook because this was so much worse than she'd thought it would be.

"It's because I care that I won't."

A sob caught in her throat, the ache in his voice a knife to her chest. The smart thing would be to let it go, to walk away, but . . . she *needed* answers. Needed to understand how it had come to this, because the paltry explanation she'd been given fell short. "You're being a coward."

"Yes."

"I'll go out into the camp." The threat slipped out, but she couldn't bring herself to regret it. "I'll scream it so that every cursed one of them knows that you aren't man enough to look me in the eye."

"Do it."

Tears trickled down her cheeks. "Look at me, Marcus, or I'll leave. And I don't mean this room, I mean this camp. Quintus will help me get out, and I'll go and do what needs doing without you."

Marcus's eyes snapped open. "You will do no such thing!"

Their eyes locked, and all the world fell away as she stared into their depths, where all his secrets lurked. All his demons. Though in truth, she suspected they were one and the same. "I am not conquered, Marcus. You have no authority over me, but I am giving you the opportunity to convince me that I can still trust your word." Not allowing him the chance to respond, she added, "My people are depending on me for this. Cassius is going to kill them if these paths aren't secured, and every day that passes, it seems less and less like you've any intention of securing them. Or maybe . . . maybe that you don't know how."

Silence stretched, and Teriana swore her heart ceased to beat while she waited for him to answer. While she waited for him to confirm the fears that had been growing in her heart.

Instead, he said, "I hate that dress." His gaze moved from her face to her throat, then down the length of her body. "One more sign that the Empire has sunk its claws into you, made you its tool, used you to achieve its ends. It's the ugliest thing I've ever seen."

Her cheeks burned, and Teriana didn't know if she was angry or humiliated or both, only that the weight of everything she felt was too great. With a noise that was half sob and half shriek, she tore at the knot of fabric at the nape of her neck, and the gown slipped down her body. She ripped the sandals off her feet and hurled them across the room, then snatched up the dress to scrub away the cosmetics she'd so carefully applied before tossing it aside as well. "Happy?"

"No," he answered. "I'm not."

Though she stood nearly naked, wearing only her plain cotton undergarments, it struck Teriana that it was not her who was exposed. That, for the first time since they'd been reunited, his walls were down, and the misery she saw in his eyes was a vise around her chest.

"Why didn't you stay in Celendrial?" Marcus whispered. "Why couldn't you let me do this for you?"

Her lips parted to say that it had been because she didn't trust him to do it, except had that really been the reason? "I don't know why. I just . . . I couldn't."

His head tilted. "Did you really believe I'd abandon your people?"

So much was on the line, and it all felt like it hung on what was between them. Countless lives and the liberty of nations sitting on a knife blade formed of sentiment. "The only reason you had to risk so much for them was me, and—" Her voice cracked. "And your plan to *ask* Kaira to give you Emrant was destined to fail. They'd never give up territory based on a threat, and it wasn't just me who knew it. Everyone is speculating that you haven't recovered from the xenthier. That you've lost your nerve. That you just want to sit in Arinoquia forever."

If her words surprised him, Marcus didn't show it, for he only reached around her to pick up his bottle of wine and drained it. "I didn't *ask* Kaira to cede me territory. I asked her to work with me to trick the Senate into believing that they had their paths, securing the liberty of your people, after which I'd withdraw. For obvious reasons, that wasn't a plan I shared with anyone."

All the blood drained from her face. "But . . . but when they learned what you'd done, they'd have you arrested. Executed for treason."

"Doesn't matter." Picking up a folded piece of paper, he handed it to her. "Kaira declined."

Unfolding it, Teriana scanned the single line.

You, and the Empire, can kiss my ass.
Kaira

Teriana's lips parted, speechless despite the thousands of thoughts she wished to voice.

"So now it will come down to force." He set the bottle down with a loud click. "Invasion. Siege. More death than you can imagine, because there is no other way to achieve our ends within such a short timeframe."

A timeframe she'd agreed to. If only she'd stayed out of it, if only she'd *listened,* then maybe he'd have had longer.

Seeming to sense her thoughts, Marcus said, "Six months is important to Cassius, which is why he chose it. Even if you'd stayed with Valerius, he'd have found a way to impose the timeline on me. That's not your fault. But your choice to return to Arinoquia was the biggest mistake of your life."

The room was beginning to spin, yet Teriana sucked in a breath, then held it.

"If you had stayed in Celendrial, none of this would be on your conscience," he said. "But now you are here, and this is only the beginning. The Empire's war machine will pour into the West, and it will be like a tide of rot spreading across the world, corrupting and consuming everything to feed the insatiable greed of the men who sit upon a hill in a city most will never see. I would have carried that blame. I would have been the villain whose name was cursed, but you insist on being complicit. Why?"

He half shouted the word, and Teriana twitched, feeling suddenly so very cold, her lips numb. "I . . ."

"Because of me?"

He caught hold of her hips, jerking her onto his lap, her knees slipping to either side of him. Teriana bit down on a gasp as his arm pulled her against him, his other hand tangling in her braids. "You don't need silks and cosmetics to seduce me." His breath brushed her ear. "Because I'm already in love with you. So in love with you that sometimes I can't breathe when you step into the room. Yet it's the thought of you leaving that makes my heart stutter in my chest, because I don't know how to live without you."

A thousand words filled her head, yet Teriana spoke not a one as his hand abandoned her hair to catch hold of her chin, lifting her face so that their eyes locked.

"Except I *am* the Empire." His eyes were like fire and frost, burning and chilling her in equal measure. "My love is a blight on your soul, changing and spoiling and ruining you. I am the worst thing that has ever happened to you, Teriana, and you should stay as far from me as you can get."

Time seemed to stand still, and her mind spun down and down, trying to imagine what had happened in those brief moments they'd been apart in Celendrial that had somehow changed everything. How the man who'd held her in his arms and smiled at her stories had been consumed so easily by this cold creature she barely recognized. What had been said to him? What had been done to him? What threats had been voiced to make him believe the words he was saying to her?

She must have spoken the questions aloud, because he gave the slightest shake of his head. "Nothing was done to me. I was only reminded of who I am."

"And who is that?"

Silence.

His lips parted, and Teriana's pulse roared with anticipation and terror because this felt like a confession. Like the moment when he'd finally give her the reason why everything had fallen apart.

But all he said was, "Your enemy."

The weight of those two words had been chained to her for so long, and yet Teriana found herself wondering if they were true. Cassius was the enemy. The Empire was the enemy. And not just hers, but Marcus's. He had as much cause and more to hate them, to resist them, and the only reason he wasn't was because of *her.* That they were losing to their enemy did not make them less allied, and if she'd learned anything in life, it was that losing a battle was not losing the war. Marcus said that nothing had happened to him, yet somehow the ever-victorious commander had conceded defeat.

Except she refused to let him go without a fight.

Curling an arm around his neck, she stroked the side of his face, feeling the prickle of a day's worth of stubble. Trailed a finger down the scar that marred his cheek. "You say you are my enemy, but how can that be when we both want the same thing?"

She brushed her lips across his, her body heating as his fingers tightened against her back. "What is done cannot be undone, but our future is uncertain. The only control we have is the moment that is upon us, and it is in this moment where I want to *live.*"

To prove her words, she kissed him. No soft brush of the lips, but with the ferocity of everything she felt for him. Not just love and lust, but anger and frustration and hurt. Everything that had been building up in her heart since that fateful night in Celendrial when he'd told her he loved her and then walked away.

And was met in kind.

She felt the remnants of the walls he'd built up fall away, unleashing him. His tongue parted her lips, and she tasted the wine he'd been drinking even as she felt his fingers trail down her spine to cup her hip, pulling her closer.

Except it wasn't close enough.

She wanted his skin against hers.

Teriana pulled at his clothes. Felt him lift her, so she could drag his tunic over his head, the fabric joining her dress on the floor. Then her breasts were pressed against his naked chest, her fingers tracing over the black tattoos on his skin as he kissed her jaw, her neck, drawing moans from her throat.

Because he *knew* her.

Had mapped every curve of her body, memorized every place she liked to be kissed, to be touched.

Just as she knew him.

Her name was a growl on his lips as she moved her hand between them, taking hold of him even as she bit his bottom lip hard enough to taste blood. The Empire had not won. The moment was theirs. The future was theirs—she just needed to make him see it. Just needed to beat back his demons with the force of everything that she felt for him, and then—

Marcus abruptly broke away from her kiss, his cheek resting against hers.

Unease ate at her lust, growing to fear as she felt dampness where their faces touched.

Tears.

Oh gods.

"I need you to stop." His voice was rough. Broken. "Please stop, Teriana."

Her body started to shake, her stomach roiling with sudden nausea as he pulled back to meet her gaze. His eyes were liquid with grief.

"I can't say no to you," he said. "I won't say no to you. Except if this happens, I won't be able to live with myself. Do you understand?"

Teriana felt her heart seize in her chest at the horror of the unspoken promise, and she lurched to her feet.

Marcus scrubbed a hand across his face, then reached to the floor to retrieve her dress and handed it to her. Then he retrieved something from the box on the table and pressed it into her palm. "For all the hair ornaments you sold back east. We're even."

Teriana opened her palm and looked down. Her breath caught at the sight of the hair bead, which was an identical golden replica of the *Quincense,* complete with enameled blue sails. Miniature and perfect. "This is worth ten times what those beads were."

He lifted one shoulder. "For your birthday, then."

She stared at the tiny ship, every part of it perfect. Every part of it carving out her heart.

"You should go," he said.

To respond was impossible because Teriana could barely breathe. Holding the hair ornament tightly in one hand, she pulled the dress over her head. Fastened it around her neck. Retrieved her shoes.

Marcus said nothing as she left the room.

If the men on duty outside the door acknowledged her, Teriana couldn't have said, for her eyes were fixed blindly on the stone floor. Every part of her wanted to break into a run. To flee not just this cursed fortress, but the camp. To race as fast and far as she could despite knowing that the horror in her heart was not something she could outrun.

Humidity struck her in the face as the men guarding the exterior doors opened them for her to exit, rain misting down from the dark sky. Teriana saw none of it as she hesitated on the steps, the tiny ship clutched in her hand.

I don't know what to do.

The thought threatened to turn into a scream, so Teriana forced herself to move. Her bare feet splashed in the little puddles accumulating on the boardwalk, the water warm against her chilled skin.

It didn't matter. She didn't care. Couldn't even think, her mind's eye full of the raw despair in Marcus's eyes. The grief in his voice. And she had no more answers as to the cause than she'd had before.

Only certainty that it was specific to her.

Her feet took her back to the fire in front of the tent she shared with Quintus, her friend on his feet in a flash at the sight of her. "Are you all right?" he demanded, voice full of panic. "What happened? Did he *hurt* you?"

"I'm fine." Her lips were numb, making it hard to speak. "He didn't do anything to me."

Teriana stood for a long moment in the rain, then shook her head, ducking inside the tent.

Quintus followed, pulling the flaps shut behind him.

Catching hold of her arm, he pulled her down onto her pallet. "What happened in there? What did Marcus say?"

"More of the same." The tiny gold ship was digging into her flesh, but she couldn't seem to loosen her grip on it.

"He's an asshole, Teriana. I've told you that." Quintus gripped her hands. "He doesn't care about anyone's feelings."

She felt cold again, the wind from the storm coming through the tent flaps and drawing gooseflesh to her skin. Lightning flickered, and a heartbeat later, thunder boomed, causing the men in the camp to shout and laugh. Quintus was trying to make her feel better, but he was also so far from the truth. The proof of that dug into her palm with sharp edges of gold and enamel. "After we crossed the Teeth, we stayed in a tiny town during solstice and there was a fair. Did I tell you that?" When Quintus shook his head, she said, "There were games. I kept spending coins to try to solve this puzzle to win candy, but I couldn't get it. No one could. Only Marcus solved it on the first try."

"Probably to show how smart he is."

She gave a slow shake of her head. "No, I think he played because he knew I wanted the candy." Tears dripped down her cheeks. "He was so different than he is as legatus, but every day that passes, what I remember feels more like a dream. Like something that I made up, except . . . except . . ." A sob tore from her throat, and Teriana rested her forehead on her friend's shoulder. "I don't know what I'm doing. I thought I could influence the direction of events, but I feel like a toy boat in a hurricane, entirely powerless about what direction I go. I feel like an absolute idiot believing that I was a player, because it turns out I'm just a pawn."

Quintus was quiet for a long time, then he said, "We could leave. It's not like he didn't give you the option. You *do* have a sea serpent at your beck and call, and with him, we could free your ship and crew, load up Miki, and sail away."

"You want to be a sailor?" she asked, wiping at her tears.

"I want to be with the man I love. Nothing else really matters."

The sadness in his voice broke her already fractured heart, and Teriana moved so their foreheads were pressing together. Remembered the first time she and Quintus had spoken, when Cassius had paraded her through the streets of Celendrial. Remembered his grin when he'd told her that the legionnaires gossiped worse than a knitting circle, for it had been the first moment she'd seen one of them as human. As a person.

And now a friend. One of the closest friends she'd ever had.

"Don't stay just because of me," she said quietly. "If there is a moment where you think you can get away, when you think you can steal Miki off that island, do it. If you need my help, ask, because I'll do anything and everything in my power to help you."

"Except come with me."

She bit her lip, her shattered heart desperately wanting to say *yes*. To race away with her friends and her crew and leave all of this behind. Except how much longer would there be a place for all of them to hide? How much longer until the Empire's reach had grown so great that deserters were hunted to the ends of Reath? Maybe she was only a pawn in this mess, but if she didn't at least *try* to contain the Empire's dominion, there would come a moment when she cursed her cowardice.

"I can't. For the sake of my captive people, I have to see this through." It was bigger than that, a compulsive sense that she *needed* to be here that she hadn't been able to explain to Marcus and couldn't explain now, so Teriana didn't bother to try, only said, "Marcus said he plans to take Emrant by force, so in truth, it won't be much longer until I'm free. If you're still here, I'm going to take you with me."

"I'll still be here." She felt Quintus's brow furrow where it was pressed against hers. "I've lost too many close friends. First Yaro. Then Agrippa. And nearly Miki. I'm not going to abandon you in this underworld of a camp, Teriana. You need someone at your back. As it is, if Miki learns that I abandoned you, he'll send me right back."

She squeezed her eyes shut, seeing a small glow of light in the sea of darkness trying to consume her. "Thank you."

32

MARCUS

He awoke to a splitting headache and Amarin banging loudly around his room as he set the table for breakfast.

"It's past dawn," his servant said at a volume that felt closer to a shout, and Marcus winced. "Your officers are already in the command room, possessed of the full faculties of those who did not consume half our wine stores."

"You say that as though this were a regular occurrence." His mouth tasted like death, the light seeming to pulse as his brain dragged itself out of its stupor. "I took a night off."

"Well, I hope you enjoyed it, because now you have a mess to clean up."

For a heartbeat, Marcus thought Amarin meant a *literal* mess, but then memory washed over him. Not his conversation with Austornic, although there'd be repercussions to that, but Teriana.

Teriana in a Cel dress.

Teriana in his lap.

Teriana's lips on his.

And her face . . . eyes pooling to the deepest grey of hurt and grief and horror as he'd begged her to walk away. As he'd . . .

"*Fuck.*"

"Indeed. I am sympathetic to the challenges you have faced in recent months." Amarin shoved a cup of water into Marcus's hand. "But you need to remember who you are, else you will soon find yourself supplanted. Titus was a *boy*, and yet look at the grief he caused you. If Cassius decides to send grown men, equally experienced, equally well trained, you will be in their sights because their minds will be *wholly* focused on achieving glory, not heartache over a girl."

Marcus flinched.

"Austornic smells weakness and fears for his legion, much as you once did for the Thirty-Seventh beneath Hostus. Like you, he'll conspire to better his situation, likely by appealing to the Senate to replace you. Cassius will capitalize on that in a heartbeat and send someone of his choosing, and it's unlikely to be someone you like. Do you want to go back to being told what to do by another, as you were under Hostus? To have the Thirty-Seventh used as fodder against the enemy because you don't have the clout to protect them? To participate in brutal strategy with no regard for human life simply because it's the easiest path to victory? To have another legatus applauded in triumphs through Celendrial's streets despite it being your strategies that led them to victory?"

"When have I ever cared about *triumphs*?"

The blow came without warning. One moment Marcus was sitting on the bed, the next, his water cup was rolling across the floor and his jaw was screaming from the impact of Amarin's fist.

"Pull your head out of your ass," Amarin growled, the submissive man who'd served him gone, a harder, unfamiliar one standing in his place. "I've invested too much in you to watch you throw it away."

Wiping the beads of blood from where he'd cut his lip on his front teeth, Marcus eyed the older man with a wariness he'd never felt before. He knew Amarin's history. Knew that he'd been a rebel warrior in Sibal, captured and forced into indenture, his defiance supposedly assimilated out of him, as he'd been the model servant for close to two decades. Marcus now wondered how much of that was an act.

Rising to his feet, he kept his eyes on Amarin and ignored every instinct telling him to go for his weapons on the far side of the room. "Investment implies a goal, Amarin. Which makes me question just what you hope to achieve."

A flicker of frustration moved through the older man's eyes, regret over having spoken in haste. But then Amarin's shoulders squared. "To keep the Senate from turning you into the most terrifying weapon it has ever possessed."

Marcus didn't answer, only held his ground, and waited.

"Ever and always, you've had two halves," Amarin finally said. "The capacity to do the greatest and worst of deeds, and while once you always reached up, the Senate wants you to sink down and *down and down.* They surrounded you with the darkest of men to destroy your every moral so you would do the Empire's villainy without argument. For my part, I tried to temper that. To keep the defiance alive in you, so that . . ."

"So that *what*?"

Amarin looked away. "So that you would have a choice of what sort of man you wished to be." Amarin picked up the fallen cup and refilled it, then handed it to Marcus. "What you told Teriana is true. You've done dark things. What is false is your belief that your past deeds condemn you to a future of doing the same. You believe you don't deserve her because of the things you have done and think to prove it by becoming even worse. Perhaps instead you might try to be worthy of the way that girl feels about you."

Without another word, Amarin left the room.

As if it were that simple. He'd *tried* to do the right thing by enticing Kaira into a scheme that would have freed Teriana's people at a cost to no one but *him* and been told to kiss her ass for his troubles. What other solution was left to him but force?

Anger simmering in his veins, Marcus went to the table on which sat a map of the coast, glowering as he stared down at it. Trying and failing to force the older man's words out of his head.

Was Amarin right? Could good deeds outweigh the horror of his past? It seemed lunacy to think that it could be so, greater lunacy still to think that there was a path forward for him that was *good*.

Except if there was a lesser evil . . .

Resting his elbows on the table, Marcus reconsidered what he aimed to achieve. Secure Emrant, yes, but that was only half the battle.

Atrio was not his only spy in Gamdesh. Retrieving the reams of reports that had come in during his absence, Marcus read through the updates, speculation, and details his men had noted. In one that had arrived a week ago, his eyes snagged on a few sentences about some construction that had taken place in the middle of Emrant. It had been worth noting because the military had cordoned it off and no civilians were allowed near. What made it more interesting was that the spy subsequently discovered that an old stone structure of seemingly no purpose had been rebuilt, but larger. It was now kept under guard.

Marcus's mouth turned up in a smile.

Kaira had already cracked open the xenthier encasement, and she wouldn't have bothered refortifying so excessively if she hadn't found compelling evidence it posed a risk to the city. Bodies of pathhunters, no doubt, which meant she'd known it was a viable path from the Empire long before he'd sent his letter. And yet . . .

Atrio's voice filled his head. *Kaira doesn't reside in Emrant but in a fortress about two hours north. Must be worried about assassination attempts, because the garrison in her fortress has twice the number of men they need.* Marcus flipped through the reports, searching for anything that suggested that hadn't changed, but all indicated that Kaira remained in her fortress, and every spy believed it was out of fear of Cel assassination.

Fear.

Marcus frowned, instantly rejecting his spies' suppositions. Kaira was marked by a god to fight, and Marcus did not think that created a woman who hid behind soldiers and walls. He picked up the bowl of porridge that Amarin had brought, and his smile grew as he formed his own theories about Kaira's behavior. The problem would be in proving them.

Marcus mechanically spooned the cold food into his mouth, losing himself in the problem, adrenaline having driven away the fog of both hangover and his ever-present headache. A conversation he'd had with Agrippa what felt like a lifetime ago rose in his mind.

"Do you think that if someone on guard duty at the genesis farts that we'd smell it here?"

The question had been so unexpected that Marcus had struggled for a response. *"I . . . I . . . I suppose it would stand to reason, though I've never seen it documented. Certainly, there have been complaints of other foul odors emanating from other terminus stems."*

Agrippa had pursed his lips, giving a slow nod. *"Would have to be sustained, I imagine. No one is going to report a passing whiff."*

It had been hard not to laugh. *"Agreed. Sustained and concentrated enough to note, else the fortress's commander would be inundated with endless reports on smells."*

"Would make an interesting experiment. The collegium is always interested in our discoveries, after all."

As the memory faded, Marcus considered the theory and how to execute it. As always, solutions rose, his mind picking apart the flaws and rebuilding them, the strategy growing and evolving into the combination of certainty and luck that he liked best. Pulling blank paper in front of him, he wrote two copies of the same letter to be delivered to the spies in Emrant, with specific instructions. Then another in code to Wex with more instructions. He included a recommendation that the collegium take note of the strategy, giving credit to Agrippa because Wex had endlessly bumped heads with him at Lescendor and had questioned Marcus's choice to make Agrippa primus.

Rising to his feet, Marcus flung open the door to his room and said to his guards, "This letter needs to be sent through to the Atlia terminus. And I need both Felix and Rastag."

Going back into his room, Marcus examined the map as he ran through his plan, intending only to reveal it in parts to those who needed information to play their role.

"It smells like a bottom-of-the-barrel wine house in here," Felix said, and Marcus turned to find his friend coming through the door, Rastag on his heels. The Thirty-Seventh's engineer stumbled, his spectacles slipping down his nose, and Felix caught his arm by reflex before fixing Marcus with a glare. "How much did you drink?"

"Irrelevant. Sit down." While the two moved to take stools around the small table, Marcus went to the door to speak to Gibzen, who stood outside. "No interruptions. Short of this camp coming under attack, I don't want to hear so much as a knock on the door. Understood?"

"Yes, sir."

Slamming the door shut, he strode to the table and flung himself on a stool. "I've a plan. A plan that must stay between the three of us, is that understood? Because all it will take is a whisper in the wrong ear, and it will fall apart."

Felix's brow furrowed, but he nodded along with Rastag.

"All right." Smoothing the map, he tapped a finger atop the major crossing on the river Orinok. "Rastag, I need you to build me a bridge."

"Not feasible," his engineer snapped. "Truly, sir, it often feels you allow your imagination to take precedence over the realities of—"

Marcus held up a hand to cut him off. "Hear me out."

They sat silently as he explained his plan, then leaned back. "Well? Can it be done?"

Rastag crossed his arms, scowling through his smudged spectacles. "I don't like it."

"I realize it lacks your usual elegance, but will it *work*?"

The Thirty-Seventh's engineer glared at the scratchwork of calculations in front of him. Then he looked to Felix. "As many men as I want?"

"Within reason."

"Can we afford it?"

Marcus cleared his throat. "That's my problem."

Rastag's sigh was long and dramatic. "It *should* work."

Those words from anyone else would have filled Marcus with doubt, but from his engineer's mouth, they amounted to absolute certainty. "Good. Get underway."

Rastag saluted and left the room, leaving Marcus alone with Felix. He waited in silence as his second-in-command examined the map, and then Felix finally said, "There is no room for error in this. It will require perfect execution for everything to go exactly as you planned, or it will explode in our faces."

"But do you think it will work?"

"Yeah." Felix shook his head, chuckling. "You haven't proposed something this mad since we took Hydrilla."

"I walked in Hydrilla's shadow on my way to the Bardeen stem. It still looks the same, though now it flies Cel banners." Marcus hesitated, his mind drifting back to a memory of a different time, when the defiance Amarin spoke of had burned strongly in his blood. "Do you remember our goals during that siege?"

Felix nodded. "We were a different legion, then."

They were harder now. Stronger. More skilled. Yet that wasn't what Felix meant. "I think perhaps it's time the Thirty-Seventh becomes that legion again."

A slow smile formed on his friend's face. "Agreed. But it has to start with you." He rose to his feet. Reaching into his belt pouch, he extracted a heavy gold bracelet and set it in front of Marcus. "I found this in the command room. I know Austornic has been meddling, but his intentions are in the right place."

"I know." Taking another drink of water, Marcus said, "Assemble the Thirty-Seventh outside of camp. I need to talk to them."

After Felix left, Marcus picked up the gold bangle, turning it over in his hands. There was nothing he could do that would ever make him worth Teriana. Nothing that he could do that would ever outweigh what he'd done to Lydia, and even without the rules imposed on him by the Empire, no future possible while he held that secret from her. He needed to stay away from her because he didn't trust himself around her.

Yet that didn't mean he needed to make her life worse.

Donning his armor and weapons, Marcus shoved the bangle into his belt pouch. Flinging open the door, he said to Gibzen, "Get Teriana and Quintus a room inside the fortress."

The primus's mouth twisted. "But you—"

"Do it. And someone get me my horse."

Men hurried to obey as Marcus strode through the fortress, then out the doors. His hangover reared its head as brilliant rays of sun stabbed him in the eyes, but Marcus ignored the pain and shoved his helmet on his head. The camp was a flurry of activity as his men flowed out the gates, the men of the other legions watching with interest.

Descending the steps, Marcus found Servius standing at the base, holding the reins of a mare with a coat of an alarming shade of gold.

"Your old horse is lame," his friend said. "So I bought you a new one. Isn't she a beauty? They breed them in Gamdesh."

Marcus stared at the tall mare. Her coat was so shiny she reflected the sunlight as though she were made of metal in truth. "Interesting choice."

The horse stomped her feet and squealed, then tried to bite Servius's arm. He only laughed. "She's got good spirit, and she'll make you look good."

What she looked like was a mount that was likely to toss him into the mud at her earliest convenience. "Maybe—"

Servius leaned closer. "What I'm told is that there's something special about this breed. They don't make people sneeze."

That was an enticing attribute. Marcus frowned at the horse, wondering if not sneezing after every ride was worth the target such a mount would paint on his back. Taking the reins, he said to her, "You cause me trouble and horse meat will be on the menu."

She pinned her ears and tried to bite him, Servius laughing as Marcus scrambled into the saddle. He ignored the wave of dizziness that came over him, and urged the mare into a trot toward the gates, his bodyguard formed up around him. Felix was waiting, his friend reining his own mount between Marcus and Gibzen. "Nice horse."

"Servius's choice."

Felix laughed, then heeled his mount through camp. From the back of the tall mare, Marcus saw Teriana's familiar form. She held a gladius in one hand, and Quintus was gesturing wildly as he explained something to her. Though she no doubt had seen the party, her eyes remained fixed on Quintus, chin bobbing up and down as she listened to his instructions.

"You know who she reminds me of?" Felix asked, and Marcus winced internally that he'd been so obvious.

"No."

"Agrippa's girl. The laundress. She used to watch us train for hours on end. I always figured she had a thing for legion boys, so I never did anything about it. You remember her name?"

Marcus blinked, seeing the pretty Bardenese girl in his mind, her eyes wide with fear because she'd just dumped a bucket of water on his feet.

"Silvara," Gibzen said from where he rode next to them. "We used to see the little chit mimicking us in the woods when she thought no one was watching. Agrippa even let her play dress-up in his gear one time; I heard Yaro and Quintus talking about it."

To do so was against legion law, so Felix surprised Marcus by snapping, "You're awfully well informed of other people's business, Primus. Move off—this conversation doesn't involve you."

Gibzen's glare was murderous, but he moved back a few paces. Only then did Felix retrieve a page from his belt pouch. "I bring it up because more supplies arrived via the Bardeen stem, including an update on the security at Hydrilla. The rebels have been increasing their attacks on supply caravans, which is why we only received half of what we should've. They're led by a young woman who fights with a Thirty-Seventh gladius, and you'll never guess what her name is."

"You aren't serious?" Marcus snatched the page, scanning the report, none of the decidedly bad news resonating as his eyes stalled on the description of the rebel leader. *Prisoners were given over to questioners, who discovered the rebel leader goes by the name Silvara.*

"Do you think Agrippa is helping them?"

Marcus reread the page, then shook his head. "No . . . No, they'd know these supplies were for us, and while it's one thing for Agrippa to have deserted, it's another thing for him to willfully attack the Thirty-Seventh's supply lines. That's no better than sticking knives into our backs."

"So you think he's dead?"

Marcus glanced at Gibzen, remembering the moment he'd delivered Marcus the news of Agrippa's desertion. "Yes. There's not a girl on Reath he'd be willing to raise arms against us for. Servius, update the books."

"That he's dead doesn't change that he left us for her."

A prickle of gooseflesh broke over Marcus's skin, and he looked to the skyline above Aracam, the black tower looming. "Change the books."

"Will do," Servius replied. "But on a more pressing note, what's this gathering about?"

"Unity." Marcus nudged his horse into a canter in the direction of the orderly ranks of the Thirty-Seventh forming up on the planes before Aracam. Arinoquian civilians outside the walls watched nervously, many of them hurrying inside the city, but Marcus paid them no mind as he glanced to the ridge where Titus's pyre had stood, the young legatus now nothing more than an urn of ashes to be delivered to Celendrial. Yet in his mind's eye, Marcus could see the black plume of smoke that had stained the air, smell the stink of burning flesh, and feel the pain of knowing he'd failed Titus as thoroughly as Titus had failed him.

He'd not make that mistake again.

The Thirty-Seventh was watching him as his attention turned once more to their ranks, and he called out, "At ease."

Men glanced between each other, but then relaxed their stances, watching him with curiosity. Heeling his horse, he rode slowly between them, feeling his cloak billow out behind him as the wind rose. "The Senate has tasked us with a campaign far beyond the scope of anything we've undertaken before!" he shouted, allowing the wind to carry his voice. "We face an adversary of a strength Celendor has not faced since the dawn of the Empire. Never have we needed fortitude more than we do now, and yet the only reinforcement the Senate has sent us is the greenest legion in the Empire."

The men shifted restlessly, none of this having been lost on them.

"Thirteen years old," he said. "They've never seen real combat. Everything they know about battle is theoretical. Skirmishes fought on the plains before Lescendor with dulled blades and catapults filled with paint. Children who have only played at war, and yet here they are in the midst of the biggest campaign of the Empire's history."

He wove through the ranks, watching their faces, feeling the tension rise, then he shouted, "Little boys stand at our backs, my brothers! Soldiers whose faces won't need a razor for years to come. Soldiers whose faces *never fucking will* unless we teach them right."

The legion collectively stiffened, his words not what they'd expected.

"We are the Thirty-Seventh!" His voice carried over their heads.

"Undefeated champions of the Empire, and if we fell today, oh what glorious speeches would be given about all the things that we have done. Of the endless foes who have fallen beneath our feet, banners flapping and horns blaring triumphantly. Of how we never once fell back." He took a breath, watching them watch him. "But it was not the men we are now who were cast into battle and blood, told to fight or die. It was little boys who'd only fought with dull blades and paint, who'd only played at war."

Passing Servius, he took the Thirty-Seventh's standard from his friend, hooking the base of it into his stirrup. Sunlight glinted off the gold, sending little beams of light bouncing off the armor of his men.

"You all know I've been in Celendrial," he said. "Meeting with the Commandant. The Senate. The Consul. What you don't know is that while there I encountered some old *friends* of ours. The Twenty-Ninth."

Faces soured, dozens of men spitting into the dirt at the mention of the legion that had been supposed to finish their training. The legion that had been the architects of the Thirty-Seventh's misery for years.

"Do you remember life under Hostus's command? Do you remember being tethered to them with apron strings of razor wire? What it was like to fear the teacher more than the enemy? Many would say that it was because of their methods that we are who we are, but I ask, how many of our brothers would stand among us today if not for the *lessons* of the Twenty-Ninth?"

"Yaro!" someone shouted, but the dead legionnaire's name was only the first, dozens more filling the air as the Thirty-Seventh screamed the names of those who'd died because of the older legion, every man present remembering their own personal suffering beneath the Twenty-Ninth's fists.

"Our blood is on their hands!" he roared over their voices. "Will the Fifty-First's be on ours?"

"No!" they screamed back at him, ranks abandoned as the men pressed around his horse. The animal's eyes rolled in panic, but Marcus only checked the reins. "Who are we?"

"The Thirty-Seventh!"

The noise was deafening, his horse twisting in circles as he lifted the standard into the air. The dragon was the symbol of the empire they served, but the 37 it clutched in its talons? That number was *theirs*.

Urging the horse forward, he led his legion back to their camp, his friends falling in alongside him.

"Well," Servius said. "It's been an age since you gave a speech that pretty. What was that all about?"

Marcus glanced back at the ridge, seeing imagined smoke rising black as night. "A different kind of legacy."

33

LYDIA

"I wish I'd fallen," Baird groaned. "I wish I was a splatter on the rocks or crushed to pulp by blighters, because at least it would have been quick. Not this slow, miserable march toward death, like being cooked on a low-burning fire."

"Quit complaining," Agrippa answered. "The heat forestalled pursuit, and honestly, it's not even that hot."

It absolutely *was* that hot, and in Baird's defense, he'd been tasked with carrying the bulk of the supplies that they'd retrieved from the underground storage room where she and Killian had hidden during the storm.

Lydia's cheeks warmed as she thought of that moment, and she glanced at Killian, who walked to her left. His face was concealed by a length of fabric to block the sun, but it did nothing to block her imagination. It had been days since they'd fled the escarpment and into Anukastre, but the time had done nothing to diminish her memory of the feel of his hands on her naked skin or the feel of his lips pressed against hers. The weight of him on top of her as he'd held her down, his muscles like steel beneath her hands.

Gloved hands.

She scowled beneath her scarf, painfully sick of wearing the sweat-soaked leather gloves day and night, but there was no helping it. The moment she took them off, the dark side of her mark reared its head, and it wasn't worth the risk. Agrippa was convinced it was all in her head, reminding her ad nauseum that gloves were easily removed and therefore did not prevent her from doing anything. In her head or not, there was no denying that they kept everyone safe.

Most especially Killian.

There was no privacy for them to pick up where they'd left off, for they were primarily traveling at night and sleeping under the cover of a single piece of canvas during the day, which meant eyes were always on them. They'd had to content themselves with sleeping fully clothed in each other's arms, and for her part, her mind happily supplied detailed fantasies of what would have happened if Agrippa hadn't walked in on them. Lydia allowed her mind to drift, vanquishing the toil of walking over endless dunes with the imagined feel of Killian's skin against hers, nothing left between them.

You are mine. Every part of you, light and dark.

Her toes curled in her boots as she remembered his words, then Agrippa said, "Honestly, Lydia, we could charge money to watch what's going on inside that head of yours."

Bending to pick up a handful of sand, she threw it at him. "You're the most obnoxious individual I've ever met. Do you ever shut up?"

"Silence is not a strength of mine." He hopped over a rock in his path with no sign of the exhaustion everyone else suffered. "Especially when my words yield such amusing results."

"You're the only one laughing," Killian pointed out, but Agrippa only shrugged.

"No accounting for humor."

"And it is that hot," she snapped at him, knowing that she was giving Agrippa exactly what he wanted by arguing but unable to stop herself. "I grew up in Celendrial, which is miserably hot, and this is worse."

"Oh, please." He turned so that he was walking backward and facing her and Killian. "You lived in the cool rooms of a villa on the Hill, with servants to supply you with endless iced drinks and fan you while you drank them. Were carried about in shaded litters by sweating peregrini while you lounged on silken pillows. Were treated to cool baths with water brought in from the countryside in the aqueducts. Were allowed to sleep through the heat of the day because your only responsibility was to exist and look pretty doing it."

"What does a legion boy know of life on the Hill?" she demanded, hating that he wasn't wrong.

"Contrary to what you seem to think, I wasn't born in Campus Lescendor. I was, in fact, born on the Hill and lived the first seven years of my life as a spoiled patrician brat until the law required my father to deliver me to legion training."

She blinked. "Who is your father?"

"The late Senator Egnatius. You're likely more familiar with my brother, Tiberius." He frowned. "If he's still alive, that is."

"You can't be Tiberius's brother. I knew his parents before they died, and they were both Cel through and through, whereas you are—"

"Ilithyia wasn't my mother, nor was she Tiberius's," Agrippa explained, and with the revelation, Lydia put another familial connection together, though she said nothing.

"My mother was a Bardenese indentured servant my father took a shine to," Agrippa continued. "Ilithyia was barren, so she passed us off as her own, which was easier to accomplish with my brother as he favored our father's complexion."

"You can't be serious." Killian looked between them. "That matters?"

"I expect Lydia knows all too well how much it matters."

She gave a tight nod. "I didn't look like them, and they never let me forget it. I was unmarriageable, which was how Lucius Cassius roped my father into a betrothal, never mind that Lucius never intended to follow through."

"Your bloodline is impeccable," Killian said with a scoff. "Your father was king."

"Doesn't matter," she and Agrippa said at the same time, though Agrippa added, "The key to Celendor controlling the East is every other nation perceiving it as stronger, richer, and more powerful. As elite and untouchable. Maintaining that illusion requires everyone to believe the same of the people: that those with Cel blood are *superior.* Obviously that's total horseshit, but given none of the provinces have the strength to stand against the Senate, it's a belief that is never challenged. And because it's never challenged, there is no reason for patrician Cel to believe it anything less than the truth. They really do believe they are superior, and once I was at Lescendor, I had my ass kicked, more times than I care to count, for thinking myself better than the boys from the provinces, because in the legions, you're supposed to forget who you were and where you came from. We were all the same, all equal, until we proved ourselves within that framework, which is how boys rise to officer status.

"Which . . ." Agrippa drew in a deep breath. ". . . is also horseshit, because patrician boys arrive with the advantage of being well fed, educated, and raised from the tit on the exact sort of politics that sees a boy to command of a legion, which is to say the power of manipulation. That's why there is a disproportionate number of legati who have a very patrician look to them despite the vast majority of legion ranks being made up of men from the provinces."

"Does your . . . *legatus*"—Killian stumbled slightly on the Cel word—"fall into those numbers?"

"Marcus?" Agrippa laughed, but there was an edge to it. "Without a doubt. I never heard him admit to anything, but if his gilded ass wasn't born on the very top of the Hill, I'll eat my own boot. We probably crossed paths with him as children, Lydia, we just don't remember."

"Domitius."

"Pardon?"

Lydia didn't answer, her mind's eye filled with memory. Of Marcus's hand on her jaw, ready to break her neck as he said, *I do know you. I didn't remember until Cassius mentioned your library. Though I remember it as your father's library.*

"He's Senator Domitius's son. We were neighbors." She shook her head, pressing fingers to her temple because it had been so long ago. Almost another life. "I suppose that doesn't much matter."

"Doesn't matter? Have you lost your mind?" Agrippa shouted. "That means the eldest Domitius daughter is Marcus's sister. She's married to my brother, which makes us family! Oh gods, that information will annoy him to no end. When we inevitably go to war against him, we should find a way to tell him. Will put him out of sorts for days."

"If we go to war with him," Killian said softly, "I'm going to kill him for what he's done."

Despite the heat, a shiver ran over her skin. Lydia rubbed at her arms, noting that Agrippa had fallen silent, humor gone.

"Here," Malahi abruptly announced, rising from where she'd knelt a dozen paces ahead in the dry creek bed they'd been following. "There is plant life underground here, so start digging."

Agrippa didn't answer, only moved to where she pointed and began to dig. This was how they'd been surviving in the barren lands that made up Anukastre. They'd raced south, following Agrippa's mental map from explorations that had been ordered by Rufina until they reached the creek that apparently only ran above the surface once a year, then headed east toward the southern Liratoras, where they'd eventually cross back into Mudamora. Malahi's gift allowed her to sense plant life surviving on water deep underground, though it often required hours of digging to reach.

Malahi dusted her hands on her trousers as she rose, saying something to Agrippa that Lydia couldn't quite make out, though it made him smile. Then she walked over to where Lydia had seated herself on a rock.

"Agrippa says it won't be long until we reach the mountains," Malahi said, sitting on another rock. "He and Killian think we should be able to see them by tomorrow."

Lydia nodded, toying with a tear in the knee of her trousers, deeply aware of Agrippa's scrutiny and of how Baird had moved within reach.

"Do you worry what we'll find on the far side of them?" Malahi asked, and when Lydia didn't answer, she added, "I'm afraid we'll find nothing but blight. Nothing but death. Afraid that we're too late."

"If we were too late, Rufina wouldn't have bothered pursuing us," Lydia said, though her dreams were filled with the same. A world of blighted earth and dead things walking. "If there wasn't something we could do to help, we wouldn't be worth chasing."

Malahi sighed. "Validation of our value from our enemies is not much comfort, though part of me wishes they still pursued, because then we'd know there was hope." Unhooking her waterskin from her belt, she took a sip and then passed it to Lydia. "I know the expectation is that I'll kneel before the blight and know instinctively how to send it away or destroy it, but I don't. Killian took me out to where it had spread near Mudaire to see if I could remedy it, but I couldn't. There is nothing living in it to make grow. It's dead."

"The blighters are the same." Lydia took a mouthful. "They might walk and talk, but they're dead. There's no more life to them than the rock I'm sitting on. Less, in a way."

Malahi nodded, seeming to understand.

"I was able to help Lena when she was infected because it hadn't killed her, but doing so nearly killed *me*. Maybe I could save a few dozen over a stretch of time, but the thousands, the tens of thousands, who've already died? I think they're lost to us forever."

Malahi sucked in a ragged breath, and when Lydia looked at her, it was to find tears rolling down the queen's face. In an instant, Agrippa was at her side, his hand curving around her face, wiping away her tears. "What's wrong? What happened?"

"Nothing." Malahi smiled up at him. "We are just talking about the blight. Trying to figure out how it can be reversed."

Agrippa made a noncommittal noise, then said, "Don't make any plans together. The last one was nearly the death of me."

Malahi rolled her eyes, watching as he retreated to where Killian was now shirtless, olive skin glistening with sweat as he worked. Agrippa said something to him that earned a dour look, then Agrippa pulled off his own shirt and started helping.

They sat in silence, watching Agrippa and Killian dig, and Lydia took the opportunity provided by the dim glow of the rising sun to examine the other woman's face. Her injuries were no longer raw and livid, but without a healer's intervention, the scars would remain for the rest of her life. Her blond hair was growing back where it had been torn out, but it was a far cry from the waist-length locks she'd once had.

"I haven't seen my reflection since Helatha," Malahi said, and Lydia flushed, realizing her scrutiny hadn't gone unnoticed. "I don't mean in mirrors. Even when I wash my face, I keep my eyes shut so that I won't have to see myself. Rufina used to make me look at the ruin of my face, but I like living in the delusion that it will all heal away. Seeing otherwise would be worse than the pain itself."

Reflex demanded that she say that Malahi wasn't ruined, to spew forth platitudes, but Lydia kept silent, instinct telling her that wasn't what the other woman needed.

"It's probably terrible to be so vain, but I liked being beautiful," Malahi said, watching Agrippa throw wet sand at a scowling Killian. "I liked the power it gave me and the way it caused people to treat me, and knowing that I'll never experience that again makes me want to scream and scream."

Lydia could feel Malahi's grief, the weight of it, and she said, "I—"

The queen held up her hand. "I know what you're going to say, and while I appreciate the offer, I need to be this way. Need to have the scars of this war written on my face because my kingdom has the same wounds. I need the rage I feel every time I look at my hands or touch my face, because it gives me the strength I need to keep fighting. Perhaps one day I'll come to you to heal the trauma inflicted upon me, but it won't be until I've—until *we've*—healed the trauma inflicted upon Mudamora. Perhaps not even then, because I never want to forget what I survived. Remembering what I can endure gives me strength."

They'd been right to save her.

"Don't look at me like I'm brave." Malahi met her gaze. "For all my words, I can't look in the mirror."

Lydia smiled. "I can't take off my gloves."

"Aren't we a pair?"

A laugh tore from her lips, and the men broke off their conversation to look at them before going back to whatever Agrippa was sketching with his knife in the dirt, both of them looking decidedly guilty.

"What are you talking about?" Malahi asked.

"Peaceably assailing a fortress," Agrippa called back. "Killian's never done it, so I'm imparting my extensive wisdom."

Killian gave Agrippa a furious shove, the pair arguing under their breaths before going back to Agrippa's drawing, and next to her, Baird gave a soft chuckle.

"What's so funny?" Lydia asked the giant, whom she'd thought had been asleep.

"The four of you make me feel old," he answered. "And young."

He closed his eyes, seemingly unconcerned with leaving Lydia unsupervised with Malahi, which gave Lydia a strange sense of peace in her heart.

"I looked for answers in the library at the healing temple," she told Malahi. "I couldn't find anything, but it was disorganized and there wasn't time to read everything." Shaking her head, she added, "It made me wish for the Great Library in Celendrial with its endless librarians who, between them, have read every tome. Research takes time, and time is the one thing we don't have."

"There is such a library in Revat," Malahi said. "I've seen it myself. More books than you can imagine and countless librarians holding court within its walls, many of whom are marked. We could appeal to the Sultan for their help, for if there is an answer written, it is surely there. Once we reach Serlania, we should send word."

To call it a plan was a mockery of the word, but it was *something.* Something where moments before, there had felt like nothing.

Lydia smiled and stretched her legs out before her, only for every instinct in her body to flare as Malahi's eyes widened with fear.

A cold blade pressed against Lydia's throat, and then a male voice said, "Some might say it is brave for Mudamorians to walk these lands, but I? I say it is very, *very* foolish."

34

TERIANA

Teriana leaned on the ramparts, her eyes staring north. Not at the endless swathes of jungle, but at a vision in her imagination of the Orinok river. A river wider than any in the world, yet not an hour ago, Marcus had ordered hundreds of men to accompany Rastag to its banks.

Where they were instructed to build a bridge.

Not just any bridge, but a bridge over a river that increased to three times its width each rainy season. Which meant that it was a bridge that never had a hope of being completed because it would be washed away as soon as the heavy rains began to fall.

"Could be a floating bridge," Quintus had offered when they'd heard about the *new plan*. "Those don't take long to build."

Except floating or otherwise, Marcus had ordered the bridge built exactly opposite the Gamdeshian fortress on the far bank. A fortress with *catapults* that would make short work of any construction that reached past the midpoint of the river.

Even Quintus seemed worried. He no longer clung to his unfaltering faith that no matter Marcus's flaws, he'd never lead the Thirty-Seventh astray. This was unease that was clearly shared, for through her tent walls, Teriana heard mutters about the lunacy of it all. Most of it came from the Forty-First and Fifty-First, but the unease in the Thirty-Seventh was palpable even in their silence. Marcus was the reason they were considered the most dangerous legion in service, ever undefeated, but if he'd lost his nerve, that would swiftly change.

It was as though in their erosion of faith in him, they'd lost faith in themselves. While on duty, they seemed calm, but the moment the legionnaires were left to their own devices, violence ensued. Most especially when men ventured into Aracam. She'd have thought it because of the tension of the war they all knew was coming, but the civilians were as bad, if not worse. She'd heard that last night the legions had broken up dozens of fights, and this morning, no less than six bodies had been found in alleys.

Friends killing friends.

Husbands murdering wives.

Mothers turning on children.

To top it off, disease was taking a toll. Not on the legion camp, but on the civilians, and Teriana had heard that Racker and his medics frequently went into Aracam to treat illnesses common to the Empire that had never been seen before in the West.

Because all the healers were absent.

All the *marked* were absent.

Shaking her head to clear her thoughts, Teriana returned to watching the Thirty-Seventh train the Fifty-First.

It was the one thing that did seem to be going right in a sea of wrong, and Teriana thought that might be because it was the one order Marcus had given that made sense.

They'd spent the day in endless exercises and drills, the older legionnaires seeming to take their duties to the boys as a personal mission after Marcus's speech late that morning. The boys had come out of Lescendor supposedly knowing everything, but even her inexperienced eye could see the superior skill of legionnaires who'd been blooded in battle more times than they could count. "Could they win a battle on their own?"

Quintus yawned. "That's too vague a question. Give me a situation. Numbers."

"The battle on the plains beyond the ridge." She shoved her hand in her pocket, gripping the hair ornament, the tiny mast digging into her palm. "When the Thirty-Seventh was attacked from the rear."

"Wasn't there," Quintus said with another yawn. "I was getting stitched back together."

She opened her mouth to mumble an apology for her poor choice of example, but then a voice said from behind, "If they kept their nerve."

Nic, his bodyguard shadowing him, moved to stand next to her at the wall.

"Any updates?" she asked, squeezing the ornament again.

Nic shook his head. "He met with Rastag and Felix in private. What I know is only what everyone else knows. That his new plan is to build a bridge over the Orinok. When it is complete, we'll invade by land. That this entire camp, including the engineers, knows that building a bridge there is impossible doesn't seem to matter to him."

"He's got a plan," Quintus said. "He's not stupid, you know."

"Or it's busy work because he doesn't have a plan. Or doesn't have the nerve needed to invade Gamdesh and this is his way of delaying."

"Sir!" Pullo hissed, and Teriana turned around to find Marcus standing behind Nic's bodyguards, his arms crossed over his breastplate and his expression unamused. She squeezed the ornament in her pocket, wincing as the mast cut her palm. This was the first time she'd seen Marcus since last night, and it felt hard to breathe in his presence.

I need you to stop. Please stop, Teriana. She flinched as his voice filled her thoughts, then shoved her hands in her pockets to cover the reaction.

"Thank you for your defense of my intelligence, Quintus," Marcus said. "Though I understand your sentiment is not shared."

Quintus shrugged even as Nic stammered, "Sir . . . I wasn't . . . I didn't . . ."

Anger flooded her veins, and Teriana stepped between Nic and Marcus. "Don't you dare punish him just for talking to me. He didn't say anything that everyone else isn't saying."

The moment the words left her mouth, she regretted them, but Marcus only glanced over his shoulder at the camp. "Yes, I've heard the gossip."

No one spoke. No one even seemed to breathe.

"That's the reason I'm here," Marcus finally said. "We're just going to do an exercise. One I think you could stand to participate in, Teriana."

He exuded an almost frenetic energy, blue-grey eyes slightly bloodshot. Yet he was steady on his feet.

"Fine," she muttered. "I have nothing better to do."

"Let's go." Marcus motioned them to follow him down the steps. Gibzen and his men pressed around them as they exited the gate, the primus eyeing her coldly. An expression she returned, for while Marcus seemed content to forgive the man for nearly bashing his head in with a rock, she was not.

As they entered the muddy plain, the men training all ceased what they were doing and saluted.

"Austornic," Marcus said. "Three hundred of your finest, if you would. Four lines."

Then he called to Servius, who was watching over the training. "Five hundred."

"That's not fair," Teriana snapped. "Whatever you're planning, don't. You can make whatever point you need to make another way."

Marcus ignored her, and Nic, looking like he was ready to be sick, motioned for his men to approach.

Marcus gave a slight nod to Nic, who called out an order, and boys moved into tight ranks, shields interlocked and spears bristling outwards. It was all done within moments, with the coordination of a well-trained dance troupe, every boy knowing exactly where he was supposed to be. Nothing Teriana hadn't watched a dozen times or more from atop the wall, but it felt different down here on the ground. Despite knowing she was in no danger from them, her pulse escalated.

Marcus motioned for her to walk in front of them, and a bead of sweat rolled down Teriana's spine as she stared into a mass of razor-tipped spears, steel shields, and gleaming armor. Gone were the faces of the boys of Nic's legion, only hard eyes visible beneath their helmets as they stared her down.

"Would you attack them?"

"Obviously not," she grumbled, glancing sideways at Quintus, who stood a dozen paces away, watching with his arms crossed. "I'm alone."

"How many soldiers would you need surrounding you to charge that line?" Marcus asked. "Fifty?"

She snorted. "Not unless I'm at the back."

"Let's assume you're at the front."

"Then no."

"One hundred?"

Teriana looked at the razor-tipped spears pointing outwards and shook her head. "Everyone in the front will get impaled."

"Only if Austornic's lines keep their nerve and don't break. But answer the question. How many men would you have to have to charge them with some certainty that you'd survive? Five hundred? A thousand?"

Her fingertips felt like ice, for it seemed no number would make running into those sharp points *safe*. "I'd go around. Attack them from the rear."

"Let's make it interesting and attack them from both sides. Austornic, your men are your own to command."

Nic called an order, and with terrifying precision, the last rows turned to face the rear. It took them seconds, which meant unless they were truly caught by surprise, they'd meet the attack.

"What's the point of this?"

And why does Nic look so worried?

"My point is that sometimes it's not about size or numbers or skill, it's about nerve. And *nerve* is something I understand to be the forefront of everyone's minds these days." Marcus walked the length of the line, then turned to the mass of Thirty-Seventh. "You all know this exercise. No weapons. They break, you can give a good thrashing to everyone you get your hands on. As usual, anyone who gets overenthusiastic and maims someone will be docked six months wage. Clear?"

The Thirty-Seventh all nodded, even as Teriana blurted out, "Pardon?"

Marcus ignored her, turning back to the Fifty-First. "They are going to charge you. A few are a bit thick in the head, but generally speaking they won't impale themselves for the sake of an exercise. So if you hold your lines, it will be them who lose their nerve. Of course, if even a few members of your line break and make a run for it, you'll have gaps that these men are experts at breaching, never mind what they'll do if your lines get snarled. That said, if you do choose to run and make it to the wall, you're free and clear. You're all young and nimble, while this lot," he gestured to the Thirty-Seventh, "have years of war injuries. You might be able to outrun them, but if they catch you, well . . ."

The Thirty-Seventh all laughed. The Fifty-First did not. As Racker approached, in the company of both Thirty-Seventh and Fifty-First medics, Teriana felt ready to be sick. She opened her mouth to argue against it, but Nic's hand closed on her arm, the young legatus shaking his head.

"Now, there would be a reason your commander would ask you to hold a line against a greater force," Marcus said. "Else he'd pull you back. So let's create some stakes."

Gibzen approached with a large rock, around which was wrapped a chain, a pair of manacles fastened to it. Shouldering among the Fifty-First, he dropped it in the middle of their ranks.

Marcus gestured to the rock. "Austornic."

Without argument, Nic walked to the rock and allowed Gibzen to shackle him to it.

"Every last one of you might be able to break and make it to the wall, but not your legatus," Marcus said. "So for his sake, I suggest you hold your lines or Nic is going to be black and blue for a month."

"All right," Servius bellowed. "Only what's in it for us?"

Marcus walked over to Nic and fastened the other manacle to his ankle, which resulted in the Thirty-Seventh all hooting loudly.

"If any of you hit him in the head, I'll castrate you!" Racker shouted. "But feel free to nominate one of your ranks to kick him in the balls since they are what keeps getting him into trouble!"

The Thirty-Seventh all roared with delight, then howled, "Servius! Servius!" The big legionnaire held up his hand. "Would be my honor."

Marcus gave a nod of agreement, then fixed his eyes on Teriana. "Willing to test your nerve?"

This was madness.

Racker approached. "A reminder, sir, given you clearly are feeling more yourself: head injuries compound. Another blow to the skull might render you jabbering and drooling, unable to wipe your own ass. Show some care."

Marcus shrugged, then shouted, "Teriana is a civilian, so no one can hit her. But if she breaks and runs for it, I've heard that a certain outhouse isn't up to camp standards."

All the men screamed their approval.

She couldn't very well decline when Nic faced a beating and she only faced scrubbing shit. "Fine."

The boys parted to allow her to stand next to Nic, then tightened the formation around them. Teriana sucked in a breath as she looked out from behind three rows of spears. Three rows of shields. Three rows of armored bodies. With another behind her to protect her back.

None of which meant a gods-damned thing as Marcus shouted, "Remember the rules!" and the Thirty-Seventh retreated down the field.

"This isn't for real, is it?" she asked Nic under her breath. "They won't actually hurt you?"

"If we break, they'll beat the ever-loving shit out of us," Nic answered. "They must. Because if we break in battle, lives will be lost."

"That's not fair," she hissed. "Because they're sure as shit not going to kick him in the balls."

Nic looked at her as though she'd just spouted pure idiocy. "He gave them permission. You really think they're going to pass that opportunity up?"

Oh gods.

"This is stupid. This is reckless. Marcus, they are just children."

"No," he replied. "They are legionnaires of the Celendor Empire."

Then he lifted his hand.

The Thirty-Seventh broke into a running charge toward them, a mass of muscle and armor, their faces twisted with grim determination. The ground shook, and behind her she heard one of the boys whisper, "Shit."

Run.

Teriana's body swayed, the instinct to shove her way through the boys and flee hitting her like a battering ram, only pride keeping her in place.

It's fine, she told herself. *This is just to scare Nic. To scare me. He'll stop them. There is no danger.*

Except they were coming closer with each passing second. Hands clenched into fists, mouths opened as they screamed, their faces a frenzied blur.

"Steady," Nic said, and Teriana first thought the word for her but then she saw two of the spears waver. Saw hands flexing on weapons. Saw jaws tighten.

All while the Thirty-Seventh drew closer. Legionnaires who were older. Stronger. Infinitely more deadly.

"Steady."

Oh gods, this is real.

He's going to hurt them.

He's punishing Nic for talking to me.

They were close enough now that she could see the sweat on their faces, their bared teeth, the marks in their armor.

"Stop this," she whispered.

Marcus's expression was impossible to read: impassive but not. Like there was no doubt in his mind that the boys surrounding him would follow his orders. "You are legionnaires of the Celendor Empire!" he shouted. "You do not break."

The gap between the forces narrowed, raw terror pulsing through Teriana's veins. Several of the boys near her were shaking.

"Steady!"

"Stop this!" she gasped, the wind blasting the smell of sweat and steel and impending pain over her face. "Don't do this. *Please!*"

Her plea came out as a shriek of terror a heartbeat before the legions collided. Teriana threw herself through the line behind her, falling between two boys. Crawling on her hands and knees, every instinct demanding that she run.

Except instead of the thud of fists and screams of pain, laughter and shouts of congratulations reached her ears. Teriana stopped crawling.

It's fine.

It was just a demonstration.

Yet she couldn't move. Couldn't stand up. Couldn't gods-damned *breathe.*

"You all right?" Nic moved as far as the chain would allow him and reached down to pull her upright. His face was unmoved, but she didn't fail to notice that his palm was slick with sweat. Off to the right, one of the boys was puking, several others sitting pale-faced in the dirt, barely seeming to hear the congratulations ringing in the air as they warred with unspent adrenaline.

"Well done," Marcus said to them all, the manacle still locked around his ankle. "You kept your nerve, which means you live another day. And I don't have to piss blood for a week, for which I am profoundly grateful."

She hadn't kept her nerve.

"Back to drills!"

The legionnaires all returned to what they'd been doing under Servius's command, leaving her alone with Marcus and Nic.

"There are plans in play," Marcus said to the younger legatus. "But if you wish to be privy to them, I have to be able to trust that you'll keep my confidence. Lives are at stake, and loose lips might cost them. Earn my trust and you will be brought into the fold. Understood?"

"Yes, sir." Nic saluted sharply. Catching the keys Gibzen tossed him, he unlocked the manacle, then the one around Marcus's ankle before he straightened. "Thank you, sir."

Teriana was certain Marcus would leave then. Would walk away, because it felt like every interaction caused the gulf between them to widen. Instead, as the manacle fell from his ankle, Marcus approached her.

"It is going to be hard," he said so softly that none of the others would be able to hear, though they were surely trying. "Violent. Ugly. And you won't be the same after it's over. Do you still want to go through with it?"

"Will you win my people free?"

"Yes." There was no arrogance in his voice, no vaingloriousness. Just utter certainty.

"Then do it," she whispered.

Marcus's eyes searched hers for a long moment, then he took her hand and uncurled her palm. The hair ornament had dug deep into her flesh, her sweat tinged with blood, but he picked it up without comment. Though hundreds, no, *thousands* of legionnaires watched on, he unwove one of the braids nearest to her face and strung the bead on her hair.

Her body trembled as he swiftly rebraided it, knotted the end, and stepped back. Showing not a care for the thousands of eyes judging the exchange.

Marcus had not lost his nerve.

Far from it.

"One last thing." His voice was low, and Teriana couldn't help but sway closer to him, anticipation burning in her chest as he said, "Make sure you do a good job. Servius will inspect after you're finished, and it will need to be up to Thirty-Seventh standards."

Her jaw dropped. "You aren't serious? I'm not cleaning that mess."

"Fair is fair." He scrubbed a hand over freshly cut hair, surveying the training men before he met her gaze again. "I've requested the

Thirty-First legion be sent to reinforce us. When they arrive, I'll invade Gamdesh."

Teriana's heart lurched. *Oh gods, it's happening.*

Marcus turned to walk away, but then paused and said, "Teriana, next time, don't break."

35

KILLIAN

"If there is one good takeaway from this disastrous turn of events," Agrippa said, "it's that I now know it's not just us mere mortal men who make mistakes while consumed with thoughts of a woman—even god-marked men with magical instincts are vulnerable."

"There is truly not a day that goes by that I don't regret not killing you." Killian again tested the ropes binding his wrists, and again found them secure.

"Don't bother," Agrippa advised. "The Anuk know their knots. And you'd be consumed by guilt if you killed me."

"I would not."

"Be silent," their captor snapped, and Killian shot him a look that promised death, and not a quick one.

Prince Xadrian's face was concealed by his face coverings, but the gleam in his brown eyes betrayed the smirk beneath them. Killian remembered that smirk and added another regret: not killing this little prince when he'd had the chance in Rotahn.

"While it's tempting to attribute this ill will to patriotism," Agrippa said, "I have a growing sense that there is something of a personal grievance between you and the dear prince."

"When I was stationed in Rotahn defending the Rowenes gold mines, he and I encountered each other a few times." Killian cast a sideways glance at Agrippa. "You're familiar with him?"

"In the early stages of planning the invasion, Rufina sent messengers to the Anuk to curry their favor, given Mudamora was a mutual enemy. All that came back were their heads. Queen Ceenah of Anukastre is apparently a faithful follower of the Six, and the chance to strike a blow at Mudamora was not worth endangering her immortal soul."

"Be silent," Xadrian ordered. "I grow weary of your ceaseless commentary and have a growing sense that your presence would be improved by the loss of your tongue."

"You aren't alone in that," Killian muttered, but Agrippa only sighed and said, "It would be a loss that would ripple across all of Reath."

For all Agrippa's commentary, Killian didn't miss the way the other man's arms flexed, testing his bindings. He'd already escaped once, dislocating his own thumb to do so, and though it had to hurt, Agrippa showed no more reaction to the pain than he had when he'd knocked out one of their guards and broken the arm of another earlier. The only reason he hadn't made a second attempt was because Xadrian now walked with his sword resting against the back of Malahi's neck.

Killian did not envy the boy his death if Agrippa escaped a second time.

Baird and Lydia walked unbound, their marks seeming to earn them courtesy. In truth, Malahi might have secured the same treatment if her mark was known.

Maybe.

The bad blood between House Rowenes and Anukastre was so thick it all but stained the land between their borders red with blood.

A fair bit of it, Killian had shed himself.

His eyes flicked to Lydia for the hundredth time, his fear that she'd risk the darkness to break them free more terrifying than the thirty armed Anuk who surrounded them. Yet her eyes were quartz-green and steady, as was her voice as she asked, "Where are you taking us?"

"To his mother," Agrippa said. "Isn't that right, Xadrian? You don't fart without asking Mummy which direction to blow your wind."

The Anuk prince appeared to have discovered some level of self-control in the time since Killian had last encountered him, for he only snorted in amusement. "You think to bait me into making a mistake, General? Because, yes, we do recognize the commander of Rufina's armies. I'd ask *why* you are fleeing in the company of Mudamora's queen, but I've already come to my own conclusion." He curved his blade, forcing Malahi's head to drop. "It's because the ugly shrew pisses gold."

"You're never going to know what it's like to shave more than peach fuzz, boy," Agrippa said, his voice light. "Nor hear your voice change from that of a child's to a man's. Certainly never enjoy the pleasures of desired company."

"Why, because you're going to kill me?" Xadrian asked with a laugh.

"Not kill, no," Agrippa said with a toothy smile. "I'm just going to cut off your balls and slow roast them over the ashes of your kingdom after I burn everyone within it alive."

The prince's smile fell away, and he shoved Malahi forward. "I think it will be you who burns, dog."

Agrippa opened his mouth, but Lydia said, "It is urgent that we return to Mudamora to combat the blight. While I understand you are motivated by past grievances, you put all of Reath in jeopardy by waylaying us."

"With respect, Marked One," Xadrian said, "I fail to see how *any* of you will halt that tide given that all of you are complicit in the hold it has over the wetlands."

Lydia was quiet for a long moment, then she said, "It is in Mudamora now. How long until it crosses the Liratoras into Anukastre, or drifts north into Gendorn? How long until it flows beneath the seas to the Southern Continent and the rest of Reath falls to the Corrupter? This isn't just Mudamora's fight—all of Reath needs to go to war against the evil threatening us."

Silence stretched, then Xadrian said, "The queen will decide. Now be silent, or you will be gagged."

Then one of the soldiers gave Killian a shove, sending him marching over the endless sea of sand in the exact opposite direction of Mudamora.

* * *

They were marched for days, the Anuk driving them deeper and deeper into the dunes. While Killian and the others flagged in the deep sand and unrelenting heat, their captors showed no ill effect from the toil of their journey. Baird suffered the worst, and although the Anuk gave him special care in deference to his mark, the giant collapsed several times, rousing only when they poured precious water into his mouth.

Even Agrippa relented on his attempts to break loose, seeming to recognize that it would be suicide to escape into the endless sand under the ceaseless burn of the sun.

After days of walking, Killian saw something in the distance, smelled moisture in the air. At first, he was certain it was a mirage, until he noted how the Anuk quickened their step. Anticipation filled their eyes, the only part of their faces he could see given the scarves they wore to protect their skin.

The distant shadow grew, the towering sandstone walls of a city emerging out of the heat waves that swayed across the dunes like a mirage. Yet what captured Killian's attention was the greenery beyond the walls. An oasis, there was no doubt, and his lips parted as he tasted the sweet moisture on the air.

"Welcome to Obarri," Xadrian said as gates opened in the walls ahead of them. "Heart of Anukastre. Very few foreigners have seen our city, so you should consider yourself privileged."

"How many have lived to tell the tale?" Agrippa muttered, and Xadrian laughed before he said, "None."

"Shocking." Agrippa's hazel eyes flicked to Killian's, and he knew the other man was already planning an escape. Except even if they could steal supplies and water, they had no knowledge of this part of the desert, so Killian couldn't help but wonder if escape would only be a slower death.

After days of sand and clothing designed to blend into it, the color of Obarri was a shock to the senses. The narrow, winding streets teemed with people dressed in every hue. Awnings stretched between buildings and shaded the Anuk from the oppressive sun as they stopped in their work to stare at the group. Around nearly every turn was a small courtyard filled with towering palms, their fronds swaying gently on the desert breeze and providing shade to pools of precious water ringed with emerald foliage. The walls of the building were adorned with cascading vines and blooming flora, the air infused with the heady fragrance of unfamiliar flowers in a multitude of colors, which mixed with the scent of grilling meat and spice. Music emanated from several of the buildings from some sort of stringed instrument, and silver chimes hung at the center of every intersection, their gentle metallic rhythm adding to what felt like a cacophony after the silence of the desert.

They wove their way into the heart of the city, to what Killian could only assume was the palace. It had no walls separating it but was surrounded by an open space paved with sandstone cobbles, a massive balcony on the third level of the structure overlooking it. The building itself was all straight lines and narrow windows, obviously built to withstand the intense heat, but the sandstone glittered as though it had been dusted with gold. They passed through the archway forming the entrance, the relief from the sun immediate, though it took Killian's eyes a long time to adjust to the dim light.

The gurgling fountain in the center of the foyer was the only sound to break the silence, and Killian's eyes skipped over the walls, which were decorated with elaborate motifs depicting the Six, a blank space left to acknowledge the Seventh. Except there was no time to appreciate the work, for Xadrian kept walking.

Two women bearing spears stood to the sides of a large set of bronze doors, the first sign of any guards or soldiers Killian had seen since they'd entered the city. Killian had no doubt that the lack of defenses was nothing more than an illusion, and judging from Agrippa's furrowed brow, he believed the same.

A dais sat at the far end of the room, on which sat an elaborately carved wooden bench. A small woman dressed in russet robes sat upon it, and her dark eyes glittered with interest as they approached. Xadrian's soldiers shoved Killian and Agrippa to their knees, doing the same to Malahi, although with less force. Lydia and Baird were left standing in deference to their marks.

"Your Majesty." Xadrian bowed low. "These individuals were captured within our borders. Because of their identities, we believed it prudent to bring them for your personal judgment, as for some, their crimes against Anukastre are beyond number." He gestured to Malahi. "The Rowenes vermin queen of Mudamora, who is apparently not quite as dead as her people believe." Then Agrippa. "Rufina's general, who has apparently abandoned his post for the sake of golden Rowenes—"

"Mind your tongue, my son," the queen cut him off.

Xadrian shrugged, then pointed to Killian. "Killian Calorian, the marked of Tremon responsible for the massacres along the border in the name of Ria Rowenes, who is said to be—"

"None of that is true," Killian interrupted before Xadrian could go the direction he knew the boy was going. "I'm guilty of plenty, but not that."

"You—"

"Xadrian, I know who he is. What of the others?"

"Lydia, marked healer of Hegeria," Xadrian muttered. "And Baird of Eoten Isle, marked by Gespurn."

The queen rose to her feet, a beam of sunlight from a window illuminating her face. Her skin was light brown, her hair black with only a touch of grey at the temples. For her to be Xadrian's mother, she must have had him at a very young age; only the faintest creases marked the corners of her eyes. "I am Ceenah," she said to them, progressing down the steps to move among them, sandaled feet making soft pats against the stone floor. "Interesting that the Six saw fit to deliver you all to me. They are not normally so reckless with their Marked Ones, so there must be some purpose to it."

"So that you can execute them for their crimes," Xadrian snapped.

"Countless of our people are dead because of them, and I would have vengeance."

Ceenah made a soft humming sound, and Killian couldn't help but wonder how such a seemingly levelheaded woman was responsible for an impulsive brat like Xadrian. Her eyes fixed on Malahi, and she said, "I see you suffered greatly as Rufina's prisoner, Your Grace. The majority of my people would see you suffer to the grave for the blood your family has on its hands. Given your own people believe you dead, I think you will not be missed."

Agrippa's eyes darkened, and before Killian could stop him, he moved.

Xadrian shouted a warning, but the ex-legionnaire was quick.

In a heartbeat, he had Ceenah's arm twisted behind her back, his other hand gripping her by the chin. Killian took advantage of the distraction, pulling Malahi and Lydia away, Baird backing up to the opposite wall.

"This is how it's going to go," Agrippa said to Xadrian and his men, who all had their weapons out, eyes full of fury. "You're going to back away from my companions. Then you're going to get us the supplies we need to leave this gods-forsaken dust bowl, and we're going to take Mother dearest with us. You do the smart thing and don't follow us, and I'll let her go. You test my patience, and I'll snap her neck. Now back up."

"I will gut you like a pig for this." Xadrian held his ground. "There will be no forgiveness for this insult."

"Gutting me won't bring her back to life. Now back out that door and get us what we need." Agrippa forced the queen's chin higher, and Ceenah grimaced in pain, though she said, "Hold your ground."

"Now is not the time for bravery, Your Grace." Agrippa's bicep flexed, pushing her head back to the point her neck would be on the verge of breaking. "Your threats make it clear that we have nothing to lose."

"Don't you?" Her tone was acidic, brown eyes narrow, and Killian tensed, every part of him screaming *danger* as she added, "There are many ways to die."

"I will gladly die for the sake of those who have the power to stop Rufina."

"Then you won't begrudge me this." Ceenah closed her hand over his wrist.

She didn't move, but Agrippa's face abruptly drained of color and Killian *knew.* "Corrupted!"

Agrippa attempted to rip free of Ceenah's grasp, but she held on even as his fist slammed into her cheek, then his foot into her knee. Malahi screamed, and Killian tried to go to Agrippa's aid, but Xadrian was already between them, weapon raised. "Let your foolish friend meet his end. It is what he deserves for serving the Seventh."

The ground abruptly shook and vines exploded into the room. Through the doors and windows and up from the floor. They wrapped around Ceenah, wrenching her away from Agrippa, who had aged fifty years in a matter of seconds. He fell backward, his head striking a step with a terrifying *crack*.

"Agrippa!" Malahi howled.

Xadrian lunged at her, but vines wrapped around his ankles and pinned him to the ground, then grew to form a wall blocking the rest of the Anuk soldiers.

Malahi's face was twisted with fury and grief. "You will die for this, corrupted!"

Ceenah's eyes were wide, but it wasn't fear that shone in them. "You're—"

Whatever she'd been about to say was cut off as the vine wrapped around her throat, strangling her.

Killian's skin crawled as though a million spiders danced across it, instincts screaming. This was wrong. This was a mistake. One he'd made before and wouldn't make again. "Malahi, stop! Don't kill her!"

She ignored him. Her eyes were on Baird, who'd reached Agrippa's side. The giant pulled his friend into his arms, tears streaming down his face, and Malahi howled with grief.

"Malahi!" Killian grabbed her shoulders, but a vine wrapped around his leg, jerking him off his feet.

Snatching up a sword one of Xadrian's men had dropped, Killian chopped at the vine, but more rushed to replace it. "Malahi, don't kill her!"

But Mudamora's queen was lost to grief and deaf to his words.

Ceenah was purpling as she clawed at her throat, but Killian couldn't get loose. Every time he cut a vine, another wrapped around him. Through the chaos, he saw Lydia edging toward Agrippa.

You cannot heal the dead. Death to the healer who tries. "Lydia!" he screamed. "Don't do it!"

The masses of vines were starting to take on a familiar shape, cocooning around Malahi like the corrupted tenders in Deadground, and through them, he saw Malahi's amber eyes had pooled black as voids.

"Malahi, stop!" He slashed at vine after vine but more kept coming. Pinning him down, smothering him. "Lydia!"

She didn't answer, and Killian didn't know if it was because she hadn't heard him over the noise, or if . . .

The vines abruptly went still.

Time seemed to stand still.

In the silence, Killian heard Agrippa say, "This is not who you are. You aren't a killer."

Agrippa was alive.

But at what cost?

The vines trembled, and then as one, began to retreat. Escaping out the doors and windows, back into the earth. Leaving behind a fractured mess of sandstone. Wide-eyed Anuk soldiers. A gasping Ceenah. And Malahi, shoulders shaking with sobs as she clung to Agrippa. Who looked not a day older than he ever had.

Which was impossible.

Killian's eyes skipped to where Lydia knelt next to Baird on the floor, pale-faced but very much alive.

What had happened?

Ceenah was the first to react. She pushed herself onto her hands and knees, eyes fixed on Malahi. "You're marked by Yara. A tender."

When Malahi didn't answer, the Queen of Anukastre said, "I think we need to set aside old grievances. There's something you must see."

36

LYDIA

Lydia's knees shook beneath her as Baird helped her to her feet, the giant's eyes wide as he asked, "What did you do?"

"Later," she replied, though the real answer was, *I don't know.*

"I don't want to see anything that you have to show me!" Malahi snarled at Ceenah. "I want you to allow me and my companions to leave with the supplies we need to cross the desert."

"So you can fight the blight."

"Yes," Malahi said from between her teeth. "It was created by corrupted tenders, so it stands to reason that a tender can drive it back."

"You're right," Ceenah said. "That's what I wish to show you. Come."

With seemingly no regard for the fact they'd nearly all killed each other or that Malahi had torn apart Ceenah's throne room, the Queen of Anukastre guided them through the palace to a wide set of stairs that led down into darkness.

Agrippa drew to a stop, keeping between Malahi and Ceenah. "If after all we've been through I discover that there is a prison down here, I'm not going to be happy, Your Grace. Do recall that I just saved your life."

"After you threatened to kill me," Ceenah answered, shooing Xadrian away as he started to draw his sword.

"Only because you *planned* to kill me."

"Which I'm considering again." Ceenah threw up her hands in annoyance, and Lydia noticed the bruising around her throat was already gone. That she healed as quickly as any corrupted. "It's the way to the underground lake, not a prison."

"Fine." Agrippa swept a hand toward the staircase. "You go first."

The queen looked to the stone stairs, then back at Agrippa. "I'm not going anywhere with *you* at my back."

"Together, then?" Agrippa held out his arm. Frowning, Ceenah took his elbow, the pair of them walking side by side down the steps. Malahi and Xadrian eyed each other warily before following them.

"What in the name of the Six happened?" Killian asked, stepping close to Lydia as they followed, Baird and the rest of Xadrian's soldiers taking up the rear. "Are you all right?"

She gave a tight nod, though in truth, she was rattled. Agrippa's head wound had been bad, it was true, but when she'd first set eyes on him, he'd been old. Frail.

Which she shouldn't have been able to do anything about.

Except there had been a pool of life floating in the throne room, and though she could not quite explain how, Lydia had known it belonged to Agrippa. She'd been able to put it back into him, using herself as a conduit rather than a source of life. It was a miraculous discovery, yet it was not lost on Lydia that the only thing that had made it possible was that Ceenah hadn't kept any of the life she'd taken from Agrippa. She'd pulled it out of him and released it into the room. Anukastre's queen had used Hegeria's mark as a weapon, but by not keeping it for herself, seemed to have avoided corruption. Her eyes hadn't turned to black voids with a ring of flame, only remained the solid brown they were now.

Lydia had a thousand questions she wished to ask the woman, but would Ceenah be forthcoming given the violence that had erupted between the two groups? Would she be willing to teach Lydia the secret to weaponizing her mark given they were from enemy nations?

As they descended, a hallowed stillness enveloped Lydia, soothing her frantic need for answers. The stairs ended, revealing a grand cavern, its walls bearing oil sconces that reflected off the perfectly smooth surface of the lake. The air was saturated with the aroma of damp stone and clean water. As she stared into the midnight pool, Lydia was struck with the sense that if she dived in and swam down, she'd never find a bottom.

"This way." Ceenah led them along the water's edge, the glow of her lamp revealing that the walls of the cavern had been used as canvases: each panel depicted a different scene rendered with skillful strokes that seemed to breathe life into the stone.

"This place is old," Ceenah said. "Far older than Obarri itself, which was built upon the ruins of a civilization whose name has been lost to time. Yet the paintings remain, telling us the stories of the people who have come before."

Lydia took in the artwork, tales of this long-forgotten civilization unfurling as they circled the lake. Paintings of men and women traversing the lands, their shadows elongated by the sun. Warriors battling enemies wearing helmets in the shapes of beasts. Stories of love and loss, wars waged in defense, and tender moments between people whose names were as lost as the civilization itself. Each brushstroke was imbued with a whisper of forgotten history, and the academic in her longed to pause and drink them in, but Ceenah kept walking.

The cavern narrowed, then opened up again into another grand space, the only light from the lamp Ceenah carried. The images here were of the gods and their marked, the scenes seeming to serve the same purpose as Treatise of the Seven in that they depicted the acts of the marked in service to the people.

No one spoke as Ceenah finally stopped, holding up her lamp to reveal a series of scenes.

"This is not the first time the land has been infected by blight." Malahi reached out to touch the winding black snakes branching through the ground, originating from a ball of vines painted in the same sickening green that Lydia had seen in Deadground. Men, women, and children were shown on their knees, black lines running across their skin, and then again dead at the feet of warriors. But the tableau grew grimmer, mountains of corpses, trees and plants the color of ash, the hopelessness making Lydia's eyes burn with tears of empathy, for she knew well how they had felt.

Yet it was the last scenes that stole her breath. Three people knelt with their hands to the ground, the blight retreating, to end with a scene of life teeming in an oasis.

"They defeated it," Lydia whispered, moving to stand next to Malahi. "This room holds stories of the marked, so those have to be tenders driving back the blight." Rounding on Ceenah, she asked, "Is there a similar depiction for one of Hegeria's marked? Something that shows those infected by blight being cured?"

The queen shook her head. "No. This is the only record I've seen of it. The only record, I believe, that has survived the intervening time. That we know of, at least."

"Why didn't you bring this information to Mudamora the moment you learned the blight had invaded us?" Malahi demanded. "If you knew there was a way to stop it, why not share the information?"

"I did," Ceenah answered. "Via the Maarin, who are ever impartial, I sent a letter to King Serrick. Your father either dismissed it as false information because we are enemies, or his tenders tried and failed. I suspect the former, but only the Six can say."

"Perhaps it is false," Agrippa abruptly said. "You say this painting is ancient, yet it is unfaded as though it were painted ten years ago. Or *yesterday.*"

Lydia winced, and next to her, Killian muttered, "Why can you never be silent, Agrippa?"

"Are you accusing me of deceit?" Ceenah's tone was icy. "Accusing me of fabricating images of Marked Ones in order to mislead a young woman I didn't even know was one of Yara's until she tried to kill me?"

"When you put it that way, it seems unlikely," Agrippa conceded. "Except it's still not proof of anything. Perhaps the artist was depicting drought or locusts or any number of natural things. How can we know for sure that these black squiggles"—he gestured to the walls—"are blight?"

"Look around at all the pictures you've seen." Ceenah rested her hands on her hips. "Tell me, do any of them look like the Anukastre you've journeyed across?"

"They're all green," Malahi breathed. "The ground is lush and full of life."

"These paintings are all that remain of that era," Ceenah said. "Yet I believe that so much was lost to the blight that the land never recovered. That despite the myriad of underground rivers that flow down from the mountains, Anukastre turned to sand."

"But the same tenders who defeated the blight could have brought life back to the lands. Why didn't they?" Malahi asked, and Lydia could feel the other woman's worry, because most of Mudamora's population wouldn't survive life in a desert.

"I have no answers," Ceenah said.

"What of your own tenders?" Malahi pressed her hands flat against her trousers as though wiping away nervous sweat. "If they were able to create the life we've seen in Obarri, why not expand their reach? Why not make Anukastre green again?"

"We have no tenders." Ceenah looked away. "Yara has cast her eyes away from Anukastre, and all that you have seen was built and cultivated by mortal hands and talent. You are the first of Yara's marked to step foot here in living memory."

Not for the first time, Lydia wanted to scream that she'd not asked more of Hegeria when they'd spoken. The Six had witnessed all this, knew the answers, knew what was to be done, yet they seemed content for their marked to flounder in the dark. Why was that? They obviously did not want the Corrupter to consume Reath, yet they refused to reveal the information needed to drive it back.

"I . . . I could try," Malahi offered. "There is much to work with here in Obarri, and a great deal of water. Maybe I could make Anukastre look like this again." She gestured to the paintings.

"I thank you, Your Grace, but no." Ceenah inclined her head. "We are accustomed to our way of life, and the desert protects us from our enemies to the north and to the east."

Malahi gave a slow nod, then said, "Perhaps a better path would be for those in the east to be your enemies no longer. My father is dead, Your Grace. I am the High Lady of House Rowenes and the Queen of Mudamora. It is within my power, if you will it also."

"It is something to be considered," Ceenah admitted.

"Would you also consider lending your army to the fight?" Killian asked. "We have a common enemy, and if Mudamora falls, it will not be long before that enemy turns on Anukastre."

"The blight needs life to consume in order to spread," Ceenah answered. "The same dunes that protect us from human enemies will protect us from the corrupted use of tender power, for there is nothing here for them to take. My people are already few. I'll not risk them fighting Mudamora's battles."

"But—"

"No." Ceenah's voice brooked no argument. "I will aid you in returning to the coast, where you will surely find a Maarin ship willing to deliver you back to Mudamora. But I will not involve myself or my people in this fight."

"Coward," Agrippa muttered, but Ceenah only replied, "We will grant you time to eat and rest, then my son will escort you to the coast. That you keep your lives is concession enough on my part, and one I make only in deference to the gods who marked you or"—she cast a cold glare at Agrippa—"those protected by the marked."

"This is all well and good," Baird said, speaking for the first time since they'd entered the caverns. "Except you have weather rolling in from the west, and in Anukastre, that means a sandstorm. None of us are going anywhere just yet."

37

TERIANA

It all happened with what felt like impossible speed.

Logically, Teriana knew speed was the Empire's greatest weapon, their control over countless xenthier paths allowing them to transport both men and information so quickly that their enemies had no chance to prepare. Yet even with Quintus filling her ears with information about relay systems and men trained to find the fastest route for information to travel, her stomach still dropped when word came that the Thirty-First legion had crossed through the Bardeen stem and were on their way to Aracam.

Marcus didn't even give them the opportunity to unpack. He allowed the older legion only part of a night's rest, the majority of which they spent fraternizing with the Thirty-Seventh, and then the entire camp began the process of readying to board the fleet of ships waiting in Aracam's harbor. The plan to invade via a bridge over the Orinok was apparently only a ruse so that Kaira would send soldiers to defend the fortress there, lessening the defenses of Emrant. Though last she'd heard, five hundred of the Thirty-Seventh remained there with Rastag, working steadily on the bridge.

Though this was the path Teriana had chosen to walk, there was a part of her that desperately wished to backtrack and find another road, especially once she got a look at the Thirty-First. Well into their twenties, the legionnaires were *hard* in a way that even the Thirty-Seventh hadn't achieved, but it was how they interacted with Marcus's legion that made the reality of what she'd unleashed so terrifying. The Thirty-Seventh treated the Fifty-First like little brothers. The Forty-First like an irritation they had to put up with. But the Thirty-First? These men they treated like comrades, for they'd fought side by side more than once.

She'd watched Marcus walking with their legatus, Zimo, who was a tall man clearly born to Faul Province, judging from his midnight hair and the shape of his eyes, and they clearly got along swimmingly.

"They were a few years ahead of us at Lescendor, and Marcus is friendly with Zimo because of a deal they made over soap," Quintus had told her with a yawn when the Thirty-First arrived. "Good men to have at your back. Even better to share a drink with, but don't gamble with them. Notorious cheaters."

"Noted." She'd watched the older legionnaires pass their tent, eyes raking over her with cool curiosity. This was what would be invading Gamdesh. This was the force she'd brought to the West.

Her allies.

Yet as the thousands upon thousands of Empire legionnaires made their way to Aracam's harbor, Teriana knew it was too late to go back.

Though the shocking inefficiency of the process was giving her many more hours to come to terms with it.

"This is a mess." She wiped sweat from her brow as she watched two groups of men from different legions trying to converge down a street, their centurions barking at each other that they had the right of way. Where hours before they'd been friends and comrades, the disorganization, compounded by the incredible heat of the day, had several of the centurions looking close to blows. And noise of the same was coming from across Aracam as Marcus's army, nearly twenty thousand men, all tried to move toward the harbor to be loaded onto the waiting ships. It was already late afternoon, the sun low on the horizon, and only a third of the Thirty-First legion had been loaded onto the ten newly arrived Katamarcan ships. At this rate, it would be past midnight before the fleet could set sail.

Quintus pulled off his helmet to wipe sweat from his brow, which was furrowed as he panned the chaos of shouting, sweating legionnaires. "The signals are all conflicting," he said. "Whoever is giving out the orders must be drunk. I don't envy the punishment Marcus will dole out, because this will have him right pissed off."

Teriana was inclined to agree. Yet as she shaded her eyes to better see Marcus where he stood at the end of the dock with a group of officers, the only sign he gave that he was aware of the disorganization was the scowl on his face each time he glanced toward the city. Her instincts jangled in her head, *nothing* about this process a reflection of Cel efficiency, and certainly none of it a reflection of the way Marcus ran his legions.

"Why isn't he doing something about this?" she grumbled to herself, touching the tiny ship resting against her cheek, where it had been since Marcus had put it there. "If this carries on, we're going to have legions fighting legions in the streets of Aracam."

"It is a bit out of character." The amusement in Quintus's voice caused her to glance sharply at him as he added, "One might almost wonder if it were by design."

"To what end?" she demanded. "Is he trying to convince any spies watching that he's so disorganized that he's not a threat? They've been watching this camp for months; there is no chance that they're going to be fooled."

Quintus lifted one shoulder. "How should I know? It's not like Marcus shares his plans with me."

Or with her.

Teriana's already tense muscles balled into tighter knots of anxiety. "Don't give me excuses, Quintus. You have fought under his command all your life—you have at least an idea of what he's planning."

Quintus shoved his helmet back down on his head. "The only thing I know for certain is that the plan that was communicated to the legion *isn't* Marcus's plan. Other than Felix and Servius, and possibly Nic, I suspect not a single soul knows the entirety of what he's got cooked up in his head. I'd hazard that even Zimo has only been given instructions pertaining to his part in all of this. All we can do is wait and see how it plays out."

Out of the corner of her eye, the black tower of the Seventh moved.

Teriana stumbled into Quintus, a gasp of horror tearing from her lips because the tower was leaning over Aracam, the eyes carved into it watching the legions with cruel malevolence. Then she blinked, and it was standing straight again.

"Did you see it move?" Quintus said quietly.

"Yes." It felt like lunacy to admit, but though the legionnaires were all carrying on as they had, Teriana had seen what she had seen.

"I've seen it." Her friend eyed the tower. "And I've heard others muttering the same. The Arinoquians say it is sentient, a vessel for the Seventh god, but the centurions say it's just heat sickness getting to those on duty."

"It's not heat sickness." Her throat was dry. "Tearing down the other towers gave the Seventh god power here. They need to be rebuilt."

"That's not going to happen."

Teriana rubbed her hands up and down her arms, chilled. All of this was on her. All of it.

Turning back to the harbor, she asked, "How long has he been negotiating with Queen Erdene?"

How long has Katamarca been an ally of the Empire?

"Queen Erdene made overtures to Titus not long after you two disappeared," Quintus said. "She wanted formal trade terms with the Senate once paths between the East and West were safely established, likely assuming that the best terms will go to the first movers."

"What's in it for her?"

Quintus shrugged. "The Katamarcans seemed eager to be the Senate's new allies. Titus suggested they become the first Cel province in the West."

"I take it Titus failed to mention that Erdene would be deposed so a Cel senator can assume governorship?"

"I'm sure he kept that to himself," Quintus answered. "Though it's possible she knows. The Maarin aren't holding back, if the rumors coming into Aracam's ports are accurate. Katamarca's military is weak, so she likely hopes by aiding the Empire in a move north, we'll spend our strength against Gamdesh, giving her a fighting chance if we ever look south. In a sea of poor options, she chose the most intelligent path."

"How is this intelligent?" she demanded, well aware of her own hypocrisy given she was *also* an ally to the Empire.

Quintus didn't answer, and Teriana glanced at Marcus, only to find him still at the end of the docks, crimson cloak swirling on the breeze, the gold thread of the dragon gleaming in the sun. His helmet was tucked under his arm, armor freshly polished, but even from this distance, she could tell he was tired. And no wonder, because in the days since he'd fired back at everyone who'd thought he'd lost his nerve, he'd not ceased working. The flow of information coming in and out of the camp had been nonstop. Messages from spies up and down the coast. Messages from the Empire, which all came via heavily armed escort. Messages he sent back, guarded with equal care. From dawn until well past the midnight hour, and though he seemed steady on his feet, the way Racker had been storming about camp recently told Teriana everything she needed to know about the surgeon's thoughts on the matter.

Teriana, next time, don't break.

She touched the tiny ship, remembering the feel of his fingers braiding her hair. He hadn't meant that he needed her to hold her ground when faced with a charge on a battlefield. He'd meant that she needed to trust that he had her back, no matter what came next. And that she had his, even if the gulf between them was as wide as ever.

She did trust him. Yet seeing those Katmarcan naval vessels sail into the harbor demonstrated just how hard rolling back this invasion would be after her people were freed. "I suppose it never occurred to me that any of the rulers in the West would ally with the Empire," she said. "I believed they'd fight until the end."

Her skin crawled, and Teriana shifted her gaze from Marcus to the Corruptor's tower, but it stood static. Nothing but stone.

Quintus sighed. "What Katamarca faces is something I've only known from the side of the conqueror. It has been so long since anyone *attacked* Celendor that, if not for history books, it would be lost to memory. We are always the attackers, always the invaders, always on the offense, so we don't even think of what it's like to *be* invaded. What it's like making choices to protect our own people. What it feels like to protect. That said, my gut tells me that Erdene took a look at the odds, and this is her roll of the dice."

Teriana watched the Thirty-First slowly board the massive ship. There were ten vessels, all of which would cost a small fortune to build. Katamarca hadn't rolled the dice—they were all in. The only uncertainty was how Marcus intended to use them.

Though no matter his plan, the results would be the same. Kaira had refused to deal, which meant a battle was coming. The ships would sail north, would land, would fight the Gamdeshians until one side was defeated. In her heart, she knew who would lose.

How many would die?

How many people were going about their lives, entirely unaware that these coming days would be their last? Unaware that their end was near, whether it be by hunger or on the tip of a legionnaire's gladius or beneath the heels of a thousand feet.

What are five hundred lives compared to the millions in Gamdesh?

They're everything.

They're—

A piercing shriek from above ripped Teriana back into the moment. Her heart leapt to her throat as the giant hawk circled low above the massed legions with no care for the danger they posed to her.

Marcus glanced upward, then shouted, "Shoot her, you idiots! She's a spy for the enemy!"

The legionnaires within earshot were all boarding, but they scrambled for weapons. Arrows were fired, but all too late, for Astara had already soared out to sea, heading north to report what she'd seen to Kaira.

"Interesting that he didn't anticipate she'd be watching," Quintus murmured. "Now if I were a betting man—"

"Which you are," Teriana snapped.

"—I might suggest that he *wanted* her to fly north to give Kaira a report on our activities." He hesitated, then nodded and pointed. "Look."

A flicker of light flashed across the sky, as though a bit of glass were catching the light of the setting sun.

"Past the first scout." Quintus lifted a hand to shade his eyes from the sun, nodding as another light flashed. "And the second."

Teriana's eyes moved to Marcus, who was berating the legionnaires boarding the ship for sluggishness and seemingly not paying the slightest bit of attention to the scouts' signals.

"And the third," Quintus said.

Felix reached out to touch Marcus's arm, and what had obviously been false outrage at the men's failure to shoot Astara disappeared. He and Zimo exchanged swift words. Zimo nodded with an approving expression, then he called out orders and a centurion strode up and down the dock, screaming more commands in the aggressive fashion every man of that rank seemed to use.

Teriana felt the *shift*.

Where they'd been dragging their heels, now the Thirty-First moved with the speed and efficiency the Cel were known for, every man knowing exactly what he was supposed to be doing and where he needed to be, all while Marcus continued to instruct the officers, each of them nodding in approval of what she could only assume was his explanation of his *real* plan.

It was happening.

Gods help her, it was happening.

Teriana's heart was in her throat, pulse roaring, but there was nothing she could do but stand there as Marcus and Zimo clasped arms. The latter laughed with obvious delight as he turned on his heel to stride up the gangplank, the ships at the neighboring docks already running out sweeps to move the vessels into deeper waters.

The *underloaded* ships.

Rather than the waiting vessels moving into empty berths to be filled with more legionnaires, they raised their sails. "What is . . ."

She trailed off as Marcus started walking down the dock, Nic and Felix following at his heels.

The wind from the water caught at Marcus's crimson and gold cloak, sending it floating out behind him as he walked. Face expressionless, he said something to Felix, who lifted an arm. A signalman from the Thirty-Seventh hurried up the dock, listened to Felix's orders, and then lifted a signal flag, the fabric slashing this way and that in such rapid motions that Teriana couldn't parse the meaning.

"It would appear we aren't sailing to Gamdesh after all," Quintus said, and Teriana's stomach twisted into knots even as the horns that had been blasting through the city all afternoon echoed the signalman's orders.

"He's ordered a march north," Quintus continued. "Double time, no torches."

Teriana barely heard her friend, for Marcus had reached the end of the dock. His eyes went first to the hair ornament resting against her cheek and then to her eyes. "Last chance. Do you want to join the *Quincense* or march?" He hesitated, then added, "Quintus will go with you, regardless of your choice."

Guilt made her chest clench, because if she said yes, Quintus would be reunited with Miki, but as she met her friend's gaze, he shook his head. "Don't make the decision because of me."

"Can't he go without me?" she asked.

"No."

"You're an asshole," she muttered.

"An asshole on a schedule." Marcus mounted his new golden mare. "Quintus, if it's to be a march, take one of the horses. Otherwise, safe travels. You'll receive word when we've taken Emrant." Then he dug in his heels and trotted his mount after Felix.

She touched the miniature ship that brushed her cheekbone, swallowing hard. She'd told Astara that the legions were her weapon to wield to free her people, and she'd soon discover how deep that weapon cut.

The legions flowed out of Aracam with all the precision and discipline the Cel were known for. What had moments before been a harbor market teeming with angry legionnaires was now empty except for the few hundred men from the Forty-First who would remain to hold Aracam.

One of them approached with a horse, holding out the reins to Quintus. Mounting, he held a hand down to her. "What do you want to do?"

She stared at her friend's calloused hand, part of her wondering what the point was in marching with the legions given that she could not affect the plans nor control the outcome of the war that *she* had set in motion. That part of her wanted to scream, to throw herself into the surf and rage at Madoria for setting her on a path too steep to climb. A path that seemed destined to destroy her.

Yet the other part, the *stronger* part, curled its lip in disgust, because in all her life, Teriana had never once given up. She'd faced insurmountable odds before and persevered, and she refused to concede now. So she grasped Quintus's hand. "I'm sorry. I need to see this through."

"Nothing to be sorry for." He pulled her behind him in the saddle and heeled the horse into the fading glow of the setting sun.

38

LYDIA

Baird's warning about a coming storm proved to be accurate, for as soon as they exited the underground caverns, Lydia heard the wind. Servants ignored the mess that was the throne room in favor of hurrying about the palace to pull shutters into place over the narrow windows, casting the whole building into darkness broken only by the lamps on the walls. They were led to a series of neighboring rooms. Baird disappeared into one, Agrippa and Malahi into another. The servant directed her and Killian to the last, the man clearly of the belief that they desired to share.

With what had happened between them during the sandstorm at the base of the escarpment, Lydia knew there was no lack of *desire* on either of their parts, yet both of them stood outside the door, the awkwardness so intense that Lydia's cheeks burned. To cut the tension, Lydia blurted out, "I want to talk to you about what happened with Agrippa."

"About how he can't keep his gods-damned mouth shut?" Killian muttered.

"More about the part that he's not an old man." She reached for the handle, and opened the door.

The large bedroom was beautifully appointed, with a floor set with tiles of rich amber, gold, and terracotta laid in a pattern that resembled the dunes outside the oasis. The walls were decorated with vibrant tapestries depicting the six but her eyes went to the large bed. Low to the ground and made of sandstone, it had silk covers of a bright azure blue and pillows embroidered with golden thread, the mattress beneath plump and inviting.

"The spoils of war," Killian growled. "I can't begin to tell you how much gold they've stolen from Rowenes mines. It makes me wonder how much of Ceenah's murmurs of peace are just talk, because without plunder, they have no economy."

"They may have other resources we don't know about." She took a seat on a low cushion before an equally low stone table. It had writing tools on it, along with glasses and a carafe of water, and she drank from it greedily.

"That could be poisoned," he muttered.

"Poison doesn't really seem like Ceenah's first choice."

"The best choice is the unexpected choice." Killian dragged over another large cushion and sat down awkwardly. "They still haven't returned our weapons."

"Would you?"

He sighed, then poured a glass of water. "I saw what happened with Ceenah and Agrippa. She aged him like a corrupted would, but her eyes didn't change. Which is interesting in and of itself, but more interesting is that you aren't supposed to be able to put life back into a person who has had it stolen, yet Agrippa looks the same age as he did yesterday."

"Because she didn't keep the life she took out of him," Lydia explained. "She just dumped it into the room. I could see it floating like a cloud, and I was able to draw it in and give it back to him."

"I've never heard of such a thing." Killian rubbed his chin, stubble having grown into a short beard during their travels. "But when Agrippa paid that corrupted in Deadground to heal me, the man took some of Agrippa's life to do it. Acted like a conduit. Agrippa said something about Rufina forbidding the practice, but that many of the corrupted bent the rules for gold. We can ask Agrippa if he knows more."

"That's almost exactly what Ceenah did." Lydia traced the design carved into the tabletop with her finger, noting that her gloves were getting worse for wear. "It seems that by using her mark as a weapon to protect herself rather than for personal gain, she doesn't invite the Corrupter in." Giving a sharp shake of her head, she added, "That seems too insignificant a loophole to pass the scrutiny of the gods, though."

"Is it?" Killian sipped on his water, brown eyes thoughtful. "I use my mark to defend myself and others constantly. Have used it to injure and kill countless people. We've seen Malahi turn plants into a weapon and Baird do the same with the weather. Why shouldn't you be able to use your gift to protect yourself?"

"I . . ." Lydia swallowed hard, feeling incredibly overwhelmed with the possibility. The ability to defend herself had become almost an obsession in her mind, but she did not want strength to come at the cost of being a monster. If there was another path . . . Her eyes burned, and she squeezed them shut before tears could spill down her cheeks.

She heard Killian move next to her, then his arms were around her body, pulling her against his chest. "I know what this means to you," he said. "You don't need to hide that from me, because it means a lot to me as well."

A sob tore from Lydia's lips, and she twisted to bury her face in his neck, feeling the prickle of days away from a razor as his chin brushed her forehead. His hand moved up and down her back in wordless comfort as she cried. The revelation of hope for Mudamora, and for herself, was somehow more overwhelming than all the horror they'd faced.

Only when all the tears in her were spent did her sobs cease, and Killian said, "Do you know how to do what Ceenah did? Can you replicate it?"

"I'm not sure." She wiped her nose on her filthy sleeve, well aware that she was desperately in need of a wash and fresh clothes. "I know how to take the life in. I know how to put it into a person. Only I've never tried to do one into the other, and certainly not to take and just . . . dump it into the air. Yet obviously it's possible."

"Ceenah may be willing to teach you," he said. "For all she has denied us an alliance and the army that would come with it, it doesn't seem she's willing to withhold knowledge of the workings of the gods, good and bad, else why did she send information about the blight to Serrick? The worst thing she might do is say no, and then you can figure it out yourself." He hesitated. "You can try it on me, if you want."

Lydia's breath hitched as he lifted one of her hands, slowly peeling up the leather of her glove. It was sticky with sweat, her hands dirty and her nails ringed with grime. To cover her rising panic, she choked out, "I really need a bath."

"We all need a bath," he murmured, removing his own glove, and holding his hand up so that there was only an inch between her palm and his. "I trust you, Lydia. If you can't trust yourself, trust that I can take care of myself. Or at the very least scream for Agrippa to rescue me."

There was a sudden thump against the wall, then another and another, and Lydia's cheeks colored. "I think perhaps he's occupied."

"I was wondering when he'd find the courage," Killian said with a laugh, glancing at the wall separating the rooms and shaking his head before returning his scrutiny to her. "Truthfully, I might rather die than scream for his help, because he'd never let me live it down."

"True." Her laughter faded as she examined their hands, her focus shifting to the brilliant light of life surrounding his skin, the allure of it palpable, even now. "I don't know if I can do it again."

"I won't make you."

"I know."

Quivering, she slowly pressed her palm to his larger one. Killian's skin was warm, callused from a lifetime of combat, and her breath hitched as their fingers interlocked, because she wanted this so badly. Wanted to be able to touch him, to show with her hands, her lips, her body how she felt in her heart.

Take it.

The voice entered her thoughts like poison, and she jerked away. "I can't. I just can't."

Snatching up her glove, Lydia twisted away from him, pacing the room. Furious at herself for not being able to do such a small thing. For being weak. For having no self-control. She pressed her forehead against the wall, seeking calm, only for the sounds of Agrippa and Malahi doing exactly what she wanted to do with Killian to invade her ears. Their freedom to do whatever they wanted with no consequence sent a sudden rush of jealousy through her veins, a scream rising in her throat to tell them to *shut up.*

Killian's hands pressed down on her shoulders. "Think of how far you've come in such a short time," he said. "Not so long ago, you could barely look at me without feeling the Corrupter's pull. Now you can sleep at my side with no fear in your heart." He rotated her and pulled her into his arms, pressing his lips to her forehead. "Your hands are just the last little piece you need to gain victory over."

"They aren't a little thing."

"But they are the last thing." His voice was steady as he gently pushed her across the room. "There's a bathing chamber in here. Go get cleaned up, put on the clothes the Anuk have given you, and then go ask to speak to Ceenah. Listen to what she has to say before you leap to conclusions."

"What are you going to do?" she asked, unable to keep the misery from her voice.

Picking up a banana from the tray of fruit that had been left for them, Killian said, "I'm going to find Xadrian."

"Why?" She made a face. "He's awful."

"Because my gut tells me it's the right thing to do." He walked backward toward the door. "You know I always trust my innards when there is an important decision to be made."

Lydia smiled, unable to help herself because it had been so long since she'd seen him smirk like that. "Be careful."

"Unlikely." He winked at her, and then disappeared out the door.

* * *

In the bathing chamber, she discovered a narrow tub filled with cool water, along with several choices of soap, and the pleasure of washing away days upon days of filth from her skin and hair did much to ease her distress.

As she dressed in the loose trousers and tunic made of linen that had been left for her use, Lydia put her mind to all she'd learned in the space of a day that could change everything. They finally had proof of their suspicions that Malahi had the power to drive back the blight, if not exact answers as to how. Yet the knowledge that it had been done before, along with how aggressively Rufina had first tried to corrupt Malahi and then fought to get her back, was a glowing beacon of hope where once there'd been only a candle.

Lydia pulled on her worn boots and then went to the door. The corridor was empty. Baird's snoring emanated from the room down the hall, along with the faint howling of the wind outside the thick sandstone of the palace, but she heard no other sign of other people. Lydia felt an abrupt sense of claustrophobia, knowing they were trapped inside the building for some time, at least according to

Baird. She brushed away the sensation and tentatively knocked on the door to the room shared by her other two companions.

"Who is it?" Agrippa asked from the far side.

"Lydia."

The door cracked and the ex-legionnaire peeked through, what looked like a candlestick held in one of his hands. Seemingly satisfied, he opened the door and stepped out, closing it most of the way behind him. "She's asleep," he said in Cel, showing no discomfort about his shirtless state, the 37 tattoo on his chest black against his golden-brown skin. "Where's Killian?"

"He went to talk to Xadrian. Is Malahi well?" She answered in Cel too, in case anyone was listening to them.

Agrippa scrubbed a hand through his brown hair, then shook his head. "Worried. I think it's safe to say that tenders have the power to cure the blight, but she has no idea how to do it, as her previous attempt yielded nothing. There's always trial and error, but that takes time we don't have."

"And you're worried that she'll be harmed in the process?"

He eyed her for a long moment, the intelligence that he usually hid behind sarcasm, insults, and jokes peeking out. "Yeah. Malahi says that the blight can't harm the marked, but . . ." He shrugged. "She says the library in Revat has the largest and oldest collection of books in the West, so it might have answers. But having done my own fair share of library research while at Lescendor, that's going to take time, even if the Gamdeshians help. Needle in the haystack, and all that."

"You have a better idea?" she asked, the visual of him sitting in a library doing research odd to her even though she knew all legionnaires received more education than just how to kill.

"No. Those are the two options; I'm just acknowledging that both are shitty and that the odds are not in our favor." He gave a soft laugh as she scowled at him. "You're far too easy to provoke, Lydia. You really need to work on that if you want to be my friend."

"I don't." She crossed her arms. "And I didn't come here to hear your opinions on my character."

"I'm not waking up Malahi. She's exhausted."

"I'm here to talk to you. Specifically, about how for a moment in time, you looked around ninety years old and ready to breathe your last, and I was able to return you to a man of . . ."

"Twenty years," he supplied. "Thank you for that, by the way. For all my grand speech, I'm not actually looking to die right now. I've a fair bit to live for." He glanced back into the room, then his eyes returned to Lydia's. "Ceenah seemed a bit put out to be referred to as corrupted, though they are the only ones I've ever seen use their marks to both heal and kill. And when they did heal, it was never their own lives that they used. They always took from someone else. Rufina forbade the practice."

Lydia perked up at that reminder, because Derin's queen did little without reason. "Did she give a reason why?"

"She wasn't in the habit of explaining herself, but I always figured it was because she wanted her minions fully committed to the Corrupter. Though in all honesty, sucking the life out of a prisoner in order to heal the injuries of a soldier willing to pay was plenty corrupted."

On that count, she agreed. "Did you ever see one of them take life out of a person but not keep it? I don't mean pass it on to someone else for coin, but just . . . dump it out into the world?"

Agrippa barked out an incredulous laugh. "Are you joking? They're all addicts, Lydia. You know that. That's the last thing one of them would do."

"Well, it's what Ceenah did, and it's why you're still good-looking enough to interest Malahi."

"Thank you for the compliment." He smirked, but then his brow furrowed in thought. "If you could learn to do that . . . Lydia, if you could learn to take life in the defense of your own without getting all punch drunk on murder and falling back into bed with the Corrupter, you'd be a force to be reckoned with." He smiled, and this time it was genuine, with not a hint of mockery. "It's been an age since I lost a fight, but I lost to Anukastre's queen sure and true. You should really talk to her."

"I was planning on it."

"Good." He stepped back into the room. "Now if you'll excuse me, I'm going to go make good use of my second chance at life." Agrippa shut the door in her face.

"Ass," Lydia muttered, not remotely willing to admit she was becoming fond of the ex-legionnaire in the way one might feel about a particularly irritating brother. Then she started down the corridor, searching until she found a servant, who inclined his head respectfully. "Marked One."

Nerves flooded her, making it hard to speak. If Ceenah refused to see her . . . Lydia shoved away her insecurities, and said, "I would like to request an audience with your queen."

39

KILLIAN

Killian didn't like the palace.

It made sense that the building could be shut in against the sandstorms, but with every window and door sealed, not an ounce of natural light to be seen, it felt to Killian like a tomb.

The Anuk gave him wide berth as he passed, eyes full of equal parts distrust and dislike, which he supposed was fair. The blood between Mudamora and Anukastre had been bad for generations, and while it was primarily heated between them and the Rowenes family, Killian had made his own reputation. Some of that had been lies and deception perpetuated by Malahi's cousin, Ria Rowenes, but not all.

He'd let his own darkness take hold of him in those endless weeks spent defending the border. Angry about Lydia's choice to join Hegeria's temple. Guilty about not being there when Malahi was taken by Rufina. He'd been harder because of it. Crueler when he'd fought. Only Sonia and Finn had kept him from crossing the line, and it was the latter who now consumed his thoughts as he searched the sprawling palace for Xadrian.

He trusted Sonia. She'd served under his command as one of Malahi's bodyguards, then remained at his side as his lieutenant when he'd traveled to Rotahn to guard the Rowenes gold mines. She would do her best to keep Finn safe, but the orphan and self-styled king of Mudaire's sewers wouldn't make it easy on her. Finn was used to going his own way. Though Killian had made him his squire, he'd left the boy behind when he'd ventured into Derin, and Killian remembered the hurt on Finn's face when he'd left. How long would he stay with Sonia before going back to his old habits of crime and life on the streets? Streets that had to be even more dangerous than when Killian had left Mudamora, because he had no doubt that the Corrupter's influence had only spread.

Please keep him safe, he silently prayed, picking up the sound of clashing blades and following it. *Protect him, especially from himself.*

Turning down a corridor, Killian stopped in front of an open door, watching Xadrian spar against two men and a woman. The prince had discarded the garments the Anuk wore to protect themselves from the desert, head and chest bare, and Killian marked him at fifteen. Killian was only five years his senior, yet watching the skinny boy fight, he felt old.

Xadrian disarmed all three of his warriors, but rather than seeming pleased about the win, he threw his practice blade across the room with an angry shout. Only for his eyes to finally fall on Killian. "You're supposed to stay in your rooms."

"Then you should've locked me in."

The prince scowled as Killian entered the room and picked up the wooden practice blade. The soldiers all tensed, but Xadrian only said, "What do you want?"

Killian tested the balance of the weapon. "Strange how always winning is a frustration, isn't it?"

The boy didn't answer, only took up one of the other practice swords and motioned for the soldiers to leave.

"It gets boring," Killian continued. "And to alleviate the boredom, one hunts out greater and greater risks."

"The only thing I risk right now is the boredom of your prattle," Xadrian retorted, though his feet were moving. Circling. "What do you want, Lord Calorian?"

"That's why you started leading the gold mine raids when I came to Rotahn."

Xadrian snorted. "I was there because *you* were raiding our villages and killing my people."

"I wasn't, but even if I was, the point stands." Killian gestured at the boy with the sword. "The real threat was in the north along the border with Derin. That's where you were, where you should've remained, but instead you came looking for a fight. Or more accurately, a challenge."

They circled each other.

"Ria Rowenes deceived both of us," Killian said. "Sent her men across your border to attack villages under my banner only to turn around and weep on my shoulder that Anuk raiders were terrorizing Rotahn. She did so because Serrick wanted my reputation ruined, and she aimed to be his heir. The future Queen of Mudamora. Never mind how many people died as a result."

Xadrian's brow furrowed, but he didn't accuse Killian of lying.

"Except while Ria fanned the flames, it was you and me who did the killing, Xadrian," he continued. "It was you and me who chomped at the challenge, never once seeking a solution other than a fight. So I think we are just as at fault as she was."

Tossing aside the practice weapon, Killian said, "If you want a fight, then let it be between the two of us. Leave our people out of it."

Not waiting for the boy to respond, Killian left the room.

40

LYDIA

The chamber she was brought to was large and circular, the walls carved in swirling curves to depict the dunes and illuminated by sconces burning a scented oil that immediately calmed Lydia's rapidly beating heart.

"Wait here, Marked One," the servant murmured, shutting the doors and leaving Lydia alone.

But not in silence.

At the center of the chamber, a large fountain made of silver rose nearly to the ceiling, the water flowing to strike shining basins that each produced a different tone, creating a strangely hypnotic music that drew Lydia closer. Crossing the space, she watched the water flow with fascination, marveling at the craftsmanship it had taken to produce such a sound.

Which was why she didn't hear Ceenah enter, nor sense her presence until the Anuk queen said, "Beautiful, isn't it? Xadrian's father gifted it to me. He purchased it from the Maarin, who said it was made in a far-off land. It took our own craftsman a year and a day to align the pieces so that it would play the music that was intended rather than the noise of falling water."

Lydia cleared her throat. "It's from a place called Faul, across the Endless Seas, Your Grace. I've seen its like before." In a senator's villa, the fountain taken in lieu of taxes owed during the man's governorship of the province. "They are both rare and precious. A generous gift."

"He gave me many gifts, including my son," she answered. "Then I caught him in bed with one of my servants and I gifted his soul back to the Six."

Lydia blinked at the revelation but held her tongue.

"I was only seventeen," Ceenah continued. "Newly queen after my mother's death, the Six protect and keep her soul, and I was accused of being impulsive and emotional in my reaction to his betrayal, for his family was a tribe of great importance. Yet fifteen years have passed, and I'd make the same decision today. I will suffer much but never a liar in my house. Why did you wish to speak to me, Marked One?"

Lydia bit the insides of her cheeks, hearing the warning. "I wish to speak to you of how you used your mark on Agrippa, Your Grace. I . . . I want to know how you took the life out of him without succumbing to the Corrupter's influence."

Ceenah made a soft humming noise, circling the fountain. "Why do you wish to know?"

Don't lie. "Because I've never seen it done in that manner. The corrupted take, but they keep it, whereas you just tossed his life out into the room. My hypothesis is that by not keeping it for yourself, you avoid inviting the Corrupter into your heart."

"The Corrupter is in all our hearts, as are all the Six, to a greater or lesser extent." Ceenah cocked her head, brown eyes considering. "It seems you understand very well what I did, so what is your question? Or did you merely wish to have your hypothesis confirmed?" There was a hint of sarcasm in her voice that reminded Lydia of Xadrian, the apple clearly not falling far from the tree.

"I want to understand how you expelled the life into the room," Lydia said, palms slicking with sweat.

"The same way I would put it into someone to heal them, which you clearly know how to do."

Lydia clenched her teeth, frustration rising in her chest because she knew the woman was baiting her. "I mean, how do you overcome the urge to keep it?"

"The same way I overcome any urge. Willpower. Morality. Dedication to the Six."

So it was as simple as that. Lydia's shoulders slumped with the confirmation of what she'd suspected in her heart. There was no trick, no technique, no skill to be learned. She succumbed to the Corrupter because she didn't have the willpower to overcome her own urges. Because she was weak. Tears welled in her eyes, and Lydia scrubbed them away furiously.

Ceenah kept circling the fountain, only its music breaking the silence between them until she said, "There is a reason why the Corrupter made the keeping of stolen life the sweetest of pleasures. Temptation is his weapon, and he wields it with a mastery very few can resist. That is why it is taught that the corrupted have a separate mark, not that they were marked by Hegeria and turned to darkness. It is easy to resist temptation when you do not realize it exists. Except it does leave Hegeria's marked woefully unprepared if they stumble across that line. Which is why in Anukastre, we teach our children the truth. Teach them how to be strong. How to be true to the Six, and to themselves. Most choose never to cross the line, for it is also easier to resist a temptation you've never tasted."

Lydia knew the taste far too well. "But some cross the line? Like yourself."

"Yes."

"Do . . . do many of them succumb?"

"Yes. And they are executed."

Lydia closed her eyes, knowing the question that was coming.

"Have you crossed the line, Lydia of Mudamora?" The cold blade of Ceenah's sword pressed against her throat. "Have you succumbed?"

Lie lie lie! "Yes."

Lydia squeezed her hands into fists, waiting for the cruel slice of the blade that would end her life, but Ceenah lowered her sword. "Only you fought back to yourself, which means you are strong indeed."

Her eyes shot open. "But—"

"I return to my first question," Ceenah interrupted. "Why do you wish to know how to take life without keeping it? Why not instead ask how to avoid taking it at all?"

"Because I want to be able to defend myself and my friends," Lydia answered. "I have little martial skill, but my mark is as dangerous as any blade. If I could use it as you do, I'd be a different sort of warrior."

"You speak the truth." Ceenah's fingers flexed on the grip of her sword. "Yet not the whole truth."

"That is the whole truth!" Her frustration was rising on a tide of anger because she'd already confessed so much. Yet it wasn't enough. "That is the reason. I want to be strong but not at the sake of my soul. I don't want to be used but I also don't want to use others. What more is there to say?"

"You tell me."

Lydia's anger was taking over, and the ever-present darkness that lurked within her was using it to rip down the walls of her control, the Corrupter's voice whispering up out of the darkness. "I want to be strong enough that the Corrupter can't control me. Can't make me serve his will."

"None of the gods can control you," Ceenah said. "None of them make you serve their will, least of all *him*."

That wasn't true. She could hear him, hear his cursed voice whispering for her to take, to kill, to revel in the strength of stolen life.

Understanding struck her like a slap to the face. It wasn't the Corrupter's voice she heard in her thoughts.

It was her own.

"I want to be master of myself," she blurted out. "I want to be in control of myself. Not by hiding from what I'm capable of, but by using my power on terms I can live with."

"Good," Ceenah said. "Then let me teach you how."

41

LYDIA

"Ceenah says she won't teach me with so many vulnerable people within reach," Lydia told Killian the moment she returned to their room. "She plans to travel with us and teach me on the road, because we'll be surrounded by those who can stop me, like you and Xadrian."

Killian stared at her, then said, "It seems like a good way to get yourself killed. All it takes is one slipup, and either Xadrian or one of his soldiers will cut off your head. I already have enough problems keeping Agrippa from killing you."

"Agrippa isn't going to kill me."

"I might," came a muffled response through the wall, and Killian cursed and kicked at the bed frame. Then cursed again, this time in pain, because the bed frame was made of stone.

Lydia crossed her arms. "I want to learn from her, Killian. I need to. If this is the risk, I accept it. It's my decision."

Drawing in a slow breath, he said, "I . . . I know that you don't want to be protected, Lydia, but standing back and watching you risk your life makes me feel sick. It makes me feel powerless and useless."

Any anger she might have felt at his protest faded away. "You can't fight this battle for me, but I can't fight it without you with any hope of victory." Closing the distance between them, she slipped her arms around him. "I should say that it's for the sake of Mudamora. For the sake of defeating Rufina and the Corrupter. Except the truth is that I want to win this battle for *us*."

His hands closed around her waist, pulling her closer, and heat flared in her core.

"I have your back," he said, drawing her over to the bed and pulling her down. "But right now, I think we both need some rest."

Rest was *not* what Lydia wanted, but she kicked off her boots and rested her head on the pillow. Killian lay at her back, arm wrapped around her waist and the heat of his breath on her hair. "I spoke to Xadrian."

Lydia wrinkled her nose. "He's obnoxious."

"It's an act, I think," Killian said. "He's worried. He feels the threat, the same as I do, and it has him on edge."

"He said that?"

"No, but I can tell. It's why he can't sit still and is looking for a fight."

Unease pooled in her stomach, and she rolled so they were facing each other. "Rufina? The blight?"

"Undoubtedly." Killian stroked her spine. "Yet this feels like something else. It's hard to put into words, but it feels like there has been a shift and a threat is rising."

Her tongue felt thick with sudden fear. "The Empire?"

Killian's silence was all the confirmation Lydia needed, and she pressed her forehead to his chest. "Teriana is in the thick of it, and there is nothing I can do to help her."

"She's resilient." His hand continued to stroke up and down her back. "Madoria herself said that Teriana is where she needs to be. I don't know why, but my gut tells me that in the fight to come, Teriana might well be the most powerful weapon we have against the Cel."

"But at what cost?"

Killian didn't answer, only pulled her closer. She allowed his touch to sooth her fear. To drive away thought. Except in its absence, the ache in her core rose again. An almost painful need to be closer. For there to be nothing between them at all.

Only that meant she needed to be able to take the gloves off.

* * *

The sandstorm faded overnight, and they left just before dawn the next day in the company of Ceenah, Xadrian, and a dozen Anuk soldiers.

They made camp to rest through the heat of the day, and no sooner were they settled in the shadow of an enormous dune did Ceenah snap her fingers at Lydia and say, "We begin now. Xadrian, you will be prepared for the worst, but you will only act on my signal or if I fall. Understood?"

Lydia expected the prince to protest, but Xadrian only rose to his feet and drew his weapon, saying to the soldiers, "Be at the ready." They drew their weapons, as did Agrippa, who added, "Our friendship has been short, Lydia, but as Xadrian severs your neck and your head flies through the air, I hope you remember how much I treasured our heartfelt conversations."

"Not helpful, Agrippa!" Malahi shouted at him, but Lydia barely noticed the argument that ensued as Killian grimly drew his own blade.

She wanted to tell him to allow Xadrian to do what needed to be done if she lost control, except it would be wasted breath. Killian would try to stop him, and with a dozen deadly Anuk warriors, including several archers, watching him as much as her, it was not lost on Lydia that Killian's life was as on the line as hers.

Was it right to tempt fate? Was it right to test herself when she'd failed to control herself every time in the past? It was one thing to gamble with her own life but the thought of Killian falling, body full of black fletched arrows, made her heart skitter and her breath come too quickly. "I . . ."

"To master yourself, you must have faith in yourself," Ceenah declared. The other woman pulled off her scarf and tunic, leaving her in only loose trousers and a thin undershirt that left her arms bare. Her brown skin gleamed in the too-bright sun, arms corded with muscle that suggested she was equally deadly with the sword at her waist as she was with her mark. "Bare skin, girl."

Lydia reluctantly removed her gloves, scarf, and tunic, folding them before setting them on the sand. The sun baked into her skin, but it was only partially the cause of the sweat that ran in rivulets down her back. Killian was speaking to Xadrian in low but heated tones, but the prince only shook his head.

"Ignore them," Ceenah said. "There is no one here but you and me and the gods."

Lydia's skin prickled, the hairs on the back of her neck rising. She rubbed at her arms, and Ceenah gave a nod. "Yes, they are watching."

The older woman moved closer. "When was the last time you lost total control?"

"Baird was shot by an arrow in our escape down the escarpment," Lydia answered. "Healing him took more life than I'd anticipated, and I fainted. When I roused, I . . . I panicked at how weak I felt."

Ceenah made a clicking noise of disapproval. "Healing using only that which is in oneself is a limitation of those who do not test the boundaries of their gift. Even here, surrounded by sand, there is life that is free for the taking that you might use rather than render yourself weak."

Ceenah wasn't wrong.

As Lydia allowed her mark to control her gaze, she saw not just the life glowing around the living but that which was present in the air. Not a fraction of what she would find in a city, but there nonetheless.

"Take it."

Lydia reached out a hand to the mist, attempting to draw it into herself as she had when she'd healed Agrippa. "I can't. I . . . I don't need it."

Ceenah nodded. "That is why the corrupted can't sate themselves without taking from the living. To take from the world around you requires a *need*. So let's give you one. Lord Calorian, if you would."

Killian approached, his wariness palpable. Especially as Ceenah drew a knife. "Just a little nick. It's nothing to the likes of you."

"What are you going to do?" Lydia demanded.

"Create a need that you don't just see but that you also *feel*."

Anxiety sent bile burning up Lydia's throat because that would mean touching Killian without her gloves. "Not him. I . . . I don't know why, but it's hard with Killian."

Ceenah grunted. "Because he's marked." She shoved Killian back and then leveled a finger at Agrippa. "You. Come."

To Lydia's surprise, Agrippa didn't argue, only motioned to Baird to sit next to Malahi and approached, silently pulling up a sleeve and holding out a bare arm. Ceenah drew the blade across the thick part of the muscle, not a nick but a deep slice. Agrippa didn't flinch.

"Do you feel it?" Ceenah demanded.

Lydia could see the life trickling out with every drop of blood, but she felt nothing except irritation at the woman for hurting her friend.

"I feel it," Agrippa said. "Terribly painful, and if I'm stuck with it because you can't get this right, Lydia, I might need to reconsider our friendship."

The queen made a noise of annoyance, then caught hold of Lydia's hand and clapped her palm on the bleeding wound. "Do you feel it now?"

It struck Lydia with a familiar jolt. The compelling need to remedy the injury beneath her hand, but the need to *take* was also there, the two warring with each other. "Yes."

"Most healers would take from themselves to fill that need," Ceenah said, "leaving them in a deficit and weaker as a result. Their mark would passively draw life from all around them to eventually fill that deficit. Those like you and me need not wait. Take what is needed from around you and heal the wound."

Lydia lifted her free hand, and Ceenah said, "That's not necessary."

"It helps," Lydia growled, her heart thundering because trying to *take* from what floated around her was like trying to drink from a thimble when an entire well was beneath her opposite hand.

You can do this, she told herself. *You will do it.*

Looking away from Agrippa so as to not be distracted by the glow of life around him, she *pulled*, her breath catching as the glowing mist sped toward her outstretching fingers and into her. She immediately shoved it into Agrippa, her brow furrowing because the effort had barely slowed the bleeding.

"Again."

Sucking in a breath, Lydia drew in life and shoved it into him, seeing some of the flesh begin to knit when she examined the wound.

"Now at the same time, and do not stop until the need is gone."

Closing her eyes, Lydia turned her focus inward. On the beat of her heart. The rapidness of her breath. The pulse in her throat.

The need created by the wound beneath her hand.

And then that which would sate it beyond.

It came slowly at first, then faster and faster, like a river pouring into her left hand and out her right. The moment the need ceased, so did the flow.

Lydia's eyes snapped open and she lifted Agrippa's arm. The only evidence there'd been a wound was the sticky blood drying on his skin. "I did it!"

Agrippa whooped and clapped his hands, but Ceenah appeared unimpressed.

"Of course you did. A child could do as much. You may go, you obnoxious creature." She waved her hand at Agrippa.

Agrippa went to stand with Malahi, taking a long drink from a waterskin. Lydia was about to ask him for a sip of water when, quick as a viper, Ceenah caught hold of Lydia's forearm. Anukastre's queen ripped life out of her and spilled it out into the empty air.

It was like having her insides yanked out, and Lydia's panic surged. Killian took a step toward them, blade up, but Ceenah raised a hand to him even as she snapped at Lydia, "Take it back."

Lydia lunged at the cloud, drawing it back into herself, and then retreated warily from the woman.

"You need to master the panic you feel when you are in a deficit." Ceenah circled her. "There is no *need* to panic because what you require to remedy your problem is all around you. Again."

Though every instinct told her not to allow it, Lydia held out her arm. Sickness twisted her stomach as the woman took even more, casting it out above the sands.

"Wait."

Sweat beaded on Lydia's brow as she watched the life drift away, her hands trembling in fear that it would dissipate. Disappear. That she'd be left without, and she was terrified of what she might do if that happened.

"Now satisfy the need."

Lydia chased after the drifting mist, gathering it back into herself until she was whole.

"Good. That is enough. We will rest until the sun begins to descend." Turning on her heel, the Queen of Anukastre walked back to camp.

Killian watched Ceenah go with narrowed eyes, then approached Lydia. "Are you all right?"

"I think so." She snatched up her clothes, abruptly aware that she wore only the thinnest of fabric. "We should get some rest while we can."

"Not yet, Lord Calorian," Xadrian said. "I have thought about your words and we will spar now."

Killian sighed, but despite the prince's bluster, he murmured to her, "You aren't the only one with work to do on this journey," then followed Xadrian into the dunes.

* * *

For days, they traveled west over endless sand dunes, and during the height of the merciless sun, Ceenah would continue her lessons. Though it had to be the purest form of misery, Agrippa never argued about being used as Ceenah's victim, suffering endless cuts so that Lydia could practice healing him using the life in their surroundings until she could do it without thinking. She moved on to Baird and Xadrian, and though the temptation was worse with someone who was marked, their wounds closed beneath her hand.

Her friends weren't the only ones who suffered. Lydia also had to endure Ceenah draining more and more life from her, forced to sit for longer and longer stretches before reclaiming it. If Lydia cracked and took her life back before the queen ordered it, Ceenah made her do it again.

There was no denying that her control was growing in leaps and bounds with every test, but it still came as a shock when Ceenah held out her own arm. "It is time for a true test. Take life from me and put it out into the world."

Lydia sensed Xadrian and Killian tense behind her, and no part of her could blame them. Already her hands trembled, both her body and her mind remembering what it felt like to take from the living. The rush of strength and pleasure that was like nothing else in this world, and every part of her wanted it.

"Just a bit," Ceenah warned. "Do not overwhelm yourself with more."

"What if I can't stop?"

"My son will kill you." Ceenah studied her for a long moment, expressionless, then she grinned. "If you get the better of me, girl, then I deserve my fate."

Which didn't mean that Xadrian wouldn't kill her. Or try to. Lydia glanced over her shoulder at Killian, who was staring at the sand, his jaw tight. *What are you thinking?* she silently wondered. *What will you do if this goes wrong?*

There was no mistaking what Agrippa was thinking, for though his eyes were fixed on the sand in the same blank way as Killian's, he held a bow he'd borrowed from one of the Anuk warriors, an arrow loosely nocked.

Malahi stood next to him, the only person besides Ceenah who seemed willing to meet Lydia's gaze, though her amber eyes were unreadable.

"Maybe I should wait another day. We can practice you taking life from me. Take more. Take—"

"We are very nearly to the coast," Ceenah interrupted. "At which time our lessons will come to an end."

"Maybe I'll never be ready." Lydia pulled off her spectacles, wiping sweat from her face before donning them again. "Maybe I'm not one who can cross the line and come back. Maybe it's better that I forbid myself from taking."

"It is nothing to me whether you do or do not," Ceenah replied. "Yet ask yourself whether you'll be able to live with that limitation, or whether days, weeks, months from now you'll find yourself reaching across the line."

Lydia couldn't live with it. Knew in her heart that this would loom over her, not only as something she'd failed to accomplish but as a razor-sharp knife that always had the potential to fall on those she cared about most. If she couldn't master her mark, both the light and dark sides of it, she'd always be a threat.

Malahi approached, and then led Lydia a short distance away. "What are you thinking?" her friend asked her. "What is it that you worry is going to happen?"

"I think I'll lose control and come back to myself surrounded by corpses."

Malahi chewed on her bottom lip, then turned to face down Ceenah. "Lydia is not ready. Not yet."

The words were a punch to the gut because they were true. Lydia's shoulders slumped as Malahi walked back over to Agrippa, passing Killian as she did. The relief in his eyes was palpable, and somehow, that made Lydia feel worse.

Then Ceenah lunged after Malahi.

Lydia's lips parted to scream a warning, but Agrippa was already moving. Except it wasn't Malahi that Anukastre's queen attacked.

It was Killian.

Her knife slashed down across Killian's exposed forearm, the blade going nearly down to the bone. He hissed in pain, jerking away even as he clapped his other hand around the wound, arterial blood spurting between his fingers.

"Heal him, Lydia," Ceenah commanded. "It's long past due."

Lydia tripped over her own feet, nearly falling in her rush to get to Killian's side. "No," she pleaded as she took in the severity of the wound, blood already pooling on the ground. "Ceenah, help him. Please!"

The Queen of Anukastre didn't move.

"You cannot seriously be refusing to help him?" Lydia screamed, her heart rising to her throat as Killian swayed on his feet.

"It's fine," he muttered. "I'll be fine."

"You'll die if she doesn't help you," Ceenah said. "If you wish to buy yourself time, I suggest sitting."

Killian thudded to the ground, hand still gripping the bleeding wound. "Just get a lamp burning. Cauterize it."

"This is madness." Lydia reached for him, then jerked back, the sight of his life flowing out between his fingers making the voice deep inside her scream *take it*!

"It's madness to believe you can't help him!" Xadrian shouted in her face, his weapon in hand. Then he spun away. "Mother, heal him! Don't let her weakness be the death of him!"

"Lydia is not weak." Ceenah crossed her arms. "The trouble is that her adversary is herself."

Killian only met Lydia's gaze, expression steady. As though he had no doubt in his mind that she'd do what needed to be done.

Reaching out, she pulled his hand away from the injury. The wound extended up to his elbow, blood pulsing out with each beat of his heart. The life he'd lost hung around him like a cloud.

Behind her, Xadrian begged his mother to help and Malahi sobbed, but Lydia pushed away their voices, slowly placing her palm on the wound.

Take it.

"No," she growled at the voice, clenching her teeth against the compulsion within her, which grew worse with each second that passed. Like being deep underwater and desperately needing to breathe.

Take it.

"I won't." Her eyes skipped to Killian's face. His lids were closed, face drained of color. "I will not lose him."

Because she loved him. Needed him in a way that was so much greater than all the things the voice promised if she allowed her darker half to consume her. What was strength without him? What was pleasure? What was power?

Nothing, was the answer.

The glow of Killian's life drifted around them, and lifting her other hand, Lydia touched the swirling mist.

And she *pulled*.

The life that Killian had lost flowed into Lydia at her call, but it didn't stop there. From all around, it surged toward her, like clouds on a racing wind, flooding her like a breath of air.

"Lydia, hurry!" Malahi screamed. "Don't let him die!"

All around her was the chaos of her friends threatening Ceenah and the Anuk drawing blades, but Lydia tuned them out as she drew in more power.

Keep it! It's yours!

"No," she told the voice, then she exhaled and poured every drop into Killian.

The wound knit beneath her hand just as his heart began to stutter.

Her own heart caught with the certainty that she'd been too late, but then Killian's eyes met hers. "You won the battle."

Lydia didn't trust herself to speak as she looked down at their interlocked fingers and all that they promised before meeting his gaze again.

Killian gave her a lopsided grin. "If almost dying was all it took, I'd have fallen on my own sword a long time ago."

"You're mad." Tears rushed down her cheeks, but Lydia was smiling as she turned to look at Ceenah, whose eyes were wide, lips slightly parted as though Lydia had not done what she'd expected. Ignoring the woman's expression, Lydia said, "Now I'm ready."

42

KILLIAN

The rest of what Ceenah had to teach Lydia came to her easily. While Killian sparred with Xadrian, they sat on the sand to rest, one growing older only to grow young again. It never seemed less miraculous than the first time Killian had witnessed it.

Except each time Lydia walked away from the lesson with a smile on her face, Killian saw something that she did not. An uneasiness in Ceenah's eyes that made him nervous despite it seeming as though he'd been given that which his heart most desired.

Every night since Lydia had won her inner battle and healed him, she'd slept in his arms. Her hands were free of the gloves she'd worn for so long, the feel of her fingers on his skin driving him to a different form of madness, for there was no gods-damned privacy to be found on the endless dunes. So it was no small amount of relief when he finally scented the sea on the air, his eyes searching the horizon until he finally caught sight of the small port town that sat on the coastline of a white-capped ocean.

Killian had heard that the desert ran straight down to the sea along the western edge of Anukastre, yet the lack of plant life still felt strange to him, having grown up on the verdant southern tip of Mudamora. Baird muttered various explanations that attributed this to the weather, but Killian couldn't help but wonder if there was some truth to what Ceenah claimed: that the blight had wreaked such havoc on these lands that life had never been able to carve its way back.

A thought that vanished from his head the moment Killian saw the blue sails on the ship docked at the town. "The Maarin are here."

"We trade with them a great deal," Ceenah replied. "They respect our laws and keep our secrets, especially given that it gives them a near monopoly on our business."

"I recognize that ship," Lydia said, shading her eyes. "It's the *Kairense*. They rescued Dareena and me from Mudaire and took us south."

"A good omen given this is where we part." Ceenah lowered her hand, which she'd been using to shade her eyes. "May the Six be with you in your travels and in the war to come."

They all said their good-byes, Agrippa, Malahi, and Baird moving ahead toward the port town. "Go with them," Killian said to Lydia. "I'll be right behind you."

She hesitated, then followed their friends. Killian waited until she was out of earshot, then rounded on Ceenah. "She did something when she healed me. Something unexpected, and you're withholding that information. She's overcome enough obstacles, and if there is another forthcoming, I'd prefer to be prepared for it."

The Queen of Anukastre eyed him for a long moment, then lowered her scarf so her face was revealed. "You know how a lodestone can draw nearby pieces of iron to it?" When he nodded, she said, "Hegeria's marked are like lodestones for the essence of life, drawing that which is nearby into them whenever they have a need for it. When Lydia healed you, she didn't just draw the essence that you'd lost, she drew it from leagues around. I could see it racing toward her like clouds on a storm wind, and in all my life, I've never seen such a thing done. Never heard of it. It was as though her need was so great that she called for all life on Reath to aid her."

Killian's skin prickled. "What does that mean?"

Ceenah lifted one shoulder. "Only the Six can say for sure, but . . ."

"But . . . ?"

"She told me of what occurred when you escaped Rufina. How the Six stepped onto the mortal plain to stymie their brother's meddling. Hegeria herself laid hands on Lydia, yes?"

Killian nodded, his pulse roaring.

"That makes her twice touched by a god," Ceenah said. "Who can say what power that would bring, but I think what I saw when she healed you was just a taste."

"Given what we face, that seems a good thing," he said. "But that is not the sense you're giving me, Your Majesty."

“Because I feel it makes the Corrupter covet her all the more,” Ceenah replied. “He cannot force her to misuse her mark, but he will sense any moment of weakness and dangle temptation before her. I think it not your blade that you’ll use most to protect her, Lord Calorian. I think it will be your heart.”

Without another word, she wrapped her scarf around her face and retreated back into the desert. Xadrian swayed on his feet, seeming torn between holding his ground and following his mother, but then he said to his soldiers, “Stay with her. Those in the town may not take favorably to Mudamorian faces, so I will escort them to their ship.” Then he flicked his fingers at Killian. “Come.”

Casting his eyes skyward, Killian fell in next to the boy. “You know, Xadrian,” he said, “we’d get along better if you didn’t insist on treating me like I’m less than you.”

The boy lowered his scarf and frowned. “But you are. I am crown prince of Anukastre, destined to rule as king on the day the Six decide to take my mother’s soul into their embrace. You are the youngest brother of a High Lord and destined to rule nothing. I respect you for your martial prowess, like you for your wit, and honor the mark you bear, but that does not make you my equal.”

Killian sighed. “You’re hopeless. What do you want, Xadrian? Because I don’t for a second believe that you’re worried about me reaching that ship.”

The boy’s jaw worked back and forth. “My mother believes this is not our fight. That the sands and the Six will protect Anukastre, as they always have. But I’ve thought hard on your words, and I think she’s wrong. The Six do not reward those who stand back in a fight against the Seventh. I will make her see reason, so that if Mudamora calls for our aid, Anukastre will answer.”

“Thank you.” Killian rested a hand on the prince’s shoulder. “It would be an honor to fight at your side.”

Xadrian started to smile, caught himself, then shoved Killian’s hand away. “Do not thank me, Calorian. Once the Corrupter is defeated, I fully intend to resume stealing Rowenes gold and I’ll not have you weeping about alliances.”

“I look forward to it.” Killian increased his pace to catch up to his companions. “Take care of yourself, Your Highness. Look for word via the Maarin.”

But Xadrian was already walking away.

Agrippa frowned as Killian reached them. “Everything all right?”

"Anukastre will fight with us in the battle to come."

"Says who? Xadrian?" Agrippa snorted. "Ceenah seemed set against it, and last I heard, it is she who wears the crown."

"If Ceenah didn't want him making promises, she wouldn't have given him the opportunity to do so," Killian replied. "Anukastre is with us."

"What remains to be seen is how many of *us* are left," Malahi said, drawing up at the base of the singular dock.

Her unease was shared by all of them, for the Maarin would have the latest word of Mudamora's fate, and none of them were fool enough to believe what they'd learn was good.

They started up the steps onto the dock, walking down the length to where the ship was moored in the deep water, and Killian cast a sideways glance at Lydia, knowing that she'd be thinking of Teriana. "They might have news of her," he said, and she gave a tight nod.

"Madoria believed she was where she was supposed to be, and I have to trust in that, if not in those she is with."

Shouts of recognition echoed off the ship as they were spotted, Lydia's name, and Killian's own, repeated, and then a familiar face raced down the gangplank in a limping run.

"Lydia!" Bait exclaimed as he reached them. "Thank the gods, you're alive!"

Lydia hugged him tightly. "Bait, what are you doing here? How did you know where to find us?"

"We didn't," Bait answered. "But Dareena Falorn has asked every Maarin vessel sailing the coast to keep eyes out for you. You too, Killian. And for . . ." He faltered as his eyes landed on Malahi's scarred face, though he recovered by bowing low. "For you especially, Your Grace."

"What news do you have?" Malahi demanded. "Has the blight spread?"

Bait hesitated, eyes skipping between their group. "Nearly half of Mudamora is lost to it, and every day, the blight presses south."

Killian's stomach plummeted, everything they feared swiftly becoming reality.

Bait gestured for them to cross the gangplank. "Rufina has traveled back to the eastern side of the Liratoras to take her place at the head of a new army."

"The Derin blighters?" Agrippa demanded. "She's moved them across the Liratoras already? That's not possible."

Bait's brow furrowed as he looked the ex-legionnaire over. "No," he finally answered. "They aren't from Derin."

Drawing in a steadying breath, Baird said, "Her army is made up of Mudamorians, all raised from the dead."

43

LYDIA

No one spoke, the only sound the slap of water against the hull of the ship and the distant conversation of the Anuk watching from shore.

"What do you mean, dead Mudamorians?" Malahi finally asked.

"The blight spread swiftly and poisoned many rivers." Bait pursed his lips, clearly hating to be the bearer of the news. "Thousands perished only to rise again as the Corrupter's puppets. And even knowing the risk, many refuse to flee south because they don't wish to abandon their holdings, so with each passing day, Rufina's army grows."

"The gods have mercy," Baird growled. "That woman's villainy knows no bounds."

Lydia's hands were cold as ice. "What are Dareena and the other high lords doing to fight back?"

"They are trying to force civilians to evacuate south with promises they'll be cared for, and Dareena is marshaling the Mudamorian army to create a front to hold the blighters as far north as possible." Bait sighed. "But my information is a fortnight old. Come aboard, and I'll tell you what all we know away from listening ears."

The group climbed the narrow gangplank onto the *Kairense*, Lydia's nose filling with the familiar scent of tar and brine. The deck boards creaked beneath Baird's weight, audible because all of the crew were silently watching them, their anxiousness palpable. Even after this ship had plucked her and Dareena from disaster in Mudaire, the Maarin had been bright and carefree, but that was gone now.

More had changed than just the spread of the blight, and nerves turned Lydia's stomach sick with nausea as Bait led her past coils of rope and barrels of supplies. "What of Teriana," she made herself ask him. "Have you had word of her?"

"Yes." He spoke under his breath. "But best not to mention her name until we're alone."

Her heart leapt into a gallop, but Lydia bit her tongue to stay silent. The captain, whose name she recalled was Vane, gave a tight nod to Bait and then began shouting orders to his crew to finish their business, for the ship was leaving *now*.

Bait waited until everyone was inside the captain's quarters, then shut the door firmly behind himself. "After we spoke in Mudaire, Lydia, I journeyed to Arinoquia to tell Teriana that you were alive and what had happened to you. But when I arrived, she was missing." Bait's throat moved as he swallowed. "Missing with *him*."

There was only one *him*, but Lydia said, "Marcus, you mean?"

Agrippa stepped closer, expression intent.

Bait grimaced. "Yes. His legion was in a frenzy trying to find them, and I ventured back to Revat to see if maybe she'd somehow escaped, but the Gamdeshians had heard nothing. I waited for weeks upon weeks for news, going back and forth between Revat and Taltuga, only for a ship full of my people who'd been imprisoned in Celendrial to arrive. They told us that Teriana had been in Celendrial and negotiated with Cassius for the release of a hundred prisoners."

In exchange for what? Lydia wondered, but stayed silent.

"Not long after, the Gamdeshians learned that the Thirty-Seventh's legatus had returned to Aracam, and on his heels, Teriana arrived with another legion. The story Kaira's shifter spy heard was that they were separated from his men in the inlands of Arinoquia and came under attack. They escaped by way of a xenthier stem that apparently delivered them somewhere back East, and they were able to get back to Arinoquia through a stem originating in—"

"Bardeen," Agrippa finished. "Shit. So they've mapped paths, then?"

"Who are you?" Bait's eyes darkened to a deep grey, waves rolling violently across them and betraying his unease.

"Legion deserter," Lydia answered. "Former Thirty-Seventh."

"I'm not—" Agrippa started to say, then he sighed. "Well, I suppose I am at this point, given I'm not going back." Malahi touched his arm, and Agrippa's eyes flicked to the queen, something unspoken passing between them before he said, "There's a genesis within spitting distance of Hydrilla fortress in Bardeen that crosses to the inlands of Arinoquia. I was half dead when I crossed, but the inlanders took it upon themselves to heal me up. I took a liking to them, so I warned them to make short work of anyone who ever came through that stem. They've shifters aplenty among them, so they were well equipped for the job, though from what you're saying, they got lax and it's costing them."

Bait was quiet for a long moment, then he shook his head. "The stories are conflicting. There were a lot of accusations in the legions that he deserted."

Agrippa laughed. "Marcus would cut out his own heart and eat it for lunch before he deserted. That's bullshit."

"Why would they think Marcus deserted?" Lydia asked, something in Bait's expression suggesting there was more to this than he'd admitted. "And why was it that only the two of them were caught alone?"

Captain Vane walked in right in the middle of Lydia asking the question, slamming the door behind him. "Because it's rumored that the legatus of the Thirty-Seventh has taken Teriana as his lover. She's a traitor."

The blood drained from Lydia's face even as Agrippa burst into laughter. Pounding the table with his fist, he said through guffaws, "Not a chance. Please, allow me to put these rumors to rest, because there is not a *chance* that Marcus has taken a lover, much less taken his *prisoner* as a lover. You will never meet a man more enamored with rules than him, and relationships with anyone outside the legion are forbidden. I don't care if this girl is the most beautiful thing to ever walk Reath; even if he took the time out of his busy schedule to notice, he'd not act on it. If Marcus is keeping Teriana close, it's likely only that he's trying to dissuade anyone else from taking a crack at her."

Bait shifted restlessly. "It's what everyone says. That's why they were caught alone."

Agrippa made a face, then waved a dismissive hand. "Marcus always wanders off alone, especially if he's brooding about something that displeases him. Was the bane of my gods-damned existence when his safety was my responsibility because he had a habit of strolling about enemy territory as though he were invincible. He probably wanted some information out of her that he didn't want prying ears to overhear, and whatever jackass has my job is doing a piss-poor job of minding him."

Agrippa's words were noise in Lydia's ears.

Lover.

Traitor.

No. There was no chance that Teriana would want anything to do with a Cel legatus, especially given that he'd . . .

Lydia struggled to swallow the lump that had formed in her throat as she realized that Teriana still had no idea what Marcus had done on Lucius's orders.

"I hope you're right." Bait exhaled between his teeth. "But regardless, the Cel's hold on Arinoquia has only strengthened."

"Which legion has joined them?" Agrippa demanded.

"A young one," Bait said. "But there are rumors that before he was killed, Legatus Titus of the Forty-First negotiated an alliance with Queen Erdene of Katamarca, who seems to be of a mind to get on the Empire's good side."

"Smart in the short term," Agrippa muttered. "But it won't save her in the end."

Lydia rounded on Captain Vane, not interested in alliances. "Why did you call Teriana a traitor?"

"Because she gave the legions information of where they might find terminuses in Gamdesh," he answered. "Kaira cracked open the structure encasing the one in Emrant, and it's full of dead pathhunters. If the Empire gains control of Emrant, the legions will spill forth from that stem in a tide as dangerous as the blight."

Lydia's skin abruptly began to crawl, and her eyes shot to Killian, who gave a tight nod. This was the threat that he'd sensed; it could be no other.

"Teriana didn't have a choice!" Bait's hands balled into fists. "Cassius has our people locked up, and she's trying to get them free. It's not her fault the Senate didn't think the paths she found were *good enough*. She's trying to save Maarin lives. You know that it is so from her own hand." Yanking a stained piece of paper from his pocket, Bait shoved it at Killian. "She wrote this to you. The *Kairense* might be here for Malahi, but I'm here for you."

Killian unfolded the page, but he said nothing as he read.

"I know Teriana's justifications but also that the price the West will pay for them is too high!" The captain slammed his hands down on the table. "We've argued this before, Bait, and I'll not waste breath on it now. The shifter Astara communicated the decision the West has made, and Teriana responded with threats! And I, for one, think there's a reason why she's not even attempted to contact Magnius since her return. That she chose to write a letter to Lord Calorian rather than face the judgment of her own people."

Killian was still staring at the page, his jaw tight, but he said nothing of the contents.

"Just what are you implying, Captain?" Lydia couldn't keep the acid from her voice. "Because if it's that you believe Teriana is willingly aiding the Cel, you are *wrong*. She'd never betray her people like that. *Never*."

"Lydia . . ." Killian handed her the page, which was water stained and appeared to have been unfolded and refolded many times. It also bore Teriana's familiar delicate handwriting.

Killian,

I won't waste time on preamble, because I suspect you are well informed on recent events. I know the situation in Mudamora is dire, but I desperately need your help. Five hundred Maarin souls remained imprisoned in the worst of circumstances, and if I don't give the Empire what they want, less than six months from now, they will begin executing them. One hundred souls for every month of delay. I've appealed for help from the Arinoquians, the Gamdeshians, and from my own people, but everyone has declined. They see the five hundred as casualties of war, but I refuse to give up on them. I know you have influence with the Gamdeshians. If you are able, please speak to them and see if they will see reason. Otherwise I fear what lengths I will have to go to to free my people, because I will not accept their deaths as certain.

All my love,
Teriana

Emotion overwhelmed her, and Lydia didn't argue as Agrippa plucked the letter from her hand. Through the lines on the page, she had felt her friend's fear and desperation, especially knowing Teriana stood alone. "How can you read this and think that these are the words of a traitor?" she hissed. "Teriana isn't motivated by lust! She's trying to save five hundred lives, and *no one* is helping her!"

"A loss that we, as a people, have agreed to accept," Vane snapped. "Do you think we don't grieve it? That we don't hate the Empire for its evil? But to save them would mean setting the legions loose on Gamdesh, and you of all people, Lydia Valerius, know the cost of that. Thousands will die. Tens of thousands. And if the Empire is victorious, every nation will be enslaved to the Senate. Yet Teriana spits in the face of the desires of the Gamdeshians and the Maarin to pursue her own ends—it's treason. She needs to be stopped, permanently, if needs be, because she's a tool for the Cel. They control her."

"You don't know that."

"Teriana is young!" Vane crossed his arms. "And young people do foolish things when they are enamored. It may be as you say"—his eyes flicked to Agrippa—"and the Thirty-Seventh's legatus would not break legion laws. Yet I doubt it's beneath him to use charm and good looks to his advantage. Who is to say that he has not played her like a fiddle on the orders of the Senate, filling her with the idea that she will be the savior of her people if she does this."

"He wouldn't . . ." Agrippa shook his head. "I don't know if he'd agree to it or not, but I can tell you that Marcus can lie through his teeth with no one the wiser. He is as much a politician as he is a commander, and if he thought pulling the heartstrings of a girl would get him what he wanted without casualties . . ." He turned away. "If he's willing to do that then I'm not sure how well I can claim to know him anymore."

Bait looked ready to be sick, and Lydia's temper snapped. "Everyone can quit acting as though she's some brainless twit to be manipulated by a pretty face. Teriana is not that easily fooled. If she's aiding them, it's *only* to free her people, because what I do believe is that she's not willing to sacrifice the lives of the few to avoid risking the many." Catching hold of Bait's arm, she squeezed tightly. "She's a gambler. I'd bet my life that she's willing to go to the brink to save those imprisoned on the belief that a united West has the power to force them back."

"Which we would," Malahi said quietly, "if not for the fact that the Northern Continent is fighting its own war. Teriana may not know how dire our situation is and may be making decisions on the belief that Mudamora will sail to Gamdesh's aid, for we have long been allies. If she's guilty of anything, I suspect it's that she's had information kept from her that might cause her to alter her course. Efforts should be made to get this information in her hands."

"Is it possible to speak to her, Bait?" Killian asked. "For one, I'd like to hear from Teriana's own mouth the full truth about both her actions and intentions before jumping to *any* conclusions, but I also think it's important to make certain that she knows *all* the information, including certain facts about her captor."

"I can try," Bait said. "If it's anything like before, she's with him at all times, always under guard. Astara is the name of the shifter who keeps an eye on the legions. She can take on the shape of a hawk, so she was able to speak to Teriana once in the middle of the night. She might help me get in."

"If maintaining Teriana's value as an asset requires keeping her in the dark, they'll make sure that no one gets near her," Agrippa said from where he was now sitting on a chair in the corner. "You try to sneak past, they'll catch you and kill you. Better to get this bird to drop her a note."

"They aren't half as clever as they think," Bait retorted. "I'll just watch for the right opportunity."

Agrippa rolled his eyes skyward. "Your funeral. Oh wait, there won't be one, because they'll dump your body where it will never be found."

Bait's hands balled into fists, but Lydia tightened her grip on his arm. "Maybe a message. Or paying off someone they trust near her. Either way, I think you need to try."

The whole room fell silent, and Lydia said, "Madoria told me that Teriana is exactly where she needs to be." When Bait opened his mouth to ask the obvious question, she added, "That's a long story for another hour, but I personally choose to have faith in Madoria. And faith in Teriana."

"Regardless of what the truth of Teriana's situation may be," Malahi said, "we cannot aid Gamdesh. Captain, what can you tell me of Mudamora? Where are the high lords and ladies? Who leads?"

We cannot aid Gamdesh, Lydia thought, *yet the first thing we intend to do is to ask them to aid us.*

She didn't envy Malahi's role. Always having to weigh the needs of one group against another, which inevitably required hard choices. Much like Teriana. Lydia's heart demanded that she try to save everyone despite knowing that walking that path risked catastrophe for all involved.

"I think the question you are asking, Your Grace, is whether you're still queen." Vane rocked on his heels. "When we left Serlania, you had not been replaced, but I think that more to do with the fact they can't agree on who should rule than any loyalty to House Rowenes. They were all in Serlania, but Hacken Calorian holds the most influence and seems content to rule in proxy given your absence."

"Oh, I'm sure he does." Malahi turned away and walked to the windows at the rear of the cabin, watching their wake.

Lydia bit the insides of her cheeks as she met Killian's gaze. While Malahi had released him from both an unwanted engagement and his oath to protect her, Hacken was likely to have different views on the matter. She had not forgotten how Killian's older brother had manipulated circumstances the night of that awful ball, making his support of Malahi's rule conditional on an engagement to Killian, and there was nothing to stop him from doing the same again. For Lydia didn't for a heartbeat think that the spreading blight or an army of the dead were enough to curb Hacken's desire for power.

Judging from the anger seething from Agrippa, Malahi had already shared Hacken's previous schemes with him, so Lydia said, "It's a different circumstance now, if all the High Lords are together. You don't need his vote, Malahi. Once everyone knows what we learned from Ceenah and that you are marked by Yara, they'll support you." Both Bait and Vane raised their eyebrows in surprise, but they said nothing, and Lydia added, "We support you."

Malahi cast her a small smile over her shoulder, then went back to her contemplation of the wake. Agrippa moved to her side, his murmured words too low for Lydia to hear, though she expected it was something related to cutting the throats of anyone who didn't bend the knee, for Malahi laughed softly and shook her head.

"There is little to be done other than to sail to Serlania with all haste," Vane said. "Your Grace, I will gladly give up my cabin for your use on the journey, and we will attempt to make your companions as comfortable as possible. What information we have, we will freely give to you, and I hope you will extend the same courtesy."

Malahi turned around to face the captain. "Our conversation has been grim, Triumvir Vane, but we have learned information in Anukastre that gives us hope the blight can be defeated. The sooner we can return to Mudamora, the better."

"I believe I can help with that," Baird said. "All I need is some space and a drum."

Vane gave the giant a wary look but led him toward the door. Before he disappeared, the captain called back, "I'll have someone bring up food, drink, and water for washing. I imagine your journey has taken its toll."

"Hacken is going to be a problem," Malahi said once he was gone. "He was already the most powerful high lord, and given the Calorian lands are the most removed from the blight's progress, his strength will have only grown."

"Fortunately, no one likes my brother." Killian was staring at Teriana's letter, smoothing the creases. "And they trust him even less. He can plot all he wants. Once you return, they'll turn to you to lead."

"Perhaps." Malahi met Lydia's gaze. "Vane called you Lydia Valerius. I've never thought to ask, but do you wish to be known by your birth name?"

Malahi may have forgotten to ask, but in truth, Lydia hadn't given the idea much thought. "No," she said. "It doesn't feel like who I am anymore."

"I understand." Malahi reached over to squeeze her arm. "It will remain between us unless you wish it otherwise. Though I think if Dareena knew the truth that she'd welcome you."

An image of the High Lady of House Falorn filled Lydia's eye. Her aunt. Her only blood relation left living, and yet Lydia recoiled from the idea of Dareena learning the truth because it felt like a betrayal to the father who had raised her. "I'll think about it. But for now, we'll give you some space to rest. Bait and I have a great deal to catch up on."

She, Killian, and Bait departed the cabin, leaving Agrippa and Malahi standing by the window in quiet contemplation of the ship's wake.

"Birth name?" Bait asked once they were on decks, but Lydia shook her head. "I'll explain later."

The Maarin who weren't busy sailing the ship were all watching with interest as the captain handed Baird a drum, the giant frowning as he eyed the sky overhead. With a slow, deliberate motion, Baird lifted his hand and began to beat the drum. The sound was thunderous, vibrating through Lydia's bones, the rhythm a call to the skies above and the god who controlled them.

"Marked by Gespurn," she said by way of explanation as Bait gaped.

Baird circled the mainmast, his movements fluid and graceful, belying his immense size. Each step reverberated through the deck, sending shudders through the timbers. His feet pounded out a rhythm that grew faster and more insistent with every beat. The wind began to rise, dark clouds gathering on the horizon, swirling in response to the giant's summons.

"It's going to get gusty," Killian said. "Is there somewhere we can talk?"

"Galley." Bait led them below and down a narrow corridor to the ship's kitchen, which was empty but for a cook busy with a half-dozen fish. They took a seat at a scarred table on stools that were bolted to the floor, the clatter of copper pots hanging from the ceiling over the cook's workspace more than serving to drown out what words they might say.

"I was looking for Killian, but I'm glad I found you, Lydia." Bait rested his elbows on the table, head in his hands. "I'm gods-damned terrified. I have no idea how the legions are treating Teriana, whether she's been harmed, or . . . or anything. The Gamdeshians are furious with her. Our people are furious with her. Everyone is acting as though she's on the Empire's side, mostly because—" He broke off, throat moving as he swallowed. "Marcus is the Empire incarnate. He represents everything Teriana hates, and I can't believe that she'd—Gods, I can't even say it."

"I agree." Lydia's chest tightened at the tears gleaming in Bait's eyes. "Lucius is evil, and what he's using Marcus and the legions to accomplish is no different than what the Corrupter is using Rufina and the blight to accomplish. Everyone is looking for someone to blame, and it's falling on Teriana, but the truth is that she got into this mess trying to help me out of a horrible situation. It was *my fault* that Vibius found *Treatise of the Seven* in my library. I should have hidden it better. Or destroyed it. Instead, it landed in Cassius's hands, and while his discovery of the West may have been inevitable, if there is anyone who should be blamed for setting these events in motion, it's *me*."

Killian's hand rested on her back. "We know that the Corrupter has some form of connection with this Lucius Cassius, and if the Six were aware of who you were, and where you were, the Seventh surely was as well. You were involved even before Teriana gave you that book, so I think that even if you'd shown every caution, events would have transpired in much the same way. Regardless of who did or didn't know, it's still easier to blame Teriana because her actions are visible."

"I love her," Bait whispered. "I've loved her since we were children, and I know she doesn't feel the same way but that doesn't change how I feel. I want to get her out of this mess but I don't know how."

Madoria believes Teriana is where she needs to be.

Lydia jerked as Magnius's voice invaded her thoughts, as did Killian, though Bait only scowled. "Quit eavesdropping, you overgrown snake." He pressed his hands to the table. "Madoria may be correct that Teriana is best placed for whatever the Six hope will happen, but that doesn't mean she won't get hurt. Doesn't mean that she hasn't *already* been hurt, and I'm not willing to sacrifice her on the basis of vagaries. Give us a reason, Magnius. Something concrete that explains what Madoria thinks Teriana will do. A reason why she needs to be with those Cel dogs."

Show more faith in the goddess. You yourself are proof of her power.

Bait snorted in annoyance. "Right. You don't know either."

Lydia blinked. "You're marked by Madoria?"

"Oh. Well, yes." Bait seemed surprised she didn't know. "Most Maarin ships have one of Madoria's marked aboard because we are good for salvage, among other things. Fara is the *Kairense*'s diver."

Lydia had met Fara, the marked girl who was part of the *Kairense*'s crew, when she'd traveled with Dareena. Fara had calmed the seas when they'd escaped from the opening in the cliffs beneath the palace in Mudaire, but the girl had kept to herself during the journey, so Lydia had learned nothing more about her mark. "This seems a foolish question, but what does your mark allow you to do, Bait?"

"Breathe underwater." He hesitated. "Control the tides, though we avoid that if at all possible as it has unintended consequences."

"You should just flood the legion camp," Killian grumbled. "Drown the lot and steal Teriana back in the chaos."

"As tempting as that is, a lot of innocent people would drown as well." Rising to his feet, Bait went to a storage cabinet and extracted a bottle and three glasses. "The wave that I'd have to form to reach that far inland would be immense and far reaching. It would flood all of Aracam, which is full of civilians, killing many and then dragging more back out to sea when it retreated. I'd consider it a tool of last resort."

Lydia took the glass Bait offered her and sipped the wine, recognizing it as Atlian vintage. "What about the *Quincense* and the rest of the crew? Where are they?"

"On an island off the coast of Arinoquia," Bait said. "It's where the legions keep their injured, all under heavy guard. They know about Magnius, so they keep several crew members under heavy guard far away from the water as hostages."

"Are they well treated?" Her mind went to Teriana's aunt Yedda, the old woman near and dear to her own heart.

"Yes." Bait gave a sharp shake of his head. "But still prisoners, just like Teriana."

Lydia ran a fingernail down a scratch on the table, thinking. "Madoria's words make me wonder if Teriana has a strategy in play. I think it needs to be her choice whether to leave the legions, not ours. We focus on ensuring she has all the information she needs, and then trust her to make the right choices with it. Agreed?"

Bait nodded. "Agreed. I'll get you to Serlania and then travel to Revat to learn what has developed, then I'll go find her."

"We will travel with you," Lydia said. "Malahi needs to rejoin the High Lords, but I need to seek the aid of the library in Revat. What we learned in Anukastre is only part of the picture, and everything depends on the Gamdeshians having the final piece, even if they don't know it."

Killian abruptly stood, rubbing at his arm where Ceenah had cut him, his jaw tense and his eyes distant.

"What is it?" Lydia asked, her unease rising.

"My skin is crawling," he muttered. "Every instinct in my body is telling me that something is happening and that I need to act."

Her heart lurched. "Teriana?"

"Maybe. Bait, I know you have means to travel faster than any ship. Could you go ahead and track down Teriana?"

"Yes. Magnius can carry me, and we can use the ocean paths that ships can't access."

"I think you should go ahead of us," Killian said. "I can't give a reason, but I sense that speaking with Teriana can't wait."

"I've never known your gut to be wrong. I'll leave tonight." Bait gestured to the wineglass. "But first I want to hear of everything that has happened since we parted. I might only have one chance to speak to Teriana, and I want to be able to tell her everything she needs to know. Everything. Magnius will listen as well, because he doesn't believe in private conversations."

He gestured at the porthole in the polished wooden walls, and Lydia nearly choked on her wine when she saw an enormous eye looking through. "Is he the only one of his kind?"

We are three.

"Magnius, Aspasiana, and Lysander," Bait clarified. "One for each of the Maarin triumvirs. Aspasiana is nearby, because Vane is a triumvir, but Lysander has been moving back and forth between Revat, Serlania, and Taltuga."

Taking another sip of her wine, Lydia mused over how deeply everyone underestimated the Maarin. For all they were relegated to the role of traders and messengers, they held more power at sea than all the navies of the world combined, for she'd no doubt that Magnius and his kind were more than capable of sinking ships. But rather than saying as much, she rested her elbows on the table. "Let's start from the beginning."

* * *

Hours later, when they'd exhausted both wine and conversation, they stood next to the railing with Bait and Vane. "Be careful," Lydia warned her friend. "You heard Agrippa. The legions won't hesitate to kill you if they believe you're a threat, and you know better than to underestimate them."

"I won't let them catch me," Bait promised.

"And when you see Teriana, tell her I love her." Tears pricked in

Lydia's eyes because it felt so profoundly wrong that she wasn't going to her friend's rescue. That she was, for all intents and purposes, turning her back on her best friend in favor of other priorities. "No matter what has happened, she is my sister until the end."

Bait nodded, then clapped Killian on the shoulder. "Take care of her." Then he leaned closer and muttered something in Killian's ear, earning a soft laugh and a thanks.

"Fast winds and smooth seas," Bait said to Vane, then he dived off the ship, disappearing into the black waters.

"The winds we have thanks to Baird," the captain said. "If the seas remain our friend, we will be in Serlania in less than a week, the Six willing."

Lydia inclined her head, watching as Vane retreated into the quarters he was sharing with his first mate while Malahi had his cabin. "What did Bait say to you?"

"That instead of a hammock with the rest of the crew, we can have his room," Killian replied. "Let's go have a look."

With a flush of anticipation, Lydia lifted her bag over her shoulder and followed him inside the ship to where the quarters for the higher-ranking crew members were located. Bait's quarters were tiny, little more than a narrow bed, a wardrobe, a washstand, and a sea chest. There was a distinct lack of personal touch, which made sense given that this ship wasn't Bait's home, but Lydia felt the hollowness of it. Knew that for all his bluster and focus on Teriana, Bait grieved his absence from the *Quincense* and her crew, whom she knew were a family to him.

Setting her belongings in the corner, Lydia poured water into a basin, distinctly aware that this was the first time since they'd been in Obarri that she and Killian had been alone. The first time they'd had any form of privacy since she'd mastered her mark and removed her gloves, and her nerves warred with her anticipation as she washed her hands and face. The former won the battle, and she turned and blurted out, "What did Ceenah say to you before she left?"

Killian was busy checking the lock on the door, but he went still at the question. "She had a few thoughts about you," he finally said. Instead of elaborating, he unbuckled his sword and put it near the bed, then removed his coat and hung it on a hook.

"Are you going to tell me?" Uneasiness added to the mix of emotions running laps in her stomach.

"She said you didn't just draw upon the life nearby to heal me." Killian went to the porthole and looked out at the night. "She said you drew upon all the life of Reath, and she's never seen that before. Didn't know it was possible."

In her mind's eye, Lydia saw the glowing clouds of mist that had surged toward her, far more than she'd needed to heal Killian's wound. She'd known what she'd done, but not the extent of it, and Lydia wasn't sure how she felt about being different from other healers.

"Ceenah thinks it's because Hegeria has touched you twice. First to mark you and then again to aid you against the Corrupter, and that it has given you more power than other healers," Killian said. "Her fear is that your strength will only make the Seventh work harder to tempt you, because your power can do as much harm as good."

She bit the insides of her cheeks. "Did she say anything else?"

"Yes. But it was for my ears, not yours."

Curiosity bit at her insides, but Lydia left it alone as she watched him pull off his shirt and hang it on the hook with his coat. Crossing to the washstand, he began to scrub away the dirt and sand of their journey across the desert.

Realizing she was staring, Lydia dug her comb out of her bag. She unfastened the tie holding the end of her braid and began to unravel the lengths, sand coming loose as she did. But she scarcely noticed, for it was impossible to tear her eyes from Killian's naked back.

The lamplight cast shadows across his broad shoulders and tapered waist, taut muscles testament to a lifetime of trials and training, the long grueling weeks on the road ensuring that there was not a spare ounce of flesh on him. Her eyes roved over the scars from battles, the white lines stark against his olive skin, which had grown darker in the unforgiving sun of Anukastre. Without his belt, his trousers hung low on his hips, and as he twisted to scrub the washcloth across his shoulder, the lamplight illuminated his stomach, the hard V of muscle drawing her eyes downward. Lydia busied herself with combing out the tangles of her hair.

It was nothing she hadn't seen before, both in her mind and in the flesh, yet there had always been something that had stood between them. First Malahi, then Lydia's lack of control of her mark, then the presence of their companions.

But now? There were no obstacles between them, yet Lydia felt paralyzed by uncertainty over how to claim the moment she'd dreamed of for so long.

Wait to see what he does, her nervous mind cautioned even as her heart told her that Killian would not instigate. How could he, given what she'd put him through? Either by shoving him away or trying to kill him. Killian wasn't afraid of what she'd do to him, Lydia knew that, but he was afraid of the consequences to *her* if he pushed too far. And she desperately wanted him to push all the way. Which meant she needed to take the first step.

"When I returned to Mudaire after Alder's Ford, I missed you so much." She toyed with her comb. "I used to imagine you coming into the temple to find me. The sound of your boots coming down the hall to my room. What you'd say. What you'd do." She lifted her head to meet his gaze. "What it would feel like to be yours in every possible way."

She saw Killian's throat move as he swallowed, blindly setting the cloth behind him on the washstand, though he said nothing.

"I swear I imagined being reunited with you in every possible way, which means little given that I know *nothing* about what happens in such moments," Lydia said softly. "Yet when we finally found each other, it was nothing like my dreams. Instead, it was battle and blood and fighting for our lives, the distance between us vanquished only to be replaced by what has oftentimes felt like insurmountable obstacles. All of which we've conquered, and though I know no more than I did in those cold dark nights alone in my room in that tower in Mudaire, what I want is the same." She hesitated, then said, "I want you, Killian. All of you. And I want you to have all of me."

Killian made a low noise, then dropped to his knees before her, his hands on her hips. "You are my everything, Lydia." He pulled her to the edge of the bed. "There is nothing I wouldn't give you, least of all myself. I love you."

Her heart was beating so hard it threatened to tear from her chest, and Lydia tangled her fingers in his dark hair, the silky strands longer than he normally wore it. "I love you," she whispered. "But for all my imaginings of this moment, I . . . I don't know anything. I need you to show me how."

Killian let out a choked laugh, then lowered his head to rest it against her thigh. "What makes you think that I know more than you?"

She bit her lip. "I thought . . ."

"My reputation with women is grossly exaggerated, Lydia. I've never . . ." He exhaled a shaky breath. "That's what I was asking Agrippa about when we were captured by Xadrian, because he knows a lot about . . . Well, suffice it to say that he knows a lot about a lot of things."

"Oh, gods." Her face burned. "I'm terrified to think of what he had to say."

"He said, 'You two are forever, which means there will be countless times. But only one *first time*, so don't rush it.'"

Forever.

"Oh." Lydia frowned and caught hold of his chin, lifting his face. "But that's not all he told you, was it?"

Killian's mouth turned up in a half smile, even as his eyes darkened, his hands tightening on her hips. "No, it wasn't."

He removed her spectacles and set them next to the washstand. Catching her by the waist, he lifted her to her feet, then his hand curved around the back of her head as he kissed her. Softly at first, and it gave Lydia the chance to do what she'd wanted for so long, which was to *touch* him. His skin was smooth beneath her fingertips, and she trailed them over the hard curves and valleys of the muscles forming his shoulders. His arms. His back. Downward until they snagged on the waist of his trousers, stopping there half for nerves and half for the intensity of his kiss, which was soft no longer.

His tongue parted her lips, and Lydia gasped as it stroked into her mouth, stoking the heat in her core. Then he abandoned her lips, kissing down her jaw, then her throat, his fingers catching the hem of her tunic and lifting it over her head, casting it aside. The air in the room was cool, and with only a thin camisole to cover her torso, Lydia's skin pebbled.

All thoughts of the cold vanished from her head as his hands drifted over her sides, his mouth raining kisses on her collarbone and shoulders, then down farther still, claiming the peak of her breast through the thin silk.

Lydia gasped, her knees shuddering at the sensation, only her grip on his shoulders keeping her from losing her balance. He moved to the other breast, the heat of his mouth making her ache, though nothing could prepare her for him lifting the camisole over her head and the feel of his tongue against her naked flesh.

"If you want me to stop, just tell me to stop," Killian said as he moved down the flat expanse of her stomach, tongue catching on her navel and making her shudder.

"Don't stop," she breathed, for her imagination had fallen far short of reality, every part of her quivering with the need for *more*.

Killian unfastened her belt, and her trousers slid over her hips to pool at her feet. She stepped on the heels of her boots to drag them off, kicking leather and fabric away as he dropped to his knees before her. His breath was hot just above the top of the undergarments, his hands equally so as his fingers stroked her legs before catching on that last scrap of clothing she wore and tugging it down, leaving her naked before him.

"You're so beautiful." Killian looked up at her with reverence. "The bravest woman on Reath, and you are mine."

"Yours," she repeated, running her fingers over his high cheekbones and strong jaw, stubble rough beneath her fingertips, face so perfect that it made her breath catch. "Forever."

He kissed one of her hipbones and then the other, pausing a heartbeat before his hands closed around her thighs and his mouth claimed her as his.

A sob tore from her throat; there was no room for thoughts, only sensation. Her hand braced against the wall for balance as she drowned in the feeling of finally having what her heart longed for. In finally erasing all distance between them, leaving nothing behind but breath and touch and love.

When she crested the edge, pleasure she'd never known possible crashing over her like a wave, the strength of her knees finally abandoned her, and Lydia collapsed into Killian's arms. Clung to his neck while she remembered how to breathe, her skin slowly cooling where it wasn't pressed to his.

Yet no part of her felt sated. Not with Killian still half dressed, his breath ragged against her temple, his desire pressing against her through his clothes. For all her inexperience, Lydia knew enough to move against him, her heart skipping as Killian groaned.

"I want to know what you want," she breathed, trailing her tongue around the rim of his ear and feeling him shudder.

"You."

She trailed her nails down his back, tracing the hard lines of muscle and old scars. "Be more specific."

"Lydia . . ."

A smile curved onto her lips, because she knew that he was warring with the propriety that was engrained with him. She kissed him, stroking her tongue over his, then murmured, "Tell me."

Propriety lost the war, and his dark eyes locked with hers. "I want to be in you. I want to claim every part of you."

Lydia's heart accelerated with anticipation, and planting her feet on the floor, she rose to her feet, drawing Killian with her. She kissed his throat, his chest, struck by how in control she felt despite being so small relative to his muscled bulk. His fingers tangled in her hair as she unfastened the laces of his trousers and drew them down, Killian kicking them aside so that he was naked before her.

Nothing between them, and there never would be again.

She took hold of him, her breath catching at the heat of his skin. "Show me how."

Killian's hand wrapped around hers, and desire pooled in her core as his head tilted back at her touch, pulse throbbing in his throat. "Oh, gods, Lydia."

Her skin felt on fire with need, her toes curling against the rough wood floors. Every part of her wanting more. Wanting everything.

She pushed him down onto the bed, then straddled him, her knees to either side of his narrow hips. "I want this," she said between kisses. "I want to give you this."

Killian's strong hands gripped her hips, moving her. Lifting her.

A whimper pulled from her lips as they came together, kisses desperate and frantic with a need that surpassed the need to breathe, nothing mattering but each other.

"Don't stop," she sobbed, her body teetering toward climax again. His teeth scraped her throat, the bite of pain making her dig in her nails.

Her darkness was still there. The need to *take* that would be with her all her life, Killian's life coating her hands and daring her to claim it.

Yet rather than tearing away from her, Killian only flipped her onto her back, his hands pinioning hers to the mattress. "You're mine, Lydia," he growled. "No one else's. Not ever."

A wave of pleasure rushed through her, driving away darker needs as her body shuddered beneath him. Killian groaned, his fingers tightening, her name on his lips as he pressed his cheek to hers.

There was no sound but that of their breath and the creak of the ship.

"Are you all right?" he asked, lifting his head to meet her gaze.

Lydia smiled up at him, the love of her life. The one she trusted above all else. "Yes."

Killian laid her down on the narrow bed, curling around her back and then pulling the blanket over them both. The *Kairense* rocked on the swells, the rhythmic slap of the waves against the hull lulling her to sleep. Lydia's last thought was that now that they were together, there was no power on Reath that would separate them.

44

TERIANA

Logically Teriana had known that the Cel legions moved faster than any army on all of Reath, but she'd always assumed it was because of their access to xenthier stems.

She'd been wrong.

The legions moved quickly because their commanders made them *run*.

It reminded Teriana of her trek with Marcus across Sibern, except this was *thousands* of men, all stretched in a winding snake down the lone road leading north, sunlight glinting off weapons, armor, and sweat-soaked skin. There was no stopping, everything—and she meant *everything*—done in the all too short moments when the centurions allowed their men to walk. Which meant there were things Teriana bore witness to that she sorely wished she could expunge from her brain. The road both looked and smelled like a latrine from the men ahead of them, and she swiftly came to understand why Quintus had told her there were benefits to being in the front of the line.

"I'm not pissing off the side of a horse!" she'd snarled at him early in the journey, forcing him to veer into the jungle, where she'd crouched behind a tree to do her business, her eyes all for the endless ranks of men who were given no such grace.

"This is inhuman," she'd added when she was once again behind Quintus on the horse, cantering up the sides of the column to regain their position. "No one should be treated like this. Not even animals are treated like this."

Quintus had only laughed. "Welcome to the hard march, Teriana. But trust me when I say, Marcus is actually going easy on us, likely in deference to the puppies. The Thirty-Seventh has done worse, in far worse conditions. At least we get breaks to sleep."

The longest *break* was four hours, each of those hours spent curled up next to Quintus's back pretending she wasn't fully aware of the filth around her, her lids no sooner shutting as some ass of a centurion was shouting the order to rise. The order to march. The order to move faster or *else*.

The *else* would have quickly made itself clear even if Quintus hadn't explained. "The ruse that all four legions are on those ships will only work for so long, then the Gamdeshians will discover we're marching to the Orinok ford and whatever bridge Rastag has conjured. The Gamdeshians have access to cavalry, and Kaira will send reinforcements, so unless we want to fight ten times the current number defending that crossing, we need to beat them there."

"How is this even going to work?" Her ass ached from bouncing on the horse's back. "From what I've heard, the bridge doesn't even reach halfway across. Rastag had to stop construction because the Gamdeshians were throwing rocks at them with their catapults."

"Boats, I assume. I don't recommend trying to swim in armor, plus I've heard that river has all sorts of creatures that bite swimming around in it."

She'd heard the same. "But won't the Gamdeshians use the catapults to hit the boats?"

"It's harder than you'd think to hit a moving target." Quintus rolled his shoulders, grumbling about how his back hurt, then he added, "Might be why the Forty-First is the vanguard and not the Thirty-Seventh. Though in truth, it's out of character for Marcus not to put us front and center of the attack. He trusts us more than the others. At any rate, he and Felix will have an idea of the cost we will incur taking the northern banks, and they obviously reckon it less than us trying to land by sea on a heavily defended coastline."

Not cost in gold. Cost in lives.

"Then what is the Thirty-First doing?" It didn't make sense that Marcus hadn't brought the older, stronger legion for this task. "Are they just sailing about, sunning themselves on the decks of the Katamarcan ships?"

"You're asking the wrong person," Quintus answered. "Though I suspect the right person isn't going to be forthcoming."

That conversation had been on the second day of the march, and the days since had proven Quintus's words to be more than accurate, for Marcus hadn't so much as glanced her way. Most certainly hadn't spoken to her. All he'd done was ride down the muddy road looking straight ahead, showing little sign that the high stakes weighed upon him at all.

Trust him, she reminded herself over and over, touching the tiny ship bouncing against her cheek. *This is what he does. This is what he's famous for.*

Yet for all her admonitions, it still hurt that Marcus refused to bring her into the fold. That they weren't together, and never would be again.

Nic trotted his horse along the ranks of men, his bodyguard keeping tight ranks around him. "Nic!" she called out. "Come here."

His mouth twisted, and Teriana could see the boy was thinking of ignoring her.

"My how things have changed since the prodigy decided to give him the time of day," Quintus said with a chuckle, but then fell silent as Nic reined his horse next to theirs.

"Don't ask me anything you know I can't tell you."

She gave Nic a long look. "Hello, Austornic. How is the march treating you?"

The sigh he gave her was world-weary. "Well enough. Is there something you need?"

Teriana wanted to press him for information. To dig Marcus's plan out of him. But instead she asked, "Are you worried?"

"Why would I be?"

Quintus gave a soft snort of amusement and Teriana punched him in the side, then cursed as her fingers clanked against steel. "It's your first real battle, and I assume you have no idea what the plan is."

The muscles in Nic's jaw flexed, but his tone was bland as he said, "I know what I need to know." He dug his heels into his horse and continued up the line of men.

"He doesn't know shit," Quintus cackled. "But I see that Marcus is already starting to rub off on him. Poker face and nonanswers. I wonder how much longer until we find the puppy disappearing for solo jaunts where he stares broodingly off into the distance."

Teriana watched Nic straighten his cloak and square his posture as he rode up next to Marcus's golden mare. "I don't want Nic to get hurt trying to impress him. He's just a boy."

"Don't worry," Quintus said. "Marcus will keep them out of the thick of it."

"How could that possibly go wrong given that we all *know what we need to know.*" Teriana couldn't keep the sarcasm out of her voice.

Her friend laughed, but there was no humor in it. "Welcome to the life of an Empire legionnaire, Teriana. Go where you're told to go. Do what you're told to do. Try not to die while doing it. It doesn't matter how terrifying the enemy is, because the senate looking down from their hill is far, *far* worse."

Sighing, Teriana rested her forehead against Quintus's back. The uncertainty exhausted her. Made her want to lie down and curl in on herself, allowing sleep to take her away from all the troubles of this world. As if sensing her thoughts, Quintus took hold of her interlocked hands where they rested against his armored stomach. "Have a nap," he said. "I won't let you fall, and when you wake, we should be there. Then the interesting part will begin."

"Interesting isn't the word I'd use." Yet the swaying motion of the horse lulled her, and she slipped into a shallow sleep.

Lydia sat on a bench next to her, the Valerius gardens a riot of green and color, dappled light drifting through the trees that shaded them. "How long will you be here?" Lydia asked.

The question felt more important than it should have been, but Teriana didn't know why. So she only said, "I don't know."

"It feels as though your visits grow shorter and shorter." Lydia sipped at her lemonade, green eyes unfocused behind her spectacles, as though she were seeing something that Teriana did not.

"My mother's decision." She pressed fingers to her temples, the reason for her mother's behavior lurking just beyond reach. "Or maybe your father's. I . . . I can't remember."

Footsteps thudded down a path in the distance, an angry voice filling her ears.

Curious, Teriana rose and went to the wall that divided the property from the neighbors. As she rested her elbows on the ancient stone, the world abruptly fell dark, and Marcus stood before her.

"I knew her," he said. "When I was a small child. I used to play with her in her father's library. She was kind."

"Teriana?"

It brightened to daylight again, Lydia leaning against the wall. "That's Gaius Domitius," she said, and Teriana's eyes tracked to the young man storming through the shaded gardens.

Marcus.

Except no . . . It wasn't. This young man had longer hair and the soft arms of one who did no labor, the petulant expression on his face not an expression Marcus ever wore.

"We were playmates as children," Lydia said. "He'd read books to me in my father's library, as I didn't yet know how. Then he went away for a time, and when he came back, he'd grown cruel."

Teriana frowned. "You're mistaken. It was Marcus you knew, not Gaius. He told me."

"He lied," Lydia replied, her voice strange. Teriana turned to look at her, only to jerk back, because Lydia's eyes were inky dark and rimmed

with flame, her skin marred with black veins that pulsed with the beat of her heart. "The dead are never mistaken."

Teriana jerked awake and would have fallen off the side of the horse if not for Quintus's grip on her hands.

"Oh good, you're awake," he said. "We're here."

Teriana blinked against the brilliant brightness of the midday sun. Quintus had reined in the horse at the top of a ridge, and her jaw dropped at what lay before her.

She'd known the Orinok was vast, but from the sea, it merely looked like a hundred dark mouths emerging from the vast mangrove swamps. Whereas from this vantage . . .

Teriana swallowed hard as she took in the wide snaking path of brown river. It was the border not just between Gamdesh and Arinoquia, but also the border between Gamdesh and the wild expanses of jungle that made up the Uncharted Lands. The monstrous river was the only break in the canopy of forest, although the jungle had been aggressively cleared on both sides of this section of the river. Which meant she had a clear view of the bridge Rastag had been charged with building, which stretched about half of the way across.

While she knew that there used to be a ferry system here with barges attached to ropes that stretched between the multiple rocky outcroppings, Teriana couldn't help but question the choice to build a bridge at this location. The river at this point appeared twice as wide as it did just a little bit farther upstream and downstream.

Frowning, she slid off the side of the horse and removed her pack. She removed her spyglass, and lifting it to her eye, Teriana examined the bridge.

Which was no bridge at all.

It was a *dam*.

Taking a step closer to the ridgeline, Teriana examined the structure, which looked to her as though the legionnaires had been dumping rock and rubble into the river, then building a boardwalk of wood over top of it. Not only was it nothing like the feats of architecture that the Cel were known for, but there was a gods-damned reason you didn't use a dam to make a bridge, because it would—

"Oh." She blew out a long breath between her teeth. "I see."

The river was wide here because Rastag's dam bridge had caused it to overflow the northern banks. The small fortress town of Rita had flooded, so only the upper halves of the buildings were visible above the flow of water. The Gamdeshians had formed a tent camp beyond the edge of the flooded river, complete with swiftly constructed wooden fortifications and catapults, the latter what had stopped the construction perhaps eight hundred feet from the northern bank.

"Rastag, this is your best work yet! A true thing of beauty!" Quintus shouted with a laugh, and Teriana lowered her spyglass to see the Thirty-Seventh's engineer standing with his arms crossed in front of a large white pavilion. Rastag scowled at Quintus, shaking his head in disgust before retreating to the shade. He somehow tripped over his own feet, only saved from a fall by one of the legionnaires tasked with watching over him. His other minder retrieved Rastag's spectacles from the ground, placing them back on his face before guiding him into the pavilion. A flicker of memory of Marcus saying that the engineer vied with Racker as the most valued member of the legion filtered through Teriana's mind. She glanced back at the dam, not seeing the genius of it given that it had not remotely solved the issue of crossing the river.

But Teriana's instincts were still firing, telling her that she was missing something. She turned in a circle, searching for the man who held every answer in his head. But Marcus was nowhere in sight.

"What's going to happen now?" she asked, rounding on Quintus, who only shrugged and said, "We'll fight. Hopefully they surrender, but if not, they'll die. What remains to be seen is the numbers we'll lose getting to that point."

Despite the obvious challenges, his confidence seemed reasonable. The seemingly endless line of legionnaires snaked out of sight down the road, but those who had arrived were already forming up in neat ranks on either side of the road, rows and rows of carts that had transported rubble only to be abandoned filling the banks before them. Centurions barked orders, and some of the men began removing the wheels from the carts. Teriana's heart skipped as she realized they'd been designed to serve the double purpose of boats.

Quintus gave a soft laugh. "Ah, Rastag, you are a genius."

Sunlight glittered off shields, weapons, and armor, and as she lifted her spyglass back to her eye, it was to watch the Gamdeshians racing to prepare for an assault they had no chance of holding against.

Run! she wanted to scream. *Retreat!*

But there was a grim determination in the faces she saw through the spyglass, a willingness to die for the sake of killing as many of the invaders as they could, despite the outcome being inevitable.

You did this, her conscience accused. *You brought this down upon them.*

Which meant the blood of all who fell today was on her hands as surely as if she'd wielded a weapon herself. A painful throbbing pulse formed in her skull, and Teriana pressed fingers to her temple, the sun abruptly seeming too bright. *Retreat,* she willed the ranks of Gamdeshians on the distant bank. *Live to fight another day, because we will need every one of you.*

Except that day would come all too soon, for once the legions gained the bank and took Rita, they'd begin the march on Emrant. The port city held the xenthier stem that she and Cassius both desperately sought, albeit for entirely different reasons. A city with a hundred thousand Gamdeshian civilians, which Kaira would not concede without a fight. It would be bloody and vicious, the armies nearly matched in size.

And to save her people, Teriana needed Marcus to win.

Thousands of lives for five hundred Maarin souls.

Teriana's eyes burned, the world spinning until she remembered to take a breath. Then another. *You chose this,* she reminded herself. *You bet the many to save your few. Now is not the time to lose your nerve. You cannot break.*

"You all right, Teriana?" Quintus's voice was filled with concern.

"Fine." She swallowed. "It's hot."

He caught hold of her arm and steered her toward the pavilion. Rastag was sitting inside reviewing pages of drawings in the corner under the watchful eye of his bodyguard, but other than Amarin, who was filling cups with water and setting them out on the table, the pavilion was empty.

Where was he?

"Giving last-minute orders," Quintus answered, and Teriana realized she'd spoken aloud. "He won't arrive until everyone is in position."

A practiced routine, and sweat dripped down her brow as she considered the number of times they'd done this. The number of battles they'd fought. The number of nations they'd invaded. This was the well-oiled machine that ruled the East with organization and an iron fist, and though she'd eaten and drunk and *lived* with them for a year, this was the first time she was truly seeing why the Empire *ruled.*

She'd made a mistake.

Unleashed a force she hadn't really comprehended.

A force that couldn't be pushed back, couldn't be stopped.

Teriana's body trembled as she watched the slope below her filled with men. Filled with *legion.*

The Forty-First.

The Thirty-Seventh.

And lastly, the Fifty-First, who formed a perimeter of defense around the pavilion, no longer children but smaller versions of the men arrayed before them.

They all fell still, no one speaking a word, not even a whisper, the only sound the faint rushing of the Orinok and the wind blowing through distant trees.

Then she heard the drum.

A repeated rhythm, ominous in its simplicity, and as Teriana watched, a drummer leading a procession of mounted legionnaires appeared.

Astride the golden horse, Marcus followed the drummer, Nic and Felix behind him, the rest of their officers following, but Teriana barely noticed them, her eyes all for *him*. His crimson cloak billowed behind him on the breeze, golden dragon dancing as the ranks parted to make a path before stepping back into position after the procession had passed. His expression was hidden by the nose and cheek pieces of his helmet, but his posture was confident. Relaxed. As though he were on a ride through a park, his only care what food had been packed for a picnic lunch, not the thousands of men about to cross a river in a battle that was sure to turn the water red straight down to the sea.

"What's he doing?" she muttered, for while Nic and the others were making their way to the pavilion, Marcus had continued riding through the ranks. "What's the point of this?"

"Showmanship," Quintus replied. "A show of confidence that boosts morale of the men, while at the same time putting the fear into the enemy. Look." He lifted her hand and aimed her spyglass toward the northern bank. Teriana's chest tightened, for the Gamdeshians had stopped their flurry of activity and were silently watching, arms slack at their sides. "I hate this," she said, ignoring the officers dismounting their horses and walking into the pavilion. "Why is the world this way?"

"Greed." Quintus's eyes tracked Marcus as he finally began to weave his way up the slope toward them. "Men who seek power and wealth and glory are never satisfied. They only want more, and they believe it is their right to walk upon the backs of those they use to achieve it, for it keeps their feet out of the mud."

Teriana bit her lip, silent as Marcus reached the open space before the pavilion. He dismounted, handing the reins to Amarin and moving to stand at the edge of the ridge, surveying the gleaming ranks of his army.

No one moved.

No one spoke.

All the world seemed to be holding its breath, the only motion the ebb and swirl of Marcus's cloak in the wind, and the only sound Teriana's thundering heart.

Marcus cleared his throat, then said, "Proceed."

The hornblower standing to the side lifted his instrument to his lips.

The sharp blast echoed into the river valley, and as its note faded, Marcus turned on his heel and strode past Teriana and Quintus into the pavilion.

"He isn't going to watch?" she hissed, torn between gaping at the flow of ranks moving down to the water's edge and Marcus, who had handed his helmet to Amarin and then seated himself on one of the stools.

"Doesn't need to." Quintus drew her forward so they stood on the ridgeline. "There will be a constant stream of reports. Besides, watching implies interest, which suggests concern that the battle won't go exactly to his plan, which gives the enemy confidence. Even if everything is going all to shit, to the enemy's eyes, he'll always appear cool as a cup of water on a hot day."

Marcus might be cool, but Teriana was dripping sweat. Below, the first ranks were already in the boats, oars in hands as they pressed laterally across the river. The rest of the army remained still and unmoving as statues.

"What's interesting," Quintus said, "is that he told the Forty-First that they were the vanguard, but it's our boys getting into those boats. Also, we appear to be missing a century of men."

"What does that mean?"

Her friend shrugged. "I'm sure we'll find out soon. This won't take long."

On the northern bank, the Gamdeshians were a flurry of activity. Smoke from fires rose into the air, great vats steaming above them, and piles of stones rested next to fifteen catapults, all armed and ready to deploy when the boats came into range.

"They're going to die." Horror built in her stomach. "Quintus, he needs to stop this. This is wrong, they're all going to burn or drown, and he's just sitting there"—she wheeled around to look at Marcus—"eating a fucking apple!"

The last came out more shrilly than she'd intended, and all eyes in the pavilion went to her. "You can't do this. You can't let hundreds of men die just to gain a riverbank."

"Thousands of men have died for less," Marcus responded around a mouthful of apple. "But thousands of men won't die today. Felix, are they in position?"

"They're approaching the Gamdeshians' range, sir," Felix said, and Teriana's stomach plummeted as she realized the boats were well past the halfway point, rowing hard.

"Good." Marcus abandoned his apple core on Amarin's tray. "Rastag, shall we see what fruits your efforts yield?"

The engineer was clutching his papers in the corner, sweat beading on his brow. "I should perhaps accompany it, sir. To ensure the calibrations are correct."

"The Gamdeshians are deploying their catapults, sir," Felix said.

"Range?"

"As anticipated."

"Good. Signal to hold position." Marcus grasped Rastag's elbow and led him out of the pavilion. "You're too important to risk," he said to the engineer, giving Teriana a look she couldn't parse as he passed her. "You selected the men yourself, and they *will* follow your instructions."

"If it's the slightest bit off—"

"It won't be."

All the officers moved out of the tent, and Teriana stood frozen, not wanting to watch. Not wanting the horror of witnessing so many deaths under a storm of rock and fire, their bodies left to float down the river to the sea. But she made herself walk back to the ridge to stand next to Quintus.

Below her, the ranks remained still and unchanged where they were arrayed on the slope, but on the water . . . there were dozens upon dozens of boats, the legionnaires in them rowing hard to keep in position just out of reach of the Gamdeshian catapults. There was a loud *crack* as one deployed, a stone the size of a man's skull soaring through the air. It exploded into the water, spraying the men in the nearest boat, having barely missed.

Yet that wasn't what held Marcus's attention.

Teriana frowned, following his line of sight. A group of legionnaires was carefully moving a catapult down the hill, the war machine larger than she'd ever seen. Even so . . . "What are they going to do with the catapult?" The river was too wide to fling rocks across.

"Trebuchet," Quintus corrected, then whistled between his teeth.

"See that big block of stone waiting at the end of the bridge? That's not building material, it's a counterweight."

Teriana watched in silence as the war machine was pulled down the length of the bridge, which brought them just outside the range of the Gamdeshian catapults.

Her concern for the legions had been misplaced.

Lives would be lost.

But it wouldn't be theirs.

You did this, her conscience accused. *You brought them here because your few mattered more than Gamdesh's many.*

The Gamdeshians saw the threat and turned their own catapults on the Cel trebuchet, but the rocks fell short.

Just as had been intended.

Out of the corner of her eye, Marcus nodded once, then a horn blasted. A heartbeat later, a deafening *crack* split the air, the monstrous war machine hurling a stone at the northern banks with deadly aim.

It slammed into one of the Gamdeshian catapults, wood flying every direction.

It was not the only victim.

Teriana hugged her arms around her body, unable to look away from the writhing forms of those who'd been injured. Or the still ones on the ground next to them.

Yet the others didn't run, choosing to hold their ground.

Crack!

Another rock hurled through the air at a catapult, and tears trickled down her cheeks as it struck true.

"Surrender," she whispered. "Put down your weapons."

But as the legions carefully destroyed the catapults one by one, the Gamdeshians only pulled their weapons, staff and bow and sword, all held at the ready.

Marcus nodded again, and the cursed horn blew a series of notes. The legionnaires in the boats began to row hard for shore, those without oars lifting shields overhead as sheets of arrows fell.

Teriana's body shook with tension, breath coming in rapid pants. "Surrender," she pleaded, willing her words across the massive river. "*Please.*"

"They may not," Quintus said, then, softly enough that only she could hear, he added, "You don't need to watch, Teriana."

She realized now that *this* had been the point of Marcus's demonstration with the Fifty-First's test of nerve. To show her what it would be like.

But this time, she refused to run. "I have to watch."

Teriana clenched her teeth as the first boats neared the banks. But just before they hit the shore, another horn sounded from the north.

"Oh gods," she whispered. "Kaira didn't fall for the trick."

Horns from the north meant Kaira had arrived with reinforcements, and the outcome of the battle suddenly became much less certain. Teriana's heart threatened to tear out of her chest, the war of emotion in her making it very clear that she didn't know whose side she was on.

Lifting her spyglass, she sucked in a deep breath and *looked*.

Only for her breath to catch, because it was not Gamdesh's familiar banners moving to reinforce their countrymen, but the crimson and gold dragon. Legionnaires with a 37 on their breastplates. Only a hundred men, a pittance compared to the numbers on the field, and yet at the sight of them, it was as though the flames of the Gamdeshians' defiance had been doused with water.

They went still, looking between the dozens of boats hitting the bank and the deadly lines that had come up from their rear, the centurion leading the Thirty-Seventh shouting something at them.

The Gamdeshians lowered their weapons.

"Felix, have centurion Qian accept their surrender and ensure they are secured. Then have our medics brought over to see to their injured." Marcus turned back to the pavilion. "Rastag, I want the floating bridge in place within the hour and the fortress drained within two."

"Yes, sir." Felix motioned to signalmen and gave them orders that Teriana barely heard.

It was over. The Cel had won.

She had won.

Unspent adrenaline still surged in Teriana's veins, and with no outlet, it left the world spinning. One minute she was standing, the next she was on her ass, forehead pressed to her knees.

Quintus flopped down next to her, silently watching masses of men moving to follow orders in the river valley below. "You all right?"

Teriana shook her head.

"We couldn't have asked for a much better outcome," he said. "It could have been a lot worse, trust me on that."

She stared blankly at the dirt.

"It's one step closer to securing the xenthier stems and freeing your people." He bumped her elbow with his. "In a few weeks, the *Quincense* will be sailing to retrieve you and Cassius will have no choice but to liberate your imprisoned people."

"And then what?" The question sounded like it had been dragged over gravel.

Quintus didn't answer.

Gods help her, she'd tried. Tried to get help from Kaira. From Ereni. From her own people. No one had been willing to risk saving her five hundred.

And for the first time ever, Teriana thought perhaps they'd been right.

She'd bet everything on the belief that if it came to it, the West would have the collective strength to force the Cel back, if not across the seas, then at least to Arinoquia.

But it was now very clear to her that she'd underestimated the Empire.

That she'd underestimated *him.*

We do not fall back. That was the Thirty-Seventh's motto, and yet that was the very thing she was trusting them to do once this was over.

A hawk screamed overhead. Teriana's eyes jerked skyward to find Astara circling above, the shape-shifter's cries filled with anger and grief as she took in the scene. Teriana could only imagine how the Gamdeshian woman felt, knowing that she'd been duped by Marcus's ploy in the harbor and that the northern bank had been lost as a result.

And Emrant, a city filled with innocent civilians, would be next.

Laughter from behind caught Teriana's attention, and she turned her head to see the officers all filling their cups with drinks, toasting an easy victory, platters of food already filling the table of the pavilion. Nic was speaking excitedly with Felix, his face flushed with excitement, whatever frustration he'd felt about not knowing every step of the plan clearly erased by the glow of victory.

Marcus stood apart from the rest, and though there was a cup in his hand, he did not drink, only watched Astara circle, his face expressionless.

Teriana's heart stuttered, and a fresh wave of adrenaline surged through her veins because every instinct in her body warned that what she'd just witnessed was the tip of the iceberg.

Warned that Marcus's strategy had only just begun, and that she had only his word and a hair ornament to support her faith that he'd know when to finish it.

With his face still tipped to the sky, Marcus said, "If Astara comes within range, shoot her down, else she'll carry word of our victory here to Kaira, and I want their focus on Zimo."

Nic moved to give the order to the Fifty-First surrounding their position, and several of the boys turned their eyes skyward, weapons at the ready.

Another gods-damn trick.

Teriana clenched her teeth, knowing damn well that if Marcus actually wanted Astara dead, there'd be archers hidden and watching for her. Knowing, with the same surety that the underworld would take her soul for her role in this, that Marcus *wouldn't* have looked up at the sky as he gave the order to shoot her down, allowing the farseeing hawk to read his lips.

Nic watched Astara circle, hand shading his eyes against the sun. "Doesn't look as though she's going to come in range, sir. Orders?"

Face twisting in annoyance, Marcus drained his cup, then looked back up at the sky. "It's of no consequence. Let her flap back to her mistress and tell Kaira of how easily the northern bank fell. If Kaira knows what's good for her, she'll surrender Emrant, else they'll soon discover what it's like to be under siege by the Empire."

Was it a threat or a warning? Teriana's blood chilled, every part of her hating the cold expression on Marcus's face.

We do not fall back.

Then his face blanched, and Marcus screamed, "Shoot her!"

Teriana's eyes shot skyward to find Astara dropping with deadly speed, talons outstretched.

Not for Marcus.

For her.

A weight struck Teriana's side, all the air rushing out of her lungs as Quintus slammed her into the ground. An ear-piercing screech of talon against metal filled the air, then Quintus was twisting. Sun glinted off a blade. Blood splattered Teriana in the face. The hawk shrieked, wings pounded, wind sending feathers swirling.

And Astara was gone.

Quintus made an *oof* sound as he was yanked off her, then Marcus's face was inches from hers, blue-grey eyes wide with panic. "Are you hurt? Do you need a medic?" Without waiting for an answer, he shouted, "Get Racker!"

Gasping for breath, Teriana managed to say, "I don't need him. I'm . . ."

She trailed off as Marcus lifted her upright. His palms were hot through her clothing, his breath rapid as his eyes roved over her body, checking for injuries.

"I just had the wind knocked out of me." Her braids made little clinks as her beads swung against the metal of his breastplate. It seemed both a lifetime and a heartbeat ago that he'd last touched her, and the world faded away as his eyes locked on hers, the emotionless commander gone and the man she loved once again before her.

"I'm sorry," he said, and Teriana instinctively knew it wasn't for Astara's attack.

It was for everything else. What she knew. And what she didn't.

"I'm fine, too, sir," Quintus said. "Thank you for inquiring."

Marcus ignored him, as well as the officers in the pavilion who watched with keen interest. Like they were assessing the level of sentiment between them. "She did that to get back at me." He growled the words. "This is why I didn't want you involved."

And yet he hadn't sent her away.

Teriana shook her head. "Here or not here, it doesn't matter. My people have named me a traitor and put a target on my back. I think it fair to say the Gamdeshians have done the same."

"Traitor?" Marcus's eyes blazed with terrifying fury. "After everything you've done for your people?"

"It's because of what I've done." She hung her head, unable to meet his gaze. "They see those five hundred as casualties of war. The cost of saving them too high to pay."

"Teriana, why didn't you tell me any of this?"

She laughed because the alternative would be to cry. "Because you never gave me a chance. And because it doesn't change anything." She lifted her face and stared Marcus down. "I'm not going to break."

His eyes searched hers. "I know you won't."

Climbing to his feet, Marcus pulled Quintus upright and inspected the gouges in the metal on his back. "You'll need to have that repaired. And I'm assigning you more men."

"That bird should never have gotten so close." Quintus glared down the slope at the Fifty-First archers, who were shifting uneasily as though anticipating reprimand. "They stop teaching boys how to aim at Lescendor? How did every single one of you miss?"

"Because they were under orders to miss." Marcus took another step away from Teriana. "I wanted Astara to deliver a count of our numbers and position. But now . . ." He turned to Felix, who was tracking Astara through a spyglass. "How badly did Quintus wound her?"

"Can't tell." Felix lowered the glass. "But she's not struggling to fly, and I assume one of their healers will mend her." His eyes flicked to Teriana, and she nodded confirmation even as she hunted for her composure.

"She's passed the third marker, sir," Nic said from where he stood on the ridgeline squinting after Astara. "Do we continue with the plan?"

Marcus had known Astara would track them down. Had wanted her to see all this and bring the news back to Kaira. Teriana swallowed hard, her mind racing through what he could possibly be planning next.

"Do you still wish to pursue the same strategy, sir?" Felix asked.

Marcus exhaled slowly, watching the progress in his directives the legions were making, expression distant. "Yes. Proceed."

Teriana's heart beat wildly as Felix stepped close to a signalman, who nodded several times as he was given lengthy instructions, which Teriana couldn't overhear. But immediately, the boats that had been used in the attack began returning to the south side of the river even as more that had gone unused were dragged down to the water's edge.

And the Forty-First finally began to move.

Gear slung over their shoulders, they marched down to the water's edge and began loading into the boats by the dozens. The hundreds. The *thousands.* Not to row across to the north bank, but to float downstream.

As she watched, Marcus stepped close to Felix, their foreheads pressed together as they spoke. Then Marcus clapped him on the shoulder, and Felix said, "Take care of him, Amarin. Food. Water. And at least some sleep," before starting toward the river. Within moments, Felix was in one of the vessels and drifting out of sight.

"Where are they going?" she demanded. "What's going on?"

Marcus didn't answer, and taking a few quick steps, she grabbed his arm. "What are you doing, Marcus?"

But the man she loved was gone again, the Empire commander firmly in control as he said, "What I do best."

The men all raised their full cups in toast, then they walked down the slope to Rastag's bridge, leaving Teriana and Quintus with a handful of the Fifty-First on the ridgetop.

We do not fall back.

45

MARCUS

He lingered only long enough to allow Rastag the manpower he needed to modify his bridge to allow the river to flow beneath. The floodwaters drained swiftly out of the Gamdeshian fortress of Rita, though getting rid of the mud would more than occupy the small force he left behind for the days to come.

Then Marcus ordered his army to march.

It felt peculiar marching without Felix at his side, though Austornic was eager to take up Felix's usual duties, which meant he never left Marcus's shadow. The boy desired to endlessly rehash the mechanics of the battle on the Orinok, picking Marcus's brain over how he'd coordinated each step, how he'd kept the trebuchet a secret, and how Rastag had determined distances. Though Marcus's focus was the strategy to come, he forced himself to answer the endless variations of the same questions, knowing he'd been equally inquisitive at that age. It wasn't until Hostus had gained authority over him that he'd stopped asking questions, because firstly, the legatus of the Twenty-Ninth had little to offer, and secondly, Hostus had had a tendency to answer questions with violence.

The strain of the journey didn't seem to touch the boy. Whether it was because Nic was physically eight years Marcus's junior or because he didn't carry the mental weight of those eight years, Marcus couldn't have said, only that as day after day passed, Nic happily took on a greater workload, managing hours of administration, often from the saddle of his horse, while Marcus slipped deeper into grim silence as he contemplated what lay before him.

And behind.

Neither were allowing him any peace.

What Marcus needed above all else was *sleep.* The schedule of the hard march didn't allow him the ability to use narcotics to pull him out of the reach of nightmares. Nightmares that had only grown worse since the battle to cross the Orinok. Night after night, he was plagued with visions of Teriana being torn apart by the enormous hawk. Of Gamdeshians and Maarin cursing her name. Of an ocean of dead men and women, all with their mouths open to scream one word.

Traitor.

Astara's choice to attack Teriana instead of him was the first sign his greatest fear was coming to pass.

Gamdesh didn't blame him for invading.

They blamed Teriana.

You should kill them for threatening her, a dark voice demanded from the recesses of his mind. *The shifter first and foremost.*

Marcus shoved away the thought, then swayed in the saddle as a sudden wave of exhaustion poured over him.

Why hadn't she stayed in Celendrial? Why hadn't she gone to join the *Quincense*? The questions repeated in his head, and he knew that he was piling blame on Teriana for a decision he'd been unable to make.

And now her life was on the line because of it. She'd been named a traitor because of it.

Shifting his weight in the saddle, Marcus glowered at the ranks of marching men ahead of him, sick with rage at himself. For not being able to turn off sentiment as had always been so easy for him in the past. For not making logical decisions.

For not making himself stop loving her.

His love was poison to her, even if Teriana didn't realize it. Better for her to hate him. Better for her to think the absolute worst of him. Because even if all this worked exactly as he intended, there would come a day when Cassius revealed to her the truth of what Marcus had done to Lydia.

Yet for every step he took to drive her away, he took two closer. Unwilling to let himself have her. Unwilling to give her up.

Teriana had his heart and there was no force on earth that would put it back in his chest. The only release for both of them would be the inevitable moment that she'd choose to crush it beyond repair.

You murdered her best friend.

You murdered her best friend.

You murdered her best friend.

Marcus shook his head sharply to clear the refrain, then caught sight of smoke in the distance. The land here was tropical, but great swathes of forest had been cleared to make space for farmland, allowing one to see a fair stretch in either direction. Miles and miles of black ground, the stink of wet ash heavy in the air, for the skies had unleashed heavy rains the night prior.

A scout approached. "There's another small town ahead, sir. The civilians have already fled, but they burned what they had to leave behind."

They'd passed many villages and towns on the road that had been burned, but Marcus still found he couldn't tear his eyes from the column of smoke as they drew closer. It wasn't long until his eyes picked out the smoldering buildings, little left but the stone encircling wells that had undoubtedly been poisoned or fouled.

And one small black column.

Guiding his snorting mare into the ruins, Marcus stopped before the monument to the Seventh god, which stood no higher than the average man. Around it were the toppled remains of six more columns. "Did the Gamdeshians pull them down?"

The scout shifted in his saddle. "No, sir. We did."

He hadn't given the order for this, but Marcus held his tongue. Word of this would reach Kaira, and it would serve his purpose well. Besides, these small shrines were easily replaced. Nothing more than piles of stone. Meaningless, really.

Tear them all down, the voice ordered.

Marcus froze, abruptly realizing that he'd dismounted his horse and now stood with one hand pressed against the black column of stone, though he had no memory of doing so.

Shaking his head, he stepped away. "We don't have time to waste on this sort of destruction. Speed is of the essence."

"Yes, sir." The scout dug in his heels and galloped ahead to relay the message to the advance force.

Mounting his mare, Marcus headed back to the road where Austornic waited and fell in alongside the boy.

"Sir?"

Marcus twitched, looking sideways at Nic. Realizing the boy had asked him a question, possibly more than once, he said, "Pardon?"

"I can lead your horse if you want to get some rest."

It was something Felix would have done, the two of them trading off wakefulness during a hard march, but something in Marcus recoiled from the idea of showing any weakness to the thousands of men marching around him. "I'm fine."

Nic shrugged. "As long as you know that I can do more, if you want me to. Since Felix isn't here."

"Nothing to do but ride and hear reports."

"I can take the reports, sir."

"I need to hear them, unfiltered." To soften the rejection, he added, "I'd tell Felix the same."

Silence stretched, the only sound the steady thump of marching feet.

"I know you're keeping your plans close, sir," Nic said. "But I'm curious as to the central motivator behind your choices given that overly complicated plans invite error. Particularly in circumstances such as these, where we are . . ." He hesitated. "Flying in the dark."

"My central motivator is the desire to win." Yet as Nic fell silent, Marcus was reminded of his speech to the Thirty-Seventh. These boys were his responsibility, his younger brothers to teach and protect.

Clearing his throat, he said, "You know how to play the game. What you still need to learn is how to play your opponent, which in this case is Kaira. We not only know her to be a warrior nearly without equal but also that she's been granted some level of supernatural intuition by the grace of the god Tremon."

Nic wrinkled his nose, not having been in the Dark Shores long enough to overcome his Cel prejudice against paganism, and Marcus gave him a half smile. "Believe what you will, but trust that her intuition will sense that we . . ." His exhausted brain struggled for words. ". . . are up to something. Which of course we are."

"I can accept that," Nic said.

"The key to achieving victory with minimal loss of life is not an application of our force of numbers, but an application of cleverness and guile. Of using the strengths that are, if not unique to Celendor's legions, at least unequaled, to facilitate our trickery. Except one such as Kaira will suspect a trick, which she most certainly did upon learning our entire force was sailing north. That is why Astara came in search of us, arriving in time to witness us use yet another trick with Rastag's bridge. Astara will report that I have three legions with me on the northern bank, my intent to march on Emrant. Kaira will suspect that this is only the first of my gambits and Astara will once again be sent to spy. A quick survey will show that the Forty-First is not marching with us, and she'll track them down. Will watch them travel by boat down the river to load onto the waiting ships, which will sail north with Zimo's Thirty-First, suggesting we are reverting, at least in part, to what is perceived as my original plan."

"Not the final trick, I take it."

"Of course not." Reining his mare around a pile of rocks, Marcus said, "Kaira's instincts will again be warning her that what I appear to be doing is not my end game. Except how many times has she redeployed her soldiers to face my perceived shift in tactics? Soldiers who haven't trained as we have to switch strategy on the spin of a copper. Who haven't been drilled to endure hard marches on thin rations, as we have. Who haven't the discipline of a lifetime of training, as we have. Not only are they likely to be tired and frustrated, they may well be spread thin covering the multiple fronts where we *might* attack."

"The Gamdeshian army is said to be extremely well trained."

"There is well trained," Marcus said, "and there is indentured to the Empire at age seven to become weapons."

He allowed Nic to quietly contemplate that fact before he added, "The trouble with instincts is that while they may warn you of threats"—he moved his hand in a circle in front of him—"at a certain point, there is too much warning, an overwhelming of the senses, and the inability to determine the greatest threat. Or at least, a reduced ability to move forces to meet that threat. It is at that point my blade will fall."

Nic was quiet as he thought, then he said, "So all of this complexity and additional cost, it's for Kaira?"

It was for Teriana.

And for himself.

But Marcus said, "Kaira is my opponent, the woman sitting across the game board from me, and every decision must be catered to what I know of her. And I'd be a fool to underestimate or discount her rumored abilities."

He could see the frustration in Nic's demeanor, the boy trained to make decisions based on facts, not intuition, and sure enough, he muttered, "Then it's all a roll of the dice. An entire strategy based around some girl's supposed magical powers, which could easily blow up in our faces."

"*Woman*," Marcus corrected. "Kaira is no child. Unlike yourself."

Nic scowled at him, and Marcus laughed to soften the blow. "Think what a fool she'd be to underestimate you because you are young," he said. "Then imagine how much a fool it would make you to underestimate *her* because of what is between her legs. She is a legend in this half of the world, her reputation only rivaled by Dareena Falorn and Killian Calorian in the north. The Sultan of Gamdesh has given her full control of his military, which means that he trusts her prowess. The Empire might have taught you that martial skill is the domain of men, but keep in mind that it behooves the *men* in the Senate to propagate information that allows them to maintain their power, even if that information is lies. We are bound to their will, but that doesn't mean we are bound to believe everything they tell us."

Not waiting for Nic to respond, he added, "As to the roll of the dice, all strategies are, to a greater or lesser extent. Even a plan formed entirely on facts and certainties can and will go awry, which is why we must examine every possible way the die may fall and create contingencies. I plan to be right. But I also plan to be wrong. So rest assured, I have strategies in play in case I have misjudged Kaira."

"Strategies that you do not share." Nic cast a sideways glance at him. "Except with Felix. The commandant warned us of the consequences of not trusting our officers."

Marcus took a long mouthful from the waterskin hooked on his saddle. "It's not a matter of trust, Nic. Or at least, it isn't entirely. For these gambits of deceit to work requires a collective poker face that is impossible to achieve if the men are aware of my actual plan. We are always watched by our adversaries' spies, and they aren't idiots. They are trained to read emotion and nerves, so I must play our men as pieces on the game board. They must believe, or the spies will sense the ruse. And . . ." He gave a slow shake of his head. "We don't know the limits of the magic given by the gods. Who is to say that Astara is limited to the shape of a hawk? Perhaps she might become a mouse or even a fly, perched and listening on the wall while I explain the full extent of my plans. Or listening to you discuss the plans with your second. She could have taken the shape of my horse here and might well be listening to our conversation even now."

Nic's eyes went to the silly golden mare, eyeing her suspiciously, then he said, "Isn't that something Teriana would know?"

At her name, tension sang through Marcus's veins, causing the horse to sidle and snort. "I don't want her involved."

"Why?"

"She's here under duress."

"Except she isn't," Nic argued. "You told her to stay put in Celendrial, and instead of doing so, she went behind your back and cut a deal with Cassius that meant coming back to the Dark Shores with me and ensuring our success. That was *her choice,* and if we fail, her people will suffer the consequences. Arguably there is no one we should trust more, because the stakes are higher for her than any of us. But more than that, she *knows* our adversary better than any of us, for she knows Kaira *personally.* Yet you have not once asked her for information that might aid us. Which, given circumstances, would be understandable, except you have also forbade the rest of us from asking her for insights."

Marcus's temper flared, and he bit down on sharp words because Nic was justified in questioning him. He was responsible for the lives of those in the Fifty-First, and Marcus's reasons for keeping Teriana as clear of this campaign as possible ran counter to that because they put her wellbeing above all others. "We don't need her insights. As much as it might seem as though our goals are aligned, once she's free and clear of us, there is *nothing* to stop her from taking everything she's learned and giving that information to the other side."

"Then why not put her on the island with the rest of her crew we keep under guard? Why is she here?"

Why is she here? Reasons exploded across Marcus's thoughts, turning his head into a kaleidoscope of painful colors, his grip tightening on the reins as a scream threatened to boil out of him. *I cannot let her go.* "My reasons are not your concern."

Silence stretched.

"Fine," Nic muttered. "If you'll excuse me, sir. I would ride with my men."

Marcus didn't answer, only watched with dull eyes as the boy trotted his horse away, grief filling his core. Not for himself, but for Nic. Because the Empire had no use, nor desire, for idealism, and bit by bit, year by year, all that was good about the young legatus would be erased until he, too, would look in the mirror and see a stranger staring back at him.

A chill abruptly ran over Marcus's skin, a motionless wind with a coldness that belonged in Sibern, and his mare pinned her ears and squealed.

"Easy," he muttered, not sure if he was talking to himself or the horse.

What good is idealism? a voice whispered. *What matters is results.*

Marcus frowned at the thought, disliking the callousness behind it, but trying to push it from his mind made his head pound. Shoving his fingers under his helmet, he rubbed his temples, the world swimming around him.

"You all right, sir?" Gibzen asked, moving his horse right next to the golden mare, who immediately tried to bite the gelding.

"Tired. But so is everyone."

"Yeah, but everyone else *sleeps*. With respect, sir, don't think I haven't noticed your lack of shut-eye. You need more?"

"No," Marcus muttered. "I don't have time for it. I can't command an army with my head in a fog, Gibzen."

"Seems to me that's exactly what you're doing."

Irritation flooded Marcus's chest, and he turned to meet Gibzen's brown eyes. "I'm not putting us off schedule so that I can get a full night of rest."

"Of course not, sir." Gibzen broke away from Marcus's stare. "But there are other options."

They rode in silence for a long time, and with each step Marcus's horse took, his head pounded harder. Finally, he said, "What options?"

"Racker's not just got narcotics to make you sleep," Gibzen answered. "He's got some that keep you sharp." Reaching out a hand, the primus handed Marcus a vial. The glass was cold as ice. "I got your back, sir. Only one drop."

The slippery slope he walked upon grew steeper by the day, but Marcus tucked the vial away. He considered pressing Gibzen as to whether he'd made progress on his hunt for the traitor, but given how hard the march was, he doubted much investigation was possible.

"I know you're not going to want to hear this," Gibzen said. "But the pup has been meddling again. Saw him talking to Quintus more than once, which everyone knows is the same as talking to her."

Marcus curbed the urge to look backward, his anger rising.

"Pup wants his name to go down in the history books for this campaign," Gibzen said. "Which means he needs to make a mark in some fashion. That's why he's pressing for information—to find a way to influence how all this goes down."

To steal your glory. The thought rose in his mind, and Marcus shook his head to clear it, because none of this was about glory.

But it is about it going your way, the voice asked. *Austornic might ruin your plans if he interferes.*

Except that didn't make sense. Marcus had involved Nic more than anyone other than Felix and Servius. Marcus had told him that the Fifty-First would be given credit for their part.

What if that isn't enough?

"He's not stupid enough to mess things up," Marcus growled at the voice, but it was Gibzen who answered, "Take a look, sir."

He glanced backward just in time to see Nic rein his horse away from Quintus's mount, and Marcus snapped his gaze forward again, clenching his teeth against his rising anger.

You were teaching him. You brought him into the fold. And this is how he repays you?

"He might only be being courteous." A wave of exhaustion rolled over him. "Teriana is a woman, and thirteen or not, he's got eyes."

Gibzen responded, but all Marcus heard was the voice. *Austornic is jockeying for power, just as you did. He sees you're exhausted and aims to take advantage.*

"He's not me. He's better than me."

Gibzen said something, and Marcus turned his head to look at him, seeing the primus's eyes were narrowed, the predator in the man smelling Marcus's weakness.

"Keep an eye on him."

"Yes, sir. Will do, sir."

Gibzen backed off his horse. Keeping the vial concealed by his hand, Marcus took a drop. Moments later, the world seemed to sharpen, his thoughts along with it. Just in time for a scout to approach.

The man saluted, his exhausted horse lathered with sweat. "No signs of evacuation, sir. She's emptied the garrison north at Imresh to man the walls of Emrant and put up the harbor chain."

Even though Marcus knew that Kaira would have to be mad to concede the city easily, part of him had hoped that they'd arrive to find Emrant empty. Yet as Astara shrieked, once again above him and watching, Marcus said, "If it's a fight that they want, a fight they shall have."

46

KILLIAN

Killian couldn't recall the last time he'd really *slept*. For months upon months, he'd spent his nights at least partially alert, always ready to act if attack came. But on the Maarin ship, with Lydia in his arms, Killian finally allowed himself to relax.

They spent their days with Agrippa and Malahi, often with the captain and other members of the crew joining in for games of cards and dice, the food fresh caught from the sea and the wine the best vintages from across all of Reath. And their nights . . .

Nights were for him and Lydia to explore each other in ways that they'd been so long denied, the noise of the waves mercifully drowning them out, though if the entire ship had heard, he wouldn't have cared. Lydia was his. *His.* And though they sailed toward war and worse, it would be at each other's side, because he wouldn't allow anything to come between them again.

Not rushing hadn't been the only piece of Agrippa's advice he'd taken, for his friend's admonition of "For the love of all Six of the gods, do not get her pregnant" motivated Lydia, in the company of Malahi, to consult with the Maarin women about preventive measures. They'd both returned with herbs that were brewed into a tea that they were to drink daily.

"Smells like feet and tastes worse," Killian had told her when he'd tried a sip of the tea. To which Lydia had only shrugged and said, "Be thankful I'm the one who has to drink it." Then she'd removed her spectacles and given him a dark smile that made him want to drag her back into bed. "And I think it will be well worth it, don't you?"

He most definitely *did*, though as they rounded the peninsula that formed the southernmost point of Mudamora, it was not lost on him that this respite from the world was rapidly coming to an end.

Serlania appeared in the dawn light, and Killian rested his elbows on the rail, watching the city his family all but owned grow in the distance. Agrippa joined him, a cup of some dark bitter drink they apparently drank in the East clasped in his scarred hands.

"Where is Baird? I haven't seen him all morning."

Agrippa laughed. "He's below fretting about his appearance and the state of his clothes. Apparently there is a chance he might cross paths with his estranged wife, and he's hoping to regain her favor. I understand you know the lucky lady."

"Bercola." Killian sighed. "We had a falling out, but in hindsight, I might have been as much in the wrong as she was. I hope she's in Serlania so that I can make my own amends. Do you know what he did to piss her off?"

"Apparently he was quite the ladies' man in Eoten Isle," Agrippa said. "Sowed oats in the wrong field and she washed her hands of him. It's the reason he abandoned his duties maintaining the doldrums, so it isn't just her who is angry at him, it's his entire people. Honestly, new clothes are probably the least of his concerns, but he told me I wasn't being helpful and kicked me out of his berth."

"Have Malahi test the waters. Bercola is fond of her, so Malahi might be able to forestall her putting a sword through his stomach. As far as forgiveness goes, that's Baird's battle to fight."

Agrippa shrugged. "Serves him right for stepping out, if you ask me."

It was a struggle not to smirk, because Killian remembered just how many of the tavern girls had seemed intimately acquainted with Agrippa in Deadground. But the smile kept rising despite his best efforts, so he changed the subject. "You been to Serlania before?"

"Briefly," Agrippa answered. "The Gamdeshians were after me

for debts considered unpaid, and the fight pit masters have a lot of friends in Serlania."

"True. My sister-in-law is the Sultan's niece, but she loves the fights. I've been to a few with her."

"Box seats, I'm sure." Agrippa laughed. "Sometimes I forget that you're highborn. You looking forward to going back to being a lord?"

"No." Killian opened his mouth to elaborate, then his eyes snagged on the golden band encircling Agrippa's ring finger that had most certainly *not* been there the day before.

Noting his scrutiny, Agrippa took a sip of his drink. "Oh, by the way, Malahi and I got hitched last night. Sorry for the lack of invitation, but she was of the opinion that you'd be against it. She's telling Lydia right now."

Killian turned and found both women standing on the quarterdeck. Lydia was staring wide eyed at Malahi, whose chin was raised in defiance. "Agrippa, she's the Queen of Mudamora. You can't just . . . *marry the queen*!"

"Actually, you can." Agrippa took another sip of his drink. "Captain Vane officiated, and Fara and Baird witnessed, which is why he's so morose about matters of nuptials. Malahi and I did the rest, so it's done and can't be undone. Anyone who tries to claim otherwise will find said claims pouring out of a hole in his guts."

There was a hint of a threat in Agrippa's tone that made Killian tense. "You barely know each other."

"If you weren't so caught up in your own love affair, you'd know that's not the case." Agrippa tossed the dregs of his drink overboard, hazel eyes frosty as he said, "She's got reasons, if you care to hear her out, but for my part, I love her. Malahi had my heart the moment she spit in Rufina's face. Where she goes, I go. What she fights for, I'll fight for. Given that I've had your back while you pined over a girl who wanted to suck the life out of you, I hope you'll do the same for me because I'm well aware that I've painted a target on it."

That was an understatement. Malahi might well rule, but the High Lords, most especially his brother, would take significant issue with their queen making such an important decision without them, most especially given that she hadn't chosen one of them. Which Killian strongly suspected was the primary motivation behind the midnight nuptials.

A thought swiftly confirmed by Malahi as she approached, pulling Lydia bodily by the arm. "Killian, whatever opinions you are voicing, keep them to yourself. I'm not allowing Hacken to try to force me into a marriage that I don't want in order to secure his vote." She lifted her chin, staring him down. "This protects Lydia and you from his manipulations as much as it protects me, and . . ." Her voice faltered as she looked to Agrippa. "And I have spent my whole life doing what others wanted. Just this once I want to do something for myself."

Killian could think of a dozen reasons why the decision was a bad one, but it was difficult to argue with that statement. And it wasn't that he thought the choice was wrong, only that he knew the High Lords would hate that she'd made any choice at all. Still, Malahi was more a politician than he'd ever be, so she didn't need him to explain the potential consequences of her actions. "Then I suppose the only thing to say is, congratulations."

"Congratulations." Lydia kissed both of Malahi's cheeks. "I wish you both a long life filled with happiness."

Vane approached. "The Serlania harbor is overcrowded with refugees from the north," he said. "It will be a day or more before we can secure a berth."

"We can't wait." The words slipped out of Killian, voiced by instinct rather than thought. "Row us to the beach outside Serlania."

Vane shrugged, then shouted the order.

While the anchor was lowered, Killian and Lydia went to retrieve their meager belongings, as did their friends, and when they returned to the deck, a longboat was waiting for them.

"We'll make port as soon as we are able," Vane said to them. "I'll gather the supplies that we need to be ready to take you to Revat."

"Thank you," Killian said. "We won't linger. I . . ." He trailed off, shaking his head. "I think we might be running out of time."

Vane's brow furrowed. "Then we will make all haste."

Baird chose that moment to come on deck. "I'm of a mind to stay on the *Kairense*," he said. "You'll need swift winds when you sail to Revat."

Agrippa started flapping his arms and squawking like a chicken, but Killian gave him a shove. "We'll see you soon, then."

Killian, Lydia, Agrippa, and Malahi climbed into the longboat, and two of the Maarin crew members rowed them to shore. Yet as they approached the white sand beach, Killian spotted a blue carriage with a team of white horses stopped on the road up the slope, his horse, Seahawk, tethered to the back of the carriage. A man sat on the beach, boots off and bright blue trousers pushed up to his knees, the position quite at odds with the man's flamboyant attire. Killian smiled.

"Do you know him?" Lydia asked, shading her eyes. "Wait . . . Is that . . . ?"

"Seldrid." Killian lifted his hand right as the other man did. "The brother I actually like."

Jumping out of the boat as it hit the sand, Killian strode up the beach to where the middle son of House Calorian now stood. "How did you know we were coming?"

His brother held out his arms. "Hacken manipulates things. You kill things. But I, little brother, I *know* things." Then Seldrid wrapped his arms around Killian, half lifting him off the ground in a hug. "Gods, but it's good to see you alive. When my watchers said that *Kairense* had been spotted with you on it, I was afraid to believe it lest I be delivered disappointment, but here you are."

"Here I am." Killian stepped back. "Though it was a near thing more times than I care to count."

Seldrid straightened his coat, which had an obscene amount of gold embroidery, his eyes moving past Killian to the others. If he was shocked at Malahi's changed appearance, he didn't show it as he bowed low. "My lady. It is my greatest honor to welcome you back to Mudamorian soil."

"Seldrid." Malahi stepped forward to kiss both his brother's cheeks. "It is good to be welcomed by a friendly face. How fare Adra and your children?"

"Both are well, though Adra will be furious that she wasn't here to greet you properly, for of a surety, this would not pass muster. But she's at Teradale with the children, assisting my mother."

Killian's skin abruptly prickled, his mark warning that trouble was coming, and he frowned at his brother.

"I'm sure I'll see her soon enough." Malahi gestured to Lydia. "This is Lydia, Marked of Hegeria and . . ." Her throat moved as she swallowed. "My husband, Agrippa Egnatius."

Killian felt his brother's shock only because of how well he knew him, for Seldrid betrayed nothing on his face as he inclined his head. "It is my honor to make your acquaintance, Agrippa. Correct me if I'm mistaken, but is that not a Cel name?"

Agrippa blinked. "Likewise. And yes, though I'm surprised you know it."

"I'm in the business of making money," Seldrid replied, "and though I question Celendor's methods of achieving the trade it seems to desire, that does not mean I haven't investigated its business potential. Any chance you are of relation to the senator of the same name? Tiberius Egnatius is quite the rising star, I've heard, though it's all hearsay and gossip at this point."

Agrippa's jaw dropped, his eyes snapping to Killian's, the question in them quite clearly: *How does he know?* Killian only shrugged, because Seldrid never disclosed his informants, *Bad for business* always being the excuse he gave.

"My brother," Agrippa finally answered. "Though he'd be quite shocked to learn I'm on this side of the world."

"And rising high within the Mudamorian aristocracy, no less," Seldrid said with enthusiasm, clapping a hand on Agrippa's shoulder. "I hope you won't mind if I pick your brain? I would like to know more about what the Empire has to offer, since it is looking less and less like we'll be easily rid of them."

"Of course." For once, Agrippa seemed lost for words. "Whatever you want to know."

"Wonderful!" Seldrid gestured to the carriage. "Shall we? It's something of a journey to Teradale, and it's always best to get it over with before the heat of the day. We'll be a bit pressed for space, but Killian can ride his horse while you catch me up on your adventure, Your Grace."

Killian caught his brother's arm. "Lydia and I aren't going to Teradale. We need to travel to Revat to consult with the librarians. We hope they might have information to supplement what we learned in Anukastre about the blight."

"Whatever you need, write it down and I'll send it to the Sultan himself," Seldrid said. "But you need to come to Teradale."

"What is happening there that is more important than the blight?" Killian asked the question even as his instincts told him Seldrid's urgency wasn't misplaced. "Has something changed?"

"Yes." Seldrid pulled Killian toward the carriage. "Ria Rowenes has a document signed by Serrick before his death declaring Malahi dead and Ria his heir. She claims the title of High Lady Rowenes now."

Fury washed over Killian, because this was exactly the sort of thing that Ria would do. "Well she only has a few hours to enjoy it, because Malahi is very much alive."

"Alive or not matters little," Seldrid said quietly. "He clearly named Ria as his heir. As of this moment, Malahi is not High Lady, and if she is not High Lady—"

"She's not queen."

Seldrid gave a tight nod. "But it gets worse."

"Of course it does," Killian growled, watching Malahi climb into the carriage. "What has Hacken done?"

"Betrothed himself to Ria, for starters," Seldrid said. "And with her support, he's gathered the high lords and ladies at Teradale. You've arrived just in time to watch them vote for Hacken as Mudamora's next king."

47

LYDIA

The carriage bounced over the heavily rutted road, everyone inside bracing hands against the interior to keep from being tossed onto the floor.

"Does no one on this continent know how to build a proper road?" Agrippa muttered. "My ass is never going to be the same after this."

"If you don't quit complaining, I'm going to make you ride outside with the driver." Malahi wore a silk dress gifted to her by Vane, and it had a matching fan, which she snapped open and used to fan herself vigorously. It was hot and humid, there was no denying that, but the sweat beading on Malahi's brow had everything to do with the fact that the crown had been removed from it.

Seldrid had relayed everything that had happened in their absence, including the gathering of the Twelve Great Houses at the Calorian estates of Teradale. Even if they reached them in time to prove Malahi was alive, it would not change the fact that she was no longer High Lady. Her cousin Ria now held that honor, and had used her newfound power to cement a union with Hacken Calorian.

It was no shock that Hacken desired to rule Mudamora, and while there'd been a time when the high lords would have refused to bend the knee to him, much had changed in the intervening period. House Calorian was the wealthiest of the houses, after House Rowenes, allied to Gamdesh by way of Seldrid's marriage to one of the Sultan's nieces, Lady Adra, and Calorian lands some of the few untouched by blight. All of which placed the house as the most powerful in all of Mudamora.

"Tell me, what is the name of the Cel Emperor?" Seldrid asked, clearly making chatter to ease the tension. "I've heard much of this Senate but little of the man who rules it all."

"Celendor has no emperor," Agrippa replied, his eyes full of concern as he watched Malahi.

Seldrid frowned. "So it's a republic?"

Lydia opened her mouth to answer his question, then bit her lip, her knowledge likely to raise questions she wasn't interested in answering.

"It's ruled as a republic," Agrippa answered. "But it's never been formally declared as such. The throne of the emperor still exists, but it remains empty. The last emperor was assassinated, along with every individual who might claim any form of relation to him, and no one has ever gained enough personal power to claim it."

"Fascinating." Seldrid cast a sideways look at Malahi, who stared out the window where Killian rode alongside the carriage. "Malahi, what are your thoughts about republics?"

Sighing, Malahi turned to meet Seldrid's gaze, having apparently been listening more than Lydia had realized, for she said, "Mudamora needs unity above all else. If there is a better path to that than me as queen, I will gladly support it, but I know those men and women. They want the crown for themselves, whereas those who work to the benefit of Mudamora avoid the role that would allow them to achieve those admirable ends."

"You've been dealt a bad hand, Malahi." Seldrid's tone was grim. "But it would be a disservice for me to lie to you. You have very few true friends among the Great Houses."

"I think the only friends I have in all the world are those surrounding me now." Malahi reached for Lydia's hand.

"A not unformidable company." The carriage slowed, and Seldrid squared his shoulders. "We're here. Allow me to formally welcome you to Teradale."

They passed through a set of gates connected to a low stone wall, and beyond, Lydia saw rolling green fields filled with long-legged horses, the vibrancy of the scene making the blight seem a distant threat. The carriage carried on down the road, finally slowing as it eased around a large fountain surrounded by beds of brilliant tropical flowers. Killian's dog appeared from around the building, racing at top speed toward them and barking with excitement. Killian dismounted and met the dog with equal enthusiasm before approaching the door to the carriage.

"Welcome." He took Lydia's hand, and she gave him a tight smile that conveyed the tension of the conversation that had taken place inside of the carriage. Agrippa helped Malahi out, Seldrid following. Lydia turned to look at the beautiful palace, but her admiration was cut short as Lady Calorian flew out the front doors.

Killian's mother raced down the steps, elegant skirts hiked up to her knees. "Killian!" she cried, then her arms were around her youngest son's neck. "Oh gods, they said you were alive, but I could barely bring myself to believe it. But you're alive. My baby is alive."

Seldrid laughed, and Lydia didn't fail to notice how Killian's cheeks colored as he patted his mother on the back. "I'm fine, Mother. You don't need to act as though . . ." He trailed off, finally seeing the tears on her cheeks as he pulled away. "Truly, I'm fine. I'd have sent word, but we were in Derin and then Anukastre, so it wasn't possible." And then, as though it were a remedy for Lady Calorian's emotion, he added, "I've brought Malahi back."

At Malahi's name, Lady Calorian seemed to recall herself, straightening her skirts and wiping her cheeks dry as she surveyed their company. To Lady Calorian's credit, she did not react to Malahi's appearance, only inclined her head. "Your Grace. It is a blessing from the Six to see you returned to Mudamora. Our house is yours."

Malahi kissed both of the woman's cheeks. "It is good to see you, Lady Calorian."

The silence stretched a heartbeat too long, then Lady Calorian said, "Please come inside. The journey from Serlania is unpleasant in this heat."

Malahi swayed as though to follow, then in a flurry of words, said, "First, I would like to introduce my husband. Agrippa."

Though he surely felt the awkwardness of the moment, Agrippa bowed low. "A pleasure to meet you, my lady. Thank you for welcoming us into your home."

Lady Calorian's face blanched, but she only said, "How lovely to meet you. That's a Cel name, is it not? Seldrid is endlessly curious about your countrymen, though in truth, my sentiment toward the Cel and your invasion of Gamdesh is somewhat darker. Though this wouldn't be the first war to be tempered by unions between enemies. Was that your goal? Or did you even have one?"

Anger washed over Malahi's face, her lips parting to retort, but Killian's mother only lifted a hand. "What's done is done, girl. If you were still available for marriage, there might have been some hope for you regaining your position, but no longer. You've secured Ria's claim, sure and true."

She rounded on Lydia, her eyes immediately falling to where Killian's hand grasped hers. "Spare me from the impulsivity of youth. Who, pray tell, are you, young lady?"

Killian kept his grip on her hand. "This is Lydia. She's one of Hegeria's marked."

Lady Calorian's eyes narrowed slightly, though she only inclined her head. "You are welcome, Marked One."

"Just Lydia." Her cheeks warmed under the woman's scrutiny; she was certain that Lady Calorian knew *exactly* the nature of Lydia's relationship with her son. "Thank you for your hospitality."

"Well, well," a familiar voice said, and Lydia's gaze tore from Killian's mother to rise the steps, where she found Hacken standing with a blond woman on his arm. "The prodigal son returns."

Killian stiffened, a scowl rising to his face as his eyes fixed on his brother. She squeezed his hand to urge him to remain calm, because there was no doubt that Hacken was trying to provoke him.

"Cousin Malahi," Ria said, "it is a gift from the Six to see you alive and . . ." She looked Malahi up and down. "Alive, that's what matters."

Lydia had met Ria in Rotahn and her opinion of the woman was not improving.

"You overstep, Ria." Malahi smoothed her skirts, fussing with the lace detail as though this conversation was of only minor interest. "I would see this document you claim names you my father's heir, for I do not believe he'd disinherit me in favor of *you*."

Ria sighed. "I'm sorry, cousin. This must be painful for you, but I'm afraid that I must honor my uncle's wishes, which he sent to Rotahn just prior to his death. Truly, it was the greatest foresight on his part to send them to me. He must have known that his end was coming."

"He didn't see it coming." Lydia's tone was cool. "He had no notion that Rufina and Cyntha were one and the same until nearly the moment he died."

All eyes went to Lydia, then back to Ria.

"A tragedy, truly. Mudamora was robbed when that monster stole Serrick's light from us." Ria lifted a handkerchief to her eyes to dry false tears. "I have his letter here if you wish to read it. It has been verified by the lords and ladies present as written in his hand. He . . . Well, I do not wish to cause strife, but he claims that you were marked by Yara yet begged him to hide your gifts so that you would not have to serve. Allowing you to do so was his greatest regret, and he did not want the heir to House Rowenes to be faithless."

All the color drained from Malahi's face. "He made me hide my mark. I didn't want to. This is lies."

Ria made a small noise of sympathy that didn't reach her eyes.

"Malahi's telling the truth," Killian snapped. "She told me about her mark after I came into her service, and also that Serrick had made her swear to hide it. This is nothing but his resentment toward the Marked revealing itself, and the Great Houses should not allow this mockery of our laws to stand."

"Serrick died from blight poisoning," Lydia said, though it was apparent their protests were doing little good. "He rose as one of the Corrupter's puppets before my very eyes, so I think it possible that this letter was written not by Serrick but the Seventh himself."

Ria ignored her. "Malahi hid her gifts. To do so is not only faithless but a crime."

"You misrepresent circumstances in the pursuit of power!" Malahi retorted. "My father—"

"I can understand your distress, Malahi," Hacken interrupted. "But you may atone for your choices by serving Mudamora, for we need a tender's mark more than ever. This is your chance to make things right, not your chance to grasp for the throne."

"The only one doing any grasping is you, Hacken," Malahi spat. "Have the Great Houses voted yet or are you merely pretending at being king while you wait?"

Hacken's jaw tightened ever so slightly, which told Lydia that the votes were not as certain as he wanted everyone to think. A fact confirmed as said lords and ladies came outside, expressions tight and unreadable.

"Mudamora needs unity, now more than ever," Hacken said, Ria nodding along with him. "We cannot waste time on infighting over who rules while the blight consumes our lands. Not when Rufina and her army of blighters marches ever closer. You broke faith and the law, Malahi. You are not the right choice to lead our people out of darkness."

"Perhaps you are right in that," Malahi replied. "But neither are you the one who should rule, for you care only for power."

"Then who?" Hacken threw up his hands, turning in a circle to address his peers. "We have argued for weeks now over who is the best choice, and there is no agreement, only a thousand reasons against each of us. Ria and I have united with the intent to lead together in order to gain a consensus, but if there is someone you feel better suited, name the house now."

"House Falorn!" Malahi shouted, but Hacken only waved a hand dismissively in her direction.

"Dareena has already declined."

"Good." Malahi drew in a steadying breath. "Because Dareena is not the rightful High Lady of House Falorn. Kitaryia is."

Killian stiffened as Lydia sucked in a sharp breath, panic rising in her chest.

Malahi turned, her amber eyes pleading for forgiveness even as she said, "The Six returned Kitaryia to us. Hegeria has chosen her as one of her marked. And I, for one, would gladly bend my knee to her so that she might lead us through the dark days to come."

48

LYDIA

Lydia felt all the blood drain from her face, the eyes of the most powerful men and women in Mudamora all fixed on her.

She did not want this.

She did not want to be queen.

She did not want to rule.

"Kitaryia Falorn is dead," Hacken snapped. "And don't think I don't see through this ploy. Having one of your bodyguards, or whatever this girl is to you, ape the dead princess is beyond the pale."

Betrayal turned her stomach to ice, because Malahi knew this wasn't the life Lydia wanted to live, but she'd told everyone anyway. *You were my friend,* she wanted to scream.

"It is no lie." Malahi surveyed the onlookers. "Camilla fled with her to Celendor, where Kitaryia was raised under a different name."

"Is Camilla still alive?" a familiar voice asked, and Lydia turned to find Dareena approaching. Her aunt, she realized, but also the woman who had most to lose from Malahi's revelation.

Malahi's lips parted, but Dareena interrupted. "You've said your piece, Malahi. Allow Lydia, or Kitaryia, as the case may be, to answer for herself."

Lydia's hands fisted. She wanted no part of this, least of all talking about her mother's death in front of a crowd.

"Camilla was like an older sister to me," Dareena said. "I've never once forgiven myself for not being there to protect her."

"You were just a girl, Dareena," Lady Calorian murmured. "Do not take that blame."

"She died." The words were choked, the admission unleashing a torrent of grief in her stomach. "Rufina stabbed her, but she managed to escape through the xenthier beneath the palace to Celendrial. My fath—the man who found me raised me as his own until . . ." She trailed off, shaking her head. "It is a long story."

Dareena closed the distance between them, her eyes cold and expression unreadable. Killian stepped in her path, and the High Lady's eyes fixed on him. "If it's the truth, it would explain your behavior."

"It's the truth." Killian's voice was low. "But don't forget that it was Malahi who revealed the truth, not Lydia, so if you have grievances, take them out where they are deserved."

"Noted," Dareena said, then shoved him out of her way. "I suspected. Mark or blood, I can't say, but my instincts put the idea in my heart. Though there is only one way to know for sure."

Her eyes flicked to Lady Calorian's. "Do you remember how she screamed when the artist did the work?"

Killian's mother nodded. "Camilla wanted to wait but Derrek insisted."

"Insisted, then couldn't bear to be in the room to hear her weep, so he went hunting with his friends." Dareena sighed. "Few knew that the work had been done, because the attack happened not long after."

"What are you talking about?" It struck her then that Dareena's was the first Mudamorian face she'd ever seen, illustrated in Teriana's copy of the Treatise, and she remembered how long she'd stared at the portrait.

Dareena turned, tapping at the tattoo of the Falorn falcon on the back of her head. "I held Kitaryia while she was inked."

She pulled a knife, causing Lydia to jump and Killian to tense. "If you are her, you have the tattoo under your hair."

Lydia felt paralyzed, because on one hand, proof would give her back the family she'd lost. But on the other . . .

Malahi stepped closer. "Do not let those two rule, Lydia," she murmured. "Give the Great Houses another option."

All she wanted to do was reach for Killian's hand, but instead Lydia said, "All right."

Unraveling her braid, she separated the top section and knotted it atop her head, trying not to flinch as Dareena cut away the length at the base of her head, then shaved it close. Lydia stared at the long black locks falling to the ground at her feet, the hair reminding her of strands of blight against the white stone.

Lydia heard the High Lady's breath catch as the truth was revealed, but she said nothing until the work was done. Dareena turned Lydia to face her, murmurs of shock running through the onlookers as they saw the falcon inked in black on the base of Lydia's skull.

"The cat is out of the bag, girl, and there's no shoving it back in," Dareena murmured. "So I'll give you the choice. Claim your legacy or take Killian and run. Run as far as you can and find happiness for as long as you can."

"There is nowhere to run," Lydia replied. "And even if there were, I won't abandon my friends."

"So be it." Dareena dropped to one knee, lowering her head. "I swear my service to you, High Lady Kitaryia. My blade is yours."

That's not my name! Lydia silently screamed, but she only gave her aunt a tight nod before turning to face Hacken. As she watched, he smiled and pulled Ria's hand from his arm, dropping it like a dead fish before he said, "This is a sign from the Six."

His words made Lydia profoundly nervous, because moments ago, he'd been ready to declare himself king.

Rounding on the watching High Lords and Ladies, Hacken said, "Will you also bend your knee to Kitaryia as queen? Will you give Mudamora the ruler it needs to defeat its enemies? For she"—he leveled a finger at Lydia—"is the only healer to save the life of one of the infected."

Brows furrowed with interest.

"The heir to House Falorn has been returned to us, albeit under a different name than when she left. Yet there can be no denying her heritage. House Falorn is a house of warriors, and I think it fitting that it should be them who lead us to victory against the minions of the Corrupter. Will you kneel and name High Lady Kitaryia Falorn your queen?"

Lydia didn't believe that these men and women looked at her and saw someone they intended to follow. What they saw was an option who was not Hacken. An option they could potentially control.

But if she had to do this, it would be on *her* terms.

Hacken lowered to one knee. "In the long tradition of unity between the Houses Falorn and Calorian, I, High Lord Hacken Calorian, swear fealty to High Lady Kitaryia Falorn."

That's not my name.

Ten lords and ladies stood behind him on the steps. Ria grimaced, but then curtsied deeply. "House Rowenes swears fealty."

Three of the men dropped to one knee, swearing the same, while four more shook their heads and stepped back. Leaving only High Lady Helene Torrington.

Lydia stared into the eyes of the young woman who was no friend of hers, and who never would be. The swing vote that would decide her future, and Lydia remembered the endless callous words that had come from Helene's lips. Her utter indifference to the suffering of others. To have the fate of so many held in the hands of such a woman seemed the purest form of injustice.

Yet rather than stepping back, Helene stepped forward, her arms crossed.

"You still have that ring?" she asked. "The black diamond one you sold to me? The one Killian bought back?"

Lydia could feel it hanging on the silver chain that Killian had taken from Malahi what seemed a lifetime ago, a familiar presence yet one she paid little mind to. "Yes."

"If you gave it to me as a symbol of goodwill, I might be inclined to vote in your favor."

Next to her, Lydia felt Killian tense and curse under his breath, but the faintest breath of warmth filled the cold hollow in her chest, because this wasn't greed. Wasn't bribery. High Lady Torrington was giving Lydia one last chance to make this step her own choice rather than something that was forced upon her.

Rufina was coming, marching at the head of an army of the dead, leaving a blackened wasteland in her wake, and someone had to stand against her. Lydia's eyes moved over the men and women standing before her. All of them feared what was to come, but every last one of them was also driven by the desire for power, not the desire to protect the people whose lives stood in the balance. When Hegeria had told her that she'd be walking a hard road if she accepted her mark, Lydia had never imagined that it would take her here.

But she'd made it through every trial, and she refused to break now.

Drawing the silver chain over her head, Lydia walked up the steps and handed it to Helene.

"I'll treasure the gift." The High Lady shoved the ring onto her finger and then dropped into a low curtsey. "House Torrington swears fealty to you, Queen Kitaryia Falorn."

That's not my name.

Behind her, Dareena said, "As a representative of the Six, I swear that this vote has been conducted lawfully and that all have acted of their own accord and without compulsion."

Lydia turned on the steps, refusing to look at Malahi, who had stepped back in the crowd, Agrippa grim-faced at her elbow.

Hacken snatched hold of Lydia's wrist and raised it into the air. "All hail Queen Kitaryia Falorn, Marked by Hegeria and chosen by the Twelve to lead Mudamora to war!"

"All hail the queen!" everyone shouted, but all Lydia heard was her own voice in her head.

That's not my name.

49

TERIANA

With a speed beyond anything Teriana had dreamed possible, Marcus had marched his army around the mangrove swamps that ringed the mouth of the Orinok, then up the road leading to the port city of Emrant.

Farms and towns and villages emptied ahead of them, the scouts reporting that the Gamdeshian civilians were evacuating north under Kaira's directive. They took their flocks and herds with them and razed the land in their wake, making it seem to Teriana that they rode through an underworld. *Scorched earth*, she'd heard Servius call it, and understood it as a strategic term. Yet it also described the ground itself, which was blackened and devoid of life. Useless to the legions, but also so ruined that it was a struggle to envision how the Gamdeshians would ever go back to life as it once had been. Even the gods felt vanquished, for while she'd heard that Marcus had told the front-runners to leave the small shrines to the gods be, she'd also heard that those in the rear ranks had taken matters into their own hands. Though he surely knew what they were doing, Marcus did not take action, only steadily rode toward Emrant with Gibzen constantly at his side.

You cannot break, she chanted to herself. *You must trust him.*

But every day her faith faltered. Every day her fear grew that, because of her, all of Gamdesh would burn.

Scorched earth.

The words repeated over and over in her head, feeling like a description of what she left in her own wake. Chaos and ruin and unforgivable hurt, and Teriana knew that she'd never be able to go back. Knew that in walking this path to free her people, she'd ensured she'd forever be a pariah in the West. What a disappointment she must be to Madoria, for this could not be what her goddess had hoped for.

But Teriana no longer apologized. No longer spoke silent words in prayer to the Six, because she did not deserve absolution and therefore would not ask for it.

It made her feel cold.

And so very, *very* alone.

As miserable as it was, Teriana wished the ride would go on forever because once they reached the end of this long march, there would be war.

Yet what were wishes but prayers? And for her, no one was listening.

50

LYDIA

"Let us get in out of the sun, Your Grace." Lady Calorian tugged at Lydia's elbow. "A chilled wine and a moment alone, I think."

Lydia allowed Killian's mother to draw her forward, but it was Killian's arm she latched onto. "I want Killian with me."

"Of course." His mother looked between them, then shook her head. "Like yesterday, I remember him practicing the words to swear his oath to you. Dozens of times he said it, and though he never spoke it to your face, the spoken word binds. It is no surprise the Six saw fit to have you reunited."

"Have her made presentable to the people in Serlania," Hacken said, ignoring his mother's comments. "And there must be a ball."

"It is not a fitting time for dancing," his mother retorted. "We're at war."

"It's a show of strength." Hacken's brown eyes were cold. "And I will be obeyed in my own house."

Lydia's lips parted to remind the High Lord that he'd given her authority over him, but nothing but breath escaped.

"If I had not birthed you, I would deny that you are my flesh and blood," Lady Calorian said between her teeth. "Death snaps at our doorsteps and still you think of politics."

Hacken only rolled his eyes, then took the steps two at a time, disappearing inside with the other high lords. Malahi started after him. "I'm still a Rowenes, and until they convict me of crimes, I have the right to be here. I'll endure their abuse for the sake of monitoring their plots."

"Or we could just kill them all," Agrippa suggested. "Nothing like a massacre to change up the political landscape."

Lady Calorian muttered, "Just make sure you do it outside."

As Malahi passed, she paused before Lydia. "I'm sorry. I know this isn't what you want, but Mudamora needs you to do what I cannot. Please forgive me."

Lydia didn't answer, and Malahi sighed, climbing the steps into the palace.

Dareena waved a hand, and Sonia approached with two former members of Malahi's guard, Lena and Gwen, all women Lydia counted as dear friends. Yet she felt nothing at seeing them; all her emotions drowned each other out so that all Lydia felt was numb. And though she'd just been made into the most powerful woman in Mudamora, never had she felt more powerless.

Shade fell over her as she entered the manor, the air smelling like wood polish and fresh-cut flowers, the floorboards creaking slightly beneath their feet. The foyer was large, with a twin staircase curving up the sides to the second level. A delicate chandelier hung over a table at the center, which held an enormous arrangement of roses. Lydia was led up the right-hand staircase, then down a hall. Bright light filtered through windows to make rainbows across the whitewashed walls, which all bore watercolor paintings in vibrant hues.

"In here." Lady Calorian opened the door to a room, but Killian said, "Wait outside. I need to speak to Lydia alone."

"Not possible," his mother said curtly. "And most certainly not appropriate."

"Please tell me you're joking, Mother," Killian snapped. "I'm gods-damned oath sworn to protect her and have traveled across the whole bloody continent with her. The propriety ship has sailed."

"Of that I have no doubt," she retorted. "But I know that every High Lord has predicated his or her support on the potential union with an unwed queen, most especially your brother. He already sees you as an obstacle. I didn't get you back only to lose you within the day." Then she smacked him on the back of the head. "And mind your language, boy, or I'll have Dareena hold you down while I wash that filthy mouth out with soap."

Dareena burst into laughter. "He learned half those words from me, Anne, so that hardly seems fair."

"Fair punishment for both of you, then."

"They don't honestly think I'll marry any of them, do they?" Lydia asked, her tongue finally loosening, though her voice sounded strange in her ears. And her question was foolish, because she'd seen Malahi in this exact same position. Gods, she herself had been forced into a betrothal before.

"Inside," Lady Calorian said. "The halls have ears and not all of them are friendly."

It was a finely appointed bedroom, the balcony doors on the far side flung open, diaphanous curtains blowing inward on a breeze that smelled of greenery and horses. A large fireplace made of white stone dominated one wall, and the opposite held open doors leading to a bathing chamber with a large copper bath and another fireplace. The furniture was all polished teak, the bedding and upholstery all a pale blue that would have been serene if Lydia weren't drowning in anxiety.

"This is Teriana's favored suite when she visits," Killian said, then led her to a sofa and sat next to her. Lydia leaned against him, the heat of his shoulder through their clothing causing her to realize how cold she was. Like ice had seeped into her bones.

Dareena went to the sideboard, where she bypassed the chilled wine and retrieved a decanter and four glasses, carrying them to the low table like a barmaid. She sloshed a generous amount of what smelled like whiskey into all of them. Snatching hers up, Lydia gulped the contents, the burn making her eyes water.

"Feel better?" Dareena asked, but Lydia only shook her head.

The High Lady of House Falorn sighed and leaned back in her chair, muddy riding boot resting on her knee. No . . . not High Lady. Because Lydia was High Lady now, on top of being queen, and Dareena was . . . "You suspected who I was?"

"Yes," she answered. "You look like how I *think* I look, though the mirror tells a different story. The years have taken more of a toll than I care to admit. I'm not nineteen anymore." Her green eyes fixed on Killian. "The blight has crossed the River Aln and presses south by the day. There is no containing it. Ditches and fire accomplish nothing, and while stone and mortar hold it for a time, we can't build a wall across the entire kingdom. There are branches that feed north, but it seems whatever force drives the blight is focused on pressing south. Likely because Rufina and her army follow at its heels."

"Corrupted tenders," Killian said. "We saw them in Deadground before we crossed the Liratoras into Derin. They're more plant than human now."

"You killed them?"

"Just one," Lydia said softly, and the story of all that they'd learned poured from her lips.

Dareena muttered a string of colorful curses under her breath, then shook her head. "Even if Anukastre does join forces with us, it may not be enough. Rufina's army of blighters is in the tens of thousands. Gamdesh would have been able to turn the advantage to us, but they are in no position to offer aid, as the Cel invaders from across the seas are marching north as we speak, their eyes on Emrant."

Lydia's thoughts went to Teriana, who was a prisoner of that army. Who'd be in the midst of those battles. Her chest tightened with a sudden flood of fear tempered only by her memory of Madoria's words. *Teriana is where she's supposed to be.*

"Kaira is near Emrant with a large portion of her army, with more mobilizing to aid. Emrant might well suffer under a siege, but there is no reason they shouldn't be able to hold against the Cel until reinforcements arrive."

Lydia exchanged a tense look with Killian, then said, "I wouldn't underestimate the Cel army. If they gain control of that xenthier stem and the path is good, more legions will come. Tens of thousands of trained soldiers. Gamdesh needs to know what they're up against."

"The Maarin have warned them," Dareena replied. "But the fact of the matter is, Gamdesh lost the majority of their fleet to Rufina's attack on Mudaire. They don't have the ships to move soldiers at speed and it takes time to march an army across a third of Gamdesh."

A wave of unease passed over Lydia, and she pressed fingers to her temple. These decisions were all now hers to make, and she felt woefully out of her depth.

"Gendorn has refused our requests for aid," Dareena said. "They think they can hide in the frozen north, failing to realize that while Rufina's personal goal is the destruction of Mudamora, the Corrupter won't be content until all of Reath is under his sway."

Everyone was quiet.

"I've seen her host," Dareena finally said, her green eyes haunted. "When they aren't marching or fighting, they lie on the ground in heaps where they fall. Like mass graves of men, women, and children."

Her throat moved as she swallowed. "When it is time to march, they rise as one under the singular will that binds them. The blighters don't fight well and are not unreasonably strong, but they also don't feel pain. They keep fighting despite catastrophic injuries. The only way to stop them is to take off their heads or burn them."

"She did the same thing to her own people," Lydia said quietly. "Poisoned thousands then animated them to hunt for us. They are dead, though. Their souls are with the Six."

"Tell that to the soldiers who have to cut them down." Dareena passed a hand over her face as though trying to wipe away a memory. "We're losing men to desertion by the droves, though where they think they can flee to, I don't know. The whole gods-damned world is at war."

Draining her cup, she said, "So to answer your question, no. We can't defeat them by strength of arms, so all our hope depends on our ability to destroy the blight. Malahi's ability, if what you say is true. Without it, Rufina loses her ability to raise the dead as blighters and we might have a chance at defeating them."

"We believe Malahi can do it," Lydia said. "There are ancient paintings in Anukastre that show as much. Beautiful artwork that has stood the test of time by virtue of being underground, and it shows people with branches for hands standing before rivers of black. The Anuk believe they were tenders of old."

"But no records of exactly what they did?"

"No, the Anuk believe the paintings are a thousand or more years old, and any record that might have existed has been lost to war, fire, or time. Our hope is that the library in Revat will still have some record. Seldrid plans to send word to the Sultan requesting that he have the librarians assist in the search, but my plan was to go look myself, because it isn't just the land that has been corrupted. My plan . . ." Lydia trailed off, reality slapping her in the face. "But that's no longer possible, is it? The High Lords aren't going to allow their puppet queen to traipse off to Revat to dig for answers in the stacks."

Everyone's eyes turned to Lady Calorian, whose glass was empty in her hand.

"Hacken aims to be king," she said quietly. "But though he holds a great deal of sway over the High Lords and Ladies currently sipping wine with him in his study, they refuse to kneel to him, which is reason for the betrothal to Ria. A betrothal that I expect will never see a wedding, for of a surety, his eyes are now on Kitaryia."

That's not my name.

"If he aims to try to marry me, he's in for a harsh rejection," Lydia muttered.

"You say that now, but you forget the power he wields," Lady Calorian said. "Our lands are the few untouched by blight or war; our crops and water are nearly all that Mudamora has to feed the people. What if he makes his support, and all that comes with it, conditional on a betrothal? Will you say no? Because if he removes his support, you will be queen no longer."

Lydia's lips parted to unleash an angry retort, but instead said, "He wouldn't do such a thing. It would be madness to risk the entire kingdom on a bid for power."

"All my sons are gamblers, in their own way," Lady Calorian responded. "Seldrid with his gold and Killian with his own life, but Hacken? Hacken gambles with the lives of others, and he does not much care how many he loses if it helps him achieve his ends."

Killian abruptly rose to his feet, going to the balcony, and Lydia followed him. The rear of the manor overlooked a dense canopy of trees, the sunlight dappling the leaves and the air alive with the hum of insects, though she could also hear the horses in the pastures whinnying beyond.

"I don't know what to do," she said. "This is the last thing I wanted. But for all Malahi violated my trust, I understand her motivations. If I don't wear the crown, they *will* vote for Hacken, and I do not think he will act in the best interest of the people."

"I know." His brown eyes fixed on the trees, though she doubted he was seeing them. "But that doesn't mean I'm happy to dangle you before all those High Lords as a future wife for them or their sons."

She wrapped her arms around him, pressing her head to his chest. "I'm yours. There is no future for me without you in it."

"But . . ."

Growing up in Celendor had trained her in the arts of politics, and like it or not, the lessons she'd learned in the East had left their mark. "I think we need to string them along with the potential of marriage until we're on the other side of it."

"And what am I supposed to do?" he snapped. "Be your shadow, guarding your back while you lead all these men into thinking you aren't mine through and through?"

Lydia flinched, hearing the hurt in his voice. Feeling it in her own heart, because they'd fought their way to each other only to have yet another obstacle drag them apart.

"I think you're getting ahead of yourself," Dareena said. "All of this is speculation and theory, not a demand that anyone has made of you. I'd suggest we appease Hacken by playing along. We dress Lydia like the Falorn queen he wants her to be while working to achieve our own goals."

Lydia turned around, latching onto Dareena's words because at least they offered hope. And all at the cost of wearing certain clothes. "Do you have a dress I can borrow?"

"I don't wear dresses."

"Let me see what I can do." Lady Calorian rose to her feet. "Excuse me."

After she left, Lydia said, "Do you think Hacken can be persuaded to allow me to travel to Revat? If there is an answer to be had, it *will* be there."

"I think that's a task Malahi will have to manage," Dareena said. "She's learned enough to work with the librarians, and if what those paintings in Anukastre indicate is true, it's her mark that will defeat the blight. Unless there is another reason you believe you'd be an asset in the search?"

Lydia hesitated, reluctant to put words to the hope in her heart. "I wanted to speak to the librarians to see what could be done for those who have succumbed to the blight," she finally said. "Not just those infected, as Lena was, but . . . but those we've lost to it."

Killian shifted behind her, his distress palpable. "Healers cannot bring back the dead, and it's death to those who try."

"I know that." She rounded on him, her hands balled into fists. "And maybe Malahi is the answer for those who have fallen. Maybe in pulling it from the land, she'll pull it from the infected as well, but I don't think so. The body is Hegeria's domain, so I truly do believe it needs to be a healer who saves them."

"But their souls are gone," he said. "Even if you remove the poison from their bodies and the Corrupter along with it, that doesn't change that their souls are with the Six."

"Then maybe that's all I accomplish." Lydia knew it was a long shot, but it still hurt that he wasn't willing to support her attempt. "Maybe all I can do is give them peace, and in doing so, take away Rufina's army."

"Well, that's not nothing given that they outnumber us four to one," Dareena said. "I'll think on it."

A knock sounded on the door, and when Killian opened it, Lady Calorian stood outside with a large box in her arms. "This was mine, once," she said, crossing the room to set the box on the bed. "When

I was in service to Queen Camilla. I dare say, I could not fit into it now."

Feeling uneasy for reasons she couldn't quite explain, Lydia pushed her spectacles up her nose and then lifted the lid off the box. Inside was an elaborate corseted gown made of leather dyed green, the neck high and the sleeves long. A gown fit for a warrior and a queen.

"You'll sweat like mad in that," Dareena said. "That's a gown for the north. Should we cut off the sleeves so your armpits can breathe?"

"You will do no such thing!" Lady Calorian snapped. "Put away that knife."

Lydia drew Killian aside. "Will you go speak to Malahi and Agrippa? Explain the situation and have Seldrid make arrangements for passage to Revat? We have no time to lose."

Killian nodded, then said to Dareena, "Don't leave her side."

She only grunted at him, her focus on the dress.

Lydia went back to the bed, then lifted the garment, the rich leather nothing more than beautifully made shackles. "Turn me into a queen worthy of Mudamora."

But as Killian shut the door behind him, she heard him say, "You already are."

51

KILLIAN

He'd known trouble had been coming, but this . . . this was the last thing Killian had anticipated.

Striding through his family home, he fought to keep the rage burning in his heart in check. Killian was not one to hate, but gods help him, he hated his brother right now. Hated that despite Mudamora falling beneath the heels of an enemy that they had a minimal chance of beating, his brother was jockeying for power with a total disregard for who he hurt in the process.

His hands fisted, his body needing the physical release of a fight to ease the tension singing through him, because Lydia did not want to be queen. Did not want to embroil herself in the politics of rule, where the choices for the many always outweighed the needs of the few. Especially given that Hacken and the rest of the High Lords were unlikely to give her any power, no doubt intending to use her as only a figurehead. A puppet queen, and it would be Hacken who held her strings.

"Killian?"

Finn's voice caught his attention, and he lifted his head to see the boy waiting just outside the doors to the drawing room. Relief flooded Killian, but also guilt, because he'd not thought about his young friend once since they'd arrived at Teradale. He'd been too consumed with everything else, but seeing the boy was well was a weight lifted off his shoulders.

"I'm glad you're back," Finn said, pushing dark curls out of his eyes. "Everyone was worried. Not me, though. I knew you'd fight your way clear of anything Rufina threw at you."

"It was a close thing at times." Killian gripped Finn's shoulders and then pulled him into a tight embrace. "Gods, it's good to see you here. Are you well?"

"Living like the king I am."

Killian grinned. "I'm looking forward to hearing your stories and telling you my own, but I need to speak with Malahi now. What has happened with Lydia needs my focus. I'll find you later?"

Finn shrugged, then looked away. "I'll find you."

Killian pushed through the doors, a wave of laughter and the scent of wine washing over him. The High Lords all stood about with glasses in their hands, servants circulating with trays of food, and guards stationed like pieces of furniture around the large room. Malahi stood with Seldrid and Adra off to one side, Agrippa at her elbow. His expression was bland to anyone who didn't know him, but to Killian, it was obvious that everyone in the room was lucky to still be alive.

At the sight of Killian, Adra started toward him, the Gamdeshian woman a froth of bright pink silk and gold. While his brother always looked ridiculous in his extravagant clothing, the Gamdeshian woman looked like a work of art. Nearly as short as Malahi, she had to stand on her tip toes as she caught both sides of his head, pulling him down to kiss him firmly on the cheek. "I am so relieved that you are alive," she said. "Let's keep it that way. Do not lose your temper."

"No promises," he muttered under his breath, then added, "It's good to see you well."

Adra gave a soft laugh as though he'd told her something witty, then murmured, "Malahi has told me of your need for aid from the librarians in Revat. I will send word to my uncle on the next ship detailing your requests, as well as the urgency of the situation. I'll choose my most trusted messenger."

"Thank you, though it may be that Malahi serves the role of messenger." He could feel eyes on him and Adra, the men in the room not hiding their curiosity. "A conversation better suited to a location with fewer ears."

"Of course." She giggled and batted eyelashes so long they brushed the tops of her cheeks, the consummate courtier given she'd been raised in the Sultan's palace in Revat. From across the room, Seldrid called out, "Adra, love, you know it hurts my feelings when you flirt with Killian. He already makes me feel woefully inadequate whenever he walks into the same room."

Looping her arm through his, Adra tugged Killian in Malahi's direction. "I have eyes only for you, my darling."

"It *is* hard to miss you, Lord Calorian." Agrippa examined Seldrid's clothing. "I should really consult your tailor. That's a splendid coat."

"People have a habit of underestimating men in bright colors," his brother replied. "Whereas if you walk around wearing black, as Killian does, everyone immediately suspects you are a threat."

"Clever." Agrippa crossed his arms. "How is Lydia holding up?"

"Trying to see her way forward." Killian fixed his anger on Malahi. "You should have asked her first. She trusted you and you betrayed her confidence."

Malahi's voice was tired. "If I hadn't done it then, rest assured, Hacken would have seen himself voted king on those very steps. I know it wasn't fair, but do not pretend it wasn't the right choice for Mudamora."

Malahi always chose Mudamora, no matter the cost to those around her. No matter the cost to herself. It might have made her a good queen, but gods help him, it made Malahi a poor friend indeed.

"It's done, so what I think doesn't matter much at this point." Out of the corner of his eye, Killian saw Hacken approaching. "We need to go somewhere to talk. Lydia thinks you two should head to Revat immediately."

"Agreed," Malahi said. "I have no power here. At least in Revat I might be able to do some good."

They all fell silent as Hacken stopped before them. "Where is Kitaryia?"

"You know how women are, brother," Killian answered, not

bothering to turn around. "Never quick to get ready. I suggest you be patient."

"Mind your tone." His brother's gaze darkened. "Your value here is limited, and do not think for a heartbeat that I won't send you to join the front lines if you cause trouble. You've always been a tool to be used by those in power, Killian, and that hasn't changed. Remember that the marked *serve*."

"The Marked are also to be respected," Malahi snapped. "We were chosen by the Six, Hacken, whereas you demand respect for no reason other than that you were born *first*. And lest you forget, the woman you bent the knee to is also marked."

The room went silent.

"I haven't forgotten." Hacken gave Killian a slow smile. "And I have no doubt that Kitaryia will serve well."

Killian's temper snapped. With no thought for the consequences, he struck, his fist connecting with his brother's cheekbone and sending Hacken staggering.

Then Agrippa and Seldrid were on him, hauling him backward.

"He's baiting you," Seldrid hissed as they struggled. Killian only shoved him away. But as he did, Agrippa's foot caught Killian's ankle, sending him staggering. Both men leapt on him, pushing him to the floor.

"Don't give him a reason to send you away," Agrippa hissed into Killian's ear. "Lydia needs you."

His friend's words made sense, but Killian couldn't hear them through the noise of his rage at what his brother intended. Not only to use Lydia as a puppet, but to . . .

"Her Most Royal Majesty, Queen Kitaryia Falorn," a voice announced, and Killian went still, his eyes shifting to the doorway.

A woman in a green leather gown appeared, her dark hair twisted into a complicated series of braids interwoven with a tiara, the tattoo on the base of her skull visible where the hair was freshly shorn, the mark of Hegeria a black half-moon on her forehead. Her face was concealed by the traditional dark green war paint worn by the warriors of House Falorn, and on her nose perched a pair of wire spectacles, the green eyes behind them deeply familiar to Killian. His heart skipped, then sped.

Every man in the room bowed low, murmuring, "Your Grace."

She surveyed them all, then said softly, "I would hear how best I can serve in our fight against our enemy."

Showing no care for his already swelling cheek, Hacken approached her and bowed low. “It would be my pleasure, Your Grace.” Taking her arm, he led her to a table containing several maps, but as they walked, Dareena glanced back at Killian from behind Lydia’s spectacles.

And she winked.

52

TERIANA

The legions hummed with a different energy, a tense *readiness* that made Teriana feel as though static danced across her body. She wanted to brush it off, to shirk the sensation, but it only grew worse as horns blew and the legionnaires tightened ranks, feet stepping in a rhythm pounded by dozens of drummers.

The noise was terrible, not only in volume but in what it promised.

“It’s an intimidation strategy,” Quintus said. “Kaira won’t lose her nerve but the people of Emrant might, if they are afraid enough.”

“And if they don’t?”

“Then their army will either ride out to fight or will man the walls while we lay siege.”

Teriana glanced back at the trebuchet the oxen pulled, only one of the many war machines the legion carried with them. All things designed to pull down walls or go over them.

Endless scouts brought information to Marcus where he rode not far ahead of her in the company of Nic and Servius. Close enough that she overheard some of their reports, and with Quintus interpreting some of the signals, she gathered that Kaira had heavily armed the walls of Emrant and arrayed the rest of her army before the main gates. Seven thousand soldiers was the number she kept hearing. An enormous host by most standards, yet smaller than the one Teriana rode with.

And a spec of sand in the numbers at the Empire’s beck and call.

Thud.

Thud.

Thud.

The merciless rhythm of thousands of marching men took control of her heart, forcing it to beat to the same relentless pace, and nausea rose in Teriana's stomach. "Tell me how this will go," she whispered to Quintus, trepidation overwhelming her. "Tell me what he's planning. Tell me what will happen."

"I don't know." Quintus's whole body was tense. "I don't think anyone does except for him."

Thud.

Thud.

Thud.

It sounded like death was on the march, and Teriana could only imagine how those in the city felt, the very ground trembling as the legions moved ever closer. Families hiding in cellars, clutching each other tight while those who could fight raised what arms they could to join the trained soldiers on the wall. *Gods* . . . just imagining civilians trying to fight the legionnaires surrounding her made Teriana want to vomit.

It was not right.

It was not fair.

"Why didn't Kaira evacuate?" Tears dripped down Teriana's cheeks as she watched the vanguard disappear over the rise of a hill, war machines pulled by oxen trundling between the lines of men. "So many people are going to die, Quintus."

"Evacuating a city this size is next to impossible," Quintus said. "Especially one that has never known a threat. People aren't afraid enough to abandon everything they own, everything they've worked for, and by the time they realize that they're going to lose it all anyway, it's too late. Either that, or Kaira has reason to believe she can win the fight."

A scout approached on horseback, falling in alongside Marcus. Teriana leaned around Quintus to watch them, heads bent together. Marcus nodded slowly at whatever information the legionnaire conveyed before the man sped north again.

"As anticipated, Kaira emptied the military fortress of Imresh, which is about three miles from here." Marcus spoke loud enough for the officers around him to hear over the noise. Loud enough for Teriana to hear, though she was not certain whether that was his intent. "An extra thousand soldiers, whom we should see"—his horse reached the summit of the hill—"now."

The officers stopped their horses on the ridge, Gibzen's men forming neat ranks around them while the rest of the army kept marching onward. Teriana held her breath as Quintus guided his horse to stand at Nic's left. Sliding off the side of the animal, she stared at the scene before her.

It was all she could do not to fall to her knees.

Emrant sat on the edge of the azure sea, the towers of the seven gods rising from the center of the city. The tops of the city's high walls were elbow to elbow with men and women. Before the walls stretched ranks and ranks of Gamdeshian soldiers, their armor glistening in the sunlight, banners flapping on the breeze. Teriana's eyes went unerringly to the armored figure mounted on a black horse at the center, the Gamdeshian royal crest embossed in gold on her breastplate. Kaira wore no helmet, and as Teriana lifted her spyglass, it revealed the princess's dark hair fluttering in the wind, lovely face grim and unyielding in the face of the thousands of Empire legionnaires marching toward her.

On the water, the ten Katamarcan vessels with decks filled of legionnaires blocked the harbor.

But where were the Cel ships? Where was the Forty-First?

The question vanished from her head as Marcus said, "A bit of noise, if you would."

Gibzen chuckled and said, "Put the fear of the Empire in their hearts."

If Marcus answered, Teriana didn't hear, because a second after a horn blew a series of notes, the marching men began to beat their weapons against their shields in the same rhythm, the voices rising in unified shouts.

It was wordless and terrifying, fifteen thousand voices promising death.

Row after row of them, and though she knew the legionnaires were flesh and blood, they looked to her inhuman. Like some many-headed beast that had come across the seas not in search of power and gold, but of *blood*.

And Kaira's army seemed child-sized standing before it. Insignificant and pitiful.

Teriana's heartbeat was a riot in her chest, a scream rising in her throat because she'd fought for this moment. This was the battle that would see her people freed but would be her damnation. She could not watch Marcus slaughter this city and then go on breathing. Go on *living.*

Thud.

Thud.

Thud.

The horns blasted, the sound echoing like a god screaming his wrath.

The legions stopped marching as one.

And they fell silent.

The only sound was the whistle of the wind and the rustle of banners, the whole world seeming to hold its breath.

Then Marcus's horse started down the slope, the Thirty-Seventh's standard braced in his stirrup.

The legions parted ranks to allow him to pass, the golden mare walking sedately downward, Marcus's crimson and gold cloak billowing out behind him.

"Shit," Quintus muttered. "I haven't seen him do this since Hydrilla." From Servius's muttered curses, Gibzen's open-mouthed gape, and Nic's expression of horror, *none* of them had expected this, either.

"What is he doing?" she demanded.

"Offering her the chance to surrender without a fight, is my guess," Quintus said under his breath. "But he's not supposed to do it himself. He's supposed to send someone we can afford to lose. He's . . . he's also supposed to do that under a white flag."

Teriana's head snapped sideways at her friend's tone, and she saw Quintus's face was drained of color under his helmet. His blue eyes met hers. "If she tries to kill him, no one is close enough to stop her."

53

MARCUS

After days of smoke and ash, the scent of the sea breeze was a welcome change, and Marcus inhaled deeply as he walked the golden mare down the slope toward the Gamdeshian army, a fresh dose of Gibzen's narcotics flooding his veins, making colors brighter. Sounds louder, most especially the thundering beat of his heart.

The Thirty-Seventh parted to make a path for him, and though he could feel their anxiety over his choice to step out from the safety of their ranks, he paid them no mind. His eyes were all for the army before him. The ranks and ranks of men and women who'd fight him to the death to protect a city full of those they loved.

They'd fight harder than his men would.

Would press through terror and pain and embrace death, because the consequences of giving up were so much worse in their eyes than falling beneath legion blades.

Those with something to protect, someone to defend, were the most dangerous opponents—not soldiers fighting because rich men on a hill told them to.

His horse stepped into the open, the mare prancing like a peacock beneath him as he crossed the distance to the Gamdeshians. A woman of perhaps thirty years of age broke away from their ranks to ride toward him. Her black mount was perfectly behaved, and for the hundredth time, he cursed his stupid horse for her foolishness. "Steady," he muttered, patting her neck. "It's not you she wants to kill."

He'd read descriptions of Kaira, which were all accurate. Skin of a medium-brown hue, dark brown hair most often worn in a long tail at the back of her head, though it was woven into a coronet today, and brown eyes. She was pretty, but the heavy plate armor she wore turned her beauty fierce. Yet what his spies' reports had failed to capture was the gravitas the woman possessed. Almost as though she were not quite mortal, but rather something nearer to the gods of this land. Every instinct in his body screamed *danger*, but Marcus kept his posture as relaxed as possible while supporting the blasted weight of the Thirty-Seventh's golden standard.

They both reined their mounts in at the midpoint between the two forces, and Marcus inclined his head. "Your Highness."

Her mouth twisted into a cold smile. "Spare me the pleasantries, Cel dog."

Marcus let out a soft chuckle. "You've been spending time with the Maarin, I see."

"Not as much time as you, though I understand Teriana's mouth is too preoccupied for insults."

Though he'd anticipated similar comments, Marcus's temper swelled at the slight.

Kill her, the voice ordered. His mare squealed and pinned her ears, stretching to snap at Kaira's mount.

"Control your animal," she growled.

"She's looking for a fight." He allowed the mare to keep pawing the ground with one foreleg. "Though we've yet to find one."

Kaira's jaw tightened. "Then why are we talking?"

"I thought I'd give you another chance to do the right thing. Surrender. Save lives. This is a courtesy, nothing more." He used the hand holding the reins to pat the mare's neck, and she used the freedom to rotate in a circle, giving him a quick glance behind him before facing Kaira again. *Where are you?* he silently screamed. *We're running out of time.*

"I already provided an answer to your *courtesy*," Kaira replied. "It still stands, though perhaps your lips are too preoccupied with Teriana's backside to deliver."

The black horse was pawing now, sensing his rider's unease. *She's on to you,* his instincts warned. *You're out of time!*

"Teriana is not your enemy." His defense of Teriana would fall on deaf ears, but given Kaira seemed intent on bringing her up, the topic might serve to stall her a little bit longer. "My masters in Celendor have her people imprisoned, and her actions are driven only by the desire to free them. Teriana has done a great deal to try to protect your people, whereas you have done nothing to spare hers, which suggests you are more her enemy than she yours."

Kaira tilted her head, considering his words. "What would you do, were you in my shoes, *Legatus*? Would you sacrifice a city of one hundred thousand innocent souls for the sake of five hundred?"

"I'm not here to murder your people," he answered. "The exact opposite, in fact. The Senate has no interest in trade with corpses, and indeed, they would be most displeased if I destroyed the market they desire to trade with. Whereas I can assure you, the lives of the imprisoned Maarin are very much on the line."

"Yet you come with an army." She gestured toward the ranks standing a hundred paces behind him. "You come to lay siege."

"You are the one who invites a siege in your unwillingness to compromise, Kaira." He allowed his mare to spin again, seeing no motion in the Thirty-Seventh's ranks. "We can only hope that a taste of it will cause your people to reconsider their options. Mutually profitable trade with the wealthiest nation on Reath or starving to death to satisfy your pride?"

"Mutually profitable?" Kaira spat on the ground between them. "Lies. Your Senate desires to turn Gamdesh into another of its *provinces*. To control it in every possible way."

Marcus shrugged. "True. Yet these people are already controlled. Already pay taxes to your father and bend to his whim. Will changing the face of the collector change their lives enough to risk war for the sake of keeping your father on the throne?"

"Taxes are the least of it," she retorted. "We know what was done to the god towers in Aracam and Galinha. Know you'll do the same here."

"Also true," he said. "But will that matter when Emrant's supplies run lean and children with empty bellies begin to cry? Will your voice of warning about what Celendor may or may not do *matter*? Or will the propaganda the Katamarcans have been spreading of the glorious opportunities for trade be the louder voice? Will your merchants scream loyalty to your father or"—he hefted the standard—"will they clamor for Cel gold?"

Her gaze jumped behind him, then back to his face. "They are not so weak as you seem to think."

"Neither were the people in the other cities and fortresses I have laid siege to over the course of my service to the Empire," he replied. "And yet all now pay taxes to the Senate, and I remain undefeated. Perhaps Emrant will be different." Her eyes shifted past him again, brow furrowing. "Then again, perhaps not."

Kaira wasn't listening to him, her gaze on the scene behind his back. The shifting of soldiers filled Marcus's ears, along with the tread of dozens of feet and panted breaths, but Marcus didn't turn, only sat on his horse as Gamdeshians with bound wrists plodded past him, their heads down. Some wore uniforms, some civilian garb; all wore the same grim expression of bitter defeat.

A horse's hooves thudded, and Felix reined in his ambling mount next to Marcus. "A fine afternoon for a ride, wouldn't you say, sir?"

"It is." Marcus waited until the masses of prisoners had passed, disappearing into the ranks of the Gamdeshian army where they'd have to explain how easily they were defeated. "Though tell me, do I have a feather bed waiting for me at the end of it?"

"You do, sir," Felix replied. "And the nicest bathing pool you could want. The view looks over the sea. Nothing like a bath after a long march, am I right?"

"I look forward to it and the sleep to follow."

Kaira's eyes burned with fury, and her horse half reared beneath her, snorting loudly.

"You'll sleep easily, sir, for Imresh is as solid a fortress as you could want to have. If the walls had been properly guarded, I dare say we'd have lost a few men trying to take it. Was lucky for us that the general here decided those soldiers were better off watching your little chit-chat."

"Do we rely on luck, Felix?"

"No." Felix laughed. "We don't."

Kaira seethed with barely checked violence, but she held her ground.

"Felix, order the men to withdraw to our new accommodations." Marcus waited for Felix to ride back to the ranks before he said, "To answer your question, Your Highness, I don't know what I'd choose to do if my home and family were threatened, because it's never happened. This"—he gestured to the ranks of men slowly retreating back up the slope—"is my family, and where they are is my home. Which makes my choices much easier than yours. That said, I hope that given more opportunity to consider said choices, you'll make the correct one. Good day to you."

Reining the mare around, he turned his back on Princess Kaira of Gamdesh and rode after his army.

"Tell Teriana to watch her back," Kaira called after him. "There will be a reckoning for what she's done!"

A chill ran across his skin, but Marcus didn't stop his horse. Didn't turn around. Only trusted the wind to carry his words as he said, "You harm a hair on Teriana's head, and you'll no longer be dealing with the Empire, Kaira. You'll be dealing with me."

54

TERIANA

"What is happening?" Teriana demanded of Felix as he gave the order for the legions to withdraw and march north. "Where are we going? Who were those prisoners?"

"The Forty-First captured Imresh," Felix answered, and Nic slapped his hand against his saddle and whooped with delight.

"Those prisoners were the skeleton guard and serving staff that she'd left behind," Felix continued, giving the boy an amused glance. "As to why, you'll have to ask Marcus."

Who was trotting his horse up the slope toward them.

"Let's go see if this gambit was worth it," was all Marcus said as he rode past them, forcing Teriana to scramble up behind Quintus on their horse. With uncharacteristic urgency, Marcus wove through the ranks of marching men, then heeled his mount into a gallop down the road.

"Bring the ranks to Imresh and watch our heels," Felix snapped at Nic, then he broke into a gallop after Marcus, as did Gibzen.

"Go!" Teriana shouted at Quintus, thumping her heels against their horse. "Catch them!"

They galloped down the road, and what terror Teriana might have felt at the speed was eclipsed by a desperate need to discover why Marcus had done this. To learn what his strategy was to have marched so far, to have pushed his men so hard, only to have taken a location other than their target.

Crimson and gold Cel banners were already draped from the walls of the forbidding grey fortress of Imresh as they approached, legionnaires patrolling the ramparts and manning the gates as though this stronghold had been theirs for months rather than hours. Marcus disappeared beneath the portcullis just as she and Quintus reached the drawbridge over the moat. How Felix and the Forty-First had taken Imresh so easily she couldn't have said, for the murky waters below were filled with wooden spikes with no evidence of casualties.

The horse's hooves clattered over the cobbles as they entered the courtyard. Marcus was already dismounted, and she heard him bark, "Please tell me that someone has found something of worth in this place?"

"Yes, sir," one of the Forty-First answered. "It's this way, sir."

Slipping off the side of her horse, Teriana hurried after them, ignoring Gibzen's glower. They wove through the interior of the fortress, which, unlike its austere exterior, was painted in vibrant colors, the walls decorated with elaborate wooden carvings and woven tapestries. It smelled heavily of the incense that the Gamdeshians burned.

"In here, sir," she heard someone say, then Marcus's cloak disappeared into a room, a shattered wooden door propped against the wall.

"I knew it!" Marcus shouted, and Teriana broke into a run, ignoring Quintus's protests as she spun into the room.

To find Marcus staring at a glittering stem of xenthier.

"Is that—" She broke off, needing to swallow down the tightness that had formed in her throat.

"A genesis? Yes. Yes, it is." Marcus turned away from the stem of crystal, and pulling off his helmet, he tossed it aside before crossing the room to grip Teriana's shoulders. "I knew they were hiding something in here. Something important, else Kaira would have been in Emrant itself."

His eyes were almost manic, a combination of exhaustion and euphoria and . . . something Teriana couldn't put a name to.

"I couldn't get a spy into the bloody place, but then I remembered a conversation I had with Agrippa in Bardeen about farts."

"Farts?" She stared at Marcus in bewilderment, feeling a slight shake in his arms that filled her with fear, because he wasn't talking straight. "I don't understand."

Marcus shook his head. "That doesn't matter. What matters is that I had my spies burn pitch and sulfur upwind of this fortress. The smell is distinct, and the fires are hard to put out. Wex had trusted men sitting next to unmapped terminuses all across the Empire, smelling the drafts that came out of them, and this? This path leads to a stem in Celendor itself. And that"—he jabbed his finger in the direction of Emrant—"is its gods-damned mate. There are always two, Teriana. Always two; that's what keeps things in balance."

"All right." She hated how pale he was, eyes so dilated she could barely see the iris around them. "Do you know the location of the Emrant path's genesis?"

"Yes, because of the firecrackers. At least, we think so." He looked around wildly. "I need to confirm it. I just need to—"

Firecrackers?

He spun away from her, digging in his belt pouch. "I have the instructions ready. I wrote them just in case." Pulling a packet of paper free, he sent other objects flying, including a familiar glass vial. She didn't have the chance to think about why he was carrying around narcotics, because Marcus was walking toward the xenthier, hand outstretched. "No!"

She flung herself at him, grabbing hold of his cloak and wrenching him back even as Gibzen and Felix caught his arms.

"I'll do it." Felix pulled the letter from Marcus's hand. "I just need something heavy." Spotting a candlestick on the lone table in the room, he secured the letter to it with a piece of twine. Taking a deep breath, he cautiously lobbed it at the xenthier.

It disappeared.

No one spoke. No one moved. No one seemed to even breathe, then Marcus abruptly pulled out of the grip of his men and raced toward the door.

"Shit," Felix hissed, bolting after him, and Teriana was forced to wait while his anxious bodyguards fell into pursuit before following.

"Something's not right with him," she said to Quintus. "Someone should get Racker."

"He's with the Thirty-Seventh," he said. "And I don't think Marcus is going to let a medic near him. He's manic."

She followed the clatter of steel tread back into the courtyard, then up the stairs leading to the ramparts. Marcus was leaning on the stone, staring fixedly in the direction of Emrant. "Come on," he muttered. "This should be quick. Red smoke."

"Sir?" Gibzen came up next to him. "What are we looking for?"

"An explosion with red smoke," Marcus said, his nails scratching at the stone of the battlements. "Wex is sending just enough black powder to crack open the casement they've put around the stem without doing irreparable damage. Once we've confirmed it, we'll send a messenger to Kaira telling her that she's got a day to remove her forces from the city or Wex will send through a wagonload of explosives."

"Shit," Gibzen mumbled, and the look on his face turned Teriana's blood cold. "I'd like to see that."

"Obviously the hope is that it doesn't come to that. The whole point of all this was to secure the paths without casualties, and using explosives with xenthier is risky at the best of times!" Felix snapped, though Teriana could tell from his expression that even he hadn't known this part of the plan. No one had known more than what was required to do their part, it seemed.

"Yeah, *our* casualties," the primus said. "This will make a point. Will put that bitch they call a general in her place. She'll be kissing our asses at the end of the day, begging us not to do it."

Though Teriana knew there was a lot that wasn't right in Gibzen's head, horror still filled her chest at the primus's total lack of empathy for those in the ill-fated city. It seemed she was not the only one to feel that way, because Felix shoved Gibzen with such force that the other man nearly fell. "You are relieved from duty until I say otherwise!" Felix snarled. "Take a walk until you learn to keep your opinions to yourself."

"You can't relieve me!" Gibzen shouted. "Only Marcus can do that!"

Except Marcus seemed oblivious to what was going on behind him, his eyes fixed on the city, mouth moving as he silently repeated, *red smoke red smoke*.

"And yet I just did." Felix took a step closer to Gibzen, mouth twisted with disgust. "Walk of your own accord or I'll have your corpse tossed over the wall to feed the carrion. Your. Choice."

Gibzen's hands balled into fists, and Teriana held her breath, certain it was going to turn violent. Then the primus shrugged. "Fine. I could use a break."

Giving Felix a sarcastic salute, he turned on his heel and strode away, passing Racker as he came up the stairs.

The surgeon stepped sideways, expression wary, but Gibzen ignored him as he disappeared from sight.

"What's wrong?" Racker asked as he approached, eyes narrowing on Marcus. "How long has he been like this?"

"Since he spoke to the Gamdeshians," Felix said. "It's getting worse. Did she do something to him? Everyone was watching but . . ."

"Kaira didn't do anything to him." Teriana held out the vial she'd picked up off the floor. As Racker plucked it from her hand, she moved beside Marcus, riffling in his belt pouch until she found another, which she handed to the surgeon.

Racker opened the bottle, sniffed it, and then swore. Giving it to Felix, he grasped Marcus's shoulders. "Sir, I need you to look at me!"

Marcus didn't even seem to hear.

"What is it?" Teriana demanded. "I know the first one is for pain, but what is the other?"

Felix sniffed the contents, then in one violent motion, smashed the bottle on the stone. "It's a potion cooked up by chemists in Celendrial. Men use it to stay awake on guard duty, but it's banned because it's dangerous. Some of the Thirty-First must have brought it over with them because I doubt the Fifty-First has yet crossed paths with it."

Something to make him sleep.

Something to keep him awake.

It was no wonder he wasn't making any sense, and sickness pooled in Teriana's stomach because how long had this been going on? How long had he been poisoning himself for the sake of bearing the full weight of this mad strategy?

"Sir!" Racker shook Marcus hard, but he only shoved the surgeon away, then returned to gripping the balustrade, knuckles bleached white and nails scratching the stone.

"Restrain him," Racker ordered, and with grimaces, Felix and Quintus grabbed hold of Marcus's arms. They were stronger than him, yet Marcus fought them like a thing possessed. "I have to watch!" he screamed at them, the pupils of his eyes drowning out the irises despite the brilliant sunshine. "I need to see the smoke!"

"We have time." Felix forced him to his knees. "Wex will need time to set up the explosives. They'll need to do it carefully or they'll take out the entire stem—you know that."

Yet it was as though Felix hadn't spoken, for Marcus only fought harder, desperately trying to look over his shoulder even as the worst sort of threats poured from his lips.

Teriana's pulse roared with fear, and heedless of the jostling men, she threw herself at him. Catching hold of the sides of Marcus's face, she forced him to look at her. "I'll watch. I'll watch the city for any sign of smoke. Red, right?"

He stared at her, and it felt like staring into a void. "Red, yes. But the size as well. If the explosives go off at the wrong time, this will be for nothing. We'll have to start over with a new stem." He sucked in a breath. "You can't look away. We can't miss it."

"As though we'd miss that earthquake," Felix muttered. "Marcus, we're watching. Answer Racker's questions, all right?"

Marcus only stared at her.

"I won't look away." Taking hold of his hand, she stood up and fixed her gaze on the city sprawled in the distance, never mind that tears were streaming down her face.

"How long have you been taking the narcotics?" Racker asked, voice calm. "And how frequently?"

Silence.

Teriana clenched her teeth, almost afraid to blink lest she miss whatever signal Wex would send, though she knew that was irrational given it was to be an explosion.

"I can't sleep," Marcus finally answered. "Too many dreams. It takes away the dreams."

"How long? How often."

"The night Titus died. Every . . . every night I had enough time."

Racker let out a long breath. "I knew someone was stealing from my stores, but I thought it was one of the medics. Not *you*."

"I can take what I want."

The surgeon huffed out a breath, but only asked, "What about the stimulant?"

Marcus didn't answer him, only said, "Teriana, are you watching?"

"Yes." It was a struggle to stifle her sobs. "I'm watching."

"Marcus, how long?" Racker repeated.

"I don't know. A week, maybe." His voice was bitter as he added, "I needed to be able to *think*."

"The thoughts of the dead have little value," Racker snapped.

"Better to be dead than for this plan to have failed."

There was a flash of light in the center of the city, and a heartbeat later, a *boom*. Teriana blinked, watching as a stream of crimson smoke floated up into the sky. "Red," she said. "Red smoke."

But Marcus was already on his feet, staring out at the plume. "Padria. The genesis is in Padria."

Teriana looked to Felix, who said, "It's an hour's hard ride east of Celendrial. Wex must have had a signal chain waiting for this to have happened so quickly. Using black powder with xenthier can go . . . badly."

"Will . . ." She swallowed hard. "Will the Senate deem Padria secure?"

"There could be no more secure a location," Felix replied. "We'll send terms to Kaira to remove her army from the city. She'll have no choice. Once we hold Emrant, the Senate will send a few individuals back and forth to confirm, and then—"

"It's done." Marcus turned away from the city, then slid down the wall to sit on the stone. She dropped to her knees next to him, her heart aching as his bloodshot gaze met hers. "It's over, Teriana. These paths are good, which means Cassius has no grounds to deny your people their liberty. They'll be free in days. So will the *Quincense*. So will you."

Why doesn't this feel like victory?

She was spared speaking as Racker knelt before Marcus. "I should have you restrained in medical. Should remove you from command, for as it stands, you are not fit to serve."

Marcus's eyes narrowed. "Don't test me, Racker. I need to be in control of this."

"You're not even in control of yourself." The Thirty-Seventh's surgeon radiated disgust as he looked Marcus up and down. "Give me one reason why I don't go to Zimo the moment his ships make port and ask him to assume command."

"That would be unwise of you." The threat in Marcus's voice sent a chill over Teriana's skin, and she fought the urge to rub her arms.

"Let's not allow this to get out of hand." Felix pushed between them. "We've won the day, and we're finally going to get the chance to breathe."

"He won't be breathing long if he keeps this up."

"Marcus," Felix said, "just promise you won't take any more. Please."

Silence.

"Fine."

"You have to look me in the eye every morning and every night," Racker said. "Submit to search every day until I say otherwise. Agree, and I'll hold my tongue."

Marcus's voice was half growl as he said, "Fine."

Racker sat back on his heels, and Teriana couldn't fault him for the distrust painted across his face, for Marcus's tone implied everything but concession. But he gave a slow nod. "I'm only agreeing to this because I believe you are capable of pulling yourself straight, sir. And because, while I don't agree with your choices, I do support the reasons you made them." His brown eyes fixed on Teriana. "Assuming the Gamdeshians yield control of Emrant, which I suspect they will, the cost of this mission was ten Gamdeshian lives taking the Orinok ford and perhaps two dozen injured, who will all recover. The historians prefer to write about victories that are bloody and brutal, but this was truly an undertaking that should be remembered for all time."

Rising to his feet, the surgeon saluted, then departed.

"Felix, get word to Kaira that I want her out of the city within twenty-four hours," Marcus said. "And I don't want her army within fifty miles of Emrant until we come to terms on how this will go."

How would it go? Teriana couldn't help but wonder. And would she even be part of that conversation? Her people would be free, her ship and crew set loose upon the seas, which meant there was no reason for her to remain. "What if she refuses?"

"She'll do it," Marcus answered. "Everything Kaira does is to protect her people. That's why she lost to us today."

Felix inclined his head. "I'll have a message sent. I trust Wex will wait for word from us before taking action."

"That was the plan we agreed to, but I'd rather not trust to chance. Go now."

"I'll stay," Quintus said to Felix. "You do what needs doing."

Teriana could see that Felix was torn between doing his duty and remaining with Marcus, but he gave a tight nod. "I'll post guards."

After Felix left, Quintus said, "I'll be in earshot. But short of our flying friend making an appearance, you should be safe enough up here."

Shifting so she was sitting next to Marcus, Teriana rested her head against the stone and stared up at the sky. Not a single cloud marred the blue. Seagulls danced above them, filling the air with their cries, the sun warming her skin.

There was so much to be said. Weeks and weeks of words that

both of them had locked in their cores that needed to come out, but Teriana said nothing for a long time.

Just breathed and breathed, waiting for elation to set in. Yet despite the legionnaires cheering victory in the fortress below, Teriana's heart ached as though she'd suffered the greatest loss of her lifetime.

"I'm sorry."

Teriana turned her head to look at Marcus, who had his head in his hands, elbows resting on his knees. She took the opportunity to take him in, to memorize everything, though she knew that his face was burned upon her soul. That even if she lived to be a hundred, she'd be able to close her eyes and trace the hard lines of his jaw, the scar crossing his cheek, the swell of his bottom lip. The blue-grey eyes that saw everything and betrayed nothing.

From the beginning there had been an ending. This had never been destined to be a forever. Yet faced with the end, her heart wanted to dig in its heels in a desperate attempt to stall time. "For what? Because of you, my imprisoned people will be freed, and it was accomplished in such a way that they'll not feel their lives came at the cost of others."

At least, not yet.

Marcus was quiet for a long time, then he said, "I thought if I just did everything perfectly that, at the end of this, you'd be able to walk away untouched. That you'd be able to sail away with your crew and have your name untarnished by the Empire, your conscience clear. These long months of your life would be but a brief ordeal that would fade with time because your hands wouldn't be stained with innocent blood. But it seems I'm destined to claim every *fucking* victory but the one I care about, because even though it's me who has done every wrong, it's your name they curse. It's you they blame."

A fate Teriana had long since accepted, but apparently Marcus had not. Teriana slowly came to terms with the understanding that *all* of this, all the tricks, the endless marching, and risks to his men's lives had been in a pursuit of an impossible victory.

Because what the world thought of her wasn't his battle to fight, it was hers. What mark she left upon Reath was of her own making, and it was time for her to quit dwelling on the scorched earth behind her and turn to the future she could help shape.

"It's not about what historians choose to write in their books," she said. "*We* know the truth. The world holds up those with no stains upon their hands as heroes, never stopping to think that their hands are clean because they never had to fight for their lives. They never had to stand in the mud, with every path leading to blood, and make a choice. Sometimes there is no right choice. Sometimes there is only the choice you can live with. And sometimes there isn't even that."

Her voice caught on a sob, and Teriana sucked in a ragged breath because she needed to get the words out. Needed to make him understand.

"I made the choice to help find these xenthier paths," she said between tears. "Kaira refused to help. Ereni refused to help. My own people refused to help. So I chose to make my name anathema to the West for the sake of five hundred prisoners, and I did it knowing that there was the potential for thousands to die. I rolled the dice, but my bet was on you." Moving onto her knees in front of him, she took hold of his hands. "I bet right."

Marcus lifted his head to look at her, eyes searching hers.

"I can live with this," she whispered.

Leaning forward, she kissed him. Nothing more than a brush of her lips against his, but it sent sparks across her skin, every beat of her heart a thud of certainty that of all the choices she'd ever made, loving him was the most right.

Marcus's hand curved around her cheek, then tucked the braids that had fallen forward behind her ear. "There's something I have to tell you," he said in a hoarse voice. "Something you need to know."

Time seemed to stand still, because Teriana knew that he was going to tell her what had changed in Celendrial. The reason he'd ended things between them. For so long, she had been desperate to know what had the power to turn him from her in the space of an instant, but now faced with it—

She pressed a finger to his lips. "No."

Grasping her hand, he said, "Teriana, I—"

"I don't want to know." She moved so that her knees were to either side of him, her body pressed against his armored chest. "Cassius made me look at so many horrible things that you have done in the legions. Not just the reports on battles, but the assassinations. The tortures. Gods, Marcus, the first time we met was in a cellar where you stood and watched a questioner kill my people. I know who you were, but what I care about is who you are now." He looked ready to argue, so she swiftly said, "We stand at a critical moment where we can either step toward peace or submit to war, because this isn't over. You have the power here to hold the Senate in check, and I have the power to try to make peace with Kaira. The doors between East and

West have been blown open and there is no going back, and we are uniquely positioned to control the outcome."

"You are suggesting that you want to stay?"

"Yes."

"With . . ." His throat moved as he swallowed hard. "With me? Despite who I am? What I am? All that I've done?"

A sudden flood of uncertainty filled her. "If you want me."

"If I want you?" His laugh was half sob. "I do not deserve you, Teriana, but that has never meant I didn't want you. I could live a thousand lives and never earn your love, but I swear on all that I hold dear that I am willing to try."

The elation that had been absent flooded her soul, and Teriana wrapped her arms around his neck, kissing him. Losing herself in the moment, because this wasn't just about a future with him, it was about finally seeing a path out of the mud for both of them. Something worth fighting for.

Marcus pulled back, holding her face with his cupped palms. "Not until it's certain. Not until Kaira has left the city, the Senate has confirmed the paths, and Hostus has opened the prison gates. I need documents in hand saying that your deal with the Senate has been fulfilled." He hesitated. "You need to be certain this is what you really want."

Teriana had never been certain in her life, but there was something right about embarking on the next journey of her life on the heels of her people's liberation. With the past firmly in the past and their eyes only on the future.

She curled against him with her head resting in the crook of his neck and her fingers locked with his. Listening to the seagulls and the cheers, the sea breeze blissfully fresh after so many long days of nothing but the stink of wet ash and sweat.

Then a soft whistle caught her attention, and she looked to see Quintus jerk his chin in the direction of the city. Unease filled her chest, and Teriana climbed to her feet, pulling Marcus with her.

Riding out of the city was a column of soldiers. For a heartbeat, she was certain they intended to attack the fortress, but horses and men alike were laden with packs, weapons all in sheaths. Kaira's familiar form rode at their head, and as they passed the fortress heading north, the Gamdeshian Princess looked up at the ramparts to where they stood and pointed a finger at Teriana.

55

LYDIA

"This is an unnecessary risk," Lady Calorian growled angrily. "I can convey your plan to Killian just as easily as you can. All it takes is one of Hacken's little spies catching sight of my son speaking to you, and this entire ruse will be for naught."

"No." Lydia made her voice as firm as possible, trying to hide the churn of apprehension in her stomach. "I need to make him agree to stay with Dareena, because that's the only way this will work. If I just leave, he'll come after me."

Killian's mother sighed. "I can't argue that point."

They both fell silent as they heard a scuffle of noise outside Lady Calorian's rooms, and a heartbeat later, Killian landed on near silent feet on his mother's balcony. "Have you lost your gods-damned minds?" he demanded. "There is no way this is going to work."

"People see what they want to see," Lydia said, her anxiety immediately diminishing as he pulled her into his arms. "Dareena is only a decade older than I am. With my spectacles, plus the right clothes and a generous amount of war paint, we look strikingly alike. She is going to be everything Hacken wants me to be. He can call her Kitaryia and tour her about, but if you aren't at her side, he'll be instantly suspicious. I don't need to fool him forever, but I do need to fool him long enough to get on a ship to Revat."

The color drained from Killian's face. "You're not actually suggesting that you intend to go to Revat without me? Malahi and Agrippa have already left for Serlania, where they'll board a ship to sail south. It's Malahi who needs to find instructions in that library, not you."

"This sort of research is my speciality," she said instead of addressing his concern. "Malahi and Agrippa will board a Maarin ship in the harbor, as a distraction, but the *Kairense* will retrieve me from the beach, and we will sail in their wake. I won't arrive more than a day after them."

"Sail alone."

"Sonia will come with me, and the crew of the *Kairense* are no strangers," she said, a band of grief squeezing around her chest because the last thing she wanted was for them to be apart. "And I'm not entirely helpless."

"I know that." Killian blew out a long breath, then said, "Mother, would you go elsewhere?"

Lady Calorian snorted but crossed the room and disappeared into the bathing chamber, calling out, "Be quick. Dareena will have to play both Lydia and herself, and she'll need our help to make it work."

The door shut.

"Hacken is many things, but not a fool," Killian said. "Dareena might be able to trick him for a few days, but he's going to figure out she isn't you."

"So what if he does?" Lydia leaned against him, trying to project confidence that she didn't feel into her voice. "All he wants is a puppet anyway, and Dareena can play that role just as well as I can. It isn't as though he's going to send someone to drag me back from Revat."

"Don't be so sure."

"We are desperate, Killian," Lydia said quietly. "All we learned in Anukastre is that it's *possible* to destroy the blight, but not how. Just as I know that it's possible to draw it out of those who are infected but not on the scale we need. Revat's library is our best hope at finding the answers." She bit her lip because she'd said nothing that he didn't already know. "No one has a future if we don't find a solution, including us."

He twisted away from her. "And even then, we may not, because some other obstacle will fall between us."

Lydia's heart ached, because she understood how he felt to have climbed over so many barriers to find their way into each other's arms, only to be torn apart again. She followed him across the room, pressing her forehead between his shoulder blades, feeling the rapid beat of his heart. "No matter where I am, no matter how many leagues between us, my heart is yours, Killian Calorian. And I will always fight my way back to you."

"I'm the one who is supposed to do the fighting."

For a long moment, she didn't speak, only focused on the steady throb of his heart. "The fight is coming for all of us. I can feel it, and I know you can as well." She tightened her grip on his waist. "The Corrupter has planned this for a very long time, and we are outmatched on every front. You have had faith in me in my darkest moments. Please don't lose faith in me now."

"Never." He turned in her arms, lowering his head to kiss her. "I'm with you, no matter what the end."

Lydia kissed him back, wanting desperately to lose herself in him. His tongue stroked across hers, his hand running down her back to curve over her bottom, then jerking her closer. Her fingers tangled in his hair, and she wanted so much more than was possible. Wanted one final moment with him before they raced off to fight separate battles. But they had so little time.

Lady Calorian knocked softly on the door, and Lydia reluctantly stepped backward as Killian's mother reentered the room. Her eyes were red, as though she'd been weeping. "You need to return to Dareena, Killian. You are as critical to her act as all the war paint she's using to conceal her identity, and I fear she'll already have ruined the ruse with her incessant cursing. Go."

Killian sighed, then bent to kiss Lydia one last time. "I love you."

"I love you, too," she whispered, then watched him escape back out the balcony.

Lady Calorian went to the door, and Sonia entered, carrying two travel bags slung over her narrow shoulders. Though she nearly always wore a shirt and trousers, her friend was dressed in a simple dress with scarf concealing her short brown hair. "We should go," her friend said. "Malahi has already left in Seldrid's coach, and we'll go cross country on foot. Seldrid's sent word ahead to Captain Vane to meet us on the same beach where they brought you to shore."

Killian's mother approached Lydia, gently taking her by the shoulders. "Your mother was my friend," she said quietly. "And I know Camilla would be so very proud of the woman you have become."

The words were unexpected, and a jolt of grief hit Lydia in the chest. "She died bringing me to safety in Celendor. She . . . she could have been saved if she'd stayed in the West and found a healer."

"If given the chance, I know she'd have done the same thing all over again because protecting you was what mattered most," Lady Calorian said, her eyes liquid with tears. "It is what mothers do."

Rising up on her toes, she kissed Lydia's cheek. "Please come back to my son, Your Grace. He needs you."

56

KILLIAN

How anyone believed that Dareena was Lydia was beyond Killian, because every time he looked at her, it was screamingly obvious she was not.

And yet they did.

As the Teradale ballroom filled with nobility all intent on meeting the new Falorn queen, it was very clear to Killian, who dutifully stood at Dareena's elbow the entire time, that everyone was seeing exactly what they wanted to see.

Even Hacken.

His brother fawned over Dareena, who, at his mother's suggestion, said little. He introduced her to men and women who'd known Dareena her entire life, none of them seeing the decade of age difference behind the heavy war paint that was starting to bleed in the extreme heat.

"Dance with her," his mother hissed. "You look miserable."

"I am miserable." But he dutifully took Dareena onto the dance floor, then pretended to teach her steps that she knew as well as he did, the watching lords and ladies smiling and laughing in delight.

It was with the greatest relief to both of them when he finally delivered her to Lydia's room, where Gwen and Lena had resumed their duties. His mother, who'd taken on the role of Lydia's lady in waiting, disappeared inside with his mentor, who started cursing about skirts the moment the door was shut.

Leaning against a wall, Killian drew in a steadying breath. Lydia would already be aboard the ship and heading to Revat, which was a short journey. Sonia was with her, and he knew the Gamdeshians would do everything in their power to protect her. Yet he still hated not being at her side, because it was where he was meant to be.

"Killian?"

He lifted his head to see Finn standing in the corridor, expression full of uncertainty, and he silently cursed himself for forgetting to track his young friend down. "I'm sorry, Finn. I meant to find you earlier, but . . ."

Finn shrugged. "It's fine. I had other business."

The other business was likely theft of some sort, and Killian made a note to have the boy turn out his pockets later. But not now. They'd been too long apart for him to start with criticism. "Sonia took care of you?"

"Sure. Seldrid lets me have the run of his palace. He's got fewer rules than you."

"Probably because he doesn't know the half of the trouble you get into. Come on." He slung an arm around Finn's skinny shoulders, heading toward the kitchen. "Let's get something to eat."

The kitchens were still warm and scented with food from the banquet, but only a few servants remained cleaning up. Killian knew all of them, and they smiled and pretended not to notice as he piled a plate high with cuts of meat left over from the banquet. He started to pour a glass of milk for Finn, then eyed the boy for a moment and gave him half a glass of ale. "Don't tell Sonia."

The corner of Finn's mouth turned up as he took the glass, and then he followed Killian to the scarred table the cooks used to prepare food and sat down on a stool.

Finn sipped at his ale, then asked, "Where's Lydia?"

"In her room," Killian answered, taking a mouthful of ale himself. "She's tired."

The boy cast a sideways look at the servants, then leaned his elbows on the table, voice quiet as he said, "That's Dareena. Those puffed-up nobles might not be able to tell the difference, but I ain't fooled by a bit of face paint."

Killian blew out a slow breath of air, not certain whether he was anxious or relieved that Finn had seen through the act. "How can you tell?"

"By the way she looks at me," Finn replied. "Or, more accurately, doesn't look at me."

Killian's skin prickled ever so slightly, and he flicked a glance at the servants, but they were all on the far side of the room.

"Also because Dareena stomps like she wants to murder the ground beneath her feet, and Lydia—"

"Glides," they both said at the same time, and Killian gave a soft laugh. "I told Dareena as much."

He eyed Finn for a long moment, noting that the boy had grown taller in the time they'd been apart, yet somehow skinnier. "You cannot tell. Not anyone."

Finn snorted. "You think I can't keep my mouth shut? I'm a collector of information, not a spender of gossip."

Seldrid had clearly had an influence on him. "Sorry for the offense."

"So where is she?" Finn asked. "And why aren't you with her?"

"Because no one would believe this ruse if I left." Killian stared at his glass, unease rising. "She's on a ship to Revat. Sonia's with her."

"Why Revat?"

"Because she and Malahi hope to find answers as to how to defeat the blight," he replied. "If we can't do that, the war is lost."

Finn was silent, and when Killian lifted his gaze, it was to find the boy staring at him intently. Almost . . . angrily. "What's wrong?"

"It can't be defeated," Finn snapped, then shook his head. "Everyone says so. She should be here. With you."

"I should be there. With her." Draining his glass, Killian waited for the servants to abandon the kitchen, then said, "We learned in Anukastre that the blight has come before and been defeated by tenders. It can be done, we just don't know how."

"And you think the Gamdeshians do?"

"Revat has the oldest and largest collection of information. If there are answers, the answers are there."

"Makes sense." Finn took another small sip of his drink, then pushed it aside. "So there's hope? What about the blighters? Did the Anuk know anything about stopping them?"

The most tenuous strands of hope, but Killian nodded. "The Anuk didn't have any knowledge about the blight infecting the living. But Lydia is twice touched by Hegeria, Finn. She can . . . do things that other healers can't. If there is a way to help them, she'll find it."

Finn gave a slow nod. "I believe you. Kitaryia has always been special. I knew from the first moment I met her."

Killian rubbed at his arms, abruptly tired of the endless tension. Of always sensing the threat but unable to do anything about it. "Don't call her that."

"But it's her name. Kitaryia Falorn."

"Once, but no longer." Sighing, Killian said, "She has been Lydia most of her life, and to call her something against her will strips away her identity."

Finn shifted restlessly, then said, "Makes no difference to me, especially since it's going to be my lady this and Your Grace that. Though she ought to do me the same favor, king of the sewers that I am."

Killian laughed. "You've claimed Serlania, then?"

"Of course. Your mum shipped my old crew down here and they've been running wild. They needed me to put things to right, so it's well and good that I didn't go with you."

There was a trace of bitterness to Finn's voice, and Killian said, "It was miserable. Like journeying into the underworld itself."

"No place for a child."

Irritation filled Killian, impatience that Finn was attempting to make him feel badly for not bringing him despite it being almost certain he wouldn't have survived the journey. "No place for anyone."

Finn didn't answer.

Rising to his feet, Killian pushed in his stool. "I need to get some sleep. If you'd like, we can find some time to work on your swordsmanship."

The boy nodded sullenly, but as Killian moved away from the table, he said, "How did you get your sword back? Sonia was sick with worry when it went missing. Thought it had been stolen."

"Tremon."

Finn's head snapped up, eyes filled with shock. "How?"

"Handed it to me himself," Killian answered. "Good night."

Walking through the kitchen to the main door, Killian paused, knowing that he needed to do better by him, especially with Sonia already gone. "Finn," he started to say, but when he turned, it was to find the boy already gone.

All that remained was the tray on the table, the food on it entirely untouched.

57

MARCUS

He slept for two days straight, his last moments of consciousness filled with the distant cheers of the legions shouting his name—they, at least, saw this as a victory.

Marcus wasn't quite ready to cheer just yet.

"Look straight at me," Racker ordered, and Marcus dutifully looked the surgeon in the eye. Racker grunted, then said, "Amarin, you searched everything?"

"Yes." His servant gave Marcus a dark glare. "And I'll do so twice daily until you tell me otherwise."

With no parting words, the surgeon left, and Marcus walked to the table where Teriana sat with a mountain of food before her. "I cooked," she said. "I'm sick of cold porridge and the kitchen here is well stocked." Then she frowned. "Perhaps you might consider hiring a proper chef."

"That's not really how we do things." He took a bite of some sort of grilled meat. The spices on it instantly made his eyes water. "Although I might consider it."

"You're an ass."

He smirked before downing a mouthful of water. "That's unlikely to change."

Teriana only rolled her eyes, then ate a forkful of eggs from her own plate. While he'd been asleep, Felix had given her the royal suite of rooms, and Teriana had apparently availed herself of the much-discussed bath. She smelled of lavender, all the dust and grime washed clean of her long black braids, the tiny ship woven onto one of them resting against her right cheek. She wore a dress made of bright blue linen trimmed with an elaborate pattern of golden thread, the fabric ever-so-slightly sheer, which he'd noticed when she'd walked in front of the window, the outline of her legs tantalizingly visible. Her eyes were a brilliant blue of nearly the same hue and the waves rolling across their depths were calm, although the color deepened to indigo as she caught him staring, her cheeks coloring.

"I found it in the wardrobe," she said. "Thought it would do until I could secure new clothes."

"Take whatever you want." The pleasure Marcus felt over seeing her in the spoils of victory was not anything he'd admit, but he felt it anyway. "Everything in that room is yours."

"Temporarily," she said. "I'll pack up Kaira's things and arrange for them to be sent to her."

Marcus highly doubted that the princess cared about dresses, and after that pointed threat to Teriana, he wasn't inclined to allow Kaira within a hundred paces of her, but he only said, "Let me settle things with the Senate first." He coughed on an extra-spicy mouthful. "If I survive eating this breakfast, that is."

Teriana flipped up her middle finger on the hand holding her fork, but there was laughter in her eyes. If her smile was the last thing he ever saw, Marcus swore he'd die happy.

This could be your life, a voice whispered up from his thoughts. *Once the Maarin are freed, Cassius can't use them as leverage against you. You hold the power here, which means the rules are yours to make.*

His mind drifted as he ate, imagining going to bed with her in his arms every night and not having to hide it. Spending each day united in purpose, keeping the peace between the Empire and the West.

For how long? And how much will it cost you?

He shoved away the thought. This victory would bolster sentiment toward Cassius enough to ensure the citizens would vote him in for another term, and with trade from Katamarca, Arinoquia, and southern Gamdesh filling Senate coffers, they'd be content with what they had. He could make a life that didn't endlessly revolve around war, and his mind's eye filled with a future that he'd never dreamed possible, every vision with Teriana at his side.

When is the Senate ever content with what they have?

The answer was never, but what could they do if he held the gates between East and West?

Tell your secrets.

Teriana had absolved him.

Are you sure?

He wasn't.

She doesn't even know your real name . . .

The fork slipped from his hand to clatter against the plate, and Teriana jumped.

"You all right?"

"Fine." He covered his reaction with a sip of water, appetite gone. "I should hear what Felix has to say. Amarin?"

"I'll fetch the Tribunus, sir."

Felix must have been on his way, because moments later, he appeared in the door. "Looks like all you needed was a feather bed," he said, then inclined his head to Teriana. "Morning."

Marcus gestured for him to sit, and Felix waved away Amarin's offer of food. "The civilians haven't caused us much in the way of trouble. Seems your Katamarcan propagandists did their duty spreading word of the virtues of trade with the Empire, though we'll want to make good on that soon to keep the peace. Buy up everything they sell so that they're too busy counting their coins to worry about the Senate's longer game."

"Tell Servius to start spending," Marcus said. "What did you find when you opened the casement around the Emrant terminus?"

"Was a thing straight out of anyone's nightmares," his friend replied. "Wex's smoke explosion cracked open the extra stone they'd put in place, and when we pulled it open, it was still full of corpses. Some were nothing more than bones, but a few were fresher, all carrying path-hunter gear. The insides of the walls were covered with scratches from dozens of men trying to chop their way out, though with all the bodies, they had to have known their fate the moment they arrived."

"An awful death." Teriana pushed away her plate. "Why would anyone volunteer to map a stem when that's the risk?"

"Gold," Felix said. "The answer is always gold."

"It's all cleared out now, though?" Marcus asked. "Secure?"

"Yes, the Senate has sent no fewer than six pairs of mappers back and forth to prove it's good."

Marcus tensed. "So it's done? We're good? Cassius is happy?"

"Not quite." Felix cast a sideways glance at Teriana. "They're sending us a senator to serve as governor."

"Gamdesh is not a province, and one city doesn't need a bloody governor." Marcus was on his feet though he didn't remember standing. Already it was happening. Already the Empire was flexing its muscles of control. "Who?"

"Grypus."

Of course it was him. Why wouldn't it be, with Hostus rearing his head and all of Marcus's old enemies coming back to haunt him? "Please tell me this is a jest?"

Felix shook his head, and Teriana said, "Who is Grypus?"

"A bloody pain in the ass is what he is," Marcus muttered, circling the room.

Drinking from the glass of water Amarin had poured for him, Felix said, "Senator Plotius Grypus. He was the proconsul lording over us while we were in Bardeen, which meant he took credit for the taking of Hydrilla. The man looks like a potato with legs and fights about as well, but he's got a taste for war, so he is often sent where the fighting is thickest. Zimo mentioned in passing that Grypus was in Chersome, but I guess even that wasn't far enough from Lucretia."

"Who's Lucretia?" Teriana asked. The calm seas had turned turbulent, blue fading to grey.

"His wife," Felix told her. "Grypus likes to keep something of a harem of women about him, and she puts a damper on that. Fortunately she's got a patrician's taste in all things, so she won't go anywhere that doesn't meet her exacting standards."

"Right," Teriana said, and Marcus felt her gaze tracking him as he paced. "Marcus, do you care to elaborate on why you're so unhappy about this particular man, or should I ask Felix?"

They were all a problem. Every last cursed individual living atop

Celendrial's mountain of wealth, and every last one of them would try to stymie Marcus's plans. But Grypus—"Because he's not stupid!"

Teriana lifted her teacup and took a mouthful, then raised an eyebrow. "I see."

Sucking in a breath to calm his temper, Marcus rested his hands on the back of the chair he'd been sitting in. "Most patricians are inbred imbeciles."

"*You're* patrician."

Felix choked on his water, then covered his mouth to contain a mixture of coughing and laughter.

Marcus glared at him, then refocused on Teriana. "Grypus isn't just smart: he's clever, ruthless, and he knows me."

Which was likely the real reason Cassius had chosen him.

"You know him, too," Felix said. "He's worked with you rather than against you in the past, so there is no reason he won't be amenable again. Either way, he's arriving in a matter of hours, so we need to go into the city to meet him."

Abandoning the table, Marcus went to the balcony and breathed in the fresh air. Below, his men were going about their assigned duties, but his eyes were all for the sea in the distance. He searched it for familiar blue sails but saw nothing but Cel and Katamarcan vessels.

He'd hoped for more time. Time to focus on the immediate complications before turning his eye back to the problems breeding in Celendor, but the Empire moved with the speed of a plague, meaning he'd be fighting a two-fronted battle from the moment Grypus arrived.

He's going to ruin your plans.

He's going to take control.

He's going to drive her away from you.

The voice in his head was so loud it made his skull throb, and Marcus pressed fingers to his temples, desperate to silence the voice and its endless fucking orders.

The voice went quiet, his mind still, and then it softly said, *It doesn't have to go that way. You command the legions. You could make the Empire bend to your will.*

It was madness to consider. And yet . . .

You are the one in control. You are the one who will decide how this will go.

Schooling his face, Marcus turned back around to face them. "We should get ready to greet him."

58

TERIANA

Leaving Marcus and Felix to their plans for the senator's arrival, Teriana stepped out into the corridor where Quintus waited with the rest of Marcus's guard, none of which were Gibzen's men. She'd not seen the primus since Felix had dismissed him, and she wondered if Marcus would allow the order to stand when he learned of it.

Either way, it was a problem for another hour, and catching hold of Quintus's arm, she hauled him around the circular corridor of the tower to where her own rooms were located.

Kaira's rooms, her conscience reminded her. *Which you stole from her.*

Shoving away the thought, Teriana said, "What do you know about Grypus?"

Her friend blinked. "Plotius? That old fart is still alive?"

"Apparently he's arriving in Emrant in a matter of hours." She slammed the bedroom door shut behind them. "Marcus isn't happy."

"Of course he isn't. Grypus outranks him. By a lot, if he's still a proconsul." Abandoning his helmet on a table, Quintus flopped onto a divan, nearly disappearing into the pile of pillows decorating it. "He has good taste in wine, women, and olives, but I don't think that's the information you're interested in."

Exhaling a steadying breath, Teriana perched on the edge of a chair and shook her head.

Quintus extracted himself from the pillows and rested his elbows on his knees. "Hydrilla was a long siege. The rebels holding the fortress went into it well-supplied and their defenses were good. They repelled our attacks at every turn, although months in, they were starving. Most of what I know is rumor and hearsay, but apparently Marcus was of the opinion that the rebels would surrender, and it was only a matter of waiting them out, but Grypus wasn't satisfied with that approach. He wanted a glorious battle that would be talked about in Celendrial, never mind how many of us had to die to achieve it. Hostus was primed for a big attack, and the Thirty-Seventh would've been on the front lines. Marcus went to Grypus behind Hostus's back and convinced him to allow Marcus to direct the attack. No one knows quite how, but Hostus found out about it. Cut Marcus up good and he nearly bled out, but he rallied enough to command the battle, which went exactly as planned. The victory was one for the history books, which made Grypus happy. He granted the Thirty-Seventh autonomy from the Twenty-Ninth, and we set off for Chersome."

An old memory of the conversation she'd had with Marcus after she'd been caught climbing into her mother's room in Celendrial rose in Teriana's mind. When he'd bandaged her injured hand. *It wasn't until we were stationed in Bardeen that I had moved up enough in the Senate's eyes to take command,* he'd said. *It was an easier campaign than any we've had since—quite clear what had to be done from a tactical standpoint.*

Only Marcus would claim a campaign was *easy* when he'd been half-dead while orchestrating it. "How did you win it?"

"By being smart." Quintus explained what had happened, and Teriana's eyes widened as she listened.

"There's a whole lot more to the story," Quintus said. "But if I had to hazard a guess, Marcus is unhappy because Grypus cares more about glory than he does lives, legion or otherwise. Grypus can't claim this victory as his, so he'll be looking for something else to fight over that will make him the talk of the Hill." Quintus sighed. "It means expanding our reach, probably using force because Grypus hates negotiation."

Which was the exact opposite of hers and Marcus's goal to negotiate a peaceful arrangement with Gamdesh. And it was all happening so quickly. Teriana pressed her fingers to her temple, feeling panic starting to rise. "Is there a way to control him?"

"I imagine that's the exact thought running through Marcus's mind right now."

A knock sounded at the door, and Quintus rose, hand going to the weapon at his belt. "Yeah?"

"Senator came early," a male voice called through. "He's on his way to the fortress with his escort. Legatus wants Teriana with him."

Quintus glanced at Teriana, and after she nodded, he called back, "All right."

Sweat broke out on her palms, and Teriana glanced at herself in the large mirror on the wall, taking some confidence from the composed woman looking back at her, even if it wasn't how she felt. "Let's go, then."

Quintus donned his helmet, then opened the door. Glancing in both directions, he nodded and led her down the corridor. The sandals she'd taken from Kaira's closet made soft pats against the stone as they descended the tower stairs, walking through the maze of corridors until they reached the courtyard. Marcus stood with Nic and Servius, heads bent together in discussion, expressions grim.

Servius raised an eyebrow at the sight of her. "Enjoying the spoils of war?"

Shame over her decision to wear the Gamdeshian princess's clothing flooded Teriana's veins, and she quietly prayed that word of it would never reach Kaira's ears. She'd needed clean clothes. Had wanted to look pretty. Hadn't even considered the signals that it would send, and her naivety abruptly caused her to call into question whether it was madness to believe she could take on this role. To believe she could stand between the most powerful nations in the world and move them to peace rather than war.

Someone called down from above that the party was approaching, and the chaotic mass of legionnaires and officers moved without hesitation into position in the courtyard. Marcus stepped to the center before the closed gates, Felix and Nic just behind him.

"Over here." Quintus pulled her over to where Servius had taken up the Thirty-Seventh's standard.

Outside, horns blasted a series of notes, and Marcus said, "Open the gates."

Drying her sweating palms, Teriana squared her shoulders and stared forward as the towering twin gates swung open, the portcullis beyond rising to reveal a large procession of legionnaires. The front ranks were all Thirty-Seventh, but behind marched men who had to be well into their forties.

"He still has the Ninth with him—I recognize them," Quintus muttered. "Shouldn't they be retired?"

"Could be he hired them privately afterwards," Servius answered. "It's good pay."

"But they're wearing their number."

"Yeah." Servius's tone was grim. "I see that."

"What's that mean?" Teriana asked Quintus under her breath.

"It means that the Senate has extended the mandatory years of service. Which they'd only do if they had reason to think they needed them."

She needed no explanation for why *that* was a bad development.

The ranks of the Thirty-Seventh split to form up along the bridge, those of the Ninth marching into the courtyard to form neat lines with just enough space for a golden litter enclosed with crimson silk to press through. The eight white-clad servants carrying the thing were dripping sweat and panting, their arms shaking as they slowly lowered it to the ground.

A servant with an impressive head of blond curls and golden Cel skin stepped forward and announced at top volume, "Our most esteemed proconsul, Plotius Grypus!"

Another servant moved aside the curtains, extending an arm to assist a Cel man in his sixties with standing. The proconsul wore a gleaming white tunic and toga, the hem trimmed in crimson and gold to mark his office. He was, as had been described to her, possessed of incredibly skinny limbs and a round torso, with beads of sweat dampening his brow and thinning grey hair. A woman not much older than Teriana wearing a nearly transparent silk gown stepped out of the litter after him. She straightened his garments, then retreated. A mistress, no doubt.

Every legionnaire in the courtyard thumped a hand to their chest in salute, then Marcus stepped forward. "Greetings, Proconsul. Welcome to Gamdesh."

"Marcus!" Grypus closed the distance, and to Teriana's shock, embraced Marcus, pounding him on the back. "It's good to see you, my boy. And well done in your efforts. You are the toast of Celendrial." Then he gripped Marcus's shoulders, looking him up and down. "Though not a boy anymore, are you? With your boldness, I'd half thought you'd never grow to be a man, yet here you are. It's no wonder all the ladies stop to admire your statue in the Forum."

"It is good to see you well," Marcus replied, and Teriana wished she could see his expression. "Would you care to move out of the heat? My men will see to your escort, as well as to your belongings. I think you'll find Gamdesh more suitable to your exacting standards than Chersome."

"Let's keep that to ourselves. If word reaches the wrong ears, we'll be subjected to the company of my wife, and that would not spell good things for any of us." Grypus looked past Marcus, eyes latching onto Felix. "Felix, my boy!" Then he lunged at Felix as though in a duel. "Here's one who deserves a statue! I look forward to resuming our practice sessions. I think you'll find I've become quite the force to be reckoned with in our time apart."

"It would be my honor and pleasure, Proconsul," Felix said. "I've always said you had the finest form of any man in the Senate."

"That's not saying much," Quintus said softly, only for Servius to mutter, "Keep your bloody mouth shut."

Laughing, Grypus looked around the yard, his lip curling. "Where is Zimo?"

"Harbor," Marcus answered. "He's responsible for the Katamarcans."

"Tell him to keep his distance," Grypus growled. "I caught him with one of my girls in Chersome and told him if he ever got handsy again, I'd cut off the problem. She was one of my favorites, and I had to get rid of her after that."

Teriana struggled to keep her disgust off her face.

"Zimo will abide by my rules of conduct," Marcus replied, but Grypus was already eyeing Austornic.

"What a first campaign to have!" the proconsul said. "Making a name for yourself on the battlefield already and not even fully grown. You'll do well to learn from Marcus, and if you're as clever as Wex claims, perhaps one day Marcus will be reporting to you."

"I don't foresee him reporting to anyone until after he retires," Nic said, and Teriana could feel the boy's admiration, which had only grown once he'd understood the full scope of Marcus's strategy to capture the stems. "It is an honor to serve."

Marcus's jaw tightened ever so slightly, but he said nothing.

Grypus patted Nic on the shoulder, then said, "I would take refreshment out of the sun. Cassius is eager to hear of your plans to secure further territory now that we have the capacity to adequately reinforce."

Teriana's stomach plummeted at confirmation of Quintus's prediction, but Marcus only said, "Of course. But there are other matters to be addressed, first. Commitments that both the Consul and the Senate need honor."

"Ahh, yes. The Maarin girl."

Though Teriana hadn't thought the proconsul had even noticed her presence, Grypus's eyes found her with unerring precision. Within them, she saw not just intelligence but cunning, and Teriana instinctively understood why Marcus was worried. Grypus crooked his finger at her, and she reluctantly approached.

"Teriana of the Maarin." He looked her up and down. "Cassius sends his well wishes and his congratulations on your success. It seems any concern over your ability to deliver on your promises was misplaced, for you have delivered with time to spare."

"Have my people been freed?" she asked, not interested in his games.

"Not yet." His gaze flicked to Marcus, who had moved within arm's reach. "It is my duty to confirm that Emrant is indeed securely under Celendor's control, at which time I'll send a missive formally declaring you have fulfilled your obligations. Though I do understand your impatience given Hostus's control of Celendrial's prison. Vile piece of work, that man, and while I understand the reasons Cassius had for selecting him, I cannot say that I support the decision. Hostus is a feral dog that should be put down before he bites the wrong hand."

She shivered, and Grypus smiled, eyes cold. "But let us take these matters to more private accommodations. Preferably with chilled wine and food. Travel always leaves me famished." He took hold of her arm. "Lead the way."

His palm was warm and surprisingly calloused on her bare arm, and Teriana curbed the urge to pull away from him. The proconsul was baiting Marcus, that much she could see, and though Marcus showed no reaction as he fell in next to Grypus, she could feel his tension. Understood it, because while a matter of hours ago it had felt like they were firmly in control of the situation in Emrant, it now felt as though that control was slipping through their fingers.

If they'd ever really held it at all.

"I imagine you're eager to be away from the legions, Teriana," Grypus said as they stepped into the cool corridors of the fortress. "They serve an important purpose, but legionnaires are base creatures. We train them to be that way—to be more animals than men. Though I've spent years in their camps, I've never enjoyed it. It is only out of loyalty to Mother Empire that I endure their coarseness. I can only imagine what it has been like for you, as a young woman."

There was no good answer. "They've treated me with courtesy."

Grypus made a soft humming sound of amusement. "Yes, yes. I've heard about your indiscretions. Marcus is something of a different creature, patrician born as he is. You remember how I speculated that your blood was blue, Marcus? Everyone else was squawking with surprise when Domitius finally claimed you, but not me. I sensed your superiority in breeding from the moment I met you. Good patrician stock rises to the top of every legion at Lescendor." Then he cast a glance in Nic's direction. "Though not always."

Nic did not so much as blink at the slight.

"The best of every year at Lescendor rises to command." Marcus's tone was bland. "As to my own blood, it is as red as any other man in the Thirty-Seventh's. The Empire is my father and my mother. The men of the Thirty-Seventh are my brothers. I am a legionnaire."

Grypus laughed at the refrain all the legionnaires were taught to say when asked about their parentage. "Oh, what a glorious politician you'd have made, Marcus. Mark my words: you'd have risen to the consulship itself had you not had the misfortune of being born second. Your father's misfortune as well, for your brother is an idiot of the first order. Even your sister has a better mind than him, though she's tarnished by her husband's weak politics." He cast a sideways glance at Marcus. "Your mother is busy making matches for your younger sisters, aided by your status, to be sure. I'd half considered putting Lucretia in the grave so that I might secure one of them, but the blasted woman will likely outlive me, if not kill me herself with her ceaseless badgering."

"My sympathies for your plight." Marcus gestured to an open door. "In here, if you would."

The large room had been largely cleared of furnishings and décor to be used as Marcus's center of command, but traces of the wealth of Gamdesh still remained in the heavy rosewood table, matching chairs upholstered in brilliantly patterned silk, and ornate molding. The walls were painted deep plum, one wall dominated with a heavily gilded mirror. The rectangle of unfaded paint on the opposite wall suggested that the mirror had once reflected a piece of art.

Amarin waited with his arms crossed behind his back, though he swiftly moved to pull out a heavy chair for the proconsul, who wrinkled his nose at the expensive furniture and stayed standing. "Wine."

Amarin poured him a glass of chilled wine, and then said, "Food is being prepared and will be brought shortly."

"It should be ready now," Grypus muttered with no regard for the fact he'd come early. "It is well that I brought my own servants, else this would be a truly miserable experience. Pour the girl some wine."

Amarin handed Teriana a glass, and she took a sip, barely tasting it. "Are you satisfied with the paths, Proconsul? As you say, I do not wish my people to spend any more time in Hostus's care."

"You're a pretty one, aren't you." Grypus looked her over. "You must have been quite a distraction."

He reached out to touch her face, but just before his fingers brushed her cheek, Marcus's hand closed over his wrist. "Do not touch her."

Grypus's jaw hardened. "You forget yourself, boy. You've been given too long a leash for too long a time and have it in your head that you possess real power. Remember that the Senate owns you. I *own* you. You have no more say than a dog, and like a dog, you will be put down if you choose to bite."

"I've not forgotten anything." Marcus's voice was frigid, but the murder in his gaze made Teriana clench her teeth in fear of what he might do, so she swiftly said, "Is the Senate's word good or not, Proconsul? Because I think you'll find your power to negotiate much reduced if you withhold approval of these paths when they are clearly viable."

"You trying to goad me with threats, girl?" Grypus spat.

"I'm not threatening you with anything," she replied. "But ask yourself if stringing me along or provoking *him*"—she nodded at Marcus—"is worth sabotaging your ability to achieve much larger goals."

She watched the wheels turn in the proconsul's gaze, then he jerked out of Marcus's grip. "Cassius has already claimed the glory of conquering the Maarin. You are worth nothing." Turning to the table, he snapped his fingers. "Paper and ink."

Amarin swiftly obliged, and Grypus wrote a message that the paths were secure and would serve the Empire well, and that Teriana's obligations were fulfilled. He signed it and waited for Amarin to add a blob of red wax, which he stamped with a golden seal. "Here." He shoved it at her. "Go collect what remains of your miserable people."

Marcus gave her a tight nod, and Teriana snatched up the page and hurried to the door, Quintus opening it ahead of her. "Come on." He hauled on her arm. "We need to go."

She tripped over her sandals, uncertain why such haste was required but knowing that it was. Quintus pushed between Grypus's servants, who approached with trays laden with food and wine, and it felt like Celendor was already assimilating its new conquest.

Teriana looked down at the expensive paper she clutched in her hands, trusting Quintus to guide her through the corridors as she read and reread the words.

Her people would be freed.

She'd done it. Done what Madoria had asked.

Yet as she reached the bedroom she'd taken from Gamdesh's princess, Teriana felt a rising unease that the worst was yet to come.

59

MARCUS

Marcus sat across the table, watching Grypus stuff his face with food being fed to him by one of the many young female servants he always kept around him. The young woman masked her revulsion well, but Marcus could see it in her eyes. In the way her jaw imperceptibly tightened every time the man touched her, leaving grease marks on the silk of her dress.

The same grasping hands Grypus had tried to touch Teriana with, and it took all of Marcus's willpower not to draw his gladius and use the hilt to smash every one of the proconsul's lecherous fingers to pulp.

"We can have another three legions here within the week," the proconsul said, wine dribbling down his chin. The young woman wiped it away with a cloth, then refilled his glass. "We couldn't have asked for a better staging point with Padria, it being a port. Food, weapons, men, *women*"—he leered at the servant woman—"all at our fingertips. Let the Gamdeshians scorch their earth. The only impact it will have is them starving themselves while we feast like the emperors of old."

You sick piece of shit. Marcus's jaw flexed, his control over his hatred for this man fracturing.

Running a finger over the map, Grypus added, "We could control Revat within the year. Governor of Gamdesh has a good ring to it." He grinned, then took a mouthful of wine. "We will all be legends. And the gold . . ." He drained his glass. "You get your head on straight and some of that can go in your direction, Marcus. The Maarin girl has what she wants, which means she'll be on her way. Might already be gone given the speed with which she sprinted out of the room."

Marcus didn't answer because he didn't trust what he might say. Didn't trust himself not to reach across the table and tear out Grypus's tongue so that he might never speak Teriana's name again.

Grypus belched loudly. "I was a fool when it came to girls when I was your age, boy, so don't think I don't understand it. The difference is that I was the heir to one of the greatest patrician families on the Hill, whereas you are property. I could do what I wanted, whereas you, if you know what's good for you, will do as you're told." His eyes flicked to Nic. "I'm sure you've seen the consequences of his weakness, so hopefully you'll be wise and not make the same mistakes."

"Yes, Proconsul," Nic said, and Marcus's irritation grew with the flicker of judgment in his eyes.

"Smart boy." Grypus rested his elbow on the table, and said, "I've already begun putting things in order. My Ninth engineer brought enough black powder to make short work of the pagan nonsense looming over Emrant. He's a man with talent—something of an expert when it comes to destroying unwanted xenthier paths, which he claims is all in the timing of the blast. He'll have those towers down by now—I'm surprised we haven't heard the explosions."

Before Marcus could react, the ground trembled and a loud *boom* filled the air.

Grypus cackled, but Marcus only closed his eyes for a heartbeat. This was only the beginning if Grypus remained in control.

He shouldn't be in control.

The trembling ceased, and a cold breeze blew beneath the heavy door to fill the room.

"The Ninth is a legion that follows orders. Good men who understand the way of things." When Marcus didn't respond, Grypus made a face and slapped his servant on the thigh. "More wine, woman."

As the woman poured, Marcus shifted his gaze to the map, feeling his control over the situation slipping between his fingers. With it was flowing the dream he'd had for such a precious short time. A dream where he wouldn't be a blood-soaked conqueror but rather a peacemaker. A dream where Teriana didn't get on the *Quincense* when it arrived in port but remained with him. A dream where it was her voice negotiating across the table from him on behalf of the West, and every night they'd fall asleep in each other's arms.

He wanted that dream, wanted it more than he'd ever wanted anything, and this gluttonous piece of shit was going to take it away. Grypus was the Senate's hand reaching across the seas to move pieces and manipulate players to the Empire's advantage, and Marcus hated him.

A rising tide of frustration and rage swelled in his chest. And the voice asked, *Who is this man to tell you what to do? Who is he to ruin all that you've worked for?*

"Austornic," Marcus said softly, "would you please go ensure that the proconsul's quarters are in order."

Nic frowned. "Servius—"

"Is occupied. And I don't want anything not to the proconsul's standards."

"I will have the royal chambers," Grypus said around a mouthful of food. "No doubt they are base compared to what I'm used to, but I will make do." He jerked his chin at the concubine. "Go with him. I want you waiting."

Teriana's rooms.

"Yes, Proconsul." Nic was nearly at the door as Marcus added, "Please ensure those on guard know that we are not to be disturbed, under any circumstance."

The boy gave him a curious frown but nodded and left the room, the solid oak door thudding behind him.

Grypus, Marcus noticed, was no longer chewing, but was instead watching him warily. "You have a matter you wish to discuss?"

"You might say that," Marcus said. Then he was across the table, his hand closing around Grypus's throat to silence the scream.

Grypus struggled, but Marcus forced him to the ground, fingers like vises around the man's throat.

Kneeling on Grypus's chest, Marcus eased his grip to allow him to gasp in a single breath before squeezing it again. "Having listened to your plans for Gamdesh, Proconsul," he said, "I find that you and I are not in alignment, for I have a very different vision of how this will go."

He eased up his grip and Grypus gasped, "You're a fool if you believe—"

"That I have a say?" Marcus finished for him, having tightened his fingers. "Oh, but I do have a say, Grypus. I hold the power here, not you, and yet you come into my camp and think to tell me how things are going to go. Allow me to clarify for you: things will go *my way*."

Grypus's face was purpling, so Marcus allowed him another breath, and time to say, "Cassius will kill you for this. He already wants you dead, but I can protect you."

"I don't need protection," Marcus said. "What I need is control, and that is the one thing you'll never give me." He smiled, leaning down to meet Grypus's eyes. "So I will do what I do best and take it by force."

"You won't get away with it," Grypus wheezed. "They'll hang you for murder."

"True," Marcus said, grabbing a handful of olives, "which is why I'm going to make it look like an unfortunate accident."

Easing his grip on the man's throat, he waited for Grypus to open his mouth to gasp in a breath and then dumped the olives into his mouth. Grypus's eyes bulged as his desperate breath drew in more than just air, but Marcus only kept him pinned to the carpet.

He watched Grypus purple, then, when he was certain it would be too late for salvation, he released him. "Help!"

The door exploded open, and Marcus shouted, "He's choking on an olive! Get a medic!"

Men of the Ninth surged into the room, lifting Grypus and smacking his back, trying to dislodge the olive.

Grypus raised a hand to point at Marcus, but then his bloodshot eyes rolled backward and he slumped in the men's arms.

"Medic!" Marcus shouted again. "Get a medic in here!"

One appeared, Felix on his heels. "What happened!" he demanded.

"He choked on one of those stupid olives he loves so much."

Silence.

But it was a silence that spoke volumes, for Felix was never easy to fool.

A medic arrived and knelt next to Grypus, pressing fingers to his throat and shaking his head. Marcus watched as the medic stuck his fingers into Grypus's mouth, extracting an olive, then attempted to get the man breathing again before turning to look at Marcus. "Dead."

Everyone stood staring down at Grypus's corpse, his face purple, and unseeing eyes shot with blood.

"Have the body prepared and sent back to Celendor," Marcus finally said, then looked to the members of the Ninth Legion who served as Grypus's guard. "You can communicate what happened, yes?"

"Choked on an olive," the centurion muttered, none of the Ninth appearing remotely sorrowful over the proconsul's passing.

Turning on his heel, Marcus started down the hallway only for Felix to grab his arm and yank him into an antechamber, slamming the door shut. "What did you do?"

Marcus crossed his arms. "Solved a problem."

"By murdering a proconsul in cold blood?" Felix threw up his hands. "Have you lost your mind?"

"You know what a warmonger Grypus is." *Was.* "His plans were for us to immediately begin a campaign to press north and take Revat. No negotiation. Only force. We didn't nearly kill ourselves with this gambit to take Emrant without a fight only to turn around and slaughter our way north!"

"And you think that killing Grypus will spare us that fate?" Felix hissed. "If his plan was to press north, that means it's Cassius's plan. And he'll just send another senator to take up governorship with the same mandate and more bodyguards, because while they might not be able to pin this murder on you, do not for a heartbeat think that they won't suspect! You've bought us days of peace. Maybe weeks. But unless Cassius loses the consulship race, the Empire's plans for us have not changed!" Felix gave an angry shake of his head. "Maybe you ought to go back to bed. Maybe you're not ready to be making decisions."

He's trying to take your power, the voice said. *The Senate will make him give up command of the Forty-First, but in truth they were never enough. Felix commanded the Thirty-Seventh while you were gone, and now he wants it back.*

A sudden rush of anger turned his skin hot and Marcus shoved Felix. "I'm in command here!" he snarled. "Things will go how I want them to go, and anyone who has a problem with it can follow Grypus to the grave. We will make peace with Gamdesh, establish trade with the Empire, and the Senate will have to be content with that."

Felix stared at him. "Is this because of Teriana? Has she put it in your head that this is possible?"

"She hasn't put anything in my head."

Felix scrubbed a hand over his face, then said, "No one wants a war with Gamdesh, Marcus. We'd all be happy to sit tight here in Emrant for the next five years, but it's not going to happen. They won't let us. And if you refuse to follow Cassius's orders and are named a traitor, they'll either find a way to drag you back to be executed or send assassins to take care of the job. Peace is a dream but never our reality, and you of all people should know that!"

The voice reared in Marcus's head, repeating Grypus's words. *You've been given too long a leash for too long a time and have it in your head that you possess real power. Remember that the Senate owns you.*

Not anymore.

"I will make it our fucking reality!" he snarled at Felix. "And may this land's gods help anyone who gets in my way."

60

TERIANA

"We'll get you your things, then you need to go," Quintus said, hurrying her up the steps. "When Marcus comes up, ask him to arrange the release of the *Quincense* and an escort through the xenthier stem. I'll go with you. We'll get your people released, you on a ship that will take you to the *Quincense*, and all of this will be a bad memory."

"What about you?" she asked, feeling oddly unwilling to tell her friend that she'd be coming back to join the legions. The plans she had with Marcus seemed tenuous and new, and putting voice to them felt like tempting fate.

"He said that once you were freed, he'd fake my death and arrange for me to take Miki." His eyes roved for anyone who might be listening. "And then I was hoping we'd be able to join up with you." He was quiet for a minute, then added, "You said one of the healers in the West might be able to help Miki."

Teriana bit the insides of her cheeks because her new plans changed things. But that didn't mean she wouldn't be able to help her friend. She could make arrangements for the *Quincense* to take them aboard, have Yedda bring them somewhere out of reach of the Empire, and help Miki find a healer. "Healers can mend any injury. I'll speak to Marcus before I go and ensure he's thinking of a plan. It's . . ."

She trailed off, because it was all happening so quickly. As they reached the top of the tower and headed to her room, Teriana stared at the precious letter. It seemed like a lifetime ago that she'd first set sail with the legions because she'd believed it was the only way to save her people, and now she had accomplished what she'd set out to do.

But she wasn't done.

Teriana shut the door to her room behind them, then said, "After my people are released, I'm coming back to Emrant."

"Pardon?" Quintus turned to stare at her.

Her tongue felt thick, every word needing to be dragged from her lips. "Marcus thinks he can hold the Senate in check. That together we can negotiate peace between Celendor and Gamdesh, as well as mutually beneficial trade terms. I'm going to stay with him. Be with him."

Quintus stared at her, eyes full of shock. "Teriana, that's *madness*.

I don't know what he's said to convince you such a thing is possible, but he doesn't have the power to hold the Senate in check. You heard what Grypus said. What they think of us. Marcus's days of controlling everything are *over.* The Senate is going to roll right over whatever dreams you two have concocted, because they don't want peace. They want profit."

Her lips parted, harsh words rising in response, but Teriana bit down on them. Taking a deep breath, she said, "Quintus, I have to try. I . . . I've never told you this. I've not even told Marcus, but I was chosen by our goddess. Madoria. I was supposed to find a way to defeat the Empire."

Before he could speak, she continued, "For the longest time, I thought that meant finding a way to sabotage the legions so that you'd have to retreat, but maybe . . . maybe it doesn't mean defeating the Empire in battle but rather defeating the Senate at their own game. Forcing them to play by our rules." She exhaled a shaky breath. "It sounds mad saying it aloud."

"Because it *is* mad." Quintus gripped her shoulders, staring into her eyes. "What you are proposing is not possible, Teriana. Are you hearing me? You're grasping at straws in order to keep this ill-fated romance you have with Marcus alive."

"It's not about that." She twisted away from him, angry that everyone believed her sole motivation was Marcus. He was important to her, but he wasn't what drove her to make every choice. "What would you have me do, Quintus? Sail into the sunset and leave the West to deal with the consequences of every decision I've made? Abandon Marcus to stand between Celendor and Gamdesh alone?"

"Yes." Quintus's tone was cool. "That's exactly what I think you should do. But hearing you, I can't help but wonder if half the reason you plan to stay is that you're afraid of what he'll do if you go."

Teriana's heart slammed into her throat at his words, shock rippling over her and leaving her shaky. "You're wrong! I've made my choice. I will hold to every promise I've made to you and will ensure Marcus does the same, but right now, I want to be alone."

"Fine. I'll be outside, waiting for you to see reason."

The ground trembled beneath her as he slammed the door, and for a long time, Teriana didn't move because it felt as though the world around her was crumbling.

It's fine, she told herself. *He's just angry that you changed the plans and afraid he's losing his chance to be with Miki.*

"Breathe," she muttered. "Just keep breathing."

Yet the conversation with Grypus reared in her mind. The proconsul had not hesitated to claim authority, and with the Senate having such easy access between Celendor and Gamdesh, he had every right to. He was the voice of the Senate.

But Marcus controlled the legions. He had won their loyalty and admiration, which was no small thing. Surely the Senate would recognize that level of power for what it was? Surely they could be made to see reason? All it would take was showing them how they could make a hefty profit even if they weren't in total control, and she was well equipped to do that.

Walking to one of the many tables, she carefully put the letter down and then began stripping off her clothes. She could still feel the proconsul's gaze, and though Marcus had not allowed Grypus to touch her face, she felt dirty. Needed to be clean.

Teriana climbed into the cool waters of the bath and sank beneath the surface, the water muffling all the ambient sounds and giving her peace. She stayed under for as long as she could, then floated on her back, staring at the mosaic design of the tile on the ceiling, endless fears and doubts consuming her. Though none more so than the doubt she had in herself.

A knock sounded, then the door to the room opened with a click, and Marcus said, "Teriana?"

Her heart immediately accelerated, because for better or worse, the next part of her journey would begin now. "Come in. I'm in the bath."

There was silence for a long, painful moment, and Teriana squeezed her eyes shut, abruptly afraid that everything had already fallen apart. Then Marcus's familiar tread filled her ears, moving through the expansive room, and onto the balcony that held one half of the pool.

"Beautiful view," he said softly. She opened her eyes, expecting to see him admiring the sea. Instead, Marcus's eyes were on her.

Teriana's cheeks warmed. "You're looking the wrong direction."

"I'm not."

His tone made her breath catch, but she managed to say, "Is everything all right? Grypus—"

"Don't worry about Grypus," Marcus replied. "He's not going to be a problem."

How that could possibly be, Teriana wasn't sure, but before she could ask, Marcus said, "The *Quincense* should reach the harbor soon."

She sat upright in the pool, splashing herself in the face. "What? How?"

"I knew what our timing would be for taking Emrant," he said. "I left orders for them to be allowed to set sail to join us, along with our injured."

"Miki?"

"He'll be aboard," Marcus answered. "I haven't figured out how I'm going to do it, but I'll honor the agreement I made with Quintus. Hopefully he'll agree to go with you and your escort through the xenthier path back to Celendor before he goes his own way." He hesitated. "I would go with you myself, but—"

"You need to stay here," she said. "There is no question of that. Our position is too fragile, and the last thing we need is Grypus making decisions in your absence."

Marcus grimaced, and not wanting to hear him argue, Teriana added, "Let's be realistic; if it comes to a violence, Quintus is better able to fight me out of a bad situation alive than you are."

"If it comes to a fight, one man isn't going to do much good."

Teriana sighed. "Perhaps. But I haven't forgotten that Cassius tried to kill you. He's had plenty of opportunity to kill me but has never lifted a finger against me."

Marcus's silence was the closest he'd ever get to admitting she was right.

"I still wish there was a way I could go with you." He scrubbed a hand over his hair, which had grown longer during the march from Arinoquia. "I don't trust that Cassius won't find a way to twist circumstances to get out of freeing your people."

"He has no argument," she said. "There is no safer route than this, and it isn't as though he's an emperor to change his mind on a whim. He is still beholden to the Senate and—"

"A senate he controls by blackmail and bribery."

"And to the citizens," she finished, raising an eyebrow at the interruption. "The Cel are a political people, and while they know every man in the Senate is at least a little bit crooked, they won't accept a consul so overtly breaking his word. At worst, they won't vote him in again. At best, they'll riot."

"Would you riot against the Twenty-Ninth?"

"There are more than a million people in Celendrial," she said. "If Hostus starts killing them, every man in that legion will be strung up in the Forum. I've been to very nearly every major city on Reath, and I can tell you with confidence that no one riots like the Cel.

Do not stand there and attempt to argue that keeping five hundred Maarin in prison to maintain a leash on me is worth that risk."

"But it might be worth it to leash *me*."

Teriana bit the insides of her cheeks. "You just gave Cassius exactly what he wanted. There's no reason for him to suspect that you won't continue to do so."

Marcus didn't answer.

"Even if he suspects there might be a risk you won't be compliant, is keeping my people in prison really how he'd choose to manage you?" she asked. "Would he really risk riots and losing the election for such a tenuous method of control?"

"It's not tenuous." Marcus's tone was clipped. "It's proven to be incredibly effective because he knows I'll do anything for you."

Her chest tightened as emotion swelled within her, and Teriana waded to the end of the pool where he stood, resting her elbows on the edge. "Cassius is extremely intelligent, Marcus. Until now, using me has cost him nothing, but all of Celendrial knows that we delivered on our promise. What we really need to worry about is what new form of leverage he's got up his sleeve."

Marcus looked away, the muscles in his jaw clenching. "I don't want you to go. Let me send someone on your behalf. It doesn't need to be you."

Annoyance rose in her that he didn't understand why she had to go, why she had to liberate her people.

"I know what you're thinking." His voice was soft, his eyes on the ceiling as though looking at her would fracture what remained of his control. "That you feel this is your responsibility. That you need to see it through. That you refuse to let that letter out of your sight. But"—his throat moved as he swallowed—"I'm afraid that you'll step through that xenthier stem and I'll never see you again. That Cassius will hurt you if for no better reason than to hurt me."

It was possible. They both knew it. Yet she said, "I will come back."

"If he hurts you," Marcus whispered, "I will take this army back across the seas and burn him alive."

Shock radiated through her. For the depth of his sentiment. For the gravity of the threat. But most of all because she finally realized what Cassius was so afraid of.

Standing upright, she curved a hand around the side of his face, her sodden braids clinging to her skin. "I will come back to you." She pressed her forehead to his. "I swear on the Six, no matter what happens, I will come back to you."

"There is no one in the world with more power to hurt me," he said. "Yet no one I trust more."

Then his lips were on hers, and all the emotion that had been locked up in their hearts for so many long weeks was unleashed.

He half lifted her out of the bath, and her breasts pressed against the cold steel of his armor, a gasp tearing from her lips as his hands slid down her naked back to grip her bottom, holding her against him.

"Are you sure?" she asked between kisses. "I need to know this is what you want."

"You're what I want."

Teriana wrapped an arm around his neck, biting at his bottom lip even as she fumbled with buckles and straps. Metal clanged against the floor, some of it falling into the water, but she didn't care. All that mattered was tearing away the last of the obstacles between them. All that mattered was making him entirely hers.

"I need you," he said between kisses, letting go of her long enough to pull his tunic over his head. "You are everything."

Words she'd dreamed of him saying, and to hear them from his lips made her heart accelerate, the swell of emotion making it hard to breathe.

She tipped her head back, the sensation of his lips on her throat sending sparks through her body, tension building in her core. It went beyond want, because in this moment, the need she had for him was like the need she had for air. Bracing a foot against the bath, Teriana pulled him into the water.

It sloshed over the edge from their combined weight, and Marcus laughed softly against her throat as he unbuckled the vambraces on his wrists, tossing them aside with a splash. But humor gave way to deeper sentiments as her legs wrapped around his waist. Her lips found his, their tongues in each other's mouths, it not seeming possible to be close enough.

They'd already learned every inch of each other, but it had been so long that this felt like the first time, everything touched with a thrill of nerves that made her breathless. That made her want more, so much more, so that when they claimed each other, it felt like the first desperate breath after being caught in the undertow.

She'd thought there was no future for them. That the end was an inevitability, and looking forward had been so very hard. But now? It felt like her whole future stretched out before her, and with every beat of her heart Teriana knew with certainty that her future was with him.

Her breath came in ragged little pants after they fell still, the echoes of pleasure that had rolled over her making words impossible, all the problems they faced having been vanquished if only for a moment. A moment she clung to, not saying a word lest she shatter the peace and send them both hurtling back to a world full of those who'd do them harm.

It was Marcus who shifted first, pulling away slightly so that he could look in her eyes. "I love you, Teriana." He tucked the braid bearing the tiny ship he'd given her behind her ear. "I know I don't say it enough. That I don't show it enough. But know that there is not a moment that goes by that is not touched by you."

Any doubt that she was making the right decision vanished. This was where she was meant to be. He was who she was meant to be with, and together, they would defy every odd. "I love you," Teriana said. "Now and until the end of time."

He tangled his fingers in her braids, kissing her. Teriana allowed her mind to drift into imaginations of the future, of all that they might have, only for a familiar voice to jerk her back to reality.

"So it's true."

Teriana started in surprise, then looked past Marcus's shoulder to find Bait standing next to the balcony railing, his face twisted with anger.

"You're his gods-damned lover!"

Her skin turned to ice even as Marcus snarled, "How did you get in here?"

"One of your own soldiers told me you were with her. Brought me up here and left me in another room to wait." Bait's hands balled into fists. "You idiots always forget we know how to climb."

Oh gods oh gods oh gods, was the only thought that repeated in Teriana's head because this wasn't how she'd wanted her crew to find out. This . . . this wasn't how the situation was supposed to go.

"Everyone was saying it, Teriana," Bait hissed as she scrambled out of the bath, feet slipping on the tile as she pulled Kaira's dress over her head. "Everyone up and down the continent said you were sleeping with our enemy, but I refused to believe it. I *defended* you. But it was the truth. You're the Cel dog's—"

"Insult her, and I'll cut out your tongue and feed it to you." Marcus was out of the bath as well, though he'd gone for his knife first and undergarments second.

He stalked toward Bait, seething with fury. She shoved her way between them, hands braced on their chests. "Enough. Bait, please don't jump to conclusions. There is so much you don't know, and this is not how I wanted you to find out that I was—"

"Sleeping with your best friend's murderer?"

Teriana went still, not entirely certain she'd heard Bait correctly but very certain she'd felt Marcus stiffen. "What?"

"Oh, he didn't tell you that while he was spreading your legs?" Bait leaned into her hand. "He *personally* held Lydia under the water in Cassius's fancy baths, then shoved her down the outtake drain. That's who you're sleeping with."

The world spun, her knees threatening to collapse beneath her as she slowly turned her head to meet Marcus's eyes. "Tell me this isn't true."

His face betrayed nothing, but his eyes were dull with misery.

"Marcus," she whispered, sick with desperation to hear a denial. "Tell me—"

"It's true."

She sucked in a breath, her whole body shaking, because it couldn't be true. "Why? Why would you do that to her? Why would you agree to it?" Her mind filled with Lydia's spectacled face, memories of them giggling and laughing in the Valerius library while their respective parents discussed business below. A lifetime of friendship that bound them closer than blood. "Lydia was just a girl. She . . . she . . ."

Marcus's lips parted, then he hesitated. Teriana clung to that hesitation, praying he'd give her an answer that would make sense. An answer that would make it not his fault. Then he said, "Because Cassius ordered me to do so."

Her body reacted even before the words registered, her palm cracking against his cheek and her nails raking across his skin. "She is a sister to me! I love her!"

Marcus didn't so much as flinch, only exhaled a long breath. "I know. Cordelia told me. That's why . . ." He shook his head.

This was what had changed everything back in Celendrial. This was the secret he'd wanted to tell her. This was the crime she'd unwittingly absolved him of.

"I'm sorry, Teriana."

"You're sorry?" She stared at him, waiting for an explanation. Waiting for him to give something, anything, to explain why he'd agreed to murder an innocent girl. To murder Lydia, who'd never hurt anyone in her entire life.

But Marcus said nothing.

"You lied to me." Tears dripped down her cheeks. "I asked you what had happened to her and you lied to my face. And have lied every day since. Allowed me to absolve you knowing full well that I'd never have done so if I'd known about this!"

He didn't answer.

"Say something!" she shouted. "You owe me that much!"

Marcus only shook his head. "There is nothing to say."

Which meant there was no reason that he could give. No justification. Nothing that would make this tenable or understandable. Nothing that would allow her to live with herself for having betrayed Lydia's memory in this way. It had been an order. Nothing more.

"As always, you're right," she said softly. "I have come to hate you."

And she needed to be away from this situation. Needed to escape.

Twisting away from both men, she snatched up the letter and bolted for the door. Quintus grinned at her as she jerked it open. "The *Quincense* is in the harbor," he said, then saw her expression. "Teriana? What's wrong?"

But she was already running.

61

MARCUS

"She'll never forgive you," Bait spat. "Though I don't suppose a Cel dog like you cares. You were just using her anyway."

Marcus barely heard him. His eyes were fixed on the door Teriana had slammed shut behind her, a dull whining noise filling his ears.

She was gone.

I know who you were, but what I care about is who you are now, her voice whispered from his memory. The conversation he'd known in his heart was too good to be true.

You are suggesting that you want to stay?

Yes.

With me? Despite who I am? What I am? All that I've done?

If you want me.

He'd allowed himself to be convinced because he'd wanted to be convinced. Had wanted her absolution despite being too much of a coward to tell her the truth. But the truth always came out, one way or another, and now Teriana knew.

Knew that there were some actions that were unforgivable.

Go after her, his heart screamed. *Tell her the whole truth. Tell her about Cassius's blackmail. Tell her that if you hadn't done it, Cassius would have revealed your parents' crimes. That you had to do it to protect them.*

But Marcus didn't move. All those justifications would mean little in the face of what he'd done, and in his desperate attempt to justify himself, he'd be risking the very family he'd murdered an innocent girl to protect. It was better if she thought the worst of him.

A familiar tightness squeezed around his chest, his heart rate escalating, every breath an effort.

Good, his conscience whispered. *Maybe this time it will be the end of you. A fitting punishment for how badly you hurt her.*

"But the joke's on you."

Bait was still speaking, and Marcus turned his head to stare at the boy, knowing he'd missed much of what had been said. "How so?" he asked, though he was long past caring what insults the boy might hurl at him.

"Because Lydia's still alive."

If only that were possible. Teriana would still never forgive him, but at least she'd not bear the grief of Lydia's death.

"Lydia's favored by the gods, and she escaped through a xenthier stem to Mudaire," Bait said with a vicious smirk. "She's marked by the Six. A healer, and a powerful one at that!"

Over the faint wheeze of his breath, Marcus heard rushing water. Blinked and saw Lydia's panicked face right as she was bodily wrenched from his grasp. Not into an underground stream that never surfaced, but into a stream that surfaced on the far side of the world.

"Too bad you botched the job, or she'd never have lived to tell me what you'd done." Bait reached out to shove Marcus. "If you were half as good at killing as everyone says, you might have gotten away with it."

Since the moment Cordelia had revealed to Marcus the truth of Teriana's friendship with Lydia, he'd been plagued by visions of that fateful moment in the Celendrial baths. Visions that worsened with every passing day, the events shifting, portraying him as a gleeful murderer who delighted in holding Lydia under the water. That had relished that last explosion of bubbles and the spark fading from her green eyes.

But as the room turned abruptly cold, the truth played in his mind's eye.

Of the moment he'd changed his mind.

The current surged, slamming into him with incredible force. He caught himself against the edge of the drain, but Lydia fell backward, his grip on her wrist the only thing keeping the water from sucking her down the tunnel. She reached, fingers grasping, but he was losing his grip on her. "Hold on!" he screamed at her, his voice drowned out by the raging water. He pulled, trying to drag her out of the current, her nails clawing down his arm as she tried to grab hold. Every muscle in his body screamed, but he kept his grip. Would get her out, and then face the consequences. Then the water ripped her from his grasp, and Lydia disappeared into blackness.

He hadn't been able to do it. Hadn't been able to kill her, and his morality had cost him Teriana. His vision cleared, revealing Bait's face, mouth moving in silent insults that Marcus couldn't hear above his own wheezing breath, each gasp sending a cloud of mist into the freezing air.

Why was it so cold?

Every time he tried to do the right thing, it cost him. Every time he let his morals get the better of him, he suffered. Every time he tried to resist who he really was, the world punished him for it.

Perhaps it's time you stop resisting, the voice said. *Perhaps it's time you accept who you are meant to be.*

He was so cold. So painfully cold.

Put an end to the pain. An end to the suffering, the voice said. *Claim your destiny, and all the pleasure of victory will be yours.*

Marcus drew in a ragged breath, and said, "Yes."

Bait's sneering face snapped back into focus before him, the room no longer cold and breathing no longer a challenge.

The boy frowned in confusion, and Marcus smiled at him. "In battle, Bait, I have found that nothing ever goes quite as one might have planned, but in those deviations, opportunities arise." Bait's eyes widened, and Marcus felt a stab of pleasure as the boy realized he'd erred.

As he realized that in his desire to tear Marcus's world apart, to make him suffer, to make him weep for all that he'd lost, he'd opened up a path for Marcus to do the same to him.

Slinging an arm around Bait's shoulders, he steered the boy toward the door. "So you say that Lydia discovered a genesis downstream from the baths in Celendrial? And that it took her to Mudamora? Safely, I presume, given she was well enough to tell the tale?"

"I . . ."

A sideways glance allowed him to watch Bait's throat move as he swallowed hard, and Marcus patted him on the shoulder. "When one's mission is conquering the world, it is always such a pleasure when the other side hands one the keys to their back door."

Opening the door, Marcus found Felix on the other side reaching for the handle. His second's eyes widened at the sight of Bait. "I'm not sure what's going on, but Teriana just—"

"Make sure she boards the *Quincense*," Marcus interrupted. "And make sure he does as well."

He shoved Bait out into the corridor and closed the door.

62

TERIANA

Not caring that she was barefoot, or that the wet dress was glued to her skin, Teriana raced down the stairs, barely hearing Quintus calling her name as he pursued. All that mattered was getting away, though Teriana knew that no matter how fast she ran, she'd never outrun the knowledge slowly destroying her soul.

Men of all four legions stopped what they were doing to stare as she sprinted out the gate, feet splashing in the puddles from the overnight rains as she set her sights on the harbor. On the familiar ship with blue sails.

"Teriana, stop!" Quintus shouted, but she only put on a burst of speed. She needed to go. Needed to be gone from this place.

But he was faster.

"Teriana!" His hand closed on her arm, slowing her speed, and when she tried to pull away, her friend only flipped her over his shoulder. "Tell me what happened?"

"I have to go," she sobbed, snot running down her face. "He's a murderer. Marcus's a gods-damned murderer!"

"Is this about the towers?" Quintus set her on her feet but held tight to her shoulders. "They were collapsed on Grypus's orders, not Marcus's. But Grypus is dead. Felix told everyone he choked on an olive, but the rumors are that Marcus killed him."

"The towers?" Her eyes went to Emrant in the distance, dust hanging in a low cloud over the city and the Seventh's dark tower the only one of the seven remaining. Just like in Galinha, Aracam, and all the villages they'd left in their wake. That had been what had made the ground tremble. "Marcus murdered Grypus?"

"They were alone together when Grypus choked."

That meant the proconsul had already been dead when Marcus had come to her, and he'd said not a word. So many lies. Endless *fucking* lies.

Teriana gave her head a sharp shake. "Grypus doesn't matter. Lydia is who matters."

"Who is Lydia?"

"My sister." Teriana crouched down, needing to be small as the Seventh's tower surveyed everything within its sights.

"You never told me you had a sister!"

"My best friend." She pressed her face to her knees, pulse roaring in her ears, the world spinning around her. "Marcus murdered her. I loved her like a sister and he drowned her because Cassius didn't want her. And he knew! Knew what she meant to me and he still . . ." She screamed wordlessly, holding the letter away from her lest her tears smear the ink. "I need to go!"

"Okay, okay. Shit!" Quintus pulled her upright, wiping the corner of his cloak across her face to clean it. "Walk. Try to look steady or someone might stop you on principle."

Teriana stifled her sobs, knowing that they were fooling no one as they walked down to the harbor. Not with her barefoot and splattered with mud, her cursed eyes betraying the misery that was her heart with their black and stormy seas.

"You need to come with me." She tried to stifle her sobs. "Miki is here somewhere. Find him and bring him to the ship."

"It's not that simple." Quintus's fingers tightened on hers. "I'm not even supposed to see him. If I go in there and try to take him, someone will stop me. I need time to figure out how to steal him away."

Tears poured down her cheeks, and though she hadn't thought it possible to loathe herself more, Teriana said, "I can't stay. I can't be here."

"I know." His fingers tightened again. "You get on that ship and free your people. I'll figure out things here and then I'll find you."

"I don't want to leave you." They'd reached the tiny harbor town, her toes squishing in worse than mud as they walked through the streets. "I promised you."

"Miki and I are safe enough here," Quintus said. "Whereas your people are with Hostus. Get them out and then we'll talk promises."

"I'm sorry." She could barely speak. Could barely breathe.

"You've nothing to be sorry for."

Teriana had *everything* to be sorry for. Even if she spent the rest of her life trying to atone for her mistakes, she'd still die begging for forgiveness.

Gamdeshian civilians filled the town, going about their usual business while coming to terms with their change in regime, and many of them recognized her. Spit in the mud at the sight of her. Teriana wanted to fall to her knees before them. Wanted to scream at them to run, to escape, because the man who now ruled them was a monster.

But she kept walking, the docks appearing ahead.

"Almost there," Quintus said, then a Forty-First centurion appeared in front of them, his arms crossed.

"Did *he* approve of her being here?"

Quintus dropped Teriana's hand, and she knew that he'd fight to get her on that ship. But then a voice from behind said, "It's approved."

She turned her head to find Felix striding up behind them, Bait's wrist firmly in his grip. "Get on your ship, Teriana," he said as the centurion stepped aside to allow them to climb the steps onto the dock.

The planks were rough beneath her feet, splinters digging into her flesh, but it was all Teriana could do not to run to the *Quincense*. As though being on her decks would be salvation, all her pain left behind in the ship's wake.

"How quickly can you get to Celendrial?" Felix asked, voice toneless.

"A week." She gripped Quintus's arm.

"That letter you have should be all you need, but if you run into trouble, try to get word to me. I know our help is the last thing you want, but I can force the issue." Felix shoved Bait ahead of him.

Her friend stumbled on his crippled foot, and Teriana knew that Bait had told Felix what Marcus had done.

Rounding on her, Felix caught hold of Teriana's hands. "Grypus's death has bought time, but Cassius will send another governor soon enough, and then it will be war. Get your people, and then find whatever place is left on Reath that is out of the Empire's reach." Felix's fingers tightened. "Take care of yourself, Teriana."

Turning on his heel, Felix strode down the docks. Though Teriana hadn't thought there was room in her heart for anything but grief, her chest tightened at this act of kindness from a man she'd once thought her enemy.

"Don't give anyone a chance to change their mind." Quintus nudged her up the gangplank.

Her crew waited. Her *family* waited, faces she'd not seen in so many long months, all of them staring at her as Teriana stepped onto the *Quincense's* deck for what felt the first time in eternity. They all knew what she'd done, and Teriana waited for them to turn their backs on her as her mother had. Waited for the moment she was rejected by the people she'd fought so hard to save.

"Welcome home, Teriana," her aunt Yedda said.

Teriana's knees buckled, and she pressed her lips to the deck of the ship that had been her home all her life, hearing the voices of her family welcoming her back.

They still accept me, despite everything that happened. One good thing in a sea of darkness.

"Get up, girl," Yedda said. "Those decks ain't been swabbed since those boys took their injured. Might be a good first job for you since you've likely gone rusty on gauging the winds."

"Gladly," Teriana sobbed. "I will gladly clean every inch of this ship because it feels good to be home."

Being on the decks and feeling the faint swell of the sea beneath her feet gave Teriana back her strength, and she rose. Quintus stood next to the rail, and in two steps, she flung her arms around his neck. "I wish you could come with me."

"Only because you don't realize that I don't know anything about sailing a ship."

A smile worked onto her lips. "Never in my life did I expect to call a legion boy a friend, but you have been one of the best, and truest, friends I have been privileged to have." Holding him at arm's length so that she could meet his blue eyes, she said, "Find Miki. Tell him you love him. And then get out of this nightmare and find me."

Quintus pulled her close and kissed her cheek. "You're going to regret that when you see how seasick Miki gets." He pushed her gently away and climbed onto the gangplank. "Go to Celendrial, Teriana of the *Quincense*. I'll see you on the other side."

Then he was gone.

She hated herself for letting him go, but as she stared at the single black tower looming over Emrant in the distance, Teriana knew that she could not risk remaining. Not even for a friend.

Turning back to her crew, Teriana cleared her voice, then said, "Let's go liberate our people."

63

MARCUS

Returning to where his discarded tunic lay in a pile, Marcus donned it, along with his weapons. He allowed himself one glance out the window. His eyes found the blue sails of Teriana's ship in the harbor, the wooden version of the hair ornament that adorned her braid.

A pang of grief lanced through his chest, but it was vanquished by an icy wind of composure that blew across his mind, extinguishing the rising tide of emotion as he left the room. "Who brought the Maarin boy into the tower?" he asked those on duty outside her doors. "And where is Gibzen?"

The men exchanged glances, then one said, "Legatus Austornic, sir. He put him in the antechamber there"—he pointed down the hall—"then came looking for you. We told him you were busy, and he said to tell you the Maarin boy was in there."

Austornic was to blame.

A cold wind blew down the hallway, rustling the guards' cloaks.

Is that a surprise? the voice asked. *It's not the first time Austornic used her against you.*

The men shifted uncomfortably, the bare skin on their arms pebbling against the cold. "The Maarin boy was alone in the room. He must have climbed out the balcony. Sorry, sir. We didn't think—"

"Where is Gibzen?"

"The Tribunus relieved him of duties, sir, but he was just here checking in. Might catch him on the stairs going down."

Marcus's eyes narrowed at Felix's overstep. "Go after him. He has work to do."

"Yes, sir."

Marcus walked down the tower steps to the room he'd designated as his center of command, barely pausing to note that it had been cleared of all evidence of Grypus's demise. He poured himself a glass of wine, then unrolled a map, setting markers on the edges to keep them from curling. His eyes settled upon the largest kingdom of the north.

Mudamora.

Gamdesh was his priority, yet Marcus couldn't tear his eyes from the northern kingdom.

Healer. Lydia was marked.

What she was supposed to be was dead. Drowned, her corpse lost to an underground river without end, time having eaten her down to bones.

But she was alive.

The sudden compulsion to remedy that fact washed over him like a wave, nearly driving him to his feet. Instead, Marcus moved his focus to the nation that stood between him and the northern continent, tapping a finger on the capital city of Revat.

The door opened, and Servius walked inside. "What's going on with Teriana? You've got four legions of men all gossiping like village matrons because she was seen racing to the harbor like a pack of Sibernese wolves was on her heels."

"Nothing of concern to us." Marcus rested his elbows on the table. "Felix will deal with her."

Servius was silent for a moment, then he said, "We have a Gamdeshian emissary here to speak to you. If you want me to deal with him, I will."

"I'll speak to him myself," Marcus murmured. "I'm rather interested in what they have to say."

Vaguely, he heard Servius give the orders to those outside, but his mind was all for the xenthier path Bait had revealed. It would need to be excavated given the genesis was located beneath Celendrial, then it would need to be mapped to the Senate's satisfaction. Mudaire was reported to be overrun with blight—a dead city—which meant logistical efforts would be required before it was viable for heavy traffic. No use to Marcus now, but soon enough.

Take Revat, and you can move on Mudamora.

He eyed the terrain between Emrant and Revat. A strategy began to build of how best to cross the distance between the two cities, all the information that had been fed to him by spies and reports rising from where he'd stored it away.

Men were filtering into the room, now. Zimo and Austornic, as well as other officers and guards. Austornic was looking everywhere but at Marcus, his guilt palpable.

But guilt wouldn't get him out of this.

Then a small Gamdeshian man entered, flanked by Gibzen and one of his men. His primus gave him a small nod.

"Legatus." The Gamdeshian inclined his head. "I've been sent on behalf of His Most Revered Majesty, Sultan Kalin of Gamdesh, to negotiate your exodus from our territory."

Marcus picked up his cup, taking a long mouthful while he regarded the man. "Is that what we are negotiating?"

"The Sultan has no desire for war, but to allow a foreign power to control a city full of Gamdeshian civilians is not something he's willing to accept, especially after the wanton destruction of the towers of the Six. If you do not withdraw, either to your homeland or to Arinoquia, the full force of Gamdesh's military might will be brought to bear on your soldiers, and no quarter will be given."

"That doesn't sound like negotiation." Marcus set down his cup. "That sounds like a threat."

The man stiffened, then gave a tight smile. "Whether you retain control of Emrant is not up for negotiation, Legatus. The Sultan is willing to entertain the formation of a trade agreement between Gamdesh and Celendor, and he will allow a small force of your men and administrators to form an embassy within the city to facilitate mutually profitable trade for both nations."

"Allow?"

A bead of sweat trickled down the side of the man's face. "We have reason to believe that you've no more interest in war than we do. That you are a man who does not risk the lives of his men when words will achieve the same ends."

"True."

The Gamdeshian's throat moved as he swallowed, and if Marcus had space for pity in his heart, he would have pitied this man who'd been sent to make threats by a ruler without the strength to back them up.

"The Katamarcans have suggested that your . . . Senate"—he hesitated on the foreign word—"is more interested in trade than control."

"I'm afraid that was propaganda." Marcus took another sip from his cup, feeling Austornic's scrutiny. "Lies, if we are being honest. The Senate desires profit above all else, but experience has taught them that the greatest profit comes through control. My purpose is to secure that control by whatever means necessary, whether it be words or war. So tell me, will the Sultan choose to surrender or will he choose to fight?"

"Surrender?"

"The Senate will offer Sultan Kalin and his family the opportunity to live in exile in a location of the Senate's choosing, and of course he'll be kept in the style to which he is accustomed. Should he choose to fight, he will be captured and brought back to Celendrial for execution."

"Let's not be hasty, Legatus." Sweat now poured down the man's face. "It need not come to threats."

"Yet it already has."

"You're being rash." The emissary lifted his chin. "Allowing pride and hubris to guide your tongue rather than good sense. You cannot hope to win a war against the full might of Gamdesh with the numbers you have."

"How fortunate, then, that I can double my ranks in"—Marcus snapped his fingers—"nearly the blink of an eye. And let's not waste time with you accusing me of posturing or bluffing. The Maarin will have made clear to you that the men you see in this fortress are a mere pittance compared to the might that the Senate can bring to bear, should it feel inclined. The Sultan will surrender Revat to my control, else I will raze my way north and take it by force."

He didn't miss Austornic's intake of breath nor how Servius's hand moved to rest on the boy's shoulder, cautioning him to silence. Zimo's eyebrows rose, but the older legatus said nothing.

"The Six will not allow this incursion to stand," the emissary hissed, his hands curling into fists.

"I don't answer to the Six."

You don't answer to anyone, the voice in Marcus's head whispered.

"You will soon enough," the emissary retorted. "For when you lose and Kaira puts a blade through your heart, it will be the Six who stand in judgment."

"Surrender." Marcus rose to his feet. "Sultan Kalin must surrender Gamdesh to the Senate or I will take it by force. Ride quickly. And choose wisely." He motioned to Gibzen, and the emissary was escorted from the room by one of his men. His primus remained.

"We're going to need more legions," Zimo said the moment the door shut. "You can do it with an additional three, but I'd ask for four." He hesitated, then said, "I served under Grypus in Chersome over the past year. He was a right prick, and we all had a good laugh when we heard it was the olives that did him in."

Marcus didn't answer. Zimo was no more fooled than Felix, and he waited for Zimo to name the price of his silence.

"Grypus had a girl with him. An . . . *acquaintance* of mine, who has voiced a desire to remain in the West rather than returning with the rest of his servants. That going to be an issue?"

"She's a free woman." A lie, given Grypus's women were always indentured, but Lucretia wouldn't miss her and Marcus needed Zimo's loyalty. Taking a sip of wine, he added, "I'd hurry, though. The Ninth will want to leave before rot sets in."

"Yes, sir. I'll make the arrangements now." Zimo gave a sharp salute, then left the room, leaving Marcus alone with Austornic and Servius.

"Why are you threatening the Gamdeshians?" Austornic demanded. "We marched the men to exhaustion and leapt through a dozen hoops to avoid a fight in taking Emrant, and you're just going to throw it all away? What happened to trying to secure peace between the nations? To holding our position in Emrant and proving trade with the Empire was worthwhile? We've barely unpacked and already you're looking for the next fight?"

"Nic," Servius said, "hold your tongue."

"Don't." Marcus went to the sideboard and poured himself another drink, watching the boy seethe. "If you've got something to say, then say it."

Austornic hesitated, then he said, "I know you're angry that Teriana left, but I'm not going to allow you to use my men in a quest to satisfy your spite over a girl!"

"*Allow.*" Marcus sipped at his wine. "There is something about that word that I dislike. Particularly from a boy who has been meddling where he shouldn't be."

"I haven't been meddling!"

"It wasn't you who brought the Maarin boy into the tower and left him to his own devices? Left him to spy on conversations not meant for his ears?"

Austornic's eyes skipped around the room, looking for support. "You gave the command for the *Quincense* to meet us here but no orders about keeping them away. I thought Teriana would want to see them. I thought *you* wanted her to see them."

"You need to do less thinking and more obeying."

Austornic blanched, but then squared his shoulders. "You answer to the Senate, Marcus, and they didn't give you the order to take Revat."

Get rid of him, the voice commanded. *He's caused you nothing but trouble. If not for him, Teriana would still be yours.*

"You heard the late proconsul's intentions, Austornic. His desire for us to make ready to take all of Gamdesh. And he was the voice of both Senate and Consul."

"A goal you could delay if you wanted to," the boy retorted. "Instead, you are stepping toward war before we've even received the order."

Setting his cup down, Marcus circled the table, lowering his head to look Austornic in the eye. "I find that I've reconsidered your value to this campaign. War is no place for children, and it's time you went back to Celendor where you can learn to obey."

Austornic's brown eyes went wide. "You aren't serious? You're going to punish my entire legion because I questioned your motivations?"

Marcus didn't answer, only sat and waited for the understanding that there would be no arguing his way out of this to sink into the boy.

The flush of anger on Austornic's cheeks slowly blanched. "Sir, please don't send us back. They'll put us under Hostus's command. You know better than anyone what he's like."

"I know he doesn't suffer anyone meddling in his business."

"Marcus," Servius protested, but Marcus held up a hand to silence him.

"This isn't a negotiation. Fall to command and get your ranks through the xenthier stem."

"Punish me," Austornic blurted out. "Kill me if you have to, but don't send my men away. Please!"

Servius caught the boy by the shoulders and steered him toward the door. "Live to pick another battle, Nic," he murmured, giving Marcus a dark glare. "This isn't one you're going to win."

Felix passed them as they exited, his brow creased with a frown. "The *Quincense* has set sail. You going to tell me what is going on?"

Marcus was already bent over the table, writing a letter directly to Cassius with an update, excluding any mention of the xenthier stem below the baths. The consul would not take it well to learn that his betrothed was alive and location of the xenthier would suggest as much. Besides, for all he'd used the revelation of the path to needle Bait, it was not currently a viable route. Signing the letter, he folded and sealed it, then handed it to Gibzen. "Make sure the Ninth packs Grypus's corpse on ice and have them deliver this, directly to Cassius."

"Yes, sir."

"What's it say?" Felix asked, his eyes narrowed.

"It's a request for six legions," Marcus responded. "Because very soon, the Empire will be declaring war."

64

KILLIAN

Dawn was but a faint glow in the sky when Killian left his room, buckling his sword on as he headed to the blue room to take up guard duty outside *Lydia's* door. He was halfway down the hallway, Gwen and Lena in sight where they stood at their posts, when his mother's voice called from behind.

"Killian, you've a visitor waiting in the main parlor." His mother had an armload of gowns, and he didn't fail to notice the exhaustion written across her face as she caught up to him. "A giant."

He tensed. "Bercola?"

His mother gave him a dour glare. "If it were Bercola, I would have used her name. He called himself Baird."

"I know him." Killian hesitated, then asked, "Do you know where Bercola is?"

"She did not think you'd care to see her. It is my understanding that you had a falling out, but she has refused to give any details. Always taciturn, that woman." His mother's eyes flicked up to meet his. "Resolve it. This is not a time to cling to grievances."

Giving a sharp knock on the blue room's door, she called out, "It's Anne, Your Grace. I've the dresses you requested." Not waiting for a response, she went inside.

Gwen and Lena were watching him expectantly.

"You two have it in you to keep guard for another hour?" he asked. "This can't wait."

Lena met Gwen's gaze, then shrugged. "Sure. But only if you promise to listen to your mother."

Sighing, Killian set off to the parlor, the ancient wooden floor of Teradale creaking beneath his boots as he walked. He leapt down the staircase, circling the servants replacing the flowers in the large vase in the foyer table, green fields visible through the window as he made his way to the parlor.

Baird was pacing nervously back and forth across the room, his face freshly shaven and his clothes newly purchased. Killian was struck with an overpowering wave of cologne as he entered the room, the scent of bergamot so strong it made his eyes water. "I thought you were still on the *Kairense*?"

The giant ceased his pacing, then crossed the room and lifted Killian in an embrace that made his ribs creak. "I was. Then Lydia told me the news of the progress of the blight and knew that I couldn't allow my cowardice to get the better of me. Now is the time for boldness. I wish to see my wife."

Over the bergamot, Killian picked up the scent of whiskey, suggesting that his friend's boldness was at least half liquid courage. The other half was likely encouragement from the Maarin and Lydia.

"I need to see her, too." Killian gestured to the door. "And I think I know how to find her."

They left the manor together, and once outside, Killian lifted his fingers to his lips and whistled sharply.

Baird stared at him in horror. "Are you trying to get us both killed? One does not call a woman like a—"

Socks burst around the corner of the manor, barking happily. "A dog?" Killian supplied. Bending to pet Socks's thick fur, he said, "Where is Bercola?"

The dog's ears perked up and, with a yip, he took off running toward one of the pastures. They followed Socks, the herds of Calorian horses lifting their heads from their grazing to eye them a moment before returning to the thick grass. Socks leapt between fence boards and led them into the dense forest beyond, the thick canopy of lush trees casting heavy shadows over them.

"Are you sure this is the right way?" Baird grumbled, mopping sweat from his brow and frowning at a pair of caimans in a slow-moving creek. "This seems the path to getting eaten."

"They're harmless." Killian jumped between rocks, the reptiles retreating into the depths as they passed. "Not so the snakes, so watch where you step."

Baird cursed under his breath, carefully following Killian as they wove deeper into the jungle. Ahead, a small cabin appeared through the trees, smoke rising from the chimney. Socks darted in the open door, and familiar laughter filtered out from the cabin as Bercola greeted the dog.

"This was a mistake," Baird declared, and only Killian grabbing hold of his arm and hauling the giant onward kept him from racing back to Teradale.

"It will be fine. I'll talk to her first. You wait out here and don't touch anything that wriggles."

Leaving the anxious giant standing next to a tree, Killian pressed on to the cabin. It had weathered the years surprisingly well, the heavy wooden planks so covered with moss that it nearly blended into the jungle around it. The doorframe looked new and the windows had been replaced—both likely by Bercola's steady hand. She'd built this cabin when he'd been a boy because she'd not found Teradale, which was sized for humans, particularly comfortable. He'd spent endless hours here to escape the rules governing his behavior that he'd had to endure under his mother's watchful eye, because the giantess's only rules had been not to do anything stupid and not to piss her off. Both of which he'd done continually.

Stepping up to the door, Killian knocked on the frame.

Bercola had been on her knees petting Socks, but at his knock, her head jerked up. "Killian."

"May I come in?"

The giantess got to her feet. "You shouldn't encourage him to race around the jungle. The caimans have gotten big." Then she gestured to the pair of oversized chairs next to a table. "Sit. I'll pour you a drink."

Socks leapt onto the giant-sized cot on the far side of the room with no care for his muddy feet. Killian took the time to knock the mud off his boots before he came in and climbed into one of the chairs. As tall as he was, his feet still dangled above the ground like a small child's.

"Gwen and Lena told me you'd returned." Bercola filled a cup from a small keg of ale, setting it in front of him. "They updated me about what has happened, including about Lydia's heritage."

Killian swirled the cup but didn't drink. "You were right," he finally said. "Lydia was corrupted."

Bercola didn't answer, just took a sip from her cup, her colorless eyes unreadable.

"When last we spoke, you said that there was some of the Six in us all, but also some of the Seventh," he said. "It turns out that you were more right than you know. The Seventh doesn't grant marks, he . . . corrupts them. What you were wrong about was that Lydia was hopeless and needed to be killed. She's fought the Corruptor's influence back, and with the help of the Six and then Queen Ceenah of Anukastre, she's mastered her mark. And herself."

"I'm glad I was wrong." Bercola leaned back in her chair. "I'm glad she didn't try to hurt you."

He winced. "Oh, she did. A few times."

"Good thing you enjoy risking your life, then." She sighed. "But truly, Killian, the relief I felt hearing she'd returned rivaled the relief I felt at your return. I wanted to be wrong."

Silence stretched between them.

"I love her," Killian finally said. "There's nothing I wouldn't do to protect her, and for a long time, I didn't think I'd be able to forgive you for trying to kill her at Alder's Ford. But I've come to realize that no good is coming from me holding on to my anger. If anything, it's allowing the Corrupter to influence me, because driving you away doesn't make me stronger. It makes me weaker. And I can't afford to be any weaker than I am. Mudamora can't afford it."

Bercola rested her elbows on the table, her brow split with a frown. "What's wrong, Killian? And don't say *nothing*, because I know you too well to believe that."

The question forced him to look deep, to dig beneath the confidence and surety he always wore like armor to the kernel of doubt beneath. To admit something he'd not admitted to anyone, least of all himself. "I don't think I can defeat her."

"Rufina."

He gave a slight nod. "I've had more than one chance to kill her and failed to do it. And my failure has cost Mudamora so much. Most of the kingdom lost to blight. Thousands and thousands of Mudamorians have died and risen to fight in her army. None of this would be happening if my arrow had struck true the night she attacked the wall. Or if I'd killed her the night she attacked the palace in Mudaire. Or when we escaped from Helatha. Or when she caught up to us in Derin. But every gods-damned time, she's gotten the better of me." He let out a ragged breath. "This is what I was marked to do, but I'm afraid that when it comes down to it, I'm going to fail again."

"The burden of stopping Rufina isn't all on you." Bercola's voice was filled with sympathy. "I know that Malahi is a tender and that she's in Revat for answers as to how to destroy the blight." She hesitated, then added, "And I know that's not Lydia stomping around dressed like a queen, so I expect Lydia is in Revat with her. If they can destroy the blight, Rufina will be reduced to nothing more than a Corrupted serving the Seventh god."

"She still has her blighters." He took a sip of his drink but found he didn't like the taste. "A whole army of Mudamorian dead, plus all the Derin dead that she'll inevitably bring across the Liratoras. How do we fight against an army of that size, Bercola? How do we stand against soldiers who feel no pain? How do we cut down those who wear the faces of friends and family?"

"I don't know." Letting go of her cup, she traced the scratches in the old wooden table. "But you don't stand alone. This isn't just your burden to bear—it belongs to every nation, every person."

In the full scope of it, Killian knew that was true. Malahi was the tender. Lydia the healer. Yet when it came to Rufina, it felt personal. Like ending her was his duty, and fear ate at his insides that when the moment came, Rufina would defeat him once more.

"What can I do?" she asked. "Tell me how I can best help you."

The request for alliance should formally come from Lydia, but every instinct told Killian it couldn't wait. "Anukastre has committed to an alliance. But I don't think it will be enough. I need you to journey to Eoten Island and convince the Council of Twelve to commit Eoten's army to the fight."

"The Council of Eleven, you mean." Her lip curled. "All decisions require unanimous support, and one of Gespurn's marked has long been absent. We'd hoped he'd died, but given that Gespurn has not seen fit to choose another summoner, the traitorous prick must still live."

Killian winced. "About that . . ."

"Hello, my love."

Bercola's eyes widened, then her face turned red with fury. "You fucking bastard!" she screamed, then flung herself at Baird.

Killian cursed even as he caught hold of her arm, Bercola easily dragging him across the cabin. "Don't kill him!"

"How could you!" she shrieked. "How could you abandon our people!"

"Because you left me!" Baird scrambled backward. "I couldn't bear to watch you live life apart from me, so I left."

"Coward!"

"I'm sorry!" Baird pleaded. "Betraying you was the worst mistake of my life!"

Killian managed to get between them, though the thought that he could restrain two angry giants was laughable. "Bercola, you don't have to forgive him but you can't kill him. He's a friend and he's had my back through more than a few dark hours. What's more, he's fighting on our side."

He tensed, waiting for Bercola to attack, then realized she was crying. Great heaving sobs, and it struck Killian then that this wasn't a conversation he needed to be part of. "I'm going to go," he said. "But I need you to convince the giants to fight, Bercola. We need Eoten Isle's strength."

Stepping away from them, he called Socks's name and then started the walk back to Teradale. The dog scampered ahead of him and then slid to a stop. Hackles rising, Socks growled at a dark patch of woods.

Killian's skin began to crawl, and he drew his sword. Staring into the shadows, he prowled closer. Only for a cottonmouth to lunge at the dog. Killian reacted on instinct and cut off the deadly snake's head, his heart pounding as the serpent fell still.

Socks continued to growl at the shadows.

"Get back to the house," he said to the dog. "Bercola's right that this is no place for you."

The dog barked, then bolted toward the manor. Killian gave the shadows one last look, then followed him.

Kitaryia had a breakfast to attend, and the queen needed her bodyguard.

* * *

"She doesn't play with her spectacles like that," Killian muttered. "Even when they slide down her nose, she doesn't notice."

"No one besides you will know that," Dareena answered under her breath. "And perhaps give me some credit: wearing these things is giving me a bloody headache, I've nearly fallen down the stairs twice in this dress, and these damnable heels have resulted in me cracking my head twice in doorways. You haven't had to do *anything*."

Which was entirely the problem. Lydia and his friends were risking their lives, and he was guarding the one woman in the nation who needed protection the least.

Which would have been hard enough, except every god-marked instinct in Killian's body was screaming that Lydia was in danger. And he was powerless to help her.

"I feel it, too." Dareena tightened her grip on his arm as they walked down the path running alongside the horse pasture, Lena and Gwen following behind. "We're running out of time, and instead of being north on the front lines fighting blighters, I'm attending a picnic." She shook her head. "It feels as though we are in some strange bubble, horror all around us, and that at any moment, the bubble will pop."

As Dareena spoke, a strong northerly wind blew over them, bitterly cold, and carrying with it the faint stench of rot that briefly overwhelmed the scent of flowers.

"Do you believe they'll find the information they seek?" Dareena asked, looking northward. It occurred to him that this was the first time the woman who'd mentored him had ever shown doubt. Had ever looked to him for answers.

"If there's a way, Lydia and Malahi will find it." He fell silent as they approached the pavilions set up in the middle of the garden to block the heat of the sun. Beneath stood an array of colorfully dressed nobles, all drinking and laughing as though they'd no care in the world. His mother wore a gown of midnight blue against the sea of pastels; Adra and Seldrid were also dressed in grim colors. A speck of grim reality in this farce, and Killian steered Dareena toward them, all the nobility dropping into low bows and curtsies as Her Royal Majesty, Queen Kitaryia Falorn was announced.

Dareena gave small nods as she passed them, sweat beading on the heavy paint she wore on her face. Northerners rarely tolerated the heat of Serlania well, though it hadn't seemed to trouble Lydia much. Killian's jaw tightened when he noticed a tiny smear in the healer tattoo painted on Dareena's forehead. This act wouldn't work much longer, but Lydia was already on the *Kairense* and on her way across the strait.

His mother curtsied as they stopped before her. "Your Grace."

"Lady Anne," Dareena said in a soft voice. "Your gardens are lovely."

"I confess, it feels bittersweet to stand in the beauty of nature when so much of Mudamora has fallen to blight," his mother replied. "I pray to the Six that Mudamora will soon be restored through Lady Malahi's efforts."

"I pray for this as well."

Hacken approached, Ria again on his arm. Yet it was not his brother whom Killian found his attention drawn to, but the High Lady Rowenes. Her typically sand-hued complexion was blanched of color, almost waxy in texture, and sweat dampened her blond hair. She wore a high-necked and long-sleeved red brocade gown, and her underarms were also darkened with sweat. As she curtsied, Ria swayed, appearing ready to topple over at any moment. Her voice was tight as she murmured, "Your Grace."

Dareena's eyes narrowed behind Lydia's spectacles. "Are you well, Ria?"

"Too much wine last night, I'm afraid." Ria gave a tight smile, her knuckles white where she clutched Hacken's elbow. "I now pay for the indulgence."

The musicians under one of the pavilions began to play and the servants to circulate with trays of chilled lemonade. Killian took one for Dareena, who sipped at it while beads of sweat cut marks through her face paint. Ria also took one, though she gulped it down.

"I received word that Malahi successfully boarded a ship and is journeying across the strait to Revat." Hacken extracted his arm from Ria's grip, smoothing the damp and crumpled fabric.

"My messenger will arrive in advance of her," Adra said. "My uncle will ensure that she receives the full support of the library guild. If there is an answer to be had, they will find it."

Killian barely heard him. Ria had started to tremble, and his mark was screaming warning. "Ria, have you—"

Ria abruptly groaned, then doubled over, vomiting up the contents of her stomach onto the green grass.

"My gods!" Hacken leapt back, scowling at the splatters on his shoes.

Killian ignored the mess, catching hold of Ria as she started to sway and lowering her to the ground.

"I don't feel well." Tears ran down her face. "What's wrong with me?"

"It's blight poisoning."

Killian turned his head to see Lena staring at the High Lady with a grim expression that confirmed his fears.

"No," Ria moaned, the musicians falling silent.

"Check for the black marks," Gwen said. "Lena was covered with them."

Ria was clawing at the neck of her dress, and Dareena dropped to her knees and sliced a knife down the row of buttons on the back. Ria ripped down the high neckline, and a hiss escaped Killian's lips at the black veins of blight running up her chest toward her neck.

Helene Torrington had stepped closer, and her scream was loud and shrill. "It's the lemonade!"

Glass shattered all around as those holding glasses of lemonade cast them aside in alarm. Killian snatched a glass off a tray and held it to the light, seeing none of the telltale black in the pale yellow.

"She was ill before she drank the lemonade!" Seldrid shouted. "Calm yourselves!"

His brother might as well have spit into the wind for all the good it did. Several of the women had fainted, and many of the men were forcing themselves to vomit, the stench ripe on the air as Ria clawed at her skin.

"Help me!" she moaned. "Kitaryia, help me!"

"You must help her!" Hacken shouted at Dareena. "You've done it before. You must save my betrothed's life!"

Dareena blew out a slow breath, then removed Lydia's spectacles and wiped her sleeve over the healer tattoo, smearing black across her forehead. "I can't help you, Ria. No one here can."

Ria let out a shrill scream, then curled up on the grass in a shaking ball even as the veins of black crept up her neck.

"Where is she?" Hacken reached over as though to shake Dareena, then seemed to think better of it. "Where is Kitaryia?"

"On her way to Revat," Killian answered. "She's hunting for a way to save us all."

Hacken's eyes widened in shock, but he swiftly recovered. "The queen should be in Mudamora. Her mark is needed here, and Ria's life is forfeit because you supported Kitaryia running off on a fool's errand."

His brother's words were impassioned and angry, but Killian's skin was crawling with the sense that all was not as it seemed.

Then Ria started screaming.

She clawed at her skin, vomit running down her chin. Killian grabbed hold of her, his mother stroking the High Lady's hair and whispering soothing words that he doubted Ria could hear. The veins of blight had reached her face, and sickness pooled in Killian's stomach as it started to streak across Ria's bloodshot eyes.

She shuddered and choked, then drew in one last shuddering breath.

And then fell still.

"Mother," Killian said softly as she closed Ria's eyelids. "Please back away."

She didn't argue as Adra caught hold of her arm and pulled her to the far side of the pavilion. Adra had a long, curved knife in one hand, but her brown skin was slick with tears.

Killian drew his sword.

"Take off her head now," Hacken ordered. "Don't let her rise!"

"No." Killian's fingers flexed on his sword. "I want to see what he has to say."

The Corruptor.

"He'll see us through her eyes!"

Dareena flipped the knife she was holding over and over in her hand, a nervous tic, but the green eyes that met Killian's were steady as she shook her head. *Wait.*

Killian stared down at the woman who'd caused him so much trouble in Rotahn. Who cared nothing for life and everything for power. Ria had earned death a hundred times over. Yet he still pitied her.

The black veins in Ria's skin abruptly faded. Not disappeared, but sank deeper into her flesh. Then her eyes snapped open.

Several women screamed, but Killian ignored them as Ria slowly looked up at him, expression sly. "What do you want?" His tone was flat. "Or did you kill her just to prove that none of us are out of your reach."

A slow smile worked its way onto Ria's face, but the voice that poured from her lips was like nails on a chalkboard, clawing at Killian's ears. "How does it feel to fail yet again, Marked Ones?"

Ria's eyes skipped around the watching nobles. "If those in the very presence of two of Tremon's marked cannot feel safe, then what hope has anyone else? Your faith in the Six is misplaced. They chose their champions, yet north and south, faithful followers of the Six fall beneath the heels of those who serve at my pleasure." Ria's mouth smiled again, and this time it was all white teeth. "It is not too late to switch sides. Some among you already have."

The nobility looked between each other, but then Adra shoved through them. She hurled a lamp at the back of Ria's head, and the oil instantly ignited. "Be silent!" Adra screamed. "Your words are as much poison as the blight, and we will not hear them."

Hair and dress aflame, Ria rose and turned to Adra, the stink of burning flesh greasy and choking. "You are weak, daughter of Gamdesh. Feeble in the face of what is to come, and all that you love will turn to rot and ruin. My champions will ensure it."

Adra stood her ground, expression defiant. "My faith in the Six is strong. As is my faith in the marked."

The Corrupter laughed, and Killian swung his sword.

Ria's burning head rolled across the green lawn, but the laugh still seemed to echo in the air as an icy breeze blew down from the north. The stink of rot mixed with the stench of burnt hair, and the pavilion canvas threatened to tear loose.

No one spoke, but the eyes of the nobility went from Ria's burning head to Hacken.

"Rufina did this!" he snapped. "She poisoned Ria."

"Why, of all the individuals present, would she kill Ria?" Helene's voice trembled as she asked the question everyone was thinking. "Everyone knows Ria did as you told her to do, Hacken. If Rufina wanted to kill anyone, why wasn't it you?"

"Perhaps the poison was meant for me." He took a step back. "I was with her last night. Perhaps she drank the cup intended for me."

"Or perhaps you decided she was no longer the asset you needed and you got rid of her!" Helene shouted. "Got her out of the way because you had your eyes set on the queen. Except Kitaryia isn't even here! She's chasing legends in Revat when she is needed here!"

"Be very careful, Helene," Hacken growled. "I do not take kindly to being accused of murder."

"Everyone is thinking it—though it's a shame I'm the only one with the balls to say it." Helene lifted her skirts and strode toward the manor, the rest of the nobility giving Hacken dark looks before following her.

Killian didn't move from where he stood, his eyes focused on Ria's burning head. Then he met Hacken's gaze.

Hacken looked away first. "I'll make arrangements for the body."

Killian watched him stride away, only Dareena, his mother, Seldrid, and Adra remaining.

"You also think Hacken killed Ria, don't you." His brother removed his coat and put it around Adra's shoulders. "Dosed her with blight to make it look like Rufina's doing in order to get her out of the way so that he can marry Lydia."

At his words, their mother's face crumpled, and Adra moved to put her arms around her.

"I don't think Hacken did it." Wiping Ria's blood off his sword, Killian sheathed it and turned his face into the icy wind, remembering the shock on his brother's face when Dareena's identity was revealed. "For once in his life, I think Hacken is the scapegoat."

"You believe we have a traitor in our midst?" Seldrid's brown eyes narrowed. "The Seventh said, *It is not too late to switch sides. Some among you already have.*"

"Maybe. Or maybe it's a blighter. Lydia is the only one who'd be able to see their true nature, and she's not here."

"I agree with Killian." Dareena retrieved a discarded napkin and wiped the paint from her face. "This scene was meant to undermine the Marked. Every one of those High Lords and Ladies has come away from this moment with their faith in both the Six and the Marked much reduced. Lydia should have been here to save Ria. Killian and I should have averted the threat."

"If marrying Lydia was Hacken's goal, it didn't serve his purpose to make her look bad," Killian said. "None of this served his purpose. If he wanted to break off his betrothal to Ria, he could have done it with words. All this has achieved is undermining his control."

"And now Mudamora stands without any form of leadership." Adra still stood with her arm around Killian's mother. "Like it or not, everyone followed Hacken, which allowed unity. This leaves us fractured and weaker. The enemy is clever."

"Rufina has someone inside my house." His mother spoke for the first time, her voice full of fury. "Blighter or traitor, it matters not. Someone in my house is trying to harm my family."

"I'll look into who has been around Ria over the last day," Seldrid said. "See if I can narrow down a suspect."

Dareena had moved a few steps away from the group, her eyes fixed north. "Does the blight smell stronger to you?"

No sooner had she spoken did wings flap overhead, a hawk landing and shifting into human form.

"Niotin," Dareena said. "What news?"

"None good," the shifter said. "The blight breached our barriers and got into the river Esden. The water downstream has gone foul, perhaps all the way to the sea. The towns and villages along its banks are full of civilians dying by the hundreds. They're rising as blighters."

Killian's hands turned to ice, because the Esden flowed south. Which meant all of this was happening behind the lines of the Mudamorian army holding back Rufina's masses of blighters.

"Why did you bring this message to us?" Dareena demanded. "Fly! Warn the army of attack from the rear!"

"Because it's not them the blighters are marching to attack." Niotin appeared ready to be sick. "They're coming south. They're coming here!"

And with nearly every Mudamorian soldier at the front lines of Rufina's army, there was no way to stop them.

65

TERIANA

As her crew made ready to leave Imresh's small harbor, Teriana climbed to the quarterdeck and gripped the rail with her free hand, the other still holding tight to her letter.

"I'd ask if you're all right, but the answer to that is clear enough," her aunt said, then reached over to pat her arm.

Teriana jerked away from her aunt, then cringed at her reaction. "I'm sorry. I'm so sorry, I just need to get away. I need to be on the open sea. It feels like I can't breathe, Auntie."

"I see that."

"This letter grants our people freedom." She swallowed the lump in her throat. "We need to bring it to Celendrial to give to the Senate. Get our people on ships. Retrieve Mum."

"All right. Better put it somewhere safe, then."

Her aunt stepped away from her, giving orders to the crew to raise sails. Within moments, the *Quincense* was flying away from the coast toward the ocean path that would take the ship back east. Teriana retreated into the captain's quarters, which smelled of cedar and orange blossoms. It smelled like home, and fresh tears poured down her face because this was not how a homecoming should feel. Going to her mother's desk, she unlatched the top drawer, carefully putting the letter into wax wrapping before storing it away.

Teriana turned to stare out the window, watching the coast of the Southern Continent slowly fade into the distance and then out of sight.

Yet the agony in her heart remained.

There weren't words in any language that came close to capturing the magnitude of her grief. Her rage. Her guilt. For the combination was a beast without name, consuming her and dragging her down.

The cruelty of Marcus's deception made her want to weep, but in truth it was her own actions that made her want to drop to her knees and scream. She'd fallen in love with her best friend's murderer. Had given him every part of herself, body and soul, and never once suspected the depths of his villainy. How had she not known? How had she not sensed that he'd been the one to hold Lydia under? To put her down a drain like refuse, lost and unrecoverable for all of time? How had she failed Lydia so badly?

"Oh gods," she whispered, her knees failing her. The impact of striking the deck rattled her spine.

Her braids swung back and forth, gold and blue enamel flashing in her periphery as the gift Marcus had given her brushed her cheek.

A shriek exploded from her lips, and Teriana wrenched at the hair ornament, trying to tear it from her braid. Pain lanced across her scalp, but the braid was woven tight and would not give. A moan emerged from her throat as she scrambled up, digging through the desk for a knife and finding nothing.

Bolting across the room, Teriana slammed open the door. "A knife. A knife, I need a knife!" She snatched one off Polin's belt and sliced it across her braid in a wild swipe. The tip scored her cheek, but Teriana didn't feel the pain as she sprinted to the rail and threw the length of her braid over the edge, watching the glimmer of gold disappear beneath the sea.

Lowering herself to the deck, she pressed her shoulders to the polished wood and wept.

"Teriana?" Bait's voice filled her ears. "Listen, I—"

"Leave me alone," she choked out. "I've heard enough for one day."

"What did you do, Bait?" her aunt demanded. "I knew you were looking for trouble when you sneaked off the ship while we unloaded the injured. What did you say?"

"I went looking for her," Bait snapped. "I found her in the *bath* with him. It's true what everyone is saying about her. It's worse than everyone says, because I heard Teriana tell him she loved him. So I told her that she was in love with the bastard who killed Lydia."

"Stop." Teriana squeezed her head between her hands, struggling to breathe. "Please, no more."

"You idiot!" her aunt shouted. "I don't suppose in your jealous little rampage that you bothered to tell her that Lydia survived?"

The sob exiting her throat caught, and Teriana gagged on it. "What?"

"Lydia survived." Yedda knelt next to her, gripping her shoulders. "The hot spring flowed into a xenthier stem that brought her to Mudaire."

Lydia was alive. A shuddering sob tore from her lips, because this couldn't be real. Had to be a cruel trick.

Yedda's grin widened, her eyes shifting from stormy seas of anger to bright blue in an instant. "But what should truly ease your heart is that the gods saw fit to unite her with Killian Calorian."

"She's with Killian?" Teriana sucked in a mouthful of air, the ship and sky and clouds all spinning. "Marcus didn't kill her?"

"No. Not only that, she has been marked by Hegeria and she's—"

"Kitaryia Falorn," Teriana said quietly. "Valerius knew. As did Mum." She eyed her aunt for a long moment. "As did you, I think."

Yedda gave a slow nod, her grey braids swaying. "I knew. But for all our efforts to keep her secret, I think it no coincidence that Lucius Cassius targeted her. As impossible as it might seem, the Corrupter's reach has extended to the East, using Celendor's might to aid in his bid for power. Blight spreads from the North to create armies of the dead even as the legions claim the South. Mark my words, Teriana, this is a battle for the liberty of Reath, and the Six are losing. *We* are losing."

Just like in the vision Magnius had given her so long ago. A great battlefield filled with the dead and the dying, banners of the Twelve Houses soaked in blood and crushed beneath the feet of an army with the burning circle of the Seven emblazoned on the flags they carried. A fleet of ships, the golden Cel dragon flying high in the rigging, open seas ahead of them, darkness behind. Magnius's voice whispered up from her memories, *Enemies approach from both sides.*

"It's my fault," she said. "I opened the door."

"This is a war between gods, and you are a mortal caught up in the battle," her aunt said. "There are no coincidences. Madoria silenced every one of our people who Cassius tried to question yet left your mind and voice free. She chose you as her champion, and I believe she set the stage to give you what you needed to fight."

"The last thing I've done was fight." There was no keeping the bitterness from her voice. "All I did was—"

Yedda gave her a shake. "You know the enemy better than *anyone* on this side of the Endless Seas, girl. You know how they function. How they fight. How they *think*. That is the most crucial component to knowing how to defeat them."

How to defeat *Marcus*.

"All I have learned," Teriana said, "is that beating him is impossible. Not even Kaira, who is marked by Tremon, was able to stop him. He took Emrant with a trick, Auntie. He's every bit as good at war as the Senate claims, and the forces that he can bring to bear on the rest of Gamdesh are something never seen in recorded history. If finding a way to defeat him was Madoria's goal for me, I have failed."

No one spoke, her crew all standing motionless as her words sank in. The only sounds were the snap of the sails in the wind and the slap of the sea against the hull, her hopelessness infecting her crew.

Then drops of water misted her face, and something clattered on the deck. Teriana's breath caught at the glimmer of gold and enamel, the tiny replica of the *Quincense* sitting in a puddle of seawater before her.

Madoria yet has faith in you, Magnius's voice echoed in her thoughts as she reached out to pick up the hair ornament. *You must have faith in yourself, and remember, you don't stand alone.*

The world around Teriana fell away and was replaced with a vision of the galley of the *Kairense*, where Bait sat across a table from Lydia and Killian. Lydia's spectacles didn't fit her properly, her hair was dirty and her clothes worn, but her friend was smiling. Laughing. Magnius's memory, she realized, the demigod having watched through a porthole. For a heartbeat, Teriana's grief fell away, but as the vision faded, reality returned.

"Why didn't Marcus tell me he didn't kill her?" she asked Magnius as she stared at the ornament on the palm of her hand. "Why was he content for me to believe she was dead?"

It was Bait who answered. "Because he didn't know."

All eyes turned to him, and her friend shifted uncomfortably.

"And how might you be knowing that?" Yedda asked, her voice cool. "Had a bit of an exchange of words with the legatus, did you? Thought to twist the knife a little deeper?"

"I . . ." Bait shook his head. "I wanted him to know he doesn't always win. That he didn't defeat Lydia."

Teriana closed her eyes, fear swimming in her stomach because while Marcus had said he had no interest in conquering more territory, she now wondered how much of that sentiment had been to appease her. To keep her. To control her. "So he knows about the xenthier path to Mudaire?"

"Yeah," Bait replied. "He does."

"You jealous fool of a boy." Yedda's brown skin flushed with anger. "If it were possible to drown you, I would."

Fear gripped Teriana as she understood the true reach the Empire now had over Reath. *East must not meet the West.* And yet it had.

Closing her hand around the ornament, Teriana climbed to her feet. "We sail with all haste to Celendrial to retrieve our people, but then we sail to Mudamora to warn them that the dragon has the key to their back door."

Bait stiffened, then said, "I think you know him better than you realize. Those are the exact words he used."

Right now, it didn't feel like she knew Marcus at all.

Teriana squared her shoulders, then shouted, "Full sail! The Cel legions move quickly, so the *Quincense* needs wings if we are to stop them!"

66

LYDIA

"My gods," Lydia breathed. "I've never seen anything like it."

Captain Vane sailed the *Kairense* through the gap in the sea wall, the expanse of Revat spreading out beyond and overlooked by seven towers so tall, she'd seen them when they were still hours away from the coast. Revat's sprawl of buildings rivaled even Celendrial in scope, and the capital of Celendrial had upward of a million people living in it. A backward glance revealed the sea walls were adorned with intricate carvings of sea creatures that resembled Magnius and his brethren, as well as depictions of the Six, instantly recognizable even though their visages were Gamdeshian. It had been the same in Anukastre, the Six appearing differently to different people, only Madoria and Gespurn remaining the same.

She'd learned more about the gods and their marked during the crossing, the *Kairense*'s diver, Fara, warming up to her enough that she'd explained Madoria's mark, which was only given to the Maarin. She also told Lydia that Gespurn only ever marked the giants of Eoten Isle, their number always twelve and their duty to maintain the doldrums that made the Endless Seas impassable.

"East must not meet West," Fara said, then shook her head. "Yet for all our efforts, the East is here now."

Lydia pulled herself from memory as she took in the dozens of docks in the harbor. Ships of every nation filled the spaces, the sailors working upon them of every nationality in the West. The biggest trading port in the world, Lydia had been told, the people a tapestry of this half of Reath.

Darkness was beginning to settle when she and Sonia finally disembarked, but though the harbor market was busy with trade beneath countless strings of light, Lydia immediately sensed a nervous tension to the city. As though something bad had happened and worse was expected to come.

"Marked One," said the small Gamdeshian woman waiting for them on the dock after she bowed low. "We've been expecting you. Your companions are waiting for you in the Great Library, but the Sultan sends his regrets that he cannot attend, for he is occupied with a matter of some importance."

"Has something happened?" Lydia asked, glad that Malahi and Agrippa had not revealed to anyone her change of station.

The woman's shoulders curved in a slump, expression grim. "Emrant has fallen to the Cel invaders."

"What?" demanded Sonia. "How is that possible? Where was Kaira?"

"General Kaira, may the Six protect her, was in Emrant when it happened," the woman answered. "It is a tale of duplicity that I'll leave her to tell."

Sonia's steps faltered. "She's here?"

The woman nodded. "Marshaling our forces to march on the Cel." She motioned for them to follow her into the city, three large men with heavy cudgels forming up around them as a guard. "The leader of the Cel army not only refuses to leave Emrant; he has demanded the abdication of the Sultan on the threat of war. The Cel have expanded their ranks through the xenthier stem they now control. It is said that they plan to take Revat by force, but until Astara returns, we have no fresh news."

"Astara is marked by Lern," Sonia murmured to Lydia. "She has long been Kaira's eyes in the sky, and she travels quickly."

Except so did the legions.

Lydia clenched her teeth. The timing between the Cel threat growing and Rufina marching farther south wasn't a coincidence. The Corrupter seemed intent on trapping the twin hearts of the West, Revat and Serlania, between two hosts, and if she and Malahi didn't find answers, defeat wasn't a possibility.

It was an inevitability.

"Will the Sultan evacuate Revat?" she asked, her heart aching because where could they go? Where on Reath was safe?

"It is not yet known what Sultan Kalin will do," the woman replied. "Our lives are in the hands of the Six."

"In Kaira's hands," Sonia murmured, meeting Lydia's gaze. "If the Cel march on Revat, she'll make them bleed every step of the way."

Of that, Lydia had no doubt, but as her eyes skipped around the god towers to land on the shiny black spire of the Seventh, she couldn't help but fear it wouldn't be enough.

* * *

The library was at the heart of the city, and if not for the fact it was encircled by the god towers, it might well have been the tallest building Lydia had ever seen. Made of richly hued sandstone, it seemed to shimmer in the glow of the moonlit night, a spire of knowledge that gleamed like a beacon of enlightenment—and answers—in the darkness. Expected as they were, no one moved to interfere as they passed through the ornate entrance. Like the sea wall, it was adorned with carvings of the Six but also of scenes reminiscent of the drawings in Treatise, causing Lydia to believe they were famous individuals with god marks. Teak doors swung open ahead, welcoming them into a circular space with a stone floor marked with constellations. The scent of paper and ink mixed with the perfume of incense inspired a sense of reverence within Lydia, especially as Sonia nudged her elbow and motioned up.

And *up*.

The tower was hollow, each level a ring reached by a circular staircase that wound round and round, all the way up to the glass-domed ceiling far above.

"It's an observatory," Sonia said. "With devices formed of magnified glass that allow one to see stars that are invisible to the naked eye."

"Miraculous." Lydia turned in a circle, her eyes filling with endless shelves of books and scrolls on each level, what had to be hundreds of Gamdeshians scurrying among them or seated at tables, pouring over books and scrolls and documents.

"The Sultan has ordered the library guild to hunt for information under the guidance of the Lady Malahi after she arrived this morning," the woman said. "All have been working ceaselessly, for everyone understands that the fate of Reath rests on discovering a remedy for the blight."

"I thought I heard your voice."

Lydia looked up to see Agrippa hanging over the railing on the eighth level. He waved at her. "Quit gaping; there's something we need you to look at."

With Sonia on her heels, Lydia took the steps two at a time with no care for propriety—she'd heard the excitement in Agrippa's voice.

Please be an answer, she prayed. *Please let there be hope.*

Reaching the eighth level, she didn't waste time on a greeting. "Tell me you found something."

"We did," he said. "Not a single scholar in this place can read the language, but Lydia, it has the same drawings as the caves in Anukastre."

Excitement flooded her, and she followed Agrippa through the stacks. He was visibly tired, his eyes bloodshot and marred by shadows, his normally clean-shaven skin stubbled, and his clothes and fingers were stained with ink. Yet for all of that, Agrippa moved with energy and purpose.

"Do you wish to seek out Kaira?" Lydia asked Sonia. "I think I'll be safe enough on my own, and it would be good to have information from the source."

Sonia's dark eyes went wide. "I . . . Well, I'm not certain that's the best plan. We . . . Well, I didn't say the kindest of things when last I saw her."

Lydia knew that the two had once been lovers but that Kaira's commitment to Gamdesh had driven a wedge between them. "Then perhaps it's time to make amends."

While you still can.

Sonia gave a tight nod and retreated back down the stairs. Lydia followed Agrippa inside the room, finding Malahi seated at a table surrounded by stacks of books and radiating a frenetic energy despite being as exhausted as her husband. "Thank the gods, you're here," Malahi said at the sight of her. "I was worried you wouldn't be able to get away. Where's Killian?"

"He's with Dareena, helping her maintain her disguise for as long as possible. Sonia is with me in his stead."

"He'll hate that." Malahi turned to stare at the piles of books, eyes blank, then she shook her head. "Sorry, there's so much to tell you, I don't know where to start."

"Agrippa mentioned you'd found a book with illustrations."

"Yes. Yes, that would be a good choice, though we are at a loss as to what it says. Here." Rising, Malahi tugged Lydia over to a table on which a glass case sat, then handed her a pair of white cotton gloves. "It's ancient and very, very frail. Their best guess is that it's at least a thousand years old."

Lydia donned the gloves, then carefully lifted the case. The book was made of cracked leather edged with silver, holes from a binding marring the cover though the bindings themselves were lost to time. As gently as she could, Lydia opened the volume, cringing as bits of parchment and ink flaked away. Turning the pages, Lydia held her breath as she took in images so very similar to what they'd seen in Anukastre, though these hadn't weathered the years nearly as well. Pages were cracked, some missing, the ink faded so badly that she motioned for someone to hold up better light despite her fear of flame being anywhere near the precious volume. But whereas the cave paintings had been nothing but images, this book had text.

And Lydia could read it.

"I know this language," she murmured. "In my linguistic studies, I focused on dead languages of the East. This language is called Arcanith, and it is what the modern form of Cel is derived from, though the ability to read one does not help much with reading the other."

"I knew it!" Agrippa shouted, causing Lydia to jump, the corner of the page she was holding crumbling.

He winced. "Sorry. I can't read it, but I *knew* I'd seen something like this in the library at Lescendor. That library is mostly military history and commentary, but Marcus was always digging out obscure books to read in his free time. We tried to jump him . . . Well, never mind that, but this was the language of the book I took from him. I guarantee he knows what this says, and"—he glanced at the window—"in another few weeks we can ask him to do us the favor of translating while he lays siege to the city."

"You think they'll come, then?"

Agrippa shrugged. "The trouble with making threats is that you need to follow through on them. Marcus said if Sultan Kalin didn't surrender, he'd take Revat by force. The Sultan shows no interest in surrender."

Malahi gave a grim nod. "Kaira lost Emrant to the Cel without a fight. They tricked her, and last word is that they've doubled the size of their army using a path between the Empire and Emrant."

"He didn't trick her so much as put her in an impossible position," Agrippa said, shaking his head. "Kaira is Gamdesh's protector, and Marcus marched fifteen thousand legionnaires on Emrant, showing every sign that he intended to lay siege. Even if Kaira suspected his real target, she had no choice but to put everything she had into protecting the people." He sighed. "It's always easier to be the aggressor, because in the worst case, you retreat. When you're on the defense, there is nowhere to go that won't cost you everything."

"Better to pay with possessions than to pay with lives. Why isn't the Sultan evacuating Revat?" Lydia demanded, feeling once again as she had when Mudaire had been under threat by Rufina's host. Too easily she remembered Serrick's resistance to evacuation, and so many lives had been lost as a result.

"He has faith in Kaira." Malahi sat on a chair, shoulders slumped. "And he believes that evacuating will show a lack of confidence, not just in her, but in the Six."

"It's foolish," Lydia muttered. "But we have to leave the Cel problem to Gamdesh while we focus on our own enemies. This book suggests to me that we are on the right track."

"What does it say?" Malahi asked, the spark returning to her eye. "What do I need to do?"

"It's an account of a scholar who traveled here from the East," Lydia murmured as she read. "Some of it is illegible, but it appears he was from what is now northern Celendor. And he came by ship." She shook her head, leaving that piece of information for later consideration. "And by here, I don't mean Gamdesh. He was visiting a nation called . . ." She frowned. "I can't make it out, but he describes a land once lush but now turned to rot. It has to be Anukastre."

Falling silent, Lydia carefully flipped through the pages detailing his journey and meeting with the people. "He describes certain people as 'dirt thieves,' which is perhaps not a good translation, but I think he means corrupted tenders, because he discusses them as betrayers of the land. This picture"—she gestured to a human-shaped figure with black lines spreading out from its fingers into the ground—"is one he copied from the Anuk, and this is just like what I saw in Deadground. He says that the 'dirt thieves' steal the life from the land to feed themselves, for they no longer consume sustenance as would a human. What is left behind is the . . . absence of life. The blight."

"He's right," Malahi said. "There's nothing alive within it. Nothing I could make grow."

Lydia turned another page, then another, piecing together visible words though so many were faded to nothing. "The Anuk hunted down the 'dirt thieves' and killed them, but the blight remained and it continued to spread. Continued to consume. The 'growers' gathered to combat it, which they did. It worked, and the blight was vanquished. But there was a cost."

"What cost?" Agrippa demanded. "What happened to them?"

Lydia turned to the last page, which contained no drawings, only text, her stomach hollowing.

"What. Cost?" Agrippa repeated.

"The tenders died," she finally answered, noting that the text stopped midsentence, suggesting that there'd once been more pages but that they were lost. "Every last one of them."

67

TERIANA

Gespurn himself must have put the wind in their sails, for they reached the greater ocean path in a fraction of the time it would normally have taken. Magnius opened the whirlpool to the xenthier without having to be asked, seeming to be infected by the urgency consuming every member of her crew.

Teriana included.

The *Quincense* sailed around the familiar rocky peninsula, and the gleaming white sprawl of Celendrial revealed itself. The ship lowered its sails as they moved into the harbor, which was flanked on one side by the towering statue of a legionnaire holding a standard bearing the gleaming gold dragon and the other by the villa-encrusted hill where her enemy lurked. The water was murky as always, the river Savio dumping the waste of a million people into the sea, filling the air with the stink of humanity.

"I still dislike this plan," her aunt muttered from where she stood at the helm. "We'd be better off rowing to shore at night. Sneaking into the city and finding Valerius. It's always better to test the waters before you jump in."

"I know these waters," Teriana replied. "I need the citizens of Celendrial to know I'm here. It is the people with the right to vote who will hold Cassius to his word, so I can't risk any strategy that will allow him to keep the truth from them."

Though her voice was confident, Teriana's heart raced with fear as they drifted closer, the eyes of every sailor on every ship watching them. In the distance, she could make out the magister waving his arms, shouting at one of the ships to depart to make room for the *Quincense,* but it was the flashes of crimson and steel beyond that made her palms sweat. Legionnaires, and unless something had changed, they'd be Hostus's men.

"Still time to change your mind," Yedda said, and Teriana didn't fail to notice the beads of sweat on her aunt's brow, nor the way she bit nervously at her bottom lip. "Polin and a few of the others who are handy with a blade will go with you."

"No," Teriana said. "I'll go alone. If they want to hurt me, a handful of fighters isn't going to stop them."

A berth cleared for them, and Yedda guided the ship against the towering pier, the magistrate's men catching the lines her crew tossed out to them. As soon as the *Quincense* stilled, Teriana jumped onto the pier. "Thanks for making space," she said to the magistrate. "I have business with the Consul and Senate."

The man glanced uneasily over his shoulder, then said in passable Trader's Tongue, "Word was sent the moment your ship was spotted on the horizon. We've been expecting your arrival."

It made sense that someone, Marcus or Felix, had sent word through the xenthier that she was coming by way of ship, but his words still turned Teriana's hands to ice. Especially as a familiar figure sauntered down the pier toward her, sailors shoving each other to get out of his path.

"Teriana." Hostus pulled off his helmet to reveal a white-toothed grin. "We've been expecting you."

"Hostus." She did her best to keep her terror hidden, though judging from the gleam in the legatus's eye, she'd failed. "I'm sure you've been informed, but I've delivered on my half of the bargain with the Senate, and Proconsul Grypus signed an order authorizing the release of those of my people being held hostage."

"I *had* heard that." Hostus rocked on his heels. "Such tragic news that our dear proconsul met his end moments after signing that order. Choked on his own olives, which were found still wedged deep in his throat when his body was returned to us. Not just one olive, but three! His gluttony for the finer things finally got the better of him."

"So I heard," Teriana replied. "I wasn't there to witness it."

"Shame." Hostus sighed. "I'd have enjoyed a witness account." His eyes flicked past her to where her crew stood watching. "How does freedom feel? Does it taste as sweet as you anticipated or does the price it cost the West sour the flavor?"

No one answered, and he shrugged one armored shoulder. "Magistrate, see that the Maarin vessels are readied and waiting for the hostages' arrival. We'll be releasing them after Teriana meets with the Senate, and I doubt they'll care to linger."

"Yes, Legatus," the magistrate said, giving Teriana a look she couldn't parse before hurrying off to carry out the order.

"Let's walk, shall we?"

Hostus led her down the pier, a dozen of his men forming up around them. Teriana had spent many long hours in this market, and while the civilians had always given the legionnaires who patrolled them the respect of space, it was nothing like how they reacted to Hostus's presence. Whispers of his name raced ahead of them, merchants moving into their shops, the click of locking doors like ominous music. Those without doors hurried into alleys and side streets, parents hauling children bodily by the arm to give the group wide berth.

"You're popular," she muttered, and Hostus laughed.

"I've had to put my foot down on certain behavior. The fools mistakenly believed that their opinions were relevant and needed to be schooled on their true value to the Empire."

Sickness pooled in Teriana's stomach. All her certainty had been predicated on the strength of Celendrial's civilian population and the power they held over their government. She'd not thought anyone had the power to quell the voice of the people, but it seemed she'd underestimated Hostus.

As they moved out of the market and into the city itself, the behavior was the same, but worse, for there were signs of violence everywhere. Bloodstains on the streets, smashed storefronts, and twice, still forms sprawled in alleys. There were legion patrols everywhere, and Teriana was struck by how different the energy was between these legionnaires and those she was used to. The Twenty-Ninth were *mean*, as though Hostus's cruelty had infected all of them, and there was no missing the delight they took in bullying the populace.

It made her sick, but more than that, Teriana didn't understand why Cassius would support the Twenty-Ninth's behavior. Even if he pulled the same trick as before and had the Twenty-Ninth vote for him, he still needed some Cel citizens to vote for him in order to remain consul. Typically those running for election put extreme effort and a large amount of gold into currying favor with the populace. This was exactly the opposite.

The political buildings loomed ahead. With no hesitation, Hostus led her into the Curia. The hallways, with their towering ceilings, were cool after the heat of the sun. She remembered the last time she'd been here, how she'd been relegated to sitting outside while Marcus addressed the Senate. This time, the doors swung open for her, and her ears filled with the chatter of the hundreds of men inside.

She clutched Grypus's letter tightly, her palms growing clammy as the most powerful men in the East all ceased their discussions, eyes fixing on her. Teriana was struck by how similar they all looked, dressed in the same white tunics and togas, all with golden Cel skin, the vast majority of them possessed of light eyes and hair.

Only a handful showed any sign that they had anything but patrician blood a dozen generations back. One such was an attractive man in his midtwenties with dark brown hair and skin just a shade darker than those around him. He rested an elbow on the railing before him, hazel eyes watching her with both interest and intelligence. Marcus's father and Lydia's father sat to either side of him, the latter giving her a tight smile. She was looking forward to telling Valerius that Lydia was still alive.

"Teriana, you are a sight for sore eyes!"

Cassius's voice snapped her attention to the center of the room, where the consul was rising from what could only be described as a throne. He trotted down the stairs with surprising agility, gripping her shoulders and kissing both her cheeks.

Struggling not to cringe, she said, "Consul."

He gave a tight smile. "It's *Dictator* now, I'm afraid. A necessity given we are at war and in need of stability."

Oh gods.

That was why he cared more about controlling the population than winning their favor for an election. There wouldn't *be* an election.

"War?" she managed to croak out.

"Unfortunately. The Gamdeshians are refusing to play nice, and the legatus requested more men." He lifted a page filled with Marcus's neat writing and waved it in the air. "Six legions, to be precise."

Thirty thousand men.

What had happened in the short period since she'd left Emrant in her wake that necessitated *thirty thousand* more men? Had Kaira attacked? Had the forces of the Southern Continent united to push out the invaders?

"It was fortunate that we'd already preemptively recalled a significant number of men to have at the ready, so they were able to deploy within hours of us receiving his request," Cassius said. "We thought it prudent to send our finest to ensure Marcus has all the resources he needs. Hard, experienced legions given he wasn't satisfied with your choice of the Fifty-First and sent them home. It seems he had some conflict with the Fifty-First's legatus, although that has only been fuel to the fires of young Austornic's ambition. He is keen to prove himself in other ways."

Oh gods.

"But never mind that," Cassius said. "You achieved what many thought impossible, my dear girl! Two impeccable pathways. If you were a path-hunter, you'd now be as wealthy as some of the men in this room, but gold was never your motivation. Let's make it formal, then? You have a document certifying the paths signed by the late Plotius Grypus?"

Teriana slowly lifted the hand holding the letter, her teeth clenching as Cassius plucked it from her fingers.

"Hardly necessary given the traffic these stems have already seen, but I do love the theater of you delivering the document yourself." He unfolded the paper, giving it a quick scan. "Makes it all so much more exciting."

"You're content, then?" she asked. Her emotions were running amok in her head, rendering her numb.

"Oh, I'm quite content," Cassius said. "Tiberius, for formality's sake, can you verify this is Grypus's writing?"

He handed the page to the young senator with the dark hair, who glanced at the page. "It is." He handed the page to Senator Domitius, who nodded, and Teriana thought she might vomit as the page slowly circulated to every man in the room before returning to Cassius. "Does anyone contest Grypus's statement that Teriana of the Maarin has fulfilled her agreement with the Senate, and with Legatus Marcus of the Thirty-Seventh Legion?"

She twitched at Marcus's name, her hand pressing against the pocket that held the hair ornament he'd given her.

No one spoke, likely because now that Cassius was dictator, their opinion didn't matter.

"Excellent!" Cassius clapped his hands together sharply. "Then we will see to liberating our guests. Valerius, I trust that you will arrange for Tesya of the Maarin to be returned to her ship?"

Lydia's father gave a slight nod.

"Wonderful. If you'll all excuse me, I would like to give this moment my personal attention." Catching hold of Teriana's elbow, Cassius escorted her out of the chamber but mercifully let go of her arm once they were out of sight.

They walked in silence through the Curia's halls, Hostus's men walking before and behind them, though the legatus himself was nowhere to be seen. That made Teriana uneasy because he wasn't the sort to accept giving up prisoners.

"I confess, we expected to see you sooner," Cassius said. "And via xenthier, not ship. Though the gossip courtesy of the Ninth and the Fifty-First is that you left the legions in rather a hurry after some form of altercation with Marcus. Is that true?"

"You know it is." She swallowed hard. "Why didn't you tell me it was him who did it?"

Cassius made a soft clucking noise of dismay. "The truth came out, did it? It has a habit of doing so." He was quiet as they exited the building, then said, "There is the obvious reason, I suppose. I knew you wouldn't forgive the transgression, and I needed your love affair intact to serve as proper motivation. It was truly a remarkable campaign that he conducted on your behalf—I've no doubt that young officers at Lescendor will be studying it a hundred years from now with the same enthusiasm they are now."

"And the less obvious reason?" Which she suspected was the *real* reason.

Cassius chuckled softly. "You are finally learning to play the game, Teriana. As a reward, I'll tell you the truth. Marcus is a dangerous man, and if I'd been the one to reveal his crime, he'd have blamed me. All the grief and bitterness and rage that burned in his heart would have been directed at me. Whereas by allowing the truth of his crimes to come to your ears as it did, he blames only himself."

"Clever."

Marcus's voice filled her head. *If he hurts you, I will take this army back across the seas and burn him alive.*

Cassius inclined his head.

Teriana wanted to know if Marcus had informed him about the xenthier stem under Celendrial that led to Mudaire. Wanted to know if he'd told Cassius that Lydia was still alive. But on the very faint hope that Marcus had withheld that information to protect himself from Cassius discovering his failure, Teriana wouldn't be the one to inform him. Instead, she asked, "Why did he send the Fifty-First back?"

"Depends on who you ask. We have Marcus's letter. Austornic's verbal account. Reports from the Ninth. And of course, other information from less . . . *official* channels, which is always interesting for it brings to light that which the other sources chose to leave out. The sum of all these pieces of information allows me to glean the whole of the truth, and it strikes me that Austornic was sent back to Celendrial because of his role in Marcus's conflict with *you*." Cassius crossed his arms behind his back, the heat of the sun not seeming to touch him. "But it's just as well—we've already redeployed young Austornic, whose capacity for risk was much increased after being sent home with his tail between his legs. There is always something of a rivalry between legion commanders. A desire to outdo each other that serves as greater motivation than anything I, or the Senate, could possibly achieve."

Guilt pooled in Teriana's stomach. "You gave him to Hostus, didn't you. Nic wants to prove he can survive Hostus better than Marcus did."

"Hardly. Hostus would spoil their enthusiasm." Cassius gave her a small smile. "I'm afraid I can't say more about strategy, my dear. You are soon to be joining our adversaries, and while I have nothing but the utmost confidence in Marcus's ability to bring Gamdesh to heel, I don't wish to make his campaign more difficult."

The weight of his comment threatened to drag Teriana to her knees, but she forced herself to keep walking.

"This isn't the direction of the prison," she said, taking note of their surroundings as they walked past an excavation that hadn't been there the last time she was in Celendrial. "You said my people would be freed immediately. Why aren't you taking me to them?"

"I am," he answered. "They were removed from the prison the day after you left for Bardeen and have been kept in different accommodations since."

It should have been welcome news, but Teriana's skin crawled at the revelation. "Where? And why?"

"A property I own," Cassius said. "As for why . . . Hostus is a vile creature, and often shortsighted."

"So you moved them to protect them?" She snorted. "I struggle to believe that."

"You were my leverage against Marcus, your people my leverage against you." Cassius nodded at a group of Twenty-Ninth that saluted him as they passed. "But they were only leverage if they were alive, and Hostus's nature put their longevity in danger."

Again, the knowledge that her people had not been suffering under Hostus and his men should have been a relief, but every instinct in Teriana's body screamed that she was missing something. That, much like there had been an obvious reason and a *real* reason for withholding the truth of what Marcus had done to Lydia, the obvious reason Cassius had just given her for protecting the welfare of her people was not his actual motivation.

"Here we are," Cassius said, gesturing to a large structure of the sort that held many small apartments rented by those who could not afford to own property. Older men in civilian garb but bearing gladiuses patrolled the perimeter, most certainly retired legionnaires Cassius had hired privately.

One of them unlocked the entrance, and Cassius said, "Go in, my dear. Tell your people they have been liberated. This is your moment, and I'll not steal your thunder."

Sucking in a steadying breath, Teriana stepped inside, fully expecting to be struck with the stink of decaying corpses because this was all a cruel trick.

Instead, she was greeted with the scent of gardenias from the enormous bouquet sitting on a table in the foyer. Past the open doors was a large courtyard from which both the tinkling of a fountain and laughter emanated. Teriana moved through the building, stepping out into the courtyard to find a gathering of her people, all hale, healthy, and well fed, each of them dressed in new clothes cut in Maarin style.

No one noticed her for a time, which allowed her to watch them. It seemed impossible that these were the same people who had stared out at her from behind bars in the prison, but they were.

"Teriana!" one woman gasped, recognizing her. "My gods, it's you!"

Taking a halting step forward, Teriana cleared her throat. "I have fulfilled my contract with the Senate. You are all free. Your ships are in the harbor, waiting for you to board, and then you may sail—" She broke off, having been about to say *to safety*, except that the West was no longer the sanctuary it had once been. "Wherever you wish to go."

For a long moment, no one answered, then her cousin Elyanna's husband asked, "The Empire now has land-based paths between East and West?"

"Yes." She had to tear the word from her throat.

"Do you know their plans?"

Teriana coughed to clear her throat. "My understanding is that they are now at war with Gamdesh."

Her people exchanged weighted glances, and Teriana bit the insides of her cheeks. Not once had she envisioned this moment, for she'd refused to allow herself the indulgence of considering how they might react. Even if she had, this wouldn't have been what her mind would have come up with. It wasn't that she wanted cheers or accolades or even gratitude, but she'd been certain they'd at least be *gods-damned happy* to be free of the Cel. "I suggest you move quickly," she said. "Lest they change their mind."

No one moved.

Anger boiled in her chest, and she snapped, "A high price has been paid for your freedom. Don't squander it."

"Where is it we should go?" Elyanna's husband asked. "For it seems we have not been freed from Cel control, as they now rule all of Reath."

"Not yet they don't," she retorted. "Get on your ships."

Turning on her heels, she left the building to find Cassius waiting for her outside. "It's so quiet," he said. "I expected shouts of 'liberty!' Were they overwhelmed with the unexpected euphoria of their newfound freedom?"

She didn't answer him, only sat on a curb, watching as her people trickled out of the building.

"Congratulations!" Cassius declared to each new group that emerged. "Liberty!"

None of them responded, only gave her glances containing a mix of emotions before starting their trek down to the harbor where the ships waited.

"That was anticlimactic," Cassius said once they were gone. "I'd rather anticipated that they'd be cheering the name of their liberator."

"No, you didn't."

He gave a soft laugh. "That's true, I didn't. But you did, didn't you, Teriana?"

Not cheering, no, but . . .

"Gratitude would have validated your actions," Cassius said. "Instead, you are left questioning whether you made the right choice. Perhaps even fighting the growing certainty that you have erred."

"I hate you," she whispered.

"Hate me? Why? Because I didn't leave them to languish in Hostus's care so that they would cry out your name as *liberator* when you delivered them from the dungeons? Is that what you would have preferred?" Cassius shook his head. "I had not believed you so vainglorious, Teriana."

A tear trickled down her cheek.

"That is the nature of humanity, you know," he said. "When people are put into the worst circumstances, very few of them can think beyond their own suffering and their desire to escape it, no matter the consequences. Whereas when they are treated well and live without fear, they have the privilege of imagining themselves as strong enough to endure the worst to prevent those same consequences. Most are not, but we are all guilty of seeing ourselves as altruistic warriors who will suffer for the sake of being in the right."

She wiped away the tear, but it was replaced by another.

"Every one of them owes you their lives. Yet right now, every one of them is blaming you for the burden you've rested on their shoulders." Cassius smiled. "Congratulations on your freedom, Teriana. I hope you will use it well."

Without another word, the Dictator of Celendor strolled down the street, disappearing around the corner.

Burying her face in her hands, Teriana wept.

68

MARCUS

He stood on the fortress ramparts, staring out over a sea of men standing in organized ranks. Nine legions. Over forty-five thousand trained legionnaires, all experienced. All hardened by combat in nearly every province of the East.

All his to command.

Felix and Zimo stood with him, both men silent.

"These stems are our lifeline to the Empire," he said to Zimo, whose legion would remain. "At all costs, the Thirty-First will keep the Emrant, Imresh, and the Arinoquian stems secure, understood?"

"Yes, sir," Zimo answered, watching Astara circle overhead. "Though in truth, you're the one who has the fight ahead of you. Kaira is in Revat marshaling all of Gamdesh's forces. Her numbers are significant. But there is also the force she left behind to watch us."

"I've read the reports."

"It's too early to move on Revat." Felix crossed his arms. "Even with this many men, we put ourselves at incredible risk having our supply chain extended across such a long stretch of land. We should entrench. Secure the support from those living in the region. Establish solid trade arrangements between merchants on both sides of the Endless Seas. Do things the way we always do rather than by *force.* Force means lives lost. Force means starving civilians who hate us and try to kill us whenever our backs are turned. Cassius would have us turn Gamdesh into another Bardeen, into another Chersome, and you seem content to do it."

For days, Marcus had felt numb. The towering black walls that had formed in his mind held back emotions he did not care to feel. Yet Felix's words reached across the walls, drawing up fear and guilt and doubt, and threatened to unleash them.

Marcus's heart started to race, thundering in his chest like he was fighting for his very life. Felix wasn't wrong. Doing this put the lives of all the men arrayed before him in danger, whereas if they moved more slowly—

A stab of pain lanced through his skull, and the voice snarled, *Revat is a threat that needs to be destroyed!*

"The risk is too great," he muttered. "The cost is too high. Better to wait."

Glory does not come to those who wait.

"I don't care about glory."

What about vengeance against the one who destroyed everything that mattered to you?

The words scraped through his head like claws, and Marcus pressed his fingers to his temples. It felt as though the voice was punishing him for arguing. Which was madness given that the only voice inside his head was his own.

"Neither the Sultan nor Kaira will allow us the opportunity to entrench," he finally said, aware that the others were watching him with furrowed brows. "Already Kaira is gathering resources with the intent to attack. I offered them peace and they chose war, so war it will be. But on our terms."

Time is of the essence.

Marcus rubbed at his temples, struggling to understand the urgency burning his skull, but thinking about it only brought more pain. "Every hour we delay allows them to grow their armies. To rebuild their fleet. To secure more allies. We can't afford to wait."

Felix scowled. "Their greatest ally is at war. Mudamora is beset with blight and a pestilence that is killing them by the thousands. How long until that spreads over the narrow strait and into Gamdesh? Seems to me wise to see how it progresses before we venture farther north."

Gamdesh is distracted. The voice was like thunder inside his skull, and Marcus asked, "Why? To give Mudamora time to solve their problems so that we will be facing down *two* armies when we finally grow the balls to take on Revat? No."

"It doesn't matter what I say, does it?" Felix snapped. "You're pissed off about Teriana, and despite the fact you reaped what you sowed with her, you're going to make everyone around you pay."

She brought you nothing but suffering, the voice whispered. *You did everything she asked of you and then spit in your face for something that wasn't your fault.*

"It *was* my fault," he told the voice, and though he could see Felix frowning and speaking, all Marcus heard was a drone of noise as pain shot through his skull. He tasted blood, and wiped at his nose, his hand coming away crimson.

"It is what it is, Felix." Zimo's voice cut through the drone. "Cassius wants this fight. The Senate wants this fight. We either do what they want or hang for treason while someone who follows orders picks up the reins. Every single one of the legati that Cassius sent is twenty plus years deep into service, and any resistance they ever had to the Empire's methods has long been beaten out of them. Drusus's Eleventh were supposed to be retiring this year, and now they find themselves *here.* He's not going to do anything that jeopardizes his standing with the Senate. We either do what they want or lay down and die."

"Fuck Drusus. He's a lazy old bastard," Felix snapped. "I'm not suggesting that we don't follow orders—I'm suggesting that we do so in a way that ensures the least risk."

Marcus didn't hear how Zimo responded, because the voice shouted, *She told you all would be forgiven! That the past didn't matter! She lied!*

"Some things are unforgivable," Marcus mumbled, wiping away more blood with the edge of his cloak, the taste of copper thick on his tongue.

"Do you need Racker?"

You risked the lives of your men for her. The lives of your family. Your own life.

"My life doesn't matter."

Felix caught hold of his arm. "Marcus? Someone find Racker."

How were you supposed to know that Lydia mattered to her? She was nothing. No one.

Marcus recoiled from the statement, because Lydia had been everything to Teriana. And he deserved to hang for killing her. Should return to Celendrial and confess his crimes, accept his fate, and give Teriana that peace. "I need to go back."

The voice screamed at him in wordless rage, and Marcus staggered sideways under an onslaught of pain. It was like being attacked from within, the voice clawing the inside of his skull as punishment for defying it. Marcus caught hold of the battlements, feeling compelled to hold on to the certainty in him that this was the wrong path, but the voice was stronger. Under the onslaught of pain, his will to fight drowned beneath a flood of hurt and grief until he finally conceded.

The black walls reared again in his mind, everything that mattered once again locked behind them. And then there was no pain at all.

Marcus straightened, the ranks of men once again crystal clear before him and his thoughts sharp.

Felix had him by the arm. "I've sent for Racker."

"I don't need him. It was just a headache." Marcus pulled away. "You should be with the Forty-First, not standing around arguing with me. Zimo, Imresh and Emrant are yours."

Turning away, he strode to where Gibzen waited with the rest of his guard, his primus nodding at him approvingly. "Everything is in order, sir. Your horse is waiting below."

Marcus's cloak swirled on the draft rising the stairs as he circled down the steps and through the fortress that had been both salvation and damnation, mounting his golden mare the moment he reached the courtyard. She frisked beneath him, tossing her head, and he rested a hand on her neck. "Easy, easy. This will be a short journey."

Felix silently mounted his horse, then, surrounded by Gibzen and his men, they trotted through the gates and across the bridge. Above, Astara circled far out of reach of arrows, watching their every move.

Marcus gave the slightest nod, and from the ramparts of the fortress came the retort of a crossbow being deployed. Above him, a shrill shriek of pain broke the silence.

"Got her," Gibzen said, and a second later, the massive hawk struck the ground before them.

Its shape shivered and shuddered, then transformed into a nude woman with long dark hair. Her thigh was speared through by the bolt, and she was injured from the fall, but Astara still turned her head to look at him. Marcus met her gaze and said, "Have Racker see to her, and then lock her in irons. She's coming with us."

"Want her put to question?" Gibzen asked, his eyes bright. "She will know Kaira's plans."

"Kaira's plans won't matter in another day, but a hostage might," Marcus replied. "Tell Racker I want her alive, and give the order to march."

Signal flags waved and horns blew as he rode through the ranks to join the Thirty-Seventh. His men pivoted, then began to file down the road in neat rows, the crimson and gold banners flapping on the wind. Behind them, the other legions fell in to form a deadly serpent winding itself north.

69

TERIANA

Teriana went down to the beach where she'd once abandoned Lydia to her fate what seemed like a lifetime ago. There, she watched the two ships depart Celendrial's harbor, remaining on the burning sand until the blue sails disappeared into the horizon before notifying Magnius that she was going to Senator Valerius's villa. She planned to tell him about Lydia while she waited for her mother to be brought to Celendrial.

Teriana's legs burned as she climbed the Hill, and though the trees overhanging the pathways provided some respite from the heat, she still gave a sigh of relief as a servant admitted her into the villa.

It was short-lived, for Teriana was immediately assaulted by memories of this place. So much had happened within these walls, good and bad, and part of her wanted to run away rather than remember. Instead, she perched on a divan, sipping chilled lemon water while she waited for Lydia's father to appear, wondering if her mother would be with him. Wondering if her mother would even acknowledge her, or if Tesya's back would remain turned on her failure of a daughter.

The soft pat of sandals filled the air, and Lydia's father appeared. He said nothing as he sat across from her. Though his color was infinitely better than it had been before all of this began, shadows marred the skin beneath his eyes, his hair had grown more silver than gold, and a deep crease had formed between his brows. "Your mother will be here by nightfall."

Though she was desperate to be gone so that she might find Lydia, there was a part of Teriana that was relieved she didn't need to face her mum just yet.

"Am I safe to speak freely?" she asked. "I have news to tell you."

"I've sent all the servants out," he answered. "Only the guards remain, and they are outside."

Taking a mouthful of water to wet her dry tongue, Teriana said, "Lydia's alive."

Valerius straightened. "Pardon?"

"She's in the West. In Mudamora." Taking another drink, Teriana told him everything she knew about what had happened, including the identity of the perpetrator. The spark of joy that filled Appius's gaze as he realized the girl he'd raised from infancy was still alive was a light in the dark night of this day.

"He shoved her down the drain like refuse." Appius's hands fisted. "I visited those baths so many times searching for clues. Sat in that cursed pool myself and never once considered that possibility. Never once thought to investigate where the water went."

Teriana prayed that Cassius hadn't either. Prayed that the consul remained blissfully unaware that the underground spring beneath Celendrial led to a xenthier that crossed the world to Mudaire. The only mercy was knowing that the path was not viable by any of the Senate's standards, for Mudaire was abandoned and overrun by blight.

"I didn't know it was Marcus," she said quietly. "If I'd known . . ."

"I have never doubted your affection or your loyalty to Lydia," Valerius said. "She would not hold this against you, and neither will I."

"I intend to go to her after I leave Celendor." Teriana's eyes flicked to the window, noting that the sun was drifting lower. "If you wish me to bring her a message, I would be glad to do so."

"Only that I am sorry for the grief that I caused her. And for keeping the truth of her heritage a secret for as long as I did." His throat moved as he swallowed. "I hope she knows that there is a home here for her as long as I am among the living."

"Bait told me she's in love." Teriana wasn't sure if this was her story to tell but hoped that it would ease his sorrow. "With a young man named Killian Calorian. My family is close with his, and he's been my friend all my life. I don't think there is a better man on all of Reath, and Bait says he loves Lydia with all his heart." And because Appius was Cel through and through, she added, "His family is one of the most wealthy and powerful in Mudamora."

Relief flooded his eyes, and Appius gave a nod. "For her to have found a love match is what I should have always sought for her. I'm happy Lydia found it herself."

"Dominus," a male voice called from a distance. "A word?"

"Come."

One of the retired legionnaires who served in the Valerius house guard came into the room, inclining his head. "The Domina Cordelia is here. She requests an audience."

Teriana's mood soured immediately, for though hindsight painted Cordelia in a far better light, she still wanted nothing to do with Marcus's sister.

"Tell her I am unavailable," Appius said.

The guard coughed slightly, then said, "An audience with Teriana, Dominus."

Appius looked to her, and Teriana shrugged. "Might as well see what she has to say."

The guard disappeared, and Appius said, "I will let you speak to her alone. Cordelia may be more forthcoming if I'm absent. Call if you have need of me."

He exited the room, and a moment later, the guard appeared with Marcus's elder sister on his heels.

Teriana eyed the blond woman, finding her resemblance to Marcus uncanny. Not in appearance, though they did look alike, but in the eyes. In the blue-grey gaze that spoke of unfathomable depths and cunning intelligence, Cordelia scrutinizing her in exactly the same way Marcus had.

"Why are you here?" Teriana finally asked. "Because if it's to ask me to forgive him, you're wasting your breath."

"I don't expect you to forgive my brother." Cordelia smoothed her dress over her pregnant stomach, then sat. "In your position, I wouldn't. I have a particular dislike for being lied to or misled by those I trust. Though for what it's worth, he didn't know that Lydia Valerius was anything to you until I told him. Very little rattles Marcus, but that revelation undid him." Her brow furrowed. "I found strange comfort in his distress, for part of me had feared that the legions had destroyed all that was good in him. But his guilt and grief were palpable."

"Don't," Teriana whispered. "I know you're clever, Cordelia. I know how you think because you think just like him. If you try to manipulate me, this conversation is over."

The other woman's eyes narrowed, Cordelia watching her in silence for a long moment before she said, "There is something I want from you, and in exchange for it, I'll give you the answer to the question you can't stop asking yourself."

"Which question is that?"

"*Why.*" Cordelia sipped her lemon water, then set the glass aside. "That is the question you've been asking yourself, isn't it? Why Marcus agreed to personally assassinate a girl on the request of a senator."

Teriana said nothing, only waited.

"If it were a political assassination, it would have been approved by the Senate, not a single man, and Marcus certainly wouldn't have done it himself."

He'd have sent Quintus.

"Not for gold, because my brother cares little for material things."

The only thing he spent coin on was books. And a gift for her.

"Not for the killing itself, because he takes no pleasure in it."

Was repulsed by men who did.

"Cassius was obviously blackmailing him," Teriana muttered, wanting this to be over. Not wanting to hear anything that might temper the fury that burned in her heart for what Marcus had done. For the lies he had told. For the shattered heart he'd left in her chest. "Just like he blackmails and manipulates everyone. He told me that Cassius threatened to send the Thirty-Seventh somewhere awful, and that's why he agreed to push them to vote for him in the elections. I can only assume Lydia's murder was rolled into that agreement."

Cordelia shook her head. "No. But before I tell you the information that my brother was willing to murder an innocent girl to keep secret, I want you to agree to bring a message to him."

"Not a chance," Teriana said flatly. "Have a messenger deliver it. It's not as though Marcus is difficult to reach."

"Everything is read by Cassius's spies," Cordelia said. "And this is something I can't risk him discovering. Already Cassius is at the limits of his patience with our resistance to his regime, and we do not have the power to fight back if he chooses to end us. What I need to tell Marcus is something that wouldn't just see me found murdered in my bed, but my entire family."

The thought of being face-to-face with Marcus again made Teriana feel ill, but there was no denying her curiosity was piqued. "I can arrange to have it delivered."

Cordelia shook her head. "It must be you."

"Why?"

"Because he'll listen to you."

Teriana stood, pacing back and forth across the room, every part of her sick and tired of being the tool others used to manipulate him. "And just what is it that you wish me to convince him of?"

"To come back to Celendrial and remove Cassius from power."

Shock radiated through to her core, and Teriana rounded on Marcus's sister. "Pardon?"

"Lucius Cassius is a monster," Cordelia said. "A villain of the first order who cares only for power. Total, all-encompassing power. This moment has been a lifetime in the making for him, and Cassius will stop at nothing to see it through. Those who aid him rise high while those who stand against him find themselves in a shallow grave. He's extending service of existing legions. Increasing child tithes, including paying the poor to give up more sons to Lescendor, all of which is paid for by increased taxes on the provinces. Cassius needs to be stopped, and there is no one in the East who has the power to do so."

"But you think Marcus does? You think he has the ability to, what? Lead a coup against the Senate?"

"Not the Senate. Against an unlawful dictatorship." Cordelia leaned forward. "Do you know why Celendor is called an empire despite no one having sat on the throne for generations?" Not waiting for a response, she continued, "Because it never formally declared itself a republic. The last emperor and every one of his blood relatives were murdered, but instead of formally ending the autocracy, they left the seat open, the men behind the assassination jockeying among themselves to win the throne. The Senate rose only because no one had the strength to claim power. Long has it been accepted that no one would, but Cassius clearly believes otherwise. Today, dictator, but perhaps tomorrow, Emperor. And in that role, he has the power to dissolve the Senate, creating a position for himself with total control over Celendor and her provinces. How long until he's the Emperor of all of Reath?"

"If his dictatorship is unlawful, then why doesn't the Senate unite against him?" Teriana demanded.

"Because he controls the legions," Cordelia snapped. "Or at least, enough of them that no one dares whisper a word against him. Hostus and his men freely murder citizens in the streets for speaking their mind, and while Cassius has not yet been so bold as to murder another senator, it is only a matter of time. The only person with the military strength to remove him from power is my brother, but he won't do it, for the same reason he agreed to murder Lydia. So tell me, Teriana, will you agree to speak to him on my behalf or not?"

The stakes kept growing higher, and for all Teriana desired to extract herself from this game of power, every step she took found her more deeply entangled. And always, it felt like her role was to be the tool everyone else used to control Marcus.

Yet what would happen if she said no? If she refused, and Cassius's power grew to the point that no one could stop him? The point where he became a mortal version of the Corrupter himself? What did her feelings matter in the face of that? What did *she* matter in the face of such a nightmare? "Fine."

Cordelia blinked, but her surprise lasted only a heartbeat. "You swear on all that you hold dear that you'll use this information for the good of the people of Reath, not to enact revenge for your personal grievances?"

Teriana's imagination filled her mind's eye with the vision of Marcus holding Lydia under the water, then shoving her down the outtake drain like refuse. The same hands that had touched every part of her. Her heart screamed with the need to make him suffer in any way possible.

Except Reath had suffered enough for her selfishness.

"I won't swear that I'll never take revenge," Teriana finally said. "But I do swear that I won't use whatever you tell me to do so."

Cordelia was quiet for a long moment, her fingers toying with the embroidery on her dress, and it occurred to Teriana that the woman was afraid.

More than afraid.

Yet Cordelia only drew in a steadying breath and said, "Marcus is not my father's second-born son. He was first born, after me, and his real name is Gaius Domitius."

Of all the things that Teriana had thought Cordelia might say, this had not even been a glimmer of a thought, and the shock of it rendered her speechless.

"That might seem like such a small thing," Cordelia continued. "To switch one son for the other. Except there is no law in Celendor that is more sacrosanct than those regarding child-tithes to the legions. Families *must* give their second-born son, no matter the circumstances, the only exemption being if that boy dies before the age of seven. It is a law that prevents families from cherry-picking amongst their children, that prevents them from sending their weak son to the legions while keeping their strong son as heir."

Teriana felt the blood drain from her face, her lips parting in shock, and Cordelia gave a tight nod. "He was the sweetest boy, but he was always sick. Always collapsing because he couldn't breathe, and nothing any of the physicians tried helped him. My mother nearly died birthing my youngest sister, so another son was out of the question unless my father set her aside, which he refused to do. Our brother, by contrast, was as strong as a boy could be, unlikely to die from anything but his own stupidity. An imperfect heir was better than my father's fortune going to a distant cousin, so my parents resolved to fool the system. A journey abroad before *Marcus* departed for Lescendor, and lo and behold, the hot springs healed what the physicians could not, and Gaius came back strong and healthy."

Snatching up her water, Cordelia drained the glass. "There was no question in their minds that Lescendor would kill my brother immediately, but it was a sacrifice they were willing to make. The day my father took him to Lescendor, I followed, and I heard what my father said. 'There is honor in this, my son. I will not forget the sacrifice you've made for the sake of our family.'"

Teriana abruptly wished it was rum, not water, in her glass, because, gods, no parent should ever be so cruel.

"He *knew* they were sacrificing him, but . . . but he believed they were right to do it." A tear trickled down Cordelia's cheek. "In his mind, going to Lescendor would ensure that my mother, our sisters, and I would be protected when Father passed. And once it was done, once he was enrolled under our brother's name, he knew that the secret needed to be kept at all costs. For if the truth were ever to be discovered, he, our brother, and our father would be executed in the Forum. My mother would be stripped of everything, even the clothes on her back, as would I and our sisters if we were yet unwed."

Marcus's sister wiped away the tear. "I heard my parents speaking when they thought no one was listening. Their hopes that he'd die quickly so as not to suffer. Then their fear when he didn't, because as long as he lived, the crime hung over their heads. My father was furious when Marcus rose the ranks and won the title of legatus, because he was certain the scrutiny would be our family's damnation.

There was a time they even considered paying assassins to kill him, and I begged them to reconsider. Only my absolute certainty that, even under pain of torture, Marcus would never tell convinced my father to spare his life."

Teriana's lips parted, but no words came forth, as she had none that would convey her disgust for Marcus's parents. So instead she said, "Cassius found out?"

"Yes." Cordelia stared into her empty glass. "That's how he blackmailed Marcus. Made him choose between his family's lives and Lydia's. And that's why it will not be easy to convince him to turn on Cassius, because if Cassius goes down, so does the Domitius family. Never mind that my parents deserve to be punished for what they did. Never mind that my father deserves to *fucking* hang."

Teriana picked up the pitcher and refilled Cordelia's glass.

"It's not a matter of self-preservation," Cordelia continued. "Marcus doesn't value his own life enough for that to be a factor. But it's so seared into his heart and mind that he needs to protect our family that he'll allow Reath to burn beneath Cassius's rule just to spare our lives. We are not worth it, Teriana. On my life, we are not worth it, but it's who Marcus is. Willing to do the worst of things to protect those he loves. His family. The Thirty-Seventh." Blue-grey eyes fixed on her. "But above all, *you*."

Teriana's blood chilled, and seemingly of its own accord, her hand slipped into her pocket to grip the hair ornament.

"For you, he might do the right thing," Cordelia said. "For you, he might turn on Cassius."

Teriana tightened her grip, the golden mast of the ship digging into her palm as she squeezed, every part of her hating what Cordelia was asking even though she couldn't fault the woman's reasoning. "If Marcus does this," she said softly, "and Cassius reveals the truth, what will happen to him?"

Cordelia's chin trembled. "He'll hang."

Gods help her, she shouldn't care. Should welcome him being punished, given what he'd done, but Teriana's eyes still welled. "I'll try."

Reaching into the pocket of her dress, Cordelia extracted a rolled-up piece of paper, which she handed to Teriana. "I'll lend my voice to yours. You may read it if you like, but please make sure he receives it."

Drinking the water that Teriana had poured for her, Cordelia rose to her feet. "My husband, Tiberius Egnatius, stands against Cassius in all things. He would see Celendor become a true republic, with those in office voted for not just by Cel citizens but by those in the provinces as well. It is important to him that the provinces gain a voice, and he's willing to die to see it happen. I'm willing to die for it as well, for I share his vision, but I want my death to matter. I want it to achieve something good, something that makes Celendor better, for the sake of my children and all other children."

Teriana rose, Cordelia's letter feeling heavy in her hand.

"I'm sorry for what you have endured. Sorry for what you likely *will* endure," Marcus's sister said. "But I believe you know firsthand the realities of putting the few before the many. Examine those realities as you decide how you will approach my brother."

Cordelia started to walk away, but Teriana reached out to catch the woman's wrist. "You've held all these secrets for years. Why didn't you reveal them? You had the power to stop all of this almost before it began, but you *didn't*."

Silence stretched, and Teriana could feel the tension in the other woman's slender arm.

"A decision I regret every waking hour," Cordelia finally answered. "As to why . . . I suppose the answer is that I was a coward. I was too afraid of the consequences to take action, and now it is too late for my words to matter at all. My brother has flaws beyond counting, Teriana, but cowardice is not one of them." Pulling free from Teriana's grip, Marcus's sister left the room.

Moments later, Valerius appeared. His expression was grim. Refilling his glass, he paced back and forth across the room, visibly trying to master his anger. Finally, he said, "Cordelia has known from the beginning what happened to Lydia, hasn't she? Tiberius as well? Perhaps the whole Domitius family?"

"If you were eavesdropping, you know the answer."

"I wasn't. But since learning Marcus is Domitius's son, I've had my suspicions."

"Your suspicions are correct."

He sighed. "While I'd have hesitated to ever call any of them *friends*, for there is no such relationship between those of us on the Hill, we have long been allies. Knowing they kept the information from me to protect Marcus puts a tarnish on that alliance."

"You have it wrong." Teriana stared at the letter in her hands. "They kept it a secret to protect themselves."

"A fair point." Rubbing a hand over his face, Valerius added, "I wish I could sever my relationship with all of them, but my allies against Cassius are too few to lose even one, however imperfect they might be."

Imperfect was a generous word. More like setting villains against villains. Teriana was reminded of a conversation she'd had with Marcus about lesser evils. There was no one with the power to stand against Cassius who'd she'd describe as *good*, only less horrible. "What is the status of my mother?"

"She's being brought into the harbor on a fishing vessel," he answered. "I think it best you leave Celendrial as soon as possible, so we should head to the *Quincense* now."

* * *

Dusk was falling over the capital of the empire as they reached the harbor, the city strangely quiet.

"Where is everyone?" Teriana asked.

"There is a curfew," Valerius replied. "Civilians must be off the streets an hour after sunset. The Twenty-Ninth are supposed to imprison anyone they catch out, but more often they choose their own form of punishment. As I hold political office, I am exempt, but that doesn't mean it's safe."

They crossed paths with a legion patrol, the Twenty-Ninth giving them and their private guard, who were all retired legionnaires, a cool once-over. "Pretentious pricks," one of Valerius's guards said after they'd passed. "Acting like they're titans for intimidating civilians when everyone knows they're shit in a real battle. I'd trust a row of roaches in this city's defense over those pathetic excuses for men."

"Those *pathetic excuses for men* outnumber us, so keep your opinions to yourself," Valerius muttered.

"Yes, Senator." The guard's eyes roved the darkened city, hand resting on the hilt of his weapon.

They reached the harbor market, all the shops and stalls shuttered, but Teriana didn't miss how the guards watched the shadows between buildings, weapons now in hand. As though they anticipated an attack from every angle.

The guard who had spoken against the Twenty-Ninth murmured some commands, the phrasing and tone eerily familiar, and Teriana asked him, "You were a centurion, weren't you?"

His eyes didn't break from the shadows. "Yeah, Seventh Legion. What gave it away?"

"Experience," Teriana replied, her attention stolen by shadows climbing onto the end of the pier on which the *Quincense* was moored. One of the shadows broke away, moving toward the ship. The familiar stride made her heart hitch. "Mum."

Ignoring Valerius's warning, Teriana broke into a run, heading in the direction of her mother. She heard her aunt's voice shouting as she passed the *Quincense*, but all Teriana cared about was reaching her mother. All that mattered was once again being under Tesya's wing, every decision made for her so that there was no chance of making yet another catastrophic decision. "Mum!"

Tesya stopped in her tracks, face hidden by shadows, and for a heartbeat, Teriana thought that she'd turn her back. That she'd hold to everything she'd said about Teriana no longer being her daughter.

But then her mother's arms were around her.

"Oh, thank the gods you are safe," she sobbed, gripping Teriana so hard she could scarcely breathe. "They kept telling me you were alive, but I needed to see you with my own eyes."

Teriana buried her face in her mother's shoulder. "Mum, I've messed up. I don't know what to do."

"We'll fix it. I'll fix it," her mother whispered. "I have you back and everything will be made right again."

Relief nearly caused Teriana's knees to buckle beneath her, because she'd refused to allow herself to imagine her mother forgiving her. Their relationship had always been fraught, and while she'd once thought it was because her mother didn't understand her, Teriana now realized that it was because her mother understood all too well. All her life she'd wanted out from beneath her mother's control, wanted to strike out on her own, but now Teriana clung to her, desperate for the protection she'd always railed against.

"I missed you," she sobbed. "I needed you."

"I'm here now." Her mother hugged her tight. "I am so sorry for the things I said. I was afraid, and my fear made me say things I didn't mean. There is nothing and no one in the world I love as I love you, my little girl."

Vaguely, Teriana heard several thumps, and then shouts from behind her, but it was her aunt's scream that sent a surge of fear through her.

"Tesya, behind you!"

Her mother reacted in an instant, pushing Teriana away even as she whirled.

Directly into the downward strike of Hostus's blade.

Teriana screamed as he jerked the knife out of her mother's chest. "Mum!"

Her mother didn't answer, only collapsed into Teriana's arms.

Hostus bent down and wiped the blade across Teriana's shoulder.

"I told you there would be a reckoning, little girl," he said. "And I always make good."

Feet thundered down the pier behind them, Valerius's guards shouting, but Hostus was already moving. Teriana knew they'd never catch him in time.

If he got away, he'd get away with it forever.

Yanking free the knife belted at her waist, Teriana flung it through the air.

The blade flipped end over end, embedding in Hostus's skull. He stumbled two more steps, then fell facedown on the pier.

She stared at his still form, waiting for him to rise because a monster like Hostus could not be so easily vanquished. But the legatus of the Twenty-Ninth did not move as a pool of urine spread out around him.

Dead.

"Teriana."

Her mother's voice was weak, but her grip on Teriana's wrist was strong as she said, "I'm so sorry for what I said. I didn't mean it."

"Shhh. Don't talk. We'll get help."

Valerius and his centurion reached her right as Yedda knelt next to Teriana. Her aunt pulled up her mum's shirt to assess the injury. She immediately pressed her hands to the gaping wound, trying to stem the flow of blood, but the centurion sat back on his heels. "Say what you need to say." His voice was quiet. "But be quick."

"No, no, no," Teriana pleaded. "We'll get you help. Get you on the ship and find a healer."

"Teriana." Her mother lifted her hand to Teriana's face. "You must lead, my sweet girl. Now is the time. You must lead."

"Lead who?" Teriana sobbed. "No one would follow. It needs to be you. You need to live. You need to lead our people, not me."

"It has to be you." Her mother's hand dropped, her eyes focused on something beyond. "Madoria says it must be you."

"She's wrong! She was wrong to choose me! Every choice I make is a mistake!"

Her mother only smiled, and said, "I love you, my dearest girl."

Then she was gone.

70

MARCUS

They marched for less than half a day through the Gamdeshian countryside, those in the farms and villages they passed either fleeing or watching with worried eyes. A brave few turned to shouts and taunts, throwing rotten produce, but Marcus's men raised their shields and ignored them.

Marcus took action only against those who offered violence, those fools left trussed on the side of the road to watch as thousands of legionnaires passed them by.

"Why are you letting them live?" Gibzen asked. "It pisses off the men."

"Because," Marcus answered, "if we engage with them, it makes them feel strong. Like they might make a difference if they choose to fight. Like they'll be martyrs if they die on our blades. Whereas this proves the doubt rising in their hearts that they have any power at all."

At midday, the front ranks met up with the scouts, who stood beside a copse of trees that men were working to clear. Marcus reined his horse to where a xenthier stem jutted from the earth. While he'd been waiting to move on Emrant, his spies had not been idle, digging up information on other stems within Gamdesh. None crossed the world, but a goodly many crossed Gamdesh itself, and he had a map of the results.

"This is it," said Atrio. The spy sat slouched and glowering on his horse.

Marcus gave him a long look. "You have something to say?"

Atrio's jaw was tight, the spy making no effort to hide his anger. "If you wanted her caught, I could've done it. You didn't need to shoot her out of the sky like that."

"Racker said she'll mend well enough."

"What are you going to do with her?"

"That's information above your rank, Atrio," Gibzen snapped, but Marcus only raised one eyebrow.

"Grown soft on Astara, have we?"

Atrio squared his shoulders and didn't answer. An uncharacteristic display of defiance that Marcus didn't care for.

"She's a high-value hostage," Marcus finally said. "I'll try to exchange her for their surrender."

"They'll let her die before surrendering. You and I both know that."

"Then maybe we just stake her out for the crows!" Gibzen snarled. "See how watching her slowly die eats at their morale."

Marcus shot his primus a dark look. "I've no interest in making a martyr out of Astara. If Kaira won't deal, I'll send her back to Celendrial to be kept in comfort as the Empire's prisoner."

"She won't be able to shift if you send her East," Atrio muttered. "She'd rather die than not be able to fly."

"Then let's hope Kaira deals." Marcus waved a hand to dismiss him. "Go back to your duties."

As Atrio departed, Marcus rode closer to the stem. Apprehension bit at his stomach because he remembered all too well how his last journey through the xenthier had affected him.

Before nerves could get the better of him, he allowed the horse to lower her head to sniff the stem. Her nose brushed it, and his heart lurched as the world went white.

There was no sound.

No sight.

Only the sense of being in a void beyond comprehension, and then his mare was stumbling across dirt. She gave a squeal and then a vicious buck that rattled Marcus's spine before lowering her head to eat the thick grass beneath her hooves.

His men were coming through the xenthier, enraged that he had gone first. Marcus ignored them, his attention all for the seven towers in the distance that were so tall, they seemed to touch the clouds.

Revat.

71

LYDIA

Lydia sipped her tea, trying and failing to focus on the text before her.

Once upon a time, studying in a library like this had been her dream. To spend every waking hour bent over books with no purpose other than expanding her mind had seemed like an ideal life. But under these circumstances, her dream now felt like a nightmare.

Every librarian and apprentice was here, flipping through every possible book that might contain more information about combating the blight, but the going was slow. The relevant books were ancient and crumbling, requiring the readers to handle them with care, but the greater challenge was that the languages they were written in were archaic. Only the most learned of scholars could parse the words. Their assistants transcribed any potentially relevant information for Lydia or Malahi to read, and Lydia herself was responsible for translating the handful of books written in languages of the East.

They'd found more texts confirming what they'd learned about the tenders who'd destroyed the blight in Anukastre, but the only details given were that they succeeded.

At the cost of their own lives.

Malahi was handling that certainty with the grace Lydia had come to expect, but Agrippa was another matter. In all their travels, Lydia had never seen the ex-legionnaire truly lose his temper, but she'd learned that when he *did* lose it, it was with spectacular volume.

When Malahi said she'd sacrifice herself to save Mudamora, he'd refused to accept her decision and tried to bodily remove her from the library. The Gamdeshians had tried to restrain him, but in the end, it had taken Malahi trussing him up with the roots of an overgrown potted plant to stop him. What Malahi had said to him in that moment, Lydia didn't know, only that Agrippa had ceased trying to change her mind and descended into sullen acceptance that eventually drove Malahi to ask him to impart what he knew about the legions to Kaira. Given that he refused to leave Malahi unattended for more than a few minutes, those conversations had taken place in the library, so Lydia finally met the princess of Gamdesh she'd heard so much about.

It was like having a lioness enter the room, Kaira's long strides eating up the floor. She inclined her head to Lydia. "Well met, Marked One. Please do not rise. Your work is more important than formalities."

Lydia's eyes flicked to Sonia, who nodded in confirmation that Kaira knew her true identity and accession to the throne but was keeping the information close. "Well met, Your Highness."

Kaira's attention went to Agrippa. "Sonia tells me that you are Cel and are a deserter from the Thirty-Seventh legion, and your allegiance is now to Mudamora and your new wife, Lady Malahi Rowenes. Is this correct?"

"More or less."

Kaira stared at him.

"Yes, yes. That's correct." Agrippa rose. "I grew up with your adversary and used to be high up in his chain of command. I'm not of much use in the library, so Sonia thought you might like to pick my brain about how the legions do things. Marcus, specifically."

Kaira crossed her arms. "I'm listening."

"Before you begin," Lydia interjected, "I was hoping you might have information about the well being of Teriana of the Maarin. She—"

"Do not speak that traitor's name to me." Kaira's hands balled into fists, anger seething from her. "She betrayed us all and her name is anathema."

"You don't know her reasons." Lydia rose. "Teriana is no traitor!"

"I know her reasons better than anyone." Kaira spun away and went to the window. "She refused to accept her imprisoned people were casualties of war and instead sacrificed all of Gamdesh to free them. I do not envy those souls to know what their freedom cost."

Lydia narrowed her eyes. "They were freed?"

"So I'm told. Teriana and the *Quincense* sailed from Emrant to Celendrial, and the Cel released the five hundred Maarin prisoners. A small price for the Cel to pay in exchange for all of Gamdesh."

"Where is she?"

Kaira lifted a hand. "Who can say? She's not been seen since, and my spies report that she had a spat with the Cel commander before she left Emrant. Lovers' quarrel, no doubt, and I think it not long until we see her at his side again."

It was not the first time she'd heard this rumor, but it still made

Lydia feel sick. "You're wrong about her. Teriana is loyal. She might have risked much for her people, but every action will have been to save them. Not because . . . because . . ."

"Because she's in love with the enemy?" Kaira's lip curled in disgust. "After he took my fortress in Imresh, he put her in the royal apartments. Dressed her in *my* clothes. She is no prisoner, Lydia. She is the favored mistress of the Cel legatus—treated like a fucking queen with the spoils of his war."

Lydia rubbed her arms, Kaira's words having turned her skin cold. "I will hear Teriana's side of the story before I make any judgments."

"Then let us hope that it is you she comes to, and not me, because I will slit her gods-damned throat for what she has done."

"I'm done with this conversation." Lydia sat down on her chair, her whole body trembling. No good would come from arguing, because it seemed everyone had condemned Teriana and that her friend's side of the story mattered not.

"Right," Agrippa said. "So let's talk about Cel war machines. This is going to require some maths, so if you'd join me over here, Your Highness, I'll show you how they engineer siege weapons."

Lydia said nothing more, only forced herself to focus on the book before her as Agrippa spent the next hours filling Kaira's head with relevant information. An exercise repeated the next day. And the day after that.

"Quit pacing, Kaira," Agrippa groaned from where he was sprawled on a chair. "You're making me dizzy."

"He's up to something." Kaira continued to pace. "I can sense it."

"Marcus is undoubtedly up to something." Agrippa yawned. "I'd be far more shocked if he wasn't. But unless your magical god-marked senses can be more specific, knowing that isn't terribly helpful."

Kaira didn't reply, only continued to wear a path in the carpet she traversed, her brown eyes shadowed, and her cheeks hollowed. Despite the other woman's harsh words toward Teriana, Lydia still felt sympathy for her.

Not eating, Sonia had told Lydia. *Nor sleeping.* And it was no wonder, given the fate of an entire nation rested on her shoulders. She was the princess marked by Tremon, the woman who had won every battle, who had protected her people with an obsessiveness that had cost her nearly everything. Everyone, including her father, expected Kaira to deliver them from this.

Incredible pressure, which Kaira might have been able to withstand if not for the fact that she'd already lost to Marcus once. And that loss had rattled not only the faith everyone had in her, but the faith Kaira had in herself.

Loss of faith was exactly what the Corrupter wanted.

"He has researched you, Kaira." Agrippa's tired eyes sharpened as he watched the princess. "Probably spent hours reading reports on your character and history, so he knew that you'd always put civilians first, no matter the cost. But above all, he counted on you believing that he'd slaughter a city to get what he wanted. I understand why you'd believe that, because the Maarin have been filling your ears with tales of his villainy."

"He is a villain," Kaira snapped. "And Teriana will have told him personal details about me, using the knowledge she gained from the trust between our peoples."

Lydia stiffened, annoyed that Kaira continued to paint Teriana as the enemy.

"I'm sure he mined her for information and he's definitely no hero, but . . ." Agrippa frowned. "How do I explain this? Marcus loves to win, but he doesn't love the violence. There are commanders in the Empire who will quite literally massacre a city for pleasure, then eat the victims for the thrill of it. Marcus hunts the *best* victory. The one with the least collateral damage that results in the Senate preening over his genius. The moment I learned that he boxed you in, I could have told you that Emrant wasn't his goal. He always leaves a back door for civilians to escape. Always." Agrippa hesitated, then added, "But what else could you have done, not knowing anything about him? You had an army with the worst sort of reputation on the doorstep of a city filled with thousands of innocents, and to have left them undefended based on a gut feeling? Even if you'd been right, your people would never have forgiven you for it."

Kaira stopped in her tracks, pressing her fingers to her temples. "It feels like a thousand spiders dance across my skin. A threat is near, I know it."

"Astara's last report was that they are marshaling in Emrant," Sonia said quietly, crossing the room to touch Kaira's arm. Lydia knew they had spent some time alone together, her friend giving a secret smile whenever Kaira's name was mentioned but never saying a word about what had passed between them.

"Astara is overdue."

"Perhaps so. But it's weeks of hard marching between here and there. If they move, we'll have warning. What you need is rest."

Kaira leaned into Sonia for a long moment, then sighed and stepped away. "There is no time for rest. I need . . . I need to do something."

"The best advice I can give you is to convince the Sultan to negotiate," Agrippa said. "To pursue some form of agreement with the Empire even if it only buys you time."

"Time is what we need, Kaira." Malahi closed the book in front of her. "More than anything else, we need time. If we can defeat the blight and find a way to draw it out of the blighters that form Rufina's army, then Mudamora will be better positioned to aid Gamdesh when the Cel push north. I will not—"

Malahi broke off, her face flushing, then she said, "*Mudamora* will not leave Gamdesh to stand alone. But we cannot fight a double-sided war in earnest. We need time."

"Gamdesh has not conceded territory in generations," Kaira said quietly. "And my father is proud. I don't think he can be convinced to accept the loss of Emrant to Celendor, no matter the cost of trying to take it back. He . . . *I* can't fail him. That isn't an option."

Lydia's heart ached at the hollowness in the woman's voice, though Kaira remained composed.

"We are still gathering our forces," Kaira continued. "It will be another few weeks before we have all our soldiers at the ready, as well as the ships we need to attack the Cel from both sides. We will give you every resource at our disposal until then, and with luck, we'll both make our moves against our enemies."

Two of the librarians came into the antechamber at that moment, moving slowly, a wood-and-glass case suspended between them. An open book rested in the center of it. "We've found something of interest," one of them said. "But it is fragile beyond measure. To read it through even once might see its destruction."

They gently set the box on the table, and Lydia sucked in a sharp breath at the faded illustration on the open pages, which showed a man with both hands outstretched, one with black lines trailing out from it, the other with lines of silver. Lydia read from the page: "Blessed are the marked who use the power of the Six to serve the people, for they are salvation against the endless night delivered by the Seventh."

Malahi moved to sit at her elbow, everyone else crowding around to look at the open pages.

"It was in the back of the ancient collection room," one of the librarians said. "Judging from the dust, the case has not been removed in centuries."

Lydia pulled on the white cotton gloves she used to handle the old books and then took a deep breath and lifted the glass case. Only to cringe as the pages visibly deteriorated the moment fresh air struck the book, bits crumbling from the edges and the whole volume seeming to sag. "Write down everything I say," she said to one of the assistants. "We will not get a second chance at this."

The young woman sat across from her with blank pages, ink, and a pen, the latter of which she held at the ready as Lydia gingerly slid a flat piece of metal under the page to support it and carefully turned it over. The edges crumbled into dust, bits of paint flaking away, but as her eyes moved over the illustration of a woman touching ground laced with black veins, Lydia breathed, "I think we've found it, Malahi. These words . . . They are written by the marked featured in the illustrations. These are the words of those who fought the blight at some point."

Malahi pressed close to her as Lydia translated. "Killing the corrupted tenders stopped the progress of the blight, but it did nothing to remove it from the land, and it still killed anything it touched."

"That won't do," Malahi muttered. "Mudamora is overrun. It's not livable unless we strip the blight from the land."

"Agreed." Lydia turned the page. "Especially since this says that if you leave the blight, the corrupted tenders eventually regenerate and reform. Like ripping out the head of a weed but leaving the root, they come back. Nothing those combating them did, not fire nor blade, stopped them from coming back. Which likely means the one I thought I killed wasn't entirely dead."

"The Six have mercy," the assistant breathed, writing swiftly as she transcribed Lydia's words. "An abomination of Yara's gift."

Lydia tentatively turned the page, cringing as it crumbled.

"Does it say how they were destroyed?" Malahi leaned over the illustrations. "Wait . . . did they—"

"The Anuk tenders took control of the corrupted tenders," Lydia said quietly. "Then they reversed the flow of the blight. It killed them."

Malahi sat upright, and Lydia did not fail to notice how her eyes tracked to Agrippa, who sat with his head resting in his hands. "I see. Does it say anything more?"

"Only that they crumbled to dust," Lydia said softly. "And were celebrated as the saviors of the land. But there are more pages to read. There could be more to learn."

"I don't think there is." Malahi's eyes welled with tears. "I can't do it, Lydia. Destroying *one* of the corrupted tenders and their roots of blight will kill me, and you said there were eight. By now there could be more. Which means we need more tenders willing to die to save Reath, but how many are left? How do we find them in time? What if they won't do it?"

"What if I keep you alive?" Lydia removed her gloved hands from the book. "I can draw life from all around, Malahi. All I need to do is keep you strong and alive while you destroy the plant from within."

Malahi drew in a shaky breath. "Do you think it's possible? Why wouldn't the Anuk healers have done so, if it were? Those like Ceenah?"

"Because they weren't strong enough." Lydia leaned back in her chair. "Hegeria touched me twice. *Marked* me twice, and I can pull the untapped life from all across Reath to keep you alive. This is it. This has to be the solution."

They all stared at one another, the silence broken as a soldier ran into the room. "General!" he gasped. "You must come immediately!"

"What has happened?" Kaira demanded. "Has Astara returned? Are the Cel on the move?"

"Worse." There was fear in his eyes. "They're already here."

72

MARCUS

The sun beat relentlessly overhead with the sort of heat Marcus hadn't endured since he'd left Celendrial, made worse by the fact there was no shade for miles. Every tree had been cut down to use in the siege of Revat. He stood before the pavilion currently serving as his center of command, which sat on the low ridgeline overlooking the city and the coast beyond.

At least as large as Celendrial itself, Revat was circular and surrounded by hundred-foot walls that protected the city. Walls that reached out into the sea, the only access to the large harbor through a gap protected by a large harbor chain that controlled the flow of ships in and out. The wall itself had two gates, the heavy wooden doors reinforced with thick iron and blocked by heavy portcullises, the distance between them defended by murder holes in the reinforced overhang above. The battlements were thick with soldiers, the metal of their armor gleaming in the sunlight, though the only individuals moving were those manning the one remaining catapult. The rest of their defenses were ruins of wood and steel, shattered by his own war machines, which were bombarding the walls with merciless regularity. The walls were cracking beneath the onslaught, sections crumbling, and it wouldn't be much longer until he had enough breach points to risk moving the siege towers into position.

The only other opening was a half circle barred with thick bands of steel through which the river had once flowed. An ideal breach point if not for the vats of boiling oil hanging above it. His gaze shifted past the walls to the seven god towers that reached toward the sky, then to the smaller tower at their center. He did not know what that building held, for Astara had refused to give any information about the layout of the city, yet it held his attention all the same. Like a beacon in the darkest night.

One Marcus felt an overwhelming need to snuff out.

A loud *boom* filled the air, followed by cheers from the ranks of men. Marcus's eyes flicked to the last remaining catapult on Revat's walls in time to watch the ruined machine topple to the ground, dust rising in a cloud around it.

"Move our machines in thirty paces and then continue bombardment," he ordered, then retreated into the pavilion to take his place at the table, the guards closing the flaps behind him.

"You should have moved the fleet first," Drusus grumbled. A plate with a mountainful of food sat in front of him, for the big legatus of the Eleventh Legion had an equally large appetite. "My scouts report that the Gamdeshians are pouring out of the harbor in droves, and we don't have so much as a single ship to stop them."

He doesn't like being under your command, the voice whispered. *Doesn't like being told what to do by someone younger, and he will undermine you if he can.*

"I have read all your scouts' reports." Marcus set down the page he held and then moved on to the next. "The Gamdeshians are reacting as I anticipated, evacuating those who can't fight to the western coast. Unlike her father, Kaira isn't blinded by pride. She won't risk another Emrant."

"There could be soldiers hidden within those masses of civilians," the older legatus muttered. "You're asking to be attacked from the rear."

Marcus gave a slight shake of his head. "To make a rear attack worthwhile, they'd need to pull too many soldiers from the city walls, which would risk Revat falling to us while they organized the attempt. Kaira might command the military, but it is the Sultan who rules. It was he who demanded our withdrawal from Emrant because he could not stomach being the first ruler to lose territory in generations. Do you really think he's going to risk his capital? The jewel of the West?"

Drusus accepted a glass of wine from Amarin, then motioned for him to leave the bottle. "You give too much weight to the mindset of your opponents, Marcus. One of these days you're going to misjudge your enemy and the price will be high. I'd rather my men not do the paying."

This was the downside to requesting more legions: they came with their own legati. While the men were under Marcus's command, many of them chafed against taking orders from anyone other than the Senate. Especially men like Drusus, who'd been commanding the Eleventh Legion for longer than Marcus had been alive.

"Drusus, it's your scouts watching the coast," he replied. "If I'm wrong about Kaira's strategy, they'll be the ones to deliver that news, and we'll pivot to face the threat. At that juncture, you can feel free to point out that you were right and I was wrong."

But you're not wrong, the voice whispered.

"As it stands," Marcus continued, scanning yet another report, "I think we'll have more success pushing the soldiers on those walls to surrender if they aren't fighting to protect the lives of their families trapped within said walls."

"Hunger will accomplish the same results with less risk," Drusus said. "Soldiers hate the sound of crying babies."

Since they'd left Emrant, Marcus had felt nothing but cool confidence, but Drusus's words caused the towering black walls containing every unwanted sentiment to shudder, disgust seeping over their tops. He dropped the page he was reading on the table. "As it turns out, I also dislike the sound of babies wailing. So to spare myself the noise, I'll allow them to take all the children somewhere out of earshot."

Drusus's pale green eyes locked on his in a silent battle of wills, broken only when Rastag tripped through the front entrance of the pavilion, his spectacles flying to land in the dirt.

"What is wrong with you?" Drusus snapped. "Never have I met a man with less control over his own feet."

"Apologies, sir. I've need of a new set of spectacles—these have become quite scratched."

Marcus rose to his feet and retrieved his engineer's spectacles, then handed them back to him. "I'll request a lens maker in my next report," he said, then added, "There are more than a few men in the ranks who need new spectacles."

Drusus's smirk grew to reveal his many missing teeth, and Marcus's patience for the other legatus snapped. "I can think of no other reason that the old men of the Eleventh have such poor aim. Couldn't hit a piss pot if their lives depended on it."

"That can be a problem," Rastag agreed, not noticing the tension between Marcus and the older legatus. "I have a report on the dam you requested, sir. By necessity, we are redirecting some of the water where the river branches, else the reservoir will spill over."

Marcus looked down at the pages that Rastag was smoothing on the table. "I'll speak with you later, Drusus. You're dismissed."

The older man rose, posture stiff with anger as he left the tent.

Let him leave, the voice said. *He needed to be put in his place.*

Rastag was quiet as he set weights on the corner of the diagram, which showed the topography of the land surrounding Revat, with particular care shown to the small river that branched just south of their position. One arm flowed to the sea and the other through a fortified opening in the city walls, where it wove though Revat and emptied into the harbor.

But before the engineer could jump into an explanation of how he intended to make Marcus's plan work, Amarin said, "Drusus is worried about his men."

Marcus's eyes shot to his servant, more shocked than angry, because while Amarin often commented on strategy, he never did so in the company of others. "The Eleventh are fine."

"He obviously disagrees. And he isn't the only legatus under your command who feels the same way."

That made Marcus angry. "At what point did all of you collectively decide that I no longer know what I'm doing?"

Rastag shifted restlessly, eyes wide behind his spectacles as he looked between Amarin and Marcus.

"No one thinks that," Amarin replied. "The Eleventh was due to retire, but Cassius has used his powers as dictator to extend service indefinitely."

"I'm aware."

"The Eleventh had an easy post on Atlia. They all thought that, short of accident or illness, they'd survive service and get the chance to live lives as ordinary men. Instead, they were sent across the world to fight in a war where every last one of them is at risk of dying."

"Your point?" Marcus asked the question knowing full well what his servant's point was.

"Drusus is an ass, but he's just trying to keep his men alive. You of all people should be sympathetic to that."

"I am sympathetic, but you're defending a man who just suggested that we blockade everyone in Revat because starving babies cry and crying babies harm soldier morale. The easiest path to victory is not always the best one."

"Do you think that just because those babies are out of your earshot that they don't cry?" Amarin cleared the glasses from the table. "By all accounts, there are close to a million people who live in this city, and while they may be fleeing with their lives, that is all most of them will flee with. No homes. No income. No *food*. They suffer not because they deserve it, but because men in power want more power, and while the numbers who die in the coming days, months, and years might never make it into your official casualty count, that doesn't make them any less dead."

"Watch yourself!" Gibzen snarled from the corner, and Marcus started, having forgotten his primus was even there. "You show respect for your betters."

"You are not my better, you sick creature," Amarin said softly, and Marcus tensed at the threat in his voice.

Silence him.

Marcus shook away the thought, but it was followed in rapid succession by more of the same.

He's weak.

Talk like this sows dissention.

Put him in his place.

Rising, Marcus pointed to the front of his tent. "Get out, Amarin. And reconsider your place else you will find yourself returned to the Senate in exchange for someone who knows how to hold his tongue."

Amarin's dark eyes met his. "You have become everything the Empire wanted you to be. The perfect legionnaire. The perfect weapon for the villains on the Hill and the monster who rules them."

The walls in Marcus's mind trembled as if they were being bombarded with the same relentlessness as the walls of Revat.

You are who you were meant to be, the voice soothed, and the walls steadied. *Ever victorious.*

"Get out."

Gibzen caught hold of Amarin's tunic and bodily dragged him out of the tent, leaving Marcus alone with Rastag.

"Give me your report," Marcus said to his engineer. "Have you put the explosives into position?"

The engineer's eyes were on the front of the tent, expression strange. Clearing his throat, he said, "It won't take long to do, sir, but I chose to wait until we've fully cut off the flow of water. We've allowed a small stream of drinking water to continue to flow while the city evacuates."

His actions will cause delay, the voice warned. *There can be no delays. You must take the city now or the consequences will be dire.* The structure at the center of the city filled his mind's eye, beckoning him.

Marcus blinked away the vision. "Those weren't your orders, Rastag. I want the flow entirely cut off and the explosives set so that they understand the threat is real. If they are wise, they'll surrender."

"You don't really intend to flood the city, do you? Empty casks would suffice, would they not?"

"No, I do not intend to do so. But that doesn't mean I don't want the *option* to do so."

Rastag pursed his lips. "With respect, sir—"

"Show your respect by obeying," Marcus snapped. "I've no interest in a prolonged siege. I want Revat now, which means we break their will to resist *now.* I don't want so much as a trickle running toward that city, and I want them to see disaster sitting in the form of casks of black powder at the base of that dam. Let them understand what it means to defy the Empire."

Silence.

"I used to think being under your command was a privilege," Rastag finally said. "That, for all I built machines of war that were designed to kill, I was no villain, because you were always fighting to keep casualties low, especially for civilians. Yet now I question whether that was a delusion I told myself so that I could live with what I have done. Amarin is right: What have we left in our wake but conquered people? And those who are conquered *always* suffer, even if those who do the conquering cannot be bothered to see it."

The world swam around Marcus, his head again filling with a loud hammering that was probably his heartbeat but sounded like fists pounding against a wall. Like something trying to get out, the noise making his head hurt.

"This dam you have me building is a weapon of incredible destruction. If we release that much water on the city, it will explode through Revat like a monstrous battering ram, killing everyone in its path and leaving destruction, famine, and pestilence in its rotting wake," Rastag argued. "You claim you've no intention of using it. That it's a threat to motivate them to surrender without a fight. Yet whether you use it or not matters little, for in *your* wake there will be destruction, famine, and pestilence. You think you are better than the other legati, but you are not. You are merely a more insidious breed of villain."

Marcus stared at his engineer, then pressed his fingers to his temples, the war going on inside his head so painful he wanted to fall to his knees.

Because Rastag was right.

What choice do you have? the voice screamed at him. *If you don't do it, they'll execute you for treason and then send someone else to do the job.*

This is how it has to be.

Inevitable.

Inescapable.

Blood dripped from Marcus's nose, and he wiped at it, feeling his chest tighten, each breath more difficult than the last.

"May I go, sir?" Rastag asked, gathering up his pages.

Marcus nodded, the engineer passing Gibzen as he returned.

"You all right?"

Marcus wiped at his bleeding nose, trying to get air into his lungs. "They're right."

"They're not." Gibzen knelt before him, giving his shoulders a shake. "Amarin is running his mouth, and Rastag just doesn't have the nerve? Thinking like old Drusus and his boys that things would have looked good if we'd hunkered down in Arinoquia, but you know that was never a possibility. We're raised to fight, and if we don't, the Senate puts us down. Someone has to be food for the crows, and it's either us or them."

Colors were bleeding together, the hammering fists of an ocean full of guilt and grief and fear trying to tear down the walls. Trying to climb over. Trying to get out, even if they destroyed him. "There has to be another option."

"Yeah, there *was*." Gibzen's eyes were like voids, dragging Marcus into their depths. "You gave the Gamdeshians countless chances to do this peaceably, but they chose war. They chose it, Marcus, not you."

He'd given them no choice.

"If we'd stayed in Emrant, they'd only have gathered all their forces and all their allies' forces and attacked us. It was always going to be blood."

Gibzen wasn't wrong.

"Your duty is to the Thirty-Seventh. To ensuring we aren't the ones who do the bleeding, and this is how that happens."

Each of his primus's words steadied the walls in his mind, raising them high and strong.

They calmed the raging pulse in his veins, and the breath in his chest.

Until everything was quiet again, and Marcus said, "Change bombardment from the walls to the city itself. Let's end this."

73

KILLIAN

Killian galloped through the farmland north of Serlania, his apprehension growing with every pounding hoofbeat. The sun was low, a blood-red orb sinking into the horizon, casting a ruddy glow over the land. Surly's hooves struck the damp ground with dull, echoing thuds, but though the terrain here was fertile and lush, the wind was frigid.

No one spoke. Everyone was focused on guiding their mounts as the few hundred soldiers Killian and Dareena had recruited from the High Lords' personal guards raced to intercept the blighter horde racing toward the last enclave of the living left in Mudamora.

The fields grew dark and shadowy in the fading light, the rows of citrus trees lining them looking somehow monstrous backlit by the red sunset. The sweet scent of fruit hung thick in the air, but it was made cloying and rotten when combined with the smell of blight. In the distance, a flock of birds suddenly took flight, and his warhorse tensed, muscles coiled like springs, its ears flicking back and forth. "Easy," Killian muttered, patting Surly's black neck. "It's not the living we need to fear."

Adra reined her galloping horse near his. Her dark hair was woven into tight braids and she wore chainmail over her dark blue shirt. A short sword was belted at her waist, a bow hooked around her shoulder, and a stuffed quiver was attached to her saddle. No part of Killian wanted the mother of his nieces and nephews riding toward battle, but Kaira had trained Adra to fight and his sister-in-law was a better shot than almost anyone he knew.

"Something's bothering you," she said. "You keep looking over your shoulder. And don't deny it—I spent my whole childhood with Kaira. I know how to tell when your mark is warning you." When Killian didn't answer, she added, "I have also noted that Dareena's focus is entirely ahead."

"Don't try to put her off," Seldrid called from where he rode slightly behind. "She'll just keep asking until you give her what she wants."

Surly squealed and gave a buck beneath Killian, sensing his mounting tension. "It feels like I'm being watched," he finally admitted. "Like the greater threat is behind me, not before."

Adra straightened in her saddle. "In Serlania? Teradale? My children—"

Killian wiped sweat from his brow, hot beneath his armor. "Farther. I . . . I think the threat is to Lydia."

"Revat?" Adra's tone was terse. "The Cel are in Emrant, so it can't be them. Is it assassins?"

"I don't know." His voice was sharper than he'd intended it to be, but all his willpower was dedicated to not turning his horse around and racing the other direction to find a ship to take him to Revat so that he could protect Lydia from whatever threat lurked in wait.

Sonia is with her, he reminded himself for the hundredth time. *So are Agrippa and Kaira. And Lydia is not helpless.*

Yet despite his words, Killian again looked over his shoulder. Though he knew it was only the settling shadows of night, it felt like a tide of darkness was creeping up behind him.

Dareena called a pause to light lanterns and torches, and Niotin landed among them. The massive hawk shifted into a man, and without preamble, he said, "The blighters are less than an hour ahead of you. Several hundred by my count, most armed with shovels and picks, but a few have bows and proper weapons."

"Are there children with them?" Baird asked. Killian hadn't had much chance to speak to the giant. Only knew that Bercola had gone to secure passage to Eoten Isle and that however their conversation had gone, it had not turned to violence. For which he was grateful, because they would need Baird's strength in the moments to come.

Niotin shook his head. "If there were, they've fallen behind.

The blighters are sprinting as if Rufina herself cracks the whip at their heels." His eyes turned to the dark sky. "Which perhaps she does."

"Remember," Dareena shouted at the group of soldiers massed around them on sweating horses, "only blows to the head will bring them down for good, but taking off a leg will certainly slow them! Focus on incapacitating them, and then we'll end their misery when the battle is over. These are not Mudamorians any longer! They are flesh puppets animated by the Corrupter. Soldiers of Rufina's army. They are not countrymen and women, but minions of the Seventh. Show no *fucking* mercy!"

The wind howled past them as they pressed onward, carrying a whisper of something unseen but felt. The once-familiar landscape took on an unsettling quality, as if threats lurked in every shadowed grove and beneath every silent tree. The path ahead, barely visible, seemed to lead into the underworld itself. And in the darkness, the rhythm of hoofbeats felt like a heartbeat, quickening with fear and the anticipation of the unknown.

Yet Killian still looked over his shoulder, his skin crawling as he searched the horizon for the threat. *Please watch over her,* he prayed to the Six. Yet in his mind's eye, the dark tower of the Seventh loomed, burning eyes filled with laughter.

Overhead, Niotin gave a sharp call, and Dareena drew her horse to a stop. Killian rode up next to her, both of them silently staring out over the dark field, ears filling with the growing thunder of running human feet.

"We need light," Dareena muttered. "Killian, would you oblige."

Wrapping the head of an arrow with oil-soaked cloth, Killian lit it on a torch and then sent the arrow flying overhead. As it slowly descended, it illuminated the shadows of hundreds of running men and women.

"The Six have mercy," Adra breathed, but then drew her weapon. As did everyone around them.

Killian sent four more arrows into the sky in rapid succession to give them light to fight, and then he lowered the visor of his helmet.

"We are the last bastion between the Seventh and all the souls in Serlania," he roared. "In the name of the queen and the Six, do your duty!"

And then he charged.

The blighters did not run together like soldiers, but rather spread out haphazardly across the field. Their clothes were tattered, if they wore them at all. The people who'd risen were civilians. Farmers and fishermen. Innkeepers and barmaids. All people Killian was supposed to protect.

Which made them all people he'd failed.

Yet even as guilt pooled in his stomach, Killian looked over his shoulder one last time in the direction of Revat.

Then the blighters were upon them.

His sword sheared a man's head from his shoulders, sending it flying even as his warhorse thundered over a woman, crumpling her body beneath his hooves.

What happened next was a blur of butchery that Killian wished could be wiped from his mind. The destruction of those he was sworn to protect. As the blighters fell, Killian felt his faith in his mark fading. His faith in the Six, for it did not feel right that they stood by and watched this happen.

And it was not just his faith that faltered.

Those who fought at his side destroyed a part of their souls with each blighter they brought down. Tears slicked faces as the ground was soaked in blood, and though it was a moonless night, the world seemed to darken.

Driving his blade through an injured blighter's skull, Killian paused to suck in several breaths of air, every gasp tasting like the blight on the wind. It had been too easy. Far too gods-damned easy to win this fight, and from the way Dareena's horse was frisking beneath her, she felt the same way.

"Killian!"

Adra's voice cut the air, and he turned to see a blighter driving a pitchfork toward his chest.

He sliced the man's arm from his body with a hard blow, but the blighter kept coming. Reaching for Killian with torn and ragged nails.

Only for Adra's arrow to explode through the man's throat.

Spine severed, he dropped, but voids stared out of his eyes as he laughed. All the blighters still alive on the blood-soaked field laughed in chorus, the effect horrifying.

Then they fell silent, and the only laugh came from the darkness far above, carried on the wings of a deimos.

"Well fought, Lord Calorian," Rufina called from the sky. "Even from here, I can smell the stink of Mudamorian blood soaking into the soil, the opened bowels, the first sweet scents of rot. Tell me, does this smell like victory to you?"

Killian didn't answer, only nocked an arrow and listened to the sound of beating wings.

Before he could shoot, a jolt struck his core. A violent flood of impending doom that tore his eyes from the sky and drew them south. "Lydia."

Rufina's chuckle was soft and cruel as she soared overhead. "Well fought, well fought, indeed. How unfortunate that you won the wrong battle."

74

LYDIA

While Malahi had the information she needed to destroy the blight, Lydia had still not found the answers she sought.

Taking little time to sleep and eat, she carefully moved through the pages of the book, her eyes stinging with tears of frustration whenever one crumbled beneath her touch. Many were little more than fragments, no amount of staring at the pieces with a jeweler's lens revealing the words that had been written upon them, and she cursed the knowledge lost. Cursed those who'd had this book in their keeping for millennia and never bothered to transcribe it, because the information had value beyond measure.

"Lydia!" Sonia's boots made heavy thuds as she strode into the room. "We cannot afford to linger any longer. The Sultan has refused the terms offered by the Cel commander, refused to surrender the city. With the river dammed, it's only a matter of time until Revat runs out of fresh water. The Gamdeshians have stores to feed themselves for a long time, but no one anticipated they'd divert an entire river."

"I need another day," Lydia muttered, flinching as stone flung by one of the many Cel catapults struck a building nearby. "The answers are in here, I just need to get through all the pages."

"You have the information we need." There was a frantic edge to Sonia's voice. "Malahi knows how to destroy the blight, but she needs *you* to keep her alive. What more do you need to know that is worth this risk?"

"How to save them."

"What?"

"Those infected by the blight. The blighters." Lydia gave a rapid shake of her head. "Tens of thousands have fallen to the blight. I need to discover how to bring them back."

Silence stretched, and Lydia cringed as she felt her friend's horror press down upon her.

"That is why you are risking everything?" Sonia whispered. "In a quest to bring the dead back to life?"

Yes.

"Their deaths aren't natural. Their lives were stolen by the Corrupter's poison, so it's possible—"

Sonia's brown eyes were wide. "It's impossible! Forbidden! Death to any who try!"

"We don't know that for sure."

"Twice marked does not make you a god." Sonia's voice shook. "Do not risk our only chance on the hubris that you might achieve what even the Six dare not do."

Lifting her head, Lydia met her friend's eyes. "If it is not in these pages, I'll concede. But let me at least finish reading all that I can so that I know in my heart that I did all that I could."

Boom.

Sonia flinched as another building was struck, the deafening roar of its collapse making the entire library shake. "Bring it with you."

Lydia shook her head. "It's disintegrating beneath the touch of air, Sonia. It will be nothing but dust by the time we carry it to the ship. I have to do it here. And I'm close, I promise!"

"So are they!" Sonia kicked a chair, sending it toppling. "The Cel and Katamarcan ships are moving into position to blockade the harbor, and if that happens, we are *trapped*. Do you understand that? Trapped by the man who once tried to murder you, and exactly how do you think it's going to go when he finds you?"

"Agrippa said Marcus will leave a way out for civilians." Lydia squinted through the smears on her spectacles, assessing the illustration on a page, but the paint was flaking so badly her very breath disturbed it. "That he doesn't like to box the enemy in during sieges." She gave a sharp shake of her head, struggling to remember Agrippa's explanation.

"Which he did, but now the civilians are all gone! Only soldiers remain. Soldiers and *us*! The *Kairense* waits in the harbor, but they will not wait forever."

"The words in this book have the power to save thousands, and if

I try to pick it up and take it, the whole gods-damned thing is going to turn to dust in my hands. So just let me work!"

"Killian's going to kill me if I let you die."

At his name, Lydia's heart stuttered, but she forced away the emotions in her chest.

Sonia sat on the stool across from her, hands gripping the table so hard her knuckles turned white. "You're risking every living Mudamorian to save the dead. Perhaps every living person on Reath. This is not the decision of a queen, Lydia."

"I never asked to be queen." A tear trickled down her cheek. "I can't sacrifice those we've lost to the blight without trying to win them back, Sonia. I can't."

The door to the room exploded inward, and Lydia spun in her chair to find Kaira striding toward her.

"What is wrong with you?" Gamdesh's princess shouted. "I've sent three messages warning you to get out of the city, and you ignored all of them. Do you think I have time to be here? Do you think that standing in a library is where I best serve Gamdesh?"

"No," Lydia muttered. "You should be with your soldiers."

"Wrong!" Kaira's face was a thundercloud of anger. "Getting you out alive is the *greatest* priority because Malahi cannot defeat the blight without you. If I allow you to die here, it won't matter if I defeat that Cel prick or not, for the blight will come to Gamdesh next. So get onto that ship or I'll have you trussed up and tossed aboard. Am I clear?"

"I'm not done reading!" Lydia shouted back, her whole body shaking because she wasn't ready. Wouldn't be ready until she had an answer for how to save all those who'd been lost.

Quick as lightning, Kaira reached past her and snatched up the ancient volume. Lydia gasped, "No!"

But it was too late.

Kaira flung it across the room, where it exploded into fragments and dust.

"You hunt for answers that you'll never find in the pages of a book," Kaira said. "Use what you have gleaned. Trust in Hegeria. And believe in yourself."

Rounding on Sonia, Kaira said, "They are threatening to blow the dam and flood the city if we don't surrender. But I tell you this with certainty: Revat is lost."

"Then we flee!" Sonia caught hold of Kaira by the arms, and Lydia bit her lip, seeing that the love between them endured, no matter how long they'd been apart. "Load all who remain on the ships in the harbor. Abandon the city. Live to fight another day, and we will reclaim Revat."

"There is only one ship." Kaira's voice was grim. "The ship that waits for you." She leaned forward and pressed her forehead to Sonia's. "I am sorry for pushing you away. For fearing nothing so much as I feared how deeply I cared for you. I regret little in life, but I will go to my grave regretting the time with you I lost."

"This is not the end," Sonia pleaded. "Come with us, please!"

Kaira only shook her head. "I bought Lydia the time she needed to find answers, and now I will buy you the time you need to escape. When the histories are written, let it be said that Kaira and her army died so that all of Reath could live. Now go while you still can!"

"Please," Sonia begged.

"I'm going to force my father onto the *Kairense*," Kaira said. "Get him away so that he might rally our people. Keep him safe, Lieutenant."

Then General Kaira, Princess of Gamdesh, was gone.

Tears ran down Sonia's face, but her shoulders were square as she turned to face Lydia.

"We're going. Now."

75

MARCUS

"The Sultan has rejected our offer to talk terms of surrender. Again." Felix handed Marcus a folded piece of paper. One glance revealed that Kaira's propensity for colorful language in rejections was in the blood. Something she'd inherited from her father.

"What's it say?" Drusus asked, leaning over to read the note. "Go . . ." He shook his head. "I'm too old to learn new languages."

"It says 'Go fuck yourselves.'" Marcus tossed the paper on the table, then left the pavilion to survey both Revat and his army surrounding it. The ground was churned up and muddy, little happening on the field beyond the endless loading and deployment of the catapults. Great sections of the wall were partially collapsed, and though the ridge was not high enough to see over Revat's walls, through the crumbled gaps he could see the parts of the city within range were in ruins. Yet still the Gamdeshians fought on, their numbers and positions still making him reluctant to take the city by force.

"Have to admire the old man's defiance." Felix's eyes were fixed not on the city, but on the seven god towers that reached out of the clouds of smoke and dust. They stood strong despite the one nearest to their position having taken several direct blows.

Yet it was not those towers that commanded Marcus's interest, but rather the building at the center of the circle. The library, they'd learned from prisoners that they'd taken. The largest in the West, and he wondered how it compared to the Great Library in Celendrial, which contained every important work pilfered from every province Celendor had conquered. Everything found here would eventually be cataloged and brought to Celendrial as well. As Marcus watched, the black tower of the Seventh God shifted, looming over the library as though watching something within it intently.

Or someone.

The soldiers they'd captured had revealed that there were Mudamorians in the library—guests of the Sultan in Revat seeking information of enough importance that all the librarians had remained until recently. One of the Mudamorians, he'd been told, had a tattoo on her forehead in the shape of a half-moon, which meant she was a marked healer. *Tall*, they'd said. *Pale skin. Long dark hair.*

Bait's voice rose from his memory. *She's marked by the Six. A healer, and a powerful one at that.*

Lydia, he was sure of it.

Don't let her escape.

"Signal the fleet to send ships into the harbor." The words tore from his mouth.

Felix's brow furrowed. "Why? We've intelligence that there is only one ship left in the harbor, and it's a Maarin vessel called the *Kairense*. Our ships are fighting what remains of the Gamdeshian navy, which are loaded with reinforcements. If our ships disengage, we risk the Gamdeshians landing and coming at us from the rear."

"They don't have the numbers to matter. Secure that ship!"

Panic Marcus couldn't justify was surging through his veins, along with the absolute certainty that the Maarin ship needed to be secured lest it take her out of his reach.

But Felix didn't move. No one did.

"Sink it!" he shouted at his second, fury mixing with his panic because they were supposed to obey.

Felix blew a breath out from beneath his teeth, but then relayed the order to the signalmen. The message rippled through the relay posts to the coast, where they'd be seen by the watchmen on ships. Within minutes, the message returned to them. "Two ships are moving to block the harbor entrance."

That wasn't what he'd asked for. Marcus's head was agony, and the voice shrieked, *There are other ways out! Seal them in! Catch them!*

"Increase bombardment frequency targeting the tops of the walls and begin moving siege towers into position."

He rattled off more instructions, but instead of seeing them done, Felix stared at him. Everyone was staring at him, and Marcus heard Drusus mutter, "Going through another xenthier must have rattled his skull. He's not thinking."

"You want to go over the top?" Felix demanded. "That's madness. We'll lose men by the hundreds if we do that, and there's no bloody need for it! Another few days of bombardment with no fresh water, and they'll surrender. We haven't even tried to exchange Astara yet."

"Agreed," Drusus said, and the other legati who were present gave nods of agreement, all of them staring at Marcus like he was some sort of rabid dog.

Bring them to heel. The voice was frenzied. *Make them listen. Make them obey!*

"That ship is there for a reason." Marcus forced his tone to stay cool and level because, through the throbbing pain in his skull, he could see everyone was questioning his sanity, his fitness for command, and he *needed* to stay in control. "The Maarin are allied with Gamdesh. If we don't stop that ship, they will aid Kaira and the Sultan in escape, and they will be able to rally Gamdesh against us. Whereas if we catch them now, we end this now. Gamdesh will be under the Empire's control."

Felix crossed his arms. "I'm not giving that order. No one here is. You've let this get personal and it's impeding your judgment."

Behind the walls in his mind, the fists began hammering, but Marcus still said, "Fine. I'll give the orders myself."

Drusus stepped toward Marcus as though to intervene, but Gibzen barked an order, and his men pulled their blades, blocking him. "It is the Dictator's will that we take Revat, and the legatus is the voice of the Dictator in the West," Gibzen growled. "Be the hands that see his will done or suffer the consequences."

In the recesses of his mind, Marcus recoiled from the idea of such a connection with Cassius, but the thought was too distant to take traction. Ripping the flag from the signalman's hand, Marcus relayed his own orders to the ranks of men on the field before him. Immediately, they began to move. Six legions converged on the circular wall to strike as one. The only gap in their ranks was the riverbed of slimy rock, which now contained only a trickle of water that flowed through the barred opening into the city. The Thirty-Seventh marched on the left of the riverbed and the Forty-First on the right.

Behind him, Marcus heard arguments and threats thrown between Felix and Gibzen. But his primus's hundred legionnaires stood guard around the pavilion, and they were not men to cross, so Marcus ignored the argument.

The siege towers rolled down the gentle slope of torn-up earth to the towering walls of Revat, on which thousands of soldiers waited. Legion catapults launched rocks into the walls, sending stone and bodies flying, but the Gamdeshians held their ground. All their defenses but this wall had been destroyed, so all they could do was watch while thousands upon thousands of legionnaires marched into range of arrow fire. The skies darkened with arrows, though it did little good as the ranks lifted shields over their heads.

It felt like Marcus was watching through the eyes of someone else as his army converged on the walls. His head filled not with the sound of marching men but with the hammer of fists against stone walls. Blood trickled from his nose, the coppery taste filling his mouth, but Marcus didn't move to wipe it away.

The front lines closed the distance to the wall. Arrows flew from the battlements, mostly striking upraised shields, but when they struck true, the ranks merely tightened to fill the gap, the fallen ground into the mud.

Do not let her escape.

The siege towers pressed closer.

Closer.

Yet rather than bolstering the ranks on the walls to meet them, the Gamdeshians were abandoning their positions.

"They're breaking!" he heard someone say, but that wasn't right.

Kaira would not break. She was going on the offensive.

Shoving the flags back in the signalman's hand, Marcus snapped, "Warn them to beware the gates. She's going to ride out!"

The man gave the signal, horns blasting across space to fill the ears of every man with the same message, and even from here, Marcus saw the front ranks before the gate tense in preparation.

But the portcullises remained lowered, the gates closed.

What was he missing?

Slowly, his eyes tracked to the river. The one gap in the sea of legionnaires. To the heavy bars set into the wall itself, still slick with green slime from the river that had once flowed through them. Which meant he saw the Gamdeshians inside the city racing toward them with heavy chains.

"The river!" he shouted. "They're coming up the riverbed!"

The signalman stared at him in confusion, and Marcus screamed at him, "Tell them to close the gap!"

But it was too late.

The heavy steel grate barring the river entrance exploded inward.

A heartbeat later, dozens upon dozens of horses galloped out of the opening. But instead of attacking the ranks on either bank, the horses charged up the riverbed.

At their center rode Kaira. Guiding her big black horse with her knees, she held a torch, as did several others in the company.

Instantly Marcus knew that Kaira intended to turn his own threat against him. She was going to ignite the explosives and blow the dam. With his entire army on the floodplain, thousands of men would die, dashed against the walls by the force of the water or drowned by the weight of their armor.

Terror shattered the walls in his mind, and Marcus screamed, "Stop her!"

The men closest to the riverbed were already moving, ranks pivoting, arrows and spears flying. The Gamdeshians and their horses were dying in droves, either to weapons or to falls on the treacherous rocks, but the faces of the men and women showed no fear as they pressed in around Kaira, bodies shielding her. Dying to keep her alive to strike the ultimate blow against Marcus's army, even though it would come at the cost of the city.

Felix shouted orders, reinforcements that had been guarding their rear moving to intercept, but they'd never make it in time.

The Thirty-Seventh were going to die. Were going to drown because of a mistake he'd made.

"Gibzen!" Marcus shouted. "Stop her!"

The Thirty-Seventh's primus and his men didn't hesitate. Flinging themselves onto their horses, they rode at a dead gallop to intercept Kaira.

"They aren't going to reach her in time!" Drusus shouted. "She's going to destroy the dam while our entire army is on the field. We'll lose hundreds of men! Thousands!"

Marcus barely heard him because he was already running toward his horse. He vaulted onto the mare's back and drove her into a gallop. His cloak whipped out behind him, and he pulled the catch to allow it to fall away, leaning over the mare for more speed.

Kaira and what remained of her soldiers burst past the last of the legion lines, horses stumbling on the slick rocks of the riverbed as they raced up the riverbed toward the dam. Toward the explosives carefully placed by Rastag at its base. Every one of them rode with the desperate determination of those who knew this was their only chance to strike a final blow in a lost war.

Faster, he willed the golden mare, and seeming to hear him, she put on a burst of speed and gained ground on Gibzen and his men.

Behind him, horns bellowed. Someone, likely Felix, ordering the men on the field away from the riverbed. Out of the path of destruction.

But thousands of men could only move so quickly, and Kaira had almost reached the dam.

Faster.

Kaira and Gibzen both broke ahead of their men, moving at a perpendicular course of interception, smoke from her torch trailing in the Gamdeshian princess's wake.

Her horse stumbled and nearly fell, and she reined it up the side of the bank for better ground and dug in her heels.

Only for Gibzen to ride his horse into the side of her mount.

Both went down in a tangle of limbs, the horses screaming. The torch fell to roll a distance away, where it came to rest against a pile of dirt, still burning. One of Kaira's soldiers leapt off his horse, reaching for it—

And a gladius separated his hand from his wrist, courtesy of one of Gibzen's men.

Marcus's bodyguards collided with Kaira's in a scream of men and horses.

But the Gamdeshian princess was proving all the rumors about her were true.

Sword in hand, she cut down one, two, three of Gibzen's men like they were untrained boys, moving faster than any person should, her blade a blur of steel. They tried to back off, regrouping to attack her as one, but Kaira didn't give them the opportunity, throwing herself at the men.

More legion reinforcements arrived, the ground thick with men and glittering steel all intent on killing her.

But Kaira was the heart of this city, of this nation. Their spirit and motivation, and if she died, she would become a martyr to fuel the anger of generations.

"Don't kill her!" Marcus screamed. "Kill the others, but not the woman!"

His men obeyed without hesitation and hurled spears at her soldiers, steel lengths punching through leather and armor.

Kaira fought on.

More men dropped, the ground littered with dying legionnaires. Yet within heartbeats Kaira stood alone, facing a bristling wall of shields and spears on all sides. Marcus saw the rage on his men's faces over their fallen comrades. Their need for revenge.

Kill her, the voice ordered. *She is your enemy.*

Except that would be a mistake. That would ensure a never-ending war like in Bardeen and Chersome, generations falling only for their orphans to pick up their weapons and fight all the harder.

"Don't hurt her," Marcus roared, riding his horse in a circle around the men. "We need her alive!"

Too late, he realized his mistake.

Understanding flashed in Kaira's eyes, followed with grim determination. Snatching up a fallen legionnaire's spear, she threw the weapon.

Straight at Marcus's face.

His mare reared, lifting him high even as the spear flew.

It struck him in the torso, punching through his breastplate.

Pain lanced through Marcus's body, only instinct making him fling himself clear of the falling horse.

Marcus hit the ground hard, the impact driving the air from his chest.

He couldn't breathe.

Couldn't speak.

Couldn't order his men to hold.

Wrenching the spear from his breastplate, Marcus rolled onto all fours, gasping as he staggered to his feet. "Don't . . ."

It was too late.

Kaira was on the ground, six spears embedded in her body.

"No!" He staggered through his men. "Get a surgeon! We need her alive!"

Falling to his knees next to Kaira, Marcus took in her injuries and knew there was no saving her. That even if one of the healers in Revat rode at a gallop, they wouldn't make it in time to save the woman who'd fought so hard to defend the city.

Kaira's brown eyes met his, hate filling their depths. "You might win this battle, Legatus," she whispered. "But you will not win the war. And the Six as my witness, I curse you to die gasping for breath that will not come."

Then she went still.

Marcus stared into her unseeing eyes, watching the light fade from them as death took her. Blood ran down his chest from where the spear had punctured his breastplate, but he barely felt the pain. What did it matter in the face of what was to come?

"Marcus!" Felix dropped to his knees next to him. "He's injured! Get a medic!"

Marcus ignored him, his attention snapping to Gibzen, who stooped to retrieve Kaira's still smoldering torch.

"No!" Marcus tried to shout, but it came out as a wheeze, panic and pain inviting an attack down upon him.

"Get a stretcher!" someone ordered, then he was being lifted out of the riverbed. Moved out of danger.

"Stop!" The word was nothing more than a whisper because Marcus could not *breathe.*

"It's okay," Felix said. "We've pulled the men back. They're moving out of the flood path."

Yet distant screams filled the air.

Marcus turned his head, eyes drawn to the city. One of the god towers tilted, fractured by the bombardment of the catapults.

It began to fall.

Slowly at first, then faster. Falling until it struck the tower next to it with a noise like thunder.

Yet for all the horror, Marcus's instincts screamed that the threat was behind him. As everyone moved away from the towering dam of stone and wood that held back a lake full of water, his eyes tracked to Gibzen.

He was walking toward the fuse line, burning torching in hand.

Gibzen was going to flood the city.

Marcus had to stop him.

This wasn't the plan, had never been the plan. Only a threat that he'd never intended to follow through on.

He had to stop his primus, but Marcus couldn't get in the breath to speak the order.

"Marcus!" Felix tore at the buckles on his armor even as Marcus tried to push him away. He reached out a hand toward Gibzen, who was staring in fascination at the dam.

"Stop!" Marcus gasped. "Stop him!"

But the words were just wheezes of air.

"The rest of the towers are collapsing!" someone shouted. "Look!"

Like the death of one had been the death of all, one tower hit the next and the next, laying waste to Revat until only a singular black spike reared in the air.

The Seventh God's tower trembled. Not with instability, but with laughter. It turned, flaming eyes staring into Marcus's soul.

This is who you are, the voice whispered.

A part of Marcus, deep down, wanted to rail against the voice's condemnation. Wanted to cling to the dream that there was another path forward for him. Another life. But every time he reached for that path, it hurt in every possible way.

Accept that this is what you are.

Do not resist this destiny.

Marcus tasted blood as he warred against that certainty.

Warred . . . and lost.

As he conceded to the voice, Marcus found that he could breathe again, each inhalation clearing away grief and terror and pain until only clarity of purpose remained.

He turned his head away from the towers to where Gibzen stood holding the burning torch. His Primus's eyes locked with his.

Then Gibzen lit the fuse.

76

LYDIA

Lydia shoved as many of the books as she could in her bag, abandoning clothes and necessities in favor of trying to save as much knowledge as possible, but as they started toward the door, the whole building shook.

They both staggered, catching their balance against the wall, the thunder of falling stone deafening Lydia's ears.

"Catapult," Sonia whispered. "They hit the library. We need to run."

Lydia shoved against the door, but it was jammed. "It's stuck!"

A desperate sob of fear tore from her friend's lips. "The Six have mercy, we're trapped!"

Lydia felt the blood drain from her face. Dropping her bag, she slammed her shoulder into the heavy door. The frame rattled and strained against the force of the blow, but the door held.

Sonia picked up a chair and smashed the window. "Help!" she screamed. "We're trapped!"

But as Lydia joined her at the window, she knew to call for help was hopeless. From this height, it was easy to see that the walls were thick with Gamdeshian soldiers. And beyond . . .

Was a sea of legionnaires on the march.

Thousands upon thousands, the only gap in the ranks made for the war machines pulled by oxen, the siege towers reaching high into the sky.

Marcus was out there, the master of this horror, and Lydia knew that if he caught her in this library, mark or no mark, she was a dead woman.

They needed to get out.

Now.

While Sonia kept trying to get the attention of someone who might help, Lydia snatched up the lamp and went to the door. "I'm going to try to burn the wood!" she shouted. "Weaken it enough to break through."

Splashing lamp oil around the hinges and bolt, she stepped back as flames burst bright with a loud *whoosh*.

Thick smoke began to fill the room, and the pair of them pressed to the window, coughing violently.

"We just need to wait for it to burn enough that the wood weakens!" Lydia gasped. "Then I can break it."

But the black smoke grew thicker, pouring toward the open window and leaving no air for their lungs.

"I can't breathe!" Sonia gasped. "Lydia, I can't—"

Lydia was already running across the room. Her shoulder struck the engulfed door and it broke in half, revealing the beam that had fallen in front of it, as well as the rubble beyond. Ignoring the pain, she wrenched the burning pieces of door out of the way and climbed under the beam. Her hands were an agony of burns as she rolled to extinguish her clothes. "Sonia! Crawl through!"

For a heartbeat, she thought her friend had succumbed to the smoke, then Sonia climbed under the beam. Coughing, Lydia hauled her to her feet, and they were running to the stairs.

The catapult stone had come through the ceiling, rock and timber and glass everywhere, the shelves a chaos of what had to be abandoned, for the librarians had only been able to take the most precious of volumes. It broke Lydia's heart to leave the rest behind because the Cel would steal it all.

But there was no choice. Even though nothing had changed in the rhythm of the bombardment, Lydia could feel a *shift.* A tension in the air that immediately caused her to look skyward as they exited the library tower, certain that she'd see a swirling cloud of shadow like when the Corrupter had come for her in Derin.

The skies were clear and sunny, yet the danger she saw was just as real.

"Run!" Lydia screamed as the first god tower began a slow collapse sideways like a falling giant.

She and Sonia sprinted through streets empty of people yet full of abandoned belongings. Lydia didn't dare look up lest she lose her footing in the mess, but a scream of terror tore from her as the tower struck its neighbor, the roar of falling rock crashing down on the city like knives in her ears.

"Faster!" She saw Sonia's mouth form the word but couldn't hear it over the noise of the towers descending into one another, the sky full of falling rubble.

They reached the boardwalk running down the edge of the river, the fastest route to the harbor. Yet as Lydia looked down, it was to find the riverbed totally dry.

Then another tower began to fall.

A cloud of dust exploded over them, making it hard to see, and Lydia tripped and fell. Got to her feet only to fall again a dozen steps later, her feet tangling in the piles of belongings left on the boardwalk.

Sonia caught her hand, dragging her onward, and through the dust, the familiar blue sails of the *Kairense* appeared. It was the only vessel left in the harbor.

The sailors on the *Kairense* were making ready to push away from the dock.

"Wait!" Lydia shouted. "We're coming!"

But the Maarin couldn't hear her over the noise.

"Wait!" she screamed, praying for the roar of falling rock to cease. Lydia glanced over her shoulder, seeing that only the black tower of the Seventh remained upright over the cloud of dust. It called to her, and Lydia stopped running.

"Lydia!" Sonia screamed. "Don't stop!"

The ground trembled and a loud roaring filled her ears.

Something, like a great wind, stirred the dust as it wove through Revat.

Not wind, she realized. Water.

"Run!"

The Maarin heard the river, too, and their eyes fixed on her and Sonia as they raced toward the docks. "Hurry!" they shouted. "Faster!"

Lydia's boots hit the dock. *Don't look back,* she told herself. *Just get to the ship.*

They were almost there, the ship beginning to push away, the gangplank barely bridging the gap.

"Go!" Sonia shouted, shoving her across.

Lydia's feet flew up the gangplank, but as she reached the ship, she felt the wood slip. She leapt onto the deck, then twisted and screamed, "Jump!"

Sonia leapt, their hands locking right as the river exploded into the harbor with the force of a god's fist.

Lydia screamed, holding tight to her friend's hands as the surge struck the ship and tipped it sideways, the Maarin shouting as they clung to handholds. The vessel groaned and cracked, slammed into one of the other docks, and then they were rotating out into the harbor. Lydia dragged Sonia onto the deck as Vane screamed, "Calm the seas! Calm the seas!"

But the only person who could do that was one of Madoria's marked, and Fara was lying on the deck, blood streaming from a wound on her head.

The flooding river dragged the ship across the harbor, hurling them toward the sea walls with alarming speed.

"We're going to hit the wall! Oars!"

But there was no time. And even if there were, the oars could not fight the strength of the river.

Lydia scrambled to Fara, desperate to heal her so that she might save everyone, but as Vane bellowed, "Brace yourselves," she knew it was too late.

Lydia braced, then a flash of crimson scales reared from the water. A great serpent rose into the sky, fringed and beautiful and terrifying, her teeth bared at the river.

Aspasiana.

The guardian wrapped her long body around the *Kairense,* tail thrashing as she swam against the current. But the force was too great, even for a demigod.

And the river hurled them against the sea wall.

Aspasiana screamed in pain as her body took the impact, her great form straining as she rotated the ship to pass it through the opening in the seawall before letting go. Rising from the water, the serpent screamed in wrath and agony, her body bleeding and broken, ribs puncturing her scaled hide.

All the world seemed to stand still.

Then Aspasiana collapsed across the waves, slowly sinking beneath the surge of water that flowed out into the sea.

All around her, the Maarin sobbed in grief even as they hurried to follow their captain's orders. Sails rose, and the ship raced through the gap in the Cel fleet created by the river's surge.

Aspasiana was dead and it was Lydia's fault. She'd been the one who'd demanded they stay. Who'd refused to listen to every warning in an ill-fated quest to find answers.

Grief filled Lydia's heart as she pressed her hands to Fara, healing her injury even as she looked back at the mighty city of Revat, jewel of Gamdesh and heartbeat of the West.

At the single tower remaining, the eyes of the visage carved into its onyx surface opening to reveal rings of flame, laughter chasing them as they escaped out to sea.

77

KILLIAN

Rufina laughed and laughed as she circled high above the battlefield filled with Mudamorian dead, hidden by shadow as she soared higher out of arrow range.

Then the shriek of a giant hawk cut the night, and Niotin attacked her. There was a flurry of wing flaps and Rufina shouted a curse, droplets of blood raining down on Killian's upturned face.

A crunch of bone. A cry of pain.

The hawk struck the ground in front of Killian with a heavy thump, his body shivering and then changing into the form of a man. *Dead.*

Dareena screamed curses and shot arrows after Rufina, but Killian couldn't move from where he'd fallen to his knees in the mud and blood.

Seldrid had him by the shoulders. "Are you hurt?"

Killian pulled off his helmet and cast it aside, shaking his head to try to clear the visions filling it. God towers falling one after another until only the black tower of the Seventh remained. "I think Revat has fallen."

His brother went still. "Killian, that's not possible. The Cel army is in Emrant."

"I saw it. The towers falling." He scrubbed at his eyes. "I can't stop seeing it."

Dareena knelt before him. "Has something happened to Lydia?"

"I don't know." Killian dug his fingers into the ground, a scream boiling up from his insides. "This was a trick. A ruse to keep us from aiding Revat. A gambit to keep me from going to her." He slammed his fists against the ground. "I was supposed to be with her!"

Every part of him was rage and fear and grief, and Killian wanted to lash out. To hurt and maim and do something, anything, to free himself from the horror that threatened to drown him.

Lunging for his bow, he chased after his horse to get an arrow from the quiver fixed to his saddle. "Where is she?" he screamed, aiming at the sky. "Where are you, Rufina!"

He shot arrow after arrow, howling in fury until Dareena and Seldrid dragged him to the ground.

"Rufina's gone!" Dareena's face was inches from his, hidden by darkness. "She got what she wanted and did not linger. Now tell me exactly what you saw!"

"I saw the god towers of the Six collapsing across Revat, smashing the city to ruins," he whispered. "All that remained was the Seventh's tower."

"Killian, are you certain you didn't take a blow to the head during the fight?" his brother asked.

"I didn't hit my head. It was a vision."

"I've never heard of Tremon's marked receiving visions."

"And I've never heard of Tremon taking a sword from one place and giving it to a person half a continent away, and yet he did just that for Killian," Dareena said. "Killian, when you spoke with Tremon and he gave you your father's sword, did he touch you again, as Hegeria did Lydia?"

He blinked through tear-swollen eyes. "Yes."

Dareena gave a slow nod. "Then I believe you see truly. Revat has fallen, though it remains to be seen how such a thing occurred."

Adra let out a wail of despair and fell to her knees. Seldrid went to his wife and pulled her into his arms, giving words of comfort where there was none to be had. Killian squeezed his eyes shut, allowing grief to pull him down and down, because if Lydia was lost—

"Don't even think it," Dareena barked at him. Grabbing hold of his shoulders, she gave him a rough shake. "Lydia is clever and resourceful, but more than that, she has the capacity to endure what would kill anyone else. Focus your mind instead on what Rufina's actions tell us. She clearly knew Lydia was in Revat with Malahi, and the fact that she went through this effort to keep you from going to her suggests that they were on the right track. That the Seventh perceives whatever Lydia and Malahi might learn in Revat as a threat to his plans."

"They had no time. How much could they have learned?"

"Who can say?" Dareena replied. "But we do them no service weeping in the mud. We must hold Rufina back until they have time to return with whatever they have learned. Because I choose to have faith that they *will* return."

Killian wanted to believe her. Wanted to share her hope, except his hopes always seemed to burn to ash.

"This group of blighters is but one of many forming behind our army's lines." Dareena let go of him and sat back on her heels. "We need to track them down and stop them. We must do our duty to the queen so that all is not lost when she returns. Now get up."

Killian stood, but he felt unsteady on his feet.

All around him were the soldiers who'd fought, torchlight illuminating the splatter of blood from the blighters they'd killed. They watched him and Dareena, looking for a path through the horror pressing in on all sides.

"Which way did she fly?"

"North, I think. With Niotin—" Dareena's voice broke off with a choked sob of grief, but she wiped blood off her face and steadied her breath. "With Niotin lost, we have no way to know."

Killian drew in a steadying breath and shoved his emotions behind a wall, forcing himself to focus. "Dareena, break our force into groups and start hunting down blighters that have risen behind the front lines. Use dogs to track them."

The torchlight cast dancing shadows over his mentor's face as she narrowed her eyes. "Are you going after Lydia? Are you leaving us to this fight?"

Every part of his soul wanted to go south to Lydia, but that was not how to best serve his queen. "I'm going north."

"Why?"

Killian swung into his saddle. "Because it's time that we went on the offensive."

* * *

With only Baird racing at his side, Killian rode north through the night, the thick, rotten stench of blight growing stronger with each passing hour until it became a struggle to breathe.

"Did Bercola forgive you?" Killian asked during one of the stretches he allowed his horse to walk. "I was a little worried she might kill you."

"Of course she didn't forgive me." Baird shot him a look of disgust. "Forgiveness must be earned with acts of valor, but by allowing me to live, my wife has given me a chance at redemption."

"Fair enough." Killian loosened his reins so that Surly could stretch his neck. "Well, this might be your chance."

The giant blew a breath out between his teeth. "What precisely do you intend, Killian?"

A plan was forming in his head, but Killian needed to see the scope of what the Mudamorian army faced before it would come together. "The enemy's forces keep growing. The Cel seem to be almost without limit in the soldiers they can bring over from the Empire. Every time the blight slips past our barricades, more Mudamorians are lost to rise as blighters, who join Rufina's ranks. With luck, your people and the Anuk will join our forces. With luck, Lydia and Malahi are on their way to Serlania with a solution for the blight. But we need to strike a blow that doesn't rely on luck. A blow that sets Rufina back a step so that we have time to take a breath."

"That's all wonderful," Baird said. "But not one word of that speech spoke of a specific plan."

"Soon enough." Gathering his reins, Killian drove his warhorse into a canter, the chance for conversation over.

They met the first scouts just after dawn, the men immediately recognizing Killian. Their uniforms were stained and torn, armor dented, and their dirty faces grim with exhaustion. "We heard that blighters had risen behind the lines," one man said. "Niotin brought word that you and Lady Falorn were riding to combat them."

"Niotin fell," Killian replied. "But so, too, have the blighters. Have you found the sources of the leak?"

The scout shook his head. "Near as we can tell, it wasn't the river that was infected, my lord. Our best guess is that Rufina sent agents with barrels of blight to poison wells. Every town and village is supposed to keep their water sources under guard, but one moment of distraction is all it takes."

"It's what she did in Derin," Killian muttered, remembering the glass of water that he and Lydia had found. How the blight had swirled within it, sentient.

"It won't spread through the land that way." The soldier wiped a dirty hand over his brow. "But it kills anyone who drinks it, sure and true."

Baird stepped closer to Killian, voice low. "All it will take is her agents poisoning every well they can find and this war is over."

The thought had already occurred to Killian, but it had only reaffirmed that he needed to act now.

The army's camp was quiet and grim, a sea of tents on fields so churned up that they were nothing more than mud at this point. Men and women sat quietly around fires, but most lifted their heads as he passed.

"It's the Dark Horse," he heard them say. "It's Killian Calorian."

The weight of the hope that he'd be able to do something felt like a lead shirt.

"We're holding it back with trenches and rubble," the scout told him as they walked through the camp. "We have patrols traveling east and west of our position every day, searching for veins of blight breaking off from the main stream. Dogs have proven the best at finding them, and then it's a matter of trenching and barricading it off. But it's like plugging a leaking dam with your fingers. Plug a hole and another springs open, and we're running out of fingers. And while we're doing the plugging, the blighters attack us. We're losing men in droves."

Ahead rose a wall of rubble that ran as far as Killian could see in both directions. Wagons were moving slowly toward it, men unloading what looked like the dismantled remains of homes and pasture walls. Every bit of rock that could be stripped from the land brought here to hold back the main flow of the blight.

"Lord Calorian!" A captain in a uniform as stained and torn as his subordinates approached. "Were you able to stop the spread?"

"We killed the main horde," Killian answered, deeply aware that it was Mudamorian blood that stained his own clothes. "Dareena and my brother are working to track down the rest."

There was a large structure behind the dam, and Killian felt himself drawn toward it. Baird and the others followed, the captain saying, "That's one of our lookout towers. We have five of them up and down the dam. Dogs patrol the length hourly with their handlers, looking for leaks."

Handing off the reins to his horse with an added warning to watch for Surly's teeth, Killian climbed the wooden tower. It creaked and swayed as Baird followed him, both of them struck silent as they reached the top and stared out at the lake of blight stretching out before them.

Black and viscous, it seethed and swirled, bubbles occasionally rising from its depths to pop with loud snaps. That it was sentient, Killian could not deny. Not with the malevolent purpose that radiated from it, strands rising like fingers to pick at the rocks of the dam, dragging them back into its depths with loud gulps. The captain handed him a spyglass, and Killian took in the dried and cracked land surrounding the lake, dead forests with trees that had been leached of color, black veins rising their trunks. Nothing lived: The grass, the brush, the very air seemed to be the antithesis of life.

Yet on the far side was the true horror.

Bodies lay strewn among the trees, sometimes in large heaps. People of every age, gender, and walk of life, some with clothes and some naked and filthy, no effort put into making them seem human at all. Just shells of the people they'd once been.

"They go on for leagues," the captain said quietly. "Tens of thousands of them. They rise when there is purpose for them, then return to their camp to be discarded in heaps. Niotin had reported that another horde arrived to join them from Derin but that they are broken and worn down. Their bodies don't last forever, but the trouble is that Rufina keeps finding ways to poison more of the living."

"Have you tried attacking them?"

"We used to," the captain said. "When Lady Falorn was in command. But killing them demoralizes the men, and with the losses we've taken, it's all we can do now to maintain the defense."

"Is Rufina with them?"

"Niotin was the only one who could get a look. Her camp is leagues away from the front, and it's where the corrupted and deimos are set up."

In his mind's eye, Killian watched the shifter fall from the sky, dead at Rufina's hands when Rufina should be dead by Killian's arrows. Not just a friend lost, but one of their greatest assets in this fight.

Killian gave a slow nod, allowing himself to sink further into the numb void that would be required to execute this plan. "Would you give us a minute?" he said to the captain, watching the men retreat down the tower until he and Baird stood alone.

"What are you thinking?" the giant asked, his big face full of sorrow as he stared across the black lake to the mounds of blighters on the far side.

"Can you call a storm?" Killian asked. "A strong wind that blows north. As fierce as possible."

"I'm not calling a twister, if that's your thought." Baird crossed his thick arms and glowered. "Cursed things have a mind of their own and are as likely to turn on this camp as anything. Plus the path of carnage would be too small to make much of a dent in these numbers."

"Just a strong and steady north wind, that's all I need."

Baird's colorless eyes narrowed. "It can be done. But Killian, what is your plan?"

"It's better if you don't know." Going to the steps leading down, Killian forced his voice to be steady as he said, "Just get the wind going and don't stop. Whatever you do, don't stop."

* * *

Waiting until nightfall risked being seen by the deimos and the corrupted riders on patrol. But given the blighters themselves saw no better than the living, Killian decided to wait until the sun was fully set before he made his move.

Baird had been dancing with his drum for well over an hour, and a warm wind from the south blew with such ferocity that the soldiers were losing tents and canvas, the camp in turmoil. Killian paid it all no mind as he set out alone on horseback. He rode the length of the dam, nodding at the patrols he passed when the men saluted, but once he reached the edge of the rubble, he dismounted.

Tying Surly to a post, he hefted his heavy bag. Patrols moved up and down the front lines, dogs in their ranks. He waited for a gap between them, then skirted across the stretch of open ground, feeling the crunch of bone and squish of worse as he ran. Dozens of battles had been fought here, and the land had become a mass grave of Mudamorian dead.

Open ground gave way to dead trees. Their bleached branches rubbed against each other in the wind, the land itself seeming to be moaning in pain as he pressed deeper into Rufina's territory. Killian slowed his pace, making out the forms of blighters who were alert and on guard, weaving around them and showing care not to step on those who lay slumped on the ground.

Part of him was grateful for the dark because it hid their faces. Turned them into anonymous soldiers rather than countrymen he was sworn to protect.

Reaching a particularly dense patch of dead trees and brush, Killian removed his pack and took out the first bottle of lamp oil. He soaked the deadfall and tree trunks, moving back the way he'd come, upending more and more lamp oil as he went. When his reserves were spent, he knelt next to a splash of oil and took out his tinderbox.

"The Six forgive me," he whispered, the words stolen away on the wind. Then Killian struck sparks onto the oil.

It caught in an instant, flame spreading swiftly down the trail he'd left and igniting the dead trees and foliage choking the land. The winds fueled the flames, and in what felt like both a moment and a lifetime, an inferno blazed before him.

Killian stood entranced as the flames raced from tree to tree, the roar of the fire rivaling the wind as it climbed higher and higher into the sky. A wall of death sweeping north, and though it would do nothing to the blight itself, the blighters were a different story.

Burning figures began to rise. To run.

Hundreds. Thousands. Tens of gods-damned thousands, all aflame and silently running as the Corrupter tried to move his army of puppets away from the inferno so that they still might serve their purpose to him.

But as the soldiers had said, there was a limit to what the physical form could endure, and the blighters began to fall.

Tears streamed down Killian's face, half from the heat and smoke but mostly from grief as he watched fire purge the land of his birth. Watched it steal the bodies of his countrymen from the Seventh's grasp so that they could finally be free.

Killian backed slowly away from the wall of flame, unable to look away.

Which was why he didn't hear their approach, only the sharp warning of his mark causing him to turn around in time to stop the downward stroke of an armed blighter.

There was a group of them. All fallen Mudamorian soldiers from the look of them, and they wore armor and carried the swords they'd died with.

Killian parried the blow and took off the blighter's head, but there were too many of them to fight alone.

So he broke into a run.

Coughing and choking on smoke, he raced through the dead trees, struggling to keep his bearings in the darkness.

His feet splashed into something sticky and wet, and he realized he'd reached the lake.

The blight tugged at his boots like tar as he eased backward, the blighters approaching. Some of them were burning, and they illuminated the darkness like macabre lamps. As one, they opened their lips and screamed, "Does this feel like victory, Killian Calorian? Does this feel like a battle won?"

He took a staggering step back, wading deeper into the murk even as the blighters pursued. Dozens of them, the ones charred beyond recognition crawling into the blight only to disappear beneath its surface.

One lunged at him and Killian parried, only for three more to fling themselves his direction. He couldn't win this.

Shoving his sword in its sheath, he turned and waded deeper into the lake. Deeper and deeper until it was up to his neck, the blighters that followed sucked beneath.

He could feel the blight dragging at his body. His soul. It felt like a million tiny fingers trying to pull the life out of him, but his mark stood strong. Every step was a struggle as he navigated the edge of the lake, afraid to go deeper, because there'd be no swimming in this. It would drag him beneath until he sucked in a breath of blackness, and that would be the end of him.

But then two enormous figures waded out into the lake. Blighters, yes, but also gods-damned giants.

Killian fought through the sludge toward the relative safety of the dam. Mudamorian soldiers were now fighting the blighters around the edge of the lake, but they didn't dare step into its depths. Without a mark, they'd be poisoned, sure and true.

"Does this feel like victory, Killian Calorian?" the giants repeated over and over. "Does this feel like a battle won?"

They were getting closer, their enormous height allowing them to move more easily through the slime.

His heart thundered from exertion, his breath labored. If they got their hands on him, he was dead.

Then Killian took a step back only to find nothing solid beneath his feet.

Blight flowed over his head. Killian silently screamed, trying to swim upward, but it kept pulling him down.

Down and down, as though the lake reached to the underworld itself.

Then his boot hit something solid, and bending his knees, Killian shoved upward.

His head broke the surface and he sucked in a mouthful of air.

"Killian!"

Baird roared his name, and a second later, a rope landed on top of the blight, just out of reach. Killian lunged, fingers snagging the length just before he sank beneath the surface.

He held his breath.

And he held on.

With the strength only a giant possessed, Baird pulled him through the blight, but with each passing second, the need to breathe grew.

Hold on! Killian screamed at himself. *For her sake, for Mudamora's sake, you will hold on.*

His chest was burning, every muscle in his body shuddering. But all around him was black.

In his eyes and his ears. In his mouth.

Endless little fingers clawing at him. Trying to consume him.

Then his back struck something hard.

Killian clawed his way up the crumbling side of the dam until Baird's strong hands had hold of him.

"I've got you!"

Killian sucked in a breath.

But he still couldn't see.

Cloth dragged over his face, scrubbing away the awful biting slime even as Baird shouted, "Stay away! You must not touch the blight, you fools!"

More cloth wiped over his face and, blinking away the stinging burn, Killian fixed his eyes on Baird's face.

"I've got you, friend," the giant said. "You look awful, but you'll be all right."

Killian slowly turned his head to look out over the lake of blight. Then beyond to the vast firestorm burning through league upon league of Mudamora, through thousands of blighters who had once been Mudamorians, the flicker and flash of burning figures visible through the trees.

A blow against the enemy that would take Rufina a long time to recover from.

Does this feel like victory, Killian Calorian? Does this feel like a battle won?

Leaning his forehead against Baird's shoulder, Killian wept.

78

TERIANA

Magnius delivered the news of Aspasiana's death just as they exited the greater ocean path that had brought the *Quincense* back across the world.

Her whole crew had been near silent since, the grief they all felt at the death of her mother compounded by the death of the *Kairense*'s guardian. For not in living memory had one of the demigods been lost. They were as constant as Madoria herself, bound to the Maarin people, and Aspasiana's death felt like part of their world had been destroyed.

What will happen now? Teriana asked Magnius, who had been equally silent as he grieved his sibling. Questions she'd never had cause to ask kept rising in her mind, not the least of which was how the guardian's death impacted Vane's authority as triumvir. The guardians swam with the triumvirs—that was how it had always been, and Magnius had taken up his post behind the *Quincense* when her great great grandfather was captain. *Will . . . will another guardian come into being?*

No, Magnius answered. *What were three are now two.*

Do you need to leave? she asked, desperately afraid of losing him when grief over her mother's death weighed down her heart.

You are triumvir now, Teriana. I go where you go.

I miss her. Tears rolled down her cheeks.

As do I, young one. But Tesya is with Madoria now, where the seas are ever tranquil. Grieve not for her, who is at peace, but for the living who must still fight the evils of this world.

Evils that were winning.

Fog clung heavily to the sea as the *Quincense* slowly moved between the towers flanking the harbor entrance. Teriana's stomach clenched at the sight of the crimson and gold banners flying on their ramparts, all that Magnius had told her proving true.

Revat had fallen to the Celendor Empire.

Had fallen to Marcus.

This is where Aspasiana fell, Magnius said into her thoughts. *She rests beneath us.*

Teriana wondered if Vane and the crew of the *Kairense* were safe. Wondered why they'd been in Revat. Wondered how the Cel had killed a demigod.

But if Magnius knew any of the answers, he did not voice them.

"We can still turn around," her aunt said from the helm. "There's no good to be done here, Teriana. We should sail to Serlania to join Lydia and Killian."

"I gave my word," Teriana replied. "Run up a white flag. In their eyes, we're no threat, so they'll either talk or send us on our way."

Marcus would either talk to her or send her away.

"Oh gods," Polin whispered, as a breath of wind stirred the heavy mists. "The towers of the Six are *gone*."

Teriana's breath caught as her eyes went skyward. Considered the greatest wonders of the world, the seven towers of Revat had once reached so high it was said they touched the clouds, but through the clearing fog, she saw only one remained. The black stone of the Seventh's tower sucked in the light of the sun rather than reflected it, the semblance of a visage carved into the top seeming to shift and move, watching her.

"Revat hasn't fallen to the Cel, it has fallen to the Corrupter," someone said, but it was her aunt's words that chilled Teriana's soul.

"They are allies, sure and true, even if these boys won't admit that the Seventh exists."

The *Quincense* drifted closer, the typically packed harbor now only holding the Cel fleet and a handful of Katamarcan merchant vessels, and it wasn't long until a legionnaire waved them into a space along one of the piers. Others moved to drop bumpers and catch lines, tying the ship off before a centurion approached, his breastplate bearing a 37. She immediately recognized him, for though she'd spent little time in the company of the legionnaire whose dark hair and angular eyes marked him as born in Faul province, Qian was well liked. He was also one of the few centurions who didn't feel compelled to scream every order he gave.

"Qian," she called down. "Good to see you alive."

"I have to say, Teriana," he replied, "I didn't think I'd ever see your face again. What madness brought you here?"

"I need to speak to him." She rested her elbows on the ship's rail. "That possible?"

Qian pulled off his helmet, wiped the sweat from his brow, then put it back on before he said, "You can try. Command is in the palace. I'll arrange an escort."

"Stay on the ship," Teriana ordered her crew. "If I'm not back in two hours, go to Serlania without me."

Her aunt grabbed her arm. "No. If you think he's going to hurt you, you're not getting off this ship."

"He won't hurt me." Teriana twisted her arm free. "It wasn't a request, Auntie. It was an order."

Not waiting for a gangplank, Teriana stepped onto the rail and leapt down onto the dock. "Lead the way."

* * *

The damage to the city brought tears to Teriana's eyes, for the towers dedicated to the Six were not the only things that had been destroyed. Collapsed buildings left rubble across streets. Rocks that had been flung by Cel catapults sat in smashed fountains and in the middle of courtyards, and the stink of ash clung to the air from all the fires that had begun as a result. But almost worse was the damage that had been inflicted by the flooding. Anything near the river not made of stone had been washed into the harbor, but now that the water had receded, a vile muck coated the ground and walls up to the water line, which was higher than she was tall. In the blistering heat, everything was turning to rot, and not, judging from the smell, just grain stores and property.

Marcus had done this.

"It's mostly dead livestock," Qian said from where he walked at her left. "The city was evacuated, and the military was all on high ground when the dam was burst. They surrendered not long after."

She stepped over a dead chicken rotting in the muck. "Hard to hold out in a siege when there's nothing to eat."

"Yeah," he replied, not sounding particularly happy about the victory. "Though I think it had more to do with Kaira's death than anything."

Teriana stopped in her tracks. "Kaira's dead?"

It seemed impossible. The princess had always seemed as indomitable as . . . as the god towers in Revat's sky. Teriana looked to the black tower of the Seventh, hands cold. "How?"

"She tried to destroy the dam while we were on the field, which would have killed half of the Thirty-Seventh and Forty-First. Never seen someone fight like her—she took down a lot of good men when they tried to capture her, but she was having none of being a prisoner." He cast a sideways glance at her. "She died well, if that matters."

"Dead is dead." Teriana caught sight of a man in a legionnaire's tunic hanging from the gallows in a market square. "Hanging your own now, too?"

Qian sighed. "We had Kaira's shifter Astara as a prisoner. He aided in her escape, but while she was able to fly away, he got caught."

Teriana stared at the dead man swaying on the breeze, his face having turned an awful bruised hue that made recognition impossible. "Who is he?"

"Atrio." Qian's jaw worked from side to side. "He was one of the Thirty-Seventh's spies, and Astara was his mark. Though apparently she left a mark on him. One worth dying for."

Her eyes pricked with tears, but she looked away from the dead man before they could spill and caught sight of the Sultan's palace ahead.

It was undeniably the largest palace on all of Reath, dozens and dozens of copper spires reaching to the sky, though several had fallen victim to the siege. It grew colder with every step Teriana took toward it, and she was not the only one affected. Gooseflesh had risen on the arms of the legionnaires, and she said, "The cold you feel? That's the Seventh God's influence. By destroying the other towers, you gave him control."

No one answered, but she knew they were listening.

"There's been more violence, hasn't there?" she asked. "Friends turning on friends. Everyone quick to anger. Quicker to lash out. Pestilence, too, I reckon, as well as animals dying. Crops failing. Things being born *wrong*. That's the Corrupter." She lifted her chin. "You might think you serve the Empire, but you're wrong. Right now, you serve the Seventh God."

Their silence was telling, and Teriana left it at that as a familiar large figure appeared at the palace gates, his arms crossed.

"Teriana," he said.

"Servius."

"To what do we owe the honor? I'm hoping it's not that the Senate refused to free your people, because there's nothing we can do about that."

"They're freed," she said. "They set sail from Celendrial within hours of my delivering Grypus's letter."

"Then why are you here?"

"I'm playing messenger for *his* sister. There's something she wanted him to know that couldn't go through official channels."

One of Servius's eyebrows rose. "Not what I expected you to say, but all right. I'll see that it gets to him."

"I need to deliver it personally."

"Not going to happen."

Anger rose in her chest but so did fear, because there was a part of Teriana that had been certain she could accomplish what Cordelia had asked. That she would tell Marcus to turn around and go back to Celendor to fix its problems, and that he'd do it. But having seen what he'd done to Revat? Having heard Kaira's fate? All that certainty dissolved, and Teriana's eyes skipped to the looming black tower before she asked, "Why not?"

"He's busy."

Teriana huffed out an annoyed breath. "Don't pull that shit on me, Servius. I'm sure you know everything, but in case you need a reminder, I had a good reason for leaving as I did. He doesn't deserve you protecting his feelings."

Servius motioned to Qian, who backed off, he and his men looking everywhere but at them.

"I'm not protecting him, Teriana, I'm protecting you." Servius moved closer. "He's different since you left, and not in a good way. There are moments when he's himself, but most of the time, it's like talking to a block of ice while staring into a void that looks back at you. Whatever you are expecting to get out of him, he won't give it, and you're only going to come out of the conversation feeling worse."

She shivered, and from the corner of her eye, the tower moved.

Gasping, Teriana whirled, colliding with Servius as the black tower loomed over her, descending like the Corrupter himself stood in the center of Revat. Reaching for her.

Then she blinked and it was upright again.

"Yeah," Servius said, though she hadn't asked a question. "I've seen it, too. Many of the men have, though no one feels too good about admitting it. It moved in Aracam but not like this." He was silent for a long moment, holding her arm though she didn't think it was for her benefit. "Started right after the other ones fell."

Teriana made the sign of the Six on her chest, then shoved her hand in her pockets, knuckles brushing the hair ornament. "I need to talk to him, Servius. Maybe it will amount to nothing, but I have to try."

Servius sighed. "Fine. But don't say I didn't warn you."

He led her into the palace, which appeared much as it had the last time Teriana had been inside yet felt entirely different. The Gamdeshians were an exuberant people, none more so than the royal family, and always these halls had been filled with music and laughter and *life*. Now they possessed all the life of a crypt, the air stale and the only sound their footfalls.

"How is Quintus?" she asked, hoping Servius would say that her friend had disappeared with Miki.

"Fine. Felix redeployed him to help Racker in medical, to keep guard over the narcotics. Easy work."

Her chest tightened painfully because her friends hadn't escaped. Yet more victims of her selfishness.

"You've heard what is happening in Celendor?"

"We're a bit behind on news," Servius said. "Takes at least a day for messengers to arrive from Emrant, and . . . Well, we've been occupied."

"Occupied like a swarm of locusts," she muttered. "You feel good about what you've done here, Servius?"

"I don't feel good about what we've done *anywhere,* Teriana," he snapped. "But the alternative is worse. I like being alive, and men who don't obey get their necks stretched."

His words triggered the memory of her conversation with Cordelia.

If Marcus does this, and Cassius reveals the truth, what will happen to him?

He'll hang.

"Then you probably know Cassius has assumed the role of dictator," she said. "He no longer answers to the Senate. He no longer answers to anyone. He's doubled enrollment at Lescendor and extended the years of mandatory service, so maybe it's time you asked yourself whether you want to go to the grave doing things you don't like or whether you'll risk what years you have left to make them worth living."

"Nice speech," he muttered. "But if you're looking for a martyr, I'm not it. And yes, we know. Just as we know that you killed Hostus. We should arrest you, but in honesty, not a man in the Thirty-Seventh didn't lift a cup in toast when we heard."

Their conversation stalled after that, both of them walking in silence until they reached the throne room, the entrance flanked by thrice the normal number of guards Marcus preferred. Her stomach tightened at the sight of Gibzen, who'd obviously resumed his duties.

"What is she doing here?" the primus demanded.

"Playing messenger," Servius answered. "Not that it's your business."

"She's a threat."

"That's his decision to make." Servius loomed over the other man. "Or should we tell him that you're making decisions for him?"

Gibzen glared back at Servius for a long moment, then shrugged. "Fine."

"Wait here," Servius said to her, then cracked open one of the enormous twin doors, shutting it behind him before she could peek inside.

"If you've come running back to beg forgiveness, you're wasting your time." Gibzen's mouth twisted in a sneer. "Things are back to normal, and we are winning the way we should. All you've ever been is trouble, and he finally sees that. He can have any girl on any continent, and you've already been had, Teriana."

She tensed at the crudeness of his words. Gibzen had always been an ass, but this . . . this was personal.

"Why do you hate me so much?" she asked, wishing his words didn't hurt as much as they did.

"Because he's ours and you tried to steal him!" he snarled. "He's what makes us the best, and you knew that. Knew that if you ruined him, these shithole kingdoms might actually have a chance." He leaned in close, his breath reeking and rotten as he added, "But you failed, and he's not going to fall for your tricks again."

He's jealous.

The thought roared through her skull, but before she could respond, Gibzen said, "Did you get to say hello to your friend Austornic in Celendrial? How *is* the Fifty-First?"

"Redeployed." The words came out from between her teeth, guilt still sour in her stomach. Though maybe it was for the best that the Fifty-First was out of Marcus's reach.

A slow smile formed on Gibzen's face, as if he knew something she didn't, but then Servius appeared. "He'll see her. Search her for weapons."

Teriana kept her chin high as Gibzen roughly searched her, finding nothing because she'd consciously come unarmed. "Clean," he muttered, obviously disappointed.

Clapping a hand on her shoulder, Servius gave it a squeeze, then directed her inside the gap between the doors. Teriana stepped through, every muscle in her body tensing as the door shut with a resounding *boom.*

The throne room was cold.

Not cold in the way of Sibern, where the air had seemed to press in. Rather as it had been around Cassius, a cold that stole the heat from her flesh, as though if she stood in this room long enough, it would turn her very heart to ice.

Every instinct in her core screamed *danger*, but Teriana held her ground, taking in the room. She'd been here dozens of times in her life, and much of the décor remained, the only noticeable absence the throne that had once sat on the dais. In its place sat a familiar folding table surrounded by flimsy campstools, the surface covered with maps and reports and ledgers. At its head, in his usual seat, sat Marcus.

He hadn't looked up, one elbow resting on the table, the other slightly elevated as he dipped the pen he held in a pot of ink before resuming writing on the page before him.

Everything about him looked the same.

Yet everything about him was different.

"Bold of you to be here given it's rumored you killed Hostus."

Teriana twitched, then forced herself to walk toward the table. "Are you going to arrest me?"

"I've received no orders to do so." He dipped his pen in the ink. "Servius says you have a message from Cordelia."

"I do. I spoke with her when I was in Celendrial arranging the release of my people."

Marcus didn't answer, just kept writing. He wore only a tunic, and near the neck she could see the white of bandages. *What happened to him?*

"She told me the truth." Teriana kept her pace measured as she walked the long length of the room. "Told me about how your parents switched you and your brother, making him heir while you went to Lescendor."

His hand stilled for a moment, then Marcus continued writing. "She's not in favor of this campaign, so she likely told you with the hope that you'd scream it across Celendrial and sabotage me. Which means she must be desperate, because that information is only valuable when Cassius decides it will be valuable, and Cordelia is intelligent enough to recognize that."

"I'm sure she does." Teriana's fingers turned numb. "Which is why she had a different motive."

"Do tell."

"She told me so that I'd understand why you did the things you did. Why you do the things you do."

"The answer to both is that I follow orders."

Swallowing hard, Teriana rose the three steps of the dais and walked the length of the table. Extracting Cordelia's letter from her pocket, she set it on the table next to him.

"You've done your duty," he said, still writing. "Feel free to leave."

Teriana sat on one of the stools and rested her elbows on the table, the shivers wracking her body making the glass of wine at his elbow shake. "Read it."

He sighed but set aside his pen and picked the letter up, scanning the lines. She'd read it on her journey back west. Cordelia had explained the direness of the situation in Celendor, Cassius's abuses of power as dictator, and her fervent wish that Marcus consider returning to remove him from power.

As soon as he finished reading, Marcus held the pages to a candle, then tossed them in a silver bowl to burn. "We are at war, so his dictatorship is not unlawful. If Cordelia dislikes Cassius's politics so much, she should have her husband run for consul once this war is won, and through him, she can give me orders. Until then, I'm afraid I have to decline her suggestion that I commit treason."

Teriana was no fool and had no expectation that Marcus would immediately agree to Cordelia's request, but she had expected to see a reaction. Disgust over what Cassius was doing to Celendor, his abuses of its people, and his increasingly violent tyranny. But it was as Servius had warned. Like talking to a block of ice.

"She believes the only reason you won't do it is because you know that if you take Cassius down, he'll take your family down with him."

"The Thirty-Seventh is my family, and I will not turn them into traitors for the sake of blood." He picked his pen back up. "Why did Cordelia choose to send this message with you? Because I assure you, she's rich and influential enough to have gotten this message past Cassius's censors with little trouble." He started writing. "Is it because she thought you might have sway?"

"Yes."

He stopped writing and, for the first time since she'd walked into the room, looked up at her. Her heart skittered as she stared into not the blue-grey eyes she knew so well, but twin voids that seemed portals to the underworld itself. "Do you think you have sway, Teriana?"

Her heart was racing so fast it hurt, her pulse roaring in her ears as she whispered, "No."

Marcus belonged to the Corrupter now. Perhaps he always had.

A tear slid down her cheek because if she'd stayed, could she have prevented this? Could she have kept the Seventh God from digging his claws into Marcus? Panic rose in Teriana's chest as she was drawn into the voids staring at her. This was her fault.

I failed! she silently screamed. *I walked away. I left him. I cursed Gamdesh.*

Then the sound of waves and the scent of sea washed over her, her mother's voice whispering, *It's not your responsibility to make him do the right thing, daughter, and it never has been.*

Teriana blinked and was once again staring into the voids that were his eyes, although she no longer felt like she was falling.

"I think you should go," Marcus said. "It is my understanding that your people were released, so our arrangement is concluded."

"Not all of them." Reaching into her pocket, she closed her fingers around the tiny ship. "Hostus murdered my mother. Stabbed her right in front me. That's why I killed him."

Marcus closed his eyes, and for a heartbeat, she thought some part of him still remained. Some part of him still cared. Then his lids opened, and the voids looked back. "Everyone present claims it was all shadows in the dark, so you'll likely escape punishment for your vengeance."

Teriana drew in a ragged breath, inhaling the scent of leather and steel and soap, the painful familiarity of it making her heart ache as their time together flashed through her mind. A thousand moments. A thousand emotions. Culminating in the memory of his voice whispering, *I love you.*

Had any of it been real? Or was she mourning the loss of something, of someone, who had never existed at all?

And did it matter, given where they now stood?

"I haven't had my vengeance," Teriana finally said, wiping away the tears that now slicked her cheeks. "We both know that Hostus doesn't shit unless Cassius gives the order, so it's Cassius my sights are set on, and you, Marcus, are his general." She set the hair ornament on the table but kept her hand over it. "We've always been destined to stand on opposite sides of the battlefield, and that time has come."

Lifting her hand, she watched his eyes fix on the miniature ship cast in gold and enamel and *gods-damned* love. "We're going to war, Legatus. And I think it's time you had a taste of what it's like to lose."

79

MARCUS

You don't lose, the voice whispered. *Remind her of that!*

Instead, Marcus gave his head a sharp shake, watching Teriana stride out of the throne room, not once looking back.

His gaze moved to the hair ornament sitting on the table before him, the gold glittering in the lamplight. Though there was no sound in the room, he swore he could hear the sea. Smell it. Taste it.

Reaching out, he touched the ornament, and Teriana's voice echoed through his thoughts. *Hostus murdered my mother. Stabbed her right in front of me.* Guilt flooded over the top of his walls, choking him until he could barely breathe, and Marcus jerked his hand away from the ornament, the emotion receding.

Yet despite the misery the guilt delivered upon him, he felt the strangest compulsion to invite it back. To feel it, because feeling nothing no longer brought the relief it once had. The fists began their pounding on the walls again, a vicious hammering that made his head ache. That made him reach out.

Tentatively, he picked up the tiny ship, a shudder running through him as he heard Teriana say, *We've always been destined to stand on opposite sides of the battlefield, and that time has come.* His hand trembled, the grief that consumed him a thousand times worse than when she'd left because he'd been so long without it.

The ornament dropped to the table with a metallic thud, Marcus sucking in mouthfuls of air until the numbness returned.

"Sir?"

He lifted his head to see Gibzen approaching, eyes narrowed as he asked, "Everything all right?"

"Fine."

"What did she want?"

Marcus's lips parted to tell his primus why Teriana had been here, but then he shook his head. "Nothing that is your concern."

"You sure about that, sir? Because she's caused us problems in the past."

Gibzen's eyes fell on the ornament, and Marcus snatched it up, almost sick to his stomach as emotion swelled over his walls.

"You'd better give that to me," his primus said, holding out his hand. "It's no good to you."

"No."

Gibzen's hand latched onto Marcus's wrist, squeezing. "Let it go."

He didn't want to let it go, because if he did, the hurt would go with it. And he needed that pain.

But the other man's grip was implacable, stronger than it should have been, and Marcus's fingers opened.

The ornament bounced on the table. Gibzen snatched it up and tucked it away. "You'll feel better without it."

He did feel better. Mostly because as soon as Gibzen picked up the ornament, every emotion faded until he felt nothing at all.

"Messenger arrived from Celendrial." Gibzen placed a package on the table. Then set another one next to it, the folded paper sealed with black wax. "And another fell from the sky."

"Shifter?" Marcus touched the black wax, a shiver running over him.

"I didn't see it, but the men say it was some sort of ugly flying horse. Apparently the thing had fangs like a wildcat."

Marcus opened the official letter first, noting Cassius's familiar cursive.

Marcus,

Congratulations on the taking of Revat. I have commissioned a new statue of you to grace the Forum in celebration of your victory, to be put in a place of honor. However it has come to my attention that you did not uphold your end of the deal we made before you set sail on this grand adventure, and you know how I feel about loose ends. Rectify your error, else the consequences will be as they have always been.

Marcus's stomach tightened because the words could only refer to one thing: Cassius had somehow learned that Lydia yet lived. Without Marcus's explanation of what had occurred, Cassius no doubt believed that Marcus had somehow arranged for her escape, and the Dictator would exact a toll for the perceived betrayal.

I understand that the dust has barely settled on Revat, but the cost of your efforts runs high. To ensure the continued funding for the flow of resources your legions need, I request that you secure the gold mines of Rotahn, in Mudamora. It is my understanding that they are the largest of their kind on all of

Reath (the Maarin are so forthcoming!) and having them in our control will ensure you and yours do not go without.

Cura ut valeas,
Cassius

Marcus was not well. He was not well at all.

He read the message a second time, then cracked the black wax on the other, leaning back after he read the offer.

"Trouble?"

"Orders. And an offer of alliance from the Queen of Derin." Marcus held the papers to the candle, then tossed them into the bowl to burn. "The Dictator wants control of Rotahn's gold mines. And his betrothed returned to him. To secure both, we look north to Mudamora."

80

KILLIAN

He didn't stay at the front lines.

Couldn't stay.

Not with the charred ruin of land and bodies stretched out before him every time he looked north, forcing him to remember what he'd done.

Does this feel like victory, Killian Calorian? Does this feel like a battle won?

It had been a victory, of a sort, because the blighter army had taken enormous losses. But it had not been wiped out entirely. They had moved west out of the path of the fire, which continued to rage its way north for Baird had not been able to stop the winds entirely. The deimos still took to the wind, and Killian knew that Rufina would be looking for ways to bolster her strength yet again.

He'd sent runners with orders that every well in every town and village be kept under heavy guard, always with dogs, who seemed uniquely able to recognize blighters for what they were. With the reprieve from the blighters, the Mudamorian army was able to shore up defenses against the blight without fear of constant attack.

It was the breath he'd hoped for, and yet every second Killian remained in sight of the fire, he felt strangled.

So when Dareena arrived to take command, he got on his horse and rode.

Baird came with him, but they traveled in silence. Though Killian had done what he could to be the one held responsible for the fire, the weight of it still hung heavy on the giant. In the darkness of night when they stopped to sleep, he heard Baird weeping more than once.

Yet Killian's own face remained dry, all his grief spent in the moments he sat on the dam and watched Mudamora burn.

Seldrid's spies must have spotted his approach to Serlania, because his brother himself rode out to greet him. At the sight of him, Baird muttered something about finding rest in Bercola's cabin at Teradale and headed in the direction of the Calorian estates.

"Malahi and Agrippa have returned," his brother said. "Lydia and Sonia remained behind, but with the intention of leaving soon after. I'm afraid to say the Cel have laid siege to Revat, and there was little hope that Kaira would prevail against their numbers. They stood strong when Malahi left, but it's possible your vision has come to pass."

"So Lydia was there when Revat fell." Killian stared numbly at the city as they rode closer. "Which means that the Cel have her. That *he* has her."

"We have no confirmation of that. Lydia could be on the *Kairense* sailing this way as we speak." Seldrid cleared his throat. "As it is, Malahi has returned with all we could have hoped for and more. A way to defeat the blight. She and Agrippa are staying at my home, and they will want to see you."

Killian barely listened as Seldrid filled his ears with the news while they rode through the overcrowded city, his heart consumed with certainty that the man who'd tried to murder Lydia now had her as his prisoner.

Then his ears perked. "Did you just say that Teriana is free?"

Seldrid nodded. "The Cel apparently allowed her and the *Quincense* to go. She liberated her people from their capital, although no word has been heard from her since. I have informants watching and listening north and south."

Part of Killian was overjoyed to hear his friend was now free, but the other part felt abruptly sick. If Teriana had been with the legions, it was possible she could have intervened to help Lydia if she was captive. But if Teriana was gone . . . "I need a ship, Seldrid. I need to get to Gamdesh to find Lydia."

His brother's lips parted as though to argue, then he nodded. "I'll go to the harbor to make arrangements. But speak to Malahi first."

He didn't want to speak to Malahi. Didn't want to see her face, knowing that she'd abandoned Lydia in Revat while fleeing to save her own neck.

"Hacken is in Teradale with the High Lords." Seldrid shifted in his saddle. "There was desire on their part to reinstate Malahi as High Lady of Rowenes, but Hacken has been stymieing the process, most likely because he doesn't want anyone who is loyal to Lydia to have a vote. He wants her beholden to him. But since Ria's death, the High Lords trust him even less than they did before. They see everything he does as a bid to make himself king, and rather than their focus being on the war, they've been infighting the entire time you've been gone with little care for Rufina, the blight, or the Cel. It's a gods-damned mess, and I half expect Mother to evict them from her house out of pure frustration. We don't just want Lydia back, Killian, we *need* her back. Mudamora needs a ruler now more than ever."

"I'll get her back," Killian said softly. "And the Six have mercy on anyone who tries to stop me."

Seldrid snorted. "Never mind mercy. Send anyone who tries to stop you to the Seventh. I'll head to the harbor now."

Killian carried on to his brother's manor in the middle of Serlania. The guards at the gates opened them for him without question, and Killian handed off his horse to a stable hand.

Finn was sitting on the steps.

"Why aren't you at Teradale," he asked the boy, who had a bandage wrapped around his arm.

"Adra and Seldrid brought me back to Serlania with them," Finn said. "After your dog bit me."

"Socks bit you?" Killian blinked in surprise, because the dog didn't have a mean bone in his body. "Are you all right?"

"Was nothing. We were just scrapping and it got out of hand, but Adra likes to mother me." Finn shrugged. "I like Serlania better, anyway. My subjects are all here and it's easier to keep them in line."

It wasn't safe in the streets of Serlania. Not with food scarce and the city bursting with refugees from the north. "Stay in the manor, Finn. It's not safe in the streets."

"Safer now than it was. I heard you killed the blighters that were coming toward Serlania," his young friend said. "Then burned half of Rufina's army alive."

"They aren't alive," Killian muttered, his mouth turning sour as he remembered the smell. "Just walking corpses puppeted by the Seventh."

"Still, you single-handedly killed half her army. That's a victory."

Does this feel like victory, Killian Calorian? Does this feel like a battle won?

"Finn, I'm not interested in reliving that moment," Killian snapped. "I need to find Malahi. Please stay within the manor's walls."

Leaving the boy on the steps, he went inside, a servant directing him where to find Malahi. With every step Killian took, his temper grew worse. At Finn, for celebrating one of the worst atrocities of this war. At Malahi, for leaving Lydia in Revat to be captured by the Cel. But most of all at himself, because he'd been given every power to protect those he loved and yet all he left in his wake was death.

Malahi sat in the manor's small library with Adra and Agrippa. "Killian!" She rose to her feet. "Gods, we heard—"

"Why did you leave her!" he shouted.

Agrippa was on his feet in a flash, stepping between Killian and Malahi. "Watch your tone, Killian. We tried to make Lydia leave, but she was having none of it. Short of trussing her up and dragging her onto the ship—"

"You should have. You should have made her go, but as usual, Malahi only thinks of herself and the *kingdom*. You had the information you needed, so of course you cut and run."

Malahi blanched, but swiftly recovered. "We did find the answers to destroying the blight, but I can't do it without Lydia. I didn't want to leave her, but she was dead set on hunting down a solution for the infected. And though she never admitted it, a way to bring back the blighters themselves."

Killian's stomach dropped. "What? That's . . . that's impossible. You can't cure death and it's—"

"Death to the healer who tries, I know." Malahi rested a calming hand on Agrippa's arm. "But you know how Lydia is."

Gods help him, Killian knew better than anyone. And while Lydia had been risking her life to find a way to save the Mudamorian blighters, he'd been busy burning them to ash. Endless thousands now beyond salvation no matter what Lydia had discovered.

Heedless that he was filthy, he sat on one of the sofas, shaking his head when Adra offered him a drink. "I need to find her."

Adra set the whiskey down on the table, then knelt before him. "I know you had a vision of Revat falling, Killian, but we have heard no confirmation that it has come to pass. Lydia might well be on the *Kairense* and nearly in the harbor. Or Kaira might be successfully holding off the Cel."

He lifted his head to meet Agrippa's gaze, and his friend shook his head. "Marcus has close to forty thousand legionnaires in his main force. I counted thirty catapults bombarding the walls, a dozen siege towers, and they blocked off the river that flows through the city. But worst of all, they have a good-sized fleet that looked like it was making ready to enter the harbor. It was just a matter of when, not if."

Killian's chest clenched, it suddenly so very hard to breathe.

"But we found the answers," Malahi said. "A very old manuscript that detailed how the tenders cured Anukastre. They all died, but if Lydia is with me, she has the power to keep me alive. We can win this."

He didn't care. Without Lydia, nothing mattered, and in his heart, Killian *knew* that Lydia had been in Revat when the god towers fell.

I'll get her back, he swore. *I will kill them all if I have to, but I will free her.*

Then a commotion caught his attention. Sounds of alarm.

Rising, Killian drew his sword and made his way through the manor. Only to discover the servants surrounding a naked Gamdeshian woman who was sprawled on the floor.

"Astara!" Adra shoved past him. "Get a blanket! Medicines! She's injured."

She pulled the woman into her arms, and Killian caught sight of a wound in the shifter's thigh. It had been stitched, but the stitches had torn open and blood was leaking on the floor.

Astara sipped greedily from a cup of water Adra held to her lips, then whispered, "Revat has fallen to the Cel. Kaira is dead, and the towers of the Six have fallen."

Killian dropped to his knees next to her. "Was a Mudamorian healer taken prisoner? A young woman named Lydia?"

"Sonia would have been with her," Adra added. "They were in the library."

"I don't know." Astara winced as a cloth was pressed to her bleeding wound. "I was captured in Emrant. Kept as their prisoner. I'm only free because . . . because . . ." She squeezed her eyes tightly shut for a long moment, and when they opened, her composure had returned. "I barely escaped with my life to bring word that we need your aid in our time of great need."

"Would that we had soldiers and ships to send, but all we can give is hope," Malahi said. "In Revat's final hours of freedom, it gave us the answers we needed to destroy the blight and drive back the Seventh. Once that is done, we will unite with all our allies and destroy the Cel incursion."

Killian bit back a retort that *none* of this was Malahi's decision to make, only for Seldrid to walk into his house, calmly taking in the scene as he said, "The *Kairense* has been spotted sailing this way, and Lydia has been seen on decks with Captain Vane. It will take them some time to get a space in the harbor, but our queen is here. And I, for one, think this will be the moment that the tides turn in our favor."

Relief flooded Killian with such force that he was glad he was already on his knees. "I'm going to the harbor."

Yet as he strode to the entrance, it was to come face-to-face with his mother. Her hair was tangled and her skirts stained with mud, but it was her eyes, which were red and swollen, that stopped Killian in his tracks. "Mother?"

"I bring fell news," she whispered. "The High Lords pushed a vote this morning to take the crown from Lydia on the belief she is either dead or imprisoned, and to crown Helene Torrington, who has agreed to wed High Lord Pitolt's son, Rodern. Hacken opposed it, and Helene formally accused him of murdering Ria. They had a trial and a vote, and the High Lords convicted him. All our soldiers went north with you, and there was nothing to be done to stop the lords and their men. They hanged your brother in my gardens."

It took several moments for her words to register. To make sense. For him to understand exactly what his mother had said, because it seemed impossible. Yet the tears in her eyes told him it was no fabrication.

Hacken was dead.

He'd had more conflict with his brother than not, no love lost between them, yet Killian still waited for grief to rise. Or guilt. Yet he felt nothing but numbness.

"This will be calamity." Seldrid's voice was shaky. "A war for the crown while enemies press in on all sides. Gods-damn Helene for doing this!"

Does this feel like victory, Killian Calorian? Does this feel like a battle won?

Killian took a breath, then another. Because as long as he was still breathing, he could fight. "The queen is sailing into the harbor now," he said over the tumult. "And by the Six, we will do all that it takes to keep the crown on her head."

81

LYDIA

The mood during the passage back to Serlania was somber, the knowledge of how to defeat the blight doing little to compensate for the loss of Aspasiana, the presumed death of Kaira, or the fall of the mightiest city of the West.

Rather than being angry about having been trussed up and forcibly removed from Revat, Sultan Kalin was silent. Broken. Lydia couldn't speak to what the man had been like before, but the man he was now appeared fragile and ancient. He did nothing but stare at their wake, Vane tasking two of his sailors to remain at his side lest he attempt to fling himself overboard in despair over the loss of his only child.

Sonia tried speaking to him. "Sire," she said. "All is not lost. Your civilians are gathering on the western coast, and they will fight for you. Fight for Revat. Our soldiers will rally to them and you must lead them."

"The Empire cannot be defeated without Kaira," was his response. "They are as locusts upon the land."

"You try speaking to him," Sonia had asked Lydia. "You're queen of Mudamora. The High Lady of House Falorn. Tell him that Mudamora will aid Gamdesh once the blight is defeated, which is sure to be soon. Give him hope."

Except Lydia didn't feel like a queen. Didn't know what words she could say or what she could commit to, and she badly wished Malahi were here to advise. Malahi, who personally knew Sultan Kalin and would know exactly what to say. "The Cel are just men," she told him. "Nothing more than well-trained soldiers, and though it will be difficult, they can be defeated."

"Men who topple gods," Kalin had responded. "Evil rules Gamdesh now, just as it rules Mudamora. There is no hope."

To hope felt terrifying, yet that was what they needed to cling to the most as they ventured north to do battle against Rufina.

To war against the Corrupter.

The *Kairense* was recognized on approach, space cleared for them in the overpacked harbor of Serlania. As she stood at the railing,

Lydia's eyes latched onto a familiar tall form pacing the docks and her heart skipped. "Killian."

She'd done her best not to dwell on their separation while in Revat, but the ache of not having him at her side suddenly struck her like a battering ram to the stomach, tears welling in her eyes.

"Something has happened in our absence," Sonia murmured, and Lydia's gaze skipped from Killian to Agrippa and Malahi, all three of them grim faced. "And it's nothing good."

The ship bumped against the docks, workers catching lines and tying them off even as a gangplank was lowered. Not caring about propriety, Lydia pushed past the Maarin crew and sprinted down the dock. She flung her arms around Killian's neck, a sob tearing from her throat as he wrapped his arms around her.

"I thought they'd captured you." Killian's voice was rough. "I thought I'd lost you."

"It was a near thing, but we got out in time." Her throat tightened. "But not without cost."

"We heard of Revat's fate. The Cel had a Gamdeshian shifter named Astara prisoner, but she managed to escape and make it to Serlania."

Lydia buried her face in his throat, relieved not to be the bearer of every piece of dark news. "Kaira?"

"Dead in battle. The Cel hold the city. All those who survived the battle are locked in prisoner camps."

Grief pooled in Lydia's stomach. "She put Sultan Kalin on the *Kairense* before she rode out to fight. He's here, but he's . . . grieving."

"Adra will help him through it. He needs to rally for Gamdesh."

Killian's fingers flexed against her back, and unease filled Lydia's core because tension seethed from him. Letting go of his neck, she met his dark gaze. "What has happened?"

"Ria fell to blight poisoning." His jaw was tight, and Lydia noted the circles of exhaustion beneath his eyes. "It was one of Rufina's agents, but Helene and the other High Lords blamed Hacken and accused him of murder." His throat moved as he swallowed hard. "They hanged him this morning, and they are planning to strip the crown from your head and put it on Helene's. Likely because she'll be the proper puppet that they all want."

"I'll try to intervene," Malahi said. "I've no notion if Ria named an heir, but if not, I may be able to reclaim my vote. Helene is no leader, and every decision will be subject to infighting between the

High Lords. Mudamora needs a queen who can lead, and that queen is you, Lydia."

That queen is you, Malahi, Lydia thought, but only nodded. "Any word from Teriana? Kaira told me that the Cel released her." She kept what else Kaira had said to herself.

"No," Killian said. "Nor of the *Quincense.*"

"The Gamdeshians blame her for everything." Lydia glanced over her shoulder to watch Sonia leading Kalin carefully down the gangplank.

"Everyone likes a scapegoat," Agrippa muttered. "Especially one who can't defend herself."

It wasn't fair.

"Lydia, did you find out any more information after we left?" Malahi's eyes were full of hope. "Is there a way to bring them back?"

Killian visibly stiffened, and Lydia shot a glance at him before she said, "No. I found no answers beyond what you already know." Malahi's face crumpled, and Lydia felt a surge of kinship toward the other woman, for no one desired to bring back the Mudamorians lost to blight as much as Malahi did. "We will fight for the living, and the Six willing, we'll find a way to bring the blighters back to us along the way. I refuse to abandon them."

Killian shifted restlessly. "They are dead, Lydia. You can't bring back the dead."

"Unnaturally dead. There is nothing wrong with many of their bodies, and I refuse to give up hope of a way to restore them."

"Let go of that hope," Killian said in a low voice. "Because I burned more than half of the blighter army to ash."

Shock stole the breath from Lydia's chest, but she still managed to say, "What?"

"There was no other good option. Our army at the front was losing the fight to hold back the blight, because the blighters kept attacking them. So I lit a fire behind their lines and with Baird's help, blew a firestorm north that took out half of Rufina's army. The blow put her on her heels, and our army is successfully damming all new blight flows, preventing the incursion into the south. But there is no *reviving* the blighters who burned. They are gone."

Horror soured Lydia's stomach, and she took a step away from Killian. Hurt pooled in his dark eyes, along with guilt and grief, but she held her ground. He shouldn't have done it. Shouldn't have taken such a final step.

“On that revelation, let’s not linger out in the open any longer than we have to,” Agrippa said, gesturing to the waiting carriage. “We know that Rufina has blighters posing as civilians, which means anyone around us could be ears for the enemy.”

“He’s right.” Killian muttered, his eyes roving the busy docks. Not, she thought, because he was worried about spies, but to avoid meeting her gaze. “And you’re the only one in the city who can see them for what they are.”

Lydia’s skin abruptly crawled, and she allowed her focus to drift. Her gaze skipped over the mass of humanity in the harbor and her chest tightened as she spotted a young boy disembarking one of the refugee ships with his family. He skipped down the dock but his body was as lifeless as stone. He glanced at her, then at his mother, who was very much one of the living, smiling as she kissed his forehead. “I see one.”

“Where?” Agrippa demanded, unslinging the bow looped over his shoulder. Killian drew his sword, both of them searching for that which they could not see.

“The boy with his family,” Lydia whispered, the moment dragging her back to the horror that had been her time in Mudaire hunting the blighters. “Perhaps ten years of age, green tunic, red hair.”

Agrippa trained his arrow on the child, and Lydia grabbed his arm. “Don’t.”

“If he’s a blighter, then he’s a threat.”

“He’s just a child,” Lydia hissed. “And he’s not the only one. I see . . . six. No, eight. Nine.”

And they were all watching, not making any particular effort to hide their nature from her. Almost as though they were daring her to take action.

“We can’t just start killing children in the middle of Serlania’s harbor,” she snapped. “Their families won’t believe they’re infected, and it won’t be long until the mob turns on us. Better to get the Sultan somewhere secure.”

They moved swiftly down the docks to the waiting carriages, Sonia already seated with Kalin inside one of them. Lydia and her friends climbed into the other. Except for Killian. “I’ll sit up top with the coachman,” he muttered.

A part of Lydia, a big part, wept for the tension between them, but she could not deny that a part of her was sick with anger that he'd destroyed any hope of saving countless Mudamorians in one fell swoop. That he'd made the decision without her. It felt strangely like betrayal.

"Where's Dareena?" Lydia asked once the carriage began moving.

"The front lines," Agrippa answered. "Even with the blow to Rufina's numbers, she's still pressing them hard, and the blighters from Derin joined the ranks."

"How?" she demanded. "Dead or not, they still travel by foot."

Agrippa exhaled. "If I had to guess, it's by way of xenthier, and if I'm right, the blame can be cast at my feet. I told Rufina how the Empire uses the paths and opened that door. With a nearly unlimited supply of walking corpses, it's nothing to her if they go through a bad path and end up at the bottom of a lake or in a cave with no exit. The Senate bribes people to report stems they discover, but Rufina is getting that knowledge fed to her at no cost."

"Except in lives." Malahi picked at the fabric of her dress. "Lydia, now that you are here, we need to start thinking of a way to get to Deadground. It won't be easy with Mudamora overrun with blight. Horses will be almost immediately infected, so we'll need to go on foot. In truth, no one who isn't marked should go."

"We already argued about this, love," Agrippa said. "I'm going. But I also think we should have Astara, once Lydia fixes her up, scout Deadground to ensure the corrupted tenders are still there. That's a long walk to discover Rufina's moved them somewhere else."

"I'm not sure that moving them is possible," Lydia said. "When I went into their mounds looking for Malahi, I tried to free one of them, but cutting her loose from her . . . roots? Vines?" She gave her head a sharp shake. "Whatever you want to call them, being cut away from the blight flow caused her to wither and die. According to our research, she likely regenerated or is in the process of doing so, but I don't think it's possible to move them."

All eyes went to Agrippa, but he lifted his hands in a shrug. "My command was over the living, and those parasites gave me the creeps. They were Rufina's domain, not mine, but she never tried to move them while I was there. Only sat with them, like they were some sort of sick garden she was tending."

Malahi reached up a hand to touch the livid scar on her face. "I remember when she learned from a deimos rider that one of her tenders had been destroyed. She didn't seem to know that it would . . .

regrow. She wanted me to replace the loss, and when I refused, she flew into a rage and cut my face."

Guilt soured Lydia's stomach, for she'd caused Rufina's reaction. Reaching out, she took Malahi's free hand. "I'm sorry. That was my doing."

Malahi lifted her head. "Don't be sorry. It's good information, because I'm remembering what she said in her rage. She kept screaming at me that she needed me to pick up the threads or the fruits would be lost to her. I was in too much pain to consider what she meant, but now I'm wondering what that might mean."

"I'm sure we'll find out," Agrippa muttered. "After we cut across a dead kingdom infested with walking corpses controlled by the Seventh God and destroy a parasitic garden protected by corrupted."

Everyone fell silent, and Lydia looked out the carriage window to see they were passing through the heavily armed gates of a large manor. The carriages came to a halt, a servant running up to open the door. Killian was sitting on top, eyes roving their surroundings, then he reached up to help Lydia exit. "You see anyone we should worry about?"

Lydia slowly rotated, taking in all the soldiers and servants, as well as Seldrid and Adra, who had appeared at the entrance, both dressed in black. "No. No blighters."

"Good. I'll arrange restrictions on the coming and going of the staff, but I think it best if you and I take a look around to make sure everyone on the property is of the living. I'll also arrange for dogs to join the patrols."

She nodded as Seldrid came down the steps, bowing low. Adra followed, dropping into a curtsey, but Lydia didn't fail to notice the woman's eyes were bloodshot from crying. "I'm sorry for the loss of Kaira," she said softly. "She sacrificed herself for the sake of Reath."

"A sacrifice that netted her nothing," Adra retorted. "For she is dead and the Cel army holds Revat. Better that she'd escaped to fight another day, but it was never her way to run."

"We're out of places to run *to*," Lydia said. "At some point, we need to stand our ground even if it means some of us falling. But I have good news for you. Your uncle, Sultan Kalin, is in the other carriage with Sonia."

Adra gasped, then hurried to the carriage. "Uncle!"

Sonia climbed out, her expression grim as she watched Adra help the Sultan out of the carriage, then she turned and approached. "He'll barely speak to me, but hopefully Adra will have luck. Lord

Calorian, do you know where I might find Finn? He's my responsibility and I've left him unattended for too long."

Lydia perked up at the mention of the boy, for she'd not seen him at Teradale and her young friend's humor would be welcome right now.

"I saw him in the kitchen earlier," Seldrid answered. "Though he's not one to sit still, that boy."

"He'll be here somewhere," Killian said. "I forbade him to leave."

Sonia sighed. "That will have the opposite effect you intended. I'll find him."

Lydia watched her friend, who'd not recovered any of her spirit since Kaira's death, disappear inside.

"We're glad to have you back alive and well, Your Grace," Seldrid said, and she noted the exhaustion that hadn't been there when she'd departed marring his face. "We feared the worst when Malahi and Agrippa returned without you. Did you discover more information to aid our cause?"

"Wasted time, I'm afraid." How many times would she have to admit that she had no solution? How many times would she have to admit that even if they were victorious, she'd spend every day thereafter still feeling as though she'd failed? A failure made worse by the cost of Aspasiana's life, which was a catastrophic loss to the Maarin that wouldn't have happened if she'd left earlier.

Seldrid made a noncommittal noise, then gestured to the door. "I assume you've been updated. We need to move swiftly on many things. I'll have food and drink served while we set our course."

Lydia started to follow Seldrid, but Killian caught hold of her hand and pulled her back while the others entered.

"I'm sorry," he said. "I didn't know that you hoped to save them. It seemed like the only way to buy us time, and even knowing what I do now, I'm not sure I'd do differently."

"We're at war." Lydia's tongue felt thick, her throat choked. "You did what you thought you had to."

"As did you." Killian's hand pressed against the small of her back. "Every instinct in me screams that the Corrupter didn't want you in that library for a reason."

"Because the answers for Malahi were there."

"And yet Malahi has never been his target."

"Because he knows she won't ever turn to darkness." Her eyes tracked Malahi's blond hair as she walked inside, now a neatly trimmed cap, the bald spots grown in.

"Or because you're the threat."

She sighed. "This is speculation, Killian. Whereas there are facts demanding our attention. Let's go inside."

Leaving him to follow, Lydia rose the steps into the blissful coolness of the manor, the scent of flowers filling her nose, her boot heels clicking over the tiles. It was quiet after the noise of the city, but the serenity was destroyed by a familiar voice echoing down a corridor. "Let me go, Sonia!"

"I will not," the Gamdeshian woman retorted. "Not until you explain to Killian why you were trying to sneak out past the guards."

"I have business in the city!" Finn shouted. "My subjects need to be fed, and the Calorian larders are always full. They won't miss a few sacks of food."

"You don't steal from your hosts!"

Lydia stopped in her tracks as Sonia appeared, dragging a struggling Finn behind her.

And at the sight of him, all the air disappeared from Lydia's lungs.

Sonia glowered at Killian. "He's already back to his old tricks!"

The boy stared Lydia in the eye, and she stared back, a tremble running through her, as Killian said, "It's fine, Sonia. Seldrid can handle having his larders pilfered for the good of a few children. Finn's doing the right thing, because there are many . . ." He trailed off, his eyes moving to Lydia. "What's wrong?"

She sucked in a shaking breath, still staring the creature in the eye. "That is not Finn."

82

KILLIAN

Even as his heart screamed in wordless fury and grief, his instincts took over. Killian caught hold of Finn by the arms, restraining him.

No, not Finn.

A blighter. Which meant every word Finn had said was the Corrupter's.

"What are you going on about, Lydia?" the blighter demanded, mumming Finn with such perfection that Killian knew that Finn had likely been dead for every conversation they'd had. That all the things he'd told the boy were words told to a spy. And rather than recognizing that something was wrong with the boy who was like a younger brother to him, Killian had brushed him aside at every turn.

"It's me." The blighter's face sagged with fear, his eyes skipping around the room. Everyone with a weapon held it in their hands, faces white with horror. "It is! I don't know what she's saying!"

"Stop." Lydia's voice was frosty as ice. "You will cease this farce."

All the tension in the boy fell away, and the blighter that wore Finn's face gave a sigh that was half chuckle, the voice that emanated from his lips like nails on a chalkboard as it said, "As you like, *Your Grace.* Though I would have enjoyed watching your companions tormented with uncertainty over the verity of your claim."

"You mistake grief for uncertainty, for you have stolen someone dear to us."

Killian *knew* that tone. Knew that in the depths of rage and despair, Lydia was descending to a place where she had the potential to become very dangerous. He could tell that Agrippa heard it, too, as he pushed Malahi away from the threat.

"But were you dear to him?" the blighter asked. "I dare say that even left to his devices, he'd have gladly revealed your secrets. You, who caused the only person he cared about to abandon him over and over."

"Finn wasn't like that," Lydia hissed. "I never met a more selfless person, and I will not allow you to use his body."

"Will you order Killian to cut off his head?" the voice asked, using Finn's eyes to look at Killian. "Burn his corpse? This boy, who you swore to protect but abandoned with little thought. Who you left to make his own way, fed and watered, but forgotten by the one who mattered to him most. He was easy to take given his propensity to seek out those in dire circumstances. He died alone in Serlania's sewers. Died in agony and in fear, then rose on my strings to listen to you prattle on about a thousand concerns, none of which were him. What agony for him to watch you use his corpse to unburden your soul, with no care for how he suffered."

Killian clenched his teeth, hating the awful words because they were *true.* He had abandoned Finn to Sonia's care knowing full well that she wasn't who the boy needed. Had barely given him a second thought, every part of him consumed by other concerns. And because of that, Finn had died alone.

"Finn is gone!" Lydia snarled. "His soul is with the Six and his cares no longer of this world."

The voice laughed, the sound grating and awful. "Are you sure about that, Kitaryia?"

"Yes." Lydia's voice was stalwart and certain, but Killian felt her waver. "There is no life in him."

"Is a soul alive? Or is it, perhaps, something else entirely? Something that might be chained by the very power that puppets this body, made to watch while his friends turn on him. Will you lock him up, as you did dear little Emmy? Or will you order the one he loves like a brother to cut him down? Will Finn finally bear witness to how little he mattered to you both?"

Oh gods, no.

"Liar," Lydia whispered. "You're a liar. The greatest of all liars."

The voice made a humming noise, then said, "Lies never hurt quite as much as the truth."

Killian's skin crawled, instincts screaming that the threat was no longer the blighter but Lydia. "Agrippa, get everyone out!"

A heartbeat later, Lydia lunged, wrenching Finn's body from Killian's grasp, her hands clamping on the sides of the boy's head. "Let him go!" she screamed, her voice wrath incarnate.

All around them was chaos, Agrippa forcing everyone from the room as Lydia wrestled with Finn's struggling corpse.

His eyes were bottomless pits, his screams of rage inhumanly loud, the sound piercing and cruel. Black veins rose to the surface of Finn's skin, pulsing with a throbbing beat of a dark heart, the flow moving toward Lydia's hands.

Then into her.

She screamed, and Killian clenched his teeth as black veins crisscrossed her pale hands, rising up her wrists. As she took death into herself and warred against it, drawing in life from across Reath to aid in her battle.

A battle he was helpless to help fight.

He lunged for her, but then Agrippa had him by the arm. "Don't!" he shouted. "She can do this. She can defeat him!"

Lydia howled, her voice a mix of agony and rage. Then the black veins down her arm seemed to set aflame with brilliant light before disappearing entirely.

She'd won.

Finn slumped in her arms, the Corrupter vanquished from his body, his eyes once again a soft brown. But they were also glassy and lifeless.

Yet the determination on Lydia's face remained as she reached out her left hand to the open air, her right pressed against Finn's cheek.

One cannot heal death, and death to the healer who tries.

Killian lunged, reaching for Lydia to pull her free.

But he was too late.

He could not see the life that she manipulated, but he felt it. The surge as she dragged upon all of Reath, the windows around them exploding, the pressure knocking him to the floor. Holding him down and tearing at the fabric of his clothes, glass and shredded flowers swirling around them in a maelstrom.

Then everything went still.

Killian lifted his head, relief filling him at the sight of Lydia, alive, Finn's body clutched against her.

His still body.

"Please," she wept. "Please come back to us."

Killian crawled on his hands and knees, ignoring the slice of glass on his palms, and took Finn from her.

"I'm so sorry." Tears ran down his cheeks to splatter on Finn's face. "I'm so sorry I abandoned you. That I didn't listen. But I swear on the Six, it was never because I didn't care. I failed you, and I'm sorry."

"The Corrupter lied." Lydia slammed her fists against the floor. "It was a lie, all a lie. Finn's gone, they're all gone, and there is nothing I can do to save them. *Nothing.*" The impact of her fists cracked the tiles. "What good is all this power if I cannot save those I love most?"

Killian's eyes went back to Finn's face, which was so still despite being flushed with the life that Lydia had put into him. Life that was worthless without the soul that made Finn *Finn.*

Killian knew war. Had seen so many die, yet losing Finn had cut a piece out of him that would never heal. A piece that felt far too much like hope.

There was no sound in the room but Sonia's weeping. Lydia's ragged breathing. His own heart throbbing in his chest. As though the whole world stood still, watching this moment.

As though the Six were watching as well.

Then Finn sucked in a deep breath, his back arching and eyes snapping open. A flash of fear made Killian's skin crawl, because if the Corrupter had taken Finn back again then Killian would have to take him down.

And he didn't think he could do it. Didn't think that his heart would survive turning his weapon on Finn.

Yet Killian still reached for his sword. Only for Lydia's fingers to close over his wrist. "He's alive."

Not possible.

Bringing back the dead was not a power of this world. It was a power of a god.

Lydia was no longer bound by mortal rules.

Finn's eyes met his. "Killian?"

"We've got you, Finn." His words tripped over themselves. "We got you back. It's okay."

The boy burst into tears, and Killian pulled him against his chest. "It's okay."

"It's not okay." Finn could barely get his words out between sobs. "I could see everything. Hear everything. But *it* controlled everything, and it tells everything to *her*."

"Her? You mean the Corrupter?"

"Rufina! She is twice touched by the Seventh God, and they are connected. She wields his power. Wields the death in the blight." Finn sucked in a ragged breath. "She *knows* Malahi and Lydia can fix the blight together, Killian. She knows you all plan to go to Deadground. She knows everything I saw and *everything* you told me."

Killian's hands turned to ice, his mind pouring over everything he'd told Finn. Worse still, everything that the boy would have overheard without anyone paying him any mind. The answer was damning.

"All the eyes of evil are focused on us," Finn whispered. "And they are coming."

83

TERIANA

For all that the harbor had been packed, Serlania itself was worse, the streets of the largest city in Mudamora full to the brim. Soldiers patrolled to keep order, and Teriana, Yedda, and Polin passed long lines of people waiting to be provided with food, their faces pinched with hunger.

On the lips of everyone was the progress of the blight, which had consumed the northern two thirds of the kingdom. Dareena Falorn apparently commanded the front lines, but Serlania, overflowing as it was, had become the last bastion of the living in Mudamora in the fight against Rufina's army of the dead.

Blighters, the people called them, a term Bait had made Teriana familiar with during their journey. He'd told her how those who accidentally ingested or touched the blight became sick, eventually dying only to animate under the will of the Corrupter. He told her that these walking dead possessed all the knowledge and memories of the people they'd once been, but they were no longer *them.* Just puppets that the Seventh God used to manipulate and harm the living, recognizable only to Hegeria's marked, who were now few and far between.

When Teriana had told her crew about the changes in Marcus's behavior and how his eyes had looked like voids, they'd questioned whether he might have been somehow infected with the blight, but every part of Teriana resisted the idea that Marcus had been reduced to an animated corpse. "I could see him breathing," she'd told them. "See the pulse in his throat."

"The blighters are the same," Bait had quietly told her, for he was the only person to have seen one. "It's what makes them so dangerous, Teriana. They look alive. But it's not them anymore."

"You've also told me the process of how one of them dies," she responded. "Marcus is constantly surrounded, and there is no way that the Cel would follow someone they watched rise from the dead. This is something different. He's not a puppet."

"It might be a relief for you to know that the man you loved died somewhere along the way," her aunt had said softly when she'd pulled Teriana aside. "To know that the change you saw, the cruelty, wasn't Marcus but rather the Seventh."

It was tempting to believe that notion, because then she could grieve Marcus's death even as she fought an enemy that she'd never loved. But in her heart, Teriana knew that Marcus was very much alive and that it was only the darker side of him that she'd faced in Revat. Undeniably he was influenced by the Corrupter, but where the blighters were puppets, Marcus was the Seventh's ally.

"The chatter on the docks is that Lydia is here," Bait said as they reached Seldrid's manor. A grand structure Teriana had been inside many times. Made of a pale grey stone, it rose three stories high with thick vines of ivy climbing its walls. Great sweeping balconies sat beneath enormous windows. Windows that were all shattered, glass sprayed over the lavish grounds.

"Something has happened here," she said. "And it's nothing good."

Soldiers patrolled the stone wall surrounding the property and more still guarded the gate. But next to the banner of the galloping horse of House Calorian was the familiar falcon of House Falorn.

Lydia, who was Kitaryia Falorn, and now Queen of Mudamora, was here.

"Halt!" one of the soldiers shouted as they approached the gate. "Civilians must stay back twenty paces!"

"My name is Teriana of the *Quincense*," she called back. "I bring important information for Lydia . . . er, for the Queen. I need to speak with her immediately. Just tell her I'm here."

"That's not possible," the guard replied. "Be on your way."

She took a step closer, only to freeze as arrows trained on her chest. "Be on your way!" the guard barked, and Bait caught hold of her arm, tugging her back a step.

"I need to see her!" Frustration built in Teriana's chest, because of all the obstacles she'd known were ahead of her, not being able to see Lydia hadn't been one of them.

"Stand down," a familiar voice said. Killian walked between the guards and through the gate. "You're a sight for sore eyes, Teriana."

She flung her arms around his neck, not caring about propriety as she said, "You have no idea how good it is to see your face."

"We've been worried about you. We learned that you'd managed to free those who'd been imprisoned by the Cel but that you'd not been heard from since."

"I've been in Revat," she answered. "It's fallen."

"I know," he said. "Lydia was there when it happened and only just returned. One of your triumvirs managed to get her out just before they blockaded the harbor. Aspasiana was killed protecting the *Kairense*, though I suppose you know that."

"Lydia was in Revat?" She pushed him back to arm's length, noting the dark circles beneath his brown eyes, and the thick shadow of stubble that verged on a beard covering his jaw. "Why?"

"The library." Killian scrubbed a hand through his dark brown hair, which had grown longer than she'd ever seen him wear it. "I'll explain when we're inside. There are blighters in the city serving as Rufina's spies, and Lydia is their target for reasons better explained out of earshot."

The back of Teriana's neck prickled. She glanced over her shoulder, searching the masses of people on the street facing the manor despite knowing she wouldn't recognize the enemy if they were right before her. "Inside seems wise."

The soldiers saluted Killian as he led Teriana and her crew between them, shutting and latching the gates behind them. The grounds were the same as they'd always been, feeling like one of the last places in the West untouched by war. A candle in the dark night.

More guards flanked the entrance, though they didn't hesitate to open the door for Killian, both saluting sharply.

"We'll wait here," Yedda said, taking hold of Bait's arm and preventing him from following. Giving her privacy as Killian led her inside.

"What happened?" she asked as she took in the ruined foyer and the servants sweeping up bits of glass and shredded flowers.

Killian's eyes darkened. "A battle of wills." He blew out a long breath, then shook his head. "Your arrival is good news in a sea of bad. We feared the worst with the rumors we heard."

Her palms turned cold, because if Killian had heard rumors about her and Marcus, then Lydia surely had as well.

"We put no stock in them, though. Lydia's been stalwart in her faith in you."

Teriana's stomach hollowed, for it would have been easier if they already knew. If she didn't need to confess everything she'd done. "They're true."

Killian was silent, and she risked a glance upward at him, finding his eyes forward and his jaw tight.

"I didn't know what he'd done to her until Bait told me." Her breath caught as she warred with tears, because Killian had been her friend their entire lives. "I know it doesn't change the outcome, but . . ." Teriana trailed off, knowing she didn't deserve forgiveness and that to push for it only made what she'd done worse.

"It's Lydia you need to talk to about this," he said. "Not me."

They reached Seldrid's ballroom, the guards outside the doors saluting Killian on his approach, quietly opening one of the twin doors to allow them inside. At the center of the room was a large table littered with what looked like maps. It was surrounded by people. Seldrid she recognized immediately thanks to his brilliant blue and gold coat, but Malahi took her longer. The young woman was much changed by her imprisonment, only Bait's forewarning allowing Teriana to see past the scars and short hair to the girl she'd once known. A good-looking young man with golden brown skin and dark hair was banging his fist down on a map and gesturing wildly with his free hand. His ire was directed at the tall woman who sat in a chair with her back to the door.

If not for knowing that Dareena was on the front lines, that was who Teriana would have thought it was, with her midnight hair twisted up into complicated knots, the base of her skull shaved to reveal a black falcon tattoo on the back of her skull. She wore a coat and trousers, riding boots that rose to her knees, and a knife belted at her waist.

But Lydia was her sister, and Teriana would have known her anywhere.

84

TERIANA

Killian caught hold of Teriana's arm to hold her in place by the door, then approached the table, his hand coming to rest on the back of Lydia's neck in a familiar way that confirmed what Bait had told her about their relationship. Teriana bit the insides of her cheeks to contain the swell of emotion, for a better match for Lydia she couldn't have named.

And this was possibly the last time she'd see them both, because once Lydia knew what she'd done . . . It was not forgivable.

Killian bent his head to murmur in Lydia's ear. Lydia stiffened, then turned, her green eyes locking with Teriana's. In a blur of inhuman speed, Lydia was on her feet and across the room, nearly knocking Teriana over as she flung her arms around her.

"Oh gods, you're here. You're all right. You're here."

Teriana couldn't breathe, the band of emotion around her chest even tighter than Lydia's grip, but she closed her arms around her friend's slender back. Beyond, the others at the table were watching, eyes curious.

Lydia released her grip, then clasped Teriana by the sides of her face, green eyes liquid with tears. "Where have you been? We heard that you'd liberated your people from Cassius, but then nothing. *Nothing.*"

"I was in Revat."

Lydia went still. "Why?"

Teriana's chin quivered, grief and guilt and *shame* deep as the sea trying to drown her. "To try to convince Marcus to stop this war. He wouldn't listen. He . . ." She sucked in a ragged breath. "I'm sure you've heard what I did. I'm so sorry, Lydia. I swear on the Six that I didn't know he'd hurt you—not until Bait told me. You have every right to hate me, but please know that I'd never have let him touch me if I'd known the truth."

The garbled words stole all the fight she had left in her, and Teriana dropped to her knees, sobs strangling her. "I would never hurt you on purpose, Lydia, but I know this is the ultimate betrayal, and I don't deserve your forgiveness. I don't deserve anyone's forgiveness because Gamdesh has fallen to the Empire and it's all my fault."

Silence stretched, so long and awful that Teriana wished the ground would swallow her whole.

Then Lydia was on her knees, holding her tight. "There is nothing to forgive."

"I fell in the love with the man who murdered you."

Lydia's lips pressed against her forehead. "But I'm not dead. I ended up exactly where I needed to be, as did you. As we are now."

"I gave him everything he needed to conquer Reath."

"Marcus already had everything he needed to do that." Lydia sat back, eyes thoughtful as she rubbed a hand over the shaved portion of her scalp. "We have all done things we regret. I have done things I regret."

"Hegeria marked you. You've been saving lives, whereas I've been destroying them."

Lydia was quiet for a long moment, then she said, "The past cannot be undone, so what matters is what we do in this moment and all the moments to come."

Instead of making her feel better, Lydia's words made Teriana feel worse because she didn't deserve forgiveness. "Don't absolve me." It was hard to get the words out because they kept catching on tears. "Not until you've heard everything, because it's far worse than you think."

Lydia sighed. "Don't put me on a pedestal until *you've* heard everything, because it's far worse than you can imagine."

Something in her friend's voice caused Teriana to lift her head and meet Lydia's eyes, her skin prickling as she remembered how quickly Lydia had moved. With a preternatural swiftness that was reserved only for Tremon's marked.

And . . . and those marked by the Corrupter.

Sensing Teriana's thoughts, as she always had, Lydia gave her a tight smile. "It's complicated."

"Are you all right, though?"

"I don't think any of us are all right."

Teriana realized then that everyone had left the room through another set of doors. Only Killian remained, leaning against the wall with his eyes on the floor. "You two are . . ."

Lydia's gaze moved to Killian, a smile forming on her face. "Equally complicated, but Killian has my heart."

Killian said nothing, but his cheeks colored slightly.

"I'm glad," Teriana said. "Truly. If I could have sent you to anyone on this side of the world, it would've been Killian."

Lydia leaned against the wall, then pulled Teriana against her, and she was reminded of that last night in Celendrial they'd spent together. Drunk and giggling, and though threats had loomed, neither of them had borne the weight of experience they did now.

"There is so much I need to tell you."

"Same."

"There isn't any time, though."

"No." Lydia sighed. "The source of the blight is a place called Deadground beyond the border wall. We discovered how to destroy it while we were in Revat, but we need to get to Deadground to do it."

"I'll come with you."

"No, it's too dangerous."

A laugh tore from Teriana's lips, though nothing about the situation was funny. "Everywhere is dangerous. And one of the few good things that came from my time with the Cel was that they taught me to fight. Not fisticuffs in a tavern brawl, but actual fighting. I can hold my own."

Thanks to Quintus.

"I . . ." Lydia hesitated, and Teriana's heart shriveled because she knew what her friend was going to say. That she had no place in this journey. No role in this fight. "I don't think you're meant to come with us."

Teriana looked away. Hurt, though she had no right to be.

But Lydia only tightened her arm around Teriana's waist and gave her a gentle shake. "Not because I don't want you there. It's just . . . I think you're needed elsewhere."

Teriana's skin abruptly prickled with the sensation that they were being watched, and in her periphery, Killian lifted his head.

"It's the gods," Lydia said softly. "They're with us."

Her heart was drumming in her chest. "Why?"

"Who can say?" Lydia toyed with one of Teriana's braids, her eyes distant. "In my darkest hour, they came to aid me and I spoke to Madoria. I asked her if you were safe."

In her darkest hour, Lydia had thought of her.

Teriana squeezed her eyes shut, the weight of that revelation making it hard to breathe. "What did she say?"

"That you were where you were supposed to be."

Only the marked ever saw the gods, so Teriana asked, "What did Madoria look like?"

"Like you."

Teriana caught hold of Lydia's hand, gripping it hard, because there were no words in any language that were a response to that.

"There was a reason you were with the Cel," Lydia said. "A reason you've endured all that you have."

The moment came crashing down around Teriana, and she clenched her teeth, trying to keep herself together. "Madoria wanted me to defeat them. Magnius told me so during our journey across the Endless Seas." A laugh tore from her lips. "To say that I failed is an understatement. All those months I spent with them, and I know *everything* about how they function. *Everything.* But all that's taught me is that they can't be beaten."

"He's told you how to beat him."

Teriana started at Killian's words, pulling away from Lydia to look at him. "Pardon?"

"If Marcus is as good as all of you claim, he knows exactly how he can be beaten, and consciously or unconsciously, that knowledge lurks in the back of his mind," Killian said. "Given how close you two were, there's no chance he didn't voice that weakness to you."

A wild giggle escaped her. "Killian, Marcus told me a million things, but not one of them was 'If you wish to beat the Empire, this is how to go about doing it.'"

Killian shrugged. "He told you, Teriana. You might not have recognized it for what it was, but he told you. I'd bet every coin to my name on it."

"You'd bet every coin to your name on the roll of the dice," she grumbled, clinging to humor because it felt like she'd lost everything else. "The only thing Marcus feels is confidence in his certain victory. He's got a bigger army. A better trained army. And above all else, he doesn't need to waste time worrying about civilians he needs to protect. He told me that was the only reason that Kaira lost to him at Emrant—because she needed to protect people. The only thing he needs to protect is supply lines."

Marcus's voice abruptly filled her head. *If it's a good path, I'll be able to use it as a supply line straight back to the Empire. Food. Weapons. Gold. Legions. Every resource I could possibly want, and the only way to cut the line would be at the genesis.*

Understanding came to her like a bucket of cold water over her head, realization that Marcus *had* told her the solution slapping Teriana across one cheek and then the other. "Oh. I see."

Killian's mouth quirked in a small smile that said, *I told you so.*

The rear door to the ballroom opened, and the good-looking man who'd been standing next to Malahi came inside with her aunt Yedda. "Well, everything's about to get much worse." He paused, then inclined his head. "Good to meet you, Teriana; I've heard wonderful things about you. I'm Agrippa. I'm sure you've heard of me given you've been living with my old legion, but I assure you, the stories are a pale shade compared to reality. At any rate, we're all about to get a big reunion."

Shock radiated through her. "Agrippa, as in Quintus's friend?"

He bowed. "Glad to hear they still remember me."

Yedda stepped forward. "Lysander went to see what the Cel were up to in Revat, only to discover the legions had fresh orders to move out. He sent word to Magnius."

A flicker of hope that maybe what she'd said to Marcus had made a difference burned in Teriana's chest. That maybe he was planning to return to Celendor.

Foolish hope, because no sooner had it passed through her thoughts did Yedda say, "Lysander overheard the legionnaires gossiping on the docks. Cassius is set on the gold mines of Rotahn. The Empire isn't a distant threat. Cassius not only has his eyes on the Northern Continent, he's sent orders that the legions move in pursuit of its conquest."

All the blood drained from Teriana's skin, her pulse roaring in her ears.

Marcus was coming.

"How soon will they depart?" Lydia demanded even as Killian asked, "Where do they intend to land?"

Agrippa said, "There is no way to know where they intend to land, and I'm not sure it much matters. Nearly every soldier we have is with Dareena at the front or hunting down blighters, and using everyone left to try to stop the legions from taking a beach would be like spitting into the eye of a hurricane." He shook his head. "This doesn't make sense. The Empire no doubt has ambitions to control all of the West and most certainly to take Rotahn's gold, but it is always calculated and methodical in its approach. Always ensures what it takes is firmly under its control before it takes another bite. This . . . this doesn't feel like an attempt to take control—it feels like an attempt to destroy. It feels personal."

"It is," Teriana answered, her voice toneless.

"With respect," Agrippa said, "I understand that he's angry with you, but—"

"It's not about me. At least, not entirely. It's about Lydia."

The color drained from her friend's face.

"You're a threat. A threat to Cassius's dictatorship. A threat to the Corrupter's influence. That's why Marcus intends to sail north. That's why Rufina is marching south. The two greatest evils, whom I believe are, in many ways, one and the same, want you destroyed."

Everyone stared at her.

Finally, Agrippa spoke. "That's an argument I can accept for Rufina, because her army is dead, but the legions are living, breathing men. They're not going to follow a commander whose strategies and goals don't make any sense. They're trained to obey, but there's a limit to that."

"Is there?" Teriana met his stare. "Because I think they'll follow him into fire itself. He never loses. Always protects them. They know he's acting strangely and they don't like it, but I don't think it's enough to cause them to turn on him. Especially given that these orders have come directly from Cassius. They have been trained to obey the Senate—or at least to fear the consequences of disobeying them."

Agrippa's jaw tightened, and he looked away.

"Marcus often said that Kaira's greatest weakness was that she had people that she'd sacrifice everything to protect. That she'd make bad decisions to protect. I always thought he meant civilians. But Killian was right when he said that Marcus told me exactly how to defeat him. We go after his family. After the Thirty-Seventh. The Corrupter might have his claws in deep, but the Thirty-Seventh? That's the hill Marcus will die on."

"I don't disagree," Agrippa said, "but just how do you intend to go after them?"

"Cut off their supplies. They need to eat. Need to drink. And with all the scorched earth he's left in his wake, if the Empire isn't supplying him, it will get lean mighty quick."

A short laugh burst from Agrippa's lips. "He'll have contingency after contingency protecting his food and water sources, Teriana. Might as well go face-to-face with the main army than to try to cut through the myriad of supply lines he'll have running their direction. Supply lines are a speciality for him—you won't beat him in this."

"Which is why we're not going to cut Marcus's lines," Teriana said with a smile. "We're going to destroy the source."

85

KILLIAN

Killian silently listened as Teriana explained her plan. At first, Agrippa argued but as Teriana explained details she'd learned during her time with the legions, he swiftly began offering suggestions as to how to see the plan to fruition. But conversation ceased as Sonia entered the room, her hand protectively on Finn's shoulder. "Finn has something to tell you."

Lydia murmured a swift explanation of what had happened to Teriana, whose eyes widened with shock. "You can bring them back?"

"It's possible," Lydia answered. "But extremely difficult. I'd have to fight the Corrupter's control out of each person. My hope is that if we destroy the blight that it will accomplish the same result. Or at least, that it will make it easier for me to do." Her jaw tightened. "I found no answers to that in Revat."

A twinge of guilt bit at Killian's guts at the reminder that Lydia had been fighting to save the blighters while he'd been destroying any chance of their salvation. The tension of that truth still sat between them, but now was not the time to bring it up, because Finn clearly had something important to say.

It had been a matter of hours since Lydia had driven the Corrupter from the boy, then brought him back from the dead, and the haunted expression in Finn's eyes remained. Where he normally would never stop talking, he'd been silent. Given everything that had happened, Killian was reluctant to press him about his ordeal.

But judging from Finn's determined posture, he was ready to take that step on his own.

"I could see everything that was happening when I was a blighter." Finn wiped his palms on his trousers. "Could hear everything. But it was as though I were stuck in the back of my head while this presence controlled everything that my body did and said. It's one presence that is in all the blighters, one mind. One will, to which every one of us was bound."

It made Killian ill to know that all those blighters he'd set aflame had been conscious for it. That they had suffered a moment of knowing that their own countryman had set the fire. But he shoved away the guilt. He could drown in it later. "You said it was Rufina. That in being twice touched by the Corrupter, she gained more of his power. Joined with him, in some capacity."

Finn nodded. "Mostly, the presence just made my body go through the motions. But sometimes, like when I was speaking with you, it would *focus*. The weight of it would push me so far to the back of my own mind that it was like looking down a long tunnel. But when the presence was focused like that, I knew its thoughts as well as it knew mine. Which means that I know that Rufina goes to Deadground to draw upon the life that the blight has stolen. She has some of the life of every blighter in her. I think that's how she . . . connects with us."

It was a horrifying description that Killian wouldn't have wished on his worst enemy. "This is helpful, Finn. It's horrible, and—" He broke off. "Daily? How is that possible? Not even a deimos can fly the distance to Deadground and back to her camp in a day."

"Xenthier," Agrippa hissed. "*Shit.*"

Finn gave a tight nod. "There are stems behind her lines that go back and forth between her main camp and Deadground. She had to abandon the position when the fire roared through, which infuriated her because she couldn't travel to Deadground."

"Explosives aside, fire doesn't hurt xenthier stems," Agrippa said. "The crystal doesn't burn, so now that the fire is out, she'll have access to it again."

"So will we." Killian stared at the map on the table. "If we can get to the stem, it's a direct path to Deadground."

"She'll have it heavily guarded, Killian," Agrippa said. "Especially given she knows that Deadground is our goal."

"It gets worse." Finn lifted his chin and stepped closer to the table. "Killian, after you burned part of her army, Rufina sent an offer of alliance to the Cel commander."

Teriana lifted a hand to her mouth, her distress palpable. "What did he say?"

"I don't know," Finn admitted. "She admires him, but he also makes her nervous. When she was in my head, she was fretting about what such an alliance might cost her."

"She may only have taken the step because Killian destroyed so much of her blighter army and put her on the defensive," Agrippa muttered. "She needs the legions for manpower to destroy us because we're a threat. But Finn, what did she offer to entice Marcus to risk his men to the blight? Do you know?"

Finn shook his head, but Killian knew the answer. "The age-old bribe—gold. Malahi's lands and mines are overrun by blight, and Rotahn itself is abandoned entirely. Rufina has all that gold for the taking, and if we know that's his goal, then we have to assume she does as well."

Teriana gave a soft hiss between her teeth.

"It makes sense from Rufina's logic," Agrippa said. "Better to hold her position and allow Marcus to do her dirty work, which he will do swiftly and efficiently."

"They could be readying to set sail." Teriana slammed her fists down on the table. "It's too late, and we don't have the forces to hold both him and Rufina back. By the time I cut off the supply lines, everyone will be dead or infected. We don't have enough time!"

"You will move out of my way!" A familiar voice echoed into the room. "Don't you know who I am?"

"Who is that?" Finn asked, the noise of a scuffle reaching Killian's ears, and a heartbeat later, Xadrian strode through the ballroom door.

Killian smiled at the sight of the prince of Anukastre and said, "Reinforcements."

86

LYDIA

"He's Crown Prince Xadrian of Anukastre," Lydia murmured to Teriana. "He's also marked by Tremon."

Teriana's eyes widened. "War makes for interesting bedfellows. Anukastre and Mudamora have been at each other's throats for generations. Though I suppose they mostly fought over Rotahn's gold, so it makes sense to form an alliance given that someone else has taken it."

"I think it has more to do with Killian winning Xadrian over," Lydia said, watching the boy approach Killian, who had a grin on his face. "He understands Xadrian's burdens in a way no one else does."

Just as she and Teriana understood each other, and with Xadrian's presence, Lydia revised her thought that there was no time for them to catch up on all that had happened while they'd been apart.

Taking hold of Teriana's arm, Lydia murmured, "Let's leave them to their reunion. We've other matters to discuss, I think."

Teriana didn't argue, only followed her out of the room, the doors shutting out the din of their companions arguing over strategy. Lydia linked arms with her and said, "You probably know your way about this place better than I do."

"Hungry?"

Lydia nodded, and Teriana tugged on her arm, leading her through the corridors to the kitchen. Taking a loaf of bread and a bit of butter, they sat at a worn table in the corner of the room, the silence between them as comfortable as it had ever been. As though they'd been only days apart.

"I imagine Bait has told you most of what has happened to me in the time we've been apart," Lydia said, nibbling on a piece of the bread. "Killian and I were able to tell him everything, or at least everything that was his business, before he left with Magnius to find you."

Teriana smirked, her eyes showing hints of blue in the waves rolling across her irises as she said, "He did, but now I'm interested in the *things that were not his business*."

Lydia felt her cheeks warm. "Do you believe in love at first sight?"

"Nope." Teriana's smirk turned into a wide grin. "But I believe in *lust* at first sight. Although knowing Killian as I do, he was all honor and duty and insisted on treating you like a lady, so it took him a hundred years to kiss you."

"He doesn't always treat me like a lady." Lydia gave her friend a sly wink, but then allowed her expression to grow more serious. Reaching across the table, she took Teriana's hands. "You know my story, but I don't know yours. Tell me what happened, Teriana. I've heard the speculation of others, but *no one* has heard your account."

Teriana shrugged, eyes shifting to the deepest grey. "What's the point? The road I traveled doesn't much matter—only where I ended up. I trusted the wrong man, and while it got me what I wanted in the short run, all of Reath now pays the consequences of my choices. The Six willing, I'll be able to strike a blow at the Empire to knock it back, but that won't undo the damage that has been done."

Lydia could see the weight of grief dragging Teriana down. Her friend knew that all held her responsible, but it was also very clear to her that Teriana held *herself* responsible. "Your story matters to me. I want to hear it. All of it."

Teriana's calloused hands flexed in Lydia's grip, but then she nodded. "All right."

It was a tale as unexpected as Lydia's own, and with Teriana's gift with words, it was as though she walked along at her friend's side. The story made Lydia clench her teeth with fear, laugh out loud, and weep in heartache, and by the end of it, she felt as exhausted as if she'd walked a hundred miles.

"Part of me wants to believe that he'd deceived me the entire time," Teriana said quietly. "That I was a fool who fell for a handsome face and clever words, and that once he had what he wanted, Marcus cast the mask aside and showed his true colors. But I don't think that's true. I think that in the moments after I discovered the truth of what he'd done to you and left on the *Quincense*, the Corrupter got into him. Changed him into the heartless creature that I saw in Revat."

Lydia let out a slow breath. "I know better than anyone what it's like when the Corrupter gets his claws into you, and . . ." She trailed off, hunting for the words. "My greatest fear has always been my perception that I am weak and that my weaknesses will cost those around me. I was desperate to be strong, to be able to fight, to be able to kill to defend those I love. The Corrupter latched onto that fear and offered me a way to be free of it. In a way, I became my fear. Not changed, but reduced to one awful aspect of myself with every other part of me buried deep inside. I was awful, Teriana. Crueler than you know, most especially to Killian."

Taking a small mouthful of bread, Lydia chewed as she remembered her venomous words, wishing she could pass them off as the Corrupter's but knowing that they were her own. "I know that you think that staying would have protected him from himself, and in doing so, protected him from the Corrupter. But the truth is, the Six themselves freed me of the Corrupter's claws only for me to fall right back into his embrace the moment I was put to the test. When you are your own worst enemy, no one can fight your inner battles for you. You must fight the war yourself."

She set down the bread. "I would not be here without Killian and my companions, but I also know that I am the one who decides what sort of woman I wish to be. No one else. My heart tells me it is the same for Marcus and that nothing you could have done would have saved him from himself in the end. Only he can do that, and you must accept that he might never do so."

Teriana's shoulders shuddered, a sob escaping her. Lydia pulled her stool around next to her friend and held her close.

"I loved him."

Grief pooled in Lydia's stomach, as well as anger that Teriana was suffering so much. Would suffer more still in the war to come.

Drying her eyes, Teriana straightened. "I know what needs to be done, but you're going to have to convince my people this is the right course, Lydia. And you need to do it swiftly, because they'll need to enlist the aid of every nation on the Southern Continent if they are going to make this work. You're the Queen of Mudamora, which means they'll listen to you. It's time the Cel discover what it feels like to be attacked."

It was very likely that she was queen no longer given what had happened at Teradale, but Lydia didn't add to Teriana's burdens with the plots of Helene Torrington and the other High Lords, which were likely going to descend in earnest soon enough.

Gripping Teriana's shoulders, she met her friend's eyes. "This fight is yours. You suffered through blood, sweat, and tears to prepare for this moment, and now it's time for you to strike the blow. I have my own battle to wage. Circumstance is going to pull us apart again, know that we fight at each other's back in the same war. And together, we will win this."

87

KILLIAN

"Lord Calorian," Xadrian said, "I thought your palace would be larger."

Despite himself, Killian laughed and approached the prince, embracing him tightly even as he saw Lydia lead Teriana out of the room from the corner of his eye. "It's good to see you, Your Highness. Your arrival is timely."

The boy's grip on him tightened, then Xadrian pushed him away and dusted at his coat. "It was clear to me that you would lose this battle without aid, so I gathered my best and took to ship. The Maarin were most obliging, but it is a miserable form of travel."

"How many soldiers do you have with you?"

"Two thousand." Xadrian sighed and shook his head. "I would have brought more, but it is as Malahi said it would be: the blight has crossed the Liratoras and entered the sands. My mother and the rest of our forces have moved to hold it back."

"Mudamora's army has developed some techniques for damming the blight that we will gladly share." Turning to face the others, Killian said, "For those of you who don't know him, this is His Royal Highness, Prince Xadrian of Anukastre."

In swift, terse terms, he explained the current situation to Xadrian, who, for all his youth, was experienced in warfare.

"So they'll come by ship." Xadrian rubbed his chin. "We've experience repelling invasion from the sea."

"We have a Gamdeshian shifter—Astara—who can aid in scouting where they intend to land," Killian said. "For better or worse, a fleet is difficult to hide."

"Marcus is familiar with Astara's skills," Agrippa muttered. "He knows we have eyes in the sky and will plan accordingly."

Xadrian scoffed, but Killian could feel the boy's tension. Knew his mark was warning him of what was to come. Yet the prince's voice was steady as he said, "You fear him, Agrippa. I can see it in your eyes."

"I'm gods-damned terrified of him, and you should be, too," Agrippa snapped. "But I can see in *your* eyes that you'll not believe a word I say until you come face-to-face with them."

"I fear no man."

It was bluster, Killian knew it. False confidence from a prince who'd been raised to be the backbone of his nation's army, ever confident, never failing. But bluster didn't hide the way Xadrian's dark curls were dampened with nervous sweat.

Agrippa opened his mouth, but before he could deliver whatever retort he had lined up at the prince's expense, a heavy knock sounded at the door. It opened, and Bercola entered. A pair of giants followed at her heels. Killian recognized both as members of Eoten Isle's high council. They were old and grizzled, their colorless eyes lined with deep wrinkles, but both towered over Killian and wore their weapons like they knew how to use them.

Bercola nodded at Killian, then said, "It strikes me that time is short, so I'll not waste words. Eoten Isle stands with Mudamora, and our long ships sail with two thousand warriors to aid in the fight against the Seventh's incursion. In exchange, you'll need to hand Baird over for punishment for desertion."

Agrippa's face darkened but before he could speak, Killian said, "I don't know where he is. He aided me in delivering a blow against Rufina's army and saved my life, but I've not seen him since."

Bercola's face was unreadable as she said, "He'll show up. I trust you won't stand in the way of us reclaiming him."

Killian made a noncommittal noise, then shifted the subject. "Would it be possible for one of Gespurn's marked to make the seas through the strait less welcoming? We've reason to believe the Cel intend to set sail to our shores and every effort must be made to delay them."

One of the giants gave a slight nod. "Within reason. Altering the natural course of the skies has far-reaching consequences."

"It's starting to feel like we have a chance here," Agrippa murmured. "Which means I can't help but feel that the other shoe is about to drop."

Killian felt the same way, but before he could answer, he heard a familiar sharp voice demand, "Where are they?"

Helene. Killian closed his eyes, digging deep for reserves of patience to deal with the frustration to come.

The doors swung in, Helene swanning into the room with *Lydia's* crown perched on her head, the diamond ring that had secured her vote hanging on a golden chain between her breasts. "The High Lords voted in your absence," she declared. "I now rule Mudamora, and you will cease and desist in your plotting."

"Get out of my house, you murderous bitch," Seldrid said softly. "You killed my brother, and if you don't think there will be a consequence to that, you are mistaken."

Helene shrugged. "Hacken reaped what he sowed by killing Ria. And you are High Lord now, Seldrid, so you should not complain too much."

"Get out!"

"Not while you lot conspire to make things worse. And not when I have a solution to our woes." Helene tossed a letter written on thick, expensive paper onto the table. It was sealed with crimson wax. "The Cel commander has offered us a deal, and I intend to take him up on it."

Killian's skin began to crawl, and he nodded at Agrippa, who picked up the letter.

"It's Marcus's writing." Agrippa swiftly read, shaking his head. "And it's addressed to Queen Kitaryia Falorn. In exchange for surrendering Lydia Valerius, who is the betrothed of the Dictator of Celendor, as well as ceding control of the gold mines of Rotahn, the Empire will provide aid against the Derin incursion and supply the civilian population with food and necessities until the blight can be eradicated, at which time Mudamora will be officially named a province of the Empire."

A quiver ran through him, and Killian felt the overwhelming urge to draw his sword. To hunt down that Cel bastard and run him through.

"How amusing that they don't realize that Lydia and Kitaryia are one and the same." Helene snickered. "All we have to do is give them Lydia, as well as Malahi's mines, and they will get rid of the blight for us. I say we take the deal. Lydia is from Celendor anyway, so what difference does it make to her to go back?" Her eyes flicked to Killian. "I'm sure they'll let you go with her."

"You are a profoundly stupid woman," Agrippa said. "I dare say that if we crack your skull open, we'll find nothing inside."

Helene purpled.

"Do you even understand what they are demanding?" Malahi glared at the woman. "Or were you too trumped up on your own rise in station to stop and think?"

The room devolved into accusations and arguments, but all fell silent as Lydia's voice cut through the commotion. "Helene is right."

88

TERIANA

"What do you mean, Helene is right?" Killian demanded. "You aren't honestly suggesting we agree to this?"

Teriana internally cringed at the panic in his eyes, because she'd felt the same when Lydia had swiftly communicated her plan. This sort of self-sacrifice was *exactly* the sort of thing Lydia would do.

"What choice do we have?" Lydia walked toward the group, and Teriana followed her, keeping her expression grim. "We can't defeat the blight, and Rufina's victory will cost every Mudamorian their life. Whereas the Cel only require obeisance. For the cost of my freedom and Malahi's mines, our people have a chance. The Cel are civilized, whereas Rufina is not."

Killian opened his mouth, then closed it again, his eyes narrowing. Suspecting a ploy, because the Cel were anything but civilized. Teriana moved next to Seldrid and stepped on his toes; ever political, Seldrid showed no reaction, but Teriana knew he'd understood.

"You willingly accept this?" Helene demanded. "Or is this an act and you'll flee the moment you have a chance?"

"It is no act." Lydia's expression was resigned. "This is the only way to save Mudamora."

Helene dabbed at her eyes with a handkerchief. "Your sacrifice will never be forgotten. Though in truth, you'll be able to leave this horror for the soft life of Celendor, so I do not think you'll look back."

"It is the right thing to do," Lydia replied, her jaw set and eyes resolute. "Seldrid, would you please take Helene to a quiet place and aid in drafting a response to the Cel legatus? We should not risk the opportunity with unnecessary delay."

"Of course," Seldrid murmured. "It would be my honor to aid in the drafting of this important letter, although I believe we should send for the other High Lords first."

Silence reigned after Seldrid led Helene from the room, and Teriana took in all who were present. Bercola and two members of Eoten Isle's council. Xadrian and Adra. Agrippa and Malahi. Lydia and Killian.

"I take it you have a plan," Killian said. "Because while I would not put it past you to risk yourself, Lydia, I *know* Teriana wouldn't agree to such a scheme."

Teriana shot him a smirk, but Lydia only said, "Adra, will you ensure this room is secure. We cannot afford listeners."

Adra gave Lydia a knowing smile, then strode with purpose to the doors.

Picking up Marcus's letter, Lydia tapped the edge of it against her palm. "Teriana cannot cut off the Cel supply lines in a day. She needs time. The giants"—she gestured to them—"can delay the Cel in setting sail, but the toll is high. So what we need is another tactic to delay them long enough that Teriana can enact her plan, because I cannot believe that the legions will undertake an aggressive campaign into an already starving country without the supplies sent to them by Celendor. Helene, in her quest for relevance, has provided us an avenue of delay. *Negotiation.*"

Malahi smiled. "You aim to set her to the task of negotiating an agreement with the Cel, because if they believe they can get what they want without invading, they'd be fools not to do so."

Lydia gave a slight nod, relieved her friend so easily grasped her intention. "It was only a matter of time until they learned that Kitaryia and Lydia are one and the same, and Marcus would never believe I'd negotiate with him. But Helene is another matter. It makes sense that she'd give me up. Makes sense that she'd give Malahi's gold up. Makes sense that she'd be ignorant as to exactly how much power the Empire will give her." She tapped the letter against her palm again. "We allow Helene to carry on as queen while we enact our own strategies behind her back, none more critical than Teriana's."

All eyes went to Teriana, and she gave a tight nod. "Gather all the Maarin from every ship in the harbor. I'll meet with my people tonight."

* * *

Eight Maarin ships were already in Serlania's harbor, and within the hour, the majority of their crews were crammed into a music hall that Seldrid owned. All of them answering the call of Triumvir Tesya, none yet aware that her mother was dead. If Teriana had called them herself, she suspected not a single soul would have shown up.

"I can't come with you," Lydia had said before she left. "Both Marcus and Rufina will have spies in Serlania, and if we are to make him believe Helene intends to negotiate in earnest, we must play our parts and I must remain confined. But Killian will arrange for soldiers to—"

"No soldiers. I'm not worried about my people hurting me," Teriana had answered. "I'm worried that they'll all turn their backs for all that I've done and that Reath will pay the price."

Which perhaps made her a fool given that there was an order she be executed for treason, but it was hard to fear for her life when Lydia and Killian would be baiting Marcus with their own.

"Finn is working the crowd with Killian's dog," Bait said softly. "He says he will recognize many of the blighters, and dogs seem to have some sense that they are not right. But thus far, it seems everyone here is among the living."

"Long may that last." Drawing a deep breath, Teriana stepped out onto the stage. Scowls and angry glares greeted her, but she kept her face steady as she walked to the center and surveyed the crews before her. "Thank you all for gathering."

"Where is Tesya?" Triumvir Vane demanded. "We aren't interested in what you have to say, Teriana. Only interested in how your mother is going to remedy your multitude of errors."

Teriana's chest tightened. "My mother is dead. Murdered in Celendrial by Legatus Hostus."

Gasps tore from the lips of everyone in the room, because her mother had been beloved. Yet on the heels of her words, Sultan Kalin of Gamdesh entered the room, Astara at his side.

Teriana's stomach dropped. She had known him all her life, but the bitter and angry expression on the Sultan's face made him seem a stranger. Astara appeared as she always did—ready to tear Teriana's heart out the moment she had the chance.

She deserved their hatred. Deserved their ire. But it was her people she'd gathered here, so it was her people Teriana focused on. A sea of Maarin faces, eyes all filled with tempestuous seas. Swallowing hard, she wiped her sweaty palms on her trousers.

"I won't waste words." Her voice was strong and clear, belying the tremor in her knees. "You all know who I am. You all know where I've been and what I've done, and the majority of you have condemned me for it. I can't blame you for that, because in truth, I blame myself for much of what has happened." Teriana's throat tightened, and she coughed to clear it. "But I also know that even if I'd done everything differently, we would still have found ourselves here, one way or another. Our mantra was that East must not meet West, but in truth, they've never been separated. Reath is one world, and I see now that believing its halves could be kept apart with secrets and half truths was either a delusion or a dream destined to fail. And in refusing to acknowledge that truth, we were ill prepared when the halves collided."

Her people shifted restlessly, but no one spoke against her.

"When the Cel captured our ships and put our people to question, I believed that it was my doing. Believed that Lucius Cassius had learned about the West because I'd revealed our secret to Lydia. But he already knew the West existed, as did many others, because it was no *gods-damned secret*!" Teriana shouted the last words, anger about the lies she'd been fed all her life bubbling up in her chest.

"I believed that my people were imprisoned and dying because of me, and when Madoria silenced every voice but mine, I chose to use my voice in an attempt to save those I believed I'd condemned."

Many of the elders among the crew looked to the ground, and Teriana clenched her fist at the confirmation that many of them had known the reality. But this was no time for casting blame.

"Magnius told me that Madoria had chosen me to defeat the Empire, and *gods* have I struggled with the weight of that task. Not only in how I might accomplish such a feat, but in understanding what defeat really meant. Yet through every step of that journey, what burned in my heart and drove me forward was a need to save those I believed I'd harmed. It was the great villain Lucius Cassius who made me finally see the selfishness of my motivations. Who made me see that so much of what I chose to do was driven by my own need to remedy my mistakes. To atone for the choices I'd made."

Several heads nodded, and her anger flared brighter. "But my motivations being selfish does not mean my actions were wrong. What is wrong is to condemn five hundred souls to execution because the risk required to save them is a greater bet than you care to wager. For to do so isn't just selfishness, it's cowardice. And the greatest form of foolishness, because sacrificing them would have changed nothing. The Empire would only have found another way, and every one of us would have had to live with the question of whether delaying the Empire by a day, a month, a year, was worth sacrificing our consciences."

Silence stretched, and that silence weighed on Teriana's shoulders, dragging her down and down. She knew it was her methods, not her motivations, that pitted them against her.

"I think it is easier to look at the Empire as a faceless evil," Teriana finally said in a voice quiet enough that her people leaned forward to hear. "Easier to paint every one of the Empire's people as a villain deserving universal condemnation for what their nation has done. Easier to refuse to see the individuals that make up the whole, because that would grant them humanity, which many believe is a gift they do not deserve. And perhaps that is so. Perhaps they all deserve our hatred.

"Except I question the reasons we refuse to look at the individuals who make up the whole. Is it because we fear that in understanding *why* they do the things they do, we risk absolving them? Or is it because the *why* isn't always cruelty, greed, or ignorance? Is it because the *why* is often fear, loyalty, and even love? I think maybe we refuse to see them as individuals because in knowing that such familiar motivations drive our enemy's actions, we might be forced to look at our own choices in a different light. And that terrifies us."

Lifting her chin, Teriana stared out over the crowd. "I rolled the dice to save our people, using the legions to achieve what Cassius wanted. In the beginning, I told myself that my bet was on the West's ability to drive them back once our people were freed, but in the end, I was betting on the individual men within those legions. Betting on one in particular, because I believed he was more ally than enemy." Teriana's bottom lip quivered, and she bit down on it hard. "I bet wrong, and I will bear the weight of my choices for the rest of my days and accept the punishment you feel is fitting. But before you make that decision, I wish to put before you another bet with a higher wager than before."

She waited a breath, then said, "I want you to bet your lives on the Maarin's ability to strike a blow at the Empire herself. I want you to bet your lives on the willingness of other nations to rise up with us. I want you to bet your lives that we have the ability to defeat the undefeatable."

Silence stretched, then Vane said, "What do you propose?"

Teriana explained her plan, which was beautifully simple. Excruciatingly complex. A plan that only she could orchestrate. And when she was finished, Teriana met the eyes of her people and asked, "Will you roll the dice with me?"

No one spoke, then her cousin Elyanna stepped forward. "I will roll the dice!" She gave her husband a shove, and he gave a tight nod. "I like a good wager."

More and more voices filled the air. Her people balled their fists, their need for vengeance turning their eyes into violent storms. Their need for justice. But above all, the need to reclaim their honor and pride, for it had been brought low.

Then the Sultan stepped forward, shoulders back and head high, and all fell silent. His brown eyes locked on hers, and Teriana knew he would never forgive her. But neither would he allow his anger to own him. With the voice of the warrior he'd once been, Sultan Kalin roared, "Gamdesh will roll the dice!"

89

LYDIA

On *Helene's* orders, Lydia and Killian were confined to Lydia's stateroom in Seldrid's manor while Helene and the High Lords, who'd just arrived, negotiated a response to Marcus.

"No one is going to believe that I'll agree to this," Killian said, pacing the room. "The High Lords are all going to think this is a scheme, because they know there is no chance I'd allow you to go back to Celendor without a fight. Especially given that you are supposed to go there to marry Lucius Cassius."

Lydia pulled off her boots and curled up on a sofa, a cup of tea steaming on the low table before her. "Well, either come up with a way that I can reasonably convince you or put on an act of trying to steal me away, and we can have you put in irons for the duration of the negotiations."

"There is no way I'd be convinced, so get the irons ready." Killian went to the window and stared out into the night. "I hate that we're leaning on trickery and scheming with the hopes Marcus will fall for it rather than taking concrete action. That we'll be waiting around, locked in this room, when we could be trying to reach Deadground."

Lydia understood how he felt. Strategic or not, the passivity her scheme required rubbed her the wrong way as well. "If I disappear from Serlania, I think it will drive Marcus to act. Whereas if I am imprisoned by Helene, he will perceive me as contained. Within reach. And he'll take the time to find other routes to achieve his goals. Keep in mind that Marcus was the one who initiated this negotiation by sending that letter—he wants this to work."

"Or it's a trick on his part."

"I don't think so. Or at least, not at its heart." Picking up her teacup, she sipped at it. "Teriana knows him better than anyone, Killian, and she's convinced that no matter how far Marcus has fallen, he won't willingly send his men to their deaths. He'll only come here in force if he feels there is no other avenue, and I think that reluctance will cause him to grasp at the straws Helene offers him."

"And when he comes to retrieve you?" Killian twisted away from the window. "What then? How am I supposed to stop them from taking you when I'm trussed up in irons to make this scheme believable? How far will you take this to buy Teriana the time she needs?"

He doesn't think it's a scheme. Understanding pooled in Lydia's stomach as she realized that Killian believed she'd actually let Marcus take her. That she'd sacrifice herself in truth to give Teriana the time she needed. Rising to her feet, she closed the distance between them and wrapped her arms around Killian's neck.

"I'm not going to take it that far." Rising onto her tiptoes, she brushed her lips against his, feeling a flutter low in her stomach as his arms wrapped around her and pulled her close. "I won't let him take me from you."

Killian turned his head away. "I wish I could believe you. Except I know how far you'd go to save our people."

He wasn't talking about this scheme anymore, Lydia realized. This was about him burning the blighters. About him destroying any chance of bringing those Mudamorians back while she'd been hunting for a way to save them all. About the gulf she'd felt between them since learning what he'd done, because she'd be lying to herself if she said it wasn't there. "It feels like I'm the only one who is fighting to save them. Even with what I did for Finn, it feels as though everyone, including you, sees the blighters as lost. As casualties of war. It feels like I stand alone in my fight to save them, Killian."

"How can you say that?" He pulled away from her and began pacing the room again. "Gods, Lydia, I have had your back through *everything*, and the only times I have not been with you are when you sent me away. What more do you want from me?"

"I want you to have not burned them beyond salvation!" The words tore from her throat, fueled by anger she'd been doing her best to deny. "I want you to have found another way! I want you to believe that saving every last one of them is possible!"

"Except I don't!" he shouted. "And I refuse to make bad decisions on a deluded dream that we can win this without doing harm to a single one of the blighters in Rufina's army. Do you think that I'm not haunted by what I did, Lydia? Do you think that my every moment, sleeping and awake, isn't consumed by the knowledge that it wasn't mindless husks that I burned but the souls of those I was sworn to defend?" A tear ran down his face." But the front lines were on the verge of being overrun and I had to do *something* to stop Rufina. I'll hate myself forever for the choice, knowing what I do now, so by all means hate me as well."

His words stole the breath from her chest, but before she could answer, a knock sounded at the door. A heartbeat later, it opened and a Mudamorian soldier appeared. "The Queen and the High Lords will see you now."

Lydia smoothed her hands down her clothes, hunting for her composure. Yet her voice still croaked when she said, "All right. Killian, are you coming with me?"

"No. There's no point." He cast dark eyes at her. "You've made your decision regardless of what I say."

Lydia's chest hollowed, because she could not tell if he meant the words or if it was a performance to sell the scheme. "Fine."

She strode from the room with the guard on her heels, then allowed the man to lead her down the hallway. No matter how hard she tried, she couldn't keep tears from flooding down her cheeks as she replayed Killian's words in her head, drowning in guilt and grief and anger, all in equal measure.

Guards stood outside the doors to the ballroom, which swung open on her approach. Beneath the crystal chandelier, all the High Lords and Ladies sat around the table with Helene at its head.

"High Lady Falorn." Helene inclined her head to Lydia. "We have come to an agreement on how we will respond to the Cel offer of alliance."

You mean offer of surrender.

Helene lifted her chin. "Before I sign this document and send it to the Cel, I would like for you to confirm to all here that you will willingly return to Celendor."

"Yes." Lydia wiped tears from her face. "If my sacrifice will save all of Mudamora, then it will be one that I gladly make."

"For the record, I do not support this concession." Malahi crossed her arms, playing her part, for everyone would suspect if she willingly surrendered her gold mines. "House Rowenes votes against this agreement with the Cel."

"What choice do we have, Malahi?" High Lord Pitolt took a long mouthful of his wine, which had stained his teeth purple. "We cannot win this war. Sacrifices must be made, although to call giving up mines overrun by blight a sacrifice makes mockery of the word. As for Kitaryia, it is not as though she goes to unfamiliar ground. The Cel seem civilized enough, and likely she'll be kept to royal standards for the rest of her days in Celendrial."

The Cel were about as civilized as the reptile on their banner, but Lydia gave a tight nod.

"Where is Killian?" Helene looked around the room, and when Lydia did not answer, the guard said, "He did not wish to attend. They . . ." He looked to Lydia. ". . . were quarreling."

"Lovers' spat." Helene gave a little smile. "He'll regret it when you leave to marry the most powerful man in the Empire, won't he?"

Lydia said nothing, and Helene adjusted the crown on her head, stroking the gold as though to remind herself it was still there.

"Then the letter will be sent." High Lord Pitolt pushed a thick piece of paper in front of Helene to sign. "If we negotiate with them now, we survive, and survivors can rally and fight back. With the Cel legions backing us against Rufina, you can do your own duty to Mudamora and destroy the blight, Malahi. Then it's only a matter of biding our time until the moment is right to strike back against the Empire. A long game, whereas if we carry on as we are, it will be a short match indeed."

"Do not ask me to feel good about sacrificing my friend," Malahi snapped. "This is folly."

"You make it sound as though they will lock her in a prison." Helene toyed with the black diamond ring hanging between her breasts, then lifted it to the light. "Kitaryia will live in luxury and ease. Perhaps she might even play a role one day when we overthrow them. A spy on the inside." She smirked. "Perhaps one day you'll even be able to return, Kitaryia."

"I will pray for such a fate," Lydia whispered.

"Then it is settled," Helene declared. "Let us dress you up, Kitaryia, and then we will send you over to Revat by way of ship. The Cel will then join us in our fight against Rufina, and we will be victorious."

"You're going to send Marcus what he wants without getting him to sign a contract?" Agrippa said with a laugh. "Gods, you are dense."

Helene scowled. "You will refer to me as Your Majesty or Your Grace."

"Apologies." Agrippa gave her a smile that was all teeth. "Gods, you are dense, *Your Grace.*"

"Agrippa is right," Lydia said. "You should negotiate and sign a treaty first. The Cel are beholden to law and contract, so their commander will abide by the document he signs. All of you should be there to negotiate with him to ensure the best terms."

"Civilized," High Lord Pitolt said with a nod. "Helene, you will invite the legatus to meet us for negotiations in a neutral location, and we will see this done." Then he inclined his head to Lydia. "Your sacrifice is moving, Marked One. You are Hegeria incarnate with this act."

Coward, Lydia thought to herself. *You're only doing this to save your own neck.* "It is the right choice."

"Helene, sign the letter." High Lord Pitolt clapped his hands, and Helene obediently wrote her name on the page with a flourish. "Someone find the Gamdeshian shifter to serve as messenger. Kitaryia, for obvious reasons you are to remain confined in your rooms and under guard until our negotiations are concluded."

It was cruel to send Astara back to Revat, given she'd barely escaped with her life, but Lydia made no comment. Only allowed the guards to lead her back to her rooms, fully expecting to find them empty. To find Killian gone.

A breathless panic descended on her, but as the door opened, the first thing she saw was Killian.

"Good night," she said to the guard.

He shut the door behind her, and Lydia said softly, "Helene signed the letter. They aim to have Astara deliver it."

Killian gave a tight nod, but said nothing.

Silence hung between them, tension growing with every passing second. Lydia was silent because she didn't know what to say. No part of her hated him, and certainly no part of her wanted to quarrel with him, but neither did she wish to deny the way she felt. "I love you, Killian," she finally said. "But I am angry."

"I don't want to lose you." His dark eyes met hers. "I'm afraid that what it will take to win this will tear us apart."

A knock sounded, and the door opened. Agrippa stepped inside. "Gods, that woman is an idiot. But thankfully that serves our purpose well, especially with Seldrid and Malahi able to guide the process along. Now we just wait for Marcus to fall for it."

"Do you think he will?" Lydia's uncertainty that this scheme had any hope of succeeding mounted with each passing second. Marcus was intelligent and experienced, but it also only took one word in front of the wrong ears, and their duplicity would be revealed.

Agrippa went to the sideboard and poured himself a glass of lemon water, draining it before he spoke. "If you think about it from the outside looking in, our circumstances are incredibly dire. From Marcus's perspective, we have no chance at victory." He sighed. "When faced with the might of the Empire, cities, regions, nations, they almost always hand over their rulers in the end, because people want to live. Everyone fancies themselves brave and stalwart and loyal, but when it comes between the lives of your family and the life of a stranger wearing a crown, who do you think most people choose? So while to us this seems so obviously a ploy, Mudamora will be doing exactly what Marcus expects us to do."

"But . . . ?" Killian said. "Because I hear a *but* in your voice, Agrippa."

"But he will be prepared for trickery." Agrippa refilled his glass and downed his drink. "And he will have contingencies in play. Everything depends on Teriana winning us allies tonight, on them moving with speed, on them achieving something that has never been attempted before. If we do manage to trick Marcus, and Teriana fails, there will be a reckoning. A bloody and brutal one."

"I have faith in her." Lydia went to the window and looked out, praying that her friend had come out better tonight than she had. "This is what Teriana was meant to do."

But gods, it was going to cost her.

"We could be using this time to attempt to get to Deadground," Agrippa said. "Are you sure you don't wish to make the attempt to travel there rather than sitting here as bait?"

Lydia wasn't sure. How could she be when there were so many uncertainties? "Killian struck a heavy blow against Rufina with the fires, and I believe that is what drove her to offer an alliance to Celendor. We have her on the defense right now, and she needs the legions if she wishes to defeat us swiftly. Rufina has the xenthier stem to Deadground too heavily guarded for us to reach, and even if we set out today on foot, we'd not be even halfway to Deadground by the time the legions arrive on our shores. They'll defeat our armies and take control of the south, and even if we succeed in destroying the blight when we get there, what will be left when we return but a different form of blight consuming Mudamora in the form of the Empire?

"Whereas if we buy Teriana enough time, she can prevent the Cel from setting sail from Revat at all because Marcus won't risk bringing an entire army here without a supply chain. Rufina won't have the alliance she needs to attack, and she'll be forced to remain on the defense, which is when we make our move on Deadground."

Agrippa scrubbed a hand through his hair. "I'm aware of your reasoning, Lydia. But it's a massive gamble, because if Teriana fails, we are done. The game is over. We have lost. And not to point out the obvious, but Teriana hasn't even succeeded in securing the support of her own people in this."

Nerves twisted in Lydia's guts, making her stomach ache because she was very much aware of the risk. "If the Maarin refuse to support her tonight, then we abandon the strategy and head to Deadground." She met Killian's gaze, prepared for him to look away. "We're ready for that?"

His brown eyes were steady as they met hers. "Seldrid has horses and supplies waiting. We'll ride north to the blight line, then travel onward on foot to Deadground."

And do so knowing that if they succeeded, it would be to return to find Mudamora under the Empire's rule.

"Everything depends on Teriana," Lydia said quietly. "She is the only one with the power to save us."

They fell into silence, minutes feeling like lifetimes as they waited for news from Teriana. Then the door to the room opened, and Finn entered, Killian's dog at his heels. He looked between them, then gave them a large grin.

"Teriana did it," he said. "The Maarin sail to war tonight."

90

TERIANA

"I wish there was time to say good-bye," Teriana said to her aunt as she climbed to the quarterdeck of the *Quincense*. Night was heavy upon Serlania, but the city itself glowed like a beacon. Which she supposed it was. The last holdout of the living in Mudamora.

"Not worth the risk," Yedda replied. "And we can't spare the time. The legions are quick. We must be quicker. The other ships have already headed out to deeper waters, and we do not want them making plans without us. Especially Kalin and Vane—those two both seek blood and vengeance. But this strategy is yours, Teriana."

A sharp whistle cut the air. "A boat approaches."

Teriana's heart skipped, certain it was Lydia, but as she peered over the rail into the shadows of the sea below, it was to see Agrippa looking up at her. "Drop a ladder."

Her curiosity grew as she noted the giant in the boat with him. "Let's see what he wants."

The ex-legionnaire scampered up the ladder with ease, landing with a soft thud on steady feet despite the rocking deck. She was struck by how, even with years separating him from the Thirty-Seventh, he still looked like one of them. Something about the way he moved.

"Finn told me about your speech, and it was a good one," Agrippa said. "And it's a good plan. But it's not going to work."

Teriana parted her lips to argue, but he didn't give her a chance.

"You need more allies. Allies who understand the enemy better than the Gamdeshians or Arinoquians ever will. Allies who already understand what it means to lose to the Empire but who fight back all the same."

"Who do you suggest?"

Agrippa drew in a deep breath. "You need Bardeen."

Frustration filled Teriana, because she didn't have time for this. "I'd do a great deal to form an alliance with the rebels. But not only do I not have time to forge new alliances, I have no connection to them. All I know about their leader is that she fights with a Thirty-Seventh gladius."

A smile rose on Agrippa's lips. "I knew she'd rise to the top. She was destined for it."

"You know her?"

"I'd bet every coin to my name that the Bardenese rebel leader's name is Silvara, and that gladius she carries is mine. Find her, Teriana, and you'll have a fighting chance of making this work, because however much the West hates the Empire, Bardeen's wrath is tenfold as fierce. And they know everything there is to know about fighting the legions."

This hadn't been part of Teriana's plans, her ambition limited to uniting the Southern Continent and the Maarin doing the rest. But if she could rally the provinces that already resisted the Senate in the East . . . "You think she'll speak to me?"

"Silvara's vendetta against Marcus is personal." Agrippa's smile was grim. "But to reach her in time, you're going to need full sails. Which is convenient, because I have a friend who needs to escape." He motioned to the giant standing behind him. "So how about you both help each other out."

91

LYDIA

After Agrippa departed to *kill two birds with one stone,* as he described it, she was left standing with Killian and Finn in awkward silence.

"Teriana asked me to tell you good-bye," Finn finally said. "The Maarin intended to meet on the water to finalize her plans, and she didn't want them to do so without her."

Not a full day back together and they'd already been separated again. Lydia sat down on the sofa, pressing her hands to her eyes because her friend was who she needed right now to help calm the chaos of emotion in her chest. Slowly mastering her composure, she lowered her hands. "That makes sense. In truth, I'm not certain how much liberty Helene intends to give me. She needs me to secure this contract with the Cel, and to play along, I'll likely have to remain imprisoned in my room until we've played this as far as it can go."

Finn wrinkled his nose, then said, "Well, at least you know that Teriana is getting things done while you're stuck here drinking lemonade and resting up."

She gave the boy a flat stare, and Finn laughed. "Sorry, Lydia. I know you'd rather be out there doing good works and the like, but hopefully you'll be able to endure your imprisonment in Seldrid's fancy house, with a full belly and servants to do your bidding."

"Finn . . ." Killian's tone was exasperated. "Enough. Why don't you go to bed? It's late."

Finn snorted. "Nighttime is when I hold court, Killian. Sleep is for the day." He bowed low. "On that note, my subjects await."

"Be careful," Lydia warned. "I do not want to save you twice."

Finn only laughed and disappeared out the door.

Killian wavered in the tension between them then abruptly said, "There's something I need to do. Stay here."

Lydia's stomach hollowed as he disappeared, because she'd hoped that they might resolve their argument. Might find a way to dispel the tension between them, but instead, Killian seemed content to allow the gulf to grow wider.

Tears burning in her eyes, she circled the luxurious room. Trailing fingers over the velvet cushions and silk coverlets, examining the oil portraits of seascapes, and sipping at water made sharp with lemons. *Go to bed,* she told herself. *Get some rest.*

Except the thought of getting into the massive bed alone only made her feel worse. This was her first night back in Serlania, her first night back with Killian, and she did not want to spend it away from him.

Tap.

She twitched, her eyes going to the window.

Tap.

Frowning, she went to the glass and opened it, only her god-marked reflexes preventing her from getting hit in the face by a pebble. In the gardens below stood Killian and Finn, both of them cloaked in black, the lanterns that normally lit the space conspicuously dark.

Pulling back the hood of his cloak, Killian lifted his face to the light from her room and mouthed, *Let's revisit old times.*

Understanding flooded her veins, and Lydia clapped a hand over her mouth to silence the giddy laugh that tore from her lips. Turning away from the window, she went to the door and opened it. "I am to bed," she told the guards. "Please no interruptions. It has been a trying day."

"Yes, Marked One," one of them said, and Lydia closed the door and flipped the lock. Turning all the lamps down low, she retrieved a dark cloak from the wardrobe, then went to the window.

Scanning the gardens to ensure no one was watching her darkened window, Lydia sat on the edge and then let herself drop. Killian caught her, then pulled her into the deeper shadows of some hedges. "Finn will distract the guards," he whispered. "Then we'll go over the wall. Run straight across the street and into the alley."

Lydia grinned. "All right. But we can't get caught."

His hand skimmed down her back, and her hollow stomach filled with butterflies. "I spent a lot of time in this house as a child, Lydia. Trust me, I know how to sneak out."

They watched as Finn sauntered over to the nearest guard, showing the disinterested man some treasure he'd no doubt stolen from Seldrid. They watched, waiting for the guard's attention to perk, and then Killian whispered, "Now."

He caught her by the hips and lifted her. Lydia rolled over the wall, landing on the far side with far more grace than she had in their days in Mudaire. Killian landed next to her, silent as a cat, and they both sprinted toward the dark alley across the street. Moments later, Finn joined them.

"So this is how it is going to go," Finn said, and Lydia smiled to see him returning to his usual spirits. "There are quite a few blighters in my kingdom, and I know where they tend to gather. I'll point them out. Killian will catch them. Lydia, you'll . . . do what you do. Are we clear?"

"Yes, Your Grace." Lydia dropped into a smooth curtsy. "We are yours to command."

Though it was too dark to see his face, she sensed the boy roll his eyes. "Enough of that. Follow me and don't draw attention to yourselves."

They wove through the alleyways of Serlania, and while Lydia was swiftly turned about, Finn and Killian both seemed to know the city like the backs of their hands. It had a much different feel than Mudaire, the air heady and warm and mercifully smelling of sea rather than blight. The buildings were lower to the ground, walls whitewashed and roofs made of terracotta shingles. The alleys and roads were cobbled but rough, mortar worn away by the heavy rains mercifully common to the region. On every corner were rain barrels, and fountains sprayed water at the intersections of major streets. Most people were abed and asleep, but voices and music trickled out from establishments where people gathered, Mudamorians clinging to the good things in life despite their circumstances.

Serlania had many parks and gardens, but all were full of the tents of refugees, as were many of the alleys. Finn moved through them with total confidence, and while Lydia spotted more than a few undead among the living, she said nothing, trusting that Finn had a reason for taking them so far afield.

They approached a bridge over a small creek, and Lydia picked out the glowing forms of children on the creek's banks, all huddled together. But not all of the moving shadows were alive.

"Wait here," Finn muttered. "I'll lure one of them out."

"Won't they know that you're not one of them anymore?" Lydia asked softly. "Won't she have warned them?"

"They'll know," he answered. "That's why this will be so easy."

Lydia's pulse thrummed as Finn strolled away from them, heading toward the gathered children and calling out a greeting.

"We have to assume Rufina will know it's me bringing back her blighters," she whispered. "She'll know that means we are not as imprisoned as we are pretending to be. What if she tells Marcus?" Sudden uncertainty of whether this was a good idea filled her. "Maybe we shouldn't do this."

"Your ability to bring back those who have succumbed to blight makes you valuable," Killian murmured. "Not just to us, but to the legions when they inevitably face Rufina. Why would she reveal that information to Marcus when she wants you dead?"

"He wants me dead, too, and I don't think my ability to bring his men back to life will be enough to counter that desire."

"Maybe." Killian's hand rested against her back, his palm warm through the fabric of her clothes. "But is that a risk Rufina is willing to take for the sake of a handful of blighter souls? Or is it better to stay silent over what you can do until he destroys her greatest threat?"

She leaned against him. "Not just a pretty face with a sword, are you?"

Killian huffed out an amused breath, his hand sliding lower over her hip. Then he tensed. "Here they come. He's got two. Are they both dead?"

"Yes." A boy and a girl, both several years younger than Finn.

"If I restrain the boy, can you manage the girl?"

Lydia nodded, and they slipped through the shadows toward the trio.

Defeating the Corrupter's hold on them was no easier than it had been with Finn. Like being thrown into a fighting pit and battling for her life each time, every second agonizing. Each victory ecstasy.

She slumped against Killian, breathing hard even as she heard the shouts rising in the neighboring buildings, which had shuddered each time she'd knocked back the Corrupter. The two children were alive, but both wept in Finn's arms.

"We need to go," Killian whispered. "Soldiers will be coming to investigate. And not all the blighters are children—some are a much greater threat, and Rufina will have them hunting us."

He handed something to Finn. "You know where my house in Serlania is? Take them there. I'll arrange for provisions. Go!"

Finn took hold of both children's hands and they bolted into the night.

"Can you run?" Killian asked.

"Yes."

He caught hold of her hand and led her at a sprint through the alleys of the city, away from the rising commotion. Away from those who sought their death.

And Lydia had never felt more alive.

As Killian drew to a walk in a mercifully empty alley, both of them breathing hard, Lydia wrapped her arms around his neck. "Kiss me."

He was already moving. Lifting her even as his lips claimed her, and Lydia wrapped her legs around his waist as her back pressed against the wall. Tonight was what she'd needed. A visceral reminder of the truth that had always burned in her heart: They were united and nothing in this world would ever pull them apart.

No words were needed, only breath and touch as he slid her skirt up to her waist, weapons falling to the ground with a clatter as she unfastened his belt. He claimed her, promising her with his body that she would always be his. That he would always be hers.

And as the first hint of dawn warmed the midnight skies, they held each other close. Not in the luxury and safety of a High Lord's manor but in the gritty danger of the streets, the lives of all those they'd both sworn to protect drifting around them.

"It's better if they think we are at odds," he whispered against her throat. "Then they won't question our intent."

"By day, we are separate." She could barely get the words out, pleasure still rolling over her body.

"But after sunset, you are my mine." Killian's grip on her tightened. "We'll go to war every night to reclaim those stolen from us, and after every victory—"

"—I will have you," she finished for him. "Every night, for as many nights as we have left."

Because the front lines were not just before Teriana's ships or Dareena's dams. For Lydia and Killian, the front lines were here.

92

MARCUS

Marcus stood on the main level of Revat's library, the upper half of the tower missing as though a god had cleaved it away. It had been one of the falling god towers that had done the damage, but the impression remained as he allowed the falling rain to patter against his upturned face.

"We wish to bring everything back to Celendrial with all haste," the man standing at his left said. Marcus couldn't remember his name and didn't really care to learn it. Just one more administrator that the Senate had sent to begin the process of wrapping Gamdesh into the Empire's fold.

"If you would allocate a number of your men to aid in the packing of the crates, Legatus," the man said, lip curled as he surveyed the mess. "We need to move with all speed given the damage to the structure, else we risk losing valuable material to mold."

"I'm afraid that won't be possible. My men are forbidden from pillaging."

"This is not pillaging, Legatus! This is—" The man broke off as Marcus turned his head to look at him. "I understand. I'll make arrangements with the collegium to secure more appropriate resources for the undertaking."

Marcus was already walking toward the stairs. He'd always had a fondness for libraries—for old books, in particular—and seeing the disarray in the shelves created within him an overwhelming urge to organize. Many of the books were destroyed beyond repair, ruined either by falling shelves or by water, and he wondered how much knowledge had been lost forever.

You did this. The words drifted over the walls in his mind. *Every loss Gamdesh has suffered, and will suffer, is on your hands.*

It had occurred to him more than once that he was losing his mind. That it was not right to argue with the voices in one's own head, and Marcus supposed it was an inevitable consequence of all the xenthier stems that Racker had warned him about. Something in his mind had been cracked. Broken beyond repair. That was why he heard the voices. That was why he felt as he did.

Which was to say, felt very little at all.

Marcus climbed the circular stairs and roamed the floors, Gibzen and the rest of his bodyguards trailing after him. Rastag had looked at the building and declared that it couldn't be repaired, for the foundation was cracked beyond repair. Once it had been emptied, they'd collapse it. Yet another monument lost forever.

Because of you.

He frowned at the thought, then his eyes caught sight of a burned doorway, pieces of charred wood shattered across the floor. Curiosity filled him and Marcus approached, ducking under a broken beam that had fallen across the entrance. The walls of the room were stained with soot but the fire hadn't moved beyond the doorframe.

The space was dominated by a large table covered with books, rain blowing in the broken window and chairs scattered across the floor. There were also a number of discarded female garments. A hair comb. A piece of soap that, upon closer inspection, smelled like lavender.

She was here.

Marcus dropped the soap, and it made a dull thud as it struck the stone floor. Interrogation of prisoners had netted some information about why the *Kairense* had lingered so dangerously long before fleeing with the Sultan and a Mudamorian woman.

A woman named *Lydia.*

Marcus's frustration grew that the inconsequential daughter of a senator had caused him so much grief and seemed capable of surviving his every attempt to kill her.

How Cassius had discovered that she lived, he didn't know. Possibly Teriana's outburst as she'd fled Imresh had reached the wrong ears and the individual had sent the information back. Perhaps Bait's loose lips had achieved the same result. However it had happened, Cassius knew that Lydia was still alive. Knew that Marcus had failed to kill her. And if he didn't remedy his error, all the consequences that had driven him to try to murder her in the first place would rear their heads, not the least of which would be that he'd be destined for the noose.

"Why won't you just die?" he growled, needing Lydia's death with the same desperation as a drowning man needed air. Yet from the depths of his mind screamed the thought *Haven't you hurt Teriana enough?*

His head began to throb, and he rubbed at his temples. With luck, the Mudamorians would be enticed to surrender Lydia on the nebulous promise of Empire aid against the blight; failing that, it wasn't as though he didn't have assassins at his disposal.

Kill her.

"I will," he muttered sourly, knowing he was again arguing with himself. That he needed to pull himself together so that his men, most especially the other legion legati, didn't realize that he was losing his mind and force him back to Celendor. Cassius would inevitably decide to punish him with a rope around his neck for his failure.

You deserve it.

"Oh shut up." He picked up a pair of white cotton gloves that sat on the table, the fingertips darkened with ink stains, then discarded them in favor of examining the remains of a book that looked to have been purposely destroyed. Clearly ancient, it had been hurled against the wall with incredible force, reduced to fragments that had subsequently been blown across the floor.

Sitting cross-legged before the remains, he sorted through for pieces with text, and his curiosity flared as he recognized the language it was written in. He had more important matters to attend to, but Marcus instead picked through the pieces of the broken book, examining what remained of the artwork and text. Taking in what he could about a time lost to history when another nation had nearly fallen to the same blight.

"This reminds me of Lescendor."

Marcus looked up from the fragment he'd been reading through a magnifying lens that he'd found. Felix ducked under the beam across the entrance and came into the room.

"I can't remember the number of times I found you hunched over a book in a dark corner." Felix crouched next to him. "You're the only person I've ever met willing to take a beating for a chance to keep reading."

Marcus set down the fragment he'd been translating. It was not lost on him that Lydia had very nearly sacrificed her life to read these books.

"Find anything interesting?" Felix righted two chairs and sat on one of them. Knees cracking from sitting on the floor for so long, Marcus joined him.

"The Mudamorians were researching ways to fight the blight that has consumed their kingdom. This isn't the first time it has happened. Others defeated it, though it appears to have come at great cost."

"Interesting." Felix met Marcus's gaze, visibly relaxing at whatever he saw. "Does it impact your thoughts on the Derin queen's offer of alliance? The reports coming back from Mudamora about the nature of her army grow stranger by the day."

An army of the dead.

That was what the reports said; every one of Marcus's sources claimed in no uncertain terms that anyone who touched or ingested the blight died swiftly and then rose to fight for Derin's queen. Puppets of the Seventh god. Logic demanded that he discount those reports, but Marcus had seen too many things that defied explanation to do so.

Rufina had offered an alliance, requesting his aid in quelling the Mudamorians in exchange for ownership of the gold mines on the western edge of the kingdom. The largest gold deposits on all of Reath and the very mines that Cassius had instructed him to secure. Marcus had no doubt that Rufina would throw Lydia's death into the offer to sweeten the pot, thus giving him everything he wanted.

And yet he had not yet accepted. Not yet even responded.

"I think it safe to say that the blight is poison," Felix said. "If the men come in contact with it, or if our water sources were contaminated, we'd lose men by the hundreds. Thousands. Tens of thousands, if what the spies say is true. If we do as Rufina asks, we might win Cassius those mines only to lose them back to her because we are all dead."

Those risks were not lost on Marcus. "We'll see if the Mudamorians will deal," he said. "If Queen Kitaryia gives us what Cassius wants, we can aid them in their battle against the blight. Perhaps what they gained here"—he gestured around—"was the answers they needed."

"You asked them to surrender control of their nation, their gold, and one of their marked," Felix said. "Do you really think they'll consider it?"

"It's that or die, Felix," he said with a sigh. "And people do desperate things to live. Which is why, if they decline, we'll head to Mudamora and take what Cassius wants by force. Because if we don't, he'll execute every legati who refuses and give command to someone in the ranks who obeys. If Cassius had his way, we'd already have set sail for Mudamora's shores, but I've been dragging my heels and giving every possible excuse to keep us here while we wait to see if Mudamora will give him what he wants without a fight."

Which was a lie. Marcus was dragging his heels while all the other legion legati came to terms with Cassius's goals. He hadn't been the only legatus to receive a message from the Dictator—his spies had informed him that Cassius had sent missives to the commander of every legion in Revat. While Marcus did not know the precise contents of every letter, the grim acceptance that had grown on the faces of the men told him that the crux of each was the same as what he'd been sent: do what you are told or die on the gallows. The same threat that had been dangled over every legionnaire's head since the moment they stepped through the gates of Lescendor.

Unbidden, Grypus's voice filled his thoughts. *Remember that the Senate owns you. I own you. You have no more say than a dog, and like a dog, you will be put down if you choose to bite.*

Felix had been quiet, but he abruptly said, "You seem more yourself today than you have in a long time."

Marcus wasn't himself any more than he'd been yesterday or the day prior, but knowing that he was successfully performing otherwise eased the tension twisting his shoulders into knots.

You cannot lose control! the voice shrieked, and Marcus hid the flinch of pain with a half smile. "I've been sleeping better. I think that's all I needed."

"That's good. Servius and I have been . . . worried about you. Everyone has been."

Marcus's irritation flared. "Why? Everything has gone to plan. Everything is in perfect order. I've won every fight with minimal loss and yet everyone—"

"No one is questioning your ability to win, Marcus. But don't deny that you've been different since Emrant. Since *before* Teriana bolted. If I had to peg the moment, it was just after Grypus arrived. When his Ninth engineers pulled down Emrant's god towers and you realized that you would not be able to control our presence in the West as you had up until that moment."

No part of him wanted to talk about this, but Marcus forced his temper to remain in check.

"When I walked in on you having breakfast in Imresh with Teriana, it struck me that I'd never seen you so happy in all the years that I had known you. Like you finally had everything that you wanted. And then I told you Grypus was coming, and you decided that you would do whatever it took to hold on to that happiness. That you would go as low as you needed to go to keep it, and when it all fell apart anyway, you stayed in those depths. Went deeper still."

Marcus's head was throbbing so hard that colors blurred across his vision. "What is your point?"

"This isn't you."

Yes, it is.

"I know it's easier to stay down there where the only thing you ever have to feel is anger, but I also know that you've never taken the easier path a day in your life. We need you back if we are going to survive this." Felix caught hold of his hands, and Marcus felt the walls in his mind tremble. "You've never abandoned us, and we won't abandon you."

Marcus stared at Felix's hands, locked on his, then slowly withdrew from his grip. He gave Felix a tight smile. "The sentiment is appreciated, but your concerns are misplaced. I was angry when she left, it's true, but I'm over it. When she came to deliver her message, it struck me that I no longer cared as much as I had. I know there is concern over Cassius's ambition and the risks securing his desires entails, but I've had a lot of practice achieving political ends while not getting us killed. Trust me."

Felix sighed. "I do trust you." But then he shook his head. "Which is why I think you're lying to yourself. Not even death will make you stop caring about her."

Marcus's fingers curled into fists. "From her own lips, she is my enemy now."

For a long moment, Felix didn't answer, his eyes searching Marcus's. "If you've convinced yourself of that, then may the gods of this land have mercy on Teriana and all that she holds dear."

A soft cough caught Marcus's attention, and his eyes went to the entrance, where Gibzen now stood. "A message from Mudamora, sir. *Astara* delivered it, which means she got a good look at what we do to traitors. Coward dropped it attached to a rock and didn't get close enough for us to shoot."

Marcus's jaw tightened at mention of Atrio's betrayal. He

should've known from the way the spy had reacted over the shifter's imprisonment that he might take action, but it had still come as a surprise when Atrio had arranged her escape. It had been a long time since Marcus had had to execute one of the Thirty-Seventh, and while he'd felt nothing when he'd watched the spy hanged from the gallows, it had done nothing for the Thirty-Seventh's morale. "Give it here, then."

"The Katamarcans also brought news that the Mudamorians are infighting and intend to pull the crown from the Falorn Queen's head so as to place it on someone more pliable."

Felix gave a disgusted shake of his head, but Marcus's attention was all for the letter that Gibzen handed him. He cracked the wax, and glanced at the signatory. "It's signed by a Helene Torrington."

"She's the High Lady of House Torrington," Felix said. "I'll see what else the spies know about her."

But Marcus was swiftly reading the looping script and sycophantic prose, stalling on a pair of lines, which he read over and over, shock filling his core. *Lydia Valerius, the runaway bride your ruler seeks, is an alias, for her true name is Kitaryia Falorn.*

"How is that possible?" he muttered, then forced himself to keep reading.

Kitaryia briefly wore the crown but has proven herself a liability, so we will happily exchange her for your aid against our enemies.

"What does it say?" Felix demanded.

He'd caught her.

He could end this.

"It says they'll give up Lydia Valerius."

The matter of the gold mines of Rotahn is a different matter that requires consideration. We require greater commitments from you that Mudamora will be treated with honor and dignity as a vassal state of the Empire before making such a concession. I would like to invite you to negotiate in person, so that we might come to know each other as dear friends, and sign an agreement that is mutually beneficial, at which time we will hand over custody of Kitaryia/Lydia so that you might return her to her betrothed.

He tossed the letter on the table, and Felix picked it up.

"This is good news," Felix murmured. "We might be able to satisfy Cassius's demands for Mudamorian gold without racing onto poisoned ground. Gold in exchange for shipments of grain and fresh water. And his betrothed, of course."

Time and again, Marcus had tried to kill Lydia and she'd always escaped. Now she was to be handed to him without a fight. His instincts flared with the sense that all was not as it seemed.

"It's too easy." Rising to his feet, Marcus went to the broken window. The view overlooked the brown muddy earth left in the wake of the dam's rupture. The perfect view of the destruction Lydia had barely escaped.

Felix gestured at the books surrounding them. "My guess is that they failed to find the answers they needed and they have realized they won't win the fight against Rufina. They see us as the lesser evil. At least under Senate rule, they get to live. Though if we agree to this, we are setting ourselves up for an eventual fight against the Queen of Derin, so I'd start thinking about how you plan to negotiate with her."

It could not be this easy. "Cassius won't accept a deal without the mines. And if we don't give him the gold, it will be *our* supplies at risk."

"So negotiate," Felix said. "We risk nothing by doing so."

Then why did it feel like he was risking everything? "Gather the legati to discuss the terms we'll offer. I want to get this done tonight."

As Felix went ahead, Marcus met Gibzen's eye and gave him a slight nod.

He'd get it all done tonight.

93

TERIANA

With the aid of the greater ocean paths and a stiff wind supplied by Baird's mark, the *Quincense* made good time crossing the world, and it was not long until they were anchored off the coast of Bardeen and heading inland for a meeting with the rebels. It seemed a lifetime ago that she'd been in these forests with Austornic and the Fifty-First, but the oppressive feeling of being watched by the enormous redwoods was the same.

"These trees have eyes," Bait muttered. "I swear it."

"More like there are eyes in the trees," Teriana answered. "The rebels know we are coming, and they most definitely don't trust me."

"Us, you mean?"

"No." She looked up into the shadowed branches, which were devoid of the sound of life. "It was me they saw with the Fifty-First. They know my role in all of this, so it's me they have cause to doubt."

Cause, even, to kill, but Teriana didn't allow herself to dwell on that fact.

The meeting had been set up via the network of merchant connections the Maarin had throughout Bardeen. For all her people were the enemy of the Cel, the legions who policed the province showed Teriana and her crew little interest. Not only were the Maarin not considered a threat, Cassius had named them a conquered people. So as long as taxes were paid and laws abided, no one caused them much trouble. Yet notices were posted in every port that Maarin births were to be registered, and that child tithes of second *and* fourth born sons were to begin.

Over my dead fucking body, had been Teriana's thought as she'd cemented the arrangements to form an alliance that would ensure the Empire would never dismiss her people again.

The deal was that the rebels would meet with Teriana and one other from her crew, all bets off if she brought more reinforcements, so she and Bait walked alone down the little-used road, waiting for the rebels to make contact.

"What if they don't come?" Bait muttered. "What if they aren't interested?"

"When it comes to striking a blow against the Empire, there is nothing they're *more* interested in." Teriana remembered the reports that had come Marcus's way. "Trust me."

Then an arrow struck the ground at her feet, forcing her to slide to a stop.

Out of the trees, dozens of Bardenese warriors appeared, their clothes dark browns and greens that blended into the landscape. But Teriana's eyes were all for the woman at their head.

Perhaps a few years older than Teriana was herself, the young woman was beautiful beyond measure with her rich brown skin, large eyes rimmed with long lashes, and full lips. Her dark hair was long and woven into a braid that hung over one shoulder, but it was the gladius at her waist that told Teriana she'd found who she was looking for. "You're Silvara."

"My name matters little," the young woman answered, keeping a cautious distance between them, though Teriana had no doubt Silvara was the more dangerous fighter. "Your messenger said you wished to speak of an alliance between the rebellion and the Maarin. Out of courtesy to your people, I have come, but only to tell you that

I've no interest in an alliance with a Cel puppet who wants revenge over a broken heart. Go back to the sea where you belong." Then the woman turned and walked away.

Teriana's cheeks burned with embarrassment, but the anger that roared in her heart was louder. "Agrippa told me to tell you that he's sorry. That it took him a bit of time to figure things out, but that he's now fighting on the right side. He hopes you'll join him on that side, for I do not offer an alliance with the Maarin, but with all who oppose Celendor's oppression."

Silvara froze in her tracks. "Agrippa is dead. Drowned."

"No, he's on the far side of the world by way of the same xenthier stem that the legions now use to reach Arinoquia. He could have rejoined the Thirty-Seventh, but instead he fights for those who stand against them." She rattled off a description of Agrippa, concluding with, "He can't say more than a handful of sentences without cracking a joke or insulting whomever he's speaking to. Sound familiar?"

Silvara's hand rested on the pommel of the gladius, toying with the 37 marked on it as she whispered, "Agrippa is alive?"

"Yes. And he told me about you two, so I think it's the pot calling the kettle black to name me a Cel puppet who only wants revenge for her broken heart."

Silvara didn't answer. Didn't turn around, only stood in place, finger tracing the 37 on the gladius.

"A war is being fought in the West," Teriana said. "And the side of good is very much on the back foot. If they lose, all of Reath will fall to the Empire and its dark ally. We have one chance to stop them, but we can't do it without help from those who war against the Senate in the East. Your help."

"The war in the West has been a boon to us," Silvara answered. "The Dictator's eyes, as well as the eyes of his Senate, are fixed on those distant nations, and they have weakened their defenses in order to send more and more legions across the seas in pursuit of conquest. If it continues, we'll have the opportunity to liberate Bardeen. As will Chersome and Sibern, who have rebellions of their own. The Dictator will come to regret his over ambition."

"Will he, though?" Teriana asked quietly. "The West cannot win this war. The enemy is too strong. Within months, if not sooner, the Empire will take control. Will bend the nations of the West to its will, assimilating them and stealing their children to populate its war machine, and how long until the Dictator has the power of a god?"

Silvara twitched.

"You might reclaim Bardeen for a time while they are distracted, but if you allow them to grow stronger on the backs of their conquest, how long until the heel of Mother Empire comes crushing down, more punitive and crueler than before? If you really want to throw off the yoke, you need to strike not just a blow for Bardeen but a blow for all of Reath."

Silence.

Wind moaned through the branches of the trees, the dapples of sunlight dancing across the dirt. Then Silvara said, "Walk with me, Teriana of the Maarin."

Teriana started after the other woman, and when Bait made to follow, she said, "Wait here."

Silvara led her deeper into the forest, the other woman moving silently as any predator, her eyes always roving the shadows, whereas Teriana tripped over roots and crunched branches beneath her boots. "Sorry."

Silvara gave a soft laugh. "I've never been on a ship. I've heard the motion is so terrible it drives grown men to vomit."

"You adapt."

"When your silence means your life, you also adapt."

They reached a clearing, and Silvara sat down on a rock, motioning for Teriana to sit on the one across from her. "It's true then, that you were Marcus's lover."

Teriana brushed dirt from her sleeve. "He was *my* lover, if you must know."

Silvara laughed, the sound like silver wind chimes, beautiful and haunting. "It's good that you can laugh. It took me a long time to be able to laugh after—" She broke off, shaking her head. "They get under your skin, Empire boys. The good ones, at any rate. So wonderfully fierce and dangerous, yet so incredibly sad and broken. Impossible to resist, though Marcus . . ." Silvara gave a shake of her head. "That, I can't quite understand."

"You ever meet him?"

"Yes. He was perfectly courteous and entirely terrifying."

"I had the same initial impression. Though he had hidden depths." Teriana's chest tightened. "Or at least, that's what I thought."

"I think falling for them is setting yourself up for heartbreak, because you'll always be second to their brothers. And none of them are right in the head, not really. How can they be, given the Empire turns them into killers when they are just children? They have no hope, and neither do those who love them."

Teriana considered what Bait had told her about Agrippa, as well as her own impressions, then said, "Agrippa seems to have broken out of that cycle. Although to be honest, he made some unfortunate decisions before he got on the right track. He . . . He met a girl, married her, actually, and I don't think there is anything he wouldn't do for her, including fight the Thirty-Seventh."

Silvara was quiet. "It shouldn't hurt, but it does. To know that he had the capacity to choose me over the legions but didn't." She made a strangled noise, then pressed her hands to her face. "It's been years, and I've had other lovers since, but there's something about your first. Something about *Empire boys* that latches onto your soul and never lets go, no matter how much time passes."

"Yeah," Teriana said, because there was no other response to the truth Silvara had delivered. Her truth. And, Teriana suspected, her own truth as well. "Do you wish it had gone differently? That it had been you he'd chosen?"

"No." Silvara smoothed her hand over her stomach, revealing that it was curved with early pregnancy. "I found the sort of love I needed. Someone who loves Bardeen just as much as I do and who will help me fight for the future of our nation. And the future of our child."

They sat in silence for a long time, both contemplating the past, and then Silvara said, "I joined the rebellion because I thought it was the right thing to do. That the best way I could live my life was fighting against those who oppressed my people, erased our ways, and forced us to be like them, and in doing so, made us serve them. To put my head in the sand when others face the same threat, even if they are strangers without names on the far side of the seas, smacks of hypocrisy."

Teriana blew out a long breath, then shook her head. "It's been lifetimes since someone has taken the fight to Celendor. It's risky beyond measure, and I can understand if that's not something you want to involve your people in."

Silvara looked up at the sky, then said, "Tell me your plan."

It was so simple that the telling took only a few moments, yet when Teriana finished, Silvara smiled. "Agrippa always wanted to be famous. To have a statue in the Forum for winning a battle, and for better or worse, I dream of the same. Of being the one to strike a blow against the Empire that will be felt for generations. I think, Teriana, that this is the moment to lift my weapon."

"So you're in?"

"Bardeen is in." Silvara's eyes met hers, beautiful in their defiance. "Fuck the Empire!"

Teriana smiled. "Fuck the Empire."

94

KILLIAN

Day after day, they'd kept up the act that they were at odds, but night after night, he and Lydia had done exactly what they promised. In the company of Finn, they hunted blighters down in the streets of Serlania, and Lydia liberated them from the Corrupter's hold, filled them with life, and allowed their souls to retake control of their bodies.

Not all of them came back.

Lydia had wept in his arms the first time it had happened. It had been a man with a wife and two children, the Corrupter masquerading as a loving husband and father. All had gone smoothly, but after Lydia had filled him with life, unlike the others, he did not draw in a breath. His heart did not begin to beat, and after a few moments, the life she had put into him drifted out into the world.

"I made it worse for them," she'd sobbed. "Now they have to endure without him with no explanation for how he died."

The worst part of it was that she was right. The blighter had been performing his duties so as to blend in, working and securing food for his family, and without him, life would grow more difficult. "I'll have Finn bring them food," he said. "I'll put them on his list."

Hollow comfort given that a woman would find her husband dead in an alley, but it had not been Lydia who had killed him. Killian had cupped her tear-stained cheeks, wishing he could take away the grief in her heart. "It's the risk we have to take. If we stop because we lost one, how many will lose the opportunity to get their life back? We have to keep going."

Lydia had nodded, and then asked Finn, "Find me another one."

Though more often than not, the souls came back into their

bodies, Lydia wept just as hard each time they did not. She had too big a heart for this world, but though Killian knew that it would go easier on her if she cared less, he wouldn't have changed her. It was half the reason he loved her.

Night after night, they pressed onward while Helene *negotiated* with Marcus. Malahi and Seldrid did their best to keep her from agreeing to everything the Cel wanted, but in the end, it was Marcus himself who put an end to it by sending a missive dictating a day to meet to finish the negotiations, as well as the location and allowance for numbers who would attend.

Yet they'd still heard no word from Teriana.

"By my reckoning, we have two choices," Agrippa had said. "Either we put an end to this farce that Helene rules and send Marcus a letter telling him the deal's off, or we let the game play on and give Teriana two more days to get the job done. If we go with the former, I'd suggest we light a fire under the giants and have them foul the seas to try to hold them back. Then we ride with every soldier we have to the front lines and carve our way through to that xenthier stem and get ourselves to Deadground. If we go with the latter, we need to figure out how we are going to fight two ships worth of legionnaires without losing most of Xadrian's and Bercola's warriors, because believe me, they won't go down easily. And afterwards, we'll have to ride with a fraction of the soldiers we had to the front lines to try to reach the xenthier and probably fail."

"I'm getting the impression your vote is the former strategy rather than the latter," Killian said. "Or did I misinterpret."

"You are awfully lighthearted for a man who has been sleeping alone." Agrippa's eyes flicked between Killian and Lydia, then narrowed. "Or not. Gods, I don't even want to know what you two have been up to."

Killian shrugged. "Better you don't know. But to the problem at hand, if we send a message to Marcus that the deal is off, how long until he sails in force to take what Mudamora is no longer freely giving?"

Agrippa crossed his arms and sighed. "Immediately, would be my guess. He always has contingencies, and he'll plan for Mudamora to change its mind, even if he doesn't think it's likely."

"Which brings us right back to where we stood before Teriana left." Lydia toyed with the end of her dark braid, her eyes meeting Killian's. "She needs more time. We haven't given her enough time."

"So you'll risk your ability to reach Deadground to give her two more days? Four, tops, because I suppose we can factor the time it takes for him to learn we played him dirty," Agrippa asked. "Will you risk everything for four days?"

Lydia's eyes hadn't broken from Killian's. "What does your gut tell you?"

The letter Marcus had sent Helene had said that he'd conduct the negotiations himself. Which meant that Killian might get a chance to put the bastard in the ground. "My gut says that we play this through to the end."

"You're underestimating them, Killian." Agrippa put his head in his hands. "Even with you and Xadrian fighting, the cost of this will be higher than you think."

"I'm not underestimating them," he answered. "I just have a plan."

The chance to cancel the negotiation had come and gone, and they'd still not heard any word from Teriana or any of the other groups making ready to attack at various places around the world. Agrippa believed it was because they'd failed.

Killian's gut told him otherwise.

Yet his mind was not for Teriana and the battle she faced, but for the one he would soon face, so Killian pulled his thoughts from the past and focused on the scene before him. A table had been set up on the beach under a pavilion, white sand stretching for leagues in every direction before him and pasture stretching for leagues in either direction behind. Clear and open terrain that allowed neither party to hide additional forces without the other knowing it.

Behind the table stood two hundred Mudamorian soldiers, primarily men and women taken from the High Lords' personal guards, and they stood nervously in the hot sun. Though no one spoke, it was far from silent with the way their feet shifted against the ground, armor and weapons clicking, all punctuated by the occasional cough.

At the table itself sat High Lord Pitolt, Helene, Lydia, and Killian. Helene radiated excitement, and every few minutes, she thanked Lydia for her generous sacrifice. Lydia, to her credit, hid her annoyance each time and always smiled and nodded. Pitolt was more aware of the stakes, and the man was sweating profusely and had refreshed his glass of lemonade twice.

"You are certain he will hold to the terms we have agreed to?" he asked Lydia for the third time. "The Cel abide by their word?"

"He will follow it to the letter unless we violate the terms," Lydia answered for the third time. "They take legal documents very seriously."

"Civilized," Pitolt muttered. "Honorable. Far better to deal with such men than that witch from Derin."

Helene rested an elbow on the table. "You are so fortunate to be escaping all this madness, Lydia. With how efficiently these Empire legions travel, I rather think that you'll be in the lap of luxury within the week! All of this will feel like a bad dream."

"I pray so," Lydia murmured, and to keep up his role, Killian muttered, "You don't have to do this, Lydia. You don't have to go with them."

"Have you ever thought that she might want to?" Helene snapped. "By the Six, Killian, she'll be going back to wed the *Dictator.* He's arguably the richest and most powerful man on Reath, and she'll be away from all of this."

"It is not a matter of *want*, Your Grace," Lydia said quietly. "It is a matter of doing what is right. With these concessions, Mudamora will gain a powerful ally. They will aid Malahi in reaching Deadground, and I've no doubt that the blight will soon be a thing of the past. All at the cost of Malahi's gold and my . . ." She swallowed hard. "My chance to be with Killian."

"And we thank you for your sacrifice," Helene repeated. "Truly, Lydia, you are a proper martyr. I think I will have a monument created that is dedicated to what you have done."

Instead of answering, Lydia gestured to the sea. "There they are."

Two ships approached, though one dropped sails and fell back, keeping far distant in the deep waters. The other continued on, then dropped anchor.

The wind blew vigorously, causing the Torrington banner to flap wildly, wrapping around the flagpole.

"Fix it," Helene hissed at the servants. "How are they to take me seriously if I don't appear to be in control?"

"We cannot control the way the wind blows, Your Grace," High Lord Pitolt muttered, wiping sweat from his face. "They will take you seriously by virtue of the crown on your head and your ability to make this agreement."

The wind was, indeed, beyond their control, yet Killian noticed that the crimson and gold banners on the Cel ship blew out straight, the strange serpent that Lydia told him was called a dragon seeming to writhe and dance on the wind. The ship had anchored in deep water, and he watched with interest as he got his first look at the legions of Celendor.

They were every bit as well trained as Agrippa had said they would be, disembarking in longboats with total organization and precision, armor and weapons polished and shining in the sun. They formed neat ranks on the beach, watchful and alert until the full company of two hundred had disembarked, what looked to be a hundred more remaining on the deck.

Exactly as Killian had anticipated.

The legionnaires pressed toward the pavilion, marching in lockstep to the beat of a single drummer except for the man who walked at their head, a crimson cloak floating out behind him. The legionnaires were similar in age to Killian himself, every one of them fit and hard, marked with scars that came with years of combat. It was hard to see their faces beneath their helmets, but the bare skin around their elbows and knees varied in hue from pale as Lydia to dark brown, a visible reminder that the Senate stole children from every place it conquered.

And all of them bore the same marking on their breastplates as Agrippa had tattooed on his chest.

37.

These men were Thirty-Seventh legion, yet as they crossed the long stretch of pristine white sand to stop a short distance from the pavilion, Killian did not need Lydia's slight shake of her head to know that the man at their head was not Marcus.

Not enough arrogance.

Vicious disappointment filled Killian's stomach even though Agrippa had cautioned him that it was unlikely that Marcus would come himself. "He stays behind the lines," Agrippa had said.

"Coward."

Agrippa had only rolled his eyes. "His strength is the brain between his ears, not his sword arm. You're a bit opposite in that regard."

Killian pushed the remembered conversation from his head in favor of focusing on the man who led the force before him.

Removing his strange crested helmet, the leader tucked it under his arm and approached the table. His blond hair clipped extremely short and his face clean-shaven. His skin was golden—not from the sun but almost as though he'd been brushed in golden dust—and the eyes roving for any sign of threat were a turquoise blue. He was good looking, but Killian sensed the threat beneath the polished surface—this man was dangerous.

"Welcome to Mudamora, Legatus," Helene declared. "We are most grateful to stand on the threshold of a great alliance that will see the dark queen Rufina and her forces expelled from our borders, and our lands made green again by the grace of the great Celendor Empire."

To the man's credit, he didn't so much as blink at Helene's gross misinterpretation of this situation, only inclined his head. "Well met, Your Majesty." He spoke clear Mudamorian but with the same soft accent that Lydia had when she'd first arrived. "It is my honor and privilege to accept your commitment to the governorship of the Empire. Under the Senate's stewardship, all will soon be brought to rights."

"You are a blessing in our darkest hour, Legatus." Helene smiled and fluttered her eyelashes.

"Centurion, Your Majesty," the legionnaire answered. "The legatus sends his regrets that he was not able to take this momentous meeting in person, but his obligations are many."

"I see." Helene's smile faltered, but she swiftly recovered and rose to her feet.

"What possible obligations could be greater than this?" High Lord Pitolt demanded.

The centurion gave a small smile. "Matters above my rank, I'm sure. But the legatus gave clear instructions as to my duties here even as he professed his deepest regrets for having to delegate the matter."

Helene circled the table, and as she stepped toward the centurion, his men lowered their spears and stepped forward. Helene froze.

"Apologies, Your Majesty," the centurion said, lifting a casual hand to wave back his men. "It appears they see you as a threat."

It wasn't Helene who concerned them, but Killian could sense the legionnaires' agitation. They sensed something was wrong, sensed the threat, their eyes searching for the source. Killian didn't fail to notice that it was to him their eyes moved most, despite the fact he wore no weapon.

Helene gave a nervous giggle. "They flatter me, for I've never lifted a weapon in my life." She continued her progress around the table, stopping before the centurion. "I had hoped to meet the legatus. So that we might negotiate in person."

"I've no doubt that your paths will cross in the future and that he'll be delighted to make your acquaintance." The centurion's voice was calm and steady, but Killian didn't miss his fingers moving. A silent signal to the men behind him, who all tensed. The last line of their ranks pivoted as one, spears and attention on the beach.

They sense danger.

Killian silently cursed because the giants weren't yet in position, and the other ship waiting in deeper waters was full of more men just as dangerous as these.

The centurion took a steel cylinder from one of his men and extracted a thick roll of paper. "It is my understanding that negotiations are complete. The terms have been laid out here, in Cel and again in your language, and the legatus has already signed on behalf of the Senate. If you would sign, Your Majesty, and hand over the woman known as both Kitaryia Falorn and Lydia Valerius, we shall return to Revat and make ready to take next steps."

"Yes, well, this is her." Helene had lost all her color, her motion stiff as she gestured to Lydia. "Lydia goes willingly, as does her bodyguard. They both understand this agreement is for the good of Mudamora."

One of the legionnaires said something in Cel, and the centurion gave a tight nod to Lydia. "Your face is known to us, Domina. It is my understanding that your betrothal to the Dictator still stands, and you will be wed upon your return. So it would be best if your *bodyguard* remains here. We will do you the courtesy of keeping your . . . *indiscretions* in the West."

"How kind of you." Lydia's voice was cool. "But before we take this step, tell me: How does Celendor aim to destroy the blight that plagues Mudamora?"

"That remains to be seen." The man's words were terse, his patience for this conversation fading as his instincts sensed the rising threat. "No doubt we will enlist experts in botany from the collegium to advise."

"The blight is not a *plant*," Lydia retorted. "The blight is death itself. I was not aware that the collegium had experts on such things."

The centurion eyed her for a moment, then said, "Having not seen the substance myself, it would be speaking out of turn for me to give an opinion on its nature."

"Has Marcus seen it?"

His eyes moved from Lydia to again survey the surroundings. "You might reconsider your familiarity."

"Oh, we've met." Lydia's head tilted. "I'm sure you're aware."

"I don't know if he's seen it. He does not hold me in close confidence, so to make assumptions would be a presumption."

"And yet you stand here on his behalf, and"—Lydia gestured to the document—"he has signed an agreement that says, and I quote, 'The Empire commits to invest significant resources into the eradication of the blight.'" She rested an elbow on the table, giving the centurion a small smile. "Perhaps you might explain to me what that means before I surrender my life into your care."

"Lydia, what are you doing?" Helene hissed. "You agreed to this."

"I would like to hear the answer, Your Grace." High Lord Pitolt's eyes narrowed, for while he was an ambitious coward, he was no fool. "What resources? What is the Empire's plan?"

The centurion gave an irritated shake of his head, his eyes going to Helene. "We had an agreement, Your Grace. While elements of that agreement may take time to achieve, the surrender of Lydia Valerius is not one of them. She is the betrothed to the Dictator of Celendor, which means that you are withholding his property from him."

Killian's whole body stiffened, and the centurion's eyes shot to him, civility disappearing in an instant. "Your face and name are known to us, Killian Calorian, as is your reputation. Keep your ass on that chair and you might survive this. Get to your feet, and you breathe your last, am I understood?"

Killian didn't answer.

The centurion's mouth twisted, the pulse in his throat throbbing rapidly. "Your Majesty, please sign. We have a long journey and wish to depart."

"Helene, do not sign." High Lord Pitolt rose, resting his hands on the table. "I dislike this boy's tone and find myself questioning his master's true intent."

Hurry, Killian silently begged Bercola, but there was no sign of motion in the water.

"It strikes me that you have not been negotiating in good faith," the centurion snapped. "Do you wish Celendor to deliver you from the Queen of Derin and her blight, or do you wish us to leave you to fight on alone? To *lose* alone, for that is surely what is to occur?"

"I . . ." Helene took an unsteady step backward, colliding with the table. "What is happening here? I thought we had an agreement that this would be conducted peacefully?"

Killian caught sight of movement in the water. A stirring in the depths.

"I do not think your motivations here are peaceful," the centurion said. "Either prove me wrong by signing or get on with whatever you have planned."

"We haven't planned anything." Tears of fear ran down Helene's face, and she reached up to touch the crown on her head. "If we could just sit and have a glass of wine and discuss this reasonably . . ."

The movement in the water drew closer to the Cel ship, and one of the centurion's men spotted it. Said something in Cel.

A bead of sweat ran down the centurion's golden cheek, and he slammed his helmet down on his head. Making ready to fight because one did not live and breathe war as these men did and not know when a fight was upon you.

Hurry, Bercola.

"Sign, you foolish woman!" the centurion barked at Helene, but his eyes were on Killian. "Or get on with it."

"No." Helene lifted her chin. "I don't think I will."

The centurion snarled what was undoubtedly profanity, then caught hold of Lydia's wrist. He dragged her away from the table even as six spears were leveled at Killian's throat. "That's a lot of steel," Killian said to them. "What are you so afraid of?"

They tensed but held their position as the centurion dragged Lydia across the sand, surrounded by the rest of his men.

Killian felt the *shift.* A change in air and breath, and then the water around the ship began to churn. Hooks burst out of the depths to catch hold of the Cel ship's rails, and then giants were climbing the ropes.

Just as Xadrian and his warriors exploded from the sand beneath the legionnaire's feet.

Helene screamed and Killian flung himself sideways, feeling one of the spears score his cheek. He barely felt the pain as he rolled across the sand to rip his sword from its depths.

Killian lifted it in time to slash away a downward strike, the spear sinking into the sand next to his face. Grabbing a handful, he rolled to his feet and threw it.

The sand struck two of the legionnaires in the eyes, and they stumbled into the others.

But Killian knew he'd only bought himself seconds, and he bolted toward the battle.

A spear shot past him and another sliced deep along his shoulder, but he only gritted his teeth and snatched up one of the spears from the sand, his eyes all for Lydia.

Agrippa had not exaggerated about the Thirty-Seventh's skill.

For all they were outnumbered five to one, their route of retreat being rapidly destroyed by giants, and many of their number dying in the sand, the legionnaires held their ground with grim determination.

They'd moved into a circular formation around the centurion and Lydia, shields tight together and spears bristling outward as they moved toward the longboats.

Xadrian circled them, face splattered with blood and sword slicked with gore, searching for a weakness in their ranks and finding none. To attack would cost them.

The centurion shouted something, and Killian heard the men behind him break off their chase. Heard them run in the other direction, likely to signal reinforcements.

Whirling, Killian flung one of the spears. It soared through the air and punched through the neck of one of the legionnaires. Snatching up another fallen spear, he launched it at the sprinting men. It sank into the lower leg of one of them. He went down, ripped it out, then staggered on.

"Hunt them down!" Killian roared at Pitolt's men, who flung themselves onto horseback and galloped in pursuit. Then fixed his eyes on the centurion who now held a blade to Lydia's throat.

"You're a fool for this," the centurion spat. "What do you think that killing us gains you? We're a drop in the ocean of men camped in Revat. All this will do is anger the legatus."

"Did you really think I was going to let you take my queen?" Killian asked, circling one direction while Xadrian circled the other, the Prince murmuring orders to his warriors as he walked.

Yet as the Anuk archers lifted their weapons, the centurion uttered a single word and the masses of men shifted, their shields no longer forming a wall but a dome.

"Impressive!" Xadrian shouted. "Hiding behind your wall of steel like an armadillo."

"More like a porcupine," Killian said as they crossed paths, circling, and Xadrian shrugged.

"You may be right, my friend. Either way, I question how long they'll be able to sustain this."

"As long as it takes reinforcements to arrive," the centurion answered. "Then we'll make you bleed."

Killian locked eyes with Xadrian, who shrugged. "I enjoy a challenge."

The ship was on fire now, the giants diving off the sides and swimming toward shore to join the fight. Smoke rose in a great plume, and beyond, he caught a flash of white on the water.

The other ship was approaching fast.

His eyes flicked back to the wall of steel and spears. He and Xadrian, with the giants' aid, could bring the Cel down, but it would be a bloody toll that Killian couldn't afford to pay. These men would fight to the last, and it occurred to Killian that he'd underestimated them as much as Xadrian had. "Give me the girl, and I will consider letting you go."

The centurion barked out a harsh laugh. "I'm afraid I can't do that. I'll slit her throat right before you cut me down, Calorian, so stay your hand. The only way you get her back is as a corpse. If you want the girl to live, you'll back off and let us take her to the boats. She'll make a fine wife for the Dictator."

"No," Lydia said from within the dome of steel. "I will not."

Killian's breath quickened, then from behind the shields, the centurion screamed, "Corrupted!"

The shields burst outwards, men stumbling and whirling, half to face the threat from within and half without, and the result was chaos.

Killian attacked at the same time as Xadrian did, the Anuk surging. With their lines lost, the Cel turned to hand-to-hand.

They were no less deadly.

Screams split the air, the white beach turned red with blood as the forces collided, but though Killian cut through the legionnaires, he could not find Lydia. "Lydia!"

Then he saw her. Moving like a ghost, faster than anyone had right to be. Lydia's hands found bare flesh, and the men she touched screamed as they aged, lashing out at her. But she only skipped out of reach and moved on to the next, weakening them. Terrifying them.

And Killian took advantage.

Every death was hard won, but one by one, he cut the legionnaires down. Following in Lydia's wake like death's shadow, maiming any that dared to strike at her. It was gory and brutal, but it ended almost as soon as it began.

"Victory!" Xadrian shouted, lifting his hands. The Anuk roared and the giants added their voices, but Killian only walked from dying legionnaire to dying legionnaire, cutting throats while Lydia moved among their own force's injured, saving lives.

They met in the middle and locked hands as they looked out over the sea at the other Cel ship. It had been moving closer, but had shifted course, and as they watched, it headed back across the strait. Bringing word of what had happened here.

"These were Marcus's men we killed." Lydia's voice was quiet. "Teriana told me they are like family to him. As soon as he finds out what we have done, he will come for blood."

Killian didn't answer, only tightened his grip on Lydia's hand.

"Do you think we bought her enough time?" she asked.

He sent out a silent prayer to Madoria to aid Teriana, wherever she was. "We'll find out soon enough, but for now, we need to turn our eyes to the blight."

Keeping her hand in his, Killian led Lydia up the beach. The Anuk and the giants fell into step with them, and they stopped before the overturned table, behind which Helene and High Lord Pitolt cowered. The latter spat, "You planned this behind our backs!"

"Correct." Killian reached down to pick up the crown that had fallen off Helene's head. "Because unlike you, we refuse to concede Mudamora to *anyone* without a fight."

He handed the crown to Lydia, then walked toward the two hundred Mudamorian soldiers who'd stood there and done nothing while Anukastre and Eoten Isle had bled and died to defeat the Thirty-Seventh. "It's time you start considering where you should place your allegiance!" he shouted, his voice carrying over them. "These two"—he gestured to Helene and Pitolt—"as well as some of their peers, have spent these past days not trying to save Mudamora but to save themselves. They were willing to hand over control of our kingdom to an Empire that rules with violence and oppression. An Empire that crushes the cultures and beliefs of all they take into their fold. An Empire that tears down the monuments of the Six everywhere they go but leaves the tower of the Seventh lording over all." He picked up the agreement from the sand and held it up. "That was what they were trying to do here, and you stood idly and watched without complaint."

The soldiers shifted restlessly, staring at their feet.

"Stood by idly while the warriors of Anukastre and Eoten Isle bled and died for your continued liberty. While they bled and died for the liberty of the woman who is our greatest weapon against the Corrupter." Catching hold of Lydia's hand, he lifted it high in the air. "Many of you know her as Kitaryia Falorn, but she is known to those who love her as Lydia, for she was raised in secret across the seas in the very Empire that Helene sought to surrender to. She is marked by Hegeria, and while these fools have spent recent days fighting to give her and all of our resources to the Empire, Lydia has been curing blighters by the dozens."

A gasp tore from the mass of soldiers before him, and behind him, he heard Xadrian crow with delight.

"Dozens upon dozens of men, women, and children who succumbed to the blight and were masquerading as civilians while spying for the enemy have been restored to themselves by her hand!" Killian shouted. "Yet despite knowing Lydia is one of our greatest weapons against the blight, Helene and her supporters wished to willfully hand her over to the enemy. And you stood by and watched it happen."

Silence stretched.

"We face extermination!" Killian shouted. "It is past time that we cease following those chosen by the most privileged among us. By those who have not gone hungry once during this ordeal. Instead, we should follow those who fight for our lives. Who fight for our freedom. Who are willing to lay down their own lives to save Reath from falling under the dominion of the Empire and the Seventh, for they are one and the same!"

Taking the crown from Lydia's hand, he placed it on her head. "We ride north with our allies to bring the fight to Rufina and destroy the blight. We ride north to destroy that which threatens everything we hold dear. Will you ride with us, or will you remain here to protect the likes of these two," he pointed at Helene and Pitolt, "while they host parties and laugh as your children starve outside their gates?"

"To war!" someone shouted. "We march to war!"

The Mudamorian soldiers erupted in shouts for war. Shouts declaring in Lydia's name. Shouts for Mudamora and all of Reath. The Anuk and the giants all added roars of favor, lifting their weapons in the air, but as he and Lydia led the mass of them northward, Killian's skin began to crawl and he cast his eyes back to the glittering strait and the fleeing ship.

A battle won.

But the war was far from over.

95

MARCUS

"The Dictator and the Senate are running out of patience." Drusus tossed the latest letter from Cassius down on the table. "We need to start making the motions of readying to sail to Mudamora to satisfy his spies or there are going to be consequences."

"He's not going to punish us for moving slowly." Felix picked up the letter, scanning the contents. "We're negotiating to get what he wants to avoid marching onto poisoned ground. He has to understand that we're being cautious in order to avoid high casualties."

Drusus scoffed. "He understands the whys just fine—he just doesn't give a fuck if half of us die as long as he gets his gold."

The other legatus rested his elbows on the table, head in his hands, and it struck Marcus that the Eleventh's legatus looked old. Old far beyond his years.

"We were supposed to be done," Drusus muttered. "We were supposed to retire at the end of this year. Paid out and given land and a chance at life. Now it looks as though half of my legion will die puking on foreign soil, poisoned by rotten ground, so that the other half might have a chance at what we are owed. All so that Cassius can get the gold he so desperately needs for his quest to control all of Reath."

Marcus took the letter from Felix, again reading Cassius's orders to move to take control of Mudamora. There was a hint of desperation in the prose, obvious only because it was so uncharacteristic, and it spoke to the truth of Drusus's words. This campaign had been costly beyond measure, and threats and machinations would only work so long to keep Cassius in power if the coffers ran dry.

War cost money, and this war was like nothing the Empire had ever waged.

"That's the deal he made you, then?" he asked Drusus. "Get him the Rotahn gold mines and the Eleventh can retire?"

"Yes." Drusus lifted his face from his hands, meeting Marcus's gaze. "We were supposed to be done. And now we face either life in service or stepping onto poisoned ground. Death either fucking way." He barked out a laugh. "Likely because he can't afford to pay us out, and he doesn't want the legions surrounding him to know his coffers are empty. Because they might start to question his ability to pay *them*."

Yet more proof of Cassius's growing desperation. Desperation often made men weak and foolish, but in this instance, it only made the Dictator more dangerous.

"My men will be back today," Marcus said by way of answer to Drusus's concerns. "With luck, we'll have an agreement signed by Queen Helene, as well as the bride whom Cassius misplaced. The Eleventh will have its retirement, and Cassius will have the gold to fund his obligations. A happy ending."

"We don't get happy endings." Drusus's eyes sharpened. "The Dictator has lit a fire under the ass of every legatus under your command, Marcus. Some with threats. Some with rewards. Consensus is that he doesn't trust you to give him what he wants, which doesn't make sense given you alone seem to have voluntarily cast your eyes north." His head tilted. "Unless even the prodigy has skeletons in his closet that might be used against him."

Marcus didn't answer, only traced the rim of his glass.

"Right." Drusus gave a soft snort, then shook his head. "You just like the challenge."

Gibzen entered the room, sandals clacking against the tiles as he approached. "One of our ships has been sighted."

Marcus's skin prickled. "Just one?"

"Yes, sir."

"I don't think luck is in our favor," Drusus muttered. "Nor that this will be a happy ending."

Marcus didn't answer him, only said to Gibzen. "I want an immediate report and the . . . *asset* brought here."

"Yes, sir."

It was a struggle not to pace the room. A struggle not to abandon the room entirely and race down to the harbor to finally put an end to the woman who had caused him so much trouble. Instead, Marcus went to the window and gazed up at the black tower, the tension it seethed infecting him as legion officers filtered into the room, all of the men speculating in low voices as to whether the gambit had worked.

Then everyone fell silent. Marcus slowly turned, anticipation choking him.

Centurion Qian stood with Gibzen. Of Lydia, there was no sign.

"Report," Marcus said softly, though he already knew in his heart how this had gone.

Qian didn't meet his gaze, the centurion's eyes locked on Marcus's breastplate. "It was a ploy, sir. A trick."

"Explain."

"As planned, the first ship anchored close to shore. Two hundred went to the meeting and a hundred remaining on board, while I kept my vessel well back, as was agreed. We were too distant to see clearly, but they met on the beach and conversation ensued. Then it all went to shit. Giants climbed out of the water and boarded the other ship, attacking and killing all aboard before setting it ablaze. On the beach—" He broke off, throat moving as he swallowed. "A whole other force exploded from the sand beneath their feet."

Marcus listened in silence as Qian detailed numbers and formations, the centurion's voice shaking slightly as he said, "If they'd held together a little longer, we'd have been able to reinforce, and we had numbers enough to match the Mudamorians. But our men broke apart like they were attacked from within—like it was the woman who attacked them. She had no weapon, sir, but with the speed she moved . . . The only time I've seen the like of it was the corrupted, Ashok, who killed Titus in Aracam."

Marcus had a strong suspicion of why a healer might possess that speed given his own experiences with Ashok, but he only said, "Continue."

Qian gave a sharp shake of his head. "Our boys fought hard, but they were outnumbered, sir. Badly so, especially when the giants that had attacked the ship joined the fight. The Mudamorians and their allies cut them down to the last, but there was one man who killed the most. Tall, dark hair, olive skin—I've never seen anyone fight like him, not even Kaira."

Marcus had heard that description before. *Killian Calorian.*

"Two hundred men on the beach," Marcus said. "Another hundred on the ship. All dead."

"Yes, sir. It did not seem prudent to engage, given the odds would have been in their favor with us coming in from the sea."

"It was the right choice, Centurion." Felix's voice had a slight shake to it. "If you'd attacked, your own numbers would have joined the casualties."

Behind the walls in his mind, Marcus heard screams of grief, but the emotion didn't touch him. "A ploy," he murmured. "A trick. But to what end?"

"What do you mean, to what end?" Servius demanded. "They slaughtered three hundred of the Thirty-Seventh and burned one of our ships. That's a significant blow."

"Not in the scheme of things." Then, seeing how Servius's expression hardened, Marcus added, "From their perspective, not ours." He rested his hands on the table, head lowered so they couldn't see his face or the lack of emotion he suspected was on it.

The silence stretched, and when the tension had grown thick, Marcus straightened and began to pace around the table. "We must set our grief aside and consider the Mudamorians' intentions. On the surface, all they have succeeded in doing is poking the dragon that sits outside their doorstep. What did the feigned negotiations on behalf of that vacuous idiot who wears their crown achieve besides the death of three hundred men and the loss of one ship? Three hundred out of tens of thousands, I'll remind you."

No one spoke, and as Marcus's eyes tracked over the best and brightest minds in the Empire, he did not fail to notice how none of them would meet his gaze.

Drusus cleared his throat. "Time."

"Yes, time." Marcus continued to circle the table. "But time to do what? What have they gained by delaying our attack?"

"Allies," Felix answered. "The giants of Eoten Isle have clearly joined their forces, as well as the soldiers who Qian saw on the beach. An alliance with Anukastre, perhaps."

"Likely, yet this was not the strategy of an enemy who has gained enough allies to turn the tide." Marcus took the glass that Gibzen handed him, sipping from it. "This is something else. What have they gained that is worth destroying any chance of negotiation? That is worth sacrificing any chance of mercy? What has Killian Calorian gained that is worth *pissing us off?*" He threw the cup of wine across the room, the liquid spraying the tile floor.

Silence filled the room, and in it, Teriana's voice filled his head. *We're going to war, Legatus. And I think it's time you had a taste of what it's like to lose.* "What have our spies seen of the Maarin?"

Felix cleared his throat. "The *Quincense* was spotted briefly in Serlania, as were several other Maarin vessels, but all have since departed, destinations unknown."

She was a part of this, the voice whispered. *She declared war on you. She's allied with those who killed your men.* "See what the Katamarcans can discover."

"Yes, sir."

Marcus went back to the window to stare at the tower, watching night fall over Revat as he silently waited.

"Now what?" Drusus finally asked. "The gambit didn't work, but the orders remain the same. The Dictator wants the gold mines and he wants them now. Let's not pretend that every man here doesn't have skin in the game as far as giving Cassius what he wants, even if it's just glory. What's the plan, Prodigy? What brilliant strategy do you have tucked up your sleeve that's going to ensure Cassius is satisfied but won't cost us half our men?"

"We shouldn't rush into this," Felix said. "Mudamora has a big enough army that just making a beach landing will cost us in blood, never mind the complication of running supplies into a land where the very water itself might be poison."

"Shut up, Felix," Drusus snapped. "We all know the risks, but the Dictator has our backs up against the wall. We have to do it. What we need is a plan that will ensure we survive getting Cassius his gold."

Behind Marcus, the throne room devolved into arguments and shouts between legati and officers, everyone having various opinions on how this should be done, but Marcus only cast a glance at Gibzen, who nodded, then left the room.

Everyone fell silent when the primus returned, and Marcus turned as two dozen of Gibzen's men entered the room with crossbows leveled at the man they had with them.

A man whose eyes were black voids rimmed with flame.

"Stand down," Marcus said to his men, which they did with obvious reluctance.

"Evening, Legatus," the corrupted said. "Word in the sky is that you and yours had a run-in with Killian Calorian. I imagine that my queen's offer is looking mighty fine right now."

"Good evening, Sly." Marcus circled the table and rested a hand on the corrupted's back, then shoved him down on one of the chairs. "Why don't you explain to everyone here exactly what you told me." Drawing a map in front of the man, he added, "Let's start with xenthier paths from Gamdesh to Mudamora."

The corrupted set to explaining what Rufina had offered, but Marcus only gave his words half an ear. He knew the deal, because he'd negotiated it on the chance the Mudamorians would prove difficult. One of his many contingency plans.

As Sly named the amount of gold that Rufina would pay for the alliance, the other legati leaned in, but Marcus's eyes went to the window and the distant strait.

His enemies had won the first battle.

But the war was yet to come.

96

TERIANA

Once the alliance with the Bardenese rebels was secured, Teriana and her crew moved on to the second stage of their strike against the Empire.

Theft.

"It's been ages since we commandeered a ship," her aunt Yedda said, tucking yet another knife into her boot. "I'm looking forward to it."

Teriana wished she felt the same way. Her stomach was in knots as the *Quincense* and the rest of her fleet sped along on a stiff wind of Baird's making, heading in the direction of the naval vessel that was their mark, with Magnius leading the way.

All across Reath, their allies were doing the same. A coordinated effort made possible only because her people had ships everywhere. And because all across Reath, nations were ready to strike back against the Empire. From Arinoquia to Sibern. From Bardeen to Chersome to Sibal, forces were readying to strike legion stockpiles and naval vessels, all with the same goal in mind.

The theft of the Empire's precious black powder.

Teriana had seen the legions use it. Had watched them bring down walls with it, and knew it was how Marcus had flooded Revat.

She was terrified of the black powder.

One spark and *boom*, everything near it was blasted apart. But she also knew it was the only thing that would eliminate the Empire's paths to the West. Knew it, because of what had been said during Marcus's manic episode when they'd taken Imresh and Emrant.

Wex will need time to set up the explosives. They'll need to do it carefully or they'll take out the entire stem—you know that.

If the explosives go off at the wrong time, this will be for nothing. We'll have to start over with a new stem.

Using black powder with xenthier can go . . . badly.

None of it had resonated in the moment, because she'd been too concerned about Marcus to think of anything else. Yet in hindsight, what he and Felix had said made one thing clear: black powder had the capacity to render xenthier paths unusable.

"I've never heard about it being done," Agrippa had said when they'd been coming up with the plan. "But I've been gone for years, so it's possible they've experimented. Marcus would certainly know if they had. Except the question is: if it works, why hasn't the Senate destroyed every path they consider a liability? There has to be a consequence that they don't want to pay, which Felix's comment certainly suggests. *Badly* means fatal in legion-speak."

"So you think it's too risky?"

Agrippa had only shrugged and said, "When your back is against the wall, sometimes the risky choice is the only choice."

"There it is," the lookout called, tearing her from her memories, and the doubts that came with them. Teriana lifted her spyglass. In the distance, the Cel vessel plunged up and down on the heavy seas, the crimson and gold banner flying high from the mainmast.

"They haven't spotted us yet!" the lookout shouted.

Teriana wasn't surprised. As close to Celendor as they were, no one would dare to attack one of its ships, and that made them overconfident. Lazy in their certainty that these were their waters.

The *Quincense* drew closer. Not only were the Maarin ships infinitely faster than the Cel ship, they had every sail open to hold Baird's wind, while the Cel had lost their nerve and lowered several of theirs.

"Still haven't seen us!"

Teriana shook her head because overconfidence was starting to look like stupidity on behalf of the Cel. Yet she knew that the targets on the far side of the Reath—those under Marcus's control—would be far more vigorously defended.

"They've seen us!"

Teriana watched the Cel sailors stare at the Maarin fleet with no real concern on their faces. Blue sails meant trade, not war, and they seemed more interested in the storm front rolling in behind them, nothing about it natural.

"We'll take the port side," she ordered, lifting a flag to signal one of the other ships to move in on the starboard. "They'll have the powder in the hold. Take as many casks as you can, but for the love of the Six, do not allow it anywhere near flame."

"Prisoners?" Yedda asked, and Teriana shook her head. "No. Don't mistake their confidence in their own waters for weakness. If they learn what we've stolen, they'll suspect our strategy and be ready for us. No witnesses."

Her crew gave grim nods, their fingers brushing over the hilts of their blades. Not soldiers, but life on the high seas came with inevitable conflict, so they knew their business.

But so did the Cel.

Some of her crew would be injured. Some might die. This was a taste of what it was like to be Marcus when he sent men into battle. Or what it *had* been like to be Marcus, because she doubted he cared much about casualties any more. Or anything at all.

Teriana lifted her spyglass again. As she watched, the first signs of concern began to show on the Cel crew's faces. As the *Quincense* and the *Furia* drew closer still, the Cel abruptly seemed to realize their intent. They exploded into action, readying to repel the attack.

But nothing could prepare them for what lurked in the waters below.

Teriana's vision shifted, taken over by Magnius so that she could see what the demigod saw beneath the waves: the hull of the Cel ship.

"Now," she whispered, and as Magnius put on a burst of speed, her vision became her own again. Just in time to watch as the Cel ship shuddered from the impact of Magnius's tail.

It heeled over with a groan and spilled several sailors into the water. Their screams cut off as the *Quincense* and *Furia* sailed over them—there was no room in this moment for mercy.

"Lower the sails!" she shouted. "Ready the hooks!"

Sails dropped, but the *Quincense*'s momentum kept her moving, sliding alongside the floundering ship full of stunned sailors. "Now!"

Her crew threw the hooks, the thick metal catching the railings of the Cel vessel, and men and women strained to pull the vessels together even as Teriana shouted, "Board!"

With a roar, her crew surged, leaping the gap between ships or swinging across on ropes to land on the deck amidst the Cel. Teriana ran with them, the sea a flash of white foam as she jumped, landing with a thump.

A blade flashed toward her face, but she parried. Quintus's training served her well as she fought the man before her, looking for an opening and then dragging the tip of her sword across his stomach, sending his guts spilling onto the deck. There was no time to reconcile herself to what she'd done, for another soldier took his place, murder in his eyes.

All around her was chaos as Maarin fought Cel in pitched hand-to-hand, the Maarin on the *Furia* throwing hooks on the starboard side, then swiftly boarding to add their blades to the melee. The deck was slick with blood, pitching from side to side on the rough seas, the screams of the injured and dying deafening.

Her arm shuddered from the impact of the soldier's blows, but Teriana gritted her teeth and kept matching him. His foot slipped, and she struck, stabbing him in the chest. He toppled sideways, jerking her weapon out of her hand.

Another gladius stabbed at her, and she threw herself sideways, rolling into the legs of those who were fighting before regaining her feet, her knife in hand. "Get to the hold!" Teriana screamed, and raced to the hatch, leaping over the fallen.

Not all of whom were Cel.

Her heart ached, but there was no time for grief. She reached the hatch at the same time as Yedda and Polin, the three of them pulling it up while others defended their backs.

"They're going for the powder! They're going for the powder!" the captain screamed. "Scuttle the ship!"

Teriana leapt into the hold, then barely got her knife up as a shrieking Cel sailor came running at her. His deflected blade sliced across her forearm, and she hissed in pain, stabbing him in the neck. As he dropped, she took a step forward and peered into the darkness.

The hold was full of small casks, each about the size of her torso.

"Gods," she breathed, entranced and horrified by the danger. The watertight casks packed the space, and all of it would be destined for Emrant, which meant that Marcus intended to use explosives in some capacity.

Yedda dropped next to her, her eyes going immediately to Teriana's injury. "You're hurt."

"I'm fine. We need to get these casks out of here."

Bracing, she lifted the one nearest to her, which was heavier than she'd anticipated. With shuddering arms, she lifted it to Polin's waiting hands. "Go!"

He disappeared and another Maarin replaced him, his thick arms reaching down for the cask that Yedda held up.

But they needed to be faster.

The battle still raged above, and Teriana knew that her crew was falling to Cel blades, the soldiers on this ship too well trained to go down easily.

Teriana passed another cask to waiting arms. Then another. She was raising another still when Bait's face appeared.

"You were supposed to stay put!" she shouted at him, but he gasped out, "The ship's on fire! Get out!"

"Oh, gods!" Catching hold of her aunt's waist, she lifted Yedda to Bait. "Unlash the ships! Go! Go!"

She jumped, Bait catching her wrist and heaving her up.

The deck was thick with bodies and blood, black smoke choking the air, the flames climbing the rigging. And spread across the deck was black powder from a smashed cask. The woman who'd been carrying it lay in its midst, a knife in her back.

And the flames were racing closer.

"Run!" Teriana screamed. "The ship's going to explode!"

The lines holding the *Quincense* were cut, her crew using oars to separate the ships. But it wasn't fast enough. Wasn't far enough.

"Magnius!" She sprinted toward the rail, Bait's hand clutched in hers. "Help them!"

Maarin sailors leapt off the side of the Cel ship into the water, and as Teriana climbed onto the rail, she saw Magnius below, head braced against the *Quincense,* pushing her away.

"Jump!" Bait shouted, and then she was flying, water racing up to meet her as a flash of light burst from behind.

Boom.

Water closed over Teriana's head, but the noise still rattled her skull as Bait dragged her deeper.

Because the worst was yet to come.

The force of the casks in the hold exploding was unlike anything she'd ever experienced. It ripped her from Bait's grip and sent her tumbling through the water, driving the air from her lungs.

Everything was white, bubbles and froth blinding her, and Teriana could not see which way was up.

Then an arm wrapped around her waist and heaved. She kicked her feet, desperate to breathe, but as her head broke the surface, part of Teriana wished she'd stayed under.

Burning debris surrounded her and Bait, what remained of the Cel ship sinking beneath the waves. But it was the sinking ship beyond that gutted her, because the burning sails were blue.

The *Furia* groaned, mainmast toppling slowly sideways and taking everything still vertical with it. Injured Maarin leapt off the sinking ship into the water, and though the three other ships in her fleet were moving to aid, far too many would be lost.

Slowly, Teriana turned in the water, bittersweet relief filling her as she saw the *Quincense*. Her crew raced to put out small fires, but her ship was mostly unscathed.

Please let this have been worth it, Teriana silently prayed, taking in the still forms floating among the debris. *Please don't let their deaths be for nothing.*

"Help who you can," she said to Bait. "The Cel will have seen the explosion from shore, which means we need to hurry."

Teriana swam to the *Quincense*, then climbed the ladder that had been dropped. Her guts churned with fear over who from her crew had been lost. Who she'd have to add to the list of names she already grieved.

Hands caught hold of Teriana's wrists and pulled her over the rail. She landed with a thump, then looked up into her aunt's eyes. Yedda was bleeding from a cut on her brow but otherwise seemed unscathed. "Polin?" Teriana whispered, afraid of the answer.

"He's all right."

She wanted to ask how many they'd lost. *Who* they'd lost, but Teriana forced herself to ask the more critical question. "How many casks?"

"One."

That was impossible. There had to be a mistake.

"Only one?"

"The others were on the *Furia*."

Teriana wanted to scream. And scream and scream, because so many of her people had died for so little.

"Ships incoming!" someone shouted from above, and Teriana pressed her fingers to her temples.

"There's no time to try to salvage. Get the injured out of the water."

"We can target another ship," her aunt said. "Try to steal more powder."

A raindrop struck Teriana on the forehead, then another and another until it was a deluge pouring from overhead. Baird approached. "I can't stop the storm," he said. "It will hit land in another hour, and if you wish to use it as your cover, we need to move."

All across Reath, the attacks would already be underway. Her allies stealing the legions' supplies of black powder, hopefully with more success than she had.

Teriana had watched enough battles to know that nothing ever went precisely according to plan, but Marcus had always made it look so simple, adjusting his strategy without hesitation.

This was anything but simple.

"What do you want to do?" Yedda asked. "It's your call."

Teriana drew in a deep breath. The next step would cost her dearly, but there was no turning back now. "We're going to make that cask count."

97

MARCUS

The first thing that struck Marcus was the smell.

Rot wasn't a strong enough word, although it was the best he could come up with, given his head throbbed from the strain of traveling through yet another xenthier path. A fell mixture of bog and week-old corpse, as well as something else that he couldn't put a word to.

Evil.

Marcus shoved the thought away in favor of examining the landscape, which belied the smell. The faint light of the setting sun cast a glow over lush fields of crop and pasture broken up by thick copses of trees, and the scene stretched for as far as the eye could see. Yet every time the wind blew, visions of deadlands filled his mind's eye.

"Where is it?" he asked, not bothering to specify.

"North." Sly yawned, holding a hand to his mouth. Such a human gesture for a creature who had eyes of flame. "About four hours on foot. The Mudamorian front lines are primarily engaged with holding back the veins of blight, which they do with excavation and stone. They've grown quite adept, but I don't suppose excavation and walls of stone are particularly effective against your men."

Marcus ignored the corrupted's pandering, and asked another question of his own. "You control the flow of blight? Where it goes and when?"

"Well, not *me*, personally. *They* do, and *they* do what the Queen bids."

"And who are *they*?"

"I'm sure they had names once, but they've been forgotten," Sly answered. "What they *are* are tenders who've sworn allegiance to the Seventh god."

"Just as you are a healer who has turned to the Seventh god."

Sly's jaw tightened. "You've asked all these questions before, Marcus."

Marcus turned his head to meet the man's eyes.

Sly looked away first. "That's correct, Legatus. I can take care of that headache, if you have a prisoner who'll donate a few years of life. Doesn't have to be voluntary."

"I don't have a headache," Marcus replied even as Felix leveled his crossbow at Sly's skull and growled, "Keep your hands to yourself or find yourself without them."

"They'll grow back." Sly pressed his forehead to the bolt's tip. "And it will take more than just one arrow."

"It will be far more than just one." Felix's tone was low and angry, and Marcus knew that some of the anger was at him for allying with Rufina and her creatures.

Sly's eyes shifted, finally seeing the multitude of crossbow bolts leveled at him, Gibzen's men sour-faced and watching intently. "Right. Well ease your mind—we're all friends here."

"No," Felix retorted. "We are not."

Ignoring the tension, Marcus asked, "Killian Calorian, Dareena

Falorn, and Kitaryia Falorn are all with the Mudamorian front lines?"

Sly turned back to him. "Such was the last report we received. Malahi Rowenes and her . . . *consort* are also with them. They aim to get to Deadground in the north to attack the source of the blight and destroy it, so our focus has been on protecting our xenthier paths."

"Who is her consort?" Marcus hadn't failed to notice the man's tone.

"A deserter." Sly rolled his shoulders.

It wasn't the whole truth of this consort's identity, but Marcus had larger concerns than whoever was sharing some Mudamorian highborn's bed. "Stay here."

He left Sly cooling his heels while he walked a short distance away with Felix, his second's crossbow remaining trained on the corrupted's head.

"I don't like this," Felix muttered. "These are fair-weather allies, Marcus. The moment we give them what they want, they will turn on us. The *air* stinks like death. This is poisoned ground, sure and true."

The walls in Marcus's mind had stood untested for long days, but he found himself feeling the same unease as Felix. "We are in and out. We secure the gold, then we put down the Mudamorian resistance and reclaim Cassius's woman. If this takes us more than two days, something has gone wrong."

"Lydia or Kitaryia or whatever her name is, isn't going to come easily." Felix's tone was flat. "It was her on that beach, Marcus. It was Lydia Valerius who caused three hundred Thirty-Seventh deaths. She's like *him*." He dipped the crossbow in Sly's direction.

"Which is why the only thing we'll collect is her corpse." It was a struggle to keep his tone even, the anticipation Marcus felt at finally putting Lydia in the ground as heady as the strongest narcotic. "In and out, Felix. I don't like it any better than you, but if we do this, we get Cassius off our backs and protect legion lives."

"For how long?"

Marcus didn't bother answering.

Legionnaires were coming through the xenthier stem by the dozens. The hundreds. The thousands. Interspersed between ranks came war machines, all moved out of the path of even more legionnaires with the well-trained efficiency of men who were used to the challenges of xenthier transport. The camp grew, spreading out over fields and around copses of trees as night deepened, but it was well past the midnight hour when Marcus heard the heavy flap of wings above.

The dark sky cloaked the strange flying beasts that Sly called deimos as they circled an open space Marcus's men had surrounded with torches.

Thump.

A thick wooden chest exploded against the ground, spilling bars that glittered golden in the torchlight.

Thump.

Another chest fell from the sky and exploded more gold onto the ground.

Thump.

In rapid progression, the deimos discarded their loads into the clearing until the ground was carpeted with golden bars. When the air was free of wings, Marcus watched Servius step onto the golden ground. He picked up one bar and then another, testing the weight while other men melted apart a few bars with a forge. "Solid gold!" came the chorus of reports.

It was a fortune beyond reckoning, but Marcus felt nothing as he stared at it. The fortune that he sought was to the north. "Send it to Revat and arrange transport back to Celendor."

"You are content, Legatus?" Sly asked, approaching. "There is more where this came from, I assure you. But there is a limit to what a deimos can carry."

"It is as agreed," Marcus answered. "Go tell your mistress that we will see our half of the bargain done."

Sly shrugged, then lifted his fingers to his lips and whistled. Wings flapped, and one of the deimos landed, the corrupted climbing onto its saddle and then soaring away into the night to deliver the message.

The flow of legionnaires continued, numbers swelling into the tens of thousands. A show of force that would make this campaign as short and painless as possible, but also required every legion under his command to take equal risk on this deadly ground, no one legion allowed to hide back in the relative safety of Revat.

When the flow of men ceased, it swiftly switched to an equally valuable commodity. A stream of water from a well in Gamdesh, pumps and a system designed by Rastag ensuring that his men would have a steady supply of water with no fear of contamination. Water that could be paused for the delivery of food, all coming from Celendor to Emrant to Revat and then through to them here. Every step of the supply chain from Emrant to this place under heavy and vigilant guard, because this was their lifeline.

As dawn lit the sky in the east, it revealed an army greater than had ever been gathered in the known history of Reath. Mounting his golden mare, Marcus took hold of the Thirty-Seventh's standard. His gaze was drawn north like iron to a lodestone as he rode through the lines of his men, his voice loud as he shouted, "Mudamora took the lives of three hundred of our brothers! Today, we will have blood in return! In the name of the Empire and vengeance, march!"

98

LYDIA

In the company of every Mudamorian who could fight, Lydia and her friends had ridden to join Dareena's camp in the north. It was a grueling march with little rest, made worse by her anxiety over what was to come. Anxiety that grew worse with the rising stink of the blight. Lydia was forced to remove her spectacles to wipe her watering eyes as the camp finally came into sight.

Though she desired rest and a meal, Lydia drew in her horse as the cry of a bird of prey caught her attention, and she looked up to see Astara's familiar form circling overhead. Killian drew his horse in next to her. "Pray for good news."

But prepare for the worst, Lydia thought as the shifter landed before them and approached.

"The legion ships remain in Revat's harbor or on patrol." Astara accepted the cloak that Bercola passed her, as well as a skin of water, drinking deeply before she continued. "They showed no signs of making ready, but from experience, they can move on the spin of a copper."

"Speed and organization are Marcus's greatest weapons." Agrippa toyed with the hilt of his gladius, eyes fixed south. "They don't need to prepare because they *are* prepared. Unless Teriana has succeeded, Marcus will be making ready to move. He'll send a large force to secure a landing ground and then use his fleet to transport the men he feels he needs to achieve his goals. That will slow them down, but not by much. We need to act on the assumption that our allies have failed and move with equal speed."

Lydia had more faith in Teriana than Agrippa did, but she nodded. "Astara, when you are rested, can you travel north to gain us fresh information about Rufina's numbers and position? Only travel during the day and stay high enough that you are out of range. What we need most is an exact understanding of Rufina's forces around the stem to Deadground."

The Gamdeshian woman returned the waterskin to Bercola. "I'll go now."

Lydia could see the exhaustion written across Astara's face. The toll this was taking on her, for she alone could spy on the enemy from the skies. Gripping her shoulder, Lydia said, "Rest. We cannot afford to lose you, and errors are made in the throes of exhaustion. Our forces are only just joining with Dareena's, so we have no plans to act just yet."

Astara's jaw tightened, her brown eyes flashing with defiance, but then she sighed and nodded, heading in the direction of the tents.

"Let's find Dareena." Malahi pushed a short blond curl off her forehead, her amber eyes shadowed with the same exhaustion that plagued everyone after the long ride north to join the main army. "All our information of what has been happening beyond the lines is old, and she will have fresh news."

Lydia handed off the reins of her horse to one of their soldiers, Mudamorians, Anuk, and giants alike all trudging to join the sea of tents and cook fires. Cheers rose from the lips of those who had lived long weeks, even months, in this camp, for Lydia's forces had brought what supplies of food they could without depriving those in Serlania. As it was, Lydia suspected that many of the oxen that pulled the wagons were not long for this world, for Dareena's army all bore the hollowed cheeks of those who knew hunger and knew it well.

"We'll rest tonight," Killian said softly as they walked. "If we attack when the sun is high in the sky, the deimos, at least, will be at the disadvantage and we might have a measure of surprise."

Xadrian fell in on the far side of Killian, the prince of Anukastre having grown even closer to him since the battle against the Thirty-Seventh. "I'll see to my warriors," he said. "Don't do anything without me."

"I'm not doing anything but getting rest tonight," Killian muttered, but Xadrian's eyes only narrowed, and he jerked his chin at Finn, who trailed after them carrying their bags. "If he looks to be doing anything stupid, fetch me."

Finn only rolled his eyes and asked, "Who will watch over you for the same?"

Xadrian grinned and winked, then broke into a trot to join the Anuk warriors.

The tent that served as Dareena's center of command appeared ahead. Falorn falcon banners flapped on the breeze next to the entrance, and the woman herself stood with thumbs hooked on her belt. "About gods-damned time!" Dareena shouted at them. "I hope you brought something good to drink. We've had nothing but stale barreled water for far too long, and if I'm going to meet the Six, I want to have a proper drink before I do it."

Letting go of Killian's arm, Lydia broke into a trot and flung her arms around her aunt's neck. "It's good to see you."

"Likewise." Dareena squeezed her tight. "I heard that you put three hundred of that Cel bastard's men in the dirt. Though I assume you have a good reason for pissing off the commander with an army ten times the size of ours?"

Unease pooled in Lydia's stomach, and she glanced over her shoulder before she said, "Don't say much about that in front of Agrippa. He knew them."

"Such is war." Dareena led Lydia into the tent, calling over her shoulder, "Finn, I see that you've resumed your duties. Go find us a bottle of something good in those supplies and be quick about it."

With Bercola, in the company of Lena and Gwen, standing outside to ensure that no one would listen in on the conversation, Lydia and her company settled around the table and updated Dareena on their plan.

Her aunt rested one muddy boot on her knee and sipped at a tin cup full of wine. "You held up your end by buying Teriana time, but have you received any word that she was successful? Because if not, you've made a dangerous enemy for nothing."

"He was already a dangerous enemy." Lydia leaned her shoulder against Killian's, desperately wishing for rest. "But either way, our eyes turn north. What news do you have?"

Dareena took another sip. "Rufina has not recouped her numbers in any meaningful way, but her camp remains fixed around the xenthier you claim leads to Deadground. Thousands of blighters, as well as her corrupted and deimos. The blight itself hasn't pressed much farther—namely because we've become damned good at finding incursions and damming them—but the land beyond our barriers is a wasteland. Burned trees and lakes of blight as far as the eye can see, which serve well to defend her position, because it's hard to get close without risking soldiers being infected. Impossible, in truth, unless one is marked, because you'll have to wade through that sludge to get to the xenthier."

Lydia's hands turned cold, and she looked up at Killian. His jaw was tight, and across the table, Agrippa muttered, "Well shit," even as Malahi rested her head in her hands.

"I take it attacking in force was the plan?" Dareena asked, her eyes skipping around the group.

Sudden certainty that she'd erred in guiding them down this path struck Lydia in the stomach like a battering ram and bile burned up her throat, making it impossible to speak. It had been her idea to hold off on this attack in order to buy Teriana time, and now they'd lost their chance.

Killian cleared his throat. "Yes. We'd hoped for a direct strike with the aim of getting Lydia and Malahi to the stem. They know how to destroy the blight, but we need to get them to the source. Failing the xenthier, we need to go north to Deadground on foot."

"That's four, if not five, weeks of journey," Dareena said softly.

And we could have been well into it if I hadn't steered us down a different path. Lydia's eyes stung, and under the table, Killian caught hold of her hand and squeezed. "Can we draw the blighters out?" he asked. "Move enough of them away that a targeted force might be able to reach the stem?"

Dareena gave a slow shake of her head. "Rufina knows that Deadground is your goal, Killian. She'll defend it at all costs, because all she needs to do is hold her position and wait for starvation to take its toll. Her army is dead. She has all the time in the world."

"We can't win this." Malahi lifted her head from her hands, scarred cheeks slick with tears. "No matter what we do, the enemy seems a step ahead of us, and they grow more powerful by the day while we grow weaker. Why have the Six abandoned us like this? Why do they allow the Corrupter's power to grow like this? He gives his minions every advantage while we struggle on without."

Killian's fingers flexed in Lydia's hand, and she knew he was thinking the same thing as her. That *they* were supposed to be the advantage, but had thus far failed.

Agrippa rested his elbows on the table, eyes on the map of Mudamora before them. "It's a roll of the dice, friends. Risk an attack with force to gain the xenthier knowing that many will fall to blight poisoning or ride north on the hope that we reach Deadground before Dareena's lines are overrun."

All eyes turned to Lydia, and she tensed. Though the crown was in her saddlebags, Lydia didn't feel as though she were queen. In truth, she never had, and while someone needed to lead, in this moment, she didn't want it to be her. "I . . ."

Bercola chose that moment to duck inside. "Sorry to interrupt, but there is some concern about our rear forces. Namely, that they are missing."

Killian rose to his feet, and Lydia sensed the tension rising in him. "Have we sent riders looking for them? They're only half a day behind."

"Yes." Bercola cleared her throat. "They've not returned either."

Xadrian pushed past Bercola into the tent. "Something is wrong. I can feel it."

The whole tent fell silent, but as Lydia's eyes skipped from Xadrian to Killian to Dareena, every one of them with a hand on their weapon, a sudden certainty took hold in her chest. "Wake Astara," she called to Gwen, who stood behind Bercola. "Tell her to scout south. Hurry."

Gwen took off at a run, but Killian and Xadrian were on her heels. Lydia hurried after them, hearing her friends follow. In a silent group, they wove through to the southern end of the camp. Astara called out as she took flight and soared overhead.

The midday sun cast no shadows as they stood staring at the road leading south. The heat formed beads of sweat on Lydia's back as she searched for any sign of motion. Any sign of their rear forces.

Then a wagon appeared.

There was no driver, the oxen pulling it in a meandering fashion up the road toward the camp. Then another wagon appeared over the hill, following the first. Then another, the loads of supplies they carried all covered with waxed canvas. But sign of the rest of Mudamora's soldiers, there was none.

The sunlight shifted, and as the shadows moved, Lydia saw that the canvas was stained with crimson. "Oh gods," she whispered, even as Killian and Xadrian broke into a run toward the wagons, weapons in hand.

She tore after them, a scream breaking loose from her lips as Killian drew back the canvas to reveal the bodies of their rear forces. Bloodied and glassy eyed, all dead from violence. From blades. And stabbed through the chest of one of the dead soldiers was a Cel gladius marked with a 37, a single piece of paper speared by the blade.

Killian pulled it loose, frowned, and then handed it to her. "What does it mean?"

Two words, in familiar handwriting. *Lex talionis.*

Agrippa took it from her shaking hands, cursing as he read the words. "It means *eye for an eye.*"

Teriana failed. Oh gods, Teriana failed.

A hawk shrieked from above, and Astara landed, already shifting to her human form. "They're here!" she gasped. "The Cel are here!"

"How many?" Lydia demanded, though in her heart, she already knew.

Astara's brown eyes were filled with terror as they met hers. "All of them."

99

TERIANA

Leaving Magnius to ensure no Cel sailors remained alive to tell the tale of what had occurred, the *Quincense* sailed swiftly away from the wreckage with Yedda at the helm. Teriana remained at the rail, watching until the flickers of flame from the burning debris disappeared from sight.

Baird danced about the ship's deck with his drum, encouraging more wrath from the storm blackening the skies above even as he sped the progress of Teriana's reduced fleet. As they flew across the seas, Polin came to stand with her. "Thirty-eight dead, between our ship and the *Furia*," he said. "At least twice that injured, some badly enough that I don't think they'll survive."

"Can you give me a list of names?" Marcus always looked at the names. The weight of that hadn't resonated before, but it did now.

"Might have to wait until after the battle to come." Polin rubbed at his bandaged arm, then reached over to adjust the bandage over Teriana's wound. "We're not far from Padria."

That was true, but Teriana knew the real reason: the casualty list was about to get a lot longer. "Fine."

The seas grew more violent with every passing minute, and it wasn't long until Yedda ordered some sails lowered to avoid damaging the ship. The storm was a risk for the vessels in her fleet, but it ensured the legion guarding the low-lying town of Padria would be contending with trying to protect the supplies intended for Emrant from the heavy rain. Teriana prayed to Madoria that it would keep their eyes off the seas, because she desperately needed the element of surprise.

How do you do this? She silently whispered the question across the seas to Marcus. *How do you stomach making these plans? How do you live with your decisions risking lives?*

Nausea abruptly made her head spin, and Teriana leaned over the railing and threw up. Over and over again, until her whole body ached.

"You all right?"

She lifted her head to find Bait standing next to her, easily balancing on the rocking deck. "Still don't have my sea legs back, I suppose. The waters are rough."

"Right." Bait rested his elbows on the rail. "Feels real now. I . . . I don't think I really understood what we were getting into until I watched the *Furia* sink. A lot of our people are going to die, aren't they?"

"Yeah." She wiped her mouth on her sleeve. "But hopefully the legions will lose even more."

He nodded, eyes on the coast. His irises were dark grey, the violent waves in them betraying his fear. "I wanted to tell you that I'm sorry for all the things I said to you. You didn't deserve that."

"Yes, I did."

"No." Bait turned his head to look at her. "You didn't. You've been in the thick of it from the beginning, and anyone who pretends to understand what that was like is an idiot. I'm an idiot."

Teriana opened her mouth to tell him that it was fine, but Bait held up his hand. "Just let me finish, all right? We're going into battle, and I want to say some things. Just in case."

She didn't want to think about what *just in case* meant.

"I didn't spend much time on that island with the legions' injured before I went north with Magnius, and while I was with the Cel, I avoided them as much as possible. Refused to talk to them because I hated them. But Yedda and the others . . . they got to know those men. Came to understand how those in the legions were as much prisoners to this situation as our people, because their freedom was taken when they were children. I see the legions as this faceless enemy, but you and the crew know their names. Have come to know them as individuals. I suppose I never really stopped to think about what it would be like to hurt them once you got to know them."

Bait was quiet for a long moment, then he said, "I always thought that you and I would end up together. I knew that you didn't feel the same way about me as I did about you, but I thought that would change. Hoped it would. But I think from almost the first moment I saw you look at Marcus that I knew you'd never look at me like that. Gods, you didn't even *like* him at that point and you still watched him like he was the only person in the world. It . . . hurt.

"Later, I started hearing the rumors that you two were together, and I didn't want to believe it. Not because I couldn't see it being true, but because I didn't want it to be true. I was so gods-damned jealous, and when I went to Emrant to find you, I went with the intention of making sure you knew what he'd done. Not for Lydia's sake, and not even for yours, but because I wanted to ruin it. I wanted to hurt him, and to hurt you as much as I was hurting. And like an idiot, I thought that doing so would bring you back to me. Instead, all I did was push you further away."

Teriana stayed silent because what could she say? She'd always known that Bait's feelings for her went beyond friendship but hoped that time would fade those feelings. "You weren't wrong, Bait. And I'm sorry that I've pushed you away. I . . . I don't know why I did."

"Because I hurt you, that's why. I was not your friend in that moment."

She bit her lip, seeing the truth in that statement.

"When they told me you were alone with him and that I'd have to wait, I knew what was going on," Bait said. "I didn't need proof. But I wanted to catch you in the act so that I could make you feel as awful as possible.

"But what I saw, Teriana—it was the last thing I expected." Bait swallowed hard. "The way he looked at you, it was like you were the only thing in the world that mattered. He loved you in a way that made me feel so gods-damned inadequate because it makes what I feel seem like nothing at all. It made me angry, jealous, and so I made that moment as awful as I could. I wanted to make him suffer as much as I was suffering, and I can't help but wonder if I hadn't been such an asshole, if maybe he wouldn't have marched on Revat."

"Don't you dare take blame for what Marcus has done." Teriana gripped her friend's shoulders. "No matter how you told me the truth, the result would have been the same. I'd have left him. Because no matter how you told me, the truth would've been the same. What was between Marcus and me was always destined to crumble. Not just because of Lydia, but because we stand on opposite sides of a sea that both of us refuse to cross, and to try to remain in the middle would have drowned us both."

She let go of his shoulders in favor of gripping the rail, feeling abruptly weary. "So many times, I've wondered if everything would have been different if I'd only remained. If I could have kept him on a better path and protected him from the Corrupter's influence. But it is not my duty to keep him on the side of good. It's not my responsibility to keep him on the right path."

Yet knowing that didn't diminish the pain of watching him walk down such a dark road. Didn't make it hurt less to watch him devolve into his worst self.

"I love him," she whispered, not sure if she was confessing to herself or to Bait. "Even now I love him so much that sometimes I can't breathe, but I will not sacrifice everything I am to keep him from succumbing to himself."

Bait slung an arm around her shoulders, pulling her close. "I'm sorry, Teriana. Truly."

She leaned against her friend, but what comfort could be gained from the moment was short-lived.

"Padria is in sight!" the lookout called from above.

It was time.

Squaring her shoulders, she met Bait's gaze. "This is the battle of our lives, Bait. The stem from Padria to Emrant is Marcus's most critical source of supplies, which means we *must* destroy it. Everyone who matters to us depends on our success here, and you are the trump card up my sleeve. We have the Six on our side, so let's show the Empire what comes from underestimating the Maarin."

Bait gave her a jaunty salute, then stepped up onto the rail. Lightning crackled in the sky, illuminating his form, and then he dived into the stormy seas where Magnius waited.

Teriana strode to the helm, taking the wheel from Yedda. "Baird, you keep that wind blowing."

"Yes, Captain!" The giant retrieved his drum, then began to dance in an open space on the deck, the music drowned out by wind that rose to vicious strength.

Lifting her spyglass, Teriana watched the unfamiliar legion guarding the most critical supply route to the West. The route that fed all of the supply lines that Marcus would have so carefully protected.

While Silvara's attack on the Bardeen-to-Arinoquia path was important, it was Padria, located in the breadbasket of Celendor, that was responsible for food, weapons, gold, and supplies. This was the path that Marcus's legions depended on, and it was also the path that Lucius Cassius used most aggressively to maintain his control in the West. If she failed to destroy it, the efforts of everyone else might well be for naught.

Even from here, Teriana could see that the volume of goods gathered outside the fortress was incredible. Endless unhitched wagons lined up to be unloaded—enough food, she suspected, to feed an entire city. The legionnaires garrisoning Padria were racing to protect those supplies from the deluge, frustrated men trying to tie down tarps in the gale-force wind. So entirely occupied that they didn't notice the tide as it began to retreat.

The wind was directly behind the *Quincense*, holding the ships that made up her fleet steady even as the sea began to flow backwards beneath them.

Faster and faster, the waterline retreated down the beach, and then it drew back farther still.

Revealing Bait, standing with his arms outstretched, Magnius's massive form coiled around him protectively as he used Madoria's mark to control the sea.

The water ceased withdrawing and instead rose upward to create a towering wall. On the crest of it sat her fleet, held by fingers formed of water. As though Madoria herself held the ships in place.

As the wall of water grew taller, Padria grew smaller below, and Teriana took in the totality of the newly expanded fortress built to protect the precious xenthier. The town itself was farther inland, the streets mostly empty as people had fled inside to avoid the rain. Beyond Padria, hills rose that would be salvation to any who started running now.

No one was running.

Finally, one of the legionnaires glanced out to sea and took notice of the towering wall of water beneath the circling black clouds. He pointed and shouted, his fellows turning their heads.

For a heartbeat, they all stared in horror at a scene that should be impossible. But then their training took over and they were running. Mouths moving in what she knew were shouts of warning to retreat inland. To get to higher ground.

"Proceed," Teriana whispered to Magnius, and Bait's hands moved forward.

Bringing the sea with them.

The tidal wave rolled, carrying her fleet with it at terrifying speed.

"Get ready!" she shouted, her crew racing to follow her order while the crews on the other ships did the same.

The legionnaires were sprinting inland, heading for the hills beyond.

None of them would make it.

Water slammed into the wagons full of supplies, shattering them, then it struck the wall of the fortress with a boom, spraying dozens of feet into the air. Legionnaires clung to the upper level of the fortress even as the water swept past, flowing over the running men, their heads disappearing under the churning surface, armor dragging them down.

Breaking them.

Drowning them.

Killing them.

Tears mixed with the driving rain running down Teriana's face. *This is war,* she told herself. *In war, people die.* "Get ready to disembark!"

The ships passed the beach, the wave carrying them closer and closer to the fortress. "That's far enough," she whispered to Magnius, then shouted, "Ready!"

The sea went entirely still, then began to flow backward while the hands formed of water held the ships in place high up the beach.

Abandoning the helm, Teriana moved to join the crew massing at the bow, Baird a towering pillar among them. Polin stood with their singular cask of black powder strapped to his chest. Yedda had a storm lantern in her hand. Standing with the rest of the crew, Teriana watched the water retreat, carrying both bodies and men clinging to debris.

Don't look at their faces, she ordered herself. *They are your enemy, nothing more.*

Except in her mind's eye, they were faces she knew. Thirty-Seventh faces.

It's not them!

The fingers of water disappeared, and the ships settled onto the wet sand. Before her nerve could fail her, Teriana screamed, "Now!"

With a roar, her crew, and the crews of the other ships, threw ropes over the rails and slid down to the beach. Teriana went with them, not looking back as she broke into a run toward the fortress. Bait would hold the tide back. He had to.

The legionnaires who'd been in the upper level of the fortress were already moving, the familiar bark of a centurion giving orders promising that she wasn't going to get to the stem without a fight.

"Don't let them form lines!" she screamed. "We'll never get past them!"

The Maarin around her put on a burst of speed, the front-runners slamming into the legionnaires beginning to form up at the entrance to the fortress, the heavy gate that had once barred the entrance dangling from its hinges.

Screams filled the air as her people were impaled on spears and blades. But they did not stop coming. Did not stop fighting, and the legion line began to fracture as legionnaires fell to Maarin blades. Then the lines broke entirely, the legionnaires fleeing into the fortress.

But with terrible cost.

"Go!" Baird shouted, batting at legionnaires with his enormous staff. "Run!"

Teriana screamed as she leapt over the bodies of the fallen and through the broken gates, the towering walls of heavy stone rising to either side of her. Her people ran with her, meeting the legionnaires blow for blow as the Cel attempted to reform their lines. As they attempted to prevent the Maarin from reaching the xenthier that they'd been tasked with defending.

The stone beneath her feet was slippery with seaweed and sand, the water still up to her knees where it hadn't drained. Shouts from the fortress warned her more reinforcements were coming, but Teriana splashed onward down the wide path that led to a courtyard.

The space was empty, except for one thing.

The xenthier stem jutted out of raw earth, the crystal glittering in the dim light. Rain struck it only to disappear in an instant, and Teriana could only imagine the chaos in Emrant right now from the seawater that had come through it.

More casualties.

More collateral damage.

Her heart bled for the destruction she'd leave in her wake, yet Teriana didn't hesitate. She raced toward the stem, Polin and Yedda flanking her.

Only for a centurion to step into their path.

His helmet was gone, revealing short red hair and a deep cut on his face. Teriana instantly recognized him as the man who'd terrorized the Sibernese village she and Marcus had stayed in. The one who'd brought his men to impose the Empire's might upon a celebration.

He backhanded her aunt, sending Yedda staggering to the ground. The lantern she'd held smashed and put out by water.

No.

"I don't think so, you little bitch," the centurion hissed, lifting his blade. "I won't make the same mistake as the Thirty-Seventh."

"Auntie, get it lit!" Teriana lifted her weapon and moved between the centurion and her aunt. Then she gave him a feral grin. "Which mistake would that be? Teaching me how to fight?"

Teriana attacked, blades colliding as she drove him away from her aunt. The centurion was stronger. More skilled. But she had rage burning in her heart and desperation fueling her every swing, and that gave Teriana the edge she needed to drive him back. "Get it lit!"

Yedda was on her knees, striking a knife against a flint, sparks flying.

"Hurry!"

The centurion feinted, then punched Teriana in the face. She staggered backward, barely managing to get her blade up to keep him from running her through.

"Got it!" Yedda shouted. "It's lit!"

Teriana smashed her blade against the centurion's, and then lunged. His fist struck her cheek, but then his eyes widened and he looked down to find her blade embedded in his throat. As the centurion dropped, she saw Polin light the cask's fuse. She needed to get to him. Needed to take it out of his hands—

Except Polin was already striding toward the xenthier, the fuse on the cask burning bright.

She'd meant to do this part.

Meant to take this risk herself.

Because the timing required holding the cask until the second before it detonated, or the force of the explosion wouldn't be drawn into the xenthier. "Polin, no!"

The man who had been like a father to her turned his head to grin—

And then everything turned white.

Teriana was flung across the open space, the impact driving the air from her chest. The ground bucked beneath her, the walls surrounding the courtyard collapsing as Reath herself writhed. As though the destruction of the xenthier had inflicted pain upon the land itself.

Catching hold of Yedda's arms, Teriana dragged her aunt away from the falling blocks of stone. By some miracle, Polin was alive, his hair singed off and his skin marked with burns, but breathing. The three of them clung to each other as the ground shuddered and rippled, and then, after what felt like an eternity, fell still.

"The Six are merciful!" Polin gasped. "We did it!"

Because the xenthier was gone. Nothing remained but a gaping hole in the ground. The path between Padria and Emrant was destroyed.

"I thought you were dead, you great blundering idiot," Yedda sobbed, clinging to Polin. "Thank the gods, you're safe."

No one was safe. A roar filled Teriana's ears, and she had but a second to realize that Bait's hold on the tide had been broken by the earthquake before water exploded over the rubble and slammed into her.

It flipped her over, spinning her around, debris, bodies, and other people swimming for their lives slamming into her.

Teriana clawed her way to the surface as the tidal wave dragged her inland, her body screaming in pain from the onslaught. It took her over the ruins of the town to the base of the hills.

And then it reversed course.

Teriana screamed, trying to swim against the current, but it was relentless. Sucking her toward the storm-tossed sea and certain death. Though she'd gone into this prepared to meet her end, Teriana did not want to die. Did not want this to be her last fight. She howled, fighting the current and the pain.

Fighting against defeat.

And then the water went still.

Steady as a glass pane but for the ripples caused by her swimming crew around her. Teriana turned her head, and relief flooded her as she saw Bait sitting on Magnius's back, Baird perched behind him. The *Quincense* sat in the water in the distance, the rest of the ships as well.

"Swim!" Bait shouted as Baird pulled Polin onto Magnius's back. "Get back aboard! I can't hold the waters like this for long."

All around her, bodies floated on the still water. Legionnaires and civilians and Maarin alike, dead from battle, from debris, from drowning.

Casualties of war.

"Teriana!" Yedda swam toward her. "Are you all right?"

She'd never again be *all right*. But maybe that was as it should be.

"You did it, girl," Yedda caught hold of her arms. "You did it! There is no chance they'll try to expand their reach now—they'll have to retrench!"

She'd done it, and that meant the legion that had never known defeat was about to discover its bitter taste.

Teriana waited for elation to fill her, but it did not come. She stared dully at the bodies of the innocent civilians of Padria that she'd sacrificed for this victory, their eyes glassy and lifeless.

Please let it be worth it.

Magnius's voice filled her head. *Lysander sends word. The legions have abandoned Revat.*

They've retreated? she demanded, only for realization to strike like a blow to the gut.

It was too soon.

Word of the destruction of the xenthier paths would not have yet reached Marcus to drive him to retreat. This was something else.

No, they haven't retreated, Magnius answered. *They've invaded Mudamora.*

She'd been too late. All of this . . . every life lost, and she'd been too late to save Lydia and her friends.

Despair drove away elation, making her want to scream. Making her want to weep.

Instead, Teriana said, "Magnius, instruct the fleet to regroup at our safe harbor. We need to make plans to sail to Mudamora's aid."

100

LYDIA

Lydia's horse shifted restlessly beneath her, though she wasn't entirely certain whether it was because the animal was unnerved by the steady *thump, thump, thump* of marching men or because it sensed the anxiety the noise provoked in Lydia herself.

Both was probably the answer.

An hour past, Lydia had received information on their allies' progress as they readied to destroy the xenthier stems, though the news was woefully dated. The messenger said that Teriana had secured an alliance with the rebels in Bardeen, that Sultan Kalin had rejoined his people on the western coast of Gamdesh, that Sonia had made contact with an Arinoquian warleader named Ereni, and that Vane had met with the Queen of Katamarca, who was apparently not nearly as entranced the Empire as she'd led everyone to believe. All parties had agreed to unite to fight back against the Empire's incursion. By now, all should have successfully organized attacks to steal stores of the legion's explosive powder, and they should all be readying for a united attack against the legion's supply lines with the aim of destroying the xenthier they depended on.

Should, being the operative word, because Lydia had no news as to whether either step had been successful. And even if her allies had been victorious, it was too late for Mudamora.

Because the legions were here. Even without Marcus's gruesome message, there was no doubt that the Cel were here for blood.

Astara had ascertained that the legions had traveled to Mudamora via a xenthier terminus south of their position. As to how they'd discovered it, the assumption was that Rufina had provided the information as part of her alliance with the Empire.

Agrippa had taken the development particularly poorly. "It's my fault," he'd muttered. "I was the one who told her about how the legions use xenthier. I was the one who put it in her mind that they could be used effectively for conquest."

And with endless undead blighters at her disposal, it had been no doubt easy for Rufina to send path-hunters through stems they discovered without concern for their lives. Not that Lydia thought the Queen of Derin would have shown any compunction over using path-hunters who still lived.

Regardless, what was done was done. The delays they'd bled for to give Teriana more time had not been enough, because even as Marcus had negotiated with Helene, it seemed as though he had also been negotiating with Rufina.

Every bit the Empire's perfect commander.

He'd outplayed them, and now Lydia's army—Mudamorians, Anuk, and giants—was now pinioned between two enormous, united, and incredibly dangerous hosts. The chance to get to Deadground was lost. The only options now were to fight.

Because to surrender only meant a slower death.

Dareena and Xadrian held the line against the blight, their soldiers working nonstop to hold back the flow while Lydia and Killian stood before the giants and the Mudamorian cavalry, making ready to meet the might of the Empire.

Every possible preparation had been made, and now they stood on a ridge overlooking rolling hills of pastureland. On it stood a lone white tent, Celendor's banners flying to either side, though Lydia had seen no one go in or out of it.

Killian sat slouched on Seahawk's back, and next to him was Agrippa with Malahi on his right. For what felt like the hundredth time, Lydia reached up to touch the crown sitting on her head, for she hated the weight of it.

Seldrid had addressed everyone after the fight against the

Thirty-Seventh on the beach, and his words filled her mind now. *In the coming weeks, what matters is unity. If we cannot stand together and win this, who holds the crown will not matter. Who holds anything will not matter, because all will be taken either by Celendor or the blight. Whoever wears the crown is not only a figurehead for our armies to follow but also a target for our enemies. Who here wishes to stand in that role in the fight to come?*

Not one of the High Lords, not even the vainglorious Pitolt, had stepped forward, and when eyes had gone to Helene, she'd burst into tears and had to be taken away to calm down. Lydia hadn't wanted to take the crown, either, but Malahi had spoken to her before the meeting began. "It has to be you," her friend had said. "Not only are you the twice-marked chosen of Hegeria, you know both our enemies better than anyone else."

"You know them nearly as well," Lydia argued. "What's more, you are more disposed to rule. I make every choice for those I love. To help others survive in the moment, even if I risk everyone to protect them. I'm not meant to wear a crown, Malahi."

Malahi had looked away, her face drawn with shame. "If the Cel were our only foe, that might be true. But Rufina . . ." Her throat bobbed as she swallowed. "I'm terrified of her. And even more terrified that when it comes down to it, I'll concede to the legions to evade her. Whereas you are not afraid. Please, Lydia. Please do this."

And so Lydia had stepped forward and formally accepted the crown and every burden that came with it, none of them sitting easier as she stared out over the pastureland.

The only sign of Malahi's apprehension was a slight tensing and untensing of the muscles in her jaw. Agrippa, however, was fidgeting like a child who'd been forced to sit too long, his mount pinning its ears in irritation.

"Why is he taking this risk?" Agrippa muttered. "Gamdesh was a prime jewel that would have sated the Senate for years, and he left half of it unconquered and millions of angry Gamdeshians ready to attack his rear. It doesn't make any sense. Why is he fighting Rufina's battle for her? Why is he risking the blight?"

"Revenge." Lydia coughed to clear her throat. "We killed his men."

"He's not going to risk all the rest of them in a foolish move for the sake of revenge. He's not like that."

"My gold mines," Malahi said. "We know Celendor wants them. Perhaps even needs them, given the costs this invasion will have incurred."

"I have no doubt they want the gold, but what good are mines that are overrun with poison? Everyone they send to mine them will die and rise a blighter, then join *Rufina's* army."

"Lydia," Killian muttered. "He's made no secret of his desire to see her dead."

"Then send assassins, not your whole damned army."

Lydia sighed. "The answer is evil, Agrippa. Both the Corrupter and Lucius Cassius desire to rule Reath, and they care little for the costs that come with doing so. Indeed, I think they relish it. Just as Rufina is the Corrupter's general in this fight, so too is Marcus that of Lucius Cassius. Caught in the thrall of their masters, though in truth, I think their masters are becoming one and the same. The blighters do Rufina's bidding because they must. So too do the legions. They are same."

It was nothing she hadn't said before, but even now, Agrippa struggled to believe the men who'd once been his brothers were under the influence of evil. That they would be the hammer against the anvil of the blight.

Yet as the thunder of marching men grew louder, Agrippa fell silent, the truth now impossible to deny.

The first ranks crested the hill, thousands upon thousands of men walking in neat rows, armor gleaming, and crimson and gold banners flying overhead. Centurions and the other officers rode horses, all of them straight backed, helmets concealing their faces. Drums sounded a slow, ominous beat, and behind her, Lydia heard her soldiers shifting uneasily.

"The Six have mercy," Malahi said softly. "There are so many of them."

"That's a gods-damned work of art," Agrippa said by way of answer. "Look at those ranks. I can barely get my men to walk in the same direction, much less in a straight line. We're fucked, by the way. This is what it looks like to be well and truly fucked."

Killian cleared his throat. "Is that him?"

Agrippa was quiet for a long moment, then he said, "Yeah. The Thirty-Seventh is the vanguard, and Marcus is the one wearing the red cloak riding the gold horse. I'd recognize that massive ego anywhere. That's Felix next to him. The big one with the standard is Servius. I was sure they had to be dead for him to have fallen this low—they've always tempered his tendencies."

Lydia had already seen Marcus, her eyes drawn to him the moment he'd crested the slope. He rode as straight-backed as his centurions, but he kept his horse to an ambling walk, radiating a total lack of concern even across all this distance. The nosepiece on his helmet hid his face, but Lydia could picture it easily in her mind's eye, her heart beating a rapid staccato as old fear rose in her chest.

More and more men poured over the hilltop, marching in their perfect lines, the front ranks parting in flawless synchronicity to move around the white tent. Marcus and his mounted officers and guard reached the tent, and he drew his golden horse to a stop, holding up one hand.

Horns blew, rippling over the sea of men, and as one, the marching men stopped.

"Showoff," Agrippa muttered. "He's showing off, and the worst part is that he's doing it well. I hate this. I hate all of it."

Not one of the legionnaires among the tens of thousands moved, standing still as statues as Marcus dismounted. Without a backward glance, he walked inside the tent.

One minute passed. Then two, then three, and not a single one of the legionnaires shifted from the position he'd put them in. Almost as though Marcus possessed the same power as Rufina did over her army of the dead, though Lydia could see that every one of them was of the living.

"Thoughts, Agrippa?" Killian asked, and Lydia looked sideways at him.

Killian absently twisted a lock of his horse's mane around his fingers, showing none of the agitation the rest of them were displaying. But she could feel his anger simmering beneath the calm surface. The desire to ride down and have vengeance on the one who'd done her such harm. Who'd done harm to so many people who Killian cared about.

"Slaughtering our rear guard must have sated his need for revenge, because he's giving us the opportunity to treat," Agrippa finally answered. "But what he's expecting is for us to surrender without a fight. He's putting his full might on display; no tricks, no ruses, because he wants us to see that we can't win this. That to fight would be the greatest form of stupidity. You can call it intimidation, but that's not really it. Intimidation is a strategy for an uncertain victory, and Marcus is, right now, entirely assured that he can win this."

"Fair." Killian shifted his weight in the saddle, narrowing his eyes at the gleaming ranks.

Lydia could smell the scent of sweat and men as the wind blowing over the legions reached her, humanity at its most deadly, and she wanted to scream and scream and scream because they'd fought so hard, and it had still come to this.

"Marcus speaks Mudamorian fluently, because it's a common trade language in the East," Agrippa said. "So you can send anyone. He'll give them terms and then send them back to report everything to you. Waste of time because I can tell you what he'll tell them."

Killian shifted in his saddle. "Which is why you're the one who is going to go talk to him."

Agrippa stiffened even as Malahi gasped, "No! Absolutely not!"

"She's right," Lydia said, feeling Malahi's rising panic. "Agrippa is a deserter. At best, they'll take him prisoner. At worst, they'll kill him while we watch."

"No, they won't."

Agrippa's horse began pawing the ground, ears pinned to its head as Agrippa said, "You know I'm not one to back down out of fear, Killian, but Lydia's right. The second the Thirty-Seventh realizes it's me, realizes that I'm fighting on the side that just killed several hundred of their ranks, they're going to come for blood. I'm not going to learn anything interesting for you, because I'm going to be nothing more than a red splatter across that nice green field."

"You'll be fine."

"No!" Malahi rode her horse in front of them, her back to the watching legion. "No, Killian. I'm not allowing you to send Agrippa to his death because your gut says it will be all right. I'm not risking him when you could send *anyone* with total surety that they'd come back alive."

"Marcus believes he knows everyone's hands," Killian said. "He's confident, and we need to shake that confidence with something unexpected. Something he didn't predict."

"Teriana is our wildcard."

"We've already played that card. We need to play another. We need to rattle him."

Malahi was shaking, and as her imploring eyes turned on Lydia, she fought the urge to tell Killian it wasn't worth the risk. That Agrippa's life was worth too much to throw away on a gambit. Instead, she turned to look at the man in question. "It's your choice, Agrippa."

The ex-legionnaire shook his head. "I know everything about how they fight. Having me on your side is an asset, and even if Marcus isn't inclined to execute me for desertion, he's going to recognize that having me on the opposing side is a liability."

Killian shrugged. "If his victory is assured, then he can afford to let a liability walk away to maintain face in front of his men. Killing you will only prove he's not half as confident as this little performance indicates. You aren't betting on my gut, Agrippa. You're betting on your interpretation of Marcus's show."

Agrippa looked up at the sky, countless emotions warring across his face, then he pulled off his helmet and tossed it behind him. "All right, then. Get me a white flag."

101

MARCUS

Marcus rested his elbows on the table, on which sat his helmet, a glass of wine, and nothing else.

You're close.

Lydia was here, and was once again the Queen of Mudamora, judging from the crown she wore. She was in the company of her general, Killian Calorian, as well as several others whom his men hadn't been able to identify due to their hoods and helmets.

They'll surrender.

He twitched at the certainty of the voice because surrender was never likely when a force had its back against a wall. Or its back against another army, as was the case here.

Make your acceptance contingent on them handing over their queen. Then you'll have her. The woman who ruined everything for you because she didn't stay dead.

"It wasn't her fault, it was mine," he muttered, and was rewarded with a sharp stab of pain in his head, his defiance faltering in the face of the agony.

Kill her.

The fists were pounding against his walls, and Marcus put his head in his hands, exhausted by the war inside his mind that would not end. The two halves of himself seemed not to care that their battle was destroying him. Breaking apart his mind bit by bit. Part of him welcomed the moment he'd finally collapse under the strain.

"You all right, sir?" Gibzen asked.

"Headache." He hated to admit it, but since they'd come through the xenthier and stepped onto Mudamorian soil, the pain had been intense. "Go ask Racker for something that won't numb my ability to think."

"You'll be better once we're back in Revat," the primus replied. "It's this place. I don't feel right here either—makes my skin crawl. Like I'm being watched by unfriendly eyes. I should stay with you."

Irritation filled Marcus's voice as he snapped, "Go talk to Racker. Now."

Gibzen looked ready to argue, but then shrugged and departed, leaving Marcus to rub at his temples.

Felix ducked into the tent. "They're sending a rider under a white flag."

"Good," Marcus muttered, wiping at his nose and then staring at the crimson smeared across his fingers. "Let's get this over with so we can head back to Revat. I don't want to be here. There's too much . . ." Too much of *something*, but his mind couldn't put a finger on what.

"The stink is giving everyone a headache. With any luck, being delivered their rear guard will have cracked their resolve," Felix said. "They have to know they can't win this."

Marcus was certain that they did know, but that didn't mean they'd surrender without a fight.

"Oh, shit!"

The astonishment in Felix's voice caused Marcus to lift his head, shock radiating through him as his second said, "The rider—it's Agrippa!"

"What?" Marcus stood up so abruptly that he hit the table, only quick reflexes keeping the wineglass from tipping sideways. "You can't be serious. He's in Bardeen."

"Unless he has a twin on this side of the Endless Seas who knows all the names of our men, it's Agrippa."

Kicking back his stool, Marcus strode to the front of the tent and out into the sunlight, his breath disappearing as his eyes locked onto his once primus slowly walking his horse through the gap in the ranks, a white flag on a stick resting nonchalantly against one shoulder.

"It's good to see you boys," Agrippa called out. "It's been an age, hasn't it? You all grew up! Finally put some muscles into the lines, I see!"

The Thirty-Seventh's neat ranks were now all jagged as the men stared at Agrippa in astonishment. Though he was clearly fighting on the side of those who'd ambushed their brothers, not a one of them had anger in their expressions.

"Took a fall into the river at Hydrilla after we took the fortress!" Agrippa shouted, avoiding Marcus's gaze as he drew closer. "Wasn't the most pleasant journey across the world, but I learned a very important lesson about not pissing off the wrong woman!"

"Didn't those washer women claim he'd run off to join the rebels with his girl?" Felix muttered.

Though that had been years ago, in the shadow of Hydrilla, the memory of that conversation remained vivid in Marcus's mind. "Yes."

"Didn't Gibzen also confirm their story based on tracks?"

"Yes." A suspicion he hadn't put much thought to in far too long began to grow in Marcus's chest. "Gibzen brought the women to speak to me as well. He provided all the proof that Agrippa deserted."

"I'm going to go out on a limb," Felix's voice shook with anger, "and say that Gibzen lied."

Anger began to simmer in Marcus's chest, but where the emotion usually bolstered the walls in his mind, this time it made them tremble. Because Gibzen had done more than just lie.

Marcus and Agrippa had never been friends, but they'd been brothers. Part of the same family forged in Lescendor and cemented on the battlefield, and an attack on one brother was an attack on all.

Even when the attack came from within.

"Send someone to fetch Quintus," he ordered. "And someone else to find Gibzen."

Felix muttered the order to one of the men, and Agrippa chose that moment to lock eyes with Marcus, drawing his horse to a stop. "Sir."

"You didn't desert."

"Not then, no." Agrippa dismounted, handing his reins to Felix. "I spent years trying to find my way back east without any luck. Imagine my shock to learn that you and the boys were on this side of the world."

"But you're not here to rejoin the Thirty-Seventh's ranks, are you?"

Agrippa hesitated, and Marcus saw his throat move as he swallowed hard before saying, "No, sir. I am not."

All around him, the Thirty-Seventh seemed to hold its collective breath as they waited for Marcus to react. To give the order that needed to come, given that Agrippa was now, by his own admission, a deserter. For once, the voice was silent, seeming uncertain of what to make of this moment.

And the part of Marcus that was trapped behind the walls in his mind took advantage, screaming, *He is not your enemy!*

Closing the distance between them, Marcus wrapped his arms around the man who'd been both his rival and his savior, clapping him on the back. "It's good to see you, Agrippa. You've been missed more than you know."

Agrippa stood frozen for a moment, then relaxed and thumped Marcus on his armored back. "Thank you, sir."

Letting go of him, Marcus gestured to the tent. "Should we get to business, then?"

Agrippa cast one backward glance at the ridgeline, then nodded. "Yeah. Though I think both of us know what the other will say."

Right up until the point Agrippa had appeared, Marcus had believed there was a chance that the Mudamorians would surrender and hand over their queen. But Calorian's choice to send Agrippa was not the strategy of a general who believed himself defeated. "For old time's sake, then."

Entering the shade of the command tent, Marcus returned to where he'd been sitting, then watched as Agrippa circled the tent, inspecting the contents.

"It's like going back in time," Agrippa muttered. "Everything is the same as it always was."

Not everything.

As he watched Agrippa root around in the cabinets, Marcus examined the changes that time had wrought upon his once primus. Agrippa was taller and broader. His skin, which had always been darker courtesy of his Bardenese heritage, was darker still from the sun, new scars pale by comparison. His eyes were harder, posture more wary; that might be attributed to the circumstances, but Marcus's gut told him otherwise.

"I learned something recently," Agrippa said. "We're family."

"That's not a revelation. Once Thirty-Seventh, always Thirty-Seventh."

The corner of Agrippa's mouth turned up. "True, but that's not what I meant. My elder brother is Tiberius Egnatius. Lydia tells me he's a senator now." His smile turned sly. "And married to *your* sister."

Surprise shook Marcus's already shaken composure. "Pardon?"

"Her name is Cordelia Domitius, isn't it? I always knew you must have come right from the top of the Hill."

A sudden twinge of pain struck Marcus in his chest at the mention of Cordelia, and he couldn't help but wonder what she'd say if she knew where he sat now. If she knew all the things he had done.

Though protocol demanded otherwise, he found himself saying, "I've met him. Knowing you're his blood explains his politics."

"It's the Bardenese in him. Rebel blood. How does your sister feel about that, good Cel woman that she is?"

"It was my impression that when Cordelia says 'Jump,' Tiberius asks, 'How high?'"

"It seems that the penchant for giving orders is a Domitius trait." Agrippa extracted an expensive bottle of Atlian wine from one of the cabinets and held it up. "Amarin still with you?"

Marcus tensed at the mention of his servant's name. Gibzen had somehow seamlessly stepped into the role, taking on all of Amarin's tasks. Always in Marcus's presence, driving everyone else away. What had felt like loyalty now felt like something else, but all Marcus said was, "He's around somewhere."

Agrippa opened the bottle without asking, and drank straight from the neck. "Tastes like the Empire."

Marcus rested his elbows on the table. "If it's that bitter, it must be off."

Agrippa laughed, then took another mouthful. "Good to see you haven't been so corrupted that you've lost your sense of humor."

Corrupted.

The choice of word was another blow to the walls in his mind, but Marcus only shrugged. "We're already moving on to insults, then?"

"Seems fitting, given that you've allied with Rufina. You *do* know that she's corrupted, don't you? Or does your Cel self refuse to acknowledge that there are powers in this world that can't be explained by the collegium?"

"I'm aware of what the corrupted can do, as well as those possessed of the other god marks."

Agrippa took another mouthful, his face darkening with anger. "Then why are you working with them? Because they promised you my wife's gold mines, which are currently drowning in black pools of poison."

Wife. So Agrippa was the consort Sly had mentioned, and as Marcus recalled the exchange, it struck him that Sly full-well knew Agrippa's connection to the Thirty-Seventh and had withheld the information. "I'm not that stupid, Agrippa. Rufina has already delivered enough of Rotahn's gold to pay for this campaign twice over. It's back in Revat, and will very soon be on its way to Celendrial. Congratulations on your nuptials."

"Thank you." The corner of Agrippa's mouth turned up. "So you've lowered yourself to a mercenary?"

The word turned Marcus's mouth sour and he took a mouthful of wine. "None of that gold goes in my pocket. The gold was the Dictator's goal, and I have achieved it. Now I move to achieve the rest."

Agrippa made a noncommittal noise, then sat on the stool opposite Marcus, taking another mouthful of the wine. "What terms are you offering?"

"The usual," Marcus said. "Mudamora and its allies, such as they are, must agree to surrender and lay down arms. All positions of authority are to be disbanded, and Mudamora's queen, Kitaryia Falorn, also known as Lydia Valerius, is to be returned so that she might wed her betrothed, Dictator Lucius Cassius."

"And by returned, you mean you'll kill her?" Agrippa gave him a grin that was all teeth. "Third time's the charm?"

He's defending her! the voice shrieked, fueled by mention of Lydia. *He's no brother of yours!*

Marcus shook his head. "Her fate is in the hands of the Dictator, not mine."

"Except Lucius Cassius was the man who ordered you to murder Lydia in the first place. It would be all sorts of inconvenient if the Senate learned the real story behind her disappearance. Even more inconvenient if Senator Valerius learned the truth." Agrippa laughed. "Oh wait, he already knows the truth because Teriana told him."

"Is Teriana here?" The question slipped out, and Marcus silently cursed himself for allowing Agrippa to get to him.

"No, she had other business to attend to." Agrippa grinned again and the gleam in his eyes told Marcus that whatever Teriana was up to, he would not like it.

Don't think about her! She's your enemy!

Marcus lifted one shoulder. "The life of one girl is of little consequence to the patricians of Celendrial in the face of all that they have to gain."

"But it's of a lot of consequence to Teriana."

Not half an hour ago, Marcus had felt in perfect control of the situation, everything going according to plan, and now *nothing* was.

Get rid of him!

"Did you know that I defended you?" Agrippa jolted to his feet, taking another mouthful of wine while he paced. "I called Lydia a liar. Said she was full of shit when she told me what you'd done to her. Had to eat crow on that because every gods-damned word was true. Then I said Teriana was safe with the Thirty-Seventh, that you'd treat her with courtesy, when it turned out that you were turning on the charm to get her to tell you everything that you wanted to know. Not just the Empire's favorite weapon, but its favorite *whore*."

Marcus's fingers started to curl into fists, and he pressed them flat, biting the insides of his cheeks to keep from lashing out.

"Do you know how wrecked Teriana is?" Agrippa asked. "I watched her fall on her knees before Lydia to beg her forgiveness. Watched her cry so hard she could barely breathe because she believed she'd betrayed her best friend by falling in love with you. Watched her take the blame for your cruel manipulation when it should be *you* who is on trial. It should be *you* who is begging forgiveness. And instead you're here, doubling down. Tell me, Marcus, is there anything that you *won't* do? Is there any line you won't cross?"

The vision of Teriana on her knees, the vision of her *begging* for forgiveness, exploded the towering black walls in Marcus's mind, sending shards spinning off into nothingness as emotion surged. "Teriana has *nothing* to apologize for!"

"And yet she apologized on her knees."

Marcus was on his feet, though he didn't remember standing. "Everything she did was for the sake of saving her people! A more selfless woman you'll never meet, and I'll personally cut out the tongue of anyone who says otherwise!"

"And yet you used her. Manipulated her. Seduced her for information on your opponent."

"That's not . . . I didn't . . ." Marcus pressed his fingers to his temples and squeezed his eyes shut, head throbbing and his breath starting to grow strained. "I loved her."

I love her.

It was like being drowned. Like the walls had not been walls at all but a oppressive dam that held back every awful emotion, and they flooded over him now without mercy. As did pain. Awful relentless pain in his skull that nearly brought him to his knees.

Silence stretched, then Agrippa said, "Why are you here?"

It wasn't what Marcus had anticipated Agrippa would ask, and he dropped his hands and met the other man's gaze. "Because . . . because those were the Dictator's orders."

"Yes, but *why*?"

The question provoked a frantic sort of tension in him, and Marcus swallowed hard, his mouth suddenly dry as sand.

"Gamdesh is prime territory," Agrippa said. "Rich and fertile. The center of trade. Yet you've all but abandoned it to come attack a nation that is quite literally rotting, the land left for the living being eaten away by the day. And if you win, it will only be to face down an army of the dead. Why are you here? What does Cassius want?"

A tremor ran through him. "The gold mines."

"Gold mines you can't even reach." Agrippa's gaze was steady. Relentless. "Gold isn't the reason you're here. Nor is the reason to take the surrender of a crumbling nation."

No, it wasn't.

"Is it because he needs you to silence Lydia?" Agrippa asked. "Even that makes little sense given that Teriana told Senator Valerius everything. The truth is out, and it is unlikely to cause Cassius any particular grief given the power he already holds. So why?"

Because she needs to pay for ruining your life! the voice screamed, pressure building inside Marcus's skull. *Because she needs to die!* "He wants her dead."

"Who?"

His lips parted to say *Cassius*, because it was Cassius who had threatened him if he didn't get rid of her. Threatened his family. Yet it was not Cassius who drove his desire to put Lydia in the grave.

"You?"

Marcus didn't answer. Couldn't answer.

"You say you loved Teriana, yet you have come to murder the woman she loves as a sister. That doesn't seem like love, it seems like hate."

The last thing he wanted to do was hurt Teriana. But for all the walls had crumbled, the voice still lurked in his mind, clawing at him. "Lydia ruined everything."

"No. *You* did that. Just as you sent three hundred of the Thirty-Seventh to their deaths by believing that we'd give her up without a fight." Agrippa set the bottle down on the table. "Mudamora declines your terms of surrender. We're through here."

"You can't win this, Agrippa. Do not make me kill everyone in that army for the sake of one girl. Give her to me, and we'll turn around and return to Revat. You have my word."

No sooner had he spoken did Servius entered the tent, his brown skin strangely blanched. "I need to talk to you, sir. We've had a report from Revat."

"Can't it wait?" Marcus gestured at Agrippa, irritated that Servius would interrupt this conversation.

"No." Servius's eyes locked on Agrippa, then he shook his head. "In truth, I don't think this is going to be news to him."

An equally rattled Felix entered the tent, and a sad smile formed on Agrippa's face. Marcus stomach dropped. "Well, spit it out then."

"Our supply lines have been cut."

Marcus's hands turned to ice. "Which ones?"

"All of them."

His whole body went rigid. "That's not possible. There are ones hidden in—"

"We've been cut off from Celendor. Cut off from the East entirely."

But he'd done what Cassius had wanted. He was here, had secured the gold, was about to secure everything else. "Cassius cut—"

"I don't think it was Cassius," Servius said. "The xenthier terminus stem in Emrant blew up, which, as far as I know, is only possible if you set off explosives at the genesis. Like when the Nineteenth accidentally did it and got themselves buried in a landslide caused by the earthquake they set off. At any rate, the Emrant stem blew a mile in the air and set off an earthquake that turned half the city to rubble. Zimo managed to send a message off to Revat, but then Imresh came under attack. With the damages to the fortress from the earthquake, he couldn't defend it. Gamdeshians, united with the Maarin, forced Zimo into retreat through the xenthier. As soon as the Gamdeshians and their allies had control of Imresh, they set charges on the genesis and blew it up as well. They then pursued the messenger through the stem between Emrant and Revat. Our forces in Revat have fallen under siege, and they plan to abandon the city and move to join us. Might already be here."

"They can't!" Marcus snapped into focus. "We need that water supply, or else—"

The ground suddenly shook, the tremor causing everyone in the tent to stagger. No one spoke for a long moment, the only sounds the shouts and curses of alarm from outside the tent as the men worked to calm the horses.

"I'm going to go out on a limb and say that we no longer have the use of that xenthier," Servius said in a shaky voice. "Which also means we no longer have a clean water source."

Agrippa slowly pushed his bottle of wine in front of Marcus. "Might take a bit to receive the reports, all things considered, but I suspect that the stem between Bardeen and Arinoquia is no more. The men you left in Aracam will either be dead or fled through to Sibern, which amounts to the same thing."

Marcus's ears were ringing, the world around him too bright.

Servius gave a slow shake of his head. "Someone with knowledge of our explosives coordinated an attack in the East and the West at the same bloody time. Had the audacity to attack Celendor itself—Padria's in spitting distance of Celendrial and it was attacked."

We're going to war, Legatus. And I think it's time you had a taste of what it's like to lose.

"You pissed off the wrong girl, Marcus," Agrippa said. "And while I might not live long enough to relish the pleasure of watching you come to terms with losing, it has been a delight watching you realize that Teriana has just kicked your ass."

Distantly, Marcus heard Servius tell Agrippa to shut his mouth. Heard Felix cursing, but none of the words resonated. They were cut off. Cut off from supplies, cut off from water, and trapped on poisoned ground.

He'd gotten the Thirty-Seventh killed. His brothers, the men he was sworn to protect, were all dead men walking.

You do not lose, the cursed voice in his head whispered. *Unite wholly with Rufina. Together, you can take back control of Gamdesh. You can control all of Reath.*

"Shut up!" he snarled, barely noticing as Felix, Servius, and Agrippa started in alarm. "Listening to you has killed them all. Get out of my head!"

It felt as though a beast was clawing up the insides of his skull. Like a battle was being fought, and the pain was excruciating. But whatever monster lurked behind the voice had put the lives of his men on the blade of a knife, and the Thirty-Seventh had always been the hill that he would die on.

"Get out." It was a battle of wills. "Get out of my head!"

You will suffer, the voice answered. *You will beg for respite from the pain. You need me.*

"I don't!" He could hear the faint wheeze in his voice. Knew that winning this would have a price. But it was one he was willing to pay. "I'm done with you!"

The monster within him hissed in anger, then retreated deep, deep within his core. Walled in and barricaded away, where it could do no harm.

But Marcus couldn't breathe. Couldn't get air into his lungs, because this was the cost of victory. This was the gods-damned cost.

He fell to his knees, hearing the noise of the legion outside the tent walls. Not the family he'd been born to but the one he'd made himself, and he'd condemned them.

The world was spinning, an attack constricting his chest with a violence he hadn't experienced in so long. How unfair it would be to die now, leaving his men to fight this battle without him.

"Shit!" Felix snarled. "It's one of his attacks."

We cannot fall back.

"What's wrong with him?" Agrippa demanded.

We cannot fall back.

"He can't breathe!"

We cannot fall back.

"I know what this is," Agrippa said. "I've seen it before. Felix, get Racker and tell him to bring the bee medicine!"

Marcus was on his hands and knees in the dirt, darkness pooling in his vision.

We cannot fall back.

Hands were rolling him onto his back, and then he heard the surgeon's voice. Heard him shouting instructions, faces blurring, fading.

Now everyone would know. Yet another secret he'd fought so long and hard to keep, now out in the world.

Then smoke was wafting into his face.

"Breathe, you idiot!" Racker shouted. "Breathe it in!"

He couldn't.

Agrippa slapped him. Once. Twice. Three times, the pain giving Marcus a heartbeat of clarity in which he managed a small intake of breath.

Then another.

And another.

He coughed on the smoke, the taste strange, but the tightness in his throat and chest was easing enough that he could get air into his lungs.

"How long?" Racker demanded. "How long has this been happening?"

He still didn't have the capacity to speak, so Felix did it for him. "All his life. This one was bad, though."

"And why," Racker demanded, "was this never brought to my attention?"

"Because he wanted to keep it a secret," Felix said. "It's a weakness. You know how it goes."

"So you pair of idiots have been helping him hide it? It's a bloody miracle he's still alive!"

"There's no cure," Marcus finally managed to get the words out. "Every physician in Celendor was consulted when I was a child. There is no cure."

"But there is a treatment!" Racker screamed the words. "You cursed fool of a man; did you think you were so special that you were the only one? You have dozens and dozens of men in your ranks who suffer this, and I treat them all the time with a medicine I create. All I need to make it is bees!"

"Bees," Agrippa repeated, nodding sagely. "This used to happen to one of my men. I carried a package of that stuff about with me, just in case."

"Bees?"

"Yes!" Racker looked ready to hit him. "You're too stupid to live, Marcus. I should have let you die so that you might learn a lesson about trusting the men who follow you." Then he stormed out.

"You all right?" Felix asked, kneeling in front of him.

Every breath was still a struggle, but he was getting enough air in his lungs that he was in no danger of dying. And though his head throbbed, for the first time in far too long, Marcus felt like himself again.

Agrippa sat in the dirt next to him, elbows resting on his knees. "Who were you shouting at, Marcus? Who was inside your head?"

"No one." He'd let the villain inside him rule, and now everyone was going to pay.

Agrippa's hazel eyes were shadowed, considering, then he nodded. "Right. Well, just to be clear, we aren't surrendering. We're not giving up Lydia. We're fighting until the bitter end. Do with that what you will."

Agrippa started to rise, but Marcus caught hold of his wrist. A puzzle that had once consumed him but recently been forgotten rose to the forefront of his mind, and Agrippa had the pieces he needed. "How did you end up in the river that flowed into the xenthier?" He sucked in a ragged breath of air. "It's not like you to slip."

"I didn't slip. Silvara's family was in Hydrilla. One of the other laundresses told her about my involvement in the battle, and she saw my actions as a betrayal. She pushed me into the river and I couldn't get out of the flow."

"Any chance the other laundress's name was Carina?"

"Yeah. Carina would've seen everything."

Marcus let go of Agrippa's wrist, then pushed to his hands and knees. "Get me up, Felix."

Felix and Servius hauled him to his feet, and though he still felt short of breath, Marcus walked outside with Agrippa. The ranks visibly relaxed at the sight of them both alive.

Quintus had been pacing in front of the tent. He went still at the sight of Agrippa, then in two steps, his arms were around him. "I didn't believe them when they told me, but you're here. You're really here!"

"In the flesh." There were tears in Agrippa's eyes. "Wish we weren't on the opposite sides of things, my friend."

"We aren't," Quintus said, though what came next, Marcus didn't hear, because rather than following them to Agrippa's horse, he stayed in front of the tent.

"What are we going to do?" Felix asked softly. "We're cut off from the Empire with tens of thousands of men to feed and water."

"We could move south to Serlania," Servius muttered. "Commandeer ships and make our way south."

Marcus didn't answer, his gaze traveling beyond Quintus and Agrippa to the group of riders sitting on the ridgeline. Lydia's long dark hair blew sideways in the wind, a crown glittering upon her head, and he was struck with a memory of her as a child, tucking that long hair behind her ears as she bent over a book.

How differently would things have gone if his father had not decided to send him to Lescendor instead of his brother? How differently would things have gone if Valerius had not decided Lydia should be wed? Both Marcus and Lydia would have been rendered useless to Cassius in his quest for power, and without them, would he have climbed so far? Would Reath have suffered as it had?

"Agrippa is a valuable resource," Felix murmured. "You sure you don't want to hold on to him?"

"Let him go. He's not ours anymore." Marcus drew in a breath, his chest aching. "Where is Amarin?"

Felix cast him a sideways look. "He's been keeping my tent in order, which means he's bored stiff. You of a mind to have him back?"

"I should never have let him go."

Gibzen chose that exact moment to appear, a vial clutched in one hand. "You're not letting Agrippa go, are you? He's a deserter! He's the enemy!"

Marcus rocked on his heels, eyeing his primus and finally seeing clearly. "After the battle for Hydrilla, you told me that Agrippa had deserted with Silvara."

"Because that's what the other laundress said." Gibzen scowled. "She told you herself about them carrying on. Spending nights together. The promises he made to run away with her and such."

"Carina."

Gibzen huffed out a breath. "I don't remember her name. Some old Bardenese woman."

"But you followed the tracks." Marcus watched Agrippa push his horse into a trot, heading toward the distant ridge where the Mudamorians watched on, not one of the Thirty-Seventh attempting to stop him. "You were certain that it was Agrippa and Silvara heading to rebel territory."

"Well obviously I was wrong. There's only so much a man can tell about a footprint in the snow. Doesn't change the fact that Agrippa should have come straight back to us once he learned we were here. Instead, he's filling our enemies' heads with information on our strategies. He's not just a deserter, he's a traitor!"

"Someone was giving Hostus information during the siege of Hydrilla all those years ago," Marcus pressed, watching Quintus approach. Seeing the rage in his eyes. "Hostus knew things that only the Thirty-Seventh would know. Secrets between brothers."

"Men talk when they're drunk. And this was years ago. And Hostus is dead. What does it matter?"

"Hostus knew information about my strategies, which nearly got me killed. I never did discover who ratted me out to him about my plans with Grypus. Which means the rat never got caught." Quintus had reached them, expression murderous, but Marcus held up a hand for him to pause. "And that rat went on to do what rats do best."

Gibzen went very still. "I don't know what you're talking about."

"Was Hostus paying you off?"

Such a good dog, Hostus's voice echoed up from Marcus's memories. *He'd make an excellent replacement for your deserter.* "Or did he just promise to help you move up in the ranks?"

"This is bullshit."

"You hated Agrippa. Everyone knew it."

"Yeah, because he always made *you* look bad. Doesn't mean I tried to kill him."

"I know, but you did watch someone else try to kill him and did nothing to help." Gibzen opened his mouth, but Marcus cut him off. "I can't prove you knew the truth, nor that you were on the take with Hostus, but I can't help but be suspicious given that Titus told me he'd paid off someone close to me for information. Someone he'd promised to help move up the ranks."

The men close enough to hear stiffened in shock, and Gibzen didn't miss their reaction.

"Wasn't me."

"Someone took that *freshly minted gold* from Titus and made a deal with the enemy. With Ashok, who was Urcon's puppet master.

Someone who wanted Teriana dead *so things could go back to normal*. Someone *stupid enough* not to realize just how the enemy might use her against me. Against us."

The Thirty-Seventh were all pressing closer, faces hard and eyes growing darker with each one of Marcus's accusations, his words repeated back through the ranks.

"Who knew the exact hour Teriana was returning that day?" Marcus raised his voice so that it carried over the listening men. "Me. Titus. Felix. *You*."

"You can't be serious." Gibzen's eyes jumped from Marcus to the men pressing inward, the Thirty-Seventh's lines and protocols abandoned in their desperation to hear the truth. "Those were my men who Ashok killed."

"No, they were *Agrippa's* men," Marcus said. "Over the years since Hydrilla, you've weeded all one hundred of them out of your ranks with excuses, accidents, and deaths. Don't think it hasn't been noticed."

"So? I made my century my own. Every centurion does."

"How did you find Ashok's trail so quickly? How were you lucky enough to find one of Teriana's hair beads so as to prove she'd been taken?"

"It's my job!"

Marcus had no concrete proof, not really, and while the thousand little coincidences and rising patterns painted a damning picture, Marcus wanted the gods-damned truth. "Gibzen, you're out." He motioned to Servius. "Get Racker back here. Burn the Thirty-Seventh's mark off him, then strip him and send him on his way. I'm not keeping someone in my ranks who isn't loyal to me."

"Have you lost your mind?" Gibzen twisted in a circle, looking like he might run, but the shields around them locked, spears lowering.

"Be glad I'm not hanging you for treason," Marcus said. "Instead, I'm going to allow you to make your own way. No longer primus. No longer Thirty-Seventh. A man like you is of no value to me."

Gibzen's eyes bulged. "You'd be dead a dozen times over without me! You'd never have made it out of Lescendor alive without me!"

"Perhaps." Marcus lifted one shoulder. "But any man can do what you do. You're muscle, Gibzen. Replaceable. And I don't want someone under my command who I can't trust."

Racker pushed through the shields surrounding them, his roll of surgical blades tucked under one arm. "I'll need a brazier," he said, sounding annoyed that one wasn't waiting. "Let's get this over with."

Gibzen moved to draw his blade, but Quintus and Felix were on him in a heartbeat. Closing the distance, Marcus took Gibzen's gladius and tossed it aside, then took his helmet and armor, casting them in the same pile. The smell of smoke from the brazier blew over them, and Gibzen visibly tensed.

"It's a good deal." Marcus knew his tone did not match the simmering rage that boiled his blood. "Lose a couple of tattoos in exchange for your life. I bet there's any number of men in our ranks who'd volunteer for the opportunity. No more war. No more battles. No more killing. No more bodies. It's a better life that you can look forward to."

"You need me. You need me!" Gibzen screamed as Felix and Servius forced him to the ground, tearing off his tunic.

"Why do I need you?" Marcus glanced at Racker, who'd removed a glittering scalpel.

"Keep him steady," the surgeon muttered. "Don't want him to bleed to death and waste this effort."

"To protect you!"

"I've hundreds of men who can do that." Marcus leaned over Gibzen and smiled. "Quintus would make a fine primus, I think. What do you say, Quintus? Fancy a promotion?"

The man in question didn't respond, only watched with feral eyes.

"No!" Gibzen's eyes tracked the scalpel, not fearing the pain, but what the surgeon was about to take from him. "You need me to protect you from yourself!"

Marcus caught hold of Racker's wrist just before the surgeon could cut. "And why do you think that?"

"You've got too much softness," Gibzen said. "Not your fault, but you need someone to keep you straight or you bend for people who don't deserve it. You need someone to get rid of the problems so that you can think with a clear head."

It was hard to see straight, Marcus's rage was so intense. "And how did selling me out to my enemies factor into your way of thinking?"

"Because you didn't understand what I was doing for you!" Gibzen shouted. "I needed to be closer, needed to have more power, but you kept giving it to men who couldn't do what I do. Hostus said he'd get me promoted. Titus promised the same. So I took their gold and gave them information because I knew the cost was worth the reward. You just need to think about it, and you'll understand. You'll see everything I've done was for you!"

Marcus picked up Gibzen's belt pouch and rifled through the contents. Gold Cel dragons. Vials of narcotics. And Teriana's hair ornament, the gold of the *Quincense's* hull glittering in the dying sunlight. Grief rolled over him like a tide, but Marcus clenched the tiny ship and let himself drown in it. "Let him go."

Felix gave him a look of confusion, but obeyed and pulled Quintus away. Gibzen rose to his feet, dusting dirt off himself. "I knew you'd see reason, sir," he said. "I knew you'd understand."

What Marcus understood was that Gibzen was a monster. A monster that, instead of putting down, he'd used to achieve his own ends, never once realizing that the monster was using him for the same. He was complicit in all that Gibzen had done, which meant he was responsible for so much more than just putting an end to him.

Reaching down, Marcus picked up a fist-sized rock, seeing the ranks of his men do the same. "I understand perfectly."

What came next was legion justice. It was bloody and painful, but anger made it swift, and when it was over, Marcus retreated into the command tent, knowing that it would not be long until the other legati descended upon him, wanting answers. Wanting a solution for their predicament. For while all had pushed for this step of the campaign, Marcus commanded this army.

Which meant he needed to dig them out of this mess.

They could not fall back.

Teriana had ensured that much, but she'd also learned the art of war from him. She knew that boxing an army in meant a fight to the death, and casualties weren't what she would want. Which meant she'd left him a way out, if he had the guts to step toward it.

"Felix," he said, wiping blood from his face. "Swap me cloaks. And get me a white flag."

102

LYDIA

Agrippa rode away from the white tent, but he'd not gone far when a roar of anger surged across the space between the armies. The orderly ranks of the Thirty-Seventh had fallen apart when Agrippa had ridden into their midst, but now it was a raging mass of men in front of the white tent while the other legions watched, unmoving. Agrippa himself did not look back, and Lydia did not think his grim expression was because of the earthquake they'd just experienced.

"What are they doing?" Malahi demanded. "What's happening?"

"They're tearing one of their own apart. I don't know why." Killian lowered his spyglass as Agrippa cantered up the slope toward them, his face ashen.

"Who is that man?" Malahi demanded of him. "Why are they killing him?"

"It's Thirty-Seventh business." Agrippa leaned over the side of his horse and vomited. Wiping his mouth, he muttered, "Legion betrayal. Legion justice. Not our problem."

Already the legion ranks were reforming, the only sign of the violence the swath of blood-soaked grass in front of the equally splattered tent. Of Marcus, there was no sign.

And as the sun fell behind the slope, whatever was happening within the army below was lost to shadows.

"Teriana and the others succeeded. I was there when he got the news, and that earthquake was the Gamdeshians getting rid of Marcus's path back to them," Agrippa said as they rode into their own camp, swiftly explaining what he'd learned. "Unfortunately, I think Teriana's actions, in coming a day too late, might have pulled us out of the frying pan only to cast us into the fire. All those legionnaires are totally cut off from supplies and water, which means the only way they can get it is by taking it from us or moving south and taking it from Serlania. They'll strip the land as they go, then take every ship in port and head to the relative safety of the Southern Continent. Without the Empire to supply them, they'll be like a swarm of locusts wherever they go."

"What was Marcus like?" Lydia moved her horse close to Agrippa's. "Was he himself?"

"Yes. And no." Her friend met her gaze, and in the torchlight she could see his cheeks were damp. "He reminded me very much of you when we were fleeing Derin. Different versions of himself that were very much at war with each other. How this goes for us is going to depend on which part of him wins out. Though in truth, once all the other legati learn the nature of their predicament, even if he wants to show us some level of mercy, they may not allow it. Hungry men are dangerous men."

"What else happened in that tent?" Killian asked. "We saw a commotion going in and out."

Agrippa was quiet for a long moment, then he said, "Nothing you need to know. Thirty-Seventh business."

"If he's still trying to capture Lydia, I need to know." There was a hint of anger in Killian's voice. "Don't let your loyalties sway now."

"They haven't swayed." Agrippa dismounted in front of Dareena's tent, then helped Malahi off her horse. "Cassius wants Lydia dead. The Corrupter wants Lydia dead. And Marcus . . . I think part of him wants to blame you for him losing Teriana, so he doesn't have to come to terms with it being his fault." He was quiet for a minute. "He said he loved her, and the Six as my witness, I think he was telling the truth."

Lydia slid off the side of her own horse, handing Gwen the reins. "Despite what she's done?"

"Who can say? But what I do know is that Teriana was right that the Thirty-Seventh is the hill that he's going to die on. This is no longer about conquest, it's about survival, and if it is between us and them, he'll strip us of every mouthful of food we have with no regrets."

"Then we need to move against Deadground tonight." Lydia took Killian's arm as they entered the tent. "Before he moves against us and we lose our chance."

The four of them encircled the table with the map Astara had provided of Rufina's camp, complete with pools of blight. "Our only choice is to throw everything we have at fighting through the blighters and corrupted to reach the xenthier stem," Agrippa said. "We do it knowing that many will subsequently die of blight poisoning, but if we can destroy it, we give all the civilians a chance to survive after the legions strip them of everything."

The tent flaps opened, and Dareena appeared. "I wish I had better news," she said. "But the blight has breached our lines at multiple points and is spreading south at speed. The dogs scenting the paths beneath the ground show that it is flowing southeast and southwest, suggesting that Rufina is routing it around the Cel army, but I have no doubt that Serlania is her goal."

Sickness pooled in Lydia's stomach. They were out of time.

"So far no one has presented as infected," Dareena said. "But I'm going to do rounds with Killian's dog myself. It's better than sitting. I can't sit anymore."

Her aunt twisted on her heel and left, leaving a trail of frustration and helplessness in her wake.

No one spoke, the weight of what was to come pressing down and down.

Lena stepped into the tent. "The Cel have sent a messenger," she said. "He said they want to talk terms."

"You mean surrender?" Agrippa demanded. "I already told him no!"

Lydia met Malahi's gaze. "You might be able to destroy it without me. If it's still me the Cel want, it might be that handing me over gains you the time you need."

"No," Killian snapped. "I'll not hand you over."

But Malahi gave a tight nod. For the sake of Reath, they'd both make this sacrifice, but Lydia could not deny the fear in her heart.

"Send the messenger in," Lydia forced herself to say. "Let's hear what he has to say."

Lena disappeared, and Lydia turned her back on the entrance, drawing in breath after breath to compose herself, to control the fear rising in her chest as her demons approached. "I'll talk to him, if you want. You don't have to do this," Malahi said softly, but Lydia shook her head. "I can do it."

She heard footsteps, the rustle of tent canvas, and then Agrippa hissed between his teeth, "Oh fuck me, you have bigger balls than I thought."

Dread pooling in her stomach, Lydia slowly turned and found herself staring into familiar blue-grey eyes.

Legatus Marcus inclined his head. "It's been a long time, Lydia."

In a flash of motion, Killian moved, the tip of his sword stopping just shy of Marcus's throat.

Marcus did not so much as flinch, only said, "Careful, Calorian. While I understand that cutting my jugular might provide a certain pleasure, the consequences of your impulsivity would cause you to regret the action sooner rather than later."

"I've never had cause to regret cutting off a snake's head." Killian's tone was murderous, and though Lydia knew she needed to take control of this situation, she couldn't move. Couldn't get past the fear that was drowning her like Marcus had once tried to drown her in the bath.

"Ah, but this snake is more of a hydra. Cut off this head and you'll only have a dozen more with equally sharp teeth looking to bite. Or, if you require clearer speech, there are a dozen men in my camp with the training and experience to take over my role. The change in command will happen without hesitation, offering you no opportunity to take advantage of chaos brought by men jockeying for position."

"You think your death won't matter?"

"On the contrary, I think it will matter a great deal. Rather than thousands of men amenable to negotiation, you will have thousands of men looking for revenge. But you hold the sword, Calorian. The choice is yours but make it quick. Time is short."

Killian lowered his sword, though he didn't sheathe it.

"Why are you here?" Lydia finally managed to make her tongue unfreeze, but her whole body still felt like ice.

"To talk about our mutual problem."

"Then you talk to me," Killian said. "You don't get to speak to her after what you did."

"I'm not in the habit of negotiating with the second-in-command," Marcus answered. "I will speak with your queen, or I will speak to no one. I would say the choice is, once again, yours, Calorian, but if you respect your queen's authority, the choice is *hers*."

Every part of Lydia wanted to run from this conversation, terror twisting her stomach into ropes and binding her chest like a vise. Logically, she knew that made no sense. Marcus was mortal, unarmed, and would not win in a fight against Killian. Would not win in a fight against *her*. Yet Lydia couldn't make herself answer. Could only stand in place, trembling. Because it wasn't Marcus she feared, but rather what he represented.

Her helplessness.

Her weakness.

Despite everything that had happened since, Lydia once again felt like the girl she'd been in the baths. A pawn used by Cassius, then discarded, ineffectual in all her attempts to defend herself.

The only thing that still burned in defiance was her anger. It was no longer anger at herself, but anger at those who used their power to cause terror in others.

In three steps she knew were so quick she'd seem a blur to him,

Lydia closed one hand around his neck, her dark half latching upon his life. With her free hand, she pushed Killian back, because this was her fight. Not his.

"I'm not the girl you tried to drown in a bath any longer, Legatus," she said softly. "I'm no longer weak. No longer defenseless. So show care with what you say, or this breath will be your last."

Marcus's pulse remained steady beneath her grip as his eyes locked on hers. "You were never weak."

She blinked, his words not what she'd expected.

"Weakness is giving up. You fought to the bitter end and beyond," he said. "The gods of this land might have made you physically stronger, but the will to fight was always there."

Vaguely she knew they were speaking in Cel and that Agrippa was softly translating for the others, but her focus was entirely on this conversation. This moment.

"I'm sorry for what I did to you," he said. "Cassius was blackmailing me. Threatening both my family and my legion if I didn't do what he wanted. I chose them over you but regretted it immediately. Regretted it even more when I found out what you meant to Teriana." Marcus's voice caught on her friend's name, and for the first time, his pulse sped beneath her grip. "But Cassius's blackmail remained, so I again chose my family over you rather than seeing him punished. Time and again, I've chosen my family, my legion, and myself over the justice you deserved, and that is not a reflection of your worth—it's a reflection of my weakness. A weakness that caused my regret to turn to blame for a time. A weakness that remains, in part, because despite all that I've said, you're not the reason I'm here."

Lydia let go of Marcus's throat—and his life—and lowered her arm to her side. "Why, then?"

He gave a small smile. "To be frank, it's because Teriana kicked me in the balls." His smile grew. "The entire Empire in the balls, I think, though her actions have ensured I can't confirm that." Rather than angry, he sounded almost delighted, and Lydia's shock over that overwhelmed her relief that her friend had succeeded where so many had failed.

"Teriana, and those she's brought to her cause, have destroyed the xenthier paths supplying my legions, as well as those that would have allowed us to retreat." Marcus rubbed at one temple as though it pained him. "The only path is forward. One option is to defeat your army, claim Serlania, and make use of its resources. Except

I have a great deal of uncertainty about how long those resources would continue with Rufina's last obstacle removed."

"Is Rufina your enemy?" Lydia asked. "Because there have been many times where you two have seemed very much allies, if only because the enemy of your enemy is your friend."

Marcus was silent, and he finally said, "I think for a time that we were united in our goals."

"The Corrupter's goals."

"I don't think I'm that easily absolved." He shook his head. Lydia could feel his grief, his guilt, so it was no surprise when he said, "There are a hundred good reasons that should have driven me to this conversation, but it's because of my men that I'm here. I have a duty to protect them, and instead I've put their lives in jeopardy. Which is why I'm offering you a deal."

"What do you want?" she asked. "And what are you offering in return?"

He removed a folded piece of paper from his belt pouch, then smoothed it on the table. "Rufina's agent gave me a map of all the xenthier stems she's mapped, but none of them go east." He was quiet for a moment, then he said, "Bait told me that the xenthier beneath the baths in Celendrial brought you to Mudaire. Xenthier always has a mate; it's just a matter of finding it. I think you know where it is—the route back to Celendor. Tell me where it is, and once I've proven it's good, we'll go home."

This felt too easy. "And if I refuse?"

Marcus met her gaze unblinking, not bothering to voice the obvious threat.

"It's beneath the palace in Mudaire," she said. "In the tunnels. The terminus is near Celendrial. It's how I was brought to Celendor when I was a child."

"Then we will head north." He started to lift his helmet to put it back on, but then paused. "I don't think I need to explain what will happen if I discover that path is not good."

This time, it was Lydia who didn't blink.

The corner of Marcus's mouth turned up. "Good luck in your fight against Rufina."

He moved to go, but Agrippa stepped in his path. "You could help us," he said. "Do the right thing for once."

"I've risked my men enough. It's time for me to get them out of danger. This isn't my fight."

Agrippa spit into the dirt, and Lydia looked to Killian, warning him to interfere if Agrippa lashed out. But Killian only sheathed his weapon and crossed his arms.

"A hollow excuse given all you've ever done is fight other people's fights!" Agrippa snarled. "Maybe it's time you actually pick one you believe in!"

"Maybe," Marcus answered. "But this isn't it. Move so I can get my men on the march and leave you to your business."

As he spoke, Dareena stepped inside, a scowl on her face. "He's lying. Scouts have reported that a Cel legion has joined Rufina's ranks to bolster her defenses around that stem. This is a strategy."

"Bullshit," Marcus snapped, then stepped back as Dareena's sword came to rest an inch from his neck. "All my men are in my camp."

"Astara saw them." Dareena's blade edged closer to Marcus's jugular, but he stood his ground. "A full legion of *children*. Sent her the most expendable ones, didn't you?"

Anger pooled in Lydia's chest. Rage that burned hotter and hotter even as darkness rose. "Your soul is rotten to the core."

Dareena's sword started to slide toward his neck, but Marcus caught the blade, blood running down his hand. "Which legion? What number do they have on their armor? What symbol?"

"Kill him," Lydia hissed, furious that after everything, he would still stab them in the back. "Reath is better off without him in it."

But Killian caught hold of Dareena's wrist. "Answer his question."

Scowling, Dareena dragged her foot in the dirt, making the Cel symbol for 51.

Marcus drew in a sharp breath. "Not possible. They are in Celendor. I sent them back myself when we were in Emrant."

"Well, they are here now."

His throat moved as he swallowed, his face draining of color, and unease began to cool Lydia's wrath. Because whatever was going on was not Marcus's plan.

"From what direction did they arrive?" he asked, staring at the mark in the dirt.

"North." Dareena's tone was biting. "No doubt from ships you sent behind our lines, because I don't believe your lies."

"No ships. The stem beneath Celendrial." Marcus's voice was barely audible, as though he were struggling to come to grips with this information. "Bait told me about the path Lydia took from Celendrial to Mudaire. I kept the information from Cassius because revealing it would mean revealing Lydia lived, which came with inevitable consequences. A short-lived deception, for while I was in

Revat, I received a letter from Cassius indicating he'd learned Lydia was alive. But for the Fifty-First to have marched so far, they'd have to have traveled to Mudaire almost immediately after I sent them back to Celendor. Which means Cassius has known that Lydia was alive, and about the xenthier, since right after I captured Emrant. Someone must have heard my conversation with Bait and sent the information to Cassius."

His jaw tightened, and Lydia suspected he had an idea who the source of the information was.

"But I didn't keep information about the blight from Cassius. He knew Mudaire was overrun. Knew it wasn't a viable path. Yet he sent Fifty-First anyway. The only explanation for them joining Rufina is that he sent them with separate orders, and Nic's pissed off enough at me that he might have agreed just for spite." Marcus scrubbed a hand over his hair, and it seemed to Lydia that he was talking to himself more than he was to them. "The Fifty-First are just boys. They're only thirteen."

"And that's the oldest they'll ever be," a voice said.

Lydia's eyes went to the front of the tent to find that Astara had entered, the shifter's face drawn with exhaustion. "Those boys are all blighters. Every last one."

Marcus didn't move. Didn't seem to even breathe, the only sound the dripping blood falling from his injured hand. Then he said softly, "They're dead, then."

"Yes," Astara replied, even as Lydia said, "It's possible to bring them back."

Blue-grey eyes locked on hers. "How?"

Marcus had been her enemy for so long that telling him anything should seem like a mistake, but Lydia could feel the weight of his grief over the death of this legion. A grief that was fueling a wrath that dwarfed anything she'd ever felt, making her want to step back from the silent ferocity of it. "I am able to bring those lost to the blight back by pulling out the death in them and replacing it with life, but it's impossible to do on the scale we need."

She grimaced and then added, "Their souls are still bound to their corpses, so they are aware of all that their bodies are being made to do. They can see everything, hear everything, but have no power over themselves."

His eyes darkened with a mixture of anger and horror.

"The source of the blight is in the north," Lydia continued. "In a place called Deadground. We aim to destroy the heart of the blight.

I don't know if doing so will bring back all of the fallen, but there is hope."

"You could save the Fifty-First? You could bring them back to life?"

Lydia bit the inside of her cheeks. "I intend to try."

"There's a stem that leads to Deadground," Agrippa said. "But Rufina's camped her army right on top of it."

The wrath didn't diminish, but Lydia could see the wheels turning in Marcus's eyes. A decision being made.

Then he pivoted, side stepping Dareena and going to the table that held the maps of the surrounding lands. "Where?"

Killian moved to the opposite side of the table, and a shiver ran over Lydia's skin because two such forces should never be so close together. Killian touched the map. "Here. It's surrounded by a lake of blight, as well as thousands of Mudamorian blighters who will make short work of any effort to bridge the lake." He hesitated, then added, "If we destroy their bodies, it won't matter if we pull the blight out of them. They'll be lost."

Silence filled the tent.

Lydia's heart sank because perhaps there was no solution that wouldn't have a horrible price. Then Marcus said, "This is what we're going to do."

Listening, Lydia saw why this man had come so close to conquering the world, for his strategies were a beautiful mixture of complexity and simplicity, predictable in retrospect but utterly shocking in the moment.

"Can you do it?" Marcus asked in Cel. Agrippa cast his eyes upward and then translated.

"Can you?" Killian retorted.

They glared at each other, neither bending an inch, so Lydia lifted her chin and said, "We'll be ready."

"I need to get back." Marcus put the helmet that had been tucked under his arm onto his head, obscuring much of his face. "I'll arrange to meet with her tonight."

He turned to go, but Lydia found herself reaching for his arm, stopping him. "Is there anything you want me to tell Teriana?"

For a long time, Marcus didn't answer, and then he finally said, "Everything that needs to be said needs to come from my lips, not through a messenger. I may never have the opportunity—your gods know I do not deserve it—but I'd rather it all go unsaid than for her to hear it from anyone but me."

Then he was gone.

For the longest time, no one spoke, then Killian said, "Are you all right?"

Lydia *was* all right. In a way she hadn't expected, and most certainly hadn't anticipated, but beyond the hope the legions brought, there had been catharsis in facing down the fear on which all her other fears had grown. "Yes."

103

MARCUS

The torches crackled in the mist, not a breath of wind stirring the night air. Even so, Marcus could smell the blight, every breath he took tasting like foulness and rot. Handing off his horse, he walked a few paces and then paused, his eyes catching on a narrow ribbon of black in the ground that was so inky dark it seemed to consume the torchlight. Bending low, he examined the blight, watching it shift and swirl as though it watched him back. A reminder of the stakes. What he'd lost. And what would remain lost if Lydia and her companions didn't deliver.

The Fifty-First are dead. Austornic is dead.

Grief and guilt threatened to drown him, but Marcus instead used the emotions to fuel his focus. Lydia said they could be saved, but it was only possible if he succeeded tonight.

Stepping over the blight, Marcus carried on alone to the tent that had been set up for him, aware, as he sat, that he was very much on enemy ground. Even so, there was some degree of peace in the moment, for he couldn't recall the last time he'd sat entirely alone with nothing but his own thoughts for company. Even when the legion gave him space, he was still surrounded, still watched, and though to be without them now should put terror in his veins, Marcus found himself breathing easily as he waited in the silence.

His mind drifted, as it always did, to Teriana. The hair ornament he'd taken from Gibzen was on a string around his neck, the tiny ship pressed against his chest. Little more information had been received since the moment he'd learned his supply lines had been cut off, but the fragments of information were enough for him to piece together what Teriana had done. The history books would speak of the technicalities, of how she'd coordinated the theft of explosives from multiple locations across Reath, then used the Maarin network to organize an attack on xenthier stems, severing supply lines. Of how the Maarin, a nomadic nation with no military, had defeated Celendor, who held the greatest armies in the world. But Marcus saw it differently. Where he'd gone through life making enemies, Teriana had been making friends, and the single greatest thing she'd done was make allies out of those he'd trod upon, creating a unified force unlike any Reath had seen. The technicalities paled in comparison to that achievement, though he wished with all his heart that he'd be able to hear about them from her own lips.

A sharp pain formed in his chest, and he rested an elbow on the empty table, breathing deeply until it faded. Not that it ever went away. The loss of what had been between him and Teriana was an aching wound that would never heal. He'd always associated pain with weakness, but this pain made him stronger. Made him remember himself. Made him remember what truly mattered.

A noise like a canvas tarp being snapped filled the air, followed by a faint thud. Marcus tensed, scanning the darkness beyond the tent for the source of the sound, and a deimos stepped into view.

Remaining seated, he watched the monstrous winged creature walk closer, then stop, the woman seated on its back sliding to the ground. For all the deimos was dangerous, every instinct in his body screamed that *she* was the real threat; danger seethed around her like a dark cloud.

As Rufina approached, Marcus rose to his feet and inclined his head. "Your Majesty. Thank you for agreeing to this meeting."

"Legatus." She took the seat opposite him, watching him with midnight eyes ringed with fire. "I confess I've longed to meet you for some time. Your exploits across the Endless Seas are rivaled only by your accomplishments in the south. I dare say, you live up to every bit of your reputation."

Marcus wished with all his heart that wasn't the case, but for now he needed to be the man who'd earned his repute. "You have the advantage, Majesty, for you are something of a mystery to me. Queen of Derin. Marked by the Seventh. Mistress of the blight. Bane of Mudamora. Sworn enemy of our common problem, Killian Calorian."

Rufina's jaw tightened slightly at Calorian's name, which Marcus could appreciate, because he felt much the same way about

Mudamora's general, but all she said was, "Hardly a mystery, then. What else is there to know?"

He had a thousand questions, the most critical being how well informed she was. By both mortal and supernatural sources. There was no doubt in Marcus's mind that the Seventh knew his heart and mind, but whether he'd communicated that to Rufina would only be known if Marcus was still alive at the end of this conversation. "Whether I should call you enemy or ally."

Rufina's full lips curved, and she leaned forward, the rings on her fingers glittering in the torchlight as she purred, "Which do you want to be, Marcus?"

Since it was what she was offering, he took the opportunity to look her over. Dressed in black leather that clung to every curve, she appeared little older than he was himself, though given that she was corrupted, she could be his grandmother's age and he wouldn't know it. Her long dark hair hung in silky waves and a lock of it pooled on the table next to her elbow. Ivory skin without flaw stretched over high cheekbones and a straight nose, but it was hard to see her as beautiful with eyes like the pits of the underworld itself watching his every move. Eyes that may well have watched while Nic and the rest of the Fifty-First had died slowly and painfully, and the hate Marcus felt for her and her master was rivaled only by his hatred of Cassius. Everything about this creature disgusted him, but he gave her an appreciative smile. "I think we could be friends, Majesty. But only if we come to certain accommodations."

Rufina's head tilted as she considered, and he wondered if her power allowed her to hear the too rapid beat of his heart. If she knew that his confidence was a long-practiced act that hid his fear, this would all go to shit, leaving him dead or worse. But all she said was, "I'm listening."

"Your blight is a problem," he said. "Not only do I desire to keep my men among the living, there is no profit to be had from a wasteland full of walking corpses."

"You might prefer them dead, Legatus. They are much more obedient."

He huffed out an amused breath. "Obedient to you, which I think presents obvious problems for me."

Rufina lifted one shoulder and smiled.

"Is it within your power to cease the spread of the blight?" he asked. "Or have you unleashed something that is beyond your control?"

She was silent for a moment, and Marcus waited for her to hedge, to give him a vague answer, but then she said, "It is within my control to cease the spread, should I desire to do so."

"Do you?"

"Not yet."

"That's a problem."

"Only for you."

Battles were won and lost by knowing one's opponent. In understanding what it was the other side wished to achieve and what they were willing to do to achieve it. Power. Wealth.

Revenge.

Though Marcus did not know this woman's story, the rightness of the latter settled upon him, because there could be no other motivation to justify the wasteland Rufina left in her wake. What did power mean if there was no one among the living to control? What did wealth mean if there was no one to flaunt it before? There was only one thing total destruction achieved, and it was vengeance.

The torches crackled as the tension between them simmered, and he said, "It's a problem for you as well, Your Majesty, because if you won't give me what I want, this is how it's going to go. I will withdraw my armies and cool my heels in Gamdesh while the united armies of Mudamora and Anukastre go to war against you. It will be long and taxing, but eventually they'll triumph. At which point I'll make *my* move, returning to Mudamora, crushing its weakened army until they submit to my authority and then funneling the fruits of your failure back to the East."

Rufina did not so much as blink as she said, "I've heard your *funnels* were destroyed by the Maarin."

He'd been prepared for her to know that detail, but Marcus still silently cursed.

"All the more reason for me to withdraw to Gamdesh and put my resources to securing more paths. For I assure you, the Maarin's gambit will not work twice." Resting his elbows on the table, Marcus said, "We can work together and both achieve what we want, Your Majesty. Or you can make yourself a problem that I need to solve, which will not go well for you. I will get what I want, one way or another. I always do."

Silence.

Silence was normally his weapon, but for all everything he'd said was true, Marcus felt as though he was on the backfoot, the desire to keep talking, to elicit some form of reaction from her nearly overwhelming him.

"And why is it," she finally said, "that you believe that Mudamora will triumph when their dead all rise to serve me?"

"Because the blight has risen and been destroyed before." He gave her a slight smile, then spun a lie she had no reason not to believe. "The library in Revat was a wondrous source of information, although I was not the first to discover the secrets within it. That honor goes to Kitaryia Falorn, though I have looked upon what research she left behind. Our shared enemies know how to destroy your greatest weapon, so I strongly suggest we destroy them first."

Rufina's eyes narrowed, the first reaction he'd managed to provoke.

"I've given the Mudamorians an ultimatum: hand over Kitaryia Falorn and Malahi Rowenes or die. Given the threat they are facing, I think they will leap at the opportunity."

"They can leap all they want at it," Rufina answered. "Killian Calorian will not stand idle while harm comes to his queen, and our mutual deserter Agrippa is remarkably good at causing trouble, especially where Malahi Rowenes is concerned." Her head tilted. "I heard Agrippa paid you a visit today. What did he say?"

"A great deal about fighting for the side of good." Marcus shrugged. "He's always been easily swayed by women. Likes to play hero. I think when it comes down to it, he'll show his true colors."

"Yet instead of killing him, you killed one of your own."

Whether she had a spy in his ranks or was watching from afar, Marcus wasn't sure, but he suspected lying would not serve him well. "I don't suffer those who betray me to live. Agrippa's time will come."

"They won't surrender either woman," Rufina said after a long moment of silence. "It has to be done by force. And it needs to be done now."

"Why? Time is our friend, not theirs. I'll not spend the lives of good men when time and hunger will do the work for me." He gave her a long look. "And in truth, the same could be said of you. Why haven't you attacked?"

She didn't answer.

"Afraid you'll lose to Calorian? Again."

Rufina's jaw tightened.

"I think you wear Derin's crown not because you enjoy the tedium of rule but as a means to an end," he said. "Let us ally to achieve that end, because in doing so, we will both be satisfied."

"What is it that you think I want?"

"Revenge," he answered. "Against the Six."

Rufina's breath caught.

"I'm sure you are aware of the Empire's sentiment toward paganism," he continued. "What happened in Galinha, Aracam, Emrant, and Revat. What has happened to every one of the marked who has stood in my path." Leaning across the table so that his mouth was near her ear, Marcus murmured, "We can tear them all down, you and me. You will have your revenge, and I will have it so that none stand above us, save the ones we serve."

As he sat back in his chair, Marcus could see the yearning behind those eyes ringed with fire. Part of him wondered what wrong she'd suffered to allow her desire for revenge to consume her so. To allow hate to burn away her humanity until she cared not for those she crushed beneath her feet in pursuit of her goal.

Then Rufina's gaze focused on him again, and she said, "You desire to rule the world, don't you, Legatus?"

"One might argue that I already control most of it."

She huffed out a soft breath that held grudging admiration, but then said, "You wish for everyone to dance to the beat of your drum, but what will you do when there's nothing else to conquer?"

Marcus allowed the darkness that lurked in his own soul to stare out at her. "There's always something to conquer, Your Majesty. Ally with me in this fight, and I will show you how to rule the world."

104

KILLIAN

"He was being an ass in refusing to speak anything but Cel," Agrippa said, from where he sat his horse next to Killian. "He speaks Mudamorian perfectly. He just did it to piss you off, which means he sees you as a threat. And that, my friend, is something to be proud of."

"Just because I didn't kill him then doesn't mean I won't kill the arrogant prick later."

Agrippa laughed. "I'd say he gets better the more time you spend around him, but that's how he is."

"What did Teriana see in him?"

"He *is* painfully good looking. Being stuck in the same room as you two was honestly one of the worst experiences of my life, and I hope I never have to repeat it. Spending all my days with you is already destroying my ego."

Killian cast a sideways glance at the other man, allowing himself to be distracted from his irritation about being a cog in *Legatus Marcus's* plan. "Why? Everyone is always going on about how good looking you are."

"You don't."

"I talk about how you're a great fighter."

"That only makes me feel worse. Like being the first runner up at a prize hog contest and being given a consolation pat on the head before being turned into bacon."

Rolling his eyes at the sky, Killian shook his head. "I'm not saying it."

"But you're definitely thinking it."

Despite himself, Killian laughed, Agrippa's inane chatter taking the edge off his anxiety, as the other man had intended. But for all his jokes, Killian could feel Agrippa's own tension. Tension he shared, because this entire plan hinged on their enemy holding to his word.

"How will we be able to tell that they're following through?" Malahi asked, coming up behind them and stopping her horse next to Agrippa. Lydia was next to her, both women wearing hooded cloaks with chain mail beneath.

"We won't," Agrippa muttered. "At least, not until it's too late for us to do anything about it. I doubt there are more than a handful of men in his ranks who know the real plan, so when they march, it will be with intent. He keeps his plans close. Has trust issues that I don't think have improved in our time apart."

"What if it's a trick?" Malahi asked. "What if he lied? What if he's actually allied with Rufina?"

Agrippa didn't answer, which was an answer in and of itself.

Lydia circled her horse around next to Killian's, her eyes on the army in the distance as she reached out to take his hand. "What do you think?"

Her fingers were cold in his grip, betraying the nerves that didn't show on her face.

"Marcus has a goal in mind, and we aren't it."

"That doesn't mean he's going to hold to the plan. He doesn't have to help us to achieve that goal."

"He's not helping us." Killian squeezed her fingers. "Rufina just pissed him off and made herself the common enemy. We're merely the tool he's going to use to strike at her."

Which annoyed him to no end, as did Lydia's willingness to just let what that asshole had done to her, and to Teriana, be bygones. To let him ride away on his golden horse to pursue his own ends without paying any price for the horror he'd caused. Marcus deserved to die, and to die badly, and the *only* reason Killian wasn't set on making that happen was that he *needed* the bastard's involvement if there was to be any hope of winning this. And *that* pissed him off even more.

"You're seething," Lydia said. "He's not the enemy."

"He's *my* enemy." Everything about Marcus had been *exactly* as he'd expected. Arrogant, condescending, and wholly convinced of his own superiority. Dictating the plan in Cel so that Killian was forced to rely on Agrippa's translation, as though Killian's opinion of what to do with his own army was entirely irrelevant. "He's a prick."

Agrippa gave a soft laugh, but Malahi's mutter of, "Don't make it worse," kept the man from adding further commentary.

Lydia was silent, and Killian regretted his words as he saw the tension in her expression. The uncertainty. Then she said, "I hate that this is all under Marcus's control. That we are standing here passively, hoping for the best with everything on the line while he risks nothing."

Killian felt the same way, but he also knew there was a reason it had to be this way. "For this to work, there can be no communication between camps," he said. "I don't like it, but if I were him, I'd have done the same."

"But what is your gut telling you?" she asked. "Because you wouldn't be so tense if you were certain this would work."

She carried a large enough burden, and if he could, Killian would have carried this one for her. But for all her hand was clasped in his, Lydia hadn't asked the question as his lover. She'd asked as Queen of Mudamora. "It tells me that while Marcus's goal may have changed, others in his army might feel differently. It tells me that his control over his army might not be as absolute as he believes. And without total control, his plan won't work."

Lydia exhaled a shaky breath, then gave a tight nod.

Either way, the dice had been rolled. Horns bellowed out from the Cel army, but as ranks began to march, Astara landed before Killian. The horses shuffled restlessly as she shifted into human form and Lydia pulled off her cloak to hand to the woman, though the shifter seemed as comfortable nude as not.

Donning Lydia's cloak, Astara said, "The army of the dead are on the march."

"All of them?" Killian asked, and the shifter shook her head.

"No. She kept several hundred around the xenthier stem."

Killian had anticipated that. "Have you spotted Rufina?"

"She marches with her host, surrounded by her corrupted. Her army will strike Dareena's line right as the Cel strike yours."

Killian's skin began to crawl, because it couldn't be this easy. His eyes flicked to the distant army, picking out the golden horse that Marcus sat upon, wishing there was some way to communicate with them that wouldn't risk discovery. "How long do we have until Rufina reaches Dareena's lines?"

"Half an hour, if that," the shifter answered, then to Killian's shock, the woman's face crumpled. "We cannot hope to win this. We need to flee."

"There is nowhere to flee *to.*" Killian hated that he had to deceive his people to see this through. But all it would take was one slip of the tongue to one of the blighters he was sure were hidden within the ranks, and Rufina would know their plan. "The Gamdeshians have retaken their nation, but if we run to them, the Cel will follow. As will the blight."

And all hope would be lost.

"This is where we stand our ground," he said to Astara. "Do the Six proud and take to the skies. Keep sights on Rufina for me, so that when we win this fight, her blood will be the next to decorate my sword."

Astara wiped the tears from her face. "I'll watch her."

In a dizzying blur of flesh shifting to feathers, the hawk was gone.

105

MARCUS

"Scouts are signaling that Rufina's army is on the march," Felix said. "Everyone is in position."

And everyone, save Felix and Servius, believed that the alliance with Rufina was real. There had been no way around it given how much Rufina had seemed to know about the inner workings of his camp. Which meant everything, *everything,* depended on the legions hearing and obeying his commands.

Commands that he couldn't give until the final seconds because the moment Rufina sensed his ruse, she'd fall back to protect the xenthier stem.

The first part of the plan was simple. He'd merely refused to commit to an attack unless Rufina attacked at the same time. Her urgent desire to see Lydia dead, in combination with her certainty that he wanted the same, proved worth the risk of moving her army away from the xenthier.

The second part of the plan was anything but simple.

This is what your men are trained for, Marcus reminded himself. *This is what makes Celendor's legions the best fighting force on Reath.*

Reminders that did nothing to ease the frantic gallop of his heart as he mounted his mare and rode to look out over the field. There was no mistaking Calorian standing on the ridgeline, weapons gleaming in the sun, and as Marcus watched, a massive hawk landed and shifted into human form. Even from a distance, he recognized Astara, and Marcus didn't push away the guilt he felt over what he'd ordered done to her. Calorian had tasked her with watching Rufina, which meant this would be the confirmation that the xenthier was as unguarded as Rufina would ever dare leave it.

Come on! he silently screamed, hating his lack of control in this moment.

Then Agrippa withdrew a green scarf and tied it to his right arm.

It was time.

Marcus cleared his throat to tell his men to proceed, but before he could give the order, he spotted a scout galloping toward him.

Sliding to a stop, the legionnaire said, "Sir, the Fifty-First are here. They're marching this way."

No.

Shock rippled through the Thirty-Seventh as the report spread, because the last they'd all seen of the young legion was them disappearing back to Celendor via the stem in Gamdesh. Only Marcus, Felix, and Servius knew the true fate of the Fifty-First. Only they knew that Cassius had sent Austornic and his men into a blight-ravaged land where they had succumbed to the poison. Only they knew that the Fifty-First had risen from death as puppets of the Seventh god and joined Rufina's forces.

Yet the secret of their presence in Mudamora was a secret no longer, for as Marcus lifted a spyglass to his eye, it revealed their neat ranks marching toward him. Revealed Austornic's familiar form near the head of the line, the boy heading directly toward him.

Marcus knew exactly why Rufina had sent the Fifty-First to him. The Queen of Derin did not wholly trust his intentions, so she'd sent in spies to ensure he stuck to the plan.

Felix reined his horse so close to Marcus's that their knees banged together. "What do you want to do?"

If he reacted the wrong way, Rufina would know that Marcus was aware the Fifty-First were blighters. And if she knew that, she'd suspect *everything.* Marcus watched his plan fall apart in his mind's eye, along with any hope that Lydia might, in saving her own people, save the Fifty-First as well. "Don't look concerned," he said under his breath. "Act as though we are shocked yet delighted to have them rejoin us."

"Right," Felix muttered. "Reinforcements."

The ranks parted to allow Nic and his bodyguard through. At first glance, they appeared themselves. Whole and unharmed. But as they passed, he saw frowns rise on the faces of the Thirty-Seventh.

And that was when the smell hit him.

Vomit and excrement. Marcus's eyes picked out the stains on their clothes. On their skin. Signs of how they'd perished, succumbing to blight poisoning, dying in agony only to rise again as Rufina's puppets with no bother given to cleaning up their corpses.

Did she think he wouldn't notice the wrongness in them? Had she gotten lazy? Or did Rufina want him to know they were dead?

Nic stopped before him. "It's good to see you, sir. Cassius sent us through to a terminus in Mudaire, and we've marched hard to reach you."

"Impeccable timing." Only a lifetime of practice kept the shake from Marcus's voice. Dismounting, he approached Nic, and though he knew it wasn't the boy who'd shadowed him for months behind those familiar eyes, he said, "I'm sorry I sent you back. It was a mistake."

Nic ducked his head, color rising to his cheeks, the action so painfully well mimicked that it was all Marcus could do to keep his emotions in check.

Gods damn you! he silently screamed at Rufina. *They didn't deserve this.*

And it was his fault.

In his rage, he'd sent Nic and the Fifty-First right back into Cassius's hands, and he *knew* that the Dictator had sent them through that stem into the blight fully expecting them to die.

"It's fine, sir," Nic answered. "I shouldn't have questioned you."

Marcus needed to be the heartless commander that Rufina expected because she was able to see through Nic's eyes. Able to hear through his ears.

Yet he also remembered what Lydia had told him. That while Nic was not in control of his body, he could see. Could hear.

Could feel.

It made Marcus want to fall to his knees and beg the boy's forgiveness. To tell Nic that sending him away had been one of the greatest mistakes of his life.

Instead, he said, "No time for questions now. We've allied with the Queen of Derin, and her army is on the march. Within the hour, I want the Mudamorian army and their allies either dead or offering surrender."

"Yes, sir."

Ignoring the stink and the crushing ache in his chest, Marcus slung an arm around Nic's shoulders and led him forward. "This is the plan."

106

KILLIAN

"They're dead," Lydia whispered, watching the new ranks of child legionnaires merge with the rest of the Cel army. Marcus walked with his arm slung around one boy's shoulders, their heads together. "He does realize that, doesn't he? He believed me?"

"I don't know." Killian clenched his teeth, his mark screaming *danger*, but he couldn't tell whether the threat was the dead legion or the very much alive ones.

Or something else entirely.

Panicked horns sounded from behind him, and a heartbeat later, Astara landed, already shifted before her feet hit the ground. "Rufina's army has attacked," she said. "Dareena and Xadrian are engaged, but they're outnumbered five to one!"

"Shit!" His horse pawed the ground beneath him, sensing his agitation. The plan was falling apart before his very eyes, because even if Marcus hadn't double-crossed them, his strategy wouldn't work. Not with five thousand of his ranks under Rufina's control.

"What do we do?" Malahi said. "How do we get through?"

I don't know. "I'm thinking. Agrippa, can you tell what he's planning?"

The Cel horns bellowed, the ranks beginning their slow press forward.

Agrippa lowered his spyglass, his face pale as he shook his head. "I can't tell. He put the Fifty-First behind the Thirty-Seventh. I . . . I can't imagine that he'd risk putting the walking dead at his own legion's back if he's sticking with our plan. I don't know. I . . . don't know."

All eyes turned to Killian. Expecting him to have answers.

Lydia's hand closed on his, and she said, "What does your gut say?"

Killian looked out over the approaching army, seeing the catapults being pulled into place, faces of the men so uniformly grim and resolute that there was no doubt that they, at least, believed this was real.

Then, across the field, his eyes locked with Marcus's, the other man's mouth moving in a single word.

And though Killian spoke not a word of Cel, he knew *that* order when he saw it.

Slamming the visor down on his helmet, Killian shouted, "Today we fight for the liberty of all of Reath! Follow my lead, and charge!"

Nodding once at Bercola, Killian dug in his heels and his horse leapt into a gallop.

With a roar, five hundred mounted soldiers and two thousand giants hurtled down the slope toward the army countless times their number, the thunder of feet and hooves rivaling the worst of Gespurn's storms.

Horns blew and the legion's march paused, the front ranks dropping to one knee, shields in front of them, the next row interweaving their shields above, then next row a level higher. A wall of steel out of which thousands of spears jutted forth.

A wall of death.

Toward which galloped tens of thousands of pounds of horseflesh followed by giants carrying weapons as large as Killian was tall.

This was a test of wills.

A test of nerve.

"Steady!" he shouted, seeing Marcus's mouth move, no doubt saying the same. "Steady!"

A hundred paces.

Fifty.

Yet still no signal.

Doubt screamed through Killian's veins, fear that he'd led everyone who mattered to him astray and that Mudamora's only hope was about to die on Cel steel.

Thirty.

Twenty.

This isn't going to work! his fear howled. *Your cavalry is going to die on those spears. Bercola's giants will die on those spears. Lydia will be captured. Rufina will have her victory.*

But then his eyes locked with Marcus's over the sea of shields and spears, and Killian's gut said, *steady.*

The massive legionnaire on a horse next to Marcus lifted a horn and blew a series of notes.

With no hesitation, the legion ranks parted, creating a ruler-straight path through the thousands of men. At the back of his mind, Killian marveled at the training and discipline that allowed such a feat, but there was no time to dwell on it as he galloped toward the opening of shields and spears, shouting at his lines, "Follow me! They are not our enemy this day!"

Shock filled the faces of his soldiers, but they shifted track to follow him even as Bercola roared at the giants to do the same.

Killian didn't risk another glance back to make sure that everyone was following, focusing on pure speed as he galloped down the lane the legions had made for him. In his periphery, he saw the tension in the legionnaires' faces as they waited for the order to attack. It wasn't lost on Killian that if Marcus wanted to kill him and his entire force now, it would be easy. Yet that wasn't the fear that drove him to push Surly for more speed.

It was the dead legion at the rear.

The thousands of legionnaires who didn't answer to Marcus but to Rufina.

They hadn't reacted yet, all standing stock-still in a way that no one would ever perceive as human. But Killian saw the moment that Rufina realized Marcus's betrayal, because the child legionnaires all collectively twitched.

As one, they broke ranks and began to sprint toward the lane the living legions had made for Killian's forces.

He had less than a minute to get through.

Faster.

Horns blared, the living legionnaires shifting with unease and confusion at the actions of their younger comrades.

Hold, he silently pleaded even as he watched the dead legion race to cut off his path. No part of how they moved was human—it appeared for all the world like a swarm of insects racing to a feast. If one fell, the others stormed overtop, grinding their fellow into the mud, their only care for blocking Killian's path.

Faster.

He leaned over his warhorse's neck, urging him on, counting down the lines of men left until he'd be in the open.

The horde of dead drew closer, the front-runners lifting their weapons.

Killian fought the urge to draw his sword, knowing it would only provoke the living around him.

Closer by the second, and Killian could see now how truly young the dead legion was. They'd never reach Finn's age, and though there was nothing human in their eyes, he knew the souls of the boys they'd once been were still inside. Watching their bodies being used by the Corrupter and powerless to stop it.

Killian glanced over his shoulder. Lydia was right on his heels, as were Malahi and Agrippa. But their cavalry and Bercola's giants were stretched in a long line behind them, and most wouldn't make it before the dead legion attacked.

Not without help.

"They're not alive!" he shouted at the legionnaires behind the walls of shields and spears to either side of him, all men with the 37 on their chests. "Those boys fell to the blight! The Fifty-First are dead!"

They understood his words, eyes flicking to the horde, then back to him. But for all they heard him, Killian suspected that if he attacked the dead legion, he'd be dead in an instant.

"Look at them!" he screamed, because if they didn't help, this was over. "The Corrupter killed your comrades and now uses them as puppets. Look!"

Horror was rising across their faces, grief as pure as Killian had ever seen as the truth settled upon them, but the Thirty-Seventh Legion held their ground. Held to the orders of their commander, who it seemed intended to betray them after all.

Then a horn blew.

107

MARCUS

If the boy next to him had been Nic in truth, he'd have reacted in a heartbeat as Servius blew the horn to signal a split in the ranks. But the corpse standing next to Marcus stood frozen for long seconds as Calorian led his cavalry, and a towering column of giants, into the narrow lane before it said, "What are you doing?"

Marcus clung to the plan for a moment longer to buy Calorian time. "I thought you'd learned your lesson about asking too many questions."

But the ruse was up.

The brown of Nic's eyes was consumed by darkness until only twin voids remained, then the boy's face twisted into a snarl. "This will cost you," a voice that was not Nic's hissed, and Marcus recoiled.

"The Fifty-First just broke ranks!" Servius shouted. "They're moving to block Calorian's path. Orders?"

"Hold the lines!"

Marcus knew he should be watching the field, but he couldn't look away from Nic's face, his stomach twisting with sickness at the monster who now looked out. It said, "Don't have the nerve to kill them, do you?"

"They're already dead," he answered. "You are not Austornic. You are only using his body as a puppet, and for that, you will pay a heavy price, Rufina."

"They're going to intercept!" Servius shouted. "There's not enough time!"

The monster laughed. "Your plan isn't going to work, Legatus. My puppets will make short work of your new allies unless you turn your men on them. But you can't do it, can you? Not when you hold the hope in your heart that Kitaryia will bring them all back and spare you the guilt consuming what little you have of a soul."

The mockery in the monster's voice made Marcus want to scream because no matter what he did, a toll would be paid in blood.

"You can't turn your men on the boys you were supposed to protect," the monster whispered. "You can't give the order to cut them down. Cut them up. Grind them into the mud. You don't have it in you, and so I will have my victory."

"Marcus!" Servius shouted. "The Mudamorians aren't going to make it!"

Tears ran down his cheeks because unless Lydia broke Rufina's hold on the Fifty-First's bodies and mind, they'd forever be her puppets. But if he gave the order to kill them in truth, there'd be no bringing them back.

There was no victory to be had in this war.

Grasping the corpse's shoulders, Marcus said, "If you can hear me, Nic, I'm sorry. I'm sorry for failing you, but know that I'm going to do the right thing. I'm going to do what you would have wanted. I swear it."

And before he could lose his nerve, Marcus pulled a knife from his belt and drove it up into Nic's skull so he would not have to witness what was about to happen to his men.

The corpse slumped, and Marcus caught him, holding the boy who'd been a younger brother to him as he died. Lowering Nic to the ground, he stumbled to Servius and yanked the horn from his friend's hands. Sucking in a deep breath, he blew a series of notes, knowing that in following these orders, the Thirty-Seventh would never be the same again.

108

KILLIAN

As the last note faded, the rear ranks of the Thirty-Seventh moved, intercepting the horde of legion blighters with a wall of steel and spears.

But the blighters didn't hesitate.

Killian watched in horror as they died by the dozens. Then the hundreds.

And still they came.

Killian broke clear of the Thirty-Seventh, reining in his horse even as he shouted to Lydia, "Go! Ride!"

Pale-faced, she galloped Seahawk across the open plain, Malahi and Agrippa flanking her as they headed toward the forest, cavalry galloping fast and Bercola's giants easily keeping pace. All while death unlike anything Killian had ever seen piled up not fifty paces from where his horse stood.

Horns bellowed, more ranks moving to reinforce the lines, and Surly reared, giving Killian a clear view over the sea of shifting men. Marcus held a horn, his face splattered with blood, and his mouth formed a single word.

Go.

Digging in his heels, Killian drove his horse into a gallop and chased the tail of his cavalry disappearing into the trees.

As though eager to escape the carnage, Surly put on an extra boost of speed, and within moments he'd caught up to the last riders, passing them until he was alongside his companions. Agrippa's face was slick with tears, but he only said, "We have to be quick! She'll be sending reinforcements to the stem, and we have to beat them to it!"

Nodding, Killian moved closer to Lydia, who was pressed close to Seahawk's neck with Gwen and Lena riding on her heels. "Are you all right?"

Her face turned to him, green eyes full of tears. "Rufina knows we can save the blighters. That's why she made them do that. So there is no hope of getting them back."

Having seen the looks on the faces of the legionnaires as they were forced to kill their own, Killian suspected Rufina's motivations were darker still, but he only said, "She knows we're coming for her."

And this time, he was going to kill her.

They wove through the winding paths, the air thick and humid, the stink of blight growing as they flanked the front lines and headed into Rufina's territory.

It was truly the land of the dead.

The ground was ashen from the fire Killian had sent north, the trees nothing but charred skeletons and debris thick on the ground. But worse were the streams and pools of blight. The horses attempted to leap over them, but it was not long until everyone in the company was splattered with black murk. Which meant the hours of life for anyone not marked were severely numbered.

Still they pressed onward, deeper into the deadlands that had once been Mudamora. The horses began to falter and stumble, some willfully resisting traveling farther. Knowing they were close, Killian slowed Surly's pace, then dropped his reins in favor of his bow.

Only to draw up short as they exited the charred trees.

"You're going to need more arrows," Agrippa whispered, as they looked out at a sprawling lake of blight, at the center of which sat a small island containing a glittering xenthier stem.

Far more arrows, because surrounding the lake were hundreds upon hundreds of blighters.

109

MARCUS

Marcus sat in the dirt cradling Nic's body, what should have been silence broken by the screams of the injured. By the retching of those pushed past physical endurance. And by the weeping of those whose minds had been pushed past what anyone could endure.

Under the control of Rufina's blight, the Fifty-First had fought past human capacity, crawling onward no matter how badly they were injured. Attacking and attacking, those among the living given no choice but to deliver the killing blows required to make them cease the onslaught. Men Marcus had never once seen break had fallen to their knees and let the undead kill them rather than fight on. Had turned and run, leaving their brothers to see the battle through. No matter how they'd reacted, Marcus knew none of them would ever be the same. That none of them would ever forget the horror.

Which was as it should be, because to forget would be the greatest crime of all.

The masses of men around him stirred, and Drusus pushed through them to sit at Marcus's side, his eyes taking in Austornic.

"I've been doing this longer than you've been alive," the older legatus finally said. "I've seen more than you can ever know, and I will say, it does not get worse than what you have endured today. What we have all endured today, though the Thirty-Seventh and Forty-First took the worst of it."

Marcus swallowed, his mouth dry as sand. "It was my fault."

"I know." Drusus slung an arm around his shoulders, thick arm squeezing Marcus tight in a way that made him feel younger than he had in so very long. So incredibly out of his depth, and yet it had been his actions that had brought them to this moment.

"But this isn't the time for you to break, Prodigy. You can't lead men to the edge of oblivion and then leave them hanging because it was harder than you thought it would be." Drusus sighed. "You've been scheming. You have a plan. That much was abundantly obvious to all of us, even if it didn't go quite as you had hoped."

The plan had been to give Lydia and her allies an opportunity to reach the blight. To give her a chance at destroying it on the hopes that those who'd succumbed to it might be brought back to life. Yet as Marcus stared down at Austornic's corpse, he knew that no matter how things fell for Lydia's plans, the Fifty-First would not come back from this. Knew that Mudamora and its allies might have victory, but it would not be a legion victory, for their enemy still sipped wine on the far side of the Endless Seas.

Lucius Cassius.

Marcus's jaw tightened. "We've been fighting the wrong fight, Drusus. Our eyes have been on the wrong enemy."

Drusus banged a hand against Marcus's armored back. "You'll not get any quarrel from me on that. So get up, and get us marching in the right direction, boy."

Marcus carefully set Nic's body on the ground, ensuring the boy's eyes remained closed, and then allowed Drusus to haul him to his feet. All around them, the ranks were in shambles. Men sitting in the dirt, or staring into the distance, or wandering aimlessly, all while the Mudamorians fought on against Rufina's forces. Fought for their land and the lives of those they loved.

It was past time the legions did the same.

Amarin approached, holding the reins of Marcus's golden mare. The sight of his old servant hollowed Marcus's stomach, and he said, "I'm sorry, Amarin. I'm sorry it took me so long to get to this point."

"You're here now," Amarin replied, holding the horse steady while Marcus mounted, then straightening his cloak across the mare's haunches. "See it through."

At the sight of him, the Thirty-Seventh lifted their heads. Got to their feet, and then pulled up brothers who struggled to do the same. Centurions cleared their throats and barked orders to form lines. His legion, though a shadow of what it had been before this battle, stood tall. As did the Forty-First and the other legions that formed his ranks.

Surrounded by the bodies of the fallen, Marcus set aside his grief and spoke. "We have been fighting the wrong war."

His words were carried back through the ranks, making them as loud as a storm.

"While we conquered the West, Lucius Cassius has risen as a tyrant over Celendor and its provinces, using steel and fist to beat our people into submission even as he steals their children to bolster the ranks he uses to oppress. Poverty and famine and disease run rampant through the provinces, all while the patricians of the Hill turn a blind eye to the toll, unwilling to risk themselves or their coffers to check the Dictator's deeds. A small few stand against him, but what hope do they have against the man who wields this?" He gestured out to the tens of thousands of legionnaires surrounding him. "None, is the answer. Cassius's power will only grow as he climbs on the backs of common men and women, reaching beyond the voters, beyond the senate, until he grasps the crown that has not been worn for generations. Until he is Emperor, his rule untouchable, his rule for *life*."

The men shifted restlessly, expressions grim.

"Since the day we were sent to Lescendor, we have been told our duty is to serve. To fight. To be the blade of Mother Empire. But above all else, we have been told to obey. To go where we are told to go, kill who we are told to kill, destroy what we are told to destroy, and to never question whether what we do is right. To question is to disobey, and to disobey is treason, and treason is death. Not one of us asked for this life, and if Cassius has his way, not one of us will ever escape it. There is a word for what we are, and I tell you, it is *not* soldier."

He waited for his words to travel through the bloodied men, seeing anger rise through their grief. An old anger that had always simmered but which he now fueled bright.

"For the sake of gold to fund his rise to power, Cassius ordered us onto poisoned ground using bribery and threats with no care for how many of us lived or died. If you need more proof of how little Cassius values legion lives, know that it was he who sent the Fifty-First alone into the blight. But he would not have been able to do so if I had not broken my promise to them. It was not you who killed them today—it was me." His voice cracked on the last, and silence stretched.

"I swore to protect them until they were ready to protect themselves, but instead I cast them back into the arms of Cassius when Austornic questioned my methods, my justifications, my goals. The deaths of Legatus Austornic and all of the Fifty-First are on my hands, not yours. Nic defied the Empire's desire for more conquest—my own desire for more conquest—and he died for it, sure and true."

Marcus paused, allowing his words to disseminate. Allowing them to take what he'd said into their souls, full well knowing that he was giving them the opportunity to turn their back on him. To cast him down. And that they'd be right to do it.

"There is not a one of us standing here who is not guilty of blindly following commands. Of doing the worst while washing our hands of culpability because what choice have we but to obey? None more so than me, for in recent days, weeks, months, I have embodied that belief. Embodied that villainy, all while burying my head in denial by saying *this is how it must be. I have no choice, and therefore what I have done is not my fault.* Except that I did have a choice. I did *not* have to obey, which means that every death, every hurt, every loss that has come by choosing *this*"—he gestured around—"is on me. But also on *you*, because just as I had the choice to defy the authority of the Dictator, the Senate, the Empire, you had the choice to defy *me* and did not."

His words rolled through the ranks of men like a wave, and instead of row after row of legionnaires, Marcus saw men. Individuals with their own minds, their own hearts, each grappling with the awful truth that he set before them.

We do not have to obey.

"The legions serve the Empire!" he shouted, taking the Thirty-Seventh's standard from Servius. "But the Dictator is not the Empire. The Senate is not the Empire. It is the *people* who are the Empire, and so it is the people we should serve. The people we should protect. Instead we have abandoned them to suffer while we fight to fatten the pockets of the very man who does them harm.

"We are not the sons of the Empire, we are the sons of the people. We are Bardeen, Sibal, and Phera. We are Sibern, Atlia, and Faul. We are Timia, Denastres, and Chersome. We are Celendor." Marcus surveyed the masses of men, seeing a rage long contained rising in their hearts. "I say it is time we return to the Empire to do our duty. I say we return to the Empire and remind Lucius Cassius who rules."

"The people!" the men screamed. "The people!"

"I will not ask you to follow me. I will not ask you to obey me." He lifted the standard into the air, his arm shaking beneath the weight of so much gold. "But I ask for you to march with me and return to the East. To join me in one last battle, because together, we will remind the Dictator that the legions are people. And that the people are legion!"

The roar of the men was deafening, fists and weapons and legion standards lifting in the air.

"All well and good, Prodigy," Drusus said, rocking on his heels. "But how the *fuck* are we going to get back east? Your girl blew up all our lines of retreat."

"Not all." Marcus cast a backward glance at the smoke rising in the distance where the fight raged on. But not their fight. "She left us one. Now let's march."

110

KILLIAN

Killian stared at the mass of Mudamorian undead surrounding the lake of blight. They'd have to cut through them, leaving unsavable corpses in their wake, then wade the horses through poison to get to the stem, which meant everyone in their company who wasn't marked wouldn't be long for this world.

A terrible toll, but Killian knew that every one of the soldiers in their company would ride into that lake knowing it likely meant their lives. That was not what had drawn them up short.

It was that every one of the blighters standing before them was a Mudamorian child.

"I hate her," Lydia whispered. "How is it possible for one woman to have so much evil in her soul?"

Malahi rode alongside them. She was breathing hard from the gallop, her amber eyes staring bleakly out over the dead. "How do we get through them?"

"Slaughter," Agrippa answered, ever Malahi's deadly shadow. "Rufina thinks we won't be able to do it."

Killian gave soft orders to hold back, but below, none of the blighters so much as even twitched. As though they didn't even see them, despite being only thirty yards away.

Which meant that Rufina's focus had to be elsewhere. Either on Marcus or Dareena, or . . .

"Killian . . ." Lydia whispered. "Something is wrong."

"I know." He pressed his horse close to hers, Bercola moving to hold the reins of both animals. "If this is the path to Deadground, why isn't her focus here? Why aren't there at least some of the corrupted here?"

"Perhaps she's distracted by the Cel? Or Dareena and Xadrian's forces," Malahi said. "Maybe we're winning?"

"No," Killian answered. "Rufina knew Deadground was our goal."

Lydia's face was blanched of color, and he understood why. They'd spent every tool in their arsenal to get this far, and for what?

Bercola exhaled a long breath. "Eoten Isle will deal with the blighters, Killian. Those are not our children, and while our hands will be stained for the rest of our days, the hurt will not cut us as deep."

"We can't destroy them," Lydia whispered. "If the children can't be brought back, what are we fighting for?"

"I don't think we have to. At least, not yet." Killian unhooked the bow from his back. Nocking an arrow, he aimed at the distant xenthier.

And let loose.

He watched the arrow sail over the blighters' heads without them noticing. But rather than disappearing into the stem, it struck the crystal dead on.

"Shit," Agrippa whispered. "It's a terminus. This isn't the way to Deadground. It's a decoy."

Wings flapped above, and Astara fell to the ground before them. The shifter was bleeding heavily from what appeared to be multiple bite wounds, no doubt from one of the deimos. Slipping off the side of her horse, Lydia ran to Astara's side and the shifter's wounds disappeared beneath her touch.

"It's Rufina!" Astara gasped. "You told me to watch her. I was tracking her from the air when I was attacked, but not before I saw her and her corrupted go through another stem. Worse still, now that she knows the legion attack was a ploy, her main army has disengaged from Dareena and Xadrian and is marching this way." She swallowed hard. "*Running* this way. Thousands of them. You're going to be overrun."

"Where is the genesis stem?" Killian demanded.

"East of here. I can show you."

Before anyone could move, the blighter children began to stir, heads swiveling and eyes latching upon them.

As one, they began to walk.

In the same uncanny way as the dead legion that had attacked Marcus's forces, they moved in total lockstep, any individual too damaged to move properly falling beneath the feet of the others. Faces vacant.

Eyes fixed on Killian, and he knew that it was Rufina who looked out.

"Astara, get us to that stem!"

The woman shifted, taking wing and flying low. Killian led them, but Lydia kept close to his warhorse's heels. Their friends and comrades followed, running down a narrow track through the dead woods, horses and giants leaping over the blight. All while blighter children pursued, the dead caring not for paths, instead crashing through the blackened trees.

"Keep close!" Killian shouted at her. "We're going to have to be quick."

Never mind that they'd be going through a path blind to what was on the other side. Never mind that there was nothing to stop the blighters from following them through.

As if hearing his thoughts, Bercola shouted, "Killian, get them through the path! We'll hold them off for as long as we can."

It was a death sentence.

The blighters knew no fear. Knew no pain. They'd keep coming and coming . . .

Lydia shouted, "No! We won't leave anyone behind!"

But Killian looked over his shoulder and met Bercola's gaze, giving the giantess a tight nod. A silent promise to see her one day when the gods had claimed them both, because this war would not be won without sacrifice. And it would be his old friend who made it.

Agrippa urged his mount for more speed, passing Malahi and Lydia and reining close to Killian. "Having done it more than once—those first seconds when you pass through that xenthier are when you're most likely to die. At best, she's going to have archers waiting to shoot anyone who comes through. At worst, the corrupted are ready to take your head off. Worse still, we don't know the lay of the land on the far side. Could be into a cave or into a pool of water. Could be a long drop. So what's the plan?"

"Trust the Six," Killian answered. "And myself."

"So, no plan, then?" Agrippa shook his head. "Got it."

Astara abruptly veered up, flapping a dozen feet above the ground, and Killian said, "Give me the count of two hundred to get through, then you come. Lydia and Malahi follow. We handle the killing, and they do the rest. That enough of a plan for you?"

"It'll do."

Leaping off the side of Surly, Killian checked his supply of weapons, then drew his sword as he approached the black crystal jutting from the ground. "Start counting," he called to Agrippa, then he reached out a hand and took hold of the xenthier.

Everything turned white, and Killian was struck with the sense of an endless void of nothing. Yet every instinct screamed *parry*, and as the world reappeared, he lifted his blade even as the icy cold of the north hit him in the face.

The clang of steel striking steel filled his ears, and Killian rolled, coming to his feet in time to block another blow. The impact made his arm shudder, his mind registering that one of the corrupted held the blade even as his instincts screamed of an attack from behind.

Whirling, he ducked under a swing that would have taken his head off, then plunged his blade through the woman's heart. His sword stuck on her ribs as he tried to pull it clear, and abandoning the weapon, he drew a knife and threw.

It struck a man in the eye. The corrupted shrieked and staggered back, the injury not enough to kill him. But there was no time to finish the job as another corrupted approached, her movements too quick to be human. If Killian hadn't been marked by Tremon, the slash of her knife would have opened his jugular. Instead, he got his arm in the way, wincing as the force of her blow drove broken links of chain mail into his flesh. Ignoring the pain, he drew another knife.

Their blades clashed once. Twice. Three times, each reaction faster than thought, only endless hours of training keeping him from being sliced to ribbons as she pressed closer.

Killian lashed out with his fist, taking a blow to the ribs in order to send the corrupted stumbling back. His knife followed, flipping end over end to embed in her throat.

The corrupted ripped it out, but Killian already had his bow in hand, letting loose an arrow that punched through the corrupted's skull.

Drawing two more arrows, he launched them in rapid succession into the man who was staggering in circles with Killian's knife in his eye.

But more came on.

If they'd been smart, they'd have attacked together, but their greed to be the ones to steal his life outweighed logic, and they jockeyed between each other, giving him the chance to rip his sword loose from the corpse.

Then Agrippa appeared.

The other man didn't so much as stumble. He instantly let an arrow fly into one of the black-clad corrupted, following with another and another, giving Killian room to attack.

There was no time for caution, so he dove in with force, taking off limbs to slow them down enough for Agrippa to finish them off, and within what felt like a few heart beats, only still forms lay on the ground around them.

But Lydia and Malahi had still not yet come through.

Breathing hard, Killian stared at the crystal, panic rising because if they were in trouble, there was no way back to them.

"Come on," Agrippa whispered, wiping away the blood running down his face from a cut on his brow. "I said a count of one hundred."

In his mind's eye, Killian saw the waves of blighters coming too quickly. Cutting through Bercola and her forces and rolling over Lydia and Malahi before they could go through the path. Or worse, the pair of them refusing to abandon the soldiers and staying to fight. Lydia falling into the darkness of her mark, all hope lost.

"Come on," Agrippa repeated. "Come on!"

The women abruptly appeared together, both stumbling, only Killian's reflexes keeping them from falling into the blood-splattered snow.

"I said one at a time." Agrippa leveled a finger at them, his face still pale. "That's the rule."

"Whose rule?" Malahi demanded.

"The rule of smart people who don't want to die!" He caught hold of his wife and pulled her into his arms. "Gods, Malahi. Don't scare me like that."

Gwen and Lena also broke Agrippa's rule, flying through the stem with their hands locked and landing in a heap. "Get out of the way!" Agrippa shouted. "By the Six, we need some proper training when this is all through."

A cool hand closed around Killian's wrist, and the pain of his injuries disappeared as he looked down into Lydia's green eyes. They were liquid bright as she said, "The giants and the rest of our soldiers were holding them back, but . . . Astara said a sea of blighters were coming. She went to find Dareena for aid, but I don't know how long we have. We need to make every moment count."

Killian intended to. Catching hold of her face, he lowered his head and kissed her. "I love you. No matter what happens, remember that."

"I love you, too," Lydia whispered. "Now let's go save Mudamora."

Together, the six of them pressed at a slow run through the forest of dead conifers. Thick black streams of blight spidered across the land, the air thick with the stink of rot. To the west was the wall that had once protected Mudamora from Derin before proving itself so woefully inadequate. Flakes of snow fell from the sky, the white dulling as it mixed with the bits of rot and dust that crumbled from the trees. The land was all shades of lifeless grey. As though they'd stepped into the underworld itself.

They reached the fortress that he'd once commanded. The place where it had all began, and it felt eerily like coming full circle as Killian took in the half-moon exterior wall of the fortress he'd lost to Rufina. It was much unchanged from when he and Lydia had last come through here in pursuit of Malahi.

"Do you see any signs of life?" he asked Lydia, who held her own sword at the ready, though he knew it was the least of her weapons.

She shook her head. They warily walked up the bank of the river of blight to where it flowed through the opening in the fortress's wall. There were many footprints in the snow, and Killian noted the stone structure that had been built alongside the river of death so that travelers could pass through the wall without wading into the mirk.

He swiftly took in the crumbling outbuildings in the fortress's courtyard, his memory still echoing with the screams from that long ago battle.

"There's no one here," Lydia murmured, but her eyes were on the path of footprints that ran alongside the blight to the tunnel through the wall that had defended Mudamora for so long.

"Do you think that portcullis still works?" Agrippa asked. "We get that closed, it will buy us time when the blighters break through Bercola's lines."

Killian couldn't help but flinch, because if that happened, his old friend would be dead. "If there isn't too much rust in the mechanisms."

"Leave it to us."

He turned at Lena's voice. She and Gwen stood together, as they had for almost as long as he'd known them, loyal until the bitter end.

"We'll get it shut." Gwen lifted her chin. "You go put Rufina in the ground, Killian."

Lena hurried forward to fling an arm around both Lydia and Malahi. "You two save Mudamora. We have your back."

Killian swiftly showed them the mechanism for closing the portcullis. "Once you have it closed, run."

Lena shook her head. "We're surrounded by blight for days in either direction. If we don't win this fight, there is no surviving. We'll hold our ground."

"May the Six be with you." He gripped both their shoulders. "It has been an honor to fight alongside you."

With Lydia, Agrippa, and Malahi on his heels, Killian walked on the stone walkway alongside the river of blight. In the close darkness of the tunnel, the stink was oppressive, his eyes watering by the time they reached the other side. Tracks carried on up the pass, the blight stark against the snow. At the top of the pass was a ridge, and below was the valley that held Deadground.

The town and the mounds containing the corrupted tenders were still out of sight, but Lydia lifted a hand and pointed. "I can see the life the corrupted tenders have stolen from here, it's so bright." Shaking her head, she added, "It should be drifting. Dispersing. But it's as though they've created a well from which it can't escape."

"Was it like that before?"

"Yes, but the scale . . ." Her jaw tightened. "What I saw before was a candle compared to the sun. Every life lost to the blight has come here."

The portcullis noisily rattled shut as they climbed the pass, the air thin and cold, every breath labored as they climbed alongside the river of blight. Its black tide still had the strange effect of seeming to run both directions, toward Deadground and out into Mudamora.

"Can you see any corrupted, Lydia?" Killian asked as they drew closer to the ridgeline. "Rufina?"

"Even if they are here, I can't tell among all this life. Everything glows."

"Oh, she's here," Agrippa muttered. "And she's bloody well watching."

Killian's instincts flared a heartbeat before a familiar female voice said, "How right you are, Agrippa. How right you are."

111

LYDIA

Rufina walked over the ridgeline and then down the slope toward them, two corrupted striding to either side of her. They stopped as she pressed onward, both of them drawing weapons.

"Welcome to my queendom," Rufina said. "A taste of what is to come as Mudamora falls beneath my army. And it will only be the first, for soon all the West will kneel to me, the Six forgotten to time."

She'd destroy the world to strike a blow at the gods. Lydia's mouth curled in disgust, every part of her loathing the creature that stood before them.

"It was a clever ploy," Rufina said. "After everything that the Empire has accomplished for me, I believed they'd continue to be allies of convenience. But I've lived too long and been betrayed too often not to have contingencies, and Marcus has paid a heavy price for his deception." She smiled at Agrippa. "He'll pay a heavier price still when I'm done here."

"I wouldn't underestimate him," Agrippa replied, but Rufina only laughed.

"I don't. My master believes it is his fate to serve, and it will not be only the West that falls to my master's control but all of Reath."

"It's good to have ambitions," Agrippa retorted, buying time for Killian to come up with a plan of attack.

Time that they didn't have, because Bercola and the rest of their force wouldn't be able to hold back the blighter army for long, and then the only thing that stood between them was two women and a wall meant to defend from the opposite side. If she and Malahi couldn't stop the corrupted tenders before the blighters broke through, then—

Killian moved.

One second, he was at Lydia's elbow, and the next, he'd closed half the distance between them and Rufina. Whether Agrippa had known his intent or his reaction time was just that good, Lydia couldn't have said, only that he'd already loosed two arrows, one striking a corrupted in the face.

"Go! We'll hold them off!" Agrippa shouted.

Killian's blade collided with Rufina's with a loud clang. Lydia caught hold of Malahi's hand and they ran up the slope, boots crunching in the snow.

Yet as Lydia crested the ridgeline to look down into the valley, she nearly stopped in her tracks.

Malahi snarled, "Abomination!"

The plant mounds had grown.

Rearing up from the ravine that had once held the town of Deadground, the mounds had grown into a twisted mass of vines that stretched at least a hundred feet in the air, all of it pulsing with the beat of the corrupted hearts within. The task of destroying it felt more daunting than it ever had before. Yet Lydia still looked back over her shoulder.

Agrippa engaged with the other corrupted, weapons crashing, but the one he'd shot had ripped the arrow loose, gore streaming down her face. She screamed in fury and then broke into a sprint after Lydia and Malahi.

"Get to the tenders!" Lydia shouted at Malahi, letting go of her hand. "I'll be right behind you!"

And then she turned to face the corrupted.

The woman's face was already healing, and she laughed as Lydia lifted her sword. "You can't win this, little girl. Either you give in to the Seventh's power or you die."

"I'm not a little girl," Lydia answered. "I'm a gods-damned queen."

She knocked the woman's sword sideways with a swipe, then punched the woman in the face. The corrupted staggered backward into Agrippa's blade, and then dropped, spine severed.

"Go!" Lydia shouted to him. "Keep her safe!"

He raced after Malahi, and Lydia knelt on the corrupted's chest, closing her fingers around the woman's neck.

"Can't help yourself, can you?" the woman whispered, her eyes voids rimmed with flame. Flame that diminished as Lydia pulled the life out of her. "You're his. You'll always be his. And I will be rewarded for bringing you back to the darkness."

"I belong to no one but myself." Lydia tightened her grip. "And the Seventh gives nothing. He only takes."

The corrupted's aging face paled, her eyes, now blue, fixing on the stream of life flowing out of Lydia's free hand. *Her life.* "How?"

"Because I am not weak," Lydia answered. "I have all the strength I have ever needed. Tell the Corrupter that when you meet him."

The woman blinked once, her face ancient, then the light went out of her eyes.

As Lydia lifted her head, her gaze went down the pass to the wall. From this vantage, she could easily see over it into Mudamora, and bile burned in her throat at the sight. Racing through the trees toward the fortress Lena and Gwen defended were hundreds of blighters. Behind them, more came on, like a swarm of insects flooding across the land.

Bercola has fallen.

Yet Lydia knew there was no time for grief. Killian battled against Rufina, the clash of steel loud. The Queen of Derin was his fight.

The blight was hers.

112

KILLIAN

Their blades crashed together, the ring of steel a symphony in Killian's ears, their feet moving in the violent dance of battle. Though threats pressed in on all sides, the world fell away until there was nothing but the fight between him and his old enemy.

"Will the third time be the charm, Lord Calorian? Or is it the fourth? I can't keep track of the number of times you've failed to kill me." Rufina laughed as she said the words, but he didn't miss how her eyes kept moving in the direction of Deadground. She knew Malahi and Lydia were a threat, which meant he needed to keep her away from them.

This was his battle, his purpose. All that mattered was keeping this creature at bay while Lydia and Malahi destroyed the blight.

It would be no easy fight.

Steel sparked against steel, the speed of Rufina's attack threat enough, but worse still was her skill. Long before she'd turned to the dark, when she'd answered to the name of Cyntha, she'd been a swordswoman almost without equal, and her skill had only grown. It made her a far more dangerous opponent than the corrupted that he'd just killed.

But he'd also fought her before, which meant he knew her weaknesses.

"You're not going to win this." He deflected a blow, then threw a knife with his free hand. Rufina batted it away, and the blade disappeared into the snow. "The blight has been defeated before."

"And it took every tender in Anukastre to do it," she retorted. "Dozens and dozens, all of whom fell dead to achieve the cure. Malahi is but one woman."

"Then why are you here?" He danced backward, the tip of her sword slicing through his chain mail like it was butter. "Why not send your lackeys to pick up the pieces while you face down Dareena in the south?"

Instead of answering, her eyes flicked past him, and Killian instinctively moved left to block her as she tried to race past, the impact of their blades deafening.

Killian chuckled, though he felt no humor, because in the distance, he caught side of the horde massing on the far side of the wall. It wouldn't hold them for long. "You belie your words, Cyntha. Tell me again that they're no threat."

Her eyes skipped past him again, and he moved sideways with them.

Too late did he recognize the ruse as she instead ran straight, her blade hitting his mailed side with such force that his ribs cracked. Ignoring the pain, he closed his hand on her arm, allowing himself to fall. His weight yanked Rufina back, and she whirled, stabbing the spot where he had lain only a heartbeat before.

But Killian had already let go and rolled, on his feet, sword stabbing out.

It took her in the gut. Rufina hissed, dragging herself off his blade, but she was too slow to evade his fist as it connected with her jaw.

Instead of recoiling, she flung herself at him, either not caring that she'd be injured or trusting that her mark would heal her. Or else deeming it worth the pain as her fingers closed around his throat.

Killian felt her mark catch hold of his life and yank. Panic rose in his chest, but he tamped it down and smashed his forehead against the bridge of her nose, then his fist into her chin when she reared back.

He stabbed her again, blood spraying. Rufina only pulled herself off his sword like meat off a skewer. Even stabbed twice, she was quick as a fox, and Killian sprinted after her. He pulled another knife and threw it, and the blade embedded in her thigh.

Ripping the blade free, she spun and threw it back at him. Killian batted it out of the air with his sword and then threw himself at her. They grappled back and forth, but then an explosion rattled his eardrums. Both he and Rufina froze, staring at the plume of smoke rising into the air, but then the ground shook.

The earthquake sent them rolling down the snowy slope.

Killian dropped his sword to catch Rufina's wrists, but with inhuman strength, she ripped a hand free and drove it into his ribs. Bone cracked, pain spidering across his side, but before he could grab hold of her, her fist flew out again.

It caught him in the shoulder, the joint dislocating right as their roll flung them against a boulder and broke them apart. The pain was incredible, and it shattered Killian's focus enough to hear the noise from below. Awful meaty thuds, a glance downslope revealing that blighters were coming over the walls. Were falling to form a thick carpet of broken bodies, it only a matter of time until it was thick enough that the rest could flow over like a tide.

Rufina staggered upright. Her wounds were healing as swiftly as he could inflict them, the stolen life within her seemingly endless. He'd fought her before, but those battles felt like child's play compared to this, her strength limitless.

Pulling his last remaining knife, he threw it at her exposed back, and the weapon sank into her spine. Rufina dropped, paralyzed from the waist down, but she reached over her shoulder and extracted the blade. A heartbeat later, she was standing once more.

"You cannot defeat me, Lord Calorian." Her burning eyes fixed on him. "I am death."

She was right. He couldn't beat her. But neither was he going to die easily. He'd fight her to the bitter last to give Lydia the time she needed, because once Lydia had defeated the blight, she'd come for Rufina.

And the Queen of Mudamora was more than Rufina's match.

Retrieving his sword, Killian attacked.

113

LYDIA

The ground shook violently beneath Lydia's feet. She fell to her hands and knees, a scream tearing from her lips. Her ears rang from the explosion, and as she looked back toward Mudamora, it was to see a column of smoke rising high into the sky, debris raining down.

Someone had destroyed the xenthier to prevent more blighters from passing through.

Lydia sent up a silent prayer to whichever of her comrades had struck the blow in the south, then raced down the hill to the glowing nightmare below.

Sliding to a stop next to Malahi and Agrippa, Lydia stared up into the seething mass of vines. What had once been separate mounds was now a single sphere, the vines all tangled around one another. "I just climbed in last time," she said between gasped breaths. "They each had their own connection to the blight."

"This is an abomination." Malahi reached out to touch one of the vines. It shivered like a horse trying to shake off a blackfly, and Lydia almost gagged.

"We've only got minutes," Agrippa said, his attention not on the monstrosity but back the way they'd come. It was impossible to see over the ridge to the wall far below, but even from here, Lydia could hear the noise of far too many blighters. She did not think the wall would hold them back for long.

Agrippa heaved on two vines, opening a gap that Malahi crawled into. "I'll keep watch from the outside." He caught hold of Lydia's wrist. "Please take care of her for me."

"I swear it," she promised, knowing full well that there was every chance she'd fail in her oath.

But that no one would be alive to see it.

Lydia crawled into the mass of vines, following Malahi's heels. The interior of the sphere was humid and warm and heavy with the scent of decay. It was like climbing through a ball of yarn, but the strands were as thick as her wrist and strong. Sweat poured down Lydia's face from the effort of forcing her way through.

"Where are they?" she hissed.

"They've burrowed. And not they. *It*."

Lydia understood what Malahi meant a moment later. Illuminated by the strange glow of the vines, her eyes fell upon what had once been separate human beings, now merged into one grotesque form that throbbed with a single heartbeat.

"My gods," Malahi whispered. "How do I control this?"

"Would it be easier to control it if it's injured?"

"I don't know." Malahi's voice was panicked. "Maybe?"

Unsheathing her sword, Lydia crawled next to Malahi and stabbed the creature with all her strength. It sank deep, and black blight oozed around the edges of the blade, the whole sphere shuddering.

Except rather than withering and dying, the creature began to expel her blade. Inch by inch until her sword dropped onto the shuddering vines, the creature entirely regenerated.

"I can try to pull the life out of it. Try to weaken it that way." Lydia reached for the throbbing mass of plant, but Malahi caught hold of her wrist.

"No," she whispered. "I think . . . I think if you do that, it will only expand the reach of the blight to feed itself. You can't take life from it, because it will take from everywhere else. This thing . . . it's not human. It's a plant. It doesn't think about anything beyond survival." Malahi's head tilted. "Which gives me the advantage."

Lydia did not see how, but before she could ask, Malahi pressed her hands to the mass of plant matter that had once been human beings.

Only to shake her head as she met Lydia's gaze. "I can't control them from the outside. I have to join them."

It seemed like madness, but everything they held dear stood at the brink, so Lydia only gave a tight nod. "If you start to falter, I'll keep you alive." She gestured all around her. "There is enough life here for tens of thousands of people."

"If I falter, this is over."

Her friend was right, but the blighters on the far side of the wall felt like a distant concern as Malahi pressed her hands to the creature again.

Lydia gasped as shoots sprang out from the creature and burrowed into Malahi's hands. She whimpered in pain, body shaking, only to abruptly stiffen.

"Malahi?" When her friend didn't respond, Lydia moved so they were face-to-face. Malahi's unseeing amber eyes moved back and forth. Her muscles flexed, jaw tight with strain, as though she were fighting against someone.

Or something.

"Help her, Yara," Lydia prayed as the sphere of vines trembled. "Give her the strength she needs."

As the words left her lips, Lydia found herself flung sideways, the entire sphere moving as though a god had plucked it off the ground and shaken it.

Except it wasn't just the sphere, it was all of Reath. The ground shuddered with violence that made the destruction of the xenthier pale in comparison, the roar of distant avalanches making it sound like the whole world was tearing asunder.

Which perhaps it was.

A scream tore from her lips as she was tossed sideways, her spectacles cracking, but Lydia crawled back to Malahi.

That was when she saw it.

The sickly radiance of the tenders was fading, the vines withering and slackening as it consumed itself.

The sphere began to sink into the ground.

Blight pooled around Lydia's knees, and through the vines, she saw the great river of death was pouring up the slope and into the pit the creature had dug for itself. It flowed into the thing that had once been human tenders, its strange plant-like flesh crisscrossed with inky veins as Malahi reversed its power. As she drew death into it, slowly killing it from the inside out.

Except it was not only the creature that was dying.

Malahi's skin was ashen, and the shoots embedded in her skin turned black, the flow of blight, of death, rising into her arm. Withering her as surely as it had the monster she sought to destroy.

Without thought, Lydia placed a hand on Malahi's shoulder and pushed life into her. Yet the glow didn't just suffuse the other woman, but the entire creature. Malahi and the creature were connected.

They were one.

As understanding of what was happening settled upon her like a lead weight, a vine unraveled from the withered mass and weakly shoved Lydia away.

She's sacrificing herself.

Hot tears rolled down Lydia's cheeks as her friend turned grey, her veins turned black, and her pulse slowed. All around them, the tangle of vines was doing the same. Dying as Malahi drew more and more death into it.

"Malahi?" Agrippa shouted, and Lydia choked on a sob because she didn't want him to watch this happen.

"She's got control of it," Lydia called through the collapsing sphere. "She's winning!"

"Is she all right?"

Lie, logic told her, but Lydia couldn't bring herself to do so, and her silence must have told Agrippa all he needed to know.

The dying plant mass shook as he leapt into the pit of withered vines, fighting to reach his wife, and Lydia flinched as he shouted, "Malahi, no!"

Agrippa flung himself at Malahi and tried to rip the midnight shoots free from Malahi's flesh. "Lydia, help her!"

"I can't." Sobs shook her body. "There's no other way to defeat it. If I put life into her, it will go into them. They're too connected."

"Please!"

When she didn't move, he lifted his blade so that it rested against Lydia's throat. "Help her."

"Agrippa." Malahi's voice was soft as breath but loud as thunder as she said, "Let me go."

He didn't move his weapon. "I can't." Tears slicked his face. "I swore I'd protect you until the end."

"And this is that end." Malahi's skin was withering like a dying vine, but her amber eyes were still bright. Still human. "You kept me safe so that I could do this, but now it is done. I love . . ."

Her voice trailed off as the throbbing heart of the plant stuttered, then went silent. The light faded from her eyes, and Malahi Rowenes slumped into Agrippa's arms.

Agrippa screamed her name, and the sound compounded Lydia's own grief and shattered her heart. Yet as she looked out through the pit to where the river of blight had once been, it was to find an empty trench carved into the land. No longer a wound but a scar. A scar that would eventually heal.

Malahi had done it.

Had saved Mudamora from the blight, but the cost . . . The cost would haunt Lydia for the rest of her days.

Because she feared she wasn't done paying.

Scrambling to her feet, Lydia began to climb out of the pit of dead vines. "Killian!" she shouted. "Killian!"

Resting her elbow on the edge, Lydia heaved herself over, rolling onto her hands and knees. "Kill—" She broke off. Because surrounding her were thousands of blighters.

All still very much under the Corrupter's control.

114

KILLIAN

Yet another earthquake shook the ground with such violence that Killian lost his footing, rolling on the steep slope before catching himself against a dead tree.

Every part of him was in agony, his flesh cut and torn in a dozen places, his skin sticky with blood, but he forced himself to his feet.

Blighters were racing up the pass to either side of where the river of blight had once been, now just a deep trench in the ground. A dozen paces away from him, Rufina was on her knees. "No!" she screamed, her eyes fixed east.

To Mudamora, which was now crisscrossed with empty trenches, the blight vanquished.

They'd done it. Malahi and Lydia had done it. Elation flooded him, but it was short-lived.

He could feel Rufina's rage. Feel her wrath.

Her threat.

For while the blight had been drawn out of the land, it seemed it still flowed in the veins of those that it had murdered. For blighters beyond count were running this way, all headed toward Deadground.

And Lydia.

Killian climbed after Rufina, desperation burning in his chest because she would go after Lydia for revenge. Would try to hurt Lydia for her part in destroying the blight, and he didn't know if he could stop her.

Picking up his blood-slicked sword, Killian climbed a few more steps and then fell to his knees.

"Get up," he ordered himself. "Keep going. Keep fighting."

The world was growing darker, snow falling thicker, and his fingers were numb from cold. From blood loss. But Killian made it to his feet and climbed.

Only to trip again, the ground rushing up to meet him.

And everything went dark.

115

LYDIA

The blighters continued to pour into the valley to encircle the pit, but then they parted like a tide. A figure appeared, walking through the gap her minions had formed.

Rufina stepped out of the horde to stop a few paces from Lydia.

She was covered in blood, but the sight of her didn't fill Lydia with fear. It drowned her in grief, because if Rufina was here, if Rufina was still standing . . .

"He's dead." The Queen of Derin answered the unasked question. "Or near enough to it that the distinction hardly matters."

A tear rolled down Lydia's cheek, her cracked spectacles fogging in the cold air as she let out a sob, the ache in her heart more than she could bear. A pain she'd never recover from, but she'd be damned before she dishonored Killian by giving up. Squaring her shoulders, Lydia stepped up to Rufina.

The Queen of Derin laughed, but Lydia barely noticed, her eyes all for the filaments of black spidering out from the other woman. She tried to focus on them, but rather than something tangible, the threads were the absence of anything.

They were death.

Lydia's heart began to throb faster as true understanding of what she'd done when she'd saved Finn and all the others.

She'd drawn the death out of them as surely as Malahi had drawn it out of the land. And just as the corrupted tenders had been the heart of the blight, so too was Rufina the heart of the death that had stolen so many lives. Death connected her to them, allowed her to use them as her puppets, and that link needed to be severed. Except while the corrupted tenders hadn't fought back, Rufina most certainly would.

"It doesn't have to be this way, Kitaryia," Rufina crooned. "Accept what you are and join me."

"Why do you want that?" Lydia asked, stepping closer, drawing the excess of life left by the destroyed tenders into herself. "Why not just kill me and be done with it?"

Rufina cocked her head, thinking. "Your death isn't a victory, whereas tearing you away from the Six very much is. You make them stronger, and I want them weak. I want them to fade into nothingness and be forgotten. Most especially Hegeria. I want her last thoughts to be regret for what she did to me."

Such a hollow victory. Part of Lydia pitied this woman who'd allowed bitterness and envy to consume her, to drive her to commit horror for such petty satisfaction as vengeance, because at the end of it, Lydia suspected Rufina's heart would be empty. No happiness. No joy. All of this for *nothing*.

"What's in it for me?" Lydia asked, adjusting her spectacles even as she pressed closer, pulling in more life still. Slowly, so Rufina wouldn't notice. "Why would I want immortality at the side of the woman who murdered my parents? Who killed the love of my life? Paint me a picture of a future that makes me willing to let all of this go."

"You'll be strong," Rufina answered. "No one will ever be able to hurt you again. No more grief. No more sorrow. No more pain."

"What if I don't want that?"

They were face-to-face now, Lydia just enough taller that Rufina had to look up at her, rings of fire illuminating the dark pits of eyes that flared with confusion. As if this creature who'd sacrificed all of her humanity could not begin to understand how Lydia would reject such a prize.

"Without sorrow, what is happiness?" Lydia asked, so flush with excess life that her heart fluttered. "Because I think it is much like light holding little meaning without darkness."

"Death it is, then?"

Lydia smiled. "Death indeed."

With a strength fueled by countless lives, Lydia struck, her fist lashing out with blinding speed and smashing through Rufina's rib cage. Her fingers closed around the woman's heart. The Queen of Derin screamed, a horrifying howl of pain and fear that cut off abruptly as Lydia squeezed and whispered, "I wouldn't move if I were you."

"Do it, then," Rufina retorted. "Send me to my dark master's embrace, I care not. Mudamora is a ruin of death, and the living will turn from the Six who abandoned them to such a fate. From my master's side, I will watch the Six diminish and laugh as you realize this moment was no victory, only one last gasp before defeat."

"The fight isn't yet over," Lydia said, then tightened her grip.

Just as she had with Finn, Lydia pulled the death into herself, then pushed it out into the world, the sense of touching thousands, tens of thousands, stealing sight from her eyes and leaving only blackness. And because the world demanded balance, the life that had been stolen from all those souls pushed its way into her to fill the void, flowing through the endless thousands of channels that Rufina had created and filling those souls anew. Brightness filled the darkness.

Rufina screamed as she realized what was happening, clawing at Lydia's arms. At her face. So desperate to hold on to all that she'd achieved that she didn't care that Lydia held her heart in her hand.

Lydia felt the balance right itself almost like a click in her head, and with a gasp, she let go of Rufina's heart, the last rush of life healing the wound in the woman's chest as her fingers pulled out into the cold.

"What have you done?" Rufina whispered, staring at Lydia with pale grey eyes, her face older. No longer Rufina, no longer the Queen of Derin, no longer corrupted.

All that remained was Cyntha.

All around, was a chaos of screams and tears. Some of the blighters were once again themselves—though not all, for some lay still in the snow, their souls having chosen to go onward rather than to return. And the one face she wanted to see most was painfully absent. Beyond her power to save.

The grief of that nearly brought Lydia to her knees.

"What have you done?" Cyntha screamed again. "All the Six have ever done is take from you, but you fight for them still. They rise on the back of your victory. They stand on your shoulders even when their weight is too great to bear. Don't you see that?"

"You cannot take what is freely given," Lydia answered. "Much like your freedom. Go where you will, Cyntha. The Corrupter no longer has his claws in you, so your future is what you make of it."

Turning away, Lydia took several steps, staring out over the barren landscape that seemed a mirror of her heart. Because victory felt so cold without him at her side.

Then her skin prickled, instinct warning her.

Whirling, she saw Cyntha lunge toward her, sword in hand—

Only for her head to topple from her neck, removed by a familiar sword.

Killian staggered as though the blow had taken the last of his strength, tripping over Cyntha's fallen corpse to collapse into Lydia's arms. Behind him were Lena and Gwen, both women splattered with gore but very much alive.

"You're alive," Lydia sobbed, burying her face in his shoulder even as she vanquished wounds that would have been the death of anyone other than him. "Oh gods, you're alive."

Killian wrapped his arms around her, holding her tight. "I'm sorry I wasn't with you."

"You are always with me," Lydia whispered, then kissed him fiercely. "No matter where we are, you are in my heart."

"You did it." His eyes searched hers. "You saved them."

"*We* saved them."

Their foreheads pressed together, the silence right for there was no need for words in this moment. A moment they'd been fighting for all their lives, even if they didn't know it. A moment that they'd both lost hope of ever achieving, only to rediscover it again in each other's strength. In each other's love.

But at such a great cost.

"Malahi," she started to say, then fell silent as a noise from behind caught her attention. Killian retrieved his sword, but then a familiar hand reached over the edge, and Malahi appeared. Lena rushed forward to help her up, then leaned down to pull Agrippa over the edge.

"How is this possible?" Lydia tightened her grip on Killian's hand. "How . . ."

"You saved her," Agrippa said. "I'm sorry for doubting you, Lydia."

Understanding rose in her chest how this had come to pass. Malahi had her life taken by the blight in the same way as the blighters had, but if she'd come back to the living, then—"What of the other tenders?"

"They came back to life as well," Agrippa said. "But I watched those bastards choose this path. They were corrupted in their souls, and if we left them alive, they'd have done this all over again. So I gave them a *natural* death with my blade. Mudamora is safe from the likes of them."

A ruthless act, but it was not lost on Lydia that sometimes ruthlessness was required. And deserved.

As Agrippa helped Malahi to her feet, she looked around at the sea of the living before turning her focus to Lydia. "You believed when everyone else had lost hope." Malahi's voice was choked. "You never stopped trying to help our people. Never gave up. You were the queen Mudamora needed."

Lydia shook her head. "Perhaps I was. But the moment when Mudamora needed someone like me is over. You were destined to rule, my friend. In spirit, in bravery, and, when we can gather enough of the high families to make it so, in law."

Malahi's eyes widened. "But—"

"It's not my path," Lydia said. "It's yours." She gestured to the stunned masses of surviving Mudamorians trying to come to terms with what they'd endured and said, "Our people need you now, more than ever. You are the one they know as their queen—they will not question you, especially once they learn what you have accomplished. Go to them and give them hope."

Malahi didn't move for a long moment, her amber eyes searching Lydia's. "It is a privilege to call you friend, Lydia, and it is my hope to call you so for the rest of my life."

Letting go of Killian with one arm, Lydia grasped Malahi's hand. "We will rebuild Mudamora together. I swear it."

With Agrippa shadowing her, Mudamora's rightful queen walked toward her people. Despite her scars, many of them recognized Malahi's face and called out her name, for she had always been beloved.

Malahi paused only to pick up Rufina's head, then she stepped up onto a rock and shouted, "Our enemy is dead, her hold on you vanquished, and by the grace of the Six and the bravery of their marked, you have been given back your lives! Yet not without great cost." She dropped Rufina's head into the snow. "The scars left by what you have witnessed while your bodies were controlled by the enemy will be with you all of your lives, your souls scarred as surely as the blight has scarred the land."

Her gaze went briefly to Agrippa before returning to those looking on. "But I was once told that scars are not a symbol of weakness but of strength, and to wear them proudly as an act of defiance against those who put them there. The Corrupter tried to bring you low and yet you still stand. Every day you stand strong and faithful to each other is a day that you spit in the face of the god who tried to destroy all we held dear."

Malahi lifted her chin, sunlight breaking through the clouds to illuminate her scarred and beautiful face. "We walk a hard road. A road in which we grieve for the fallen even as we piece back together a life for the living. But I swear on the Six that I will walk alongside you. That I will give all that I am, body and soul, to raise Mudamora and its people up high."

Stepping off the rock, Malahi pressed her hand deep into the snow, and from its depths, verdant grass exploded through the grey. She lifted her head and fixed her gaze east into Mudamora, and as she did, six rays of light lanced through the clouds to illuminate her face. As the onlookers gasped, green exploded down the slope toward Mudamora, creating a highway of life that would lead them where they needed to go.

Though in Killian's arms, she was already where she wanted to be.

"I'd ask if you're sure you want to give the crown up, but I know you are," Killian said quietly. "Your heart has always demanded you walk among the people, not before them. Rule would never have made you happy."

As always, he knew her better than anyone, and Lydia smiled. "Nor you."

Killian gave a rueful laugh. "Definitely not."

It was their destiny to serve the people, Lydia knew that in the deepest part of her heart, but it would not be with crowns on their heads. It would be with their marks, using the strength gifted to them by the gods to protect the people. The rightness of that settled on her soul, along with the certainty that her future was entwined with Killian's, a path they'd walk together, to whatever end.

"I love you," she said to him. "I want to spend every day of the rest of my life with you. And"—she gave him a little smile—"every night."

Killian grinned, an expression she hadn't seen in so long that the sight of it nearly brought her to tears. "Long nights behind us," he said. "But I think longer nights ahead."

He kissed her then, and Lydia melted into him. She'd fought long and hard for so many reasons, but for herself, this moment was the greatest victory of all.

116

MARCUS

It was incredibly quiet, much as it had been since they'd abandoned southern Mudamora and journeyed through one of the many xenthier paths Rufina had mapped to a location just south of Mudaire. Silent partially because nothing lived in the barren land surrounding the city, but mostly because the weight of losing the Fifty-First still hung heavy over every one of the legions.

Most especially the Thirty-Seventh.

"Have the centurions remind the men not to drink anything," Marcus said to Felix as they approached the city. "Not to eat anything. It seems the Mudamorians were successful in their attack on the blight, but we have no way to be certain that parts of it don't linger."

"Yes, sir."

Great trenches that had once been filled with blight now sat empty, as though a dark god had carved up the land with a knife, and Marcus wondered how long it would take for life to come back. Whether the power granted by the Six would reclaim this land, or whether it would remain dead for years to come. An endless reminder of the toll that evil took wherever it reigned.

Mudaire reared ahead of them on the barren plain. It was a formidable fortress city that Marcus suspected had once been a difficult nut to crack, though now it was abandoned, the portcullis open, the gates swinging gently on the breeze.

"Set up a temporary camp." Marcus tucked the Thirty-Seventh's ledger under his arm, then said, "Felix, choose twenty good men. Quintus, with me."

On foot, they entered the dead city of Mudaire, the violence that had besieged it written in the burned buildings. In the rotted corpses littering the streets. In the blackened blood that splattered far too many walls. Marcus wondered if this city would ever be reclaimed by the living or if too much horror had marched through its streets and buildings, turning Mudaire into a tomb.

"Lydia said it's beneath the palace," he murmured, gesturing toward the large structure that perched atop the cliffs overlooking the sea.

The city was not large, and it did not take them long to reach the palace, their footsteps loud as they walked up the grand staircase to the main entrance. One of the doors had been torn off its hinges and discarded in the fountain. The interior was sacked and ruined, but echoes of what it had once been still remained. Every time Marcus blinked, he saw men in finery and women in gowns dancing to music he could not hear, their mouths open in silent laughter. Ghosts, or perhaps memories that clung to the walls of this ancient palace, whispering their stories to any living person who passed through.

Marcus stepped over bones and dried blood as they ventured into the lower level. His men roved ahead to find the entrance to the tunnels, forced to move more bones and debris to clear the way.

"We should scout it first before you go down," Felix said.

"I'm not concerned." Marcus took a torch from Quintus and descended the ladder into the darkness.

The tunnels were close and oppressive, smelling of rot and mildew, and very faintly, of the sea. The latter made him press his free hand to the breastplate of his armor, under which hung Teriana's hair ornament on a string, the metal warm against his chest. He had no information about where Teriana might be or how she fared, but he hoped that she was on her way back to Lydia. That she'd find her friend victorious, and . . . and if there was any mercy in the world, she'd not think of him at all.

"Here's the branch," a voice called from ahead.

This tunnel was narrow, and he vaguely heard Felix muttering about what a nightmare it was going to be to move so many men through such a tight space, but Marcus's eyes were all for the marks of battle. Bloodstains and places where blade tips had scratched the rock, and he swore he could hear the screams. The clash of weapons. Feel the fear that had leached into the stone.

Then the xenthier reared ahead of them.

The space around it was small, but the stem itself was larger than most, jutting vertically out of the rock nearly up to his chest.

"So it's here," Felix murmured. "But does it go where Lydia says it goes, or is this just a clever attempt to have her revenge?"

"Lydia doesn't want revenge." Marcus dropped to one knee in front of the stem. "But more importantly, she doesn't need it."

"Still, her information is old. How many years ago did she travel through this? Fifteen?"

"Sixteen."

"I struggle to believe that a terminus exists this close to Celendrial and it's never been discovered. It's not on any of our maps."

"Only one way to find out. Have the men wait for us at the branch." Once Felix had given the order, Marcus straightened and looked at Quintus. "One last job?"

"Last?"

"Yes, though you don't have to do it." Pulling the ledger out from under his arm, Marcus flipped to Quintus's number, then wrote next to it, *deceased*. He signed and dated it, then did the same for Miki's number, crossing out *injured* and replacing it with *deceased*. "You can go right now and take him. Racker's with him and he knows not to stop you." Flipping through the ledger, he found Agrippa's number and scratched out *deserted* and replaced it with *deceased*. "Find Agrippa. Or Teriana. She'll no doubt be sailing to join Lydia."

"That's the first time I've heard you say Teriana's name since she left," Quintus said, then he scuffed his sandal against the rock. "I've wanted this for so long. Wanted to be done with this life, but now that it's upon me, I . . ." He swallowed hard. "This is the only life I've known. I don't know how to be a normal man."

"Normal men walk the same way we do," Marcus answered. "One foot in front of the other. Besides, I marked your death in ink, so you can't change your mind now."

Quintus choked out a laugh. "Right."

"It's your choice," Marcus said. "But there's no one I trust more to see this last job through."

No one he trusted more to find Teriana and watch her back through whatever came next.

"The return route is by way of the baths?"

Marcus nodded. "Cassius will have excavated it, but you'll need to be clever to get back through it. The Dictator can't know we're coming."

"Yes, sir." Quintus drew in a deep breath, then reached out and took hold of the xenthier stem, instantly disappearing.

Enjoy your wine while you can, Cassius, Marcus thought as he started back up the tunnel. *For the blade of the Empire is descending on your neck.*

* * *

While he waited for Quintus to return, Marcus explored Mudaire, Felix and a handful of men trailing behind him but giving him enough space that he felt alone. As good a compromise as he was going to get, so Marcus didn't argue.

He walked through the homes of the Great Houses of Mudamora, all sacked of anything valuable, though most of the artwork remained. He examined the faces, struck, as he often was, how people across Reath were so different and yet similar at the same time. He found the Calorian home, recognizable by both the familiar face in many of the portraits but also the quantity of horse statues. House Falorn also had a property, the smallest of the twelve, but it was there he lingered the longest, examining the oil paintings of Lydia's parents. He wondered if she knew they were here. If she'd ever reclaim this place and the images of the mother who'd sacrificed her life to save her daughter.

"Still no sign of Quintus," Felix murmured as Marcus exited the building. "Do you want to send someone else?"

"No."

He started in the direction of the god towers at the center of the city, hearing Felix jog to keep up.

"Marcus, listen. I support this decision you've made, nearly everyone does, but that doesn't mean we throw caution to the wind. We've got the largest army to walk Reath camped outside this city, and if this path isn't good, we're going to have problems. We quite simply don't have the supplies, especially the *water* we need to march back south. Even with the blight gone from the land, it's still a dead zone. We need to make a plan."

"It's only been a few hours, Felix. Patience. Quintus will get the job done, as he always has."

"He might be dead."

"Patience."

They walked in silence for a time, then Felix said, "May I ask you something?"

Marcus knew what the question would be, and at any other moment, he'd have run as hard and fast from it as he could. Instead, he nodded.

"You've never explained why you tried to murder Lydia Valerius. I assumed it was part of the same blackmail Cassius used to get us to vote him in as Consul—threats to the Thirty-Seventh—but recent weeks have made me question whether it was something more."

His armor pressed the sharp edges of the miniature ship into his chest, but the pain was a comfort. The pain meant he was himself. "Cassius knew my name."

Felix frowned in confusion. "Your family's name?"

"No," Marcus answered quietly. "*My* name. And in knowing that, he had the power to make me do anything he wanted."

The words were stilted at first, like turning the key on a secret so old that the lock had rusted. But once unleashed, they poured from his lips. The choices his father had made because of Marcus's illness. The endless lies that had been required to keep the deception alive. The threat that Cassius had held over his head all this time.

Held over him still.

When Marcus was through, Felix rubbed a hand over his short hair. "I wish you'd told me. Wish you'd trusted me with that truth, but I understand why you didn't. It was easier to live the lie when everyone, including your friends, believed it." His best friend sighed. "So . . . Do you want us to call you Gaius?"

Marcus huffed out a disgusted breath. "Not if you want me to respond."

Felix laughed. "Fair enough, fair enough." Then his amusement fell away. "Marcus, if we go back, we need to silence Cassius before he says anything about this. Breaking the child tithe law is not something that will be forgiven—not by the Senate, not by the people, not even by the legions themselves. If it gets out, they'll execute you."

Unease seethed from his friend, and Marcus slung an arm around his shoulder to reassure him. "Don't worry, Felix. Cassius's crimes are great and his days are numbered."

Felix left to check on the camp, but Marcus continued on. He reached the circle of towers, which were large by most standards, if those standards didn't include those that had once stood over Revat. Yet where Revat's towers had had presence, these felt like lifeless stone. Marcus wondered whether it was because the focus of the gods was elsewhere, or whether something had been lost here. Whether it could be brought back, or whether the damage was as permanent as that he'd wrought upon Revat.

Hegeria's tower was the largest in width of the seven, but as Marcus opened the doors of the entrance, a wave of rot passed over him and he quickly took a step back. A massacre had occurred here, and he closed the doors again, for this place, at least, truly was a tomb.

Servius approached. "I've bad news."

Marcus's stomach tightened.

"Someone stole your horse."

His tension evaporated. "Really? That's unfortunate."

"Is it though? Did you really need to be riding a horse that looked like she was carved out of a block of gold?"

"That mare saved my life." Marcus shrugged. "But perhaps it's for the best."

Racker approached. "I've a name to add to the list. Miki has died, I'm sorry to report. Tragic. You'll want to update your ledger."

"A true loss to our ranks," Marcus murmured, but his surgeon was already heading back to camp. "Felix, ready the men for the crossing. Double time; I don't want to lose the advantage of darkness in Celendrial."

Then he started toward the palace.

Servius fell in lock step. "Before he took off, Quintus said the terminus is within sight of Celendrial, though barely. It's hidden in a slough below water level, which is likely why it's never been found. He says the water isn't deep enough to be of concern."

"And Celendrial?"

"Tense. Hostus might be dead, but the Twenty-Ninth is keeping to their legacy. There are civilian bodies in the streets. Signs of fire. So much graffiti that you can barely see the walls, all of it espousing hate for our dear Dictator."

"The people are rising."

"And being struck down with an iron fist." Servius was quiet. "We put this man in power, Marcus. This is on us just as much as it is on him."

"Yes, it is. But we cannot undo the past, so the only avenue left to us is to empower those who will see Celendor toward a better future."

"Do such individuals truly exist?"

Marcus thought about Lydia and her companions fighting against the undead. Against the power of a god. "I think so."

As they reached the palace gates, Marcus glanced back to see the legions were on the move into the city, marching with speed that had more to do with eagerness than training. "I'll need my best hundred to go first," he said. "The rest of the Thirty-Seventh will hold the rear to ensure no one lingers behind."

A runner disappeared to enact the order. "Centurion Qian would make a good primus," Felix said. "You do need to choose someone."

"I trust your judgment."

Felix shot him a sideways look of concern that Marcus pretended not to notice as he entered the palace. Taking up a fresh torch, he motioned for his bodyguard to walk behind as he again followed the tunnels down to the xenthier stem.

"Centurion Qian should be here soon," Felix said. "We'll give them a bit of time to establish the perimeter, then begin moving through. It's going to take hours, though, so—"

Marcus reached out and took hold of the stem, his friend's exclamation of alarm cut off as the world turned white, casting him into a void for an eternity and less than a heartbeat.

Darkness abruptly fell over him as he stepped out into night air, and Marcus stumbled through knee-deep water, mud sucking at his sandals. He nearly landed on his ass in the murk, but then a cursing Felix appeared, crashing into him and knocking him onto the muddy bank.

"We shouldn't both be here," Marcus told him reprovingly as he kicked mud off his sandal.

Felix only shoved him, snarling, "You're not supposed to go first. You're never supposed to go first."

"I'll never do it again," Marcus said. "I promise."

Felix only huffed, then hauled on Marcus's arm, dragging him up the slope, the brilliant glow of Celendrial visible against the midnight horizon.

"I always forget how big she is," Felix said, their elbows bumping together as they stood staring at the city of their birth. The city that ruled an Empire.

A city that had, for a moment, tried to rule all of Reath.

They stood without speaking, the only sound the drone of insects and the distant clamor of the city, for Celendrial never slept.

Then there was a splash of water, and Qian moved silently up the slope behind them, his men arriving in rapid succession. "Sir," he said, saluting. "Orders?"

"The moment we are spotted, those who have the most cause to fear our wrath will try to flee," Marcus said. "Get into the city, and when the time is right, lock down access to the docks."

"How will I know when the time is right?"

"You'll know."

"Yes, sir." Qian hesitated, then said, "There are two legions in the city, though, sir. I might need a handful more men."

"Don't worry," Marcus replied. "You'll be the least of their concerns, and I trust you'll be creative in discouraging escape. Remember, we are here to liberate Celendrial from its tyrant, not to spill more civilian blood."

"We'll see it done, sir." Qian saluted, then he and his men disappeared on silent feet into the night.

The men began pouring through the stem, first by the hundreds and then by the thousands. They all quietly saluted Marcus as he and Felix deployed the legions in a perimeter around Celendrial, every man under orders to maintain utter silence until the moment was right.

"I can't believe no one has noticed yet," Felix muttered after the second hour. "Aren't they scouting around the city?"

"I doubt it," Marcus answered. "Celendrial hasn't been attacked in over twelve hundred years, and its hubris has caused it to grow complacent. For who would dare to attack Mother Empire at her heart?"

"Teriana."

Marcus smiled. "She taught a painful lesson, but it seems they have not yet learned."

More hours passed. The first glow of dawn appeared in the east, reflecting off the branch of the River Savio that flowed before them, but men were still passing through the stem from Mudaire. Finally, the familiar voices of the Thirty-Seventh reached his ears, and Amarin came up between Marcus and Felix.

"You didn't eat before you left," his servant said with reproach. "You will not have a clear head if your stomach is empty."

He held out an apple to Marcus, but instead of taking the fruit, Marcus leaned closer. "Thank you," he said to the older man. "For everything."

Amarin inclined his head. "Don't thank me yet, sir. I've yet to discover whether my efforts were worth it."

The corner of Marcus's mouth turned up, and he said, "Accidents happen during these sorts of moments, my friend. Hearts give out. I anticipate being informed of your untimely demise in a few hours." Reaching into his belt pouch, he extracted what coin was in there and handed it to Amarin. "I hear that the weather in Sibal is lovely this time of year."

The older man pocketed the coins. "If you don't mind, sir, my heart would like to see this through before it gives out."

"Understandable."

Amarin shoved the apple into Marcus's hand, and then disappeared back through the ranks.

"We're running out of time," Felix murmured. "Hubris or no, there are men guarding those walls, and they aren't blind. We've got minutes until they see that the whole bloody city is surrounded and raise the alarm."

"Let them raise the alarm," Marcus replied. "They're not going anywhere."

Leaving Felix to manage the influx of Thirty-Seventh, Marcus walked a hundred paces closer to the city, listening to his men form up behind him even as the light grew.

And the legionnaires guarding the city walls finally spotted the threat.

Marcus tilted his head, watching as first they stared, dumbfounded, then burst into action. Alarm bells rang, the noise spilling across the city as the sun crested the horizon. At last, Servius joined Marcus at his other elbow.

"Everyone is here?"

"To the man," Servius answered. "Thanks for waiting. I didn't want to miss the party."

"We're just getting started." Marcus took a breath, the first flutter of fear for what was to come filling his stomach.

Vaguely, he heard, "It's the commandant," muttered through the lines behind him, followed by curses, because, apparently, Wex wasn't alone.

The commandant of Lescendor rode through the Thirty-Seventh leading a white horse. The ground behind Marcus's lines was no longer empty but filled with the thousands of boys being trained at Lescendor.

"Have you forgotten to watch your rear, boy?" Commandant Wex said, drawing his mount to a halt.

"I didn't think anyone had noticed we were here."

Wex snorted. "Lescendor scouts even if Celendrial does not. You're becoming forgetful."

"I didn't forget."

"Cocky, then." Wex tossed him the reins of the other horse. "You sure about this, Legatus? Once you cross the Savio, the law will cease to be on your side. It will be seen as an act of war against the Empire, and you will be branded a traitor."

"I know the laws of the Empire, Commandant. But today, the law will bend its knee to me."

"You always were my brightest star," Wex said. "But it is the brightest that burn out the quickest. I note the Fifty-First are not with you. I'd hoped . . ." The commandant trailed off with a sigh.

Marcus shook his head. "They were lost. But they will not be forgotten." Then he called out, "Remember the Fifty-First!"

The Thirty-Seventh echoed the shout, and it repeated through the legions surrounding Celendrial, announcing to the city the reason why they were here.

Not for vengeance, but for justice.

Marcus mounted the horse, taking the Thirty-Seventh's standard from Servius and turning to face the city. "Proceed."

A horn bellowed, long and low, answered by the same note played by a hornist in each legion, then the men began to march. Drums sounded an ominous beat, the noise of tens of thousands of men loud as thunder.

They reached the branch of the Savio, which was low at this time of year, the water barely passing his horse's knees as Marcus rode into it. His men splashed through without losing stride.

"This might cost you everything and yield nothing," Wex said from where he rode next to him. "Are you certain?"

Marcus heeled his horse out of the water, his eyes fixed on the golden dragon that loomed over the closed gate. "I've already thrown the dice. All that remains to be seen is how they will fall."

117

LYDIA

A cheer broke out among the civilians as Mudaire's walls appeared in the distance. Though one of the xenthier paths that Rufina had mapped had taken them most of the distance, the several thousand surviving Mudamorians with them were still without food and water, so the capital of Mudamora was a welcome sight to all.

The scouts that had gone ahead had reported back that there were signs the legions had only just come and gone, departing through the xenthier in the tunnels below the palace, which was good news. Better news still was that they'd abandoned any of the supplies not easily brought into the tunnels, which included live cattle and casks of water.

"They left their horses as well," the scout said as they drew closer. "We should try to round them up."

Malahi reached down and pressed her hand against the ground, green grass sprouting beneath her palm and spreading until they were surrounded. "This should lure them in. Have some of the cattle slaughtered for meat and distribute the water."

"Yes, my lady."

Lydia cast a sideways glance at her friend. Malahi refused to answer to the title of queen until it was made official, though she embodied the role already. "It won't look as you remember it. Mudaire has seen a lot of horror."

"We'll rebuild." Malahi lifted her chin. "Our people are strong."

Strong, but far fewer in number. Those who'd come back from the dead had known much of what had occurred in the south due to the link the blight had formed between their minds. They'd told Lydia how Bercola and those with her had fallen, and how Astara had carried Dareena through the sky and dropped her among the masses of blighters trying to get through the xenthier. It had been her aunt who'd destroyed the xenthier with explosives, but then she'd refused to fight back against the horde that remained.

Dareena Falorn had died as she had lived, fighting for the people she'd sworn to protect, and Lydia's eyes welled at every thought of her, only the knowledge that Finn, Killian's family, Astara, and Xadrian were alive and safe kept her from falling apart entirely.

Agrippa walked at Malahi's elbow, her ever-present shadow, and he said to the scout, "Any signs of human life?"

"None, my lord."

"My lord? Well haven't you gone and gotten all fancy on us," a voice with a Cel accent said, and they all whirled around to find a man walking out of a copse of trees. He was dressed in Mudamorian attire, but Lydia knew a legionnaire when she saw one.

"Quintus?" Agrippa blurted out, then his arms were around the other man, nearly taking him over backward. "What are you doing here?"

"I'm dead," the legionnaire answered. "At least, according to the Thirty-Seventh's ledger. Can't take it back either, because Marcus signed it in ink before he departed for Celendor. Miki is registered as dead, as are you."

"He's here?"

"Back at our camp." The legionnaire hesitated, then said, "I don't know if Teriana told you, but he can't walk."

"She told me." Agrippa's gaze slid to Lydia. "Any chance I can call in a favor?"

"I don't owe you any favors," she answered, "but I'd be more than happy to have *you* in *my* debt."

Agrippa rolled his eyes. "Fine. Fine." He hesitated, then reached for Malahi's hand, tugging her closer. "Though first, let me introduce you to my wife, Malahi. Love, this is Quintus, my best friend among the living." His eyes flicked to Killian. "Hopefully that doesn't hurt your feelings."

"My feelings are intact," Killian answered dryly.

Quintus inclined his head to Malahi. "It is an honor to meet you, my lady. I know your face from across the battlefield, but I am glad circumstances have changed so that I might meet you as a friend."

"Well met, Quintus," Malahi said, then she turned her gaze on Agrippa. "You go with Lydia to help your friend. Killian and I will see to getting the people settled."

Quintus led them away from the long train of civilians, heading toward a copse of dead trees. "The city is unnerving," he said. "A lot of unburied bodies and echoes of old violence. Sleeping on the ground was preferable." Turning his head, he met Lydia's gaze. "Is Teriana all right?"

"I don't know." She bit the insides of her cheeks. "The last I saw of her was when she set sail to organize the attack on the Empire, and while we know the Maarin were successful, I've not heard from her since."

"Right." He was quiet for several strides, then he said, "I was one of her bodyguards, but we became friends. I was with her through just about everything." He again fell silent, the muscles in his jaw working back and forth. "Someone needs to tell her that he did the right thing, in the end. Doesn't undo the damage, but she should know."

"Marcus didn't want me to tell her anything," she answered. "I think he plans to tell her himself."

"No." Quintus exhaled. "That's not his plan."

* * *

After she'd aided Quintus's friend, Lydia left the three of them to their reunion. But instead of heading into the city to find Malahi and Killian, she made her way down to the harbor, stopping on the stretch of beach where she'd had that fateful meeting with Bait.

Pulling off her worn boots, Lydia stepped out into the water, knife in hand. She drew it across the back of her arm, allowing blood to drip into the froth and foam. Not knowing if anyone would hear, Lydia cast a message for Teriana out into the sea.

118

TERIANA

For all her plan had failed to come to fruition in time to stop Marcus from invading Mudamora, it had been effective in liberating the Southern Continent from the Empire.

Communication flowed between Magnius and Lysander across the Endless Seas, and information slowly trickled in that Teriana's allies had been successful in their united attacks. Silvara and the Bardenese rebels had taken control of the legion base at Hydrilla, and then detonated the path leading to Arinoquia. Facing the united force of Ereni's clans and the inlanders, the legionnaires located in Arinoquia had retreated to the dubious safety of Sibern, xenthier destroyed in their wake. Likewise after Teriana and her crew had taken out the stem in Padria, Zimo and his Thirty-First had been unable to hold the city or the fortress of Imresh and had retreated, the Gamdeshians detonating the stem in their wake. The Gamdeshians had also regained control of Revat and destroyed the stem used by Marcus to travel to Mudamora. Along with their victories, Teriana heard stories of the great earthquakes the destruction had set off. And the death it had left in the wake.

No victory without cost.

Yet what was happening in Mudamora remained a mystery, the fate of Teriana's friends unknown. There was no information on whether Marcus had attacked. No information as to whether Lydia and Malahi had made strides against the blight. It was possible that Teriana wouldn't be able to reach them in time to make a difference in their fight, but she intended to try.

"Lower the anchor," she ordered as the *Quincense* drifted close to the small island where the Maarin had agreed to meet. "Ready the longboats."

"I'll wait here," Baird said. "This is a meeting for the Maarin people." Then he disappeared below.

On the island, there were signs her people were already celebrating the victory. Bonfires burned, and familiar smiling faces danced around them with cups in their hands. Music drifted over the water, musicians moving between the fires to give rhythm to the dancers. They deserved to celebrate. Deserved to lift their glasses to toast the first victory against the Empire in generations.

Yet as she listened to dozens of voices laughing and cheering that the legions would suffer, starve, and die, cut off as they were, there was another part of Teriana wanting to scream that it was wrong to celebrate victory when it was achieved with violence and death.

So many lives had been lost, dozens upon dozens of her people dead, to say nothing of the Bardenese, Arinoquian, and Gamdeshian people who'd died in the battles. Lives lost under her command, and Teriana felt the weight of them pulling her down and down, because more would follow. And not just them, but hundreds of legionnaires. Thousands.

And the dying wasn't over yet. The war wasn't over yet.

Urgency bit in her chest, because if there was to be any chance of the Maarin helping Lydia, they needed to be making ready. Needed to be organizing supplies, not dancing and drinking their weight in rum. "This isn't right," she snapped, eyes searching for the ships' captains. "We're not done yet."

"Easy," her aunt murmured. "This is an important moment, and if you go in swinging, you're not going to achieve the goals you've set."

Teriana gave a tight nod. Catching sight of the captains, she strode in their direction. Cheers rose at the sight of her, shouts of "Victory!" filling the air. Her people pressed in, surrounding her, yet she found herself flinching every time someone clapped her on the shoulder or squeezed her hand. Found herself wondering how many of those here had once called for her death.

"We grieve the loss of your mother," one of the captains said. "Triumvir Tesya was a force to be reckoned with, a backbone of our people, and we pray that Madoria holds her close."

"Thank you." Teriana dug deep in her chest for the strength not to break down into tears at the reminder her mother was dead. The reminder that she'd never turn around to see her mum walking up the beach nor hear her shouted orders across the deck of the *Quincense*. "She will be missed."

"She will be proud of what you have accomplished. And on that note, what news do you bring us?" he asked. "We've been waiting to hear from Magnius what happened across the Endless Seas. What has Lysander said?"

"Victory in Arinoquia and Gamdesh," Teriana said. "The legions in Emrant and Aracam were driven to retreat through the xenthier."

Deafening cheers rose all around, cups lifted into the air in celebration of those great victories. Teriana lifted her hands, motioning for silence, but everyone was too busy hugging and laughing. "The war isn't over!"

The words tore from her lips in a vicious shout, and everyone fell silent.

"The legions moved by xenthier into Mudamora before we struck." Teriana's hands balled into fists, nails digging into her palms. "We need to set sail to aid Mudamora however we can."

Silence.

Faces fell, cups lowered, and heads shook, yet no one spoke in support of action.

"We have been allies to Mudamora for generations. We need to go to their aid." Teriana tried to meet the eyes of the other captains, but they all looked away. "At the very least, we can supply the Mudamorian army with food and water from the Southern Continent while they fight. Perhaps entreat the other nations to lend aid."

"Aye," one of the captains said. "We can do that. We can bring supplies."

But another shook his head. "If the legions have invaded, it's over. Mudamora was already at the brink of defeat against Rufina, and the legions will have made short work of what resistance remained. We did what we could, Teriana, but for Mudamora, it will be too late. Better now to focus on keeping the legions contained. Let them starve to death or succumb to blight in the nation they so eagerly sought to conquer."

Shock rendered her speechless, but then Teriana gave a sharp shake of her head. "No! We don't know that they are defeated! We need to set sail. There's a xenthier stem beneath Mudaire that goes back to Celendor. I'll convince Marcus to retreat."

The captain closed his hands on hers. "I respect your loyalty to Mudamora, Teriana, but you aren't thinking this through. If we can keep the legions trapped in Mudamora, we can kill them all in a matter of weeks, whether it be to starvation or blight poisoning. The Empire will take generations to recover from such a loss, whereas if we tell them how to escape, they remain as much of a threat as ever."

Her chin quivered. "You want them all dead? Tens of thousands of men, never mind the civilians trapped in Serlania."

"The civilians we can aim to help. We can bring them to Gamdesh. But leave the legions to war against Rufina and the blight. Let them destroy each other, Teriana. It's the smart thing to do."

All around her, people were nodding. Agreeing that this was the right choice. A tear slipped down Teriana's cheek.

Turning away from them, Teriana walked a few paces until she was out of the crowd and her eyes were on the sea. Her aunt came alongside her. "You grieve for those boys, don't you."

Teriana's throat tightened. "I know the legions are in the wrong. I know that they have caused harm that will take generations to undo. I know that attacking them was the right choice. But I can't feel good about killing them all like this."

Her eyes burned, and Teriana rubbed at them before meeting her aunt's gaze. "War is such a horror, Auntie. Why do people endlessly engage in it? Why are we this way? Why can't we see the harm it inflicts and say, 'Never again'?"

The seas of her aunt's eyes darkened. "There are always too many who will step on the backs of others for the sake of power and wealth, and too few who stand against them. It costs nothing to hurt people, but more often than not, it costs *everything* to protect them."

"I don't feel like I won anything." Teriana stared over the darkening sea. "I feel defeated, because despite everything, what has changed? Even if all those legions starve and die in Mudamora, the

Empire is still strong. It will rebuild. How do we stop this from happening again?"

"We can't," her aunt answered.

Behind Teriana, conversation had grown heated as to the best way to evacuate civilians while keeping the legions contained until they starved, and it made Teriana feel sick to hear it. Then her aunt said, "I think a nation is like a person, Teriana. Others can attack it, break it, burn it, silence it, but they cannot change how it thinks. That must come from within, and if the people of the Empire, and of Celendor itself, do not wish for change, then the Empire's ambitions will remain the same."

"Many of them do desire change," Teriana argued. "But Cassius and his followers are too strong. I saw resistance when I was there, but I also saw the fate of those who stood against him."

"Doing right often costs far more than doing wrong." Yedda sighed. "Just like doing *something* rather than nothing."

Lydia's face filled her vision, and Teriana's heart bled to know that her friends stood so horribly alone. She wouldn't abandon them. "I have to do something. I have to try, even if I have to go alone."

Her aunt's arm went around her shoulder. "I know you do, sweet girl. And our crew will have your back until the end."

Lysander has sent news. Magnius's voice abruptly filled her mind. Filled everyone's minds, judging by how all the Maarin across the island abruptly straightened.

The blight is destroyed, and the undead have had the Corrupter driven from their minds and have risen again as themselves. Mudamora and its allies have been victorious.

The whole island erupted with cheers. Teriana flung her arms around her aunt's shoulders, dancing in circles with tears running down her face. "She did it! Lydia did it!"

A cup of rum was pushed into her hand and she downed it, allowing herself to be drawn into the dancing crowd praising the names of the Six and victory over the Seventh. Yet as she was spun round and round, Teriana silently whispered to Magnius, *What about the legions?*

Under Legatus Marcus's command they aided Mudamora in the battle and then left, Magnius answered. *Lysander knows not where, only that they have seemingly disappeared.*

The shock of his words hit her like ice water to the face. The legions had switched sides. Which meant *Marcus* had switched sides. Her chest tightened because she hadn't thought there any hope for him. Had thought he was so lost to darkness that he'd never find his way out again, but he had.

And then disappeared.

Teriana's elation faded into a tumult of emotions, and she caught hold of Yedda's hands. "The legions are gone. Lysander says Marcus aided Mudamora's army and then vanished."

"Aided?" Her aunt's eyes went wide. "You mean . . ."

"I mean they aren't lost to the Corrupter." *Marcus isn't lost to the Corrupter.* "But where could they have gone?"

Her aunt shook her head. "That many men don't just *vanish.* They're somewhere. Let's keep this between us until we learn more."

Her people were calling her name. Teriana forced a smile onto her face as they cheered for her part in this victory, and she swiftly lost track of those who hugged her, kissed her cheeks, or filled her ears with praise. In truth, it felt like she was watching herself move through the crowd from afar, like the woman they all heralded as victor wasn't her at all. And with every passing moment, Teriana's anxiety over the fate of the legions, of the men she'd called friends, of the man she loved despite herself, grew like a beast inside her chest.

She was pulled close to the bonfire that had been built higher to light the growing darkness, and everyone fell silent. One of the captains stepped forward. "Magnius tells us that he has conferred with Lysander, and that by the traditions of our people, we convey unto you, Tesya's daughter and heir, the title of triumvir of the Maarin Trade Consortium to guide our people with strength and wisdom. Do you accept, Teriana of the *Quincense*?"

Everyone was smiling and watching, and Teriana had to force herself to breathe as the world spun.

"No," she finally answered. "I do not."

Shock radiated through the crowd, but as breath filled Teriana's lungs, so did strength. "Not only do I not desire to lead, I do not feel as though I am the right choice," she said. "This victory we have had does not erase what I have done. It does not change that my loyalties are divided. The Maarin deserve to be led by someone who is uncompromisingly committed to our people, and that is not me. It will never be me. So for the good of all the Maarin, I abdicate the role of triumvir and ask that a gathering be held in Taltuga to select a captain who will lead our people with the same spirit as my mother." Lifting her chin, Teriana added, "I will always support the Maarin. I will always fight for you. But I will not lead you."

Not waiting for a response, she turned and walked away.

"It was the right choice," her aunt said as they walked back down to the beach. "Your mother would be proud."

Teriana gave a tight nod, but rather than getting into the longboat, she waded out into the surf and waited.

Magnius did not make her wait long.

The great serpent drifted into the shallows, coiling gently around her, and Teriana rested her cheek against his massive head. "I'm going to miss you when you go on to guard the new triumvir," she said softly. "We all will."

Are you sure this is a choice you wish to make?

"It has to be." She swallowed hard. "A leader cannot be divided, Magnius. And my heart is cut into too many pieces to ever be made whole. My allegiance as well."

His great head tilted, his vast eye regarding her.

"I need to go West to find the legions. I need to discover their fate. I need to know why they helped. I need—" Her voice cracked and she swallowed hard. "I need to know if he's alive, Magnius. And if he's alive, whether he's himself again."

I'll take you wherever you wish to go.

"Thank you." Turning to her aunt, Teriana said, "Let the crew celebrate until tomorrow. They fought for this moment. They deserve it."

"What about you?"

Teriana leaned against Magnius, her gaze on the starlit sea, imagining she could see all the way across to Mudamora. "I've been too much away from the sea. I think I'll stand in the surf for a while."

To remember the past. To think about the present. And to dream about what might have been under different stars.

Magnius stayed with her long into the night, so they were together when Lydia's voice reached him through the magic of the sea. Teriana's mind filled with a vision of her friend standing in the waves before Mudaire. The truth of all that had happened—of what Marcus had done and what he intended to do—brought Teriana to her knees.

"Magnius," she finally whispered. "I need you to take me to Celendrial."

119

MARCUS

For all their initial shock at discovering his army outside Celendrial's gates, the Fifteenth and Twenty-Ninth showed their training as they moved to man Celendrial's walls. But there was no mistaking how they fumbled with aging catapults that had always been just for show. "When was the last time those things were tested?"

Wex shrugged. "Lescendor is my domain, not Celendrial, but, I'd hazard, not recently."

Marcus narrowed his eyes, marking the movements of the men on those walls, because even if only a few of the catapults worked, they could put up a decent fight. Celendrial's walls might be for show, but they were tall and thick, Cel construction at its finest. "Felix, I think it's time Celendrial gets a taste of what it's like to stare down their own war machine."

A taste of the fear they'd shoved down the throats of nearly every nation across Reath.

"Yes, sir."

The horn blew a series of notes, repeated by each legion as the message raced across the wall of men converging on the city.

Then the noise began.

Weapons slammed against shields to the rhythm set by the drums, thousands of men shouting the same wordless chant promising death. It was deafening, and his horse squealed and pinned its ears, causing Marcus to miss his golden mare. But he knew that inside the city, the ground and walls would be trembling, the noise flowing over the walls terrifying, and that panic would reign. In the distance, smoke rose from the harbor. Qian had obviously put fire to the docks to drive away ships, cutting off that line of escape for those who Marcus sought. Those who'd know that they were whom he was coming for.

The circle of death tightened, and though the noise made it impossible for him to hear, Marcus's imagination conjured visions of Celendrial's streets. Civilians screaming and racing to barricade themselves in their homes while legionnaires not on duty extracted themselves from brothels and wine houses and sleep to move to their positions, leaving the interior of the city devoid of policing.

"Signal," he said to Felix, and the horns blew another series of prearranged notes that would mean one thing to those on the walls and another to the hundreds of men he'd ordered to sneak into the city during the dark hours, all dressed in plain clothes.

Wex cast a sideways look at him. "You aren't actually planning to throw rocks at the walls, are you?"

Marcus smiled, knowing that his men inside would be racing about the city, filling the ears of every civilian they found with the same message.

The legions serve the people, not the tyrant.

"Rise up," he murmured, seeing in his mind's eye the million people in the city racing out into the streets. People from every province across the Empire, from the northern tundra of Sibern to the redwood forests of Bardeen to those born of Celendor herself, all whose backs had been stepped upon by the polished and perfumed men who lorded over them from their perch on Celendrial's Hill. Men who'd ordered them terrorized and killed for resisting a tyrant. Men who'd stood by while children were stolen from their parents to be turned into soldiers, then sent to die in order to line those same men's coffers. "This is your fight. Rise up."

His front lines had reached range of the catapults, and Marcus ordered the men to stop, but to continue with the noise. Over and over, he had the signalmen repeat the same signal. Those on the walls knew by now that the signal meant something different than their training told them, but rather than easing their fear that they were about to be hit by a barrage of rock, it increased it. Because they knew that *something* was happening, and that it would not be good. An accurate assessment, because the signal told his men inside the walls to spread the word that the legions were not here to harm the people but to defend them. A duty Marcus had shirked for far too long.

The legionnaires on the walls abruptly turned to look behind them into the city. Marcus smiled as they began to understand that the true threat was not the army behind them but the masses they'd so violently subjugated.

"Silence," Marcus ordered, and within a few heartbeats, his army was quiet. Motionless.

Waiting.

Marcus rode his horse forward a dozen paces ahead of the front line, then stopped, listening to the clash of weapons, the shouts of fear, the screams of pain, and then . . . the roar of triumph.

The gates burst outwards. Yet rather than a wall of legion spears, dozens of civilians raced out to sprint toward Marcus. "The city is yours, Legatus!" one of them shouted.

There was an undeniable allure to that statement, but Marcus only shook his head. "Celendrial belongs to no *one* man. She belongs to the people." He lifted his voice and shouted, "Thirty-Seventh, you have your orders! Root out the rats and bring them to the Curia. Alive."

His legion exploded past him, surging under the mouth of the snarling golden dragon above the gates and into the city, the centurions all carrying lists of names. Felix nodded once at Marcus as he passed, his friend's target the tyrant himself.

Once they were all through the gates, Marcus handed off the Thirty-Seventh's standard to Servius, then nodded at his guard. "With me."

They moved into the city, past the ranks of Twenty-Ninth and Fifteenth that were on their knees under the eyes of countless armed civilians, past streets splattered with blood and littered with bodies, for insurrection always had a cost. Past endless balconies and doorsteps filled with people shouting "Libertas!", their fists pumping the air, and toward the Hill that loomed over it all.

It was crawling with his legion, who were bodily dragging every senator from their villa, ignoring their screaming wives. The silence of their watching servants told Marcus everything he needed to know about what type of men they were. Only a few senators walked out of their own accord, some nodding at Marcus as they were escorted to the Curia.

Where there would be a reckoning.

He reached the Egnatius villa in time to find Tiberius leaving in the company of a group of Thirty-Seventh.

"Legatus," his brother-in-law said, inclining his head. "Bold, as always. There were better ways than this."

"The people said otherwise." Marcus rode past him. "In case I don't have another opportunity, I wanted to let you know that Agrippa is marked as deceased in my ledgers, but last I saw him in Mudamora, he was alive. Do not go looking for him—he's made a good life for himself."

Tiberius stiffened, but Marcus was already past him, riding through the gardens to where his sister, still dressed in her night clothes, stood holding a baby. Her other children clutched her skirts and wept, though they went still at the sight of him.

"Brother," Cordelia said sourly. "You have a way of doing things that I can't say that I care for."

"It's not my way," he replied. "It's the Empire's way, only this is the first time she's been on the receiving end of it. It's good for you to feel what it's like. For your children to feel what it's like. May you all remember it in the days and years to come."

She huffed out a breath, then handed the baby to her eldest child, murmuring for them to go back inside. "Spare me the speeches. Why are you here, Marcus?"

"Isn't my presence what you asked for? For me to return to Celendrial and use my power to do right by my own people rather than doing wrong against those on the far side of the world?"

"Yes," Cordelia answered. "But you aren't here because I asked you to be. Nor are you here because it was the right thing for you to do. I think not even Teriana influenced your choice to return, not her hold on your heart or the fact she defeated you. So why did you come home, brother? Because we both know that you being here will have a great cost."

Marcus considered her words, then said, "I think we all have beliefs so core to our heart that they define us. Influence every action, every choice. For me, it has always been to safeguard those who mattered to me the most: my family. To do whatever it took to keep them safe from those who'd do them harm, no matter what acts it took. No matter that those acts made me a villain of the worst sort. No matter that I left ash and death in my wake."

"You've decided to change that belief, then?"

"No. I just realized that I need to put my real family first."

Cordelia didn't answer, but he swore he saw relief in her eyes.

"When last we saw each other, you would have heard Wex say to me, 'Just because you were born to them doesn't make them your family. Look to those who guard your back, not those who throw you to the wolves.'" He glanced backward at the commandant, who sat his horse just out of earshot. "I've always known the Thirty-Seventh was my real family. My brothers. Yet that bond isn't limited to just my legion, but to all our brothers-in-arms. Not a family we chose, but a family that we made in the blood and in the mud, and Cassius delivered the youngest of our ranks to the wolves when he sent the Fifty-First into the blight alone. He did it to put me in my place. To remind me that he ruled. What he failed to remember is that I am every bit the villain that he is, and when you come for mine, I come for blood."

Cordelia drew in a deep breath, then pressed one hand to her face for a long moment. Lowering it, she said, "That isn't the answer I'd hoped for."

"Nor will this be the end you wished for," he answered. "Take care of yourself, sister."

Wheeling his horse around, Marcus rode away.

* * *

By the time Marcus made it through the packed streets, nearly every senator in the city was in the Curia. Some under their own free will, others clearly under duress, his men watching them weep and complain with unmoved expressions as they were ushered to their seats.

"This is embarrassing," Servius muttered. "Some of them had to be dragged out from under the beds. Some of them tried to hide behind their young children. And these are the men who rule us all?"

"Golden pedestals," Marcus answered. "Is everyone doing their duty?"

"So far. We've got the Fifteenth and Twenty-Ninth outside the city and under heavy guard. I don't think the Fifteenth will be a problem, but Hostus left a stain on his men that I don't think will ever come clean."

"A problem for a later hour. Sign of Felix?"

"Not yet. Apparently his rat dug a deep hole, though he's in pursuit. Forty-First is holding the perimeter around the Forum because the populace is frothing at the mouth. They're angry, and if we let them, they'll tear these men apart."

"Tempting."

"Isn't it though? There's something to be said for a clean slate."

Except it wouldn't be. Even if Marcus allowed every man in this building to be murdered, the wealth of the Empire remained in their families' hands. Sons and nephews and cousins would inherit, then rise to power, and they were likely the same caliber of men who sat on these benches. "They are supposed to speak for the people, and those who actually do so will be elevated by Celendor's citizens." His eyes flicked through the open doors. Past Appius Valerius, who'd arrived without argument, to Tiberius Egnatius, who sat quietly in the front row, expression contemplative.

Now that he knew the truth, Marcus could see the similarities in his face to Agrippa's, as well as the slightly darker hue of his skin courtesy of his Bardenese mother. "The people see now that the Senate's power is not absolute. That they are beholden to the citizens, and I think that, more than any action we take, will hold them to task."

A commotion broke out, and a dozen Thirty-Seventh appeared, Felix at their head. A struggling man with a sack over his head was being dragged between them.

"Found him in a cellar near the harbor market. His servant was trying to bribe fishermen with boats to row him out to a ship. The fishermen turned him in."

Pulling off the sack, Marcus looked into Cassius's piggish eyes. "You are going to pay for this, boy," the Dictator hissed between broken teeth. Felix had obviously taken Marcus's orders that he be brought alive as not precluding injury. "If you don't back away from this now, I'll see everyone you care about dead. Your father and brother hanged. Your mother stripped of clothes and forced to walk the streets naked, your sisters along with her, and I'll set the dogs on them. You, I'll kill last, and it will be a *short rope.* Make the smart choice while you still can."

Felix lifted his arm to backhand Cassius, but Marcus shook his head. "Gag him and bring him in."

The sack Cassius had worn was shredded, and his shouts cut off as a wadded-up ball of fabric was shoved in his mouth, another strip binding it in place. Walking into the Curia, Marcus was struck by how much smaller it seemed than the last time he'd been here. Nothing more than a small room set up like a theater with its tiered benches, the men filling them seeming smaller still. A rostra sat upon the elaborately tiled floor, and atop it sat a golden throne.

The last Emperor's throne.

Marcus stared at it for a long time as Cassius was dragged in behind him, the Dictator the only one making noise, for all the senators were silent. Yet at the sight of Cassius, Lydia's father leaned forward, his expression shifting from simmering anger to keen interest at the realization that Cassius was the target of all of this.

Tiberius rose to his feet, seeming to understand instinctively the role he needed to play here. "I would have you explain your intentions, Legatus. You have committed treason by abandoning your post in the West, by attacking Celendrial, and by doing violence upon members of this Senate. Why are you here?"

Marcus inclined his head to Tiberius, then lifted his voice. "Because the people are displeased. They are weary of being oppressed, of being trod upon, and of being taxed to fund a war they do not want. The Senate is supposed to be the voice of the people, yet its words are only to the benefit of the men in this room."

"I asked for an explanation for why *you* are here, Legatus, not an explanation of the sentiment of the people."

Marcus pulled off his helmet and let it fall to the tiled floor with a loud clang. "Am I not a person, Senator?" Unbuckling his belt, he cast aside his weapons, then the pieces of his armor, until he stood in only a tunic and sandals. "Am I not a citizen of the Empire? Cannot the reasons of the people be my reasons?"

"Curtail your theatrics, Legatus. You are no ordinary citizen, and removing the accoutrements of your rank does not change that fact. I would have justification for your actions."

"You are correct, I am no ordinary citizen, for unlike every other citizen, I am indentured. Am, for all intents and purposes, a slave to the Senate's will until I have earned back my price or until death liberates me, whichever comes first. I am *less* than an ordinary citizen, for I am not free, nor is any man in service to the Empire's legions."

"Less?" Tiberius made a face. "You hold the power. You've made that clear to us with this performance. You control Celendrial and we are all at your mercy. Except unless you intend to rule by martial force, to name yourself Dictator, to name yourself *Emperor,* then you must still answer to the law."

"And therein lies the reason I have returned to Celendrial, Senator. In answer to the call of the law."

The senators were all leaning forward now, fear replaced with interest.

"Speak clearly."

Marcus lifted one shoulder. "Is it not my sworn duty to uphold the laws of the Empire as determined by this senate?"

"It is. Yet you break them instead by disobeying the commands of the Dictator who represents us in this time of war."

"I break no law, for I have no obligation to follow the directives of a man who holds power unlawfully."

Ignoring the legionnaires training weapons upon them, the senators loyal to Cassius exploded to their feet, shouting in outrage.

Tiberius lifted his hands. "Silence! We will have order!"

The men returned to their seats, a few only under the prodding of Thirty-Seventh spear tips.

"Lucius Cassius was made Dictator by vote of the Senate, Legatus," Tiberius said. "During times of war, it is the Senate's right to suspend elections and elevate the power of the standing consul so that he might overcome the threat facing the Empire."

"I do not question the Senate's right to grant the consul a dictator's powers," Marcus replied. "However that consul must be lawfully elected by the citizens of Celendor."

"Which he was. You yourself voted for him in the same performative manner as you are using now. It is not illegal for one to incite votes with the promise to take certain actions should one win office, which one can only assume was how Cassius secured your support."

Marcus's throat tightened, his gaze going to his father, who sat quietly in the front row. Their eyes locked, and his father gave the smallest nod of understanding.

"Cassius did not gain my vote, nor the votes of the Thirty-Seventh legion, with incentives," Marcus said. "He gained it through blackmail."

The Senate was silent for a shocked heartbeat, then they were again on their feet, shouting for explanations. Shouting that Cassius be allowed to speak.

Marcus watched Cassius squirm on the ground beneath Felix's foot, the Dictator's eyes murderous with rage. And the voice, which had been quiet for so many long days, reared its head, for it was not entirely defeated. Marcus doubted it ever would be. *Silence him!* it screamed. *You earned your power! Why should you concede it to these soft and perfumed men who've never fought for anything in their lives? Why shouldn't you rule?*

He pressed a hand to the tiny replica of the *Quincense* that rested against his chest, then nodded at Felix. "Ungag him."

Felix obeyed, and Cassius scrambled to his feet, seething with anger. "Fool of a boy! Retract these false accusations and I might see fit to show mercy to you!"

Marcus tilted his head, staring into the eyes of the man who had done harm to so many. Who'd used war to achieve ultimate power, happy to step on the backs of a hundred thousand corpses in his quest to gain the golden chair behind him. For so long, he'd both hated and feared Cassius, but now as Marcus looked at him, all he felt was contempt.

"What was the nature of this blackmail, Legatus?" Tiberius asked. "Manipulating an election is a serious offense, and your accusation must be backed with details if we are to act upon it."

Marcus only vaguely heard Tiberius's question, because rising behind Cassius's anger and bluster was fear. Fear that seemed to shrink the man, making it hard for Marcus to understand why he'd ever seen him as a threat. If Cassius revealed the truth that Marcus had kept secret for so long, it would condemn them both, and Cassius feared the consequences far more than Marcus did.

"Do it," Marcus said softly. "Tell them."

Cassius licked his lips, casting a sideways glance at the watching Senate. Yet he remained silent, still banking on his certainty that Marcus would do everything and anything to protect this secret.

"As you like." Marcus cleared his throat. "I am the son of your peer, Senator Domitius. Not his second son, but his eldest son, born under the name Gaius Domitius. My health was poor as a child, my longevity uncertain, so my father made the decision to switch my identity with my younger brother's so as to retain his stronger son as heir. Cassius learned of the deception, which is easily proven by any physician, and he threatened to reveal the truth if I didn't arrange for my legion to vote for him and secure him the consulship. Given the severity of the punishment for breaking the child tithe laws, I saw no path forward but to agree to his demands."

All eyes swiveled to his father, who rose to his feet. "All that my son says is the truth. My crime was the stepping stone that allowed Cassius to commit treason, and I will accept punishment."

Marcus waited to feel something, *anything*, for his father finally taking responsibility for his actions. Yet all he felt was relief that his father had not attempted to fight him on this.

"Winning the election was not the end of what Cassius used this information to compel me to do," Marcus continued. "On Cassius's orders, I drowned Lydia Valerius, daughter of Senator Appius Valerius, whom Cassius had promised to marry in order to gain Valerius's support in the elections." He looked to Valerius, who met his gaze with an unblinking stare. "Lydia survived, finding passage through the xenthier stem Cassius most recently used to send the Fifty-First to their deaths."

Tiberius exhaled a slow breath, audible in the silence of the room. "What say you to these accusations, Cassius? For they are damning indeed."

Cassius's jaw worked back and forth, then he crossed his arms and glared in silence.

Valerius spoke. "Through other lips, I have heard this same story. That the legatus put my daughter down the drains of Cassius's *baths*, only luck allowing her to survive and bravery to see her through to the far side of Reath, where she yet lives. I would have pursued justice myself, but I did not think any of you would believe a Maarin girl over our *beloved* Dictator."

Cassius's gaze was as cold as a snake's, but he remained silent.

"I think all truths will come out in the trial, along with others I anticipate will be equally criminal in nature," Tiberius said, then he looked to Marcus. "We are all in your debt for revealing the traitor in our midst, Legatus, but it cannot be denied that you have implicated yourself as well. Not only in your role in manipulating an election, but perhaps more critically, in your breach of the tithe laws and your attempted murder of Lydia Valerius. You have right to trial, of course, but—"

"No need," Marcus interrupted. "I plead guilty to all three crimes."

Out of the corner of his eye, he saw Felix stiffen, as did all of his men in the room, their shock twisting his stomach with guilt.

"All three crimes are punishable by death," Tiberius said. "Given the extenuating circumstances, a trial might see—"

"I am guilty." Marcus kept his hand pressed to the tiny ship, needing the courage it gave him for what was to come as he said to Felix, "The Thirty-Seventh is yours."

120

KILLIAN

"You sure about this, Lydia?" Agrippa asked from where he leaned against the stone wall of the chamber. "Keep in mind that the man who rules Celendrial tried to murder you, and your reappearance, along with your subsequent accusations, are going to put you right in his line of sight."

"I don't think Cassius rules Celendrial anymore," Lydia answered, circling the xenthier.

"I wasn't talking about Cassius."

Killian's stomach tightened, because while Lydia didn't appear to have considered whether Marcus remained a threat to her, he most certainly had.

"If Marcus has decided to take control, your arrival will be a significant inconvenience for him," Agrippa said. "Don't mistake an alliance of convenience for more than it is, Lydia. He's proven what he's capable of."

"I'll be cautious," she said.

"Keep your head down." Agrippa gave Killian a once-over, shaking his head. "Shoulders, too. You're going to stand out like a sore thumb among those gilded bastards."

"Noted. You'll be all right without us?"

It was Malahi who answered. "We'll make do with the supplies the legions abandoned until ships come to bring us back south." She bit at her bottom lip. "Please be careful. We need you to come home."

Guilt bit at Killian's heart, because he and Lydia were needed here to help rebuild. But Malahi was experienced and capable, and she had Agrippa and the rest of their friends to guard her back. Whereas Killian feared that Teriana stood alone. "The Seventh himself couldn't keep us from returning."

Malahi gave a small smile. "I suspect he knows that."

"Find Finn for me," Killian said to Agrippa. "He should be with Seldrid, but . . ."

"I'll find him." Agrippa took hold of Malahi's arm and drew her back from the xenthier. "Good luck."

"Together?" Lydia asked, reaching out to take Killian's hand.

"Together," he answered, grasping it tight. Their clenched hands reached for the xenthier, and the last thing he heard was Agrippa shouting, "One at a—"

A white void surrounded him, and though Killian knew Lydia's hand was grasped in his, not being able to feel it filled him with panic.

Then he was stumbling through water, Lydia's hand tight in his as she fell to her knees in the swamp.

Killian's first impression of Celendor was that it was gods-awful hot.

The second was that he was staring down a dozen legionnaires, several with arrows pointed directly at his head.

Rising to her feet, Lydia spoke to them in Cel. Recognition bloomed on several of the men's faces, all of them bearing the mark of the Thirty-Seventh Legion. Weapons lowered, then the one who appeared to lead them said in Mudamorian, "That's a decision above my rank, Domina. I'll take you to the legatus and he'll decide what to do with you." Then he jerked his chin at Killian. "Hand over your weapons."

"You're welcome to have them if you can take them."

The man considered his words, then shrugged. "Fine. Start walking. If you piss me off, I'll have my men shoot you in the back, understood? Today is not the day to test my patience."

Helping Lydia out of the swamp, Killian started toward the enormous walled city in the distance, the legionnaires forming an escort around them. "So this is Celendrial?" he asked under his breath, and she gave a tight nod. "Heart of the Empire."

Until this moment, this place had only been a name. A dot on an unfamiliar map. His imagination had not done it justice. There was a gravitas to the city that he'd never experienced before, not even in Revat. A presence, like the city itself was alive, and Kilian fell silent as they reached the gates and passed beneath the golden reptile perched above.

People were flowing in groups toward the center of the city. They gave the legionnaires wide berth, their curious eyes looking over him and Lydia. The escort moved with the flow to a building with columns that stretched incredibly high, the ceilings above painted in vivid scenes, but the crowd carried onward.

"What's going on?" Lydia asked the centurion. "Where are they going?"

"Executions," he answered, but refused to answer any further queries as they were brought deeper into the building. Their footsteps echoed down the corridors, and a set of doors opened ahead of them, the guards to either side saying something in Cel to the centurion, who turned back to Lydia and Killian. "The legatus will see you now," he said.

Lydia squared her shoulders, meeting Killian's gaze for a heartbeat, then she stepped inside. He followed, eyes latching onto the man standing behind the table. He wore legion clothing and armor, the Thirty-Seventh's mark stamped on the breastplate.

But the man was not Marcus.

121

TERIANA

Teriana anchored the *Quincense* south of Celendrial with strict orders for the ship to flee if the navy came into sight, and even stricter instructions that no one was to follow her into the city. Yet as she entered the gates, hair and face concealed by a scarf, it was clear that the Maarin were the least of the Empire's concerns. For it was apparently an empire no longer, the Senate having officially declared Celendor a republic. Yet even that news paled in comparison to the fervor over the executions that were planned for later that day. Because she didn't know who else to go to, Teriana sought out Lydia's father.

"Teriana!" Shock radiated across his face when the servants brought her into the villa, but it was swiftly replaced with anger. "Have you lost your blasted mind coming to Celendrial, girl? No matter the reasons and no matter the outcomes, you still led an attack on Celendor and there are countless people in this city who'd happily see you dead."

"I know." Teriana was shaking, the weight of all the gossip she'd heard since she'd entered the city pushing her to the breaking point. "But I need to see him."

His expression didn't soften. "Marcus is to be executed today, Teriana. He pleaded guilty of all charges, not the least being Lydia's murder."

"Lydia's not dead, you know that."

"I know. But it doesn't change what he did."

It hurt to breathe. "I know that," she whispered. "I know everything he did, but . . ."

"But . . . ?" Senator Valerius's eyes were cold. "This is justice, Teriana. After all that you've personally endured, you should see today as a victory. You should be lifting a glass with your people on the safety of your ship, far out to sea. Not standing in my household weeping for the villain."

He wasn't wrong, but the tears spilled down her cheeks. "Please, Appius. On my life, I will never ask for anything again. I just need to see him. Please."

Lydia's father stared her down for a long time, but then looked away. "As you like. But after you say your good-byes, you need to leave Celendrial. If you have any wisdom in your heart, you'll never look back."

122

LYDIA

The legionnaire's blue eyes fixed on her, then he sighed and scrubbed a hand over his short hair. "Why are you here?"

"For Teriana," Lydia said. "Who are you?"

"Felix. His second-in-command." The man's jaw tightened. "Though not for much longer. And if Teriana is here, none of my men have spotted her. Which is just as well. I don't hold what she did against her by any stretch of the imagination, but that doesn't change that she waged war against Celendor. Many died. The Senate has been occupied, but that does not mean she is safe from them. There's no reason for her to be here and every reason to stay away."

"I think we both know that's not the case," Lydia answered. "Who is being executed today?"

Felix broke eye contact, walking to the window to look out. "Cassius."

"Who else are they executing?" she asked, already knowing the answer.

"He confessed to everything. Declared himself guilty of everything."

Lydia knew the *he* who Felix referred to wasn't Cassius.

"Marcus told me himself what he did to you, Lydia, and I was there for the rest. So I'm not going to stand here and say that he's not at fault. But so are the rest of us, because we all did as we were told. If there were justice in the world, every legionnaire who stepped into the West would be on the gallows. Every legionnaire alive, if I'm honest, because we didn't do anything in Arinoquia, Gamdesh, or Mudamora that hasn't been done in the provinces a thousand times over. Yet Marcus is the one who will take the fall, and while that may be justice to some, it doesn't seem fair given he was the one who was blackmailed."

Lydia glanced to Killian, but he only leaned against the wall, seeming content to remain silent through this exchange.

Clearing her throat, she asked, "What does Marcus have to say about that?"

"That justifications don't change outcomes." Felix shook his head. "And in less than an hour, he'll be dead for them."

The door abruptly swung open, and a large legionnaire stepped into the room. "Felix—" He broke off at the sight of Lydia, then shook his head. "Why am I not surprised?"

"Has something happened?" Felix asked, stepping away from the window. "A stay?"

The big legionnaire shook his head. "No. Teriana is in Celendrial. Valerius pulled strings and he's taking her to see him."

A sudden stab of pain hit Lydia in the heart, because she knew Teriana down to her toes. Had known exactly how her friend would feel when she learned Marcus's intentions. Had known that Teriana would come to Celendrial to try to stop it.

This war kept *taking.*

Taking and taking, and even though the side of right was victorious and would have its justice, Lydia couldn't help but feel that, at the end of it, their hearts would be hollow.

Felix exhaled a long breath, his eyes on the water clock on the table. "I wish she'd come sooner. We're to bring him to the Forum on the hour, and Marcus won't be happy if we make him late."

He started toward the door, but Lydia caught hold of his arm, pulling him back. "I think we need to give them more time. While we wait, could you please arrange for my father to join us?"

123

TERIANA

"There is not much time," Valerius said to Teriana as he led her down the corridor. "And I suggest you leave the city as soon as you say your piece. Riots are likely, and it will not go well for you if you are caught up in them."

Teriana gave a small nod, then swiftly adjusted her scarf so that more of her face was concealed. Her heart was hammering, and though logically she knew that her life was very much in danger, given the building was full of legionnaires, the twist of terror in her belly had nothing to do with threat to her own life.

A legionnaire came down the corridor, and Teriana lowered her face because there was a 37 on his breastplate. "Legatus wishes to speak to you, Senator. He says it's urgent."

Valerius made an aggrieved noise. "Where is he?"

"Down one level."

"Tell him I'll be along shortly."

One of his guards, the retired centurion who'd been with Teriana when Hostus had killed her mother, had gone ahead and was speaking to the two legionnaires standing guard outside a door. Both stiffened, their eyes jumping down the corridor to her, but then they nodded.

"You will give her no trouble, understood?" Valerius said to the men as they drew up before them. "She was never here."

"Yes, sir," one replied, but the other said, "We know we're home because of you, Teriana. Alive because of you. The Senate will do their best to erase what you did from the history books, but the Thirty-Seventh will remember."

She lifted her face to meet his gaze, lost for words because she'd been so certain they'd hate her. "Libertas."

The legionnaires inclined their heads. "Libertas."

They opened the door, and Valerius placed a hand on her back and pushed her through. It shut firmly behind her, the bolt clunking into place, but Teriana barely noticed, her eyes all for the familiar figure standing at the window. Marcus's back was to her, his elbows resting on the sill of the window she'd once climbed out of in a bid to rescue her mother. He wore only undergarments, likely in deference to the extreme heat plaguing Celendrial, the 1519 stark and black on his bare shoulders.

"Felix, they won't take you seriously as legatus if you keep coming to me for instructions," he said. "You need—"

"It's not Felix," she blurted out. "It's me."

Marcus stiffened, then slowly turned. "Teriana?"

His eyes were no longer the voids she'd seen in Revat, but blue-grey. She'd known that to have come here and done all that he had done, Marcus had to have fought his way out from under the Corrupter's influence, but seeing him once again as the man she'd fallen in love with was such a relief that Teriana nearly dropped to her knees.

"Yes." Her palms were like ice yet slick with sweat because she had no idea how he was going to react to seeing her. No idea how *she* was going to react to seeing him, because her chest was filled with every possible emotion, all warring against each other, and Teriana had no idea which one would win. "I . . ."

She trailed off, words failing her. As they seemed to be failing him, because they stood staring at each other in silence, neither of them closing the distance between them.

"Why are you here?" he finally asked.

"Why are you?" Her eyes were burning, tears barely kept in check, because on a string around his neck he wore the miniature replica of the *Quincense* that he'd given her. That she'd given back when she'd declared war upon him.

Exhaling, he ran a hand over his hair. "Cassius needed to be removed from power. I—"

"I know why you came back to Celendor," she interrupted, taking a step closer to him. "Lydia told me in her message. Though she didn't need to, because I know the reasons better than anyone. I'm asking why are you in this *cell*?"

"Ah. Well, it's because—"

"This isn't right!" She took two more quick steps. "You saved them from Cassius. If you hadn't come back, they'd still be suffering under his tyranny, and they put you in prison for it?"

"It's because—"

"And even if they do insist on this lunacy, why aren't you letting Felix get you out of here?" Another step. "Why won't you escape? Why did you plead guilty?"

"Because—"

"They're going to execute you. In the Forum." Another step. "At the same time as Cassius, like . . . like you're the same as him."

They were within arm's reach of each other. It felt too close. Too far. A tear rolled down her cheek, and Teriana brushed it away.

"Are you going to let me answer?" Marcus asked, grey-blue eyes filled with a mixture of humor and sadness that nearly undid her.

"No," she whispered. "Because I know that you're going to give me a reason I can't argue against."

He didn't reply, and Teriana found she couldn't meet his gaze, so instead she stared at his chest. Watched the 37 rise and fall with steady breath.

"Teriana, one of the crimes they're going to execute me for is trying to murder Lydia."

"I know." She balled her hands into fists, knowing that there was no justifying her hypocrisy. What he'd done to Lydia, and the subsequent lies that he'd told, had been one of the biggest hurts she'd ever endured. Part of her had hated him for it. Had wanted to put a knife through his heart for it. But this? The Empire meting out his punishment? That was not the ending she'd sought, and every part of her soul railed against this outcome. "This isn't what I wanted."

Marcus reached up and brushed away one of her tears. "I'm sorry,

Teriana. What I did to her was unforgivable, but what I regret most is deceiving you, because there was no motive in it beyond me not wanting to face your hate. It was selfish and cowardly, and you deserved better from me. And what came after . . ."

"That was the Corrupter."

"It wasn't. It was me."

Teriana gave a sharp shake of her head. "You were not yourself when we met in Revat, Marcus. The Seventh God was there controlling you."

"There, yes, but not controlling." His eyes went distant, remembering. "After you left, I didn't want to feel because it hurt too much, and he made that possible. Allowed me to wall up the part of myself that cared, which left the other part unchecked. The villain. And every time the part that cared tried to pull down those walls, I'd have to feel the hurt, and the walls would rise up higher than before. He didn't make me do anything, only gave strength to the parts of me that served him best."

The eerie similarities to what Lydia had told her silenced Teriana's argument that the Corrupter was to blame.

"That's why I'm here. Not just to be punished for all the things I've done, but because the capacity to do the same or worse again is still in me. A part that whispers, *why shouldn't I order Felix to let me out of this cell? Why shouldn't I take back command? Why shouldn't I overthrow all those men who rule from their hill, because I'd rule the Empire better than they ever could.*

Her skin chilled. "Marcus . . ."

"I've spent all my life thinking that I was powerless, but now I know that's not the case, and I am afraid of what I might do with that knowledge."

She understood what he was saying, but it still felt like conceding. Like giving up. "Then leave with me. You and I, we'll go somewhere together. An island in the middle of nowhere. Just not this."

Marcus turned away from her, going back to the window, silent for a long time before he said, "When we stood on the banks of the Savio and you asked me to leave with you, I . . . I was going to say yes."

Her chest tightened to the point she could barely breathe. "You never told me that."

"There didn't seem much point given that the decision was made for me." Marcus rested his elbows on the windowsill. "But many times since, I've wondered how it would have gone if the Twenty-

Ninth hadn't caught us. If we'd abandoned everything to hide somewhere where no one knew our names. But in every vision of that future, you always found out about Lydia. You always turned on me because I could never outrun justice. So I won't try now."

"But you are being executed for things you were forced to do." Teriana pressed the heels of her hands to her eyes, trying to contain her tears. "You were blackmailed."

"Those are the reasons the Empire will execute me, but they aren't the only reasons I deserve to die. In truth, they are the least significant." He drew in a deep breath. "Gamdesh will never be the same because of me. Nor Chersome nor Bardeen nor any other nation I've invaded. Thousands dead. Hundreds of thousands without homes. Revat is destroyed and the greatest monuments to the Six in ruins because I willed it so. If the Senate hanged me a thousand times, it would not be sufficient punishment."

"Punishment won't undo the past." The Six help her, Teriana knew her words were selfish. Self-serving. That the world should condemn her for saying them. "It won't change anything."

A lie, because it would change everything.

Marcus turned around, and when she saw his eyes liquid with unshed tears, her control cracked. "Please don't do this, Marcus. Please find another way."

His hand curved around the side of her face, and she leaned into his touch, familiar even after their time apart. In truth, she'd recognize the feel of his hand when she was old and grey, if given the chance. But there'd be no more chances.

"The world has suffered in a way that it hasn't in living memory," he said softly. "People need to see heroes like you and Lydia triumph so that they have hope. But they also need to see villains like me face justice."

"I am no one's hero."

"How can you say that when you struck the blow that changed the tide of the war? How can you say that when you united nations in order to fight back against their oppressors? How can you say that when it was *you* who put the Empire on the back foot for the first time in generations?" He tipped her face up so that she was looking into his eyes. "Real heroes aren't pristine. They're covered in blood and muck from fighting on the front lines. You fought well, Teriana, but most importantly, you kept fighting, even when it hurt."

It still hurt.

Would always hurt.

From their first moments, they'd been on opposing sides. Enemies, in every possible way. Destined to end badly. But not once had she imagined that it would end because they were finally standing on the same side.

A knock sounded through the door, and Felix called, "It's time."

No! Her heart screamed the word, but she refused to allow it to pass her lips, because she knew Marcus would not be swayed. Knew that she shouldn't try because it would diminish his sacrifice. And her own.

"Marcus, I've given you as long as I could," Felix called. "They're taking Cassius to the Forum now."

"Just . . . wait," he called back.

Not yet.

Marcus lowered his head and kissed her. The thrill of it was the same as it had been the first time, perhaps because she knew it would be the last.

"I wish I had more time." He pressed his forehead to hers. "Time to say all the things I should've said before."

"Say them now." Her face was slick with tears, the words torn out between sobs.

"Marcus!"

"I love you, Teriana." He kissed her again. "To my last breath, I will love you."

Teriana couldn't breathe. Couldn't speak. Every part of her felt broken, and she clung to his neck, not willing to let go. But then Marcus was tugging her arms loose. Pulling a plain white tunic over his head and belting it with a cord. Then he hammered a fist against the door, and Felix immediately opened it.

Yet instead of leaving, Marcus gripped her shoulders. "Live, Teriana." His fingers tightened. "And please don't watch me die."

Then he was gone.

124

MARCUS

He dragged a hand across his face to wipe away the tears as he left her, leading Felix and Servius down the corridor with long strides, because if he didn't put distance between himself and Teriana, Marcus knew that he'd turn around.

That he'd go back to her. And that no power on Reath would pull him away from her again.

"I don't want to hear any more arguments from you two," he muttered. "Let's just get this done."

Neither of his friends answered, only followed him down the stairs and out into the city—

Where the entire Thirty-Seventh waited, neat ranks packing the streets in a long column that wove through Celendrial. But painfully fewer in number than they'd been when they had set out across the world. So many of his brothers lost, his hands stained with their blood.

"Last march," Felix said quietly. "They'll follow you to the end."

Marcus's chest tightened, emotion drowning him as he stared out over the men who'd followed him across the world and back. Men who'd been his family. His brothers. He no more wanted them to watch him die than he did Teriana, but neither would he deny them this. "Then straighten up those ranks," he ordered. "Everyone in Celendrial is watching."

Backs straightened and chins lifted as he moved to the center of the column, Servius and Felix on either side of him, the Thirty-Seventh's standard in Servius's hand.

"Drums."

The drummers began to strike their instruments, the same steady beat as they'd played when they marched on Celendrial. "To the Forum."

The column began to move, the *thud, thud, thud* of thousands of feet stepping in time echoing off the walls of the building, the civilians moving onto their balconies to silently watch. No one spoke, the men all silent and grim-faced, and Marcus kept his eyes forward even as beads of sweat rolled down his back.

You can do this.

Ahead, the Forum appeared, men of the Forty-First blocking the entrance. They moved aside at the Thirty-Seventh's approach, saluting Marcus as he passed. At the far end of the space, gallows had been erected. On them stood his father, his brother, and Cassius. Nooses dangled, including the one that waited for him. Marcus's heart skittered, his nerve faltering. He pressed a hand to his chest, feeling the tiny metal ship dig into his chest.

You can do this.

The lead ranks of the Thirty-Seventh reached the end of the open space, forming neat lines with a pathway between them, allowing him a clear line to the rostra where Tiberius waited, Senator Valerius at his side. On the steps leading to the Curia crowded the rest of the Senate, Cordelia among them, her chin high though her eyes were red.

"The prisoner," Felix said coldly to Tiberius.

"Restrain him and bring him onto the gallows," Tiberius said. "We do not intend to belabor this."

You can do this.

Swallowing hard, Marcus turned to Servius and wrapped his arms around his friend. "It has been my honor and privilege to serve with you," he said, "and to call you my friend."

Tears dripped down Servius's face, and he squeezed Marcus so hard his ribs groaned. "You as well, sir."

Then Felix took his arm, leading him onto the platform.

"I have to bind your wrists," Felix said quietly. "Protocol."

"I know." He pulled the string holding the hair ornament over his head, gripping the little metal ship in his fist as Felix wrapped his wrists with rope. "Take care of them, my friend. You're the only one I trust to do it."

Felix gave a tight nod, then slipped the noose over his head, his friend's composure cracking as he tightened it. "I'm sorry," he said, wiping away tears. "I can't do this to you. I won't."

"You will," Marcus said. "Last order."

Felix was quiet, then he nodded and stepped back. "Yes, sir."

The Forum was nearly silent, not a word spoken by his men, the senators on the steps, nor the civilians that had crowded in behind the Thirty-Seventh. The only sound was his brother's loud weeping. Marcus kept his eyes forward, watching as his mother, dressed in a silk dress, was brought forward.

"You have been found guilty of treason," Tiberius said to her, and Marcus heard the faint shake in his brother-in-law's voice. "In accordance with Celendor's laws, you are to be stripped of titles and material possessions, and then made to walk the streets so that all you have wronged may see your shame."

His mother screamed, then dropped to her knees, looking up at Marcus. "Don't let them do this," she begged. "Please, stop this. I know you could stop this if you wanted. Please!"

You can do this. Marcus gripped the tiny ship tight, then looked forward, saying nothing.

The executioner stepped forward, and without hesitation, tore the dress off his mother, leaving her naked. She gasped, trying to cover herself, but the man shoved her in the back. "Walk."

His mother took one stumbling step, then another, heading down the path created by his men, who all kept their eyes forward. Slowly, she walked to the rear of the Forum, disappearing into the city. Where there would usually be shouts of mockery, there was only silence. His eyes flicked to Cordelia. She and his sisters were wed, which spared them from such a fate, but at best, the stain this had left upon them would result in ostracization for long years to come. At worst, their husbands would cast them into the streets to be rid of them. What remained of his family depended on the grace of Agrippa's brother, and Marcus could only hope that Tiberius Egnatius was as good a man as he believed himself to be.

Then Tiberius said, "Gaius Domitius, you have been found guilty of treason. In accordance with the laws of Celendor, your punishment is the forfeiture of your life."

Gaius shrieked and thrashed, then twisted to look at Marcus. "This is your fault!" he screamed. "You were supposed to die! Why didn't you die?"

"Soon enough," Marcus replied, the ship digging into his palm as the platform dropped.

Crack.

He flinched as his brother's neck snapped, then the Forum was silent again.

"Gnaeus Domitius, you have been found guilty of treason. In accordance with the laws of Celendor, your punishment is the forfeiture of your life."

His father looked at him, and said, "I'm sorry. I was a fool to have given you up."

You can do this.

The platform dropped.

Crack.

"I told you."

Cassius's voice filled his ears, and Marcus turned to meet the man's eyes, feeling a rush of cold as he stared into dark voids. Vaguely, he heard Tiberius sentencing Cassius, the crowd no longer quiet but screaming for blood. It all seemed distant as Cassius said, "I told you that if you crossed me, I'd take away everything you cared about. That I'd destroy everything you loved."

Marcus stared back, blood trickling down his fingers as the metal cut his palm under the force of his grip. "You did not choose this. *I did.*"

Cassius dropped.

Crack.

Marcus stared at the dangling corpse of the man who'd caused him such grief and pain. Cassius's eyes were now blue and unseeing, and urine dripped from the Dictator's sandaled foot to splatter the ground below.

It's over. The worst is over. The rest will be quick and easy, and then you can rest.

"Legionnaire 37–1519, you have been found guilty of treason against the Empire. In accordance with the laws of Celendor, your punishment is the forfeiture of your life," Tiberius said, then he looked to Valerius, who nodded once. "Do you have final words, Legatus?"

He didn't want to speak, but as he looked out over his legion, Marcus knew that he owed it to them, so he cleared his throat.

You can do this.

The rope of the noose was rough against his throat as Marcus swallowed hard, taking in the legion standing before him. The Thirty-Seventh. Men he'd led through countless battles, their expressions a mixture of grief and anger, but their eyes held loyalty that not even the shadow of his crimes could extinguish. "At ease."

The Thirty-Seventh all relaxed their postures, many removing their helmets, and the senators watching on all shifted nervously as though it were just occurring to them that he still held the power here. And though that power would soon come to an end, it was by his decision, not theirs.

Marcus took a deep breath, then spoke, his voice carrying over the silent forum. "It was nearly fourteen years ago that we were delivered to Campus Lescendor. Taken from the only families we had known and delivered into halls filled with strangers. Into a life of hardship and suffering and violence that many did not survive but which bound us into a brotherhood. They call us a legion, but what we are is a family that was forged with our blood, our sweat, and our tears, and it has been the greatest honor and privilege of my life to lead the Thirty-Seventh. You have all put your lives in my hands, followed my orders without question, and gifted me your loyalty. Even in the moments when I did not deserve it."

His voice cracked on the last, and Marcus squeezed Teriana's hair ornament tightly even as his composure wavered. "The Senate has convicted me of treason against the Empire, and I will not deny my guilt. Yet it is not for breaking those laws that I choose to stand here with this noose around my neck, because those crimes are paltry in comparison to the crimes I have committed against Reath."

He paused, running his thumb over the *Quincense's* sails. "From the moment we left Lescendor, we have been conquerors. Subjugators. Killers. From Bardeen to Chersome. From Arinoquia to Gamdesh to Mudamora, we have left misery and ruin in our wake all in the name of the Empire. All so the men on those steps"—he jerked his chin to the Curia—"could grow their power and fill their coffers."

The Thirty-Seventh shifted restlessly, and on the steps of the Curia, the senators all wore scowls. But from the corner of his eye, Marcus saw his sister give a sad smile.

"We say we do their bidding because we must. Because we have no choice but to obey. But that is a lie: the reason is *not* that we have no choice but that the choice to resist, the choice to say 'I will not do this,' carries with it a cost higher than we wished to pay. Higher than what *I* wished to pay, and I descended so deeply into the belief that there was no other path for me that I became no better than these Senators. Worse, in many ways, because the blood of all who have fallen beneath the Empire's heels is on my hands. Too much blood to ever atone for, so all I have left is to accept the punishment for what I have done so that Reath may at least have justice."

He drew in a steadying breath. "I will be held to account for what I have done, but so, too, must the Empire herself be held to account for what it has done. And the Empire is *not* the patricians on the Hill that looms above us, it is the people. It is *you*!" he shouted, allowing his eyes to drift over the civilians watching on, his words repeated back through the thousands upon thousands who massed in the streets. "You are all accountable for what the Empire has done in your name, and it is past time to risk the consequences that come with saying *enough*. The Empire's war machine is not faceless men birthed from a golden dragon but *your* sons. The sons of every province—the sons of Celendor herself. You do not get to give them up and then wash your hands of them, nor do you get to wash your hands of what the Empire uses them for. You are culpable."

The noose again scratched at his neck as Marcus turned his head, scanning the crowd. A visceral reminder of what was to come.

"You, the people, are what will prevent bloody conquest from happening again. You, the people, are what will prevent men like Lucius Cassius from rising again. You, the people, are who will tear down this institution of tyranny, and from its ashes, raise up a nation that is worth these legions fighting for!"

A roar of legion voices filled the Forum to be taken up by the civilians in the streets until it felt as though all of Celendrial had lifted their voices. Marcus stood until it fell silent before turning his gaze back to his legion.

"It has been my honor to serve with you, brothers," he said, then turned his head to look at Felix. "I leave you in the best of hands."

The Thirty-Seventh slammed their fists to their chest in salute, but as the noise faded, it was replaced with the sound of boots hitting paving stones. Someone running. Then a female voice screaming, "Marcus!"

No no no!

Teriana shouldered her way through the crowd, then sprinted down the lane to slide to a stop before the gallows. Her beautiful face was slick with tears as she looked up at him. "I love you," she said. "I needed to be sure you knew it."

He squeezed the ship tighter. *You can—*

stop this.

You can take control.

You can be with her.

You can—

Marcus looked at the executioner and nodded once.

Then he was falling.

Except instead of a long fall, he only dropped a few feet, the noose jerking tight around his throat, cutting off his breath.

No. Not like this.

The pain around his neck was incredible but nothing compared to the need to breathe. He gripped the tiny ship tighter.

The world was spinning, Teriana sliding in and out of his line of sight. She was on her knees. Servius was restraining her.

And he needed to breathe.

Needed air.

I curse you to die gasping for breath that will not come.

Panic rose with the memory of Kaira's dying words, then terror, because he needed air. Needed one last breath.

Darkness was rising.

His grip was slackening.

You can do this.

He couldn't feel his hands.

You can do this.

You can

125

TERIANA

She was on her knees.

Her ears were filled with a low drone, the world too bright and yet somehow the darkest it had ever been as she stared at Marcus's still form.

Dead.

Marcus was dead.

Dead, but her eyes were dry, her tears spent. Every part of her spent, her core hollow. Empty. Like part of her had died along with him.

Breathe.

She sucked in a ragged breath, her nails scratching the flagstones her hands were pressed against.

Racker stepped up, pressing his fingers to Marcus's throat. Then he nodded at Felix, who said, "We're taking him, Senator. Servius, get him down."

Tiberius grimaced. "Protocol demands that—"

"Fuck your protocol," Felix snapped. "This happened because he ordered it to happen, but now I'm in command. And if you think you can force us to leave him for the carrion, you might consider whose legion fills the Forum."

Tiberius opened his mouth, but then shook his head and walked away.

Teriana watched, frozen, as Servius sliced the ropes, Marcus's body limp as they lifted him. Neither Felix nor Servius looked at her as they carried him away, Racker following, and she did not watch them leave. Didn't move, even when she heard the centurions give orders to depart, and the Thirty-Seventh abandoned the Forum. Leaving her alone with the corpses.

Breathe.

Except how could she with him gone?

Live.

Teriana drew in another ragged breath, her eyes fixing on a glimmer of gold next to the cut length of noose. Slowly, she climbed to her feet and walked over, stooping to pick up the tiny replica of the *Quincense.* Blood glittered on the enamel sails from where the mast had cut his palm.

The gold was still warm.

A ragged sob tore from her lips, and Teriana doubled over, the hand gripping the tiny ship pressed to her stomach as she cried and cried until no more tears would come.

Rope creaked, and she turned her head to look up at Cassius's dangling corpse. His eyes stared at her, taunting.

How does victory taste, my dear, she heard his voice whisper. *Is it as sweet as you hoped?*

"Shut up," she whispered. "You lost. Evil lost."

So did you. Look around, Teriana. You're alone.

He wasn't wrong.

"I am alone." Teriana pressed her clenched fists to her ears, trying to drown out his laughter, then her eyes fixed on a pair of black riding boots approaching. Slowly, she looked up, her heart clenching as she looked into Lydia's green eyes.

"You aren't alone," her friend said, dropping to her knees to pull Teriana into her arms. "We will always have each other. Always. But I am so sorry that I was not at your side for this."

"How are you here at all?" She clung to Lydia's neck, seeing Killian standing beyond, his glower all that was keeping back those who wished to gawk at the corpses.

"It's a long story, but suffice it to say that I knew I needed to come."

If she'd arrived an hour sooner, would it have mattered? Would Lydia have had the influence to change the course of events? Teriana's eyes went to the dangling corpses, and her heart knew that nothing would have changed what happened here. Not only because the newly minted republic cared no more for the opinions of others than the Empire had, but because Marcus would not have had it any other way. "I'm so glad you came."

They clung to each other for a long time, then Lydia pulled her to her feet. "This place holds the worst of memories. I think it's time to leave it behind."

"Don't you wish to see your father?"

Lydia smiled. "I already have. He understands that Mudamora is where I belong."

They walked slowly from the Forum, arms linked, and Killian their silent shadow. People moved in as soon as they were out of the way, hands full of rocks and worse to throw at the corpse of the man who'd terrorized them. The civilians, citizens and peregrini alike, were in the streets celebrating, shouts of *libertas* filling the air, wine flowing. Part of Teriana hated them for it. Hated that they'd lift their cups and toast the worst moment in her life.

But she also understood why they did.

This was a moment that would be recorded in every history book. Celendor finally shaking off the vestiges of autocracy to step forward into a form of rule that would speak for all people in the East, not just the Cel. And most certainly not just the patricians living on the Hill.

Whether it would be a brighter future, Teriana could not say, but at least it would be a future of their own making. For all she'd played a large part in this moment, Teriana quickened her stride, desperate to turn her back on this city forever.

They left Celendrial, walking in silence to the beach where the *Quincense* was moored. It was all she could do not to run when she caught sight of its blue sails. She squeezed the hair ornament, clinging to composure as they rowed the longboat out to the ship and climbed the ladder. Though everyone should have been surprised at the sight of Killian and Lydia, no one said anything.

"Let's get underway," Teriana said quietly. "There's no reason for us to remain."

Her crew moved swiftly to follow her orders, the ship soon heading out to sea. Teriana stood silently watching the massive statue of the legionnaire that loomed over the harbor grow smaller and smaller until it finally disappeared into the horizon.

When she turned around, it was to find everyone watching her expectantly. Teriana found that she couldn't bear it. For everyone, what they'd achieved was a victory. Today *was* a victory because a tyrant had been brought to justice, but she was hollow. "I need a minute." Entering her quarters, she slammed the door shut behind her.

Resting her back against the wall, she slid down it to land on her ass, her eyes closed.

I miss you, she silently whispered. *I miss you so much.*

A breeze drifted over her face from one of the open windows, a breath of wind carrying the scent of the sea but also something else. Something that was imprinted upon her soul, and her eyes opened, gaze falling on the familiar figure outlined by the setting sun in their wake. "Marcus?"

126

MARCUS

For a long moment, Marcus couldn't answer, the weight of being back in her presence making it impossible to speak. Then he managed to get out, "It's me."

She was shaking. "You're dead. I watched them hang you. I watched you die."

"I know." The memory of that moment was not something he'd ever forget. "You did. And I was, but . . ."

"Lydia."

"Yes." Marcus didn't know whether to go to her or give her space, so he took a half step and then stopped. "She and Racker. It's a blur, but . . ." He scrubbed a hand over his hair, remembering light filling his eyes, the voices of his friends, and his chest an agony of broken ribs from the surgeon resuscitating him. The fog that had made it hard to think. "That's why it had to be the short rope."

"Did you know?" She looked ready to be sick.

Marcus shook his head. "I didn't even know Lydia was in Celendrial. She made the plan with Felix, Servius, and Racker, with aid from Valerius. If I'd known, I—" He broke off, his vision filling with Lydia's face as she'd leaned over him, her mark vanquishing the pain in his chest and the fog that had slowed his brain from too long without air.

"The dead cannot atone," she'd said softly. "I'm not letting you off so easily, Marcus. This is your chance to make things right. Make it count."

He'd been angry. Angry beyond reason, because bringing him back had felt like it had undone everything that he'd hoped his death would accomplish. In cheating death, he'd cheated justice, and part of him had wanted to stumble back out into the Forum and demand Tiberius hang him a second time.

Teriana was watching him, her eyes a pale grey he'd never seen before, as though shock had drained the color from the seas of her gaze.

"Lydia didn't tell me you were alive," she whispered. "Why didn't she tell me?"

"I asked her not to." In truth, he'd begged Lydia not to. "I thought it would be better for you if you believed I was dead. Thought it would be better if you moved on with your life not knowing I was still alive. Lydia wasn't happy, but she said the choice of what to do with my life was my own."

"But you're here."

Marcus couldn't tell how Teriana felt about that. Her eyes, for the first time he'd known her, were entirely unreadable. Sucking in a deep breath, he closed the distance between them, sitting on the floor before her. "I'm tired of lies. Tired of lying to you, because it's only ever brought us both suffering. I needed you to know I was alive."

"Why?" Anger flooded her voice. "So I could drop you off at the nearest port so that you could go back to Celendrial and have them hang you again with your conscience clear?" She slammed her palm down on the deck, revealing the hair ornament that had been his talisman so long. "Here it is, in case you need it again."

She knew him too well.

And she wasn't the only one.

Felix had sensed his intent, and his friend had rested a hand on his arm, holding him back. "Marcus, I know you're angry. I know you didn't choose this and that you have no tolerance for anything being pushed on you against your will. But please ask yourself whether you want to go back to the gallows because it's right or because you're afraid of the alternative." Felix had gripped his shoulders. "I know you're afraid. But since the day I met you, you've spit in the face of fear. Do not turn coward on me now."

Every part of Marcus had wanted to lash out. To take back control of the situation and force things to be his way. But his friend's words struck true. "I don't know how to be anything other than legion."

Felix shrugged. "Doesn't mean you can't learn."

A thought somehow a thousand times more terrifying than putting the noose around his neck again, but he said, "Take the Thirty-Seventh's mark off. If I'm going to do this, I can't have a foot in both worlds."

It was the most agonizing thing he'd ever endured, Racker's scalpel cutting away the legion numbers, the pain echoing even after Lydia used her mark to make his flesh whole.

"You need to take care of them, Felix," he said when it was done. "Tiberius has his heart in the right place, but that doesn't mean he won't lean on the legions when things don't go his way. You can't hide from the politics, not anymore."

It was Servius who answered. His big friend clapped him on the shoulder. "We'll be all right, and anyway, you don't get to order us about anymore. Go find the *Quincense,* because there are yet things you have the power to make right."

He let the memory slip away, knowing it was the last time he'd ever see his friends. Picking up the hair ornament, Marcus wiped away the blood dried on the sails, then reached for one of Teriana's braids. "I don't want you to drop me at the nearest port." Unfastening the end, he unraveled the long length of her hair, then threaded the ornament onto a strand so that it would brush against her cheekbone.

"The farthest one, then?"

"Not the farthest, either."

Teriana's breath was rapid against his face as he began rebraiding the strands, and color returned to her eyes. First a pale blue, but the hue darkened and deepened to the richest cobalt, waves gently rolling across their infinite depths.

"You deserve better than this." He knotted the end of the braid. "Better than me. I am a man with a terrible past and a dubious future. I have no coin, no practical skills, and no name. I would not blame you if you chose to cut your losses and toss me off the back of your ship."

"Say I choose to keep you," she whispered. "What *do* I get?"

"All of me, good and bad. I don't know if you want me, but I'm yours." Marcus swallowed hard. "For my part, all I want in my second chance at life is you."

Teriana was quiet for a long moment, then she reached out to pull down the neck of the borrowed shirt he wore, revealing naked skin where the 37 had once been. Her touch sent a shiver through him, the absence of the legion's mark filling him with grief over what he'd lost even as it filled him with hope for what he might gain.

Then her eyes met his, and she said, "I'll take you as you are, because you are enough. We are enough." She pressed her forehead to his. "In this life, and in whatever comes after, I will have you."

127

LYDIA

Lydia linked her fingers with Killian's, standing in silence together as they watched the sun set over the newly minted republic, but as the shadows grew, Baird approached. "I suspect you have a lengthy story to share," the giant said. "But I have to ask. Bercola . . . is she?"

"I'm sorry, Baird," Lydia said quietly. "She and other warriors from Eoten Isle didn't come through the xenthier with us. They stayed to hold back the blighters so that we'd have the time we needed."

Tears rolled down the giant's big face, but he gave a tight nod. "She died fighting. She'll be with Gespurn now. With luck, he'll tell her what I've done and when my day comes, she'll have room for me in her heart again." He wiped at his tears. "Agrippa?"

"He and Malahi are fine. We left them with the other survivors of Deadground in Mudaire, and their intent was to return south." Although what would be left, Lydia didn't know. But what she did know was that neither the Corrupter nor Cassius had destroyed the spirit of Reath. Mudamora, Gamdesh, and all the other nations that had suffered would rebuild.

"Nothing can kill that man," Baird said, fresh tears pouring down his cheeks. "I'll find him."

Polin approached and slung an arm around the giant, leading him away with a promise of drinks to toast the fallen, leaving Lydia once again alone with Killian.

"You haven't said much," she murmured. "Do you think I did the wrong thing?"

Killian lifted her hand, kissing her fingers. "I think you did the right thing for Teriana. Gave her the chance to make a choice, which is what she needed most. Now if she chooses to throw the arrogant bastard off the side for Magnius to eat, I will not shed any tears, but that's a different conversation."

Lydia smiled, squeezing his hand. "I don't think that's what she's going to choose to do. You and Marcus are going to have to make peace."

He muttered a few choice comments about Marcus's character, but Lydia's thoughts were all for that word.

Peace.

The peace across Reath wouldn't last, she knew that. Conflict would always rise between men and women who desired something they did not have, whether it be power or wealth, vengeance or justice. But peace was here now. A brief moment when the world seemed to be drawing a collective breath, coming to terms with what had passed even as it looked toward the future, and for the first time in so long, Lydia's own future held the liberty of choice.

There was something terrifying about having such an uncertain purpose, no critical goals to drive her every action, but it was thrilling as well. Especially with one certainty at her side. She rested her head against Killian's shoulder, his solid presence giving her faith that no matter what the future held, she could face it because he'd be with her.

Footsteps sounded on the deck behind her, and Lydia turned to find Teriana standing behind her. Her friend's eyes were red and puffy from tears, but she had Marcus by the hand, fingers clenched tight. Which told Lydia all she needed to know.

Bait came up the stairs two at a time, a smile on his face. "Who is up for opening a cask of ale and playing a few rounds of cards?" He caught both Killian and Marcus by the arms, and then hauled them away, saying, "Though maybe dice is a better choice. You have the instincts of a god, Killian, and I'd bet my last coin that you count cards, Marcus."

How either responded, Lydia couldn't hear over the wind, though as Bait got them ensconced on open space on the deck with full cups and a few other men from the crew to fill out the game, she could see their mouths moving. Jabs flying back and forth, she was sure, and Teriana said, "This is going to be interesting."

"They'll figure it out."

Her friend laughed, then slung an arm around Lydia's waist and pulled her back to the rail. "Thank you."

Lydia wrapped her own arm around Teriana, squeezing her tight. The sun slowly slipped beneath the horizon, but the moon was rising, illuminating them with a soft silver glow. "It isn't going to be easy. A lot of people hate him, and rightly so."

"I know." Teriana sighed. "But the same could be said of me."

"We've all done things we aren't proud of."

"Yeah." Teriana rested her head against Lydia's shoulder. "Marcus said to me that heroes are not pristine. That they're covered in blood and mud from fighting in the trenches. I know that we needed to get dirty to win this fight, but . . . I think that there comes a point when the grime is too thick to wash off. A point when you stop trying to be the hero, so that new heroes can step forward. People whose hopes and dreams and ambitions aren't yet smeared with the filth that comes with seeing them through." She shook her head. "It sounds bittersweet, but saying it makes me feel as though a weight has been lifted from my shoulders."

Lydia nodded. "Yedda told me that you declined to take on your mother's role as triumvir."

"Yes. I don't want to lead, and I don't think my people *want* to be led by me, not really." Teriana was quiet for a long time, then she said, "After Marcus and I made it through the Teeth, we sailed down the Savio on a little riverboat. Living each day as it came, seeing the world and meeting its people, and I don't think I've ever been happier in all my life. That's what I want, and I . . . I think that's what he needs. For us to go where the wind and the sea takes us, doing small goods where we can. But what about you? What will you and Killian do?"

Lydia considered the question for a long time. "We are both marked by gods. Marked to serve the people who have faith in the Six, and that is core to both of us. But I hope we can serve in a way that feels right. Many of those who'd had their lives stolen by Rufina's mark came back to us, but not everyone. And many more still were slain in combat or died from famine and are with the Six now. There are so many countless children without families, without anyone to care for them, and I think we need them as much as they need us."

"Again, our paths lead us away from each other," Teriana said with a sigh.

"But those same paths always bring us back together again."

"You're both cheating!" Bait shouted. He was glowering at Marcus and Killian, who had both already amassed piles of coins in front of them. They frowned at Bait, then leaned back over their game, and as Lydia watched, Bait gave her a sly wink.

"Look at those egos," Teriana muttered. "I think we ought to go down there so I can beat them both properly. I can try teaching you again, but we'll win more gold if you keep the cups full and Killian distracted."

Lydia laughed, everything feeling like it was settling into place. Like she was exactly where she needed to be.

"But first, I need to set a course." Teriana pulled her in the direction of the helm. "You ready to go home?"

Lydia caught hold of her friend's hand. "I'm already there."

Acknowledgments

It's been a long journey, hasn't it? There are times when I feel as though this series hit every possible obstacle, so finally getting to the finish line was a big moment. I'm so happy that readers have the long-awaited conclusion, but reaching the end is also bittersweet. I've been writing in the Dark Shores world since 2008, which means these characters are old friends to me, and it has been tough letting them go. I truly hope that I'll be able to come back to this world one day in the future.

There are many individuals whom I have so much gratitude toward for their support of this series, but before I get to them, I want to do something a little different. I want to thank myself for persevering on this series, despite every roadblock put in my way. The Danielle currently writing these acknowledgments thanks past Danielle for being stubborn as a mule and refusing to let this series fade away without a proper ending. For staying up past midnight and getting up early to work on Marcus, Teriana, Lydia, and Killian when there were a thousand other things demanding to be a priority. For never saying "good enough" and for always pushing for more. The exhaustion, missed deadlines, and total lack of social life were worth it!

Melissa Frain, there is a reason this one is dedicated to you! You are not just an editor extraordinaire, but a friend, and I will never be able to thank you enough for the love and care you put into this beast of a novel.

To my incredible agent Tamar Rydzinski, thank you for having my back through this journey. Many people would have told me to let this one go, but you never questioned my desire to see it through. Celsie Moseley, you are an organizational wonder—thank you for always being on top of things!

A thousand thanks to Amy Sarfinchan, who is the best assistant and friend to ever live. Thank you for being a daily support, because this book brought out the drama queen in me. Your love for these characters helped me through many dark moments.

To the team at Tor Teen, most especially Aislyn Fredsall, all my gratitude for the care you've put into bringing this novel to the world.

Elise Kova, my biggest sorrow is that we live so far apart, but I am thankful knowing that you are just a phone call away. Ladies of NOFFA, thank you for being there for extra support and for a good laugh—female fantasy authors for the win!

There are no words in any language that can capture my gratitude for my family. You are my biggest inspiration and greatest source of strength. Thank you for your endless love and support.

Last but not least, my loyal Dark Shores readers. Your encouragement and endless comments on social media begging for a finale were the fuel that got me to this moment. Thank you for going on this journey with me.

About the Author

Marwa Hurley

Danielle L. Jensen is the *New York Times* bestselling author of the Saga of the Unfated, as well as the *USA Today* bestselling author of the Bridge Kingdom, Dark Shores, and Malediction series. Her novels are published internationally in twenty-one languages. She lives in Calgary, Alberta, with her family and guinea pigs.

danielleljensen.com
authordanielleljensen
@danielleljensen
@daniellelynnjensen